THE GRAVEYARD: PARANORMAL
COLLECTED EDITION BOX SET
BOOKS 1-3

The Dark Man, The White Night, and The Belly of the Beast

Desmond Doane

Copyright © 2017 by Desmond Doane.

All rights reserved. No part of this publication may be reproduced, distributed or transmitted in any form or by any means, including photocopying, recording, or other electronic or mechanical methods, without the prior written permission of the publisher, except in the case of brief quotations embodied in critical reviews and certain other noncommercial uses permitted by copyright law.

Publisher's Note: This is a work of fiction. Names, characters, places, and incidents are a product of the author's imagination. Locales and public names are sometimes used for atmospheric purposes. Any resemblance to actual people, living or dead, or to businesses, companies, events, institutions, or locales is completely coincidental.

ISBN-13: 978-1981973750
ISBN-10: 1981973753

The Graveyard: Classified Series Box Set / Desmond Doane. -- 1st ed.

For those who go bravely into the dark...

GRAVEYARD: CLASSIFIED
Book 1

THE DARK MAN

Desmond Doane

Desmond Doane

1

A damp breeze pushes the rotting, translucent curtains to the side. A hundred years ago, they might have had some color. Someone's great-great-grandmother had undoubtedly hand-sewn them with pride and a song on her lips, humming as she swayed gently back and forth in her rocking chair.

Now, however, the curtains are just as faded and gray as everything else in this decrepit, abandoned farmhouse. Out here on the open land, miles away from the lights and sounds of Portland, Oregon, where it's buried under an overcast sky and the threat of rain, the night is as black as the bottom of a well.

It's hard to describe, but I feel as if my skin is starting to vibrate. That's a good sign. It means there's energy here. A presence. With the coming storm—lightning flashes in the distance, the rarest of occasions here—it'll help that much more. Those without a corporeal representation feed off nature's power; they gain strength from it, energy to communicate, and we may actually get some legitimate clues this evening. I felt that I was close the last time I was here, but it didn't happen. I went home with nothing but hours of blank tape and empty photographs, which was strange, since I was specifically asked to come here—you know, by a dead guy.

I have a new partner with me tonight. His name is Ulysses, officially, but I've decided on Ulie for short. He doesn't care what I call him. To Ulie, I'm the one and only Foodbringer. I'm the Light of His Life. I'm the One with the Stick. I am the Thrower of All Things.

I am Pillow. I am Chew Toy. I am He Who Takes Me for a Run Sometimes.

We've been together for a month, but this is the first time he's been on an investigation with me. Animals are sensitive to other realms, and I'm sure he'll be an excellent addition to my one-man team now that we've had an opportunity to connect on the appropriate levels. I went to the pound looking for company. I walked out of there with a friend.

My nose picks up on the fat scent of distant rain when another breeze rushes through the open window. Ulie lifts his head and sniffs the wind, too. Where I only smell impending precipitation, Ulie takes in the full breadth of life outside these walls. He cocks his head to the side, and I wonder what's pinging on his canine radar.

Ulie decides it's not worth more than a second of consideration. He looks up at me with an excited doggie grin, tongue wagging, almost like he's asking, "What's next, Ford? You brought me out here. Now what?"

I tell him, "Okay, Ulie, you're probably wondering why I brought you here, right?"

He closes his mouth. His ears perk up. He listens. He's probably waiting for a command, which will result in treats, but I like to pretend he's hanging on every word.

"Since it's your first day on the job, let me give you the quick and dirty. You know who sees things that other people don't? *Ghosts.*"

We're standing in the second-floor hallway of this 150-year-old farmhouse, and at the mention of the word "ghosts," Ulie flicks his attention away from me, down to the distant end where the master bedroom sits empty and, I'll admit, menacing.

Could be nothing. Could be a mouse.

I don't spook easily. You can't in this line of work. And yet, there's something about this place—something about the energy I feel—that sets me on edge more than the other times I've been here. Perhaps I should say that it doesn't feel friendly.

It never has been, honestly. Tonight, though, it feels like this could be big.

My fingers go up to the crucifix necklace I wear on nights like this. I touch it, just to make sure it's there. I'm not religiously religious, but I'm happy to call Jesus my copilot when it feels necessary.

I say to Ulie, "We're not actually on a case tonight, my friend. This is different, okay? We're looking for . . . well, we're looking for our own answers. If this works out, maybe you can start coming along with me on jobs, yeah? Local ones, at least."

Ulie grumble-whines and shakes his head, paws at his snout.

"That's easy," I say, answering an unasked question. "If you want to solve a mystery with no *living* witnesses, my dear flop-eared pal, then you have to talk to the *dead* ones."

When he turns his quizzical gaze up to me, he mutters something in dog-speak and prances in place as if he's anxious. His eyes go from me to the master bedroom and back again.

"You want to go take a peek?" I ask.

He snorts his approval and takes three tentative steps in that direction, looks back and waits, tail wagging hesitantly.

I start to say something to him, then chuckle to myself, realizing that my life has become the plot of a Carter Kane novel. It's not a bad thing by any means—Kane is a master of paranormal suspense and part of the reason I'm so fascinated with what's *out there*. He shaped my early years after many, many long, sleepless nights reading his work. And here I am, investigating the mystical with a highly intelligent mutt, having what appears to be a reciprocal conversation.

Kane would be proud.

The Graveyard: Classified Paranormal Series

Ulie takes another faltering step down the hallway. He barks once. It's not much, nothing more than a warning shot across the bow. I've heard him attempt to be more vicious with a butterfly that spooked him, but still, his caution lifts the hair on my arms.

"You think he's in there, boy?" I ask, kneeling beside the brave pup.

The *he* in question—I've spoken to him before. Carefully. I was warned before I came here. I've handled worse; you gotta be careful, though, no matter what.

My equipment case sits on the floor at my feet. It's about the size of a vintage suitcase from the 1970s, could probably double as a life raft built for two, and inside, it's packed with hard but forgiving foam where carved slots hold the items I need to conduct a proper paranormal investigation.

For a brief moment, I lament the fact that I'm down to this. One single case with five to ten devices, depending on the location and what options seem to work best after an initial analysis.

I miss my team. I miss the cameras and the cameramen. I miss investigating a single place for a week to create an hour-long slot. I even miss my producer, Carla Hancock, who was ultimately responsible for the show's demise.

"Miss" is a strong word for Carla. Perhaps it's better to say I have faint memories of the good times.

I'll never be able to explain why I let her talk me into using a five-year-old girl as a trigger object, which is something those of us in the paranormal world employ to entice spirits into communication.

Maybe it was greed. Maybe it was the thrill of the hunt. Maybe it was the potential for massive exposure. *"Tonight on this very special, live-on-Halloween episode of* Graveyard: Classified, *be prepared to witness history."*

You know how they say there's no such thing as bad press?

Apparently, there are exceptions to every rule.

Graveyard: Classified was the number-one show on cable during the coveted eight-to-nine slot on Thursday nights. We outranked every major network three-to-one. We even had more viewers than that super popular sitcom with the snippy part-time waitress who couldn't possibly afford that gorgeous loft apartment in New York City.

Top o' the world, we were.

And then, little Chelsea Hopper crawled into an attic and fell out with three massive claw marks along her cheek, neck, and collarbone. The entire crew, and millions of viewers at home and online, all heard the demonic growl during the live broadcast.

I checked. The attic was empty of anything living.

Chelsea's claw marks were real. She still bears the scars.

Graveyard: Classified wasn't picked up for its eleventh season after that, and it drifted off into the land of late-night reruns—the spirits of once-popular shows.

For the record, I questioned Carla, and myself, over that decision every step of the way, right up until the director turned the cameras on. I knew better, and I still regret it. I send care packages to the address where Chelsea lives, but I have no way of knowing if she ever gets them. Her parents did sign a contract, after all, and were awarded an incredible amount once the glory-seeking lawyers were able to find loopholes in it—yet, understandably, the Hoppers haven't chosen to forgive those who put their daughter in danger, including themselves, I bet.

A long, deep breath pushes those memories away. I choose an electromagnetic field detector—EMF for short—and a digital voice recorder, two of the simplest tools in my arsenal and often some of the best ways to detect an otherworldly presence. You almost always want to take a baseline reading with an EMF detector to make sure that there's nothing to contaminate your investigation like faulty wiring and things like that, but I figure out here, in this old farmhouse that used to be lit by candles and lanterns, there's no need.

Ulie prances some more, waiting patiently while I turn on both devices and perform one last equipment check.

The EMF detector reads "0.0" on the digital display. If it spikes while it measures the area within range, it'll give me an idea that there's something in the room making use of the available energy—energy from me, energy from the batteries in my equipment, energy from the lightning that's crawling closer.

The digital voice recorder detects what we call EVPs. Electronic Voice Phenomena, which are sounds—and voices—that aren't detectable by the human ear. Back in the olden days, and I'm talking, like, six months ago and earlier, we would run the digital recorders for hours, and then have to spend an equal amount of time reviewing the files on the back end of an investigation.

Now, however, with the BR-4000 I'm currently holding, you can do a live-stream listen. If I ask a question and something responds, I'll immediately hear it through my earbuds, rather than having to sit in my office, listening to hours of my heavy breathing, footsteps, and repetitive questions. It's a necessary evil if I'm investigating a larger place, like a hospital or warehouse, and have to run multiple DVRs at once. It can be dull, yeah, but that potential for an amazing discovery is always right around the corner.

Okay, so, with my EMF detector on and reading baseline zeroes, and the BR-4000 earbuds in and registering the ambient noise, which now includes Ulie's claws clicking on the hardwood floor, we march forward with tentative footsteps, one shoe and paw in front of the other.

Honestly, I haven't been this nervous in a while. I've been here twice. The first time, I caught two Class-A EVPs—the top of the quality charts—that spooked me to the core: "*I know what you want*," and "*Chelsea . . . Hopper.*" Both came from a deep, guttural male voice, angry and malevolent, within five minutes of each other, and I captured them in the master bedroom. After another half hour of fruitless questioning, I'd said, "If you'd like me to leave, give me a sign."

I asked for it, and I got it. I watched as a rotting two-by-four rose straight up off the floor and stood there, like a soldier at attention, for a full five seconds before it launched itself across the bedroom and missed my head by less than a foot.

The second time I was here, nothing happened. Not a damn thing. I sat and walked and perched and squatted and napped in this godforsaken place all night, alone, waiting on something to come back and challenge me again. Nothing but dead, boring silence.

Tonight, though . . . yeah, it feels different. He's here, and I plan to get some answers out of him.

These days, it's rare that I'm able to get out and investigate for fun. Now that *Graveyard: Classified* has basically gone the way of its own name, I have plenty of money that accompanies a guilty conscience; the latter keeps me from disappearing to a beach hut in the South Pacific. I can't just walk away from this life. There are promises to keep and wrongs to avenge.

What I do is, I work freelance, trying my best to assist police departments in investigations, both fresh and cold cases, in turn helping families find answers that were buried with their kin. When it comes to family matters like what a loved one intended in a will, or when it comes to proof in an ongoing investigation, paranormal evidence hasn't been officially or legally cleared for use. However, it often gives those involved enough clues or hints to proceed appropriately.

I do that kind of work to cherish the relief that I see in a stumped detective or a worried family member's eyes, and I haven't decided if I'm selfishly or selflessly building up karma.

This kind of investigation, what I'm doing here tonight, has nothing to do with an ongoing case.

The Graveyard: Classified Paranormal Series

It has everything to do with little Chelsea Hopper.

A ghostly messenger residing here requested me by name, and I think some of my answers may be on the other side of that bedroom door.

2

I had to hop on a flight early the next morning, and a day later, after some much-needed rest, I'm sitting here in a stuffy office that could double as a gym sauna.

The detective's suit doesn't fit him well. One of these days, I may introduce him to Melanie, who used to be the head of wardrobe before *Graveyard: Classified* was cancelled. She'd know exactly how to dress him properly, maybe give the poor guy an upright, professional appearance, rather than this slump-shouldered, slept-in-his-suit look he's rolling with now. Realistically, he's probably in his late forties, though the impression he gives off is, "I'm missing Bingo night and *Matlock* reruns, you whippersnapper."

He says to me, "This stuff is legit, right? What you do?"

I get this question often enough that it doesn't bother me anymore.

Maybe a little bit.

I tell him, "I've seen crap you wouldn't believe, Detective Thomas. I've watched chairs slide across rooms by themselves. I've seen an indentation form in a couch cushion, just like somebody sat down beside me to watch the big game. I've had my hair pulled, scratches and burns all over my body, cabinets flung open, knives flying at my head . . ."

"I remember, definitely. I was a big fan of *Graveyard*, back when it was still on. I just thought, you know . . ."

"That we made it all up?"

"Hate to say it, but yeah. Special effects are so good these days. I don't mean to accuse you or anything, but some of those shenanigans . . . a bit hard to swallow."

"Come with me one night. I'll show you firsthand. You guys do ride-alongs, right? Same thing."

He holds up a palm and gives me a fake frown. "Thanks, I'm good. Better for me that it stays on the other side of the TV screen. I've seen enough on *this* side of the grave to keep me awake at night."

I'm here in Virginia Beach, Virginia, this week. The VBPD called me in to see if I could do anything about this cold-case murder that recently popped back up in the national spotlight when an explicit diary was uncovered.

Apparently, the former mayor had been having an affair with his secretary—go figure—and after she floated to the surface at the mouth of the Chesapeake Bay ten years ago, nobody considered him a suspect. Mayor Gardner passed away back in 2012, according to Detective Thomas, and without any further leads, the diary was pretty much useless. There was proof of an affair in pasty, white, fleshy, gray-haired detail, but *not* proof that he murdered her, or hired someone to do it, after Louisa Craghorn threatened blackmail, the details of which she described in the final entry.

Before she was murdered, Louisa was young—thirty-two at the time—Filipina, and loved her Pomeranian. She liked taking a pottery class on Thursday nights and ran six miles four days a week. She had been married to her husband, Dave Craghorn, for just under two years when Mayor Gardner approached her about a promotion.

And, evidently, the stipulations included an inappropriate relationship, considering he had been married to the same woman for forty-nine years. She's alive and well, and also happens to be quite the public socialite around the Hampton Roads area. Ellen Gardner is still sparkling in her early seventies and loves to entertain guests, and from what Detective Thomas says, the diary revelation hasn't slowed her down in the slightest.

Detective Thomas clears his throat and takes a sip of steaming coffee. "You want some?" He holds the mug higher and tells me, "Should warn you, folks around here make it strong enough for a spoon to stand upright."

"As delicious as that sounds, I'm good. Had my fair share already." I lean back in the uncomfortable chair across from him and cross my legs. "So you explained some of the history on the phone, Detective. What're we looking at here and how do you think I can help?"

"Straight down to business. My kinda guy." He picks up a file box that's stuffed to the rim with folders and clasp envelopes. "This is the Craghorn case history. Or, well, I should say that it's the start of it. There are four more in our file room downstairs. And . . . now it might be more appropriate to call it the Craghorn-Gardner case."

My eyebrows arch at the sheer amount of it all, and my head ricochets backward like I just bumped it on a low doorway. "That much, huh?"

"Tell me about it."

"You had *that much* evidence, and the case still went cold?"

He pulls a shoulder up along with the corner of his mouth. "It happens. Sometimes you just . . . sometimes the bloodhound loses the trail."

I nod and clasp my fingers, then lean in on my elbows. Once in a while, I have to play the role of *human* investigator to get at the root of what someone is really looking for. It helps when I switch to my normal role of paranormal investigator.

I ask the detective, "What were you going to say there, just now? You stopped yourself."

The telephone on his desk rings loudly. He ignores it in favor of staring at me, waiting as if he's trying to decide how to answer.

That is, how to answer *me*, not the phone.

Five rings pass before he picks up the receiver and immediately slams it back down, hanging up on his clueless caller. "Sometimes," he says, "you just give up. I hate to admit it, but after you've exhausted every possible option, after you've got a few more gray hairs and the bags under your eyes look like they're carrying bowling balls, you have to admit defeat. Sometimes, the bad guys get away with it, Mr. Ford."

"Understandable. Who was the lead on the case back in '04? Is that detective still around?"

Detective Thomas raises his hand, almost sheepishly, without saying a word.

"You? I didn't think active homicide detectives tackled cold-case investigations. Or is that just an assumption I made up?"

"Once Elaine Lowe—that's the surviving husband's housekeeper—once she came forward with the diary she found, I requested this assignment. Immediately dropped everything I was working on because I wanted another shot, and here I am, six months later, no closer than I was back in 2004. New evidence, a new list of suspects who were cleared, and a whole lot uglier." He sighs as he flips a folder closed and drops it on his desk.

"And murder was your original conclusion way back when?"

He nods, grimaces when he sips his steaming hot coffee.

"I read the content you sent me, Detective, but from what I gathered, the body had, uh, it had decayed so much that you weren't quite sure."

He grins at me. "Then you didn't read all of it."

He's got me there. I didn't, because when he called and asked me to hop on the next flight to Norfolk International, I was bone weary after the third farmhouse investigation. The events of two nights ago had prevented sleep from coming easily, and I'm dying to get back there to follow up, but the karma ain't going to refill itself.

Part of the idea is, I feel like if I do enough of these investigations, I could look at pitching a new show idea to some producers who may be willing to overlook the fallout from the demise of *Graveyard: Classified*, but until I'm ready for that day, I'm not about to step back into prime time until I can find some peace for Chelsea Hopper, and in turn, myself. What I caught the other night could lead to a breakthrough even though I haven't had time to fully analyze its meaning.

Ulie hasn't been the same, either. The only thing I can do from here, three thousand miles away, is hope that my ex-wife, the aforementioned Melanie from wardrobe, is taking good care of him. She reports a tucked tail and whimpering, but he's finally eating again.

I say to Detective Thomas, "Guilty as charged. Although that's probably not the best thing to say to a cop, huh?"

Thankfully, he snickers. If I can get away with bad jokes, we might have a decent working relationship. Given what I do, it helps if my clients are easygoing and have an open mind. Judging by the fact that I'm here already, he's either willing to try or has crossed the DMZ into desperation.

"You're off the hook, Mr. Ford. I sent a lot, I know. Anyway, so, whenever a *naked* body pops up in the water, you suspect what?"

"Homicide. But if she was clothed, then my first thought would be an accident or suicide."

"Exactly. Could be the natural wear of the currents pulling her clothes off, but more than likely, she comes out like that, she went in like that. When her husband had reported her missing, the guys looked for her and came up with nothing. Missing Persons monitored her credit cards and bank accounts because sometimes these women—or men—they get into drugs, or they just want to be gone. Maybe they finally leave an abusive relationship behind, or they ran off with the gardener—or in this case, the Gardner. Pardon the pun."

His ambivalence doesn't sit well in my gut, but I suppose after all he's seen, it's just another day on the assembly line.

"And you found something that told you otherwise?" I ask.

"Upon deeper inspection, once the ME got past all the—you know what? I'm going to spare you the wet details. The contusions around her neck showed signs of strangulation. At first glance, you might have suspected it could have been something underwater. Seaweed. Stray rope from an anchor. Maybe she's out skinny-dipping, knocks her head against a rock, she sinks, the current drags her into something, and that's all she wrote."

"I'm guessing that wasn't the case."

"You'd be guessing correctly. The bruises revealed what we consistently see in these types of murders, and that's a really strong grip." Detective Thomas cups his hands around an invisible neck, and I have to say, it freaks me out when he grinds his teeth as if he's actually performing the act itself. I've battled demons with a crucifix, side by side with terrified clergymen, but this gives me serious goosebumps. It's almost like he's—never mind. I'm on edge after the other night. It's nothing.

"Were you able to tell, say, the size of the hands, or maybe the strength of the squeeze? Meaning, like, male or female?"

"Trust me, Mr. Ford, we went over all that during the preliminary investigations. That's the simple stuff. If you catch the deceased at the proper time, you might have a better chance of determining something like that on a good day while pulling a few miracle cards, but not after a body has been in the bay for over a week. We were lucky the ME was able to come up with what he did."

I sit back in my chair and put my finger to my lips, thinking. I'm not necessarily or inherently built with the deductive reasoning skills of a seasoned detective, but more than once, I've come up with an angle that helped spark their creative thought processes before I ever set foot in an investigation site. Beginner's luck, I guess. Often a baffled, desperate police department has begrudgingly brought me in at the request of someone at the station who was a fan of the show, and frequently, the spirits of "the deceased," as Detective Thomas refers to them, are uncooperative. I can't *make* them talk any more than I can make a proper omelet on a regular basis. If it ain't in the cards, it ain't happening that day.

I still charge them for my time. The way I see it, detectives go to work every day and don't solve cases, yet they still get paid. I could easily do this work pro bono, no problem, but I've found that if someone is paying me, they're far more likely to be reasonable and accommodating.

I stop and start a few sentences. I come up with nothing, not a single approach that I think Detective Thomas can check out. He tried it all. He's been trying again for the last six months, which means we're down to my last line of questioning for him.

"Then that leaves us here," I say, sitting up straighter. "A lot of times PDs will call me in for the novelty of it. They're out of options, and they think, 'Oh, what the hell, this guy works for peanuts. Why don't we give him a try?' I don't like those. I'm not saying you *are* one of those, I'm just saying it's hard walking onstage where the crowd hasn't been warmed up first. See what I'm saying?"

He taps a pencil against his cheek and acknowledges me by dipping his chin.

"Then, other times, some detective has seen something he can't explain and wants a second opinion, which I'm happy to help with. Those are great. It means there might be something there, and we might already have a solution to work toward. Even rarer still are guys like you, the ones who call with a little extra edge to their voices, the ones who are hesitant to say exactly *why* they're calling. Guys who are nothing but curious? They'll admit it right away. They'll say, 'This weird thing happened; we want you to come check it out.' But detectives like you, been at this twenty years or more, seen everything there is to see, all the evil in humanity . . . you don't need me. You got new evidence, fresh clues. You're not ready to throw in the towel after six months, Detective. I don't believe it when you say you're back to where you started. You called me here for a reason. Something spooked you. So let me ask you this: What was it? What did you see?"

"I'll never forget it," he answers with that somber tone I've come to recognize so well.

3

We're standing in front of the Craghorn residence. It's too damn hot in the Hampton Roads area this time of year, and I can feel the sweat beading up in places where I don't enjoy being swampy. It's part of the gig, though, and I agreed to let Detective Thomas explain himself here rather than back at the station. He said it would make more sense if Dave Craghorn, husband of the deceased, was there to back him up.

Detective Thomas tucks his hands into his pockets and looks up at the top floor of the three-story home. We're over in Portsmouth, a small city adjacent to Virginia Beach, where some of the residences are centuries old, built back when the masons didn't mind stacking stones thirty or forty feet in the air on all sides. These things were built to last.

The detective admires it, head tilted, back angled as we look up toward the hand-carved molding along the eaves. He says, "Beautiful place, ain't it?"

I lie to him and say yeah, it's nice, while I try to see it through his eyes. I get what he's saying; the place has a strong presence. It's bulky and broad-shouldered, reminds me of a middle linebacker, but I don't really see the *beauty* in it, per se. To me, it's a giant collection of rocks and cement that's covered in moss with vines climbing up the sides. Maybe it's because, over the years, too many houses have become enemies to me, burdened with evil, demonic spirits that torture families and drive them from the place where they wanted to live out their dreams. Instead, they suffer through nightmares.

So, yeah. Houses? I don't really trust them, not until I've had a chance to get to know one. Mine back in Portland, high up on the hill overlooking the Willamette River, has had so many incantations, prayers, and positive vibes bestowed upon it that you might as well say it's guarded by a soothing, white light that envelops the whole thing. That's my sanctuary, the place where I retreat after I've battled with the darkness.

Not every house that's haunted is black on the inside, just like not every spirit is a demonic, evil entity. Sometimes it's somebody's sweet old grandma who never got a chance to say goodbye before she left this world, and once I help her with that, the fog lifts.

Point is, until I know what I'm dealing with, I approach each place—each home, each train station, each barn, whatever—with full shields, and every now and then, if I've come out unscathed, I'll take a moment to appreciate the architecture, but not until I know I'm going home without any unwanted guests tagging along.

The detective clears his throat, and I can hear a bit of emotion in there, like he's trying to cough it up and maybe swallow it, down where the rest of his feelings stay buried.

I ask, "You okay?"

"Yeah," he croaks, then looks past me down the sidewalk. "There's Craghorn. I won't go in there without him, and to be honest, I don't know how he lives here by himself."

Pardon the expression, but I'm *dying* to know what happened here. After all these years and literally a thousand investigations, I still don't feel like I've seen everything there is to see, at least when it comes to the paranormal world.

I still get confused, spooked, scared, excited, and thrilled when something—notice I said some*thing*—reaches out from the other side. You'd think I'd be desensitized by now, but the truth is, this shit will never get old for me.

There's the job, then there's the wonder.

Detective Thomas doesn't smile when he lifts a hand, waves to Dave Craghorn and says, "Good to see you again, Dave. Thanks for doing this."

Dave offers a morose smile as fake as the day is long, and we shake hands. He's somewhere in his mid-forties, a little older than me, with long salt-and-pepper hair and a matching goatee that extends down past his Adam's apple. His tan jacket hangs loosely on his shoulders, like it might have fit one day, but now it's nothing more than a piece of clothing draped over shoulders as thin as a wire hanger. Which, of course, adds another layer to his odd vibe. It's gotta be well over ninety degrees out here and 100 percent humidity. He has to be swimming in that thing.

He says, "Nice of you to come, Mr. Ford. Big fan of your old show." It's a flat, emotionless voice, no heft to it at all, like he's a prisoner who's afraid to speak up in front of his captors.

"Happy to help," I respond, studying him. Let me just say this: I take my B-list fame with a grain of salt. I've been to the big parties and hobnobbed with the elites of entertainment, but I've never been one to abuse the privileges of celebrity. I'm lucky and I know it. I don't throw my soup in waiters' faces, I don't whine and complain when I'm not given the best table, nor when I actually have to *wait* for a table just like everyone else. That said, I can always tell when someone has no idea who I am, or has never seen an episode of *Graveyard: Classified*, or more than likely, just doesn't give a shit. In fact, I think I appreciate the latter the most. It allows me to investigate a site on level grounds.

Dave lifts a shaking finger, pointing up the tall set of stairs as he mumbles, "It's, um, it's right up there."

"Here we go." Detective Thomas groans, pauses in midstep, and pushes bravely forth.

Not really, but I have to give the guy credit. Whatever happened in there spooked him all to hell, and he's going anyway. I follow him up, taking the steps in twos, with Dave Craghorn following us both. I glance over my shoulder and he's climbing the steps as if each foot is encased in cement—big, heavy blocks that he struggles with as he pushes himself onward, one after the other. I can almost hear the thick clunk with each step. He's dreading this just as much as Detective Thomas is, and I feel for him. Poor guy comes home to this every single day.

The front door is thick wood, painted a shade of cloudy gray that seems to fit perfectly with the gloom and doom motif of this place. Craghorn's key makes a deep, metallic thunk, reminding me of a jailer in an ancient castle dungeon, and I immediately feel the cold of the interior racing out as the door swings inward.

Detective Thomas shivers.

Now I know why Craghorn is wearing the jacket. He says, "It's always like this now. The cold never leaves my bones. It follows me."

I don't shiver from the temperature. I do it because of the defeat in his voice.

He adds, "Come on in. Might want to say a little prayer first, if you're the religious sort."

Out of habit, my fingers go up to the crucifix dangling at my chest. It feels warmer than usual against my skin. I'm not sure if that's a good sign.

Craghorn stares down the hallway, and Detective Thomas follows with a resigned grunt. "To serve and protect," he says.

As soon as I step across the threshold, I feel it. Not just the cold, but what's buried within it. Remorse. Loss. Regret.

And so much anger.

I pause because it's been a while since I've felt such a . . . *presence* right away. Not since the Alexander house six months ago, the one up in Lansing, Michigan, with the pissed-off spirit of an ex-con who was haunting a young single mother and her three children. She'd sent me a pleading e-mail, and once in a while, I'll take on a special case pro bono, because when it comes to kids, I simply can't let that go. It's why I'm still battling with what happened to Chelsea Hopper.

This, whatever it is, actually feels stronger than the ghost of Delmar Jackson, and that's saying a lot. It took me, three Catholic priests, and enough holy water to fill a bathtub to get him gone.

My goosebumps get goosebumps. No matter how many times I've done this, the chill of evil prickles my skin. It's not the fiery, burning, licking flames of hell like the Bible and your Sunday pastor would have you believe.

Evil is the darkness. It's the cold.

It's the absence of love and light.

"Ford," says Detective Thomas, leaning back into the hallway, "you coming?"

"Yeah, sorry. Just getting a feel for the house."

"And?"

"You were right. This place is *dark*."

***

Craghorn sits on a sofa that looks like it might have been purchased at a yard sale in 1973. In fact, I'm fairly certain that my parents had this exact same couch with the exact same pattern in our living room back when Nixon was in office. Instinctively, I look at the far left cushion to see if the hot chocolate stain is there. My sister, Amy, spooked me with a Halloween mask when I was nine. The contents of the steaming mug went all over me, her, and the couch, and left behind a brown memory that refused to go away no matter how much we scrubbed.

The Graveyard: Classified Paranormal Series

It's not there, by the way, but surveying the couch does give me a chance to check out Craghorn some more while we wait on Detective Thomas to emerge from the bathroom. I can't tell if Craghorn is a small man in general, or if he's *making* himself smaller, like he's trying to hide from something. Or it could be the fact that the springs and cushions are so worn out on his couch that the damn thing is trying to swallow him whole.

I decide on a combination of all three and lean in with my elbows on my knees, asking him, "Lots of nice things here. You decorate the place yourself?" It's such a pointless, baseline question that I'm not even sure why I asked it. I think maybe I'm simply trying to fill up the sucking void in here that's taking every ounce of energy out of this room. I hear the toilet flush down the hallway and say a silent thanks. As good as I can be with people at times—you have to be in this line of work—Craghorn seems more comfortable around Detective Thomas. He hasn't said a word since the detective excused himself.

Craghorn flits a hand around the room and blandly answers, "Most of it belonged to my wife. She won't let me get rid of anything."

Present tense. *Won't let me*. It's a clear hint regarding his feelings about the situation, though I can't yet tell if he's hanging on to the past or if he means her spirit is here and dictating what does and does not go out with the garbage.

He adds, "And, really, it's all part of the scenery now. I barely notice."

Detective Thomas walks back into the living room, giving one final swipe across his mouth. I'm sure I heard retching while he was in there, or what it sounds like when someone is holding it back. His skin has turned a pasty white, and there's no life in his eyes.

"What?" he snaps when he catches me looking at him.

"Nothing. You just . . . you look like you've seen a ghost." I fake a laugh. I can't tell you how many times I've tried that joke just to lighten the mood before an investigation. I can count on one hand how many times it's actually worked over the past decade, yet it doesn't stop me from trying.

Thankfully, Craghorn snickers, and now I can graduate to counting on two hands.

I continue, trying to sound upbeat between the fearful shaking of Detective Thomas and the morose gloom of Dave Craghorn. What they're projecting doubles the effect of the blackness billowing into this room. "Normally, this is the part where I'd start out with a line of questioning to sorta gather up the history about what's going on with your property. Everybody has a story, right? Even those who have moved on. But since you, Mr. Craghorn, didn't necessarily ask me for help, and since Detective Thomas did, I'm going to let him paint the picture, and we'll go from there, okay?"

Craghorn nods without making eye contact. He almost reminds me of a witness for the prosecution who is too afraid to say yes, too afraid to point out the bad man in the room. Instead, he's focused on his fingernails and what's underneath them, and makes no further attempt at communication. His shallow breathing and a knee that bounces like chattering teeth on a cold day are enough to reveal his anxiety.

Detective Thomas coughs into his fist and then cups his hands. He blows into them, trying to warm them up and then rubs his palms together. He huffs a fat breath of air, like he's expecting it to plume. It doesn't, and he almost seems perplexed.

Cold spots are another sign of a potential spiritual presence. Normally, it's nothing more than a chilly area in the center of a warm room, maybe five, ten, fifteen degrees cooler than the ambient temperature. It's where a spirit is absorbing energy, hoping to compile enough to communicate with the living.

Craghorn's entire house feels like a meat locker.

The detective's next words drop the temperature even further.

The Graveyard: Classified Paranormal Series

4

CHELSEA HOPPER
TWO YEARS AGO
A Very Special Live Halloween Episode

"*Ford*," said Mike Long, my fellow lead investigator, "you absolutely can*not* use that little girl as a trigger object. How many times do I have to tell you? And fuck me, man, here we are! Again! It's too dangerous, like, off-the-charts dangerous. You and I both know how sensitive children are to these things. You *know* this. And at five years old? She's immaculate on the inside. There are no footprints in the mud of her mind." He said this last bit with force, tapping the side of his head as he accentuated each syllable.

Carla Hancock, my producer, put her hand on Mike's shoulder and nudged him back, just enough to distance him from the circle of trust that she was trying to establish. Carla, Don Killian, Gavin Probst, and Timothy Shearing, all of my producers and co-producers, the directors, the sound guys, the whole lot of them were crowded around me. *Graveyard: Classified* had about four minutes before the live-feed broadcast began for what promised to be the biggest, most-watched paranormal investigation ever.

Carla said, "I don't need to remind you that we're going live in forty-seven countries, do I? *Millions* of people are watching,

Ford, and they want a show. They want the goddamn Super Bowl of paranormal investigations, and if you want to keep this freight train rolling, you'll send her in there."

I shook my head. I felt the regret and remorse encroaching on my gut. I felt like, if I did it, if I really bent to Carla's will and sent a five-year-old child into an attic, to face a demon, alone, then my soul would turn as black as the creature we were hunting.

But the ratings. My God, the ratings. Astronomical.

Rob and Leila Hopper stood off to the side, near the catering truck, giving Chelsea bites of ice cream and pieces of the peppermint candy that Mike always requested before every shoot. They'd agreed to this because . . . well, one, we were offering them more money for a single night in their house than Rob earned in a year as a customer support technician. They weren't filled with bloodlust or anything like that. They weren't demented, crazy freaks that got their jollies by torturing their daughter. They weren't pageant parents who subjected their child to psychological trauma before she could even spell it.

There was none of that. They were good people, and I knew that because I'd had extensive discussions with them. They just happened to live in the Most Haunted House in America for three terrifying years after Chelsea was born. Chelsea experienced more paranormal activity in those three years than I had my entire career.

So why were her parents sending her in there? Because Carla went behind my back and convinced them that having Chelsea confront the demon would be the best way to get rid of her traumatic memories once and for all. I nearly walked away when I found out. I should've, but I didn't.

I had contractual obligations and, admittedly, once I thought about it for a little while, Carla's arguments *almost* made sense.

We were minutes away from going live, knowing there would be millions of people around the world who would judge, hate, condemn, and trash the Hoppers all over social media. They'd label them horrible parents. They'd say there was no way in hell that any self-respecting person would ever do that to a child, especially their own offspring. They'd type in all caps at them for being idiots, and likely call social services in an attempt to have Chelsea taken away. They'd tell their friends that the Hoppers were horrible, detestable, greedy human beings who were only in it for the money.

The Hoppers had hundreds of reasons to change their minds, and every single one of them was the best one. We were offering them a ton of money, yeah, but there was more to it than that.

Agreeing to something so completely ridiculous sounds insane, right? True, but think about it from their perspective.

You try watching your daughter go through what Chelsea experienced for three years and what she suffered through every night in her dreams; you try saying no when someone approaches you with promises of redemption, vengeance, and relief. Imagine having a nasty, unbearable toothache every day of your life. You can't eat. You can't sleep. You can't take a nice, long drink of cool water without blinding pain screaming throughout your body. And then one day, a nice lady with an enchanting smile shows up at your front door and says, "I've got a magic pill that'll fix what ails you. All you have to do is swallow it, and your troubles will be over. It doesn't cost anything, and, as a matter of fact, we'll *pay you* to take it."

Would you do it? Would you take the pill?

As a parent, if it were your daughter who was in pain, would you take the chance?

I'd thought about this for weeks. Mike and I argued night after night leading up to the investigation, and he was still arguing with me mere minutes before we went on air. I'd met privately with the Hoppers and explained to them what we were going up against, and they knew, they understood. The worst part about it was, they said that they trusted me, that they knew I wouldn't let anything happen to their little girl. They knew Chelsea was the vanguard in a horrifying war, and that she would win because I'd be by her side. They believed that, and I didn't try to convince them otherwise.

Why not?

If . . . no, *when* she came out the victor, I originally believed that this single investigation would seal our place in paranormal history and in television ratings. Rich corporations would lock us into sponsorships and contracts lasting as long as we wanted them to.

Big Burger City. Tire Monster. Avocado Giant. They were all standing by with ink pens and glimmers in their eyes.

Rob and Leila trusted me, but I had to wonder, did I trust myself to do the right thing? I don't know.

I had about a minute thirty to change my mind, which was insane, because it was right before we investigated the Most Haunted House in America on a Very Special Live Halloween Episode. I still had a chance to back out.

Decisions, decisions. Devil. Angel.

Nobody but the crew and the Hoppers knew what the surprise was for the viewing audience. I had it all figured out. If I changed my mind, I would just switch up the intro and catch *everyone* off guard, including the producers and directors. The unassuming house in that quaint little neighborhood on the eastern side of Cleveland, Ohio, could be the surprise all by itself, with no need to include an innocent child.

You'd never guess it, America, but this beautiful bungalow, on this quiet street where children play and puppies dance, is a place of such unimaginable horror, that I—me—Ford Atticus Ford, am terrified to go inside.

I didn't have to mention the Hoppers at all, and they understood that this was a possibility. I'd promised to cut them a check from my own bank account if I ripped up their contract in the final seconds. I couldn't leave them hanging once I learned that they planned to set up a college fund for Chelsea with the money they earned from the show.

An intern with a clipboard, an earpiece, and a puffy mic curled around in front of her lips darted over to us and tapped Carla on the shoulder. "One minute, twenty seconds, Miss Hancock."

"Thanks, Ambrosia."

Mike threw his hands in the air and backed away, shaking his head. "I can't do it, Ford. I can't. *We* can't. We're going to burn for this." He stopped his retreat and locked his fingers at the base of his skull. "Actually, you know what? *You're* going to burn for this. I'm done." He said this with all the conviction he could muster, but he didn't go anywhere. He knew that Carla Hancock had the power to ruin his career. Despite his reservations about the investigation, he loved what he did, and to have that and the money taken away . . .

Carla said to me, "Don't listen to him. You're a professional. You're a *warrior*, and we're going to make cable television *history*. You, Ford, *you* will be Monday morning's water-cooler discussion for a long, *long* time."

"Carla, I—"

"Do it for *her*," Carla said, pointing at the bouncy, happy, ponytailed child who barely had any idea what was coming next. All Chelsea knew was that her parents had brought her back to where she used to live and they wanted her to go with Mr. Ford to talk to the dark man. Aside from that, it was fun seeing all these people around. To her, it was a party.

Chelsea slurped the chocolate ice cream off her cone and giggled when Rob tried to sneak a bite. Carla pointed, adding, "Give that little girl some peace. Get her life back."

"She looks fine to me," I replied, but it was only because she had candy, ice cream, and a horde of people paying attention to her. It was a weak defense. I knew that Chelsea had been plagued by terrifying dreams, constantly waking up, screaming and crying.

Ambrosia, the intern, nudged Carla with a little extra insistence and said, "Twenty seconds, Miss Hancock."

"Ford?"

"What?"

"You heard her. What's it going to be?"

"I—"

"*Beat* this thing. Send it back to hell."

"And if I don't?"

"You're up for a contract renegotiation soon, right?"

Her question was her answer.

Carla didn't care about defeating a demon. She didn't care what happened to Chelsea Hopper or me. All she wanted was the ratings.

Ambrosia waved at me frantically, begging me to come to her, to get in front of the camera. "Five, four, three . . ."

I took one quick peek at Chelsea, and then I realized that I desperately wanted her to keep that smile. I hated to admit it, but Carla was right. We needed to defeat that thing and send it back to the darkness so Chelsea could live her life in sunshine.

I darted over to the walkway and hopped in front of the camera just as the live feed opened, clasping my hands together, fingers intertwined, giving the audience my signature bow.

"Welcome, friends, families, and to the millions of you watching around the world. This is simply unbelievable." I had to strain to keep the fake smile going. "We have the most incredible show you'll ever see on this very special, live Halloween episode of *Graveyard: Classified*. We asked for it, you delivered. After watching the ghastly evidence the Hoppers collected on their own, choking back tears during their desperate pleas for help, hundreds of thousands of votes were cast online, and you picked the winner. Let me introduce you to the Most Haunted House in America."

The Graveyard: Classified Paranormal Series

The "Most Haunted House in America" might have been a misnomer, because we had no way to confirm that, but damn, it sounded good. For all we knew, the house down the street from your grandmother might have been as scary as a spare bedroom in hell. The age-old adage for news is, "If it bleeds, it leads." In the world of paranormal reality shows, we said, "If it *screams*, it leads."

I stepped sideways, sweeping my hand back and up the walkway in the direction of the Hoppers' former home.

I felt like that was a rather anticlimactic speech, because it totally wasn't what I was prepared to say. I had something deeper, stronger, more powerful and cogent written and ready to go. My indecision cost me, because I lost every damn memorized word of it and had to concoct that bland nonsense on the fly.

Moving completely out of the way, I allowed the first camera to race up the cobblestone path to the front door, and as per the production plan, the live feed switched to a prerecorded segment. It cut to an interior tour of the house, with my voiceover in the background, as I narrated the inconceivable terrors that the Hoppers had endured while living there.

It really was a quiet, unassuming house, sort of a faded pistachio color with off-white shutters, a wraparound porch, and a front door painted soft beige. Two stories tall, with a tiny attic—where the demon lived—and colorful landscaping, the house possessed a heart blacker than coal. If houses have auras, and some of my psychic acquaintances insist they do, then that one seethed with the absence of light.

I knew that the intro piece—the tour of the home and my voiceover work—would last two minutes and seventeen seconds exactly. I used this time to dash over to the Hoppers who were standing patiently, though they looked nervous behind false grins, a pathetic attempt at convincing themselves that everything would be okay.

"You're sure about this?" I asked. "Last chance to back out."

Deep down, the part of my brain that governed *rational* thinking wanted them to. The *emotional* side was saying, "Let's go for it. I can make this better for you," and, also, "The ratings! Holy freakin' cow, the ratings!"

Rob Hopper said, "We just want it to be over, Mr. Ford."

"We trust you," Leila added. "We know you won't let anything happen to her."

I leaned down and took Chelsea's soft, sticky hands. She had a ring of chocolate around her lips. Her sweet breath smelled like peppermint candy. "Chelsea, you ready to go beat up a ghost?"

She giggled, put her chin down to her shoulder and twisted bashfully from side to side. "Uh-huh. But will it be scary?"

"Maybe a little. I'll protect you, though. If we go in there and kick this thing's hiney, all those bad dreams might go away. Does that sound like a plan?"

Chelsea scrunched up her nose. "You said 'hiney.'"

"I did, didn't I?"

Over my shoulder, I heard Ambrosia softly calling my name. "Mr. Ford? Mr. Ford? Thirty seconds. Intro's almost finished."

I stood and said to the Hoppers, "I'll protect her. It'll be fine, I promise."

Was I lying? The scary thing was, I didn't know the answer to that.

"Listen to the crew. They'll give you directions and timing. We're live for three hours tonight, but Chelsea will come in after thirty minutes—anyway, yeah. You're in good hands with these guys."

I retreated a step, ready to jog up to my next mark on the front porch, and Chelsea brought me to a heartbreaking halt when she said, "Don't let the dark man get me, okay?"

5

Detective Thomas has to sit down before he says, "It was a black mass about five feet tall, looked almost like it was flowing. Malleable, you know? Swirling around itself. It was standing there in the doorway, watching me. I took a couple of steps back, and—and I blinked really hard, kinda rubbed my eyes, thinking maybe it was just a trick of the light, but then I thought, can't be, I've already been inside for thirty minutes. You know how your eyes are sorta messed up when you look at the sun, like maybe out the window or whatever? You get those blobs in your vision? It was like that, but . . . real." He points toward the living room entryway and the hall beyond. "The thing was solid. I couldn't see past it. And I remember it as clear as day, I said, 'What the—' and before I could finish my sentence, I swear to God, I swear on the life of my poor mother, may she rest in peace, it was like this thing opened its eyes. Two red, glowing orbs revealed themselves slowly. I coulda screamed, Mr. Ford. I coulda called out to God but I was so . . . cold on the inside. Like looking at this thing froze my heart. All my happiness that I'd ever had, just *poof*, gone."

His last words come out in a whisper as he holds an empty hand over his chest, clawlike, and squeezes the air.

He adds, "In all those shows you've done, you ever seen anything like that?"

"I have in person, absolutely," I answer. "Though we were never able to catch it on film. I believe there's a variety of shadow people out there, Detective Thomas, some with less power who show up as something like a floating mass or like a misty cloud up in the corner of a room. Then you have the ones that're strong enough to appear in physical form, like being able to make out a head and shoulders, maybe even arms. I've seen those plenty of times with my own eyes, standing right there in the same room with them. I've been able to capture those on film, both with digital cameras and video recorders, plenty of evidence that those exist. But what you're talking about, the ones with the red eyes? They're too strong, too powerful, too . . . intelligent to get caught."

Detective Thomas scoffs and leans forward in the chair. "You're telling me that thing has a brain?"

"Well, there are two different types of haunts, detective. Residual and intelligent. Residual hauntings are like, say, leftover energy. Think of a tape recorder that's stuck in an infinite loop. If you're in a haunted house and you hear the same footsteps climbing the staircase every night at a quarter past twelve, that's a residual haunt. That tape recorder is simply resetting itself and playing again."

"So the ghost doesn't know it's doing it? It's totally unaware that it's stuck in limbo, repeating itself throughout eternity?"

"More or less."

"Sounds like my ex-wife." He chuckles at his own joke, and I offer a sympathy laugh. Craghorn sits patiently and quietly on the sofa, hands in his lap. His eyes keep flicking up, and his gaze lingers on something behind me. There's another entrance back there, which leads into the kitchen, and I feel a sensation of eyes on the back of my neck. A quick glance reveals nothing, and when I turn back around, Craghorn is again focused on his fingernails. The pace of his breathing has increased, but he's otherwise normal.

And, of course, I use the term "normal" loosely.

I tell Detective Thomas, "The other type of haunting is what we call an 'intelligent' haunt, and that's where the person or thing is self-aware enough to respond to questions or communicate outright. Like if I'm using a digital recorder and I ask, 'What's your name?' and upon review, I hear a response that says, 'Steve Pendragon.' And with all the research I've prepared beforehand, I know that a Steve Pendragon used to live in the location, then that's an intelligent haunt."

Without looking up, Craghorn mumbles quietly, "Episode three-oh-seven. Fort Lauderdale, October 2005."

"Wow, yeah. Exactly." It surprises me to hear that Craghorn knows the show so well.

Detective Thomas stands up and paces back and forth in front of the fireplace. "Sorry, I feel safer on my feet. So you said that a person or *thing* can be self-aware enough to communicate. What'd you mean by *thing*?"

I catch Craghorn looking over my shoulder again. Like a quarterback telegraphing a pass, his eyes follow something from left to right.

I have to look, too. I can't *not* look.

Again, there's nothing there, but damn if he's not freaking me out. I answer, "I could give you an entire history of the paranormal world, detective, from demons to subdemons, to angels, to sprites, to fairies, whatever, but my guess is, you'd only like to know what in the hell it was that you saw, right?"

He crosses his arms and waits.

"Dark, full-bodied being, clearly humanoid in shape and size, glowing red eyes? That's a top-tier demon, detective. What you saw, he's not riding the pine on any of Satan's teams; he's out on the infield playing. Front lines. The starting first baseman."

Detective Thomas snorts and shakes his head. "You're telling me I saw a *demon*?"

If he hadn't seen what he'd seen, right about now is the spot where he'd tell me that I'm a charlatan, that I'm a snake-oil salesman, and that I'm making all of this up for ratings in order to give people a thrill.

That's the thing, see—when it comes to ghosts, aliens, demons, or, hell, even Sasquatch and the Loch Ness Monster, it's easy to be a skeptic until you've actually witnessed it.

On one hand, I feel bad for the nonbelievers because they're missing out on so much. If they'd only open their minds, there's another world out there, so much more life to experience than breakfast cereal, sitcoms, and a comfortable recliner.

On the other, I feel even worse for the witnesses who are far fewer in number. They're the minority. Some have seen, and they know, and yet they hide, because they're afraid of the ridicule. They're afraid of losing their jobs or having their communities label them a freak or a weirdo.

Man, I get that. I've been there my whole life. It's not easy being an outcast. At least not until you head up the number-one paranormal show on the planet.

Then there are the brave souls who are willing to come forward and testify under the penalty of ridicule that they saw something. That's courage right there.

Detective Thomas is in this latter category, simply by calling me in, bringing me here, and telling this story, but he hasn't quite accepted that he saw what he saw.

Maybe it was my fault, his sarcastic snort just now. If I'd told him, yeah, that was nothing more than a plain-old, garden-variety ghost, he might have accepted it and moved on. However, by explaining that he witnessed something far worse, something made up of the blackest evil, a top-tier demon on Satan's council, well, I'm pretty sure I just blew his mind.

That's confirmed when he says, "I really don't know what to say to that, Mr. Ford. A demon. A demon?" He keeps repeating the word in various states of inflection, as if finding the proper way to get it out would make it more acceptable. It's only two syllables, yeah, but it's kind of amazing how many different ways he's able to pronounce it.

After roughly the eighth iteration, when he can't possibly squeeze any more inflection out of those two straightforward syllables that hold so much weight, apparently Craghorn can't take it anymore. He slings his hands up over his ears and screams, "Enough, enough, enough!" and stomps his feet on the ground like a child throwing a tantrum.

Detective Thomas freezes and turns to him. "Hey, now, ease up. I'm just trying to wrap my mind around—"

"Not you, idiot," Craghorn hisses angrily. "*He* won't shut up."

The temperature of the room drops another five degrees. I stand up and immediately turn around, searching the kitchen behind me where Craghorn's eyes had focused on something earlier. It's empty. I understand whom he means, but Detective Thomas is confused. "Who, Craghorn? Who won't shut up?"

Craghorn says in a childlike voice, "Him. There," and points.

I don't see anything. Neither does the detective because he asks, "Who are you talking about? It's just the three of us."

"No. You're wrong. Dead wrong."

I back up a step. Whatever Craghorn was pointing at is in my vicinity, and if we're definitely dealing with a "Tier One" in this house, like the filth that inhabited the Hopper home, then I should probably keep my distance. I'm not prepared for this, not in the slightest. I expected to come in here and have Detective Thomas tell me that he saw the ghost of Louisa Craghorn. I expected he'd tell me about a full-bodied apparition and that I'd do a couple of EVP sessions, ask Louisa who murdered her, and, I hope, dig up another clue for Thomas to go on.

Naively, I assumed that this would be a fairly quick one-and-done kind of moment. There's no wonder the detective was so hesitant to explain himself back at the station.

Craghorn says, "No, damn you. I will not."

"Dave," I say gently, trying to reach out to him. "Is it the demon? Do you see it?"

"He's here. He's with us now."

Detective Thomas whips his head left and right, looking for it. He retreats to a rocking chair in the corner, close to the light of the windows, and yanks his sidearm out of his shoulder holster. Even with the barrel aimed at the ceiling, I don't want this guy to get spooked and fire off a round, possibly hitting one of us in the process.

I tell him to put it away, that a bullet isn't going to stop this thing no matter what. The fact that his weapon, his shield, his security blanket, isn't going to stop what's in the room with us sends his bottom lip to quivering.

Nearly blubbering, he says, "Make it go away, Ford. You know how these things operate, right? Get it out of here."

"I wish it was that easy."

Craghorn is standing beside me now, whimpering and whining. The sounds coming out of his mouth aren't words—at least not English ones—and it takes me a moment to realize that he may be muttering in an ancient language, powerful words that died thousands of years ago. I've heard it before, but only a few times, and only in the presence of something like this.

Craghorn also attempts a pathetic escape. He stumbles and falls back onto the couch, trying to shove himself deeper and deeper into the cushions, pushing farther away from this invisible entity that's stalking him.

I can't believe that something this mighty hasn't manifested yet. Perhaps it's using the available energy to communicate with Craghorn.

Every inch of my skin prickles, and I feel the humming, vibrating sensation coursing through me. I feel weakened, as if it's stealing my energy. I'm dizzy, exhausted, like I haven't slept in days. My chest is heavy. I have an emotional anvil sitting on my heart.

"Ford?" Detective Thomas tries to get my attention. "What's going on? You okay?"

I've been in this situation before, hundreds of times, and normally I can handle this.

But when it rolls past, I know I've never encountered something as . . . as *strong* as this. Like a wave slinking toward the shore, the pressure, the sensation of death pushes by me.

Craghorn shoves his body away with a foot planted firmly on the hardwood floor, the other leg pathetically moving up and down, trying to gain a foothold and failing. He arches his back and turns his head sideways, whimpering, "No. No, please. Don't."

And then I watch as a handful of his shoulder-length hair is lifted and his head yanked to the side, pulling him from one side of the couch to the other.

I am goddamn terrified. Why? The smallest explanations often carry the most weight.

This is bad.

Very, very bad.

6

Mike Long is like a brother to me. Or he was until the night I went through with exposing Chelsea Hopper to that thing in the attic.

We built *Graveyard: Classified* up from a few piddling online videos years ago to the international powerhouse that it was before the network ripped it from primetime. We met in a junior-college film class, bonding over horror movies and the mutual adrenaline rush we got when we were trying to film our own in places where we didn't have permission. The night we sneaked into an abandoned mental hospital with six cheerleaders who were half-naked and drunk, was the last night we would ever work from a poorly written script.

When we captured that full-bodied apparition, a woman in a white nightgown, who seemed to be pleading with us to help her, that's all we needed to go back again and again, giving up on fictional stories and trying to capture real ones on camera.

We never saw her after that night. Perhaps it was enough for her to know that someone had received her message, and she passed blissfully on to the next phase of the afterlife. We, too, moved on to other decaying insane asylums and old factories, homes, churches, antique shops, and lighthouses. Anywhere that was supposedly haunted, we would ask permission and perform an investigation, then upload our videos online. Hundreds of thousands of followers would flock to them, and it wasn't long before a group of producers from The Paranormal Channel came calling, offering better equipment, an actual film crew, and contracts that promised more money than we had ever thought possible from a weekend hobby.

Mike and I, we were inseparable. He was my best man when I married Melanie from wardrobe. He made David Letterman and Ellen laugh. He was the straight man to my crazy, gung-ho attitude when it came to paranormal investigations.

We've only spoken once since the show was cancelled. His end of the conversation consisted of three words: "Go to hell."

If he sees my number on the caller ID, he might not pick up.

But, Jesus, I hope he does. After what I saw inside the Craghorn place, I don't just *want* his help, I *need* it. There's no one else in the world that I would trust with this level of evil.

Outside the house, it's 104 degrees here on the sidewalk, but I'm shivering. Detective Thomas paces back and forth, snorting like a dragon, mumbling empty, macho threats about going back inside because he never backs down from a fight. I notice he's not in a hurry to go back up the stairs.

Dave Craghorn sits on the bottom step, hunched over, cradling himself. There's a small patch of hair missing on the side of his head. I can see it from here.

My hand instinctively goes up to the back of my neck when I feel a burning sensation, but then I realize it's just the sun beating down. There's no demon out here clawing me. That's how it usually starts, though, with the scratches. You feel like a patch of your skin is on fire, it'll take on a subtle pink hue like it's a superficial burn, then the marks will gradually show up. I've had angry spirits claw me more times than I care to recall, but

I've never seen anything powerful enough to rip the hair right out of someone's head.

Well, that's not necessarily true. I can think of one other that was just as strong.

Two years ago. A faded pistachio house in Cleveland.

I stare at my phone, Mike's number is sitting there on the screen, almost as if it's pulsing, throbbing, alive and waiting on me to take the chance. I have to; Mike needs to see this. I press "Send" and hold the cell up to my ear, air caught in my lungs.

A warm breeze whips through the space between the homes to my right, pushes my hair to the side, yet offers no relief. With the temperature and humidity combined, it feels like a steaming column erupting from a kettle.

The phone rings and rings.

Detective Thomas paces. Craghorn hugs himself and rocks, muttering unintelligible words.

Finally, a voice on the other end of the line snarls, "What in the hell do you want?"

"Mike. Holy shit, thanks for picking up."

"I'm not interested, whatever it is."

"Wait. *Wait.* Don't hang up."

"In fact, I'm not even sure why I answered."

I don't believe this, not entirely. He saw my number. He could've dismissed it, deleted my inevitable voice mail sight unseen. No, he saw that it was me, and he knows I'd only call for something serious. The fact that he answered means there's a tiny bit of Mike that may have forgiven me. It's a start, at least.

"I need help, dude. I'm up against something righteous here. It's powerful. I could really use you."

He tries to stifle a laugh. "You're shitting me, right? Are you still flying around the country, feeding bullshit to whoever will listen to you? Who is it this time? Some backwoods, trailer-park sheriff in the middle of nowhere? That's what you're doing, isn't it? Consulting with law enforcement? Anybody that wants to cut you a check to hear the great Ford Atticus Ford tell them lies?"

Mike is lashing out, obviously, because he knows that none of what I do now, and what we did for over ten years together, is built on lies. Now, and in the past, I operate on solid evidence, tangible things that can't be debunked. That was the one thing I would never compromise on when *Graveyard: Classified* aired; we absolutely would *not* allow content or evidence that could easily be debunked by tricks of the light, corrupted ambient noise, or anything of that sort. It had to be inexplicable and legitimate evidence before it would air. We tossed out thousands of hours of video and audio evidence—much to the chagrin of our producers—because we didn't want to risk our reputations.

When a certain young assistant producer, Carla's original understudy, suggested we fake evidence to liven up the show, he barely had the sentence out of his mouth before I was on the phone with the CEO of The Paranormal Channel. The guy was gone the next day.

Point is, Mike knows I don't make this shit up. I tell him, "I'm with a client, yes, here in Virginia Beach."

"And you didn't call when you got into town? I'm so disappointed." The sarcasm drips so thickly, he could douse an entire stack of flapjacks.

I accepted the job with Detective Thomas for several reasons. I was intrigued by the information he presented. I wanted to help with a case that was getting some national attention, because, if I really self-analyze, I'm looking for some of that old, familiar glory and a chance at redemption. Maybe there'll be another show in my future.

And, honestly, I was drawn to the Hampton Roads area because Mike's primary residence, one of his many multimillion dollar homes, is just over an hour and a half south, down in Kitty Hawk, North Carolina. It sits on about an acre of shoreline, making the tourists just as jealous as they are curious. They filmed a movie there back in the '90s, some romantic comedy starring—hell, I can't remember who, but the guy was about thirty years too old for the young lady.

The day Detective Thomas called, I heard the words, "Virginia Beach," and immediately thought, "Hey, that's close to Mike."

So it goes.

Mike says, "I figured those big city boys would think twice about tarnishing their badges with the likes of—"

"Enough, okay? I get it. You hate me for ruining the show, you hate me for ignoring your advice, and you hate me for sending Chelsea into that attic. That's okay. That's fine. I can never apologize enough, and maybe I won't ever be able to redeem myself in your eyes, but let's put all that to the side for the moment. Please? I'm here in Portsmouth, and I've got a right-hander. Maybe the strongest one I've ever seen."

A "right-hander" is our slang for a Tier One demon that sits at the right hand of Satan. One of his go-to guys.

This grabs Mike's attention. He says, "Stronger than the Hopper house?"

"Possibly."

There's a hint of disbelief, along with a smile forming around his words as he says, "Wouldn't it be some shit if that thing was following *you*, and now it's, like, on steroids or something?"

"I . . . doubt that's the case."

The idea is both intriguing and frightening, and for a moment, I actually *do* entertain the thought. I've been through things that most people in the paranormal field haven't. Early on, mistakes were made. Mike and I both screwed up one too many times before we learned how to protect ourselves. We've been through minor possessions. Things followed us home. Our wives—Mike's current, my former—experienced too much, more than they deserved, in places that were supposed to be their private sanctuaries away from what Mike and I did publicly.

Then I remember . . . back at the old farmhouse, on the outskirts of Portland, the spirit had said Chelsea's name during the first investigation, and then the unbelievable things I caught when I was there with Ulie the other night.

I decide not to tell Mike about that yet. It'll cloud his judgment around whatever is going on here with Dave Craghorn, his house, his deceased wife, and Detective Thomas's investigation. And that's if I can talk him into helping.

I tell Mike, "Can't be. The right-hander in this house was here before they called me in. The detective I'm working with, and the homeowner, both of them, have seen a shadow figure in the past. Humanoid, about five feet tall, with glowing red eyes. That's why I'm here. This poor guy, Craghorn, he's living here all by himself and, no lie, during the interview earlier, I'm standing there in the living room with him and the detective. Neither of us can see what's going on, but Craghorn starts trying to get away from this thing—it never did manifest, but it creeps up on the guy and boom, his hair gets yanked hard enough to toss him like a dishtowel. Whole clump of it came right out of his head. Swear to God."

What Mike hears, out of all that, is this: "Did I hear you right? Did you say Craghorn?"

"Yeah. Why?"

"Oh God, Ford, you're not chasing the ambulances now, are you? That's the case with the mayor and the dead secretary? Showed up on the news again about six months ago?"

I exhale, feeling the thick, humid air escaping my lungs, then reach up and wipe a sopping layer of sweat off my forehead. "That's the one."

"And what angle are you working? Hoping to get the show back with a high profile case?"

"No, but it can't hurt." I hate to admit it openly, but there's no use in trying to hide my submotivations from Mike. He knows me too well.

"Ford, this is ridiculous."

"What happens in the future has no bearing on what's happening right now. This poor guy . . . Mike, he seriously needs our help. He needs some peace. From what I can see, he seems like he could be normal, but he also looks like an emaciated meth head just by trying to exist in his own home. I have no idea how a right-hander ties in with Craghorn's murdered wife, but I promised the detective I'd do whatever I could to help him with any possible leads.

"If this thing has been here all along, maybe it wasn't a murder. Maybe she *was* having an affair, the demon got into her head, and she threw herself off a bridge. Detective Thomas told me that her body showed signs of choking, but what if this thing got into her mind? We've seen it before—people trying to gouge out their own eyes, trying to choke themselves to death. Remember that one lady who tried to pull out her own tongue with a set of pliers? I need to get back in there. I need to ask it some questions, and I sure as hell would feel a lot better about doing it if you were here. And it doesn't have to be for me. Help the detective. Help Craghorn. That's what we used to be all about, right? At least back in the day? Whether they were alive or dead, we are always trying to give somebody *peace*."

There's a long spate of silence on the other end. For a moment, I think he might have hung up on me, and I delivered my best speech to dead air.

I'm about to ask if he's still on the line when I hear a resigned, "Text me the address. I'll be there in a couple of hours."

The Graveyard: Classified Paranormal Series

7

Mike arrives.

I meet him up the street, about half a block from the Craghorn place. Detective Thomas and Dave hang back, staring at the front door with wary glances, as if they're waiting on something to step outside and slither down the stairs.

Mike is dressed in his usual attire of khaki shorts, a T-shirt, and flip-flops. He used to be one of those heavier guys who wore shorts no matter what time of year it was, whether we were in the upper reaches of North Dakota in the middle of January, investigating a haunted ranch, or if we were down in Key West hunting Hemingway's ghost.

Used to be. I haven't seen him in two years—he was never much for Facebook or Twitter back when the show was on, choosing to keep his private life to himself—so I've missed out on the fact that he seems to have lost close to a hundred pounds. Seriously. I barely recognize the dude.

He looks healthy. Tanned. The sleeves of his T-shirt are straining against his biceps, and now, rather than stretching tight around a spare tire, the soft cotton pulls against his pecs.

"Mike," I say, unable to contain a smile, "look at you, man. You're—damn, I bet Toni *loves* this, huh?" I offer my hand to shake.

He ignores my compliment, and my hand, as he gives me one of two pelican cases, these large, black boxes that are like suitcases on steroids. They come with an interior made of forgiving foam for cushions, and over the years, they saved our sensitive equipment more times than Jesus saved souls. "Here, take this," he says, continuing his purposeful march down the sidewalk, flip-flops slapping sharply against his heels. Glancing back, he scrutinizes me and says, "Seems like we're going in opposite directions, chief. Put on a pound or twelve, huh? And what's that shit in your hair? It looks like somebody dipped a porcupine in black lard."

"Leave the gel out of this. I'm trying something new. Besides, I'm still better looking, no matter how many pounds you dropped."

"If you're desperate enough to base your confidence on the word of thirteen-year-old girls, don't let me stop you." He's not smiling. I don't think he's joking. "Anyway, I came to work. Somebody else can stroke your ego."

What I thought was a nice start, with cajoling and good-natured ribbing, might actually be Mike sniping at me, which I should've expected. I change the subject, hoping that by talking shop, he might lighten up. "You brought your own equipment?" I try to match his pace.

"Why wouldn't I? You never came prepared before, and I doubt you've changed much."

Mike's right, sort of, and I humbly admit it. "Preparation, probably not, but mentally, I'm nowhere near where I was two years ago. I can promise you that. Chelsea changed me."

"She changed your paycheck." A car honks down at the end of the block, like it's an exclamation mark at the end of his sentence.

"Come on now, that's not fair—"

"Ford, save it. I'm not here for you or to have that discussion again. I'm here to keep you from screwing up somebody else's life with another right-hander, got it?"

"I—fine." He knows I'm just as qualified as he is, even if I was unprepared with the technical stuff on occasion, but I was as equally adept at investigating—if not better—at least when it came to tapping into the emotional side of spirits and hauntings. This vitriol, it's about punishing me, and until he gets it out of his system, there's no use in trying to fight it or convince him otherwise.

When I was a kid, my grandmother used to tell me this old wives' tale about how if a snapping turtle latched on to you, it wouldn't let go until the sky thundered. That's how Mike is when he gets an idea into his head.

I think that maybe if we can get into the groove of an investigation, just like old times, he might soften a bit, and then I can have a real conversation with him.

We reach the detective and Craghorn, making quick work of the introductions. Mike is all business with the detective and soft and reassuring with the diminutive man who's been beaten down in his own home. Craghorn barely meets Mike's eyes, then he resumes the unrelenting study of his shoes.

Mike says to Detective Thomas, "Can you tell me what happened?"

"You mean now, or before?"

I start to explain, and Mike flashes me an annoyed look, holding up his palm. "I asked *him*."

"Okay. Whatever." I'd like to keep the peace here, so shutting up seems to be the best approach.

Mike listens intently as Detective Thomas goes through his story again, starting at the beginning with the original investigation as he did with me back at his desk. I've heard all of this already, and it's fresh in my mind, so I tune out their discussion. I should be paying attention. I should be listening for any more clues that I may not have picked up on earlier, but I can't help it. I'm gone, thinking about the glory days when Mike and I, and the rest of the gang, would arrive at a location and do our initial interviews with our clients.

There was always this excited hum in the air as the crew set up their equipment and we listened to the clients' stories, took notes, and crossed our fingers that, yeah, we could give them some closure, some answers, but at the same time, we were always hoping for another Holy Grail moment. Another full-bodied apparition caught on camera or a levitating dinner plate, something that couldn't be explained away by the doubters who accused us of trickery and crafty video editing.

It's hard to explain what an investigation is really like until you've done one, or several hundred, or a thousand.

Often, there's a lot of waiting, a lot of silence, a lot of waking Mike up at three in the morning when he's snoozing on a forgotten mattress. A lot of crossing your fingers that something will present itself. Sometimes it does, sometimes it doesn't. Just because a spirit doesn't provide some sort of evidence on the random Tuesday and Wednesday you're there investigating doesn't mean the place isn't haunted; it just means that the spirit world wasn't highly active that day.

Back when the show was chugging along and we were doing twenty-two episodes per season, there was a lot of down time while the crew set up and scouted angles. Mics were checked. Cameras and recorders had batteries replaced.

Oh, man, the batteries. Batteries upon batteries. We probably kept Duracell in business on our own.

With or without *Graveyard: Classified*, every investigation I've been on is a coin flip that's governed by chance, luck, and timing; life and the afterlife are bonded by those three things.

But when it all works out, and the investigation is a winner?

The Graveyard: Classified Paranormal Series

I'll take an espresso and two shots of adrenaline to go, please. Sign me up.

Things that go bump in the night have terrified people since we had to look out for nocturnal predators, praying that our campfires didn't burn out. No matter how many times you've flipped off the last switch and encased yourself in darkness, daring or begging something to show itself, there are times when you'll get spooked.

You'll hold your breath and feel every square inch of skin prickle. You'll want to scream. You'll want to run, but damn it, you have to fight that flight instinct because there's something out there, something from the other side, and it's dragging a sharp fingernail down a window, or some Civil War soldier is pleading for you to get a message to his children, or a shamed servant is apologizing for taking her own life. A piano plays by itself in another room. Footsteps echo across the wooden floor overhead when you *know* you're alone.

I've seen and heard so much. I've never faked even the tiniest of things, like a piece of dust on a camera lens. What do the hip kids say these days? Haters gonna hate, right?

Well, doubters gonna doubt.

As I daydream about past investigations, the good ol' days, my eyes drift around the neighborhood, inspecting the nearby homes.

Like I said, I normally don't pause to appreciate this stuff, but since Detective Thomas seems to be retelling his story starting with the book of Genesis, I have a couple of minutes. *In the beginning, God created demons and shitheels...*

Despite my typical reservations, the architecture here actually *is* pretty fantastic with a lot of stones and crenellations, high windows, and pure craftsmanship displayed in the front doors. These homes were built back when people took pride in their hard work. It's nothing like the homes in my neighborhood that are governed by a snippy HOA board: mow your grass to a quarter of an inch below standard; you have too many dandelions; you're not allowed to have a gnome in your flowerbed.

I swear an entire house popped up in a week around the corner from me. One day it was an empty lot, I left for an investigative trip to Lansing, Michigan, and when I got back, *boom*, house.

Anyway, if you didn't know what lurked inside his walls, Craghorn's place is beautiful and does the neighborhood justice. Minus the dying flowers and shrubs that haven't been tended to in God knows how long, minus the powerful demon controlling the interior, I'd love to call this place home.

"Ford!"

"Hmm?" I mumble, daydream interrupted.

Mike asks, "Did you see that?"

I clear my throat and cross my arms, making a decent attempt at looking like I was paying attention. "Yeah, it was up there, and, uh . . ."

"Second floor window. The curtain dropped back like somebody pulled away."

For the first time in an hour . . . no, longer, since he was attacked and we retreated to the safety of the sidewalk, Craghorn speaks a coherent sentence. He says, "That's where it likes to stay."

"It?" Mike asks. "You mean the . . ."

"Yeah. Him."

There's a layer of sharp acrimony in Craghorn's voice that I'm hearing for the first time. Perhaps he's recovering from earlier. Perhaps he feels emboldened now that the paranormal defense team is fully present.

"That was my wife's study. She used to paint in there." Craghorn clenches his jaw, the muscle rising and falling underneath loose skin. His mouth purses, his nose scrunches as he glares up at the window. I halfway expect him to make a fist and shake it like some old codger.

Mike is about to ask another question when Detective Thomas excuses himself and takes a phone call. We wait patiently while he listens to his caller, lifting his shoulders in a sorry-can't-help-it apology. Finally, he hangs up and tells us he has to go. "Wife was reminding me about my visit to the doc. Checking out the ticker today," he says, patting his chest. "After what happened in there, I feel like I should keep the appointment. Tell you what, Mr. Craghorn is in good hands here. You know what you're doing, and I'm pretty sure I'm not going back inside that goddamn place ever again. So, you do what you do, and then come meet me back at the station. That work for you guys?"

Craghorn's gaze flitters upward, looking as if he's slightly worried that the man with the gun is leaving, and I don't bother telling him that bullets would only tickle that thing inside his house.

I say to Detective Thomas, "We've got it all under control," then toss another subtle compliment at Mike. "He's the best at what he does, so if we're able to find anything for you, it'll be because he's here."

You catch more bees with honey.

The detective gives us a cordial salute and spins on his heels. He's down the sidewalk, around the corner with his step looking lighter, and gone before anyone else speaks again.

Craghorn is the first to say something. "Good thing for him."

"Why's that?" Mike asks.

"I can't repeat what the dark man inside said about the detective."

My lungs clench, and Mike flashes me a worried glance.

Maybe it's just coincidence—could be nothing at all—but it's so odd that he refers to it using the same words as Chelsea Hopper.

"*Don't let the dark man get me, okay?*"

I can see tremors of the past rippling across Mike's face. At first, I think he's reliving the moment with that little blonde angel bobbing down the hallway, excited to help and so thrilled to be with her new friends from TV. A thousand pounds of regret fill my stomach. I'm aching and anxious to get back to fighting for her retribution.

I think Mike is going to sympathize with me. He's going to tell Dave Craghorn that it'll be okay. We've fought things like this before, and we're going to get his life back. We're going to give his wife the everlasting rest she deserves. I think this, and I'm about to say something to Craghorn, but Mike's fist connects with my jaw, and I drop like my chute didn't open. I blink, trying to see around the sparkles dancing in my vision.

Before I can clear my head, there are rough hands on my shirt, yanking me up. Mike says, "You put him up to this, didn't you? The dark man? Really, Ford? Did you think I'd come running back for that?"

I taste blood. I try to tell him no, that I never said a word to Craghorn about Chelsea or the dark man, but I'm dizzy and confused. My words come out jumbled. I can make out the red hue in Mike's skin, the rage twisting his features, and then his forehead meets the bridge of my nose.

I succumb to the darkness.

8

I come to, and it takes me a second to realize that a few minutes have passed. I've been moved, and instead of lying on the searing sidewalk outside, knocked unconscious, I'm stretched out on Craghorn's couch. It's freezing in here.

I quickly sit up. A spark of fear shoots throughout my body—I'm inside, alone, where the dark man is—and then my eyesight swims just enough to send me back down, hand on my forehead and groaning. The coppery hint of blood remains on my tongue and I feel the dried, caked aftereffects of Mike's headbutt on my upper lip. My eyelids and nose are slightly puffy, and the bulge hinders my vision. When I drop my left arm, I feel an ice pack resting against my thigh.

At least they were a little considerate, and I hold the ice up to my face, wincing and hissing with the pain.

I wonder where Mike and Craghorn are, and it occurs to me that Mike might have been pissed enough to drop me off inside, alone, as a tasty, immobile sacrifice to whatever abomination inhabits this house. If that's the case, I picture myself tied to a railroad track with a locomotive bearing down on me, horn wailing, but there's no cowboy in sight coming to my rescue. There's no flying man in a cape, swooping down to sweep me away. No fireman with a ladder or a helicopter pilot with a dangling harness. You know, standard hero shit.

My mind does that sometimes, goes places. If you've spent enough time in silence, as I have, waiting on a sign from the afterlife or something to manifest, it's easy for your imagination to run unchecked. I should write books. I bet I could give Carter Kane a run for his money.

While I'm pondering my demise and picturing the dark man bearing down upon me, I hear voices in the distance, maybe down the hallway and upstairs, and I realize that it's Mike and Craghorn.

Thank God they haven't left me in here entirely alone.

It sounds like an informative discussion, but mostly it's Mike asking questions and Craghorn responding. He's such a hushed and beaten-down man, I can barely hear his replies.

Mike says, "That happened in here?" And seconds later, he follows up with, "That was only six months ago? When Detective Thomas came back? Interesting."

I make a concentrated effort to sit up, but slowly and cautiously, to give my throbbing face and woozy head a chance to catch up. One last groan, and I push myself to my feet.

You'd think I'd be used to things like this now, but there's a large mirror above the fireplace, and a peek at my own reflection spooks me. I chuckle at how ridiculous this is—the great and mighty ghost hunter scared of himself—but I wasn't expecting it to be there. Mike would probably say it's an improvement, because I really do look like Wile E. Coyote hit me in the face with a fat hammer from Acme. Blood is caked in tendrils around my mouth and crawls down my neck. Luckily I'm wearing a black T-shirt, my trademark, so you can't tell how thoroughly it's soaked, which is enough for it to pull against my skin when I turn away from the mirror. It's the same sensation you get when you pull a scab off too early.

The Graveyard: Classified Paranormal Series

***

I find them in the upstairs hallway. Craghorn is in his submissive stance, hands clasped at his belt buckle, hunched over like he's waiting to be reprimanded, examining his shoelaces.

At first, I think Mike is simply standing with his arms crossed as he surveys the photographs hanging on the walls, but upon closer inspection, I see that he's trying to warm himself. If the downstairs was cold, this is igloo territory up here. He sees me coming, drops his hands to his waist, and shakes his head. He tries to say something, but it comes out halting, like trying to start a car on a freezing day.

"It's okay," I tell him. "I probably deserved that."

Mike clears his throat. "Right," he says, then adds, "I'll buy you a beer later."

"Make it a steak and we're even."

He lifts a corner of his mouth in a genuine attempt at a smile. The steak thing, that's a running joke going back a few years, before the show was a hit, back when we were starving college students who would trade the promise of a high-dollar steak on bets and dares while we stole handfuls of coffee creamer from a convenience store just to have milk for cereal.

That's old history between us, and it's gratifying to see that he can't headbutt good memories in the face.

"You should call that detective," Mike says. He lifts a digital voice recorder and waggles it. "We need to do a full investigation. Not just an afternoon asking questions. There's no way we can properly comb this place and then meet him back at the office this evening with some answers."

I nod toward the recorder. "You catch something?"

"Class A. It's a strong one." Mike stares down at the display, breathing heavily through his nose, as he rewinds the recording to the proper timestamp.

"You think it's . . ." My words trail off.

Mike doesn't need me to finish my sentence. He knows. "Do I think it's the right-hander from the Hopper place?" He pinches his lips together, tilts his head from side to side, lifting his shoulders. "What're the odds, you know? I don't think it is. Tone is off, but then again, I was just explaining to Mr. Craghorn about how demonic entities can mimic other spirits, other animals. You know the drill. Anyway . . . honestly, I think the fact that he called it 'the dark man' was a one-in-a-million coincidence. Bad timing, whatever, and, unluckily for you, it was just the right set of words to light a fuse that I wanted lit for two years."

I chuckle. "If that's a disguised apology, I accept. What'd you catch?"

"Two voices, actually, and Mr. Craghorn, if you don't want to hear this again, it's fine if you step away."

Craghorn slowly lifts his head. "I'll be downstairs."

Mike waits until Craghorn is gone, head disappearing below the landing, footsteps whispering through the hallway, before he holds the digital voice recorder up and plays the audio file.

There's silence, followed by Mike's flip-flops slapping against his heels, and then comes the sound of a doorknob. The creaking hinges groan like they're right off a Hollywood movie. Mike's voice says lightly, "Mark time at 5:38, that was Mr. Craghorn opening his bedroom door."

Paranormal investigators tag our own noises and manmade sounds, marking the location on our recordings, so when we go back to review our tapes for evidence we don't get our hopes up if we're the cause of something going bump in the night.

Mike's voice again, saying, "The energy in here is overwhelming. It's dark . . . a dark energy. Jesus, I could cry right now."

Which is followed by Craghorn mumbling, "Welcome to my life."

I hear the floorboards screech with the weight of a step, and Mike marks the time on that one as well. Now that I conduct investigations on my own, I'll typically let some standard sounds go, rather than tagging a sniffle or something like that every few minutes. I've done this enough to recognize that my own footsteps on a creaky floor don't need to be marked. It's second nature at this point, but I get the feeling that Mike is being overly cautious, or perhaps he's skittish about hopping back on the bicycle again after a long absence.

Mike, the actual one in the hallway with me, says, "Listen. The first EVP is right here." There's more silence, with a hint of moving air in the background, and I recognize that it's Mike's anxious breathing. Something has spooked him. "Did you see that?" his voice asks. "That ball of light in the corner?"

Mike points at the recorder. "Right here."

I lean down, turn my ear closer, and hear, "*I'm sorry, love.*"

"Wow," I whisper.

"Keep listening."

The same voice, a female's, says, "*Make it go.*"

"Make it go?" I repeat.

"Yeah. That's it for those. Let me fast forward. This one comes through five minutes later."

It sounds like they're still in the bedroom. Mike again mentions the dark, suffocating energy. He feels dizzy, as if there's a buzzing between his ears. Craghorn coughs. "You good?" Mike's voice asks.

"It feels like . . ." Craghorn answers. "Feels like something is squeezing my throat. I have to get . . ."

And then the rest of his words are mumbled, because a deep, guttural voice barrels in over top of Craghorn and says, "*Guilty . . . bitch . . . is mine.*"

It's so harsh, so evil, that the words feel like rusted razor blades carving my skin, and I recoil. I feel a wetness on my upper lip and realize that my nose has resumed its bloody waterfall. Part of me thinks that's natural.

Part of me thinks it isn't.

"You're bleeding again," Mike says, with more concern in his voice than I would expect from someone who recently smashed my nose with his forehead.

I wipe my upper lip and study my slick fingertips.

This is a warning.

***

The three of us retreat to the front stoop. It's like climbing out of a freezer and stepping on the surface of the sun. The smell out here has changed. It's no longer that ever-present hint of coastal air. I think it's sulfur, or maybe it's my imagination. I could be projecting, feeling like it's trapped in my clothes. I'm trying awfully hard to convince myself that it's not, but the fact that Mike sniffs his T-shirt and grimaces is proof enough.

Craghorn again confirms that the female voice belonged to his wife, Louisa.

He hasn't fully emerged from the black, impenetrable fog that seems to be hanging around him. However, he seems slightly more willing to converse now that he's heard her voice.

Mike gently peppers Craghorn with questions, trying to coax more information out of him, while I excuse myself to call Detective Thomas. Mike is a skilled interviewer when it comes to pruning information from a flustered client, while I work best with the dead.

I move down the sidewalk until I find an acceptable level of shade, out of the direct heat, and it occurs to me that we're in a situation where "hot as hell" and "cold as hell" are *both* true and relevant. It's hotter than hell out here, and Dave Craghorn has been living inside the cold hell of his house for months.

Detective Thomas answers on the third ring. "Yeah?" He sounds agitated, but then again, that appears to be his normal state of existence. "You find anything?"

I explain what Mike caught on the audio recorder—the female voice and the demonic one—repeating it word for word. Then I add, "It's bigger than what we thought. We'd like to do a full night investigation, and as a matter of fact, I recommend it."

"What? Why? You caught Craghorn's wife apologizing, and this thing saying she was guilty. That tells me that the infidelity, the thing with the diary, it's spot on, so I should definitely be focusing on that as a motive."

"Yeah, but motive for who?"

"Craghorn, the mayor, some hired hitman."

"I don't get the sense that Craghorn is your guy."

"All due respect, Mr. Ford, but you can leave the detective work to me."

I tell him I understand, though I hold my tongue, choking down what I want to say. I get this more often than I'd like. These police departments call me in to aid in an investigation because they're stumped, I'll tell them what I learned, and sometimes they get attitude if they feel like I'm upstaging their authority and skill sets.

Sometimes it's merely pride that gets in the way, and I get that, I really do. I wouldn't want anyone making a guest appearance on *Graveyard: Classified* and telling me all about how I was screwing up a paranormal investigation as much as a detective wouldn't want anyone telling him he'd been chasing the wrong tail on a murder case.

However, there are times when I have to push back. I live with enough darkness on my conscience. It needs a little light now and then.

"Give us one night," I say. "There's more here than that."

"Look, Ford, that little hint is enough. I got what I needed."

"One night. Sundown to sunup. That's all I'm asking. Give us twelve, eighteen hours, max. Noon tomorrow."

I listen to him grunt in resignation. "It won't be on my dime. I'm sitting here getting my ass chewed for bringing you on in the first place."

I check my watch. It's three minutes to five. "Pro bono from now on. We can get you more. I know we can."

"Fine," he says. "I doubt any of this will be admissible in court, but if you come away with something solid, it'll help."

"You won't regret it."

We hang up, and I stand there feeling good about this. It's cliché, I know, but I feel like the band is back together. Well, minus all the lights, cameras, crew, and a catered service cart with a giant bowl of M&Ms and finger sandwiches. Just Mike and me, back into the breach. Old days come 'round again. History repeats itself.

A jogger trudges past me, her ponytail limp in the heat and humidity, much like the rest of her. She's cute and trim, and like a gawking fool, I'm standing there admiring her physique when I manage to tear my eyes away from her fantastic calves long enough to notice she's wearing one of the original *Graveyard: Classified* T-shirts, back from the first season when we had that cheesy font that looked like the letters were made out of tombstones.

It's a blatant reminder of the days when things were going well.

A good omen.

Right?

The Graveyard: Classified Paranormal Series

9

CHELSEA HOPPER
TWO YEARS AGO

A Very Special Live Halloween Episode

"*Enjoy Tiger Puffs, the cereal with bite!*"

The commercial ended with the large, orange cat giving a wink and a thumbs up. Off camera, Ambrosia the intern said, "You're on, Mr. Ford. Go live in four, three—"

In my head, I counted out "*Two, one,*" and then:

"Welcome back to those of you at home here in the US and the millions watching around the world. That's our one and only commercial break because we've just gotten word from our producers that we're absolutely shattering all sorts of viewership records tonight. The final numbers for our live *television* broadcast won't be in until later this week, but I can officially say that as of right now, we have over six point three *million* viewers tuned into our live-stream Internet broadcast on TheParanormalChannel.com. We can't thank our fans enough, and we certainly would not be where we are today without the Gravediggers. You're the best."

I walked down the hall of the Hopper house, my thick-soled boots clunking on the hardwood floors. The cameraman followed me, inching slowly forward.

"If you're just tuning in, we've been investigating the Hopper home, which you guys voted the Most Haunted House in America. So far, it's been wild. You heard those footsteps, you heard that faucet turn on by itself in the bathroom, and if you were paying attention, you probably noticed Mike's shirt being tugged when he was walking through the kitchen. Have another look."

A quick fifteen-second recap played on repeat three times, shown in the black-and-green light of our night-vision cameras. In the video, Mike walked across the linoleum floor, holding a digital voice recorder. He asked if the entity who made the footsteps, or turned on the faucet, would give him any further sign of his presence. Clear as could be, there was a visible tug on his collar, and it was strong enough to make Mike jump and accuse me of screwing with him, asking me why I did that, even though you could easily see that my hands were down at my sides.

It was such a great capture and we were positive that, indubitably, the doubters would be all over the Internet the next day proclaiming our heresy, trying to show how we could've pulled it off using filament line in an elaborate hoax. Whatever. It happened, *sans* shenanigans.

When the replay stopped and the cameras were on me once again, I'd taken a right turn into another hallway, where I now stood outside of little Chelsea Hopper's former bedroom. Directly above was a trap door that led to the attic, and Mike was stationed beside me with his hand on the dangling pull string. I could feel him seething, eyes boring into the side of my head. I wanted to tell him that it was too late, that he should just go with it and curse me afterward, and that I definitely regretted what we were about to do, but he should know better because we had a goddamn show to run with millions and millions of people watching.

"Ladies and gentlemen," I said, lowering my voice and pausing for dramatic effect, tenting my fingertips and holding them up to my lips, "what you're about to witness may not be suitable for young viewers."

It was tough. It really was.

Carla normally ran things from the production truck, but she was inside with us now, perhaps like a Roman emperor wanting to witness the gladiator carnage. She had this slightly psychotic, leering grin on her face, and for the briefest of moments, I thought about calling it off just to spite her.

But I didn't, because, holy shit, this was amazing television.

And I really, really *did* want to give Chelsea Hopper some tranquility in her life.

It was wrong, and I knew it, but both of those statements were true.

Ratings. Peace.

If Chelsea could beat that thing, if she could climb into the attic and face down her own personal demon and tell it to go to hell, she would come out a stronger person on the other side. That's what I was counting on.

Risky—so risky.

I paused too long, apparently, because over the cameraman's shoulder, Carla made a circular motion with her index finger, telling me to speed things up.

"Okay, here we go. You all know the story. Before our commercial break, we told you more about the Hoppers and the terror that reigned here during their time in this home. All the unimaginable horror, the torture they faced together while they tried to live their lives, but this entity in the attic," I said, angrily raising my voice, "what they called 'the dark man,' this *bastard* refused to let them live normally. We're here tonight to send this monster back to where it came from."

Carla nodded, touching the tip of her thumb and forefinger together, and if it was possible, her uncomfortable grin grew larger as she winked.

Behind me, and out of the camera's view, Mike whispered, "This is such bullshit."

I continued, "They say that the world corrupts innocence. We're all a fresh, clean canvas until life comes along and throws a smattering of paint on it like Jackson Pollock—just a crazy, wild, mishmash of experiences. That may be true, but what I like to believe is that innocence is a powerful weapon against evil. If evil has not yet corrupted a young mind, and if that young mind is given the power to face down malevolence and wickedness, then there is nothing more potent, nothing more capable of sending a demon back to hell."

I hardly believed a word of this, by the way, but it sounded pretty righteous.

However, strength, will, and determination *can* overcome the evil in our lives. And really, what's more determined than a child who hasn't yet learned to compromise?

"This is why we're trying an unprecedented tactic this evening. You all know what trigger objects are, especially if you've seen the show more than once. Trigger objects—"

The bedroom door to my right slammed shut with enough force to shake the walls and rumble the floor underneath my feet. I yelped in fear. My skin prickled.

Mike shouted, "Dude!" and moved closer to me.

The cameraman, Don, scampered away and our audience got a shaky view for a moment. Don was a professional, however, and it only took him a second to recover. Also, off camera, I'm sure those watching clearly heard Carla exclaiming, "What the fuck was that?"

Or the bleeped version of it. We were broadcasting on a five-second delay from the live feed and those audio guys out in the van had speedy fingers.

The amount of paranormal energy it took to slam that door so hard was staggering. Right then, it became completely clear that we were dealing with something significantly stronger than what any of us suspected, and again, I reconsidered sending Chelsea into the attic.

No. We *needed* to do it. We were making paranormal history. We needed it. She needed it.

Once I regained my breath, I held up a palm to the camera. "Wow. Let me just point out to you—quickly, if our cameraman, Don, will follow me here—that there are no open windows in the house, no fans, nothing that could have caused a draft to slam that door." I peeked in the master bedroom, then Chelsea's bedroom, then pointed to the window down at the end of the hallway, and had Don show the viewers that the bathroom window was also closed.

We were upstairs, and since it would take up too much valuable time, I had Mike reassure the audience that there were no open windows downstairs. "I closed them all myself," he said begrudgingly. At least he was playing along.

"That was pure, unadulterated paranormal energy, folks. All right, as I was saying—I'm just making sure that this door is propped open here—trigger objects are items we use to draw out spirits. If you'll remember from our episode in Tombstone, Arizona, we dressed up like outlaws and had a mock gunfight out in the street, shot blanks from our revolvers. That's a trigger *event* with trigger *objects*. Intelligent spirits can see us, they can interact, and it'll draw them out more if they're shown something familiar to them. That said, what we're about to do is unprecedented. Up here, directly above us in this very attic, resides one of the evilest, strongest demons we've ever encountered. We believe he—at least we *think* it's a he—has been torturing families who have attempted to live in this home for decades.

"Before the Hoppers, the Casons lived here. Before them, the Leyerzaphs, the Huttons, the Johnsons, all the way back to the 1850s when this home was built. Report after report after report, but none of them as terrifying as what the Hoppers had to endure. So what we're going to attempt is this: We're going to beat this thing with the white light of childhood innocence. We're going to send little Chelsea Hopper, who is only five years old, up into this attic. She's our trigger object. She's going to battle the demon that terrorized her for so long, and we're going to send it packing. We don't need a priest. We don't need holy water. We need unconditional love to battle the darkest rage."

I paused to take a breath. It was done. There would be no backing out.

As if he was reading my mind, Mike whispered, "Don't do this, Ford. I'm begging you."

I prayed that my mic didn't pick that up. We absolutely had to show solidarity. If we got cold feet, we'd be crucified throughout the Internet and the paranormal community. Our reputation, our credibility! Flush them like turds because we'd be a laughingstock if we lost our nerve during something so huge, right?

In my earpiece, another producer, Jack Hale, who was monitoring the feeds from the production truck, quietly said, "Holy fucking shit, Ford, we just passed eight million web viewers. Keep going. Knock this fucking thing out of the park."

Behind me, Mike said, "Ford?"

In front of me, Carla pinched her face into a point and shook her head, silently scolding him.

"Okay, let me remind you that this is live television," I said. "And here we go. Bring her up. Chelsea Hopper, ladies and gentlemen, our demon warrior."

Don panned the camera around to the stairwell, and the fans watching saw the same thing I did: a petite blonde child bouncing up the steps. It was hard to tell on screen, given the night-vision view, but she was wearing pink jeans with butterflies on the pockets, along with a white shirt bearing a rainbow-colored unicorn. Her shoes were the tiniest things, small enough to fit in a shirt pocket, and even in the pitch black of night, I could tell that she was smiling from ear to ear.

"Mr. Ford!" she said, darting down the hall toward me.

Damn it if my heart didn't turn into a mushy puddle, and I felt overpowering guilt, but the damage was already done. The boulder was picking up speed as it rolled down the hill. I squatted when she reached me and put my arm on her shoulder, turning her toward the camera. My hands were shaking.

Shy little Chelsea snickered and covered her mouth with her hands. She held them cupped together, almost like she was praying, and I wondered if she was old enough to understand the concept of God.

"Are you ready for this?" I asked. "Are you ready to go fight the—um, I mean, it's time to go beat up the bad guy, okay?"

I couldn't bring myself to say 'the dark man' because I knew she was afraid of him.

Chelsea seemed to retreat further into her hiding place behind her hands, then nodded in agreement.

"We're going to beat the bad guy together, okay? You remember what we talked about, and you'll be fine."

I stood up beside her.

Her head barely reached the middle of my thigh. She was so small.

That thing up in the attic was so strong.

I kept trying to convince myself that if she could face it down, the rest of her life would be a cakewalk. She'd be able to take on *anything*. I thought I believed it, but really, I just sounded desperate for my conscience to agree with me.

Mike slipped away like a ghost, out of the shot, leaving me to pull the cord. We'd been friends, partners, and brothers for years, and the look of disappointment on his face cut deeper than anything I could have imagined from him. It was sadness. Despair. Disbelief. I trusted Mike and his opinions. He had the right answers, always. Truth be told, I was the talent, he was the brains, and neither of us had a problem admitting it.

With my back to the camera, so that eight million people watching online and probably triple that watching on television at home couldn't see me, I mouthed the words *"I have to."* Maybe it was an apology. A poor one.

He looked away.

I pulled the cord, and then I told Chelsea, "I'll be right here. You'll be fine."

When I glanced back at the camera, I had no idea that the image would be captured and used for weeks. That single picture of my face, a helpful grin distorted into some vile sneer, would portray *me* as the demon.

And, really, who would I be to argue?

10

When I get back to Mike and Craghorn, the front door is wide open, and they're cautiously looking back inside the house.

Well, Mike is, while Craghorn stands off to the side with his arms wrapped around his body. I have to get right on top of them before I realize that Mike is whispering the Lord's Prayer, like he's a member of a SWAT team tossing a smoke grenade inside before he storms the drug czar's hideout.

I wanted to tell him about the jogger and her shirt, but it doesn't seem like the right time. I'll save it for when I need an extra dose of good karma. Or there's a chance it'll work against me if I remind him of the good ol' days.

Anyway, Mike doesn't hear me come up the steps, and Craghorn doesn't acknowledge my presence. These facts combined send Mike three inches off the ground when I tap on his shoulder and say, "What's going on?"

Once he lands and the shock has drained from his face, he punches my shoulder. "Asshole."

"We even now?"

"Even? For what?"

"Remember that old church in France, beginning of season four? You caught me napping on one of the pews, thought it might be funny to teach me a lesson?"

He nods. "One of our highest-rated episodes. Partly because a few million people watched you piss your pants."

"Hey, I dribbled. It wasn't a full stream."

I'm aware that this banter isn't appropriate in front of Craghorn, so I cut the jawing and ask Mike if they uncovered any more details while I was gone.

Craghorn says nothing, as expected, and Mike tells me, "He says the right-hander didn't show up until after that maid—what was her name?"

"Elaine," I answer.

"The right-hander showed up after Elaine found the diary. Louisa had it buried underneath a floorboard up on the second floor. So what I'm thinking is, that diary was hidden down there where nobody could find it, and all that negative energy was trapped. Yeah? Make sense? So she's up there one day cleaning, finds a loose floorboard, and being the nosy type, she decides to investigate. Pulls the diary out and boom, it's like the Ark of the Covenant in Indiana Jones when the Germans open it up. All that black energy comes surging out, and Mr. Right-Hander, maybe he's hanging around the area, looking for a fresh snack, and there you go, moth to a flame."

I have to agree with him. He makes a perfectly good case for it, and that's probably a conclusion I could've come to on my own had either the detective or Craghorn told me the diary had been buried, or that the demon had just shown up around the time the maid found it.

Pardon the pun, but the devil is in the details.

First off, spirits can get attached to objects, like something that a person had an emotional connection with when they were on this side of the graveyard soil. More than likely, Louisa Craghorn was dumping every ounce of sentiment into this diary, keeping tabs on everything she was doing with Mayor Gardner, yet she also had a tremendous amount of guilt about what she was doing to her poor husband. All that negativity was swarming around her, enveloping her body and mind, soaking into those pages.

Second, if something like that has been secured away, all of that blackness can stay contained until, you guessed it, someone disturbs it. Once it's unleashed, it's free game, and it usually results in a haunting from a spirit who's been at rest for years, decades even. We in the paranormal community see it a lot, especially when someone moves into an old house and begins remodeling.

Tear down some drywall in your grandma's old house and see what happens.

That's common. What's rare is something else, something otherworldly, being close enough to detect that fresh batch of energy. It would be like hanging out on your front porch, and a neighbor three houses down is frying bacon, and you have no qualms about traipsing right into his kitchen to feast on it.

This whole scenario is apt to be the reason we captured Louisa Craghorn's voice, and the voice of the uninvited guest in their home. Louisa is here, and she wants to apologize, but more important, I'd bet she wants forgiveness. Even still, if Craghorn says, "You're forgiven," that thing in there won't let her leave. It's feeding off of her. It's feeding off of the negative energy it's creating in Craghorn, or completely sapping what's left of the positive kind.

All of this goes through my head in a flash, and I'm immediately caught up with Mike's train of thought.

I tell them, "Totally makes sense. So here's where we move forward. I just talked to Detective Thomas, and Mr. Craghorn, if it's okay with you, and if Mike is up for it, I think we'd like to perform a full investigation. I know we captured your wife's voice, and I know we heard that evil bastard in there, but I think we can squeeze more out of it. I think we can get you some real answers."

A flicker of excitement flashes across Mike's face. Then he tries, and fails, to hide it. That's all I needed to see. The dangling carrot did its job.

Fun fact: Mike actually hates carrots.

Craghorn lifts his eyes to meet mine, but nothing else comes with it, almost as if he's glowering at me from underneath his brow. His voice is quiet, though, when he asks, "What're you hoping to find?"

"More evidence. I let the detective know about what we caught in those EVPs—your wife's voice offering an apology, that right-hander saying she was guilty. Although it's not likely admissible, and what I do so rarely is, he feels like it still gives him enough to go on. Enough to continue pursuing the murder angle."

"Hang on," Mike says. "Just because she said 'I'm sorry' doesn't mean she was murdered. He's reaching."

"Yes and no. 'I'm sorry' could be an apology for anything. But he's going on the assumption that she's apologizing for the very reason we're here—the diary, the infidelity. And if it's a true thing, then it's enough of a clue for him to keep looking. So if you couple 'I'm sorry' with the right-hander calling her guilty, it's solid."

"Ford, you and I both know demons like that, especially the powerful ones. They'll use any form of trickery and deception they can to fuck with mortals."

"Exactly, which is why we need to investigate further." I turn to Craghorn and put my hand on his shoulder. He flinches as if the act delivers a small shock. I gently squeeze fragile bones. "My hope is that we can wrangle that demon into a corner long enough to ask your wife's spirit some questions. If we can make contact and get her to communicate clearly, she may be able to tell us who murdered her."

"I would like that," Craghorn says.

There's a tiny bell ringing way deep down in my psyche. Something is trying to get my attention, a gut sensation about this beaten-down man, and I can't place what it might be.

I leave my hand on Craghorn's shoulder a second too long. He looks down at it, then at me. He's so flat and expressionless.

And then it hits me—it feels like he's hiding information, and I make a mental note to ask Mike about this later.

It's strange, the way he's acting—so emotionless—but he's also had a top-tier demon sucking every ounce of vigor and life out of him for the past six months. Could be that the poor dude's tired.

"Mike?" I say. "You're in, right?"

He hesitates long enough to act like he's thinking it over, and then says yeah, but he'll have to call Toni and let her know he won't be home for supper. I can imagine how that conversation will go, considering the fact that *I'm* involved, and it won't be pretty. My guess is, he'll spend ten minutes trying to convince her that he's here to help Mr. Craghorn, and that I can go to hell after this is done, and it's only one investigation with me. She could use a girls' night out, right? He'll tell her all of this, but if I know Mike, and I do, he's quietly wiggling his excited bottom like Ulie staring down a treat.

Ulie. *Shit*. I'll need to call Melanie from wardrobe and check in on him. I told her I'd be back by midnight tonight. There's no way that's happening now. So it looks like I might need to do a little begging, too. She's not my biggest fan, if I haven't made that clear, but she tolerates my existence when I ask for help.

Her heart is bigger than her disgust.

When Mike leaves to call his wife, I'm left standing on the stoop with Craghorn. I don't want to pepper the guy with even more questions, especially after the detective and Mike have bombarded him, but until we get a chance to compare notes, it's a necessity.

But first I say, "We won't be bringing you in tonight, okay? This will strictly be just me and Mike."

Why? Because there's no way in hell I'm making the mistake of using someone who might be susceptible to a demonic entity as bait. Not again. I learned my lesson with Chelsea Hopper, and I'm still trying to atone for that.

I add, "You got somewhere to stay? Friends with an extra bedroom?"

"Friends," he replies, as if they're something he remembers from another life. "No. Not really. None that I've seen in years."

"Family in town?"

He shakes his head. "Dead or a thousand miles away."

"Okay, no big deal." I pull my wallet from my back pocket and fish out a couple of hundred dollar bills. "I'm staying at the Seaside down at the oceanfront. They know me there. Just ask for Delane at the front desk, tell her I sent you, and then book an oceanfront room. You mention me, she'll probably comp you a nice dinner in the restaurant. Go relax, Dave. Get away from this place for a while. You could use a recharge, yeah?"

There's no need to mention the fact that Delane is one of many reasons why Melanie from wardrobe is no longer Mrs. Ford Atticus Ford.

Craghorn's hand advances and retreats toward the bills, as if he's gingerly waiting on them to bite his fingertips, and then he takes them, folds them in half, and stuffs them in a pocket.

But not before I notice the scars. No wonder he's kept his hands in his pockets this whole time.

"Whoa, let me see."

"See what?"

"Your right hand."

"I . . . it's nothing."

He shows me anyway. It's mottled pink with raised flesh, scratch upon scratch.

I grit my teeth and wince. Some of them look fresh. Others have been there awhile. You would think that you couldn't get that many scars across the back of a single hand, but they're thin lines, crosshatched, like someone has been gouging him with a stickpin. I picture the razor-sharp point of a demonic claw, slowly dragging along, splitting flesh. One single, screeching nail on a chalkboard made of skin.

I grab the stretchy jacket fabric around his wrist and pull the sleeve up to his elbow. My heart sinks. This poor man. "Oh, buddy," I say, mimicking my mother when I got hurt as a child.

Craghorn's entire arm is covered in scratches, some new, some months old, and I don't have to ask about the rest of his frail body. I can see it in my mind already. I'm sure he's covered head to toe in claw marks. I doubt there's much skin left that isn't. He's not wearing a jacket and slacks in 104-degree heat because it's cold inside his house; he's wearing them because this goddamn thing has used him as a canvas.

"Get out of here," I say. "You leave, and don't you ever come back. We'll handle this."

11

Craghorn leaves, but not without protesting as much as he can muster, and I call Melanie from wardrobe to check on Ulie. She's not pleased that I've inconvenienced her yet again, but says she's okay with it, because of this: "Ulie is just the cutest wutest puppy wuppy in the whole wide world. Yes, he is! Who's the cutest puppy?"

The conversation stopped being directed at me about two minutes ago.

I say my goodbyes to the cutest puppy in the whole wide world and promise her that it'll only be one more night. She knows me, and she knows I can't keep that promise when I'm heavily involved in a case, and says as much.

"It's fine, Ford," she adds. "He's in puppy heaven. Doesn't even know you're gone."

Ouch. That stings, but I know that she's not really referencing Ulie. I'm sure his feelings are the conduit for what she's trying to tell me.

"Thanks, Mel," I say. "I'll get back as soon as I can."

"Any word on Chelsea's story?"

She knows that any moment I'm not working for The Man—like, literally, the cops, government agents—I spend my time trying to find, and destroy, the thing that hurt that little girl. "I went back out to that farmhouse right before I came to Virginia."

"Any luck?"

"Helluva lot better than last time. Listen, Mike's coming. I'll tell you about it when I come to pick up Ulie. It's good. Big time. Could help a lot if I ever get a damn chance to follow up on it."

"Wait, hang on. Did you say Mike? As in, Mike *Long*?"

"Yeah."

"One sec, let me check the news."

"For what?"

"I didn't hear anything about the world ending."

"Funny. Oh, hardy har, hardy har."

"He's actually there. With you. On a job," she says, not like it's a question, but as a statement of absolute disbelief regarding a true fact.

"He lives down in Kitty Hawk, remember? And *this*, Jesus, Mel, this is *big*. Whatever's in this house, it's as bad as that right-hander that got Chelsea. Maybe even stronger." I almost tell her about the marks all over Craghorn's body, but I change my mind. I don't want her to worry about me. You know, since I'm foolishly thinking she'll care. "I *need* Mike's help. Seriously. So I called, and amazingly enough, he came."

I can hear her sigh. "For only the second time, the almighty Ford Atticus Ford has met something he can't tame." I can't tell if she's talking about the demon, or herself. That's a long story for another chapter. I'm still hunting the ghosts of our marriage. Maybe they can tell me what went wrong. Maybe they can give me answers.

Not about what happened, really, because I know what I did.

About why I let someone like her go.

I'd like to ask them what I was thinking, because I have no clue.

"Yeah," I say. It's the only thing that makes sense.

"Tell Mike I said hi and to behave himself."

"Apparently he's off the sauce. I don't think we'll have to worry about that too much."

"I meant for him not to kill you tonight. He wouldn't last long in prison."

"Jokes galore today, huh?"

"It's a necessary evil around you, my friend. Okay, Ford. Call me when you get into town. Ulie misses you."

And for about half a second, for the teeniest, tiniest moment, I hope that this statement might not be about the dog, either.

I hang up. It's not and never will be. I done screwed up good.

Thunder grumbles in the distance. It would be nice if a rain shower came through and cooled things down a bit, but most likely what'll happen is, it'll rain for five minutes, just enough to soak this concrete jungle. And here, this close to the ocean with the humidity sitting at about 7,000 percent, it'll do nothing more than turn all of Hampton Roads into a suffocating sauna.

I'm almost looking forward to the freezing air inside the Craghorn compound.

But not really, considering the thing causing it might finally commit me to an insane asylum.

I turn my eyes away from the dark clouds shouldering out the blue sky on the horizon and see Mike walking toward me. His expression is glum. He looks like he went a few rounds with Tyson and finally managed to crawl off the mat long after the match ended.

"Didn't go over so well, huh?" I ask.

"Well, I got permission, but if you ask me, there was another right-hander on the other end of that line. She was *not* happy."

"Not my biggest fan anymore?"

He chuckles and shakes his head. "As if she ever was."

"Good point."

"She'll never forgive you for Chelsea."

"Her and about forty million people." I let that simmer a moment. Then I ask him, "Have you?"

"Forgiven you?"

"Yeah."

"What do you think?"

His tone suggests I already know the answer. I do, but it was worth a shot, regardless.

I have to wipe the layer of sweat from my forehead. It's now mixed with hair gel that seems to be melting off my damn head and leaves my hand gooey. I fling away the droplets, and the remainder gets swiped down my pants leg. Pretty sure that my trademark black from head-to-toe outfit was the worst idea imaginable in this heat. Right about now, I'm praying that storm in the distance makes its way here. I'd love to have about five minutes of relief before we go tackle this beast.

I ask Mike if Craghorn showed him any of his scars earlier.

"Not until I asked. He wanted to show me how the doorbell would ring by itself at all hours of the night. Caught me looking at the scars on his hands, and I made him show me what else had been done to him. I wanted to ask you about it because something felt weird."

I pantomime pulling a sleeve back. "He showed you, right? Whole arm was covered, both sides."

"Not just his arms. Nearly everything."

"Yeah? I thought his entire body would be covered."

"What're we gonna do about him?"

"He's already gone." I point my chin east, in the direction of the ocean, and tell Mike that I sent Craghorn away. "Gave him money for a night's stay at the Seaside—"

"Delane still there?"

"Yeah, but that's not—forget it. Doesn't matter."

"So what's he doing after we're finished? What happens if we can't get rid of this right-hander on our own? It'll take a while to convince the Catholics to come down for an exorcism, and, even then, there's no guarantee. He *can't* come back here. Does he have family? Friends?"

"We already went over all that, and no, he doesn't. I'll figure something out."

I've been known to help out a client on occasion if I'm moved enough by their story, but rarely do I commit myself this deeply. Mike and I made a lot of money in sponsorships and advertisements for The Paranormal Channel, and, in turn, we were extremely well compensated for it. Truthfully, I wouldn't ever have to work again if I chose not to, but I have questions that remain and a little girl to avenge.

What I'm trying to say is, I have plenty of offshore accounts and investments that I can tap into. If Dave Craghorn needs a new place to live, I can afford to set him up until he gets rid of the deep shadows that are sucking away the light in his life. Nobody deserves that.

Mike says, "You know, I don't get you, Ford. I'm not sure I ever did or ever will."

"How so?"

"I get what you're saying. I know exactly what you're talking about. You'll buy that guy a freakin' house on the oceanfront if it means taking care of him. You got a good heart, but damn if it ain't tainted black once in a while."

"You mean Melanie? Cheating?"

"That's part of it, yeah. How many were there? Ten? Fifteen?"

"Six," I admit, angling the word out in a tone that suggests, 'Hey, it wasn't *that* bad.'

"One is all it takes. Anyway," he says, checking the sky as thunder barrels through, "it's more than just screwing up with Melanie. The greed, the motivation, stepping all over people on our way to the top, sending Chelsea into—never mind. This ain't about her. It's about—"

"It's *always* been about her. At least since TPC yanked the show."

"Let me finish," Mike says. A sprinkle of rain splats against my cheek. "What I'm trying to say is, it will never make any goddamn sense to me how you can buy some poor soul a house with your own money, or cut a check for a couple mil' to some kid's charity, and then you turn right around and grind something into hamburger if you think it'll get you somewhere. I don't *get* it. I don't know how you live with yourself, and I don't know what motivates you to pay attention to the angel on your shoulder one day, and the devil the next."

Mike is right. He's always right. But I'm not ready to admit it.

Plus, I don't know what the answer is either—faulty wiring, perhaps.

It's funny how this is the most he's ever opened up to me, especially on the back of a two-year separation. It sounds as if he's been practicing this for a while, and no matter how much he says he's only here to help Craghorn, I feel like he was looking for an opportunity to get this little speech off his chest. Maybe Toni got tired of listening to him recite it in front of a mirror.

No, Ford, be nice. Could be a distant attempt at forgiveness.

But, given a second to think about it, maybe I shouldn't get that confused with pity.

Whatever. I'm glad to have him back.

I spend too much time analyzing things these days.

Best to let this discussion go to voice mail.

I slap Mike on the back, heartily, like old pals, and say, "Okay then. Nice chat. Now let's go hunt some fucking ghosts."

***

Mike and I go through our standard routine, and it's fluid, like we never hopped off the bicycle. He's wax on; I'm wax off. Easy as it ever was. He runs a baseline EMF check to see if there are any unnatural electromagnetic spikes that might cause a sensation of being watched and things of that nature. You get too much EMF humming around your body and brain, there's a good possibility that it can cause visual distortions, even hallucinations. Some people are more sensitive than others, and that's the way it is. No rhyme or reason.

We had a janitor in Minnesota one time who was working around enough EMF juice to fry an egg. He never noticed. But then, there was a woman in Northern California who had a minimal spike in her laundry room whenever she turned on the washing machine. She would faint from the EMF buzzing around her and claim that whole hordes of angry spirits were trying to have an orgy with her. Fun stuff.

But, on the other hand, a hungry spirit can also soak up this EMF energy and use it to communicate. We even have what we call an "EMF Pump" that we'll deploy sometimes in an attempt to supercharge the atmosphere. Neither Mike nor I have one with us at the moment, but given the strength of this razor-clawed entity that's already here, I doubt we'll need it.

It won't be fully dark for at least another three hours, so it's beneficial to us to get all of the standard objectives out of the way while we can still see.

By the time Mike finishes the routine EMF scope downstairs and comes up empty, I already have three of his "spotcams" situated in assorted positions. Various paranormal groups have their pet terms for what they call these stationary filming units, but they're really just digital cameras on tripods that are set to record in night vision from a static location. One spot all night, thus, the *spot*cam.

We even had a group of die-hard *Graveyard: Classified* fans who dubbed themselves the "spotcamgirls." The pictures they sent to our e-mail address at The Paranormal Channel headquarters would make a porn star blush, much less the unfortunate intern who answered all of our mail for minimum wage.

Maybe he didn't mind so much.

Glory days, indeed.

"Looks like you've got them in good locations," Mike says.

"Yeah, the one there in the eastern corner picks up the entire living room where Craghorn was attacked earlier today, plus that entrance down into the kitchen where he was watching something while I talked to the detective." I move over to the next one and wave down the hallway. "This one will capture anything along this whole corridor—living room, kitchen, storage closet off in the peripheral with a direct line of sight down to the back door. It's all covered. Then the third one over here is set up in the top corner of the stairwell, looking up at where Craghorn told you he hears footsteps all night long, and then right over to the entrance. It's all set up like a funnel down here, herding everything in front of a camera."

Damn, that felt good. There for a minute, I was totally in the zone with Don the cameraman behind me and Charlie Chocolate Chip, the sound guy, standing off to the side and holding a small boom mic over my head, while I explained to the fans and casual viewers how we were setting up to conduct the investigation. Back a couple of years ago, I would've nailed the whole thing on the first take.

"Ford?" Mike says, bringing me out of the revelry in my mind.

"Huh?"

"You got a little gleam in your eye. Right there in the corner."

"Sorry. Reminiscing."

"Doesn't change anything, but I felt it, too. Did you ever think about—*Jesus Christ*"

We duck, throwing our heads down and to the side as a decorative ceramic plate hurtles past our heads.

Bewildered, mouth agape, Mike straightens up and asks, "Where in the hell did that come from?"

I look behind us. The plate lies on the hardwood floor, smashed to pieces against the grandfather clock that's been dead for decades, according to Craghorn. "That looks like the Elvis plate," I tell him. "One of those commemorative ones. It used to be in the kitchen, hanging beside the refrigerator. I noticed it because my mom used to have the same one."

In the silence between our breathing, my ear picks up an intruding sound.

It's a distant noise, the staccato rhythm of slow-stepping hooves.

Clop, clop.

Clop, clop.

I picture the demon walking down the hall behind me. I strain to listen for the hooves. The hair on my arms stands at attention. The pressing pain in my bladder builds.

Then I realize the sound isn't coming from far away. It's right beside me.

It's the dead clock ticking.

Now *that* is an omen.

The Graveyard: Classified Paranormal Series

12

We're standing up on the second floor, at the head of the stairs, looking back down toward the front entryway where the decorative plate lies in ruins. We left it alone as a small symbol of defiance, just enough to flip the bird at the right-hander to let him, or her, or it, know that we weren't going to bend to its will.

You break something and *we* clean it up?

As if.

Well, I mean, not until the investigation is over. We won't really leave a mess for Craghorn *if* he ever comes home. God, I hope he won't. I hope he listens to what I said and stays far, far away from this place.

Mike holds a thermal imaging camera, and what this thing does is, it takes all of the ambient heat in the room and projects it as an image on a small screen. All the warm stuff is displayed in reds, pinks, oranges, and yellows. Imagine the stages of a sunset; that's what the room temperature heat looks like, more or less. Now, a spiritual presence is typically cold because it's sucking energy out of the atmosphere in order to manifest, so if you're looking at the screen and you see a dark mass, or figure, whatever, as it's walking across the room, there's a damn good chance you've got company.

I wait with my arms crossed, patiently and silently. "Anything?"

Mike breathes heavily through his nose. He's always done that. That's a sound I haven't heard in a long time. It's like going home again.

He answers, "Nothing. But it's already so cold in here that it would almost be hard to tell the difference."

"Would it help to switch it over to black and white?"

Same concept, only instead of a rainbow differentiating heat discrepancies, you have a monochromatic representation. It has its uses, but I prefer all the pretty colors.

He flips a switch, turns a couple of dials and, yeah, lots of black. That doesn't do much for us.

"Should we move on?"

"Five more minutes. I want to see if that thing is stalking us."

In all honesty, we sort of *retreated* up to the second floor. That's not something I'm fond of admitting but when you have a right-hander powerful enough to sling breakable things at your head, it might be a good idea to get out of the way.

Technically, we could classify it as poltergeist activity. However, it's not like there are a bunch of cabinet doors flying open and dead-battery toys dancing around the room. This demon is strong enough, and focused enough, and intuitive enough, to lift one single object—an object that caught my attention earlier in the day—and sling it over thirty-five feet.

That's not just an explosion of paranormal energy.

That's *intent*.

Mike inhales and exhales; the tempo of his body rocks like a persistent metronome. I want to be hunting for this thing, calling it out, telling it to come fight us, but it's good to ease into an investigation like this. We have all night, and it feels like we're getting back into our groove. Mike was always the one who focused more on the technical side of the investigation. Devices, gadgets, cameras, you name it, we tried it.

Back in the day, and it looks to be shaping up the same way, he was James Bond and I was Oprah.

You know, gadgets versus emotion. He's pushing buttons, tweaking dials, and I'm riling up the crowd: You get a demonic possession! You get a demonic possession! *You* get a demonic possession! *Everybody* gets a demonic possession!

"Ford?"

"What?"

"Did you hear that?"

"No? Maybe?"

Mike hasn't peeled his eyes away from the thermal imager screen yet, but he's clearly focused on something as he lifts an arm and points over his back, which is also to my rear. I hate to be sneaked up on. Frazzles me, waiting on something to pounce.

One thing I never understood was how our cameramen, Don in particular, could stand there with a camera focused on Mike and me while we were freaking out about something happening behind them. They were brave, man. Never flinching, never wavering—it was always about the shot, capturing our reactions. I argued with the producers for over a decade that our fans wanted to see what we were looking at. They didn't want to see *us* having an absolute shit-fit when a shadow figure darted across an empty gymnasium. The spirits were the real show, not us, but the producers, Carla in particular, didn't see it that way.

I spin around and take a couple of steps to put my back closer to the wall. "What was it?"

"Sounded like a voice. Couldn't tell from where. Female, probably, and I'd bet your beach house in the Hamptons that it's Louisa again." He finally looks over at me and drops the thermal imaging camera to his side. "I got nothing downstairs. Whatever it was ain't there anymore. Should we go check out the voice?"

"Yeah. And the Hamptons house is gone, by the way. Melanie from wardrobe got it in the divorce; turned right around and sold the damn thing for about nine million."

Mike puts his hands on his hips, shakes his head like a disappointed father.

"What?"

He hooks a thumb down toward the far bedroom and starts walking. "Did you ever think that maybe one of the *other* reasons she left you, aside from cheating on her six fucking times, was because you couldn't take the relationship seriously?"

Defiant, I say, "What's that supposed to mean? Of course I took it seriously. Kinda."

"Dude, you never stopped calling your *wife* 'Melanie from wardrobe.'"

"Not to her face." But, again, he has a point. "That was habit, nothing more. That's who she was for six years before we started dating."

"And then, things changed. You didn't respect her."

"This is *not* a discussion I feel like having, okay? We're here to help Craghorn, not dissect my failed marriage. I'm not on Oprah."

"What?"

"Forget it."

As we stand in front of the bedroom door, Mike gives me a sharp look and says, "She's a good girl, Ford. You ruined it. Just like you managed to ruin everything else."

It stings to hear it, out loud, *again*, but I'm not going to argue with him. One, I don't feel like it and two, I have no counterpoint. I open my mouth, and I'm about to tell him to leave my personal life out of the hunt when we both hear it.

A soft moaning comes from the second guest bedroom at our backs. We turn, ready and guarded, cocking our heads, listening intently, glancing at each other sideways. It's definitely female, and it does indeed have the same tone and pitch as what

Mike caught on his digital recorder earlier. He lifts a finger to his lips, gently taps out a shush, hands me the thermal imager, and then reaches into his back pocket to pull out his GS-5000, which is the big brother to the BR-4000 I accidentally left at home. This thing is the Cadillac of digital voice recorders. Real time audio playback so you can ask questions while you record and hear any responses. If you do happen to catch something, you can skip back and listen to it while the secondary mic continues ahead. It's a brilliant device.

He lifts it, presses the button with the red circle on it, and pantomimes instructions. He's going to push open the door while I use the thermal imager to immediately capture what's in the room. I feel a bit like we're a couple of real badge-carrying detectives ourselves, and we're about to bust in on a most-wanted criminal snorting coke out of a hooker's butt crack.

I spend a lot of time in hotels. Maybe I watch too much television.

Mike lifts his hand, reaches for the door, and pauses. Frozen in place, he says, "Whoa, hang on," and then—"*Hungh!*"

He flies into me, sideways, and we both stumble to our left and land hard. My back crashes into a weakly constructed, triple-drawer console table, and the thing explodes under my weight, sending two picture frames and a decorative jewelry box onto my head and chest.

Mike lands off-kilter, holding his GS-5000 up high to keep from smashing it, and cracks his head against the hardwood floor.

I fling bits of splintered table and an empty drawer off me and climb to my knees, clambering over to Mike. "Holy shit. What happened? You okay?" I'm whipping my head around, trying, and failing, to see if another ambush is coming.

Instead of answering, Mike pushes himself up and crab walks back to the wall. We both know who did it—the question is where did it go? Are we still in danger?

I ask him again if he's okay, if he's hurt, either from falling or from the attack, and once he's satisfied that he's not going to get another beating, he tells me everything's fine, to back off a second.

"Okay, but just—"

"I'm good, Ford," he insists. "God, that was intense. I just need a minute. *Please.*"

I sit on my haunches and watch him, checking for anything out of the ordinary. Unusual anger, confusion, a feeling of immediate dread. You know, head-spinning, pea-soup-spitting type stuff. With a *blitzkrieg* that powerful, I'm worried that the right-hander attacked, invaded, and then put up a set of nice linen curtains in its new home, 123 Mike Long Street.

He understands what I'm doing, too, because he holds a palm up to me and says, "Just chill, man. I don't feel anything."

"Promise?"

"Yeah. It's not like that time in Miami."

Some people might go to Miami and come home with a sunburn or an STD. Mike went down for a solo investigation while I was on my honeymoon with Melanie from wardrobe—sorry, *Melanie*—and came home with a stowaway. He got careless, didn't protect himself going in or coming out, warning the entities that he was *not* a vessel, and it took days of prayer with one of the big guns from the Vatican and three Native American shamans to get his body, mind, and home clear again. Toni wasn't too happy about that, and, somehow, per standard operating procedure, she managed to find a way to blame me. Melanie and I were on a rinky-dink motorbike in the jungles of Vietnam when it happened, but, yeah, it was my fault. Thanks, Toni.

I remind him how much that experience sucked and make him promise to tell me if he feels anything out of the ordinary over the next few hours. I add, "You know the drill, Mike. Depression, murderous ideas."

He rubs the back of his head where it hit the floor and checks for blood on his fingertips. Hand clean, he says, "You mean murderous ideas directed toward you?"

"Yeah."

"That's not out of the ordinary, Ford. That's a Tuesday."

I laugh. Mike laughs.

And for a moment, it's good. That would've been a prime capture for the show. A speck of levity to break the ungodly tension right before a commercial break.

Your sheets will be as white as ghosts with new clothesline-scented Sparkle Clean.

While I'm picturing that kid in the red T-shirt and gray jeans as he runs around with the blanket on his head—acting like a ghost, as expected—Mike hums a few bars of the commercial's theme song.

Yeah. We're back. I'd like to high-five him, but it's slightly creepy how connected we are.

Are? Were? I'm not sure where we stand.

He pushes himself to his feet, and I get up with him.

"Should we check?" I ask. He's already lifting his shirt before I finish the sentence. I wince and hiss. "That's a good one."

"Burns like hell."

"Ha ha."

"No, man, I'm serious. My skin is on fire. Look at the welts."

There's a big splotch on the right side of his rib cage. It's bright pink and getting redder, along with five raised welts and a mottled mound that looks like a palm. It's a handprint, for sure, but it's not human.

"You smell that?" Mike asks sniffing the air.

"Yeah. Your skin smells like brimstone."

13

The thing about being a standard, run-of-the-mill private investigator is that they can gather *tangible* evidence, which, mostly, comes in the form of pictures, videos, testimony, and other concrete things wherein a judge will look at it, nod his bald little head, waggle his floppy, loose-skinned jowls and say, "You have proved that Bill is sleeping with Tina, and Jane is entitled to forty bajillion dollars."

Or, rather, the house in the Hamptons and other valuables.

The point is, they can collect material proof that can be used in a court of law.

Me? What I do as a *paranormal* private investigator? It requires more finesse and deductive reasoning, not to mention the fact that the field of paranormal research remains *persona non grata* in most scientific circles. I don't care how many full-bodied apparitions I've seen, how many voices I've heard from beyond the grave, or how many pictures I've taken where a translucent man is standing off to the right of somebody's kitchen table, the general public, minus our legions of believers and fans, will look down their noses at it and say, "Yeah, but you could've faked that. See right here? The bottom of the door is off camera.

Who's to say you didn't tie a piece of fishing line to it and yank it closed from across the room?"

That's what Mike and I, and the rest of our crew, had to battle every single day while the show was running, and it's what I deal with now during each investigation, and it's why my work would hold as much water as a sieve if it were taken to the US legal system.

I often spend days on location, poring over historical records, interviewing potential witnesses and clients, conducting investigations, filming dark bedrooms and hallways, taking pictures, and being sneaky. The difference is, the people I'm trying to talk to are dead.

And the dead don't always cooperate—at least not fully. It's rare that I can walk into a home where someone has been murdered, fire up the old cameras and recorder, and hear a spirit on the other end of the line say, "It was Ronald James from accounting; he's the one who slit my throat." As a matter of fact, I think that's only happened once in the two years I've been contracting as a paranormal private investigator.

And it wasn't Ronald James from accounting, actually. It was Ted, down in the mailroom, because we all know the mailroom is where the creepy people work.

Okay, so the point I'm trying to make is, sometimes during an investigation, I can say, "My name is Ford Atticus Ford, and I'm here to talk to Amanda Wallace. Amanda, if you're here, can you tell me where your husband hid your body?" and I'll get a vague response like, "He left me . . . She told him to."

Right there is an extra clue that the police can use. After friends and family members have authenticated that it's Amanda's voice, then begins the process of tracking down this "she" that Amanda mentioned. The family, the lawyers, the police, none of them had any clue that there was (potentially) a mistress or a girlfriend on the side, and if not that, a puppet master pulling the strings to help collect an insurance settlement, etc.

The courts won't accept it, but the detectives can choose to believe or ignore what I give them. Occasionally, they dismiss my evidence because even though they called me in to assist them in their investigation, they refuse to believe they could have missed something so simple. And then, when I'm out of sight, they'll follow it anyway. They're not stupid, just prideful.

If they do accept the validity of my data, it opens up an entirely new line of questioning and potential leads.

Because, like I've always said, dead people see things that others don't.

Sometimes it's that easy. Sometimes a spirit will muster enough energy and come through to our side and avenge his own death. Other times, I establish communication, but it's gibberish. Perhaps a family member can watch a video I've captured where a plant moves two inches, and then the sound of footsteps follow. It doesn't prove that Harold Bigelow choked Mrs. Harold Bigelow to death in a fit of murderous rage. What it proves, according to the family member, is that Mrs. Bigelow has come back from the grave, and she's still trying to position that plant exactly how she wanted it, against Harold's demands. It's proof that she's around, but it's not proof of her husband's guilt nor is it proof of his innocence.

Looking back on my case history, it's about a forty-sixty split between usable evidence and tangential proof of the afterlife.

I mention this because after we're finished examining the seared handprint on Mike's side, he lets me listen to the recording. He'd said, "Whoa, hang on," about a half second before the demonic linebacker caused a fumble on the one-yard line, and now, as we stand here in the hallway and listen to the rest of the recording, I get chills when the EVP comes through.

"*Ford . . . death . . .*"

It's a growl more than words, and I imagine that the voice is coated in thousands of years of soot and has been charred by the fires of hell.

Dramatic? Maybe. Sometimes I still picture myself talking to our viewership in my mind.

I cringe and lift an eyebrow at Mike. He returns it.

I take it to mean this right-hander is threatening my life, and it's freaking spooky, yet if I had given up and tucked-tail out the front door every time this happened, I would've quit, oh, about a thousand investigations ago.

We listen to it twice more and note that it comes in over top of the soft, female voice we'd heard that drew us to the room in the first place. That tells us a couple of things: one, this demonic entity didn't lure us into a trap, because sometimes they impersonate things they aren't, like children or a distressed family member, and two, that being noted, there is definitely more than one spiritual presence in this house.

We had already established this, more or less, but this is legitimate proof for Mike and me. It changes the direction of the impending overnight investigation now that we know for sure what we're dealing with.

Mike stops the playback and checks his watch. "What're we thinking? Another hour, hour and a half before total sundown? If that?"

"Probably so. I'd say we run a couple more baseline checks up here on this floor and the attic, just to be safe. Can't hurt to clear up all the variables."

"Yeah, and maybe if we find an EMF hotspot, we can target that location a little more than the dead zones. Craghorn told me that he often sees a lot of action in his bedroom and—oh for God's sake, Ford. Are you thirteen years old?"

"Sorry, it was just the way you phrased it. *Action* in the bedroom? Huh? Huh? C'mon."

"And Carla would have put that in an episode, and we would have spent the next week under a mountain of dick and fart jokes online." He scoffs, but he can't quite hide his grin. "I'm going to do the baseline EMF. Why don't you do a little recon around here and see if you can find anything he didn't tell us about?"

"On it." He doesn't have to tell me what he's thinking about, because we're operating like the machine of old, back in the saddle, and whatever cliché you can come up with. "Be careful," I add, hesitant to leave him completely alone after such a violent attack. But he's been working out, so he should be good.

Mike heads west, back in the direction of the spare bedrooms, and I go east to the front of the house. The giant bay window lets in the waning evening light, and the semitranslucent curtains hanging on an ancient iron rod do little to provide cover. They remind me of the ones back at the Hampstead farmhouse, which makes me all the more eager to get home and follow up on the leads I uncovered with Ulie the night before I came here.

A floorboard screeches under my feet, the wail of a dying animal, and I step away from it. In case Mike is running the recorder, I verbally mark the location and that it originated from me.

The odor up here is different than downstairs. Nothing bad, really, but nothing good either, like Craghorn hasn't aired it out in a couple of years. It's stale, musty, and I'm tempted to open the tall, double rectangular windows beside the big bay window, the kind that open with an L-shaped crank, and then I spot the taillights of traffic outside.

Nah, better not. The street noise could easily contaminate our investigation, so I suffer with the smell of dust and air with an expiration date from the Nixon administration.

I'm taking my time here, soaking it all up, trying to get inside Craghorn's head, hoping to give some substance to his reasons for staying here ten years after his wife was possibly murdered, and then six long months after a goddamn powerful right-hander moved in like that houseguest who never gets the hint that he needs to leave.

For as long as I have been doing this, I'll never understand why people allow themselves to be tortured. Sure, there are extenuating circumstances, like money issues, no family around, no place to go, along with a million other possibilities, but for the love of God, there *has* to be something you can do. If it were me, I would do whatever it took to get my wife, my husband, the kids, and the cat as far away from pure evil as I possibly could.

It took the Hoppers longer than it should have, but they were smart.

Eventually.

They left. They got Chelsea out.

And then this son of a bitch right here came along and brought her back.

Argh, Ford, stop it. There's nothing you can do about it this very second. You're working on fixing things. It's a process.

I have to mentally acknowledge this on a daily basis, roughly 2.3 million times. My therapist tells me it's a good thing to remind myself that we all make mistakes.

A *mistake* is putting pepper in the saltshaker.

What I allowed to happen was *unforgiveable*.

The upstairs hall seems fairly normal on this end. No new revelations into the mind of Craghorn. I hear Mike fumbling around in the office and listen for a moment. He sounds like he's fine, but damn, I'm worried. You take a hit like that from an upper level right-hander, it'll shake you for a while, especially if you've been off the bicycle for a spell like Mike has. If I send him home with a demon in his backpack, Toni might track me down and murder me.

If that happened, I'd come back and haunt her personally, because how perfect would that be?

Satisfied that my former partner, best friend, and brother-from-another-mother is okay back there by himself, I reach for the door handle closest to me. It's warm, like ten or twenty degrees warmer than the rest of this freezing house. The temperature isn't hot enough to burn me, however, but that doesn't stop me from jerking my hand away like I'm grabbing a rattlesnake by the tail. The foreign sensation—heat, I mean—is a surprise.

Normally, I'd check it out with the thermal imaging camera, but the damn thing is all the way over there on the banister, and besides, I already know it's a different temperature. I'm a bit concerned that something might be on fire in there, so rather than opening the door and fueling it with a fat, fresh supply of oxygen, I drop down to all fours and try to peek underneath the crack. I haven't done this since seventh grade when Teddy Martin's sister was changing out of her bikini.

I didn't see anything then, of course, unlike now, when a set of shadowy legs scamper across the room.

I recoil and jump back to my feet, unsure of what I saw. My hands go numb with excitement. This is it. This is the kind of stuff I live for, regardless of the investigations I'm on or what I'm trying to accomplish for some police department detective that I'll never see again. There's something in there, something otherworldly, and I can barely contain myself as I call out to Mike and tell him to hurry.

The Graveyard: Classified Paranormal Series

14

Mike touches the doorknob and feels the difference in temperature. Like me, he yanks his arm back. "Yowsa." He checks the palm of his hand, perhaps instinctively, and asks me what room it is.

"Is this the one where Craghorn said his wife painted? Maybe? And I didn't even get a chance to check out the library and the sitting room over there on the right." I look past Mike at the two rooms, whose doors are open, and don't see anything scuttling around in there. "Should we check them out before we go in here for battle?"

"Are you nuts? Why're you not in there already? The old Ford would've run in there with a Ouija board and a handful of batteries like he was handing out Halloween candy."

"That giant clawed handprint on your side makes this one a little different."

Because, honestly, while this is what I live for, I also have no intention of dying for it, either.

He nods. "Good point, but we gotta do it."

"Rock-paper-scissors?"

Mike calls me a pansy, but not in the G-rated way, twists the doorknob, and pushes it open slowly. The moaning hinges are horror-movie creepy, and I wouldn't be surprised if a rattling skeleton dropped from the ceiling. Gotcha!

Instead, ropes of heated air crawl through the space, bringing with them the scent of something ancient. I have no way to describe the putrid aroma. It's as if something slithered out of a crypt that had been buried a thousand years ago. I recognize it as the faint, musty smell I noticed earlier, only now it's overwhelmingly pungent and sends my hand up over my nose and mouth.

Otherwise, the inside of the room is perfectly normal. It's another bedroom. There's a single bed with the long side against the wall. A flowery comforter lies on top of it, pristinely pressed, and a pillow with an equally wrinkle-free pillowcase sits at the head. There's a bare bookcase that I would expect to be covered in dust. It's not. It's spotless. A clear vase, filled halfway with water, holds daffodils in front of a square-paned window.

A tic-tac-toe window.

Sometimes I'm a poet and I know it.

There's a small desk underneath, which looks to be something straight off an Ikea showroom floor. It's white, square, and plainly made. A matching chair accompanies it. The surface is also free of everything, including dust, and to our left is a 1970s-style love seat that could be nothing other than the matching unit to the couch downstairs.

Mike grunts and lifts the collar of his shirt over his nose. "Shields up."

I don't see any sign of the previous occupant—the Thing of the Scuttling Legs—and I have to admit, going against my earlier sentiments, I'm slightly disappointed. It's always such a rush when you walk into a room and either catch an entity off guard, or spook something that's hiding, and then watch as it freaks out while it tries to get away from you.

We both notice the one odd thing in the room, simultaneously, and move over to the loose floorboard beside a hole. Mike, who is never without the proper equipment, produces a miniature flashlight from his Batman-style tool belt, flicks it on, and shines it down into the orifice. It's only about three inches wide, which means that craning my neck to see around Mike is doing no good. I wait until he's finished examining it and then ask for the light.

I don't know what I was expecting. Maybe a pentagram drawn in blood or the remnants of an animal sacrifice, something, anything evil.

It's empty. Completely and entirely empty. It's nothing but a hole that's bordered by dusty joists with the splintery subflooring as its bottom.

Then it occurs to me. "Oh, shit. This is probably where the maid found the diary."

"Yeah, that's what I was thinking."

"She popped this open and unleashed all that negative energy. You think that's why it smells so disgusting in here?"

"Nah, I'd say that's the right-hander. This is where he hangs out." Mike looks around the room at nothing in particular. "You hear me, you son of a bitch? You smell like shit! A big, stinking pile of ass goo, and once we're done, we're going to send you right back to the bottom of Satan's toilet where you belong."

"Yeah, Mike. Get 'im." I can't help myself. It's the Mike that I remember. The Mike that drove the ratings through the roof for any episode where he lost his cool and got all primeval on a spirit that pushed him too far. Carla and her marketing team were brilliant when it came to teasing those episodes with dark, gritty commercials. "*On this week's very special episode of* Graveyard: Classified, *the spirit world will finally experiences the wrath of Mike Long.*"

Truth be told, the spirit world "finally experienced" the wrath of Mike Long roughly twelve times over the course of the show's run. I'm pretty sure there was only one guy who e-mailed to tell us we sounded like a broken record. I sent him an autographed headshot and never heard from him again.

"You feel that?" Mike asks.

"What?"

"The temperature. Feels like it's back to normal." He checks the black box in his hand. "EMF is back to normal. Zero-point-zero. And what's that smell? It's like clean laundry."

"We scared it out of here. Damn thing retreated."

Mike shouts, "Coward!" at the ceiling.

"What now?"

"The usual. Wait until nightfall. Then we get ready for battle."

***

I can tell that, in most respects, Mike is far from being my bestest buddy in the whole wide world again, but I do manage to talk him into joining me for dinner. After everything that's happened today, I need a break, and I'm in desperate need of some fuel before we gear up for war.

Mike balked for a bit, telling me he was only here on business, and all he wanted to do was help Craghorn get his life back. Reluctantly, he agreed to come along when I said he could pick the restaurant.

And so, here we sit at McCracken's Crab Hut.

Mike knows I'm deathly allergic to seafood.

Very funny.

While he mows down the largest bucket of crab legs I've ever seen, I convince our amazingly attractive waitress, who goes by the awkward name Caribou, to run over to the deli across the street and get me a Black Forest ham and swiss on rye. There's no denying that she recognizes the both of us, which seems to be exactly why she was willing to help me out. Or it could be the fact that if I so much as touch a plate that's had seafood on it, I'll blow up like a crimson pufferfish and go into convulsions, and that's not a good visual for the other patrons.

I'm even sitting here about a foot back from the table, trying to avoid any potential crab juice flying my way as Mike plows through the crab legs like a wood chipper shredding an oak branch.

The kind, generous, sweet, and in-no-way-trying-to-kill-me Caribou arrives with a hoagie-shaped object wrapped in white deli paper. It doesn't appear to be on rye bread, but she's forgiven when I notice that underneath the clear tape holding the wrapping closed is a perfectly smooched set of lips.

Sealed with a kiss. Nice.

She winks at me, says to enjoy my meal—on the house—and when she walks away, I can't help but notice the pert and perfectly shaped—

"Ford."

"Hmm?"

"Eyes front, soldier."

"Give me a break, dude. You're over there trying to kill me with your crab guts, the least you could do is let my eyes wander a bit."

"And isn't that exactly why you're divorced?"

"Right, and now I can do as I please."

Mike slams a half-ravaged crab leg into his metal bucket. "You don't even know, do you?"

"Know what?"

"How much that girl loved you."

"Melanie from ward—I mean, Melanie?"

"Yes, *Melanie from wardrobe*, Ford." He snatches up a brown paper napkin and angrily swipes at his juice-covered fingers. "I'm guessing you don't know she calls Toni once in a while."

"She does?"

"At least a couple times a month."

That's unanticipated, enough to stun me into silence, and I don't respond right away. Over by the bar, I watch a young boy and girl, teenagers in love it seems, giggling next to the old-fashioned jukebox. He slips a coin into the slot, pushes a button, and the speakers immediately begin gagging on the early '90s sensation, Boyz II Men. Even the girl can't handle the syrupy sweetness because she teasingly punches him in the shoulder, shakes her head like she absolutely can*not* believe he picked that song to play, and marches off with her arms crossed, feigning embarrassment. The boy comes up behind her, tickles her, and they scamper back to their table. Young. In love. Clueless.

How godawful disgustingly appropriate, too, and just another sign that the universe is out there pointing and laughing. The first night I took Melanie out, post after-party once we finished wrapping an international shoot in Prague, the discothèque we visited played nothing but Boyz II Men. All. Night. Long. On repeat.

I ask Mike, "Why would she call Toni?"

"They're talking about their cycles."

"Really?"

"No, moron, why do you think? She calls to check on you, as if I have anything to do with where you put your dick or which city you're terrorizing on a weekly basis."

"What? Why would she call Toni for that? Doesn't make any sense. I haven't seen or talked to either of you in over two years."

"I know how long it's been. Let me rephrase. Toni says that Melanie calls to shoot the breeze and catch up, but it always feels like she's somehow trying to work you into the conversation. Like no matter what they're talking about, Melanie will eventually get around to saying something like, 'Oh, speaking of the Moose Lodge, has Mike talked to Ford lately?'"

"But *why* would she do that? We talk fairly regularly. Not about anything important, just quick how-are-you type stuff."

"And you tell her how you're doing?"
I nod and mumble into my beer.
"What?"
"I said, kinda, but not really."
"And that's the thing. Toni's guess is, Melanie, she sounds like she's hoping we'll reconnect."
"You and me?"
"You and me."
"Why?"
"Because, Ford, she thinks I'm good for you. Am. Or *was*. Who knows? She knows that Toni has no idea what's going on with you, and she knows that Toni would probably pour gas on your dick if you were pissing fire—"
"Ouch."
"Yeah, ouch. Mel . . . she's planting seeds."

Caribou arrives at the table and asks Mike if he would like more crab legs since it's Bottomless Crab Leg night, which is total bullcrap because crab legs are too expensive to be bottomless anything. It's quick proof that she, and probably the manager, are former fans of the show, and they're being nice to the has-beens. Mike says he's good, then Caribou asks me if I need anything else. The look of disappointment on her face—when she sees that I've yet to open the sandwich that she so accommodatingly retrieved for me—is enough for me to thank her and pry it open. She's gone before I can look up again, and on the inside flap, I find the prize inside: her cell number, a smiley face, and a heart over the letter *i* in her name.

I fold it over before Mike can see.

"Aren't you going to eat that?"

"Later," I tell him. "But, man, I'm deliberately not being obtuse, honest to God, but why in the hell is Melanie 'planting seeds' or whatever it is you think she's doing? I don't get it."

Mike drains the last of his Budweiser and leans up on his elbows. He belches, pauses, and pinches the bridge of his nose.

"The only thing I can think of is, if she can get Toni to corral me into making amends with you, and maybe we hang out again, then that'll be good for, I don't know, future possibilities."

"What fucking future possibilities, Mike?"

"You. Her. The two of you, dipshit."

This punches me in the chest with about the same force as when the right-hander lifted Mike off his feet back at the Craghorn house. Only in a good way.

I think.

There won't be any demonic handprints left on my skin, but it hits equally as hard.

I had been holding out the tiniest bit of hope, and on occasion, had considered begging to atone for my sins, but I thought I'd have a better chance bringing some of my dead counterparts back to life.

"Melanie wants me back?"

Mike closes his eyes, lifts one corner of his mouth, and gives me a bemused, "Beats the hell out of me. I wouldn't have the slightest idea why."

"Going through you is just—"

"Ford," Mike says, stopping my blathering. "I have no clue, bro. She's obviously not going to come right out and say it to your face. You cheated on her. Many, many times."

"Six," I remind him.

"Whatever. You absolutely shredded her heart, and she can't come around asking you to try again because how pathetic would that be? No way, no how. She's not going to give up that kind of power, and, by taking the long road of, you know, trying to get us hanging out again, maybe it'll get you on the straight and narrow. You'll see how much of an idiot you were, and you'll approach her. It's the long con. She's got nothing to lose."

"That's . . ."

"Sneaky?"

"I was going to say risky. What if I didn't bite?"

"How the hell should I know? She probably would've found a different way."

My stomach is growling, yet I'm too dumbfounded to eat this hoagie. I ask Mike, "Did you figure all this out just by Melanie calling Toni and asking about me?"

"Pffffft," Mike scoffs. "Me? Fuck no. Toni said so."

"So the woman who would pour gas on my dick if I was pissing fire, your peach of a wife, she told you to come see me and tell me that my ex-wife is using this elaborate ruse to win me back?"

"Toni? Please."

"Melanie?"

"Nope."

"Then will you tell me what's going on? Enough with the twenty questions."

"I told you. I'm here to help Craghorn. That other stuff about Melanie, that's just B-roll footage. Side story. So there's that, and then there's this other thing." Mike stops Caribou as she's passing by with the remnants of someone's mangled crab. He orders two more beers, and once she winks at me and leaves, he says, "There's an offer on the table. A big one."

15

CHELSEA HOPPER
TWO YEARS AGO
A Very Special Live Halloween Episode

"You're so brave," I told Chelsea as she climbed the ladder into the attic. It's amazing how often kids are absolutely fearless unless they're taught to be afraid or something happens that dissuades any further attempts at exploring certain areas of life. Case in point, I haven't touched tequila since I took a sip of my dad's back when I was eight.

Chelsea was five. Her birthday was three weeks earlier.

The colossal fiend hiding in the space above her head had been growing in strength for thousands of years.

What in the fuck was I doing?

I reached for her on instinct, wanting to change my mind, wanting to pull her back. Then I played it off as if I was trying to steady her. Goddamn it. I was a seesaw.

She could do it. I had to *believe* with everything I had that she could. Chelsea would win and the beast would return to hell where it belonged, and she would live a long, happy life. She would be free of the black clouds because she defeated the dark man. On her own. Like a big girl.

Chelsea paused on the third step up and looked over her shoulder at me, both hands with a white-knuckled grip on the ladder. "Mr. Ford?" she said in a whimper.

"Yeah, sweetie?"

"I'm scared."

"It's okay. I'll be right here. It's your fight, your bully, honey. You beat that bully up there, and you'll never ever have to be afraid again. You'll be *so* strong, and you can fight for the other kids who are scared."

Off camera, Mike said, "For God's sake, Ford, it's not like she's getting on a roller coaster."

I couldn't hear him in my earpiece, only in my free ear. Carla must have cut the feed to his live mic. It was probably a smart decision on her part. It might have been her only one during the entire scenario.

Chelsea said, "Will you come with me, Mr. Ford? Come fight the dark man?"

"I'll be right behind you, Chelsea," I told her, but—and like the giant asshole I was—I had already decided to hang back for the sake of good television. The ratings would launch outside the stratosphere. Some cosmonaut up on the ISS would be able to reach out the window and touch the chart's arrow as it sailed by on the way to the moon.

Some time ago, Mike told me I was getting dangerously close to letting the show, the sponsors, and the money go to my head. Said it was affecting my clarity of thought, and he was sure that I wasn't the same person anymore.

Of course I wasn't.

Back when we first started, I was some goofball with a camera and a few drunken cheerleaders, who happened to get lucky by capturing a life-defining moment on film.

Fast forward to last week where I sat next to Jennifer Aniston and told a couple of funny stories to David Letterman.

I wasn't the same person, but, yeah, when Chelsea paused on the fifth step, with her legs visibly trembling and her head not yet inside the attic access above, I could see how maybe all of this had gone to my head.

What was *wrong* with me?

One minute I was standing there actually thinking that this was good for Chelsea, that she would come out of that attic as a victor who would be able to face down anything. The next minute I was waffling—my heart was melting. I was an idiot. A beat later, I'd be right back to drooling over ratings and—

"I want my mommy and daddy," Chelsea said.

I gently squeezed her ankle to encourage her. "You can do this, Chelsea. Remember how I said that if you beat the dark man, you'll never have to be afraid again?"

"Yeah." There was a quivering lip behind that single syllable.

"You, Chelsea, *you* are the monster. The dark man is afraid of *you*. Now get up there and kick his—"

"Ford! Stop it, now!" I felt a strong hand on my forearm, fingers digging into my skin, yanking me to the side. It was Mike, pulling me away, trying to get to her.

"What're you doing?"

"Get her down from there. If you don't, I will."

"Mike—" I held up an index finger to the camera. "Always nice to see on live television, folks. Anything can happen. One second, please, if you don't mind."

In my earpiece, I heard Carla whispering. "That's good, that's good. Go with it. Live TV, Ford."

Mike said, "I'm getting her out of here. We can't do this!"

Carla whispered in my earpiece, "Take him out, Ford."

"What?"

"You heard me."

Mike was reaching up for Chelsea's legs when I yanked his shoulders, spun him to the side, and sent him to the floor with an abrupt leg sweep. He cursed when he cracked his head against a dark black chest with metal bindings, and rolled over, clutching his skull.

"Chelsea, you can do this. Don't listen to Mr. Mike, okay? Don't forget, it's afraid of *you*."

Liar, liar, pants on fire because they'll be burning in hell.

"Promise?"

"Absolutely."

Downstairs, the front door slammed open, followed by angry shouts from some of the crew and the distraught voices of Rob and Leila Hopper. I was actually surprised it had taken them so long to get inside.

I found out later, much, much later, that Carla had hired security and two brutes about the size of Hulk Hogan were blocking the front door. From the moment Chelsea said, "I'm scared," the sentries had been holding the Hoppers back. It took a hidden can of mace for them to gain access.

Chelsea didn't understand what the sounds meant. Instead, she took the angry shouts to mean that she'd done something wrong, that she was in trouble, and she said, "I'm sorry, I'm sorry. I'll go!" She crawled up the last three rungs and disappeared into the gaping maw of the attic.

Downstairs, her parents screamed her name.

Mike, groggy from knocking his head, tried to get to his feet.

I looked at Carla. With every bit of sincerity, and no pun intended whatsoever, the malevolent smile slicing across her face was absolutely *haunting*.

Through the commotion, I heard Chelsea's footsteps as she cautiously crept across the attic floor.

And then it happened.

A deep, raspy growl, made of ashes and rage, poured out of the hole above us. I smelled sulfur and rot.

Chelsea shrieked and went silent, then a second later, she tumbled out of the attic, flailing head over heels along the ladder.

I lunged and caught her before she hit too hard, but the damage was already done.

Overhead, I watched a black mass, darker than the lightless attic, as it hovered there. It seemed to be mocking me, taunting me, enjoying the spoils of its effort, and then it slowly slithered back inside.

Chelsea's eyes were half-open, yet she stared at nothing.

I turned to the cameras, ashamed and horrified at what I'd done. The wavering scale of my emotions tilted back to the same caring human I had been ages ago, and I felt the softball-size lump clogging my throat.

What have I done, what have I done, what have I done?

The twenty-four-hour news channels, the nighttime talk shows, the tabloids, Facebook and Twitter, none of them used *this* image of me, so distraught and worried about that damaged angel in my arms, hating myself. No. They didn't use it at all, because to them, I was an awful, vicious, bloodthirsty devil, and I deserved the public castration of my character.

I had good intentions, though, didn't I?

Chelsea's eyelids fluttered.

I shouted at Carla, at Don the cameraman, at anyone who would listen to me: "Cut the feed. Cut the feed, goddamn it!"

Carla fired back. "No, Ford, we are staying with this!" It was unconventional for her, as a producer, to insert herself into the live television situation, but by then, it was obvious that she didn't care.

The Hoppers breached the second floor, and I moved for them.

Don, thank God, said something to Carla and lowered his camera. Even in the dim light surrounding us, barely a hint of it coming from some far off bathroom nightlight that we forgot to unplug, I saw that Don's cheeks were wet with regret.

Carla tried to block me, and I leaned into her with a strong shoulder. I was a runaway train. She was a cow on the tracks. She had no chance at stopping me. A breathy *oooph* flew out of her mouth as she careened backward, slamming into the wall. A picture frame fell and glass shattered around everyone's feet.

Rob reached us first. Leila was blubbering, bawling, and wailing her daughter's name. He took Chelsea's limp body out of my arms and handed her to his wife. Then he whipped around and nailed me with a bare-knuckled backhand across my right cheekbone.

I dropped. My face immediately puffed with fluid and split where his rigid knuckles had met skin and bone, blood trickling down while I struggled to get back up, eyes watery. It wasn't the first time I had ever been punched by a client, but it was the first time I absolutely deserved what I got.

My profuse apologies went unheard over Leila's horrified voice as Rob flicked on a hallway light. Deep, red, furious gashes arced across Chelsea's cheek, neck, and collarbone.

Three of them. A mockery of the Holy Trinity.

I couldn't help myself. I moved to the small family that had been through so much. I wanted to hug them. I wanted to apologize for a hundred years and tell them I understood that what I had done was wrong, that Carla Hancock influenced me, that I had been driven by greed and ambition, by my own stupidity. I wanted to beg their forgiveness for getting caught up in the moment, for convincing them that having Chelsea battle her demons would be a good thing.

I picked a fine fucking time to develop a conscience.

Blame the fog of war, or better yet, the fog of celebrity, but that was all bullshit. I knew better. I knew what I was doing. The catalyst was—the fulcrum to the whole state of affairs—was that I didn't stop myself, and I didn't stop Carla when I should have.

Mike was right all along. Mike was always right.

I thought about that as I bent down to the traumatized Hoppers. I put my hand on Leila's back, and she hissed, "Don't you touch me," with all the ferocity of that thing hiding in the space over our heads.

Before I was able to respond, I felt her husband's hand on my throat, grasping tightly. "Once wasn't enough?" he asked.

Through his grip crushing my windpipe, I croaked, "I'm sorr—" and then his fist centered my nose. I heard the sharp crack as the bone shattered, and then I was falling, landing on my back, choking on the blood gushing down my throat and into my open mouth.

The room flashed whiter than the hallway bulb, and I realized it wasn't my vision reacting to the blow.

I rubbed my eyes, trying to see what happened. Was it a ball of energy? Was the creature upstairs manifesting, gathering strength to attack again?

No. It was Carla, chuckling, thumbing furiously on her phone.

"You're such a dick," I said, groaning, rolling onto my knees. Behind me, the Hoppers thundered down the stairs to the first floor. "What's—"

"That's an amazing picture, Ford. So much blood. I'm thinking CNN, MSNBC. Lead story everywhere."

"Don't."

"You'll be fine," she said, without an ounce of sincerity or concern in her voice. "There's no such thing as bad publicity, right?"

The Graveyard: Classified Paranormal Series

16

Mike wants to wait until Caribou is back with the next round of beers before he explains what he means, because he feels like, in his own words, "This whole goddamn discussion needs to be numbed by more alcohol."

"I actually don't want another round," I tell him. "Not a good idea to investigate with too much of a buzz, remember? Or are you planning on ditching me?"

Mike wobbles his head as if this is something he considered. "The thought crossed my mind, but no, not after what happened back there."

I'm fairly certain that Caribou gets the beers to us in record speed, because hey, we're the washed-up superheroes from *Graveyard: Classified*, yet I'm so zoned in on Mike's revelation that I forget to thank her, and I also forget to take another glance at that perfectly cupped rear. Good on me, I guess.

"So, about this offer. You're here to, what, *pitch* me? Were you planning to do this anyway? Like, what if I hadn't called you today, then what?"

"Ease up, cowboy. I'm getting there." He takes a long pull from his bottle of Budweiser. "The short and dirty is, Carla

Hancock has some interested parties. People have been keeping tabs on you."

"*Carla?* Not a chance in hell," I say, and I'm already on my way up from the seat.

Mike pats the air, motioning for me to sit down. "Chill for a minute. Hear me out. She's got an idea for a project, and based on the feedback she's been getting—I kind of agree. I think it could be huge."

I sit, but I'm not happy about it. "Just who are these 'interested parties,' Mike?" I make sure to emphasize the air quotes around 'interested parties' and then follow that up with a quick wave to a younger boy at the next table. He's definitely interested in me. "Who's been keeping tabs?"

Mike looks confused, like I just told him that water wasn't wet. "Have you not been on the Internet lately?"

"Nope." And that's the damn truth. After the incident with Chelsea, after Wolf Blitzer, Brian Williams, Jon Stewart, and all the rest of those guys completely eviscerated me, after my sneering face was plastered all over the Internet, after the lawsuits, after everything shitty about those six months, post-live-show trauma, I needed to walk away.

"Seriously?"

"I have a phone. It rings. I have a website with my contact information so stumped detectives can get in touch. I answer e-mail from my mom and dad. I haven't tweeted, or posted, or blogged, or so much as surfed for porn in about a year and a half, so no, I haven't been on the Internet lately."

"*Really?*"

"Why is that so hard to believe?"

"Well, I mean, I figured that Captain Ego had to *look*, you know? Had to see what people were saying about him."

I have to admit, I'm curious, but after my righteous defiance just then, I most definitely can't go begging for him to tell me what's been going on in the world of social media. I make some offhanded joke about being on the psychiatrist's orders to stay away from mentally damaging material—which, honestly, isn't much of a joke.

"Folks are out there watching, Ford."

"*Again*, who are these people and what are they watching?"

"Anybody and everybody. Former fans. People like to keep up, you know? Nothing is private or personal anymore. And it's simple things, too, like hypothetically, maybe some detective took a selfie with you in Anchorage six months ago, he posts it online somewhere, some picture of you smiling and giving a thumbs up while he's got his arm around you; that thing gets a thousand likes and your name lives on. Fans get to see that the almighty Ford Atticus Ford didn't let a little bad press get him down. Some of the crazies have online maps tracking your trips."

Now it's my turn to say, "Really?"

"You still got murdered publicly for about two weeks after the lawsuits were tied up, but then they found that senator from Oklahoma with four hookers in his office and poof, you're old news. It's amazing how fast people move on."

I sip my beer. Time for a little revelation of my own. "Glad I'm no longer the social pariah—thank God—but the good thing is, I've been perfectly happy away from all that. At least for the time being. But there's always been this thing, this idea—never mind."

"What?"

I can hear myself saying it out loud, and the thought sounds insane. "I've been thinking about pitching another show when I'm ready. Maybe a show where a crew follows me around and I help these detectives solve crimes, like I'm out there doing good for society."

"Redemption."

"It's more like I'm looking at the world as a good place that I can help, but yeah, you could say redemption is a factor. I've made a couple of phone calls. Mostly it's been wishes and wants or ifs and buts." I have to take a sip of this beer. My throat has gotten dry. It's the first time I've admitted this to anyone other than Ulie.

The bottle clunks against the table, half of it gone.

Apparently I needed more than a sip.

"Could work," Mike says, "but listen to this. Since you're not public enemy number one anymore, Carla has an even bigger idea."

I haven't talked to Carla since our last day in court when the judge ordered The Paranormal Channel and its subsidiaries to pay the Hoppers 6.66 million dollars in damages.

I shit you not: 6-6-6.

Maybe Judge Karen Dunham had a sense of humor. Maybe she was trying to send a message.

Regardless, Carla tried to shake my hand, I flipped her the bird instead, and I haven't seen nor heard from her since.

"Carla has an idea," I say, "and I don't fucking care."

Mike puts his elbows on the table and leans toward me. "I completely agree."

"You do?"

"Yeah, fuck Carla. But . . ."

"Why did I know there was a 'but' coming?"

"You're hoping for redemption, yeah? Here's Carla's proposal: we make a documentary, hour and a half long, give or take, and she thinks she can get *national* theatrical distribution. The great Ford Atticus Ford is coming to a silver screen near you." He makes a wide gesture with his hands, displaying my name up on some invisible marquee. "We're talking in the neighborhood of fifteen hundred theaters on opening night. They've conducted interviews with focus groups and the tests have scored astronomically. Carla thinks she can finagle us some points on the back end, too. Ford, don't shake your head. Listen to me. We're talking tens of *millions* of dollars. All we'd have to do is spend a couple of weeks shooting, and if it does as well as they project, we'd be set for life."

I can't help but get titillated by the suggestion. My brain is buzzing with a hundred concepts already. There have been so many cases that I've worked on in the past two years that could use national attention. Hate crimes, domestic abuse, child abandonment—so many charities and organizations that need better funding and resources.

I'm not worried about the money. Regardless of what happened with the show, I walked away with plenty in my coffers. So did Mike, I thought.

"Let me think about it," I tell him, keeping my bubbling enthusiasm buried for now. "And I'll think about it on one condition. You keep Carla as far away from me as you possibly can."

Mike grins and lifts his finger to Caribou, ordering another round. "Carla suspected that would be the case, and she's already agreed to take a hands-off production credit to get you on board. You're the talent, Ford, the draw, and she knows that. I know it, too. You're the face, I'm the brains."

I don't even know how to express myself, so I hold up a saltshaker like it's a glass of champagne. "I'm not saying yes, mind you, but man, this is unreal. It's exactly what I've been wanting for almost two years now. There are so many things we can do. Wait, yeah, there's that lighthouse down in Florida. I got in good with the chief of police there—I'm sure he would love to have us work on this impossible cold case they've been looking at since 1987, and I know he—"

"Ford—"

"—would be totally cool with loaning us one of his detectives—"

"—Ford—"

"—for a couple of weeks—"

"Hey. Dude. Listen to me. We aren't going to have creative control."

My heart slams to a stop like a crash test dummy's head against a steering wheel, then sinks down to somewhere around my colon. "We don't?"

"No, they already have the concept worked up. It's the *concept* that tested so goddamn amazing."

"Which is what?"

"We go after the right-hander that hurt Chelsea. We fight back."

I'm flabbergasted that he would even suggest such a thing, let alone be on board with it. After all we went through with that family. After everything we put that little girl through. "Mike. *Mike?* You're kidding, right?" I ask this around a flabbergasted chuckle.

"It's what the people want."

"No. No, no, no. Not a fucking chance. I am not putting Chelsea Hopper through anything else. Not publicly. Never again. I can't even think of all the ways I would say no to this. And even if, by some miracle of the heavens above that I would give five seconds of thought to the possibility, the Hoppers wouldn't come within a thousand miles of me. They would rather drive a wooden stake through my heart than see my face again. Are you nuts? Is Carla nuts? What the hell?"

He scratches his forehead with the mouth of the beer bottle. "You finished?"

"I'm just getting started."

"Before you do, hear me out."

I remain silent, fuming.

Mike continues, "I don't know how she did it. Probably because she's some magical sorceress and sold the souls of a million newborns to the devil himself, but Carla got the Hoppers to agree."

"What!"

"In concept alone, nothing more. They don't want anything to do with the story, or the filming, or the production. The marketing, the celebrities, nothing. They're only granting the rights to their family's story—*because*—they have a memoir coming out this fall. They—"

"So now *they're* exploiting Chelsea? What happened to all the money they got in the settlement?"

"After all the lawyer fees and suits and countersuits and appeals, they didn't come away with all that much. Haven't you kept up with this?"

"Obviously not."

"It's how it works, Ford, you know that. That being the case, if somebody from Fifth Avenue, or wherever those big publishers live, somebody shows up on your front doorstep with a check that has two commas and six zeroes in it, and you don't have to fight anybody in *court* for it—it's easy to see how some small, tortured family like the Hoppers might hand over the rights for a bigger house, maybe a deeper college fund for Chelsea. Cosmetic surgery to conceal the scars that a fucking *demon* gave their daughter? You'd do the same, right?"

From my position, having had money, and having kept money, enough to last me for a long, long while, my answer is no. It's not worth it. However, given what I know about the Hoppers and their situation, okay, yeah. Maybe it's not necessarily exploitation if they feel like their story could serve as a warning to other families looking to cash in.

Hell if I know. People do strange things to fatten their bank accounts.

I ask Mike, "So they're on board with this whole fucked-all-to-hell idea as long as a paycheck is involved, and they don't have to look us in the eye?"

He salutes me with his beer bottle.

"And you're okay with this? You're okay coming back? Honest to God, Mike, I never thought I'd hear from you again. I called you today because I needed help, like actual, legitimate help with this badass right-hander because there's no other person on this planet that I would trust to go to war with me against something so strong, and then you show up, lying about how you just want to help Craghorn—"

"I'm not lying about that. He needs help, for sure."

"Then you drop this on me? What in the immortal fuck, dude? Do you need the money? What's the deal? Why the flip-flop? One minute you're punching me in the face and the next, you're practically begging me to come work with you again. I—I can't even fathom what's going on here."

Mike snorts and looks away; he can barely make eye contact with me. "The truth is, it took a few trips to a shrink, but I finally got around to forgiving you. And, for months now, I've been waffling about whether I was actually going to say something. I was there, man. I totally was. And then—then I showed up today, saw your face, and a whole rush of anger came on like goddamn Niagara Falls and I couldn't let it go again. Not until, well, not until we got back into the groove. By then it was just—this is hard, dude. Man to man, this opening-up thing. The doc says I gotta do it, though. Good for my head." He tips back in his chair, nibbles on his bottom lip awhile before he continues. "So there's that. And then, Toni and I, we got caught up in some bad investments," he adds, like he's already regretting the words coming out of his mouth.

"You? Captain Penny-Pincher?"

"I was stupid. Impulsive. Greedy, with a wife that wants nice things. I don't know how much cash you have left—"

"Plenty."

"You would've thought I had rocks up here," he says, rapping his knuckles against his skull. "I had all these people coming to me with 'investment opportunities,' and shit. There was this one with a salsa factory down in Guadalajara. Profit margins were supposed to be—you know what, it doesn't matter.

The money went first, then the houses, the cars. The kids are so ashamed of me, they've barely spoken to me in months. We managed to keep the beach house in Kitty Hawk, but that was because we took every single penny we found to save it. I'm talking, like, Toni and I were smashing the kids' piggy banks with a ball-peen hammer. It's been tough, bro, I won't lie. I've tried to get my own ideas made into shows, checking around with all the old contacts, ringing them up. They wouldn't touch any of my pitches, not without you. Not without the almighty Ford Atticus Ford running point. I was so pissed that I didn't even want to look you in the eye, much less be on another show with you ever again. It took a while, but I got over it."

"But why now? Why this thing with Carla and the Hoppers?"

His shoulders go up to his ears and then drop, resigned. "Same goes for me. Like I said, somebody comes at you with promises of a check that has six zeroes and two commas, it's hard to say no. I'm not proud of it."

I take a second to let this marinate. Mike's broke; he obviously and desperately needs the money, so much so that he's willing to overlook my past transgressions. He's also willing to overlook the fact that we would once again be allowing Carla Hancock to exploit the story of little Chelsea Hopper.

I want to tell him to go to hell, that I will *not* take advantage of her again, even if her parents are blinded by the dollar signs in their eyes.

But I could also get national attention for something I've been doing privately already with my own investigations. Millions of theatergoers could watch as I send that bastard right-hander back to where he belongs.

Talk about emotional wavering. I'm like a swing set in a hurricane.

Mike says, "I get it, Ford. It's a big whammy. You probably need some time. Just promise me you'll think it over, okay?"

Until I have a chance to process this, I refuse to tell him that I've already been working on Chelsea's case on the side. "Let me sleep on it. But first you have to help me beat that thing over at Craghorn's. I have a job to do, and you owe me for the surprise punch in the nutsack."

17

Mike and I remain silent on the ride back over to Craghorn's house. He tossed his idea grenade in my direction, and he probably feels like he's allowing it to do the smart thing and simmer awhile before he brings it up again. The only thing he does say is this: "Kind of a dick move to spring it on you like that."

I agree with a simple, "Yeah."

Then we pull into Craghorn's driveway. With his car gone, and Detective Thomas's unmarked sedan out of the way, I'm thankful we don't have to spend fifteen minutes driving around the block, praying someone will leave a spot open.

We slam the doors of the rented Honda closed and stroll through the gentle sprinkle, turning and climbing the steps, side-by-side. In my mind, I'm picturing us as two gunslingers in the Old West, starring in an action movie directed by Michael Bay, where we're marching in slow motion with some badass guitar riff overlaid in the background.

We did that for an episode at some ghost town in Nevada back during season five, and I'm fairly certain it was my favorite thirty seconds of staged footage on the show.

I use Craghorn's spare key to unlock the deadbolt and then reach for the door handle. It's a chunk of ice. I picture my hand getting stuck to it, ripping off a layer of skin. Instinctively I recoil, and it's nice to see that I don't leave anything behind on the metal when my hand comes free. "Jesus, feel that."

Mike touches it with the back of his hand and whistles. "That's insane. How warm is it out here?"

"Eighty-five, at least. Can you imagine the strength of that thing inside?"

"I don't want to."

"And Louisa is trapped in there with it."

"Yup," Mike says, matter-of-factly. "Ready to rock?"

I can't quite tell if his enthusiasm is manufactured so he'll be on my good side as I ponder his offer, or if he's now legitimately excited about the investigation. My guess would be a mixture of both.

"Here goes." I reach for the doorknob again and turn it gradually. I don't know why I'm trying to be quiet. That bastard inside already knows we're here. He probably sensed us coming before we hit the 1500 block on this street.

The door, weighty on its hinges and off-balance, swings inside without my help, screeching as it goes, and my thoughts instantly go back to how well that sound would've played during an episode. We would've magnified it, placed a couple of layers over it and, presto, you've got this chill-inducing shriek that sets the mood and tone for the next hour.

Mike, ever the gentleman, motions inside and says, "After you."

I actually hang back for a moment. It's not often that I get legitimately scared, but whatever's inside here has the potential to do some major league damage to our souls, and I do something that I haven't done since we went into the Hopper house for the first time years ago.

I say the Lord's Prayer, loudly, raising my voice into the long, deep, dark entryway, as if I'm talking into a tunnel that leads straight to hell. I touch my crucifix necklace, which feels warm against my skin, and make the sign of the cross over my chest.

Mike joins me, and to any of the neighbors, anyone passing by, we must be a sight. Two grown men, praying *into* a house.

When the prayer is finished, I add, "Hear me now, demon. You have no dominion over my body, or the body of my friend, Mike Long. You have no right to my soul, or the soul of my friend. We are here under the protection of our Lord and Savior, Jesus Christ. Once we enter, you are not allowed to touch us. You are not allowed to harm us in any way. We are protected by Almighty God, and you will obey us and listen to our orders. We are here to ask questions. We are here for information. And, above all, we are here to free the soul of Louisa Craghorn, and we are here to demolish your control over her surviving husband, Dave Craghorn. Do you understand us? We are protected by our faith, we are here to take back this house, and we are here to wreck your fucking ass."

Mike chuckles. "Forever and ever. Amen."

"Let's do this."

Mike and I step across the threshold. We make it three steps inside, enough to clear the path of the swinging door, and it slams behind us, the powerful shock echoing throughout the house.

We barely have time to flinch and look behind us, hoping that it was the wind, before we hear a malicious, throaty growl coming from upstairs, which is followed by the thundering sound of footsteps stampeding down the stairs.

"What the—" Mike says, unable to finish his sentence, as we're both hammered in the chest and thrown into the corner where we fall limply like old jackets.

Mike moans and sits up, rubbing his rib cage and looking like he didn't make it off the canvas after the referee's ten-count. It takes me a second, too, because I feel like I'm breathing through water. With a hit like that, who knows what's going on inside my lungs, but I can't stop now. I can't back out and run away.

"Where'd it go?" Mike asks, whipping his head around as if he can spot the next impending attack.

I do the same. For the moment, the energy in the hallway feels different, as if we just experienced a paranormal Hiroshima, and the aftereffects of the atomic blast are settling down. "Gone, I think. Feels . . ."

"Lighter," Mike says. "You're right. Hit hard and fast, now it's gone."

"For the time being."

"Oh, it'll be back."

"Gonna be a take-no-prisoners kind of night."

Mike has managed to get to his feet, and he agrees with me as he clasps my forearm and pulls me up alongside him. He says, "Three guesses what's showing up on our skin right now, and the first two don't count."

"I'll show you mine if you show me yours?"

We both lift our shirts, and, as expected, we have wide, red splotches that are condensing to claw-tipped handprints. It looks as if Mike got the left and I got the right.

"Son of a bitch. That hurt." I'm still having trouble trying to get a full breath. I double over and wobble with my head cloudy and knees weak. I count to twenty with my eyes closed, inhaling and exhaling in a steady rhythm, and when I look up, Mike is gone.

It's a weird thing, this sensation I'm feeling, because at once I'm feeling abandoned—that childlike fear of being left alone, away from my mother—and terrified of the remote possibility that our enemy has snatched Mike out of thin air.

But rather than Mike having experienced some sort of paranormal rapture, he rounds the corner from the living room, snapping his equipment belt with one hand and handing me his GS-5000 with the other. I take it from him and enjoy the comfortable bulk in my hands. It's almost like a security blanket to me. If I can communicate with what's on the other side, I'll know whether it's an entity that I can approach, or something that requires extra protection from the Big Man upstairs. Whether it was birthed from human loins or the fires of Hades, it's essential to know what's there.

Mike opens a bottle of water, and instead of sipping it, he sniffs at the opening. He scrunches his nose and asks, "Does holy water go stale?"

"What?"

"I mean, does the blessing wear off?"

"I doubt it."

"Good, because I've had this same stuff since that episode in Missouri, the one where we thought that right-hander was terrorizing the family of clowns. Remember?"

"Yeah, what a disappointment."

As it turns out, our entire crew, producers and all, were thoroughly duped by the Morgansterns, who just happened to be a family of professional clowns hoping to gain more exposure for their entertainment company. Lesson learned.

I ask Mike what our plan of attack is.

"Beats me. This is your gig, Ford. I'm just along for moral support."

I feel a cool rush of wind crawl across my exposed skin—my arms, hands, neck, and cheeks—and I know that there aren't any open windows in the house. It's almost as if this demonic entity is caressing me. "Let's move," I tell him. "Feels like it's coming back for another round."

There's nowhere to hide, of course, and I'd rather be in action than simply standing in front of the firing squad, waiting on demonic possession bullets to come flying at my head.

We coordinate our efforts around the living room, kitchen, and hallway, checking each of our spotcams. They're still working, and while I would love to spend an hour or two scanning through them to see if they picked up evidence while we were out for dinner, we don't have the downtime that we would on a normal investigation.

Mike and I, we're in an active, live-fire situation, and the enemy isn't going to sit back while we hunt for proof of his existence.

Mike says, "I don't know why, man, but I feel like this goddamn thing retreated upstairs. I feel safer down here, though."

"While the answers we *want* are upstairs."

My hands are sweaty. I wipe them on the legs of my slacks. Mike used to chide me about how my hands got wetter than a dog's tongue the first few times we filmed. It's not an easy thing, being entertaining.

Mike sees me swiping my palms and grants me a pass, because a second later he's doing the same thing. I tell him, "Here's the plan. We don't need to bother with EMF sweeps or anything generic. That's just telling a zebra he has stripes. We head up and jump immediately into the DVR. We'll do a few sprint sessions to see if we can come up with a name."

"Works for me," Mike says.

There's power in a name, which is why we'll try to wrangle it out of this sucker.

He adds, "He's not gonna give it up easily. This ain't prom night where everybody's eager."

It occurs to me that we've been wasting too much time. "Shit, Mike. Let's move. Hurry, hurry." He's chasing me up the stairs, asking what the problem is, as we take them in leaps of twos and threes. "We should've been up here right away trying to talk to Louisa while that fucking thing charges up again."

Mike says, "*I'm* out of practice. *You* should have known better."

I let the jab go because it's the truth. Then again, I haven't faced anything this overwhelming since the Hopper house. I've spent the past two years tracking down murderers and victims in the afterlife, but nothing like this.

I start the digital voice recorder in my hand, pop the earbuds in, and say, "Louisa? Are you here? It's Ford and Mike. Do you remember us from earlier? We just want to ask you a few questions. And listen to me, Louisa, you don't have to be afraid of us, but you do have to be afraid of that thing when it comes back. It knows why we're here, it knows we want to give you peace, and as soon as it can, it's going to come for us, and for you. Can you tell me if you can hear my voice?"

We wait in relative silence. I hear nothing but the thin whisper of white noise humming through the minuscule speakers wedged in my ears.

The floorboards creak underneath Mike's feet, and I don't bother to mark it on the recording because, for the time being, I don't care about reviewing these tapes tomorrow. I'm not concerned about what I'll be doing in a week. I am focused on the now.

I want this fight to end before sunrise.

I want to have some solid evidence for Detective Thomas.

I want to walk out of here victorious, with the demon gone, Louisa drifting toward the light, and Dave able to enter his own home again, without fear of pain, possession, or more scratches marking his damaged skin.

Can we do it? Can we be successful?

Or are we a couple of ants trying to take down an elephant?

18

While we wait for Louisa to make contact, I go over the details of the day in my mind, and something from earlier pokes its head out at me.

"Mike?"

He mumbles, "Mmm hmm?" in response, focused on the thermal imager in his hand.

"Didn't you say there was something weird about the scratches all over Craghorn? Did it ever come to you? I was thinking about it just now, and—"

Mike says, "Hang on, I think I'm getting something here. Take a look at this. Down there at the end of the hall. You see it?"

I lean over to look at the small screen. Just like before, it's too cold in here to get an accurate reading with the rainbow version of the heat signatures, so Mike has it on the black-and-white setting. It's almost as bad, but better than nothing.

He points to a small white blob in the doorway of the western-facing guest room. "Right there. Doesn't that look like something is peeking out at us?"

"Um, maybe a head and—whoa!" The thing, whatever it was, darts back inside the room. "Move, move, move," I tell

Mike, and we're darting down the hall, bravely running into battle. I won't say we're storming the beaches of Normandy, because yeah, we're not facing down the German artillery, but this is still pretty damn scary. You drop onto those chilly beaches in France, take a bullet to the chest, and you're a goner. Here, in this house, if it's the demon we're running toward and not Louisa, either one of us could face a full-bore demonic possession and a lifetime of sitting in a padded cell, trying to gouge out our own eyeballs with that morning's gelatin spoon.

Give me a German bullet any day. I'll take the quick road home, thank you very much.

In hindsight, maybe we should've tiptoed to the door, but son of a bitch, I'm so amped and ready to kick some ass that I don't hold back, and neither does Mike. He's taken two direct hits from this thing, and I'm sure he's itching to do some waterboarding with holy water.

We jam our shoulders together as we try to get into the guest bedroom, and it's slightly comical. Three Stooges, Laurel and Hardy, Jerry Lewis—shit like that, and it's the kind of thing that Carla would've loved to add into an episode to show the viewing audience that, yes, indeed, we are also human. Goofy ones.

Mike wrenches his body to the side, and we fall through the doorway, stumbling into the open space. It's undisturbed. Nothing has been moved. It looks exactly the same as when Craghorn showed me earlier today when I first arrived with the detective. It used to be a guest room, now it serves as a storage space, cluttered with a few cardboard boxes sitting about, some storage containers with multicolored lids, a pile of women's clothes lying on the floor, still on hangers. My guess is, those belonged to Louisa, and this empty room is as far as he made it with them.

The thing I notice right away is that there's the barest trace of a flowery smell in here.

It's a good sign.

Mike inhales deeply. "No demon farts. What is that? Roses?"

"Perfume, yeah. Anything on the therm?"

"Just the ambient room temp."

I hold up Mike's GS-5000, readjust my earbuds, and say, "Louisa? Was that you? Please don't be afraid. Do you remember us from earlier? This is Mike, and I'm Ford."

I've done this for more than a thousand investigations, but I will never get over the chills that creep up my arm when I hear a voice from beyond the grave.

Every. Single. Time.

"*I'm . . . here . . .*"

I quickly rap Mike on the shoulder. "I got her," I say, and then I offer him the right earbud. He plugs it into his left ear and leans closer. "There you are. Thank you, Louisa. Listen, this is important. We don't have much time. That thing—"

"*. . . demon . . .*"

It's a whisper from a thousand miles away, but it's right beside us, too. Distant, raspy, and full of fear.

"Yes, the demon. We're here to help you, so it's important that you listen to us."

"*. . . trapped . . .*"

"Mike," I say, nudging him. "Do you see her on the therm?"

He shakes his head, looks at me with a sharp squint, his mouth pinched, and frantically motions for me to keep talking to her.

"You're trapped, yes, and we want to free you. I absolutely promise that we're going to get you out of here, but in order to beat this thing, we need your help. We need a name, okay?" I slow down my words and make sure to enunciate. "Do you know its name?"

"*. . . name . . . Azeraul . . .*"

Mike asks me, "Did she say 'Azeraul'? I'm assuming that's the demon's name? Have you ever heard of that one before?"

"Doesn't sound familiar. Louisa? Are you still there?"

"... here ..."

"Thank you. We're proud of you, and I know it's going to be tough, but hang in there for a little bit. It won't be much longer."

Mike is panning the thermal imager around the room, trying to find any sign of our companion, and then he takes a quick look back down the hall. It's not like Azeraul would need to use the conventional methods to enter a space, but I can see how Mike would feel like it's a natural reaction.

"Ask her about the case," he says. "Ask while we have her on the line."

"It's too much. Not right now. Let's get that thing out of here and then—"

"Ford!" he barks. "We may not get that chance and you know it. She's using up so much energy already just to communicate. If this Azeraul bastard builds up enough energy for another attack, she could be too weak. This is it, bro. We gotta do it now."

"I don't want to put too much—"

Again, he barks, "Ford!"

"Okay, okay. Louisa, if you're still here, if you can still communicate, there's something else we can do for you. If you want to be at peace, if you want to go to the light, then tell us this: were you murdered?"

"... I ... was ... true ..."

"Can you tell us who did it? That's what we need to know, okay? If you want your soul to rest and finally leave this world behind, tell us now."

"... can't ... weak ..."

"Stay with us. It's okay, we're almost there."

"... demon ... here ..."

"No," I shout. "Don't go. Fight him. Fight it, Louisa. Give us the name of the person who murdered you. We're so close. Are you scared to tell the truth? Nothing can hurt you, I promise. It'll be fine. Give us a name and then go to the light."

Thinking that it may have been the mayor himself, and that he may have learned that she had kept a diary of their illicit affair and then threatened her, possibly even murdered her, I ask, "Was it the mayor? Did Mayor Gardner kill you? He's dead now. Died three years ago, and if it was him, I'm sure he's burning in hell. He can't reach you."

"... *still love ... her ... go ...*"

"No, no, stay. Please stay. We can do this together, I promise. I can protect you." I turn to Mike and order him to take out his holy water. He complies and begins saying a prayer that I don't recognize as he splashes it around on the boxes, her pile of clothing, and the curtains.

The main bulk of the approaching thunderstorm that has been threatening Hampton Roads all evening hangs in the distance, as if Mother Nature herself is too scared to approach. Small sparkles of lightning illuminate the night from the west. I'm glad the storm is hanging back because we don't need another source of energy for Azeraul.

I ask her again, "Mayor Gardner. Was it him?"

"... *her ...*"

"Her? Her who?"

"... *Azeraul ...*"

"I—what? I don't understand. The demon is a female?"

"*No ... but light ... above ...*"

"It's not a male? You're not making much sense. Can you explain what you mean? Louisa? Louisa?" And then the tape is filled with unbearable, deafening silence. I inhale the deepest breath possible, because I swear it feels like I haven't taken in oxygen in fifteen minutes.

Mike yanks the second earbud out and slings it hard enough to pull the other one out of mine. "Son of a fucking bitch," he snaps. "We *had* her. We could've solved this whole thing and been done with it, and then she tells us some crap about being in love with a demon? Are you kidding me? I mean, what is this bullshit? Something like Stockholm Syndrome?"

I put my hand on his shoulder. "Calm down. Mike. Hey. Breathe for a second."

"Bah," he grumbles, and shoves my arm away. He marches over to a window and leans up against it with his forehead, shoulders slumped, disappointed.

"You know as well as I do that we only get a small percentage of clear answers. That's how this works, and it's the same thing that I tell every single police department that I've worked with. You remember that. I know you do. You're not that far out of practice."

"Let me ask you this," he says, staring out into the night, his breath leaving small condensation circles on the glass. "How often are you *actually* able to help with an investigation, huh? How often do you come away with something tangible that they can use? Because, to me, it was always gibberish, the stuff we caught during a case, you know? At least the EVPs most of the time. When we captured apparitions on camera or saw a ball roll across the floor, that's what I could get behind. But the voices? I don't know how many times I wanted to tell you that you were full of shit, the way you tried to read between the lines and convince the audience that these random words we captured meant something. That's the part I never got, you know? Why do it? Why bother trying to force meaning onto nothing?"

"It's not nothing, Mike. It's *never* nothing. They're there. They're communicating."

"And you're making up stories around nonsensical crap."

"I'm trying to give these spirits an identity. They're people. Are. Were. Doesn't matter. They have a story and they're trying to tell it. Think of it like a coloring book. The structure was there, it just needed filling in because that's what worked for the fans. And to answer your question, I give the detectives actionable material about forty percent of the time, honestly. At least according to my case records."

"That much, huh?"

"Yeah. You want, I can sit down with you and show you all my files."

"I believe you, Ford. It's just—"

"Just what?"

"This is going to come out of left field, but I *have* to know," he says, turning to me, crossing his arms. "Here's your chance."

"For?"

"I think, maybe—look, I can't think of a way to say it without getting all worked up—but fuck me, Ford, *why*? Why did you do that to Chelsea? Huh? Can you explain it to me? I can't even begin to tell you how goddamn let down I was. You were my brother. I thought I knew, man, and then . . . *that*. I don't get it. You already had money. You already had fame. Give me a reason, not an excuse. I never gave you a chance before, so tell me now."

I sidestep over to a rickety stack of crates, grunting an exhausted old-man groan, as I lower myself onto them. I'm tired. Emotionally wrecked on so many different levels. "Really," I say, tapping the digital voice recorder on my palm. "Really, truly, and honestly, I've been trying to figure that out for over two years now. Part of me got blinded by the moment, the potential to create, what? Television history? Who would've remembered it a year later other than our fans? The other part of me—on some delusional level—actually believed that if Chelsea was able to *literally* face down her demon, then she could take on the world."

"Oh, for God's sake, don't try to fool me or yourself with that horseshit. We didn't send her in there to come out with a *win*. She was a goddamn trigger object and you know it. We sent her in there to draw out that right-hander and get some good shots for Halloween."

"Nah." I shake my head. "That was me being 'TV Ford' around the producers and the network people. I thought I was doing the right thing. You and I, the crew, the producers, we'd all been through so many investigations together and we've all seen how horribly some families can get affected by the paranormal. Whether it's a pissed-off spirit or an actual demon, everyone knows that lives get ruined all the time. I can't even describe to you just how conflicted I was, but when I looked at Chelsea and her case, the ego was on one shoulder wearing the devil horns, carrying a pitchfork, and this overwhelming need to *help* her was on the other, wearing a halo and playing the harp."

Mike moves away from the window, steps over, and sits down beside me on the wooden crates. The slats creak under his added weight. "Fine, I get *that*. Here's what I don't get. Answer this, and we can drop it, okay? I'm so fucking tired of hating you for what you did. It's exhausting carrying around so much mental baggage. I'm not saying that we can bro hug and be done with it, but what I need to know is, why bring her back to that house after they'd managed to break free? That's the part I don't get. We could have done the show without her. They were twenty miles away, and she showed every indication of being fine. Happy little kid, back to normal. Why subject her to that house again?"

Here we go. I've been holding onto this for a long time. "Did I ever tell you that I went to see the Hoppers about a week before the investigation?"

"No." He shakes his head. "Wait, was that when you said you were taking Melanie to New York City for the weekend?"

"Yep."

"Why lie about that?"

"Because, I felt like, if I took you with me to do a *pre*-pre-interview, you'd squash the whole live show, and that's kinda why I went. I wanted to gauge the situation with the family and get some feedback before we went in, right? Like you said, Chelsea seemed fine. Seemed like a normal kid, and I thought that there wasn't any use in bringing her back."

"And?"

"And she *was* fine, great, wonderful, until she said—I'll never forget the chills I got—she said, 'If you go back to our old house, can you tell the dark man to stay out of my dreams?' That's when I knew. That's when it occurred to me that we had one helluva show on our hands and that she needed to beat it if she ever wanted calm in her life again. I've regretted the decision since she fell out of that attic. You don't need to hate me. I do enough of that to myself."

"Jesus," Mike says, holding out his right arm. "Look at my goosebumps."

"See what I mean?"

"No, not from that." He snatches an EMF detector off his tool belt, flips it on, and the meter immediately pegs in the red. "Azeraul is back. Get ready."

19

We used to do that sometimes—have deep, philosophical chats during the down periods. It never made it onto the show because who wants to see two paranormal investigators sitting around, having a heart-to-heart discussion? Nah, save that for the behind-the-scenes menu item whenever the box set of seasonal DVDs comes out. We both know that after a giant explosion of energy, like our attack downstairs, it can take some time for a spirit or a right-hander to recharge itself. Depending on the strength of the entity in question, it could be a couple of hours, or a couple of days.

Apparently, Azeraul needs about fifteen minutes to recover, which is just insane. We don't have any EMF pumps running, and that approaching storm has yet to move any closer. Sure, tiny droplets of rain pepper the windows, and the lightning flickers once in a while and illuminates the house, but it's not close enough for him to recharge his paranormal batteries.

Mike hops to his feet. He's thinking the same thing because he checks his watch and says, "That was just a little over fourteen minutes since the attack downstairs. Makes you wonder if that damn thing plugged itself into an outlet."

"Plan of attack? Stay put? Or, no, we should go back to that front room where we saw him earlier. Maybe Louisa was living in *here*, and he's playing house over *there*."

"Not that I think it matters, because he'll find us regardless, but I can tell you this much: dude is gonna be super pissed that his play-toy is gone. We could probably do a quick round to check, but it sounded to me like Louisa moved on."

"Definitely. She's gone," I say. "Just like always, and I don't know how I know, but I can feel it. Heaven or hell, she went somewhere else."

"Ssshh," Mike whispers, putting a finger up to his lips. "You hear that? Footsteps?"

"I thought it was a door latch. Metallic, maybe."

"Let's go check."

From down the hall, we hear a tremendous crash. Mike and I rush for the door, allow each other to exit without a comical mishap, and once we step into the upstairs hall, I can immediately tell what happened. In the far front room, the spartan one where Azeraul had hidden earlier, a rush of water is leaking out from underneath the closed door.

"The vase," I say.

"Yep."

"God, feel the temperature in here."

"Feels like it dropped another five."

"It must be fifty degrees."

Mike turns on his thermal imaging camera. "Good call. Solid forty-nine point two, except for that bedroom."

"What's it reading?"

He holds the camera sideways so that I can see the screen. The door is glowing white hot on the monochromatic setting. A small cursor, ironically in the shape of a cross, plots around the screen, scanning temperatures and giving us an idea of what the laser is picking up with various locations. When it dances across the door, I almost expect it to read sixty-six point six. Instead, I'm blown away when I see eighty-seven degrees.

"Eighty-seven? Are you kidding me? And that's the outside of the door."

"I can't even imagine what it's like inside there."

I feel a slight rumble in my feet. It's a muted shake, almost like the platform in a subway station when the train rolls in for a stop. "Dude? You feel that?"

"Yeah."

We both look down at the hardwood flooring and retreat a step, as if that will have any bearing on our safety.

"Any trains close by?" he asks.

"Nope."

"Didn't see headlights so I'm guessing no semis come down this street."

"Residential," I remind him. "No restaurants or convenience stores for blocks."

"Then it's our buddy, or not?"

"Azeraul? Could be, but I would think—"

Something pounds against the inside of the closed bedroom door.

BOOM. BOOM. BOOM.

It's thirty feet from us, but I can feel the reverberations in my feet. They've escalated. It's no longer the rumble of an approaching subway train. Instead, it almost feels as if we're standing on top of an unbalanced washer. Almost like a rhythmic thumping under the soles of our shoes.

To our left and right, here in this cramped hall, the walls are grumbling. I put my hand out and feel the pressure being built up inside them.

"This fucking thing is *strong*," I tell Mike. "Have you ever seen anything like it?"

"Not since the Hopper house."

It's dark in here. Damn, is it *dark*. You'd think with some of the streetlights outside, there would be more of a glow, yet it feels like Azeraul is draining all the light out of this place. No wonder Dave Craghorn had such a pallid look to his skin.

Craghorn.

Craghorn's skin.

I keep forgetting to talk to Mike about Craghorn's skin. No time for that now.

We both stand motionless, like breathing cadavers, watching the room, waiting on whatever comes next.

"Mike?" I whisper with a tremor in my tone.

"What?"

"I'm not gonna lie, dude. I'm not sure I want to go in that room." I expect him to shoehorn me into attacking this demon. I expect him to say something about how the great Ford Atticus Ford of the past would never back down, and what happened to wrecking this thing's ass?

Instead, he says, "Me—uh, me neither."

"Want to stall a minute, see if it burns itself out?"

"Please."

BOOM. BOOM. BOOM.

The pounding isn't just in the door this time, it feels as if a giant is slamming the home's foundation with a monstrous warhammer.

It's not enough to make me stumble, yet I have to hold my arms out to keep my balance. The hair on the back of my neck stands up. People always talk about how that happens to them during a scary movie—maybe it does, maybe it doesn't—but wait until you're standing in a house with a demon and see what happens.

That shit is real.

"I can't breathe. Can we get out of this hallway?" Mike asks without waiting for an answer. I agree immediately and follow him, albeit forward, which is not exactly my preferred direction, until we're at the landing where it's less suffocating. The long set of stairs stretch out below us, and we both move behind the banister to our right, as if these dark-stained slats will give us any layer of protection.

"How long do we wait?"

"As long as it takes. That door," Mike says, looking down at the thermal camera, "is up to ninety-two degrees. It *can't* sustain this much—"

A violent rumble interrupts Mike. The entire house shudders.

BOOM. BOOM. BOOM.

I tell Mike, "He keeps that up, he won't have much left."

"Seems like it's getting stronger. We gotta wait, Ford. I go home with company, especially something like this? Toni will murder me before *it* has a chance to."

"Agreed. I talk a big game, but this is an entirely different sport."

We're both so caught up in the moment that I realize we're not running any equipment other than Mike's thermal imager. We never had a chance to set up our spotcams on the second floor, and I still have the GS-5000 shoved in my back pocket. I'm hoping that our cameras downstairs are picking this up on audio and capturing the shaking.

I pull the voice recorder out, offer Mike an earbud, and he declines.

"Thanks, but I'd rather not hear what that thing has to say."

I press record and wait through the rumbling of the floorboards, the rattling of the picture frames, and the erratic breathing of one Mike Long, once famous paranormal investigator. Aside from the static hiss crawling in over the top of the surrounding noises, I hear nothing. I wait and I wait, and the floor continues to shiver under our feet.

BOOM. BOOM. BOOM.

I jump. Mike jumps.

And then we're engulfed in shuddering silence once again.

I expected demonic growls. I expected this almighty right-hander to come across the airwaves, shouting vicious words of putrid hate at us. But he's not, and after witnessing this display of incredible power, I'm not ashamed to admit that I'm *still* not going anywhere near that door.

"Can we take a breather for a sec?" I ask.

"Now?"

"I need to think about something else before I piss myself."

"Fair enough."

I ask him, "Probably not the best time, but Craghorn—what was it about his skin? Something made my sixth sense tingle."

"You're right, it is bad timing," Mike says, glancing at me while keeping a wary eye on the superheated bedroom door. "But yeah, what I didn't get was, if his whole damn body was covered in that roadmap of claw marks and scratches and scars, why weren't there any on his face?"

"There weren't?" I try to picture Craghorn in my mind—

BOOM. BOOM. BOOM.

Goddamn it.

—and I see a diminutive, timid man wearing slacks, a long-sleeve shirt, and a jacket in the middle of a summer heat wave. I haven't seen him in six hours, but under such duress with that fucking thing over there, trying to rip the house off its foundation, I'm having trouble recalling Craghorn's face. Long hair. Goatee. I picture him showing me his arms and his belly, his scarred back, and then his face comes into focus. It's somewhat pockmarked from an unfortunate childhood with either smallpox or acne, but not a single series of three claw marks mocking the Holy Trinity.

"Shit. Smooth as a baby's behind, wasn't it?"

"I wouldn't go that far."

"Fine, as smooth as the moon's surface, but what do you think it means?"

"Use your head, man—"

A gut-wrenching roar emanates from the room and scrapes at my eardrums. It's the wail of a million souls swallowing acid. It's a pterodactyl being burned alive. It's Godzilla stepping on a Lego in the middle of the night.

Mike puts a hand on my arm and pulls me into a retreating step.

"You don't think he was lying, do you?"

"That's exactly what I think."

"Craghorn was making it all up?"

"Well, not all of it. I mean, witness Exhibit A behind that door."

As if on cue, and reacting to us acknowledging his presence, Azeraul pounds the door yet again.

BOOM. BOOM. BOOM.

"Goddamn, that's getting annoying," Mike says.

"He's not backing down, is he?"

"EMF meter is red-lining big time."

"Okay, so, Craghorn. You think he's using this demon as an alibi? Sort of?"

"Think about it. He's got marks all over his whole body. Even told me they're on the bottom of his feet. While you were down talking to the detective, Craghorn showed me places I didn't necessarily want to see. He's covered. All but his face."

Lightbulb. Sometimes I'm dense. "Ooooh, which he can't hide in public with long sleeves or pants."

"Ding ding ding."

"So you think he killed her? You think he found out about Louisa's affair? Choked her to death, then dumped her in the Chesapeake Bay?"

"Doesn't that make sense to you?"

The pounding hasn't happened in at least thirty seconds, and I glance at the thermal imager to see if the temperature has gone down. Fingers crossed, I'm hoping Azeraul is burning himself out again.

Nope. The exterior temperature of the door has actually spiked by another degree.

"Ninety-three," Mike announces.

"I noticed."

"He's building up."

"I noticed that, too."

The doorknob begins to rattle. I can't see it from here, but I've heard that sound enough over the years to peg precisely what it is. It's a sound that's as distinct as clipping your nails.

"*Umm*," Mike whines, retreating another step.

I follow him.

"I'm buying that Craghorn is hiding something with the claw marks, but—"

"Ford?"

"I don't understand what it could be. Your theory makes sense from every angle—"

"Ford. Look."

"I see it." The door is creeping open, centimeter by centimeter. "But the thing is, Detective Thomas told me that Craghorn has a solid alibi. He wasn't anywhere near Louisa. He was out of town on business for two weeks prior to when they found her body. Forensics said she'd only been in the bay for a week."

"Hitman?"

The bedroom door slams open, violently. There's an explosion of plaster and the door gets stuck because the handle is imbedded in the wall.

We scamper back to Louisa's room. Why? Who knows? It feels safe back there. Going forward to reach the stairs would mean going *toward* Azeraul.

No, thank you.

The Graveyard: Classified Paranormal Series

The almighty Ford Atticus Ford and Mike "The Exterminator" Long are officially terrified.

Mike admits it out loud, and I'm not entirely sure I've ever felt this level of fear.

Now I know what little Chelsea Hopper must have felt like before I talked her into climbing that ladder.

I try to make a joke. I do that in the worst possible situations sometimes. It's a defense mechanism. I say, "Hey, Mike?"

"What?"

"Don't let the dark man get me, okay?"

20

You know what's really damn eerie? Looking down an empty hallway and hearing slow, methodical footsteps coming in your direction without being able to see what's there.

This isn't just my ego talking, but it's likely that I've performed more investigations than any other working paranormal investigator, in the public eye and out, yet that gets me every single time. You'd think I would be used to it by now. You'd think that I'd be like, "Oh, shucks, there's a spirit coming, time to go say howdy."

Nope.

Each time is different. Each new experience brings new fear, new challenges.

That thing marching down the hallway? It's an approaching storm, much like the flickering lightning and distant rumbles outside, and it's about to unleash the fury of hell instead of a cleansing rain.

I duck my head back inside Louisa's room. "He's coming."

"I can hear it."

"Not it. Him."

"Whatever the fuck that thing is, Ford, it's coming, and I can hear it."

Mike tells me this as he's frantically working with his digital voice recorder, the thermal imaging camera, the full-spectrum cameras, everything we brought, all of which seem to have simultaneously lost battery power. To a ghost or a demon, a fresh battery is a protein bar packed with extra caffeine.

Azeraul sounds like he's still twenty feet down the hall, and somehow he's reached inside this room and sucked the life out of our equipment, essentially leaving us defenseless.

Mike screams, "Shit!" and slams a now-useless recorder down onto a crate. A plastic button pops off, bounces to the side, and drops to the floor.

We exchange worried glances.

Worried about demonic possession. Worried about physical damage and pain.

Worried about taking something home with us that might affect our friends and loved ones.

For Mike, he has an entire family to worry about.

For me, it's just Ulie, but I love that mutt like my own child, and I don't want anything to happen to him. Pets are sensitive, I've explained that, but I've also seen horrible cases where family pets have been mutilated by outraged, jealous, vindictive spirits and soulless demonic entities as a means of retribution or mental torture. That's not happening to my pup. No way.

I'm filled with a renewed sense of vigor, thinking about this thing trying to do harm to our families.

They say that true courage is running into the battle even when you're scared.

Well, I'm no hero, but I'm not a pansy, either.

Mike shouts, "Goddamn it!" at the ceiling. "Another one, dead in *seconds*." He pulls a rechargeable battery out of a full-spectrum camera, flings it across the room, and we're immediately greeted with the sound of shattering glass. Just a picture frame. Not a window. Though I doubt Craghorn would care much if he's never coming back here.

In addition to the footsteps, Azeraul knocks on the wall.

Tap, tap, tap.

Step, step.

It sounds like hard-soled shoes on a hardwood floor, but I know better. That's the clop of hooves.

Step, step. Tap, tap, tap.

He's teasing us.

Step. Tap, tap, tap. Step.

"Holy water, Mike."

"What?"

"Your holy water. Give it to me."

He yanks the small bottle out of his utility belt and tosses it over. "That'll probably be like shooting charging bull with a marshmallow gun, but what the hell, you can try."

Step, step.

Tap, tap, tap.

"I can do this," I say. "You just see if you can get one of those DVRs working. Or the spirit box. Something. I want to have a chat with this son of a bitch."

"Yeah, right," he says, raising an eyebrow. "Don't do anything stupid. You know how you get when—"

I hold my palm up. "I got this. It'll be okay."

Step, step.

Tap, tap, tap.

Azeraul can't be more than ten feet from us.

Outside, over the rooftop of a distant office building, a bolt of lightning shreds the sky in half, a yellow streak across a mottled black canvas.

A beat later, thunder reverberates throughout the house, rattling loose-paned glass windows.

Sure, maybe that's a subtle warning from God, but the dude ain't here right now to tell me in person, so I'm pushing ahead.

I unscrew the cap on the bottle of holy water, shove it in my pocket, and then sidestep over to the bedroom door, scooting and sliding, really, until my shoulder is just inside the opening. I lean out quickly for a peek and duck back inside. It *appears* empty, as expected. For the sake of my soul, it's better that I don't see it. My morbid curiosity, though, would like to witness a demon manifest in the flesh. Once would be enough. Once might be the only chance I'd ever get.

Mike says, "Hey, hang on. Look what I found." He hands me a crucifix, a much larger version of the one hanging on the chain around my neck. "It was over there on top of that box. Must've been Louisa's."

"Little extra ammo never hurt anybody. You should probably know that you're in my will, just make sure the lawyers know where to find you," I say, and then take three quick breaths in succession. I dart through the doorway and hold the crucifix aloft with one hand, squeezing a short stream of holy water down the hall with the other. I manage to say, "In the name of our Lord—" before I hear the same eardrum-scraping scream as before.

Only now it's directly in front of me and so loud that I can feel the sound slithering over my skin.

Before I can react, before I can dart back into the room, a searing hot hand clasps my throat, clenching tightly, sharp claws gouging my skin.

I lash out with the crucifix, trying to use it as a hammer, and sling more holy water at the invisible demon in front of me.

Another acid-drenched screech fills the hall, and underneath it, I can hear Mike shouting, "Ford! Get back in here!"

The white-hot hand is crushing my windpipe. I manage to gurgle, "Can't. Too strong."

Another stream of holy water. Another wail.

"In . . . the name of . . . God, our Father in Heaven . . . I command you . . . Get off me!" I shove the crucifix forward, in the direction where I suspect Azeraul's face might be, and I hear the crackling, hissing sound of searing demon flesh.

A howling, louder than anything I've heard so far, explodes throughout the static-filled space around me. It's hideous and coated with such vile hatred that it weakens my heartbeat.

Then, a deep, disembodied voice says, "Hell waits for you, Ford."

And then the pressure on my neck is gone.

It hurts like, well, it hurts like hell, and I feel like someone held a hot iron to my throat, but at least I can take a breath.

It's warmer, too. Noticeably warmer, as if the temperature in the hallway is clicking up a degree with each tick-tock of the supposedly broken grandfather clock downstairs.

I slump to the floor. I barely have the energy to hold my head up.

My vision swims, and Mike is at my side, hands under my arms, trying to drag me back into the bedroom. He's saying something, yet I can't make out what, because the only thing that's at the forefront of my mind is that this demon called me out by name. Again.

There's power in a name.

***

I'm not sure how long I'm out, but it's the second time I've been unconscious around Mike today. At least it wasn't his fists of fury that put me down into la-la land. I'm hoping this doesn't become a trend, because I'm not a fan of it.

Actually, before I open my eyes, I lie here for a second because I can hear Mike talking, and it's slightly amusing. He obviously doesn't know I'm conscious yet, and this might be a perfect chance for good ammunition down the road.

"Dear Heavenly Father, hallowed by thy name, your will be done on earth as . . . As what? Jesus. Why can't I remember this? On earth as in heaven! Right. That's right. And then—shit. Forget it. Amen. Just do *not* let him be possessed, okay? Please? I know you're up there, God, and I know you're listening, because there can't be good without evil and evil without good, and whatever that thing was, it was evil, so I know you're up there, too. Just—look, I'm sorry, okay? I'm sorry I didn't stick closer to my friend, and I'm sorry I abandoned him, but you gotta understand—it was harsh—*harsh*—that thing we did. *He* did. And I couldn't stand by that, and now, Jesus, who knows what's going on. All I'm trying to say is, if you'll take this off of him, get this demon out of him, we can fight it, and I'll make him, or we—*we*—can figure out what it was that attacked the Hopper girl, okay? We'll fight it for you. We'll be holy warriors, or whatever."

I open my eyes and say, "Dude, it's not your fault."

Mike yelps, lurches back, and then pulls me in with a strong hug. He's overjoyed for a good fifteen seconds before he leans into a solid punch that will certainly leave a bruise on my chest.

"Damn you, Ford," Mike says. "How long were you awake?"

"Lord's Prayer. After all these years, how it is possible that you don't have it memorized?"

"You better believe I'm gonna learn it now. Are you okay?" He helps me to my feet, hands on both of my shoulders, and starts to survey me the way a mother does when her only son gets home from the war.

"Does it seem brighter in here?"

I hadn't noticed that the storm finally arrived, but it's reached an apex. Lighting flashes and thunder bellows its damning curse. Bulging, pregnant drops of rain slam against the windows.

Yet the spare bedroom, our sanctuary, appears to be livelier. Alleviated. Unburdened.

"I swear, man, as soon as you got rid of that thing, it was almost like somebody turned on a low-watt lightbulb or lifted a blanket off the streetlights. So crazy."

Mike lets go of me and backs up a step with his hands on his hips. I roll my shoulders and crack my neck, then give him some bad news. "It's not completely gone," I say. "It's still here."

A grin spreads his lips, pulls his cheeks up until the dimples are on display—the same dimples that thousands of spotcamgirls tweeted and posted about for years. I haven't seen Mike smile like that since, well, it was a long time before Chelsea Hopper. I can remember that much.

"You're fucking with me, right?"

I'm not, and he knows it. We've been friends and partners long enough for him to understand what I'm getting at. I've mentioned that I'm 'sensitive' to spirits, for lack of a better word, and at the moment, I can feel that Azeraul remains in this house. Lurking. Holding back. Waiting and conserving his energy. If it's like before, it'll be another fifteen minutes or so before he can fully attack again.

I don't plan for us to be in this house for that long, but I'm not done yet.

"You can feel it, can't you?"

"He's weak, but he's here. I don't know where." I point to Mike's utility belt. Each of his devices hang in their slots like grenade duds, useless and weighing him down. "You got any batteries left for those?"

"Ford, no."

"Do you?"

"Yeah, one set left for the DVR. He didn't get those."

"Load 'em up."

"*Hell* no. Let's beat feet and get away from it. It's too powerful, and this is a fight we can*not* win. You *know* me, Ford. I don't ever back down from a challenge, but I know when to cut my losses and move on."

I hold out my hand and waggle my fingers. The international sign for "gimme."

"I'm telling you, don't do it. Don't risk it. Look at your neck. You're already contaminated. One more like that, and—"

"Mike! Enough. Just give me the damn DVR. You can leave if you want, but I need answers."

He relents with a huff forceful enough to knock down a Clydesdale.

"What?"

"Nothing, it's just that you remind me of somebody I used to know."

"Who?"

"The old Ford. The real one."

21

The upstairs seems dead—pardon the afterlife pun—so Mike and I move downstairs. He keeps checking his watch, every fifteen or twenty seconds, and I finally tell him to chill because the anxious repetition is driving my own angst level exponentially higher. "And besides," I tell him, "if this right-hander's recharge time is a little over fourteen minutes, then we have—"

"Eight minutes and thirty-seven seconds left," Mike says, interrupting with a voice that quakes over some obvious nervous tension.

"That's an eternity. If we were in the fourth quarter of an NFL game, we'd have, like, another thirty minutes to go."

"Shitty metaphor. We don't get any timeouts."

I smirk and see that my attempts at calming him aren't working. He's almost vibrating.

"You getting *any*thing on the live feed?" he asks.

"*Nada.* Quiet as a tomb in here."

"Are you intentionally fucking with me?"

"Probably a little." I readjust the earbuds, and if it's possible to physically do so, I listen harder. There's only the sound of our shoes on the hardwood floor, Mike's uneasy breathing, and the occasional creak of a board underfoot or a door swinging open. I don't bother audibly marking them on the recording because I'm so amped up about this moment, I'm mentally logging everything. It's only the two—well, three—of us inside this house, and the contamination from outside is so minimal it might as well not exist. We're in a vacuum, just us and him.

"Seven fifty," Mike informs me.

"Relax. *Please.*"

"I can't, man." He cracks his knuckles and wiggles his fingers. "I don't know what to do with my hands when I'm not holding something."

"Use one of them to cover your mouth. I'm trying to listen. In fact, maybe I should go a little batshit on him, huh? Get crazy aggressive and try to draw him out before the timer stops."

"Are you nuts?"

"Rhetorical question? We draw him out before he's full strength, we get control of the situation, we get some answers, and we're gone. It'll be like we're psyching him out or something. Maybe demons are just like us. Maybe they get stupid when they're all worked up."

"Seven minutes, fifteen seconds. If you're going to do it, do it now."

"There's Big Mike. Back again."

"Whatever. *Go.* Do it."

Mike is basically going into this blindfolded and wearing earmuffs since I'm holding the last working piece of equipment. It has to be slightly unnerving to simply stand there and wait on the next attack to hit without any forewarning. So I understand his hesitation, but if I get what we need, it'll all be worth it.

"Azeraul!" I call out. "Demon child of Satan! How did it feel earlier when I kicked your ass with the power of God? Did you like that? Huh? Tell me. How'd it feel when a pissant, pathetic mortal like me gave you a nice little battle scar? All the other demons around the block, laughing at you, pointing at that nice crucifix branded on your forehead. I heard it, Azeraul. I heard the hiss. I heard your flesh searing with the burn of God's love. You're weaker than I thought. You're pitiful."

"Ford—"

"I got this."

"I'm just saying—"

"Azeraul. Are you there?" I hold up a wait-a-second finger to Mike when the distant sound of a child's laughter—a young girl—comes across the earbuds. I whisper to Mike, "Laughing. He's here. Taking the form of a girl."

"Oh, shit. Okay, okay, just be careful."

"I can hear you," I shout, slipping into the living room. The clock on the wall, a plain-faced one that maybe cost Craghorn a buck at a discount store, ticks with abandon, like it's projecting through a megaphone. "Come talk to me."

More giggling, followed by the angelic voice of a young child. She sounds like she might be about five years old, but I'm not fooled. I *know* this is Azeraul. I've been doing this awhile, and there's not much creepier than a foul-mouthed, wretched, rotting right-hander trying to pass itself off as a kid.

In the girl's voice, he says, *"That's not my name, silly."*

The voice sounds as if it's on my left, so I turn in that direction and face the corner. "Yes, it is. Louisa told us. You've been keeping her hostage, and she knows you. Demon, thy name is Azeraul, and you must obey the word of—"

"*Shut up*," the girl's voice screeches. "*I . . . am not . . . Azeraul.*"

"Your lies are pathetic. We know your name. We have power over you."

Mike tugs at my sleeve. "Goddamn it, dude, don't leave me hanging. What's it saying?"

"It's lying," I tell him. "Says its name isn't Azeraul."

"Is it the same one? Maybe the big one left."

I shake my head, feel the earbud wires swaying against my neck, and say, "It's him. I can feel it. Definitely trying to disguise himself."

Mike groans. "God, I hate it when they do that."

I lift my voice to the corner and take two steps closer. "Azeraul. Tell me now. Tell me what you know about Louisa Craghorn."

Nothing. Just that fucking clock ticking like John Henry hammering a railroad spike.

I try a different tactic: flattery. "If you're so powerful, then you must know things that we don't. Doesn't that feel good? Having information? Use that power of yours. Who murdered her? If you tell us that, we'll leave, and you can have your house back. You win, we win."

Silence.

"Was it her husband? Did Dave Craghorn find out that his wife was cheating on him, and he murdered her?"

Excruciating silence.

I'm afraid I've lost him or that he's decided to retreat for now, to regroup and build up more energy before he comes back for another attack.

"Time check, Mike."

"Four minutes, eighteen seconds. Did he ditch? Should we go?"

"Calm before the storm, I think." I move around the love seat and short-step over to the corner where the demon may have been. I don't smell sulfur, nor do I see any signs of him, like floating black masses or darting orbs of light. It's times like this that the full-spectrum camera would come in handy. It's a lesson we thought we'd learned ages ago. You can never have enough batteries.

Especially against a right-hander.

Mike says, "The hair on my arms is standing up."

I look over at him, concerned. "Like, from fear, or what? A presence?"

"Maybe. I don't know. Both?"

Back when the show was running, and even before then when we were two goofy guys with a couple of cameras and a dream, the typical "sensitive" things rarely happened to Mike.

This is not a good sign. I'm worried that Azeraul is sneaking around here, trying to steal Mike's energy from him, perhaps even invade his body.

"Get out of the house."

"But what about—"

"Out the door, Mike. I'll be fine."

"But—"

I quickly remind him about his wife and kids, that he doesn't have to do this, that I dragged him into it, and it's my battle.

He closes his eyes and rubs his temples. "I feel dizzy. Weak, too."

That's even worse.

"Do I have to shove you out that door?"

"My heartbeat is going so fast."

In my earbuds, I hear a cackle of little-girl laughter, like it's the funniest thing she's ever heard. Obviously, Azeraul has absorbed enough of Mike's life force to return.

Mike whispers, "Sulfur," so quietly that it's barely picked up by the microphone. Then he adds, "Two minutes." His arm drops to his side, then the rest of his body crumples onto the middle cushion of the large couch. He sits back, eyes glazed over and staring into the center of the room as if he's catatonic.

I let loose a chorus of curse words and dart across the living room, my shin slamming against the coffee table, sending knickknacks and magazines flying as it overturns. Before I can make it to Mike, I feel a hand on my chest, hot and burning, holding me back.

The little girl's voice says, *"He's mine now, Ford."*

"Shut up. Shut up. Do *not* use my name. Get off me." I try to wrench away, but no matter which direction I turn, I can feel the pressure of the claw-tipped hand on my skin. "The power of Christ compels you, Azeraul. Get off of—"

The now-familiar screeching roar doesn't just come through my earphones, but it explodes into the entire room, so loud that I can picture it bowing the walls outward.

I trip sideways and fall to the floor, covering my ears.

Mike sits, immobile.

Azeraul's voice, as before, comes from everywhere and nowhere at once. "*I am not Azeraul. I am death. I am immortal. I am the enemy of God. I am the destroyer. I am everything you fear, child, but I am not Azeraul. This name you speak has no power over me. Master calls. I must . . . go. Light will come again, but so will I.*"

I can't actually believe what I'm about to do, because it's pure crazy-talk, but I stand up and beg for a demon not to go. "Don't leave. Please. Who murdered Louisa Craghorn? Was it her husband? Did she ever say who it was while you had her trapped? Give me some answers, please!"

Rumbling laughter that chills my spine and sends goosebumps across every inch of skin ripples around the room. And then, words follow that stun me into silence as they trail away, fading into the darkness:

"*Begging . . . beneath you . . . See you again . . . Hopper house.*"

"What the fuck did you just say?" I feel dazed, slammed in the chest by a wrecking ball. "Are you the same . . . the same one . . . the one who . . . ?"

And then he's gone.

Azeraul. Not Azeraul.

Whatever that thing's name is, it left the house. Just like before, when we initially drove him back, the room, the entirety of wood, brick, and stone in this structure, feels lighter. Brighter. Almost as if rock and maple alike are heaving a sigh of relief. The suffocating blanket that's been choking the atmosphere has lifted, too, and for the first time since I stepped in this house earlier today—soon to be yesterday, according to the ticking wall clock—it feels like I'm inhaling clean, fresh air. The hint of putrid smoke that laced the oxygen is gone, and I take deep breaths until my lungs feel washed and bleached of the demonic muck.

His final words clang around inside my head.

See you again . . . Hopper house.

I don't even—I can't wrap my mind around this possibility. We're along the coast of Virginia. The Hopper house is in Ohio, a thousand miles away.

I stand, completely motionless, considering the implications. It's not unheard-of for spirits to become attached to items and move thousands of miles, and I wouldn't imagine that demons would be confined to an area. It's not like Satan is franchising haunted houses, and these soul-sucking bastards have to set up shop in a specific territory.

But, holy shit, what are the odds that Chelsea's demon is the same one that was here? And that I would end up here investigating it as well? Mike suggested the possibility earlier, but I scoffed at him, and now . . .

See you again . . . Hopper house.

Maybe, just maybe, that's not what it meant. Maybe he was saying he'd see me there. Maybe I'm supposed to go back to Chelsea's old house for a showdown.

I honestly don't know.

Is it a sign? Should I agree to Mike's request for the documentary? Could this really be a shot at redemption?

I tell myself not to let those thoughts intrude. My redemption should not come at the hands of exploiting Chelsea's story again.

Over on the couch, Mike coughs, hard and raspy, like it's his first time smoking a cigarette, and his body is trying to reject the filth in his lungs. He leans forward, hands up over his mouth, and hacks until I go to him. I sit down on the couch by his side, fearful that Not Azeraul might still be inside Mike, having duped me with false promises about leaving. But when he turns to me, I can see the real Mike in his eyes. They're uncontaminated, unpossessed. He's looking at me by his own volition.

He says, "Did we get him?"

"To be continued."

22

Mike is beat; says he feels like he had a garbage truck run over his chest, then back up and do it again; wants to drive home and go to bed, sleep next to his wife, but I tell him it's probably too dangerous. If he's that exhausted, I don't want him passing out on the way home, crashing, and then dying. I'd be sad, yeah, and clearly I don't want Mike haunting me because that would be a never-ending barrage of practical jokes, missing keys, and general pestering until I joined him on the other side.

We made the pact to haunt each other, and to be annoyingly foolish about it back when we first started this journey together, and I'm quite positive that Mike hasn't forgotten.

Instead of letting him drive home, I convince him to come zonk out in my hotel room down at the Virginia Beach oceanfront. The couch in my room folds out into one of those grotesquely uncomfortable beds, and I remind him that it'll be like old times, back when we were on the road and filming. Me sleeping like a pampered princess with my face cream to keep the cameras and lighting friendly during the day, accompanied by a rejuvenating eye mask and earplugs, skin soaking up mist from the portable humidifier, all while Mike lay in the other queen bed, snoring, drooling, and sleeping naked.

Awkward were the nights when he'd kick the covers off.

In addition to saving his ass from turning into highway hamburger, I let him know that Detective Thomas will most likely want to speak to him again, adding, "What I do now, it's not like the old days where we'd pack up and head back to the hotel for an after-party. I usually spend a day or two with the detectives, answering questions, going over details of my investigation, maybe trying to help them piece together clues if I don't get any direct answers."

"Whatever," Mike says. "Just give me a bed and some coffee in the morning."

As we pack up the rest of our gear—my small collection compared to Mike's ghost-hunting surplus store quantity—I tell Mike what the right-hander said while he was catatonic. I add, "You're not going to believe this, but I think it's the one who hurt Chelsea."

Mike snorts. "You're shitting me."

"Dead serious, dude. It said, 'See you again. Hopper house.' Just like that."

"But that doesn't necessarily mean it was him."

"True, and I considered that, but the more I think about it, the more it feels right. Doesn't it? I mean, didn't it to you? The same type of energy, the same strength? And you know how we always talked about whether or not demons each have their own signature vibrations?"

"Yeah, I guess."

"It feels right. It feels like it was the same one."

Mike works an SB-11 spirit box into its cushioned slot of the storage case. "Feeling is a lot different than proof. You know that."

"There was something else, too, and it didn't click until it mentioned the Hoppers."

A fat rechargeable battery, now lifeless, gets shoved into its home. "And?"

"That laugh. When I told you it was pretending to be a little girl? You didn't hear it, but I swear on my mother's grave, it was copying Chelsea."

"Funny, I don't remember her laughing. Just terrified and crying."

I slam the lid closed on my case. "Low blow."

"Sorry. Old habits."

"Anyway. It was the same one. I'm positive."

We take one more quick look around the living room to make sure we didn't leave anything behind, and as we're doing so, Mike asks, "Does this mean you'll consider the documentary? Sounds like a challenge to me. Fucker is calling you out. Wants to do battle back at the Hoppers."

He's baiting me, ever so subtly, and it would work if I was ten years younger, but my mind is made up. "I told you already, no way in hell am I exploiting her again."

***

The hotel room is icebox cold since I left the air conditioner dial on the January-in-Minnesota setting, and I'm certain that Mike is asleep before I'm finished brushing my teeth. Thankfully, and possibly because in here it's as cold as a demon sucking all the energy out of the room, Mike's conked out in his clothes. The snoring and drooling haven't changed. I'm positive there's already a wet spot on the pillow.

With the temperature outside still sitting at roughly eighty degrees, even at two o'clock in the morning and a hundred yards from the ocean, it seems ridiculous to climb underneath the covers, but man, that air conditioner is top notch. So I pull all eighteen layers of blankets that come with a hotel bed up to my neck and shut my eyes.

Sleep has never come as easily to me as it has for Mike, and once again this feels like our glory days. Same old routine. Mike snoring, me struggling to doze off, only now I'm not worried about how my complexion looks on camera, and I didn't bring earplugs because I hadn't intended on having him around for a sleepover.

It's almost a comforting sound, though, because after what we just went through, it's nice to have company. I appreciate having another living soul in the room. The sound of Mike sawing logs is like a nightlight when you're afraid that something might be under the bed.

I try a variety of meditation techniques to clear my mind—tricks I learned and had to use for a long time after Chelsea's incident—but they're useless at the moment. Every time I feel the junk of the previous sixteen hours slipping away and the slow-moving calm of slumber seeping in, my mind spins back around to that thing's voice and the way it imitated Chelsea's laugh, mocking me.

Wherever it may be *now*, it was *here*, damn it, and regardless of whether it was a coincidence or not, I'm kept awake by the fact that there seems to be some sort of netherworld connection that shares information—like a ghostly Pony Express.

Or perhaps information is shared across energy.

"Energy" in the broadest sense, I guess. I'm not talking about, like, electricity or wind power. I'm no scientist, and, in fact, I could barely tell you the difference between an astrologist and an astrophysicist, but what I *believe* is this: everything, from a ladybug to a boulder, from Dick Cheney to a candy bar, from a cup of coffee to a '69 Chevelle with white racing strips, is made up of atoms and protons and neutrons, the building blocks of the universe, and whether it's inanimate or a two-year-old jumping on a trampoline, everything is made up of this interconnected web of energy. It's not necessarily the hum of life, but the hum of *existence*.

Your coffee table may not be alive, yet it *exists*, and there are billions of particles screaming around and around that make that object what it is.

Thoughts are energy. Emotions are energy. A ham sandwich on rye is energy—bear with me here—and *everything* is connected.

I've believed this for a long time, and I've also believed that spirits can somehow share information like it's a phone call or an e-mail, but I've never really seen concrete evidence of this reality until recently.

I chose not to tell Mike that I had already been investigating Chelsea's case again because, for now, I didn't want him to use it as ammo, or a bargaining chip, in his efforts to get Carla Hancock's documentary going. But in a way, I suppose he deserves to know what I learned back at the old farmhouse before I left for this case.

And, amazingly enough, it's further proof of that interconnected, subatomic layer of . . . what, invisible universe juice?

Which apparently exists on both sides of life and death.

Physically, I don't have an ounce of get-up-and-go left in me. My mind won't stop turning, in spite of this, and I'm afraid my thrashing around in the bed will wake up Mike, so I force myself to sit up and tiptoe quietly through the room. The balcony door complains loudly as the seal is broken—plastic peeling away from plastic. I cringe, but Mike only mumbles something in his sleep and rolls over while I'm greeted with the thick humidity outside our room.

I'm only wearing a pair of basketball shorts, and after the frozen tundra of the room, the warmth feels good on my skin. The concrete balcony is pebbled and prickly under my feet. The white plastic chair, still temperate from the day's heat, bends when I sit and prop my legs up on the glass table. I spot a few lights of trolling fishing vessels, along with a tanker or two heading north toward the Chesapeake Bay, and I try to sit peacefully as the waves crash against the shore.

I go over the three visits to the Hampstead farmhouse in my mind again, trying to make sense of the connection to Chelsea, the demon that affected her and Craghorn both, and the vicious, malevolent, but not demonic, entity residing there.

He, the old farmer I spoke with, may not have anything to do with Chelsea or the demon. Maybe he was just sharing information with me.

The first visit, the two Class-A EVPs: "*I know what you want*," and "*Chelsea . . . Hopper.*"

The second visit, nothing. It happens.

And then, this last visit. Wow.

How did I end up there to begin with?

The short version goes like this: I got an e-mail from a young lady named Deanna Hampstead about a month ago. She said that I should call her "Hamster," because everyone else did, and that she's our number-one fan. Or, rather, she admitted to being Mike's number-one fan, but since he wasn't available on the Internet, she figured I would be just as interested in performing an investigation at her family's abandoned farmhouse.

The thing is, I get about, oh, 437 of these e-mails each week, and it's often a huge burden on my time to sift through every single one of them myself. So I've hired a personal assistant, a young man named Jesse who lives in Albuquerque, to read through them all and pick out the ones that appear to come from actual detectives in need of assistance. He then follows up with a reply e-mail to assess the validity, and if it's a real case, he passes it along to me for review.

I was up late one night after having watched this bogus "Where Are They Now?" piece on some trashy TV show where they once again compared my good name to a certain German dictator from the past—I laughed, but it didn't mean it wasn't hurtful—and insomnia was inevitable. I decided to give Jesse a break and sort through a few hundred e-mails myself, and fifteen minutes in, I ran across a subject line that read: DON'T U KNOW SOME1 NAMED CHELSEA?

That sweet child's name might as well be tattooed on my forehead, and I hadn't had a thorough reaming in a good while, so of course I clicked. This is what it said (spelling mistakes hers):

Dear Mr. Ford A. Ford,

I am Deanna Hampstead but u can call me Hamster since all my friends do. I'm 13yrs old. My fam owns an old farmhouse close to where u live. I think. Ur in Oregon now? N E way, that's what your site says. Biggest fan here of GC and was always in luv w/ Mike Long. #1 fan on earth. I couldn't find him on the web, so I wrote 2 u. N E way, u are an inspiration and made me want to hunt ghosts. I went with my cousin Em and we hunted 1 nite. U would not believe what we caught! EVP of a man and my mom sez it's her Papa Joe, her granpa.

Truthfully, it hurt my eyes, and my head, trying to decipher what young Hamster was trying to say. Kids these days. But I've always had a soft spot for the younger fans since their minds are such clean slates, unburdened by maturity and skepticism, so I continued reading.

I nvr would have believed it if I hadn't heard it with my own 2 ears. (Y do ppl say it that way? Course u heard it w/ your own 2 ears. How else would u hear it?) N E way, it was SO cool. We listened and he said, "Ford ... ghostman" and we were like WHAT SHUT UP. And Y is that cray cray? Papa Joe died in 1983. Mom says he was a mean ol cuss.

Now she had my attention, obviously. I've had plenty of spirits and demons call me out by name, but rarely, if any, who

The Graveyard: Classified Paranormal Series

just happened to pass over to the other side twenty-plus years before the show first aired.

Me an Em—me is Em backward—funny! N E way, we asked him more ?s and all he would say was, "Ford . . . ghostman." He musta said it 8 more times b4 we left. We said, "Ford and Mike from that show, right?" And then he said, "Yes. Chelsea. Danger."

After reading that, I said, out loud, as a fully grown, adult male human being: "What?! Shut up. That's cray cray."

N E way, I have it all on tape. I dunno if u would want to but my mama says u should come talk to Papa Joe because it could be important! I think so 2 b/c Chelsea was like the gurl from that live show u did, right? Here is our phone and email but prob don't call after 9 since Dad gets up early for work. Pls tell Mike he's the best ever! And u 2 obv.

I remember checking the clock, seeing that it was half past 1:00 a.m. and contemplating calling regardless. I was so amped that I had my cell in my hand, finger hovering over the call button, before better judgment prevailed.

I waited until the next morning. I called. I spoke to Carol Hampstead, Hamster's mother, and after a few rounds of, "Holy crap, you're a celebrity! Hon, get in here! We got that Ford guy from that ghost show on the phone," it was fairly easy to get permission for an investigation. Multiple investigations. As many as I wanted, as long as I promised to give them credit or mention the family if I ever got back on television again.

Funny, isn't it? They didn't want their fifteen minutes of fame. All they wanted was to serve me a nice dinner, ask a few behind-the-scenes questions about *Graveyard: Classified*, and to hear their names on television if the opportunity ever came up.

They live less than thirty miles from my home, just outside of Portland. The primordial family farmhouse is another six miles beyond that, nestled in a field and backed up against a small, rolling hill.

And here I am. Sitting on a balcony in Virginia Beach, Virginia, roughly three thousand miles away from that farmhouse, roughly fifteen hundred miles away from Chelsea Hopper's former home, having battled the same demon, thinking about the incredible EVP that I caught on my third visit, and how it's all connected over so many miles and planes of existence:

"It's coming . . . Chelsea . . . Key . . . Save . . . the people."

What's coming? The demon? And was he saying that Chelsea is the key to something? To what?

And what am I saving the people from? And who are these people?

As the orange glow of the sun warms the eastern horizon, I'm left with more questions than answers. At the moment, the biggest one of them all is, should I tell Mike about this?

23

Mike and I each grab a handful of blueberry mini-muffins, an apple apiece, and two cups of coffee from the continental breakfast table before we dart out the door. Well, I dart, and Mike drags along behind me, grumbling about how he's not beholden to Detective Thomas, and he doesn't see why he should have to be in a hurry to get to the station.

By the time the buzzing vibration of my phone woke me up on the balcony at a quarter after nine, the detective had already left seven messages asking what had happened, and did we have any information for him. In addition to that, he had some bad news about Dave Craghorn and wanted to discuss things in person. I was to bring Mike, too, since he had become peripherally involved in the investigation.

Before I dozed off, just as the sun was peeking over the horizon, I had made up my mind to tell Mike about Hamster, the Hampstead farmhouse, and Papa Joe, yet as we whip around curves and weave through the nigh-impenetrable Virginia Beach work-commute traffic, it's clear that now is not the right time. There's too much to explain, too many implications to discuss, and I'd have to parry too many of his queries about my stance on the documentary.

Meanwhile, we inhale our muffins and apples while I curse at the other drivers, and I manage to slog through half a cup of the worst coffee I've ever tasted. Frankly, it tastes like demon piss, which I would expect to be a mixture of sulfur, charcoal, coffee beans that have been scrubbed across the anus of a dead horse, and hazelnut.

Mike's grimace when he sips at his cup is the only confirmation I need that he feels the same.

The station is pulsating with activity, more than I expect at nine thirty in the morning on a random Thursday, with hookers and the homeless, old ladies and tattooed bikers stationed throughout, and it takes a good five minutes before the desk sergeant comes back around to his post. I explain who we are and who we're there to see. He's unimpressed. I can tell by the way his lip goes up into a slight Elvis sneer along with the restrained eye-roll that he thinks I can't see.

Sergeant Hobbart—and I so desperately want to make a hobbit joke—points to a row of lime-green plastic chairs along the wall, the kind that are attached by a length of metal on the bottom, and tells us to have a seat, that someone will be with us shortly.

Before we can move to the horrid chairs that look less comfortable than a bed made of cinderblocks, Detective Thomas pokes his head through a doorway to our right. "You two, follow me." There's no welcoming smile, only the hard posturing of a serious man, and it's then that I wonder if *we're* in trouble for something.

He holds the door open farther, and Mike gives the space in front of us a wide-armed sweep. "After you."

We don't go to Detective Thomas's desk, where I expected we would be led, and instead, he points into a bare room, with a bare table, three chairs, and the sanitized glow of two fluorescent bulbs overhead. Along one wall is a giant mirror.

I haven't been in one of these since the wee hours of the morning after Chelsea's attack. "Uh-oh, what's going on?"

Mike groans and says, "Fuck me, Ford. If you dragged me into—"

"Relax," Detective Thomas interrupts. "You're not under arrest. It's just standard procedure since you two were the last to see Dave Craghorn alive."

Mike says, "Excuse me?"

And I add, "Wait. *Alive*? Like past tense? Was he mur . . . mur . . ." I can't seem to get the word out of my mouth. I cough and pretend like I have something in my throat so that the detective will finish my sentence for me.

"Murdered? No. Sit. *Sit*." He points to the two chairs on the left side of the table, the ones facing the mirror and the camera mounted in the upper corner, and refuses to sit himself until we finally relent.

We do, and the tabletop is cold underneath my forearms. Mike leans back, hands in his pockets, leg bouncing in anticipation.

Detective Thomas grabs the chair opposite from us, spins it around so that the back of it is facing his chest, and sits down, grunting as he does so. He leans forward, arms across the top, clucks his tongue like my grandma used to do. I can't help but feel as if he's disappointed in us for something, yet it's likelier that he's frustrated with the situation.

"Mr. Craghorn," he says, tapping one long, bony index finger on the tabletop, "was found last night at the first rest stop heading west on I-64, swinging from the rafters."

I don't know the area well enough to be familiar with the one he's talking about, but Mike says, "But that's a couple of hours from here, isn't it?"

"Give or take."

I can't believe this. "Hanging? Are you *positive* he wasn't mur . . . mur . . ."

Damn. Why can't I get that word out? I've talked to dead people for over ten years now, both murdered and not. Perhaps it's a different mindset, given the situation, and considering the fact that I was trying to help the poor bastard a little over twelve hours ago. I think—yeah—Dave Craghorn is the first person I've known that's died since Grandma Ford passed six years ago.

Detective Thomas clasps his fingers together, nibbles at his bottom lip, and nods. "Look, I shouldn't even be sharing this with you guys since *technically* the investigation is ongoing—and please keep your damn mouths shut since I could lose my job for this, okay?"

Mike and I nod. Of course we do.

"I just—" He interrupts himself with a cough that's designed to mask emotion that gets the better of him. "It's a damn shame, and I thought you should know. I've been working this case off and on for years now and Craghorn wasn't a friend, but I felt for the guy. Right? Every indication says that no foul play was involved and that it was a suicide. Some woman up from Charleston found him swinging. Nearly gave her a heart attack. According to the reports, Craghorn was wearing the same clothes he had on when I saw him last, there was no luggage in his car, nothing, so it appears that he left you guys and bolted. And this lady, she said in her statement that there was nothing else but an overturned chair. You gotta figure, that late at night, he could've done it hours earlier."

"Or," Mike says, "if someone did it to him, they'd be long gone."

"True, but nothing points to it."

I ask, "Aren't there security cameras there?"

"Nah, not at that one. That particular rest area probably hasn't been updated since Lee surrendered at Appomattox."

"Did they find a note? Anything like that?"

Detective Thomas nods and fishes in his pants pocket, and for a moment, I think he's going to pull out Dave Craghorn's exact suicide note. The butterflies in my gut swoop, swirl, and drop far into my nether regions.

He extracts a pair of black-rimmed, rectangular glasses from another pocket, then rests the bifocals across the bridge of his nose. "Before I let you look at this, did you notice him acting strangely?"

"You mean any weirder than he already was?"

"Beyond that. Out of *Dave's* ordinary."

I frown and tell him no. Mike does the same. I say to the detective, "No, he wasn't *acting* weird, per se, but we both noticed something about him and wanted to bring it up to you."

"Which was?"

"You knew about his scratches, right? All the supposed claw marks all over his body?"

Detective Thomas nods. "I didn't tell him to strip down and inspect him from head to toe, but yeah, that shit looked rough. And you think the, uh, the *demon* did that?"

Mike looks at me, I look at him, and we exchange a simple questioning glance, silently asking each other which one should proceed.

Mike does. It's probably better that way. He's more matter-of-fact, where I would lean toward padding what I felt was true, sorta like using the bumpers when bowling, rather than risking the wrath of the gutters. Mike says, "He was hiding something. Had to be." Mike gently strikes the table with the karate chop side of his palm once, twice, three times. "Had to be, had to be."

Detective Thomas rubs one dry, rough hand over his stubble. "Why do you say that?"

"We've been doing this a long time, and there's no way in hell that a right-hander—sorry, an upper-level demon—is going to discriminate against where he chooses to scratch somebody. Craghorn may have been marked up like the bosun's mate got after him with a cat o' nine tails—"

"Nice one," I interject.

"—but his face and neck weren't scratched at all. Any place that couldn't easily be hidden by long sleeves or jeans or pockets was clear. Initially, when Ford and I talked about it, that made me think that Dave might've had something to do with Louisa's death, and he was trying to use this right-hander in his house as an alibi. Six months ago, new evidence shows up, confirming that his wife was cheating, and now he's gotta figure out how to draw the attention away from himself. Demon comes strolling around, stops in for a visit. Craghorn figures that if he can shred himself to pieces and play the victim to a supernatural beast, he'd be the last place you'd look. That was my thought process on the whole scenario, but then Ford told me that he had a clean alibi for Louisa's murder, so that squashed that theory."

Detective Thomas lays the sheet of paper in his hands onto the table and smoothes it out. The small crinkling sound is big enough to fill the room. "Well, it would've been a perfect theory, and, yes, I noticed and thought the exact same thing because I never bought into the whole demon nonsense. At least not until the fucking thing attacked me at Dave's. I went back and tried to find a hole in his alibi. Made phone calls, tried everything I remembered. The people we questioned back then, I tried them, too, but they couldn't recall much. Long story short, I couldn't find anything. He was innocent of everything except for giving in to his emotional pain."

"Giving in?" I ask. "How?"

"Cutting." Noticing Mike's questioning squint, the detective explains. "Self-damage, Mr. Long. Some people feel that creating physical pain helps alleviate their emotional pain."

"Gotcha."

"We got a court order to search his laptop and found entry after entry on some underground website for cutters where they talked about methods and reasons, almost like it was therapy for some and sexual arousal for others. Initially, all Dave Craghorn did was talk about losing his wife. Some of the people who responded to him called him a pussy and said he wasn't worthy of being around there. Wasn't long after that he started talking about how he wasn't cutting himself, that he had a demon in his home who was doing it to him, you know? Beyond that, for the next few months, he was like a celebrity on those sites. I guess after a while he started believing his lies. He had detailed discussions with people about his rituals, how he used a Ouija board to draw it out, stuff along those lines."

I'm more than angry. I could've used this information before I went into that fucking hellhole unprepared for the strength of what we were about to face. "And you didn't think to tell me this beforehand?"

"I didn't want to cloud your judgment."

"But—"

I can hear Mike's perturbed huff as Detective Thomas holds up his palm. "That's all it was. Nothing more, nothing less. Unconventional methods call for unconventional tactics, and if you had gone in there with preconceived notions about him, then you might have approached it differently."

"Hell yes, I would have," I say. "I would've gone in with a swimming pool full of holy water and an army of Catholic priests."

"Which is precisely my point."

"Craghorn probably wasn't making that stuff up about the séances and rituals, Detective. That's how the dark man showed up at his house. And, honestly, while I don't fault your motives, that's something that would've been fucking nice to know."

Detective Thomas gives us a pressed-lip, understanding frown as he smoothes out the paper under his palms again. "All I can say is sorry, guys. Integrity of the investigation and all that. Next time, yeah?"

"Forget it. No, seriously, forget it."

He slides the sheet of paper over to us. "Here's a copy of the suicide note that was found in his pocket. From what I can tell, it proves you're right about the whole demon-summoning thing. Yet the question remains, who murdered Louisa? We brought you here for a reason, Ford. Did you learn anything new last night?"

As I scan through Craghorn's heartbreaking note, his last words scrawled out to anyone who might read it, I find a tale of misery and the need to connect with someone and any *thing* after the death of his wife. I stop for a moment and close my eyes. A sad man took his own life, and yet, the world continues to turn.

Maybe one of these days, I'll try to communicate with him. Surely that's a soul that won't rest for a long, long while.

The detective asks me again. "*Hey.* You find anything?"

So goes it. Business as usual. "Nothing that makes any sense. Not now, anyway." I had brought last night's DVR tapes along with me, just in case, and I shove them across the table. "Here. They're yours." I'm a few notches beyond pissed at the guy—let *him* sit in a quiet room for hours and review the evidence. "You can take a listen if you want, but it's mostly some random stuff from Louisa's spirit and that right-hander talking shit."

Mike says to me, "Shouldn't *you* listen to that first?"

"Nah, I'm done. Detective, I'll review the video evidence when I get a chance, within the agreed-upon time frame of our contract. I'll let you know if I find anything else." I have two weeks, officially, to get my report back to him, and given the dickhead move he made, I plan to wait until 11:59 p.m. on the due date before I send the e-mail.

Petty? A little, though I feel it's deserved given the fact that we risked a demonic possession. I've never been a doormat, and I have no plans on becoming a possessed doormat, either.

Speaking of, what would be printed on a possessed doormat?

"Hellcome" to our home?

I continue, "However, I feel like if you're going to find any new evidence, anything you can use, it'll be on the audio." And, I've always wanted to say this in a snide, movie-star tone, but I've never really had the chance. I push myself up from the table and look down on him. "Good *day*, sir."

Mike slaps the table and says, "Hell, yeah. Billy Badass," as he stands up beside me.

24

It's a quiet ride in the rental car back to the oceanfront hotel. It feels like Mike and I had our moment, together again, and now it's over. I don't know what he's thinking, but I have a little bit of, "Well, now what?" going on.

I have a long flight home, made bearable by first-class seats paid for with points, even though I could afford my own small jet. Truth is, I enjoy the company of my fellow travelers, along with the recognition of "Hey, you're that guy, right?"

I don't hide from my fading celebrity status. The "used to be" doesn't bother me, no matter how much fun it would be to get back to zero and beyond. I'm looking forward to hanging out with Ulie, giving belly rubs and rawhide treats. I'm already thinking about taking him back to the farmhouse to see if Papa Joe will give me any more information.

And when I go to pick him up from Melanie's place, given what Mike told me about her, I may ask her to dinner—you know, as a way to say thanks for watching the Best Dog in the World.

Maybe it's the right time to tell Mike what I know, that I've already been peripherally reinvestigating the Hopper house and Chelsea's tormentor, and that we just encountered the rotten asshole again and didn't even know it until the end. Mike is silent, though, leaning on the armrest, propping his chin up, and staring out the window. He looks pensive, and I leave him alone. Traffic rolls by. A naval jet carves a path across the blue sky.

I'll keep it to myself for now. I'm still not ready for the back-and-forth about the documentary, and he's not badgering me, so I'm cool with letting this car ride be what it is—a short end to another chapter.

Brake lights pinball across the highway in front of us, pinging from car to truck to delivery van, and four lanes ease into a slow crawl.

"Accident?" Mike asks. "You see anything?"

"Not yet."

"Shit. I better call Toni." He does, and I listen to him cajole her into forgiveness for having spent the night, and for having entertained my tomfoolery.

He actually uses that word.

Tomfoolery.

Funny. He doesn't look like he's eighty years old.

Mike Long, Taker of No Shit, King of You Can't Tell Me What To Do-ville, has always been humbled in the presence of Toni, whether she's in the same room or on the other end of the line. I'm sure it would drive me nuts, but he likes the challenge.

When he promises he'll be home as soon as he can and hangs up, I ask him a risky question. "Do you miss it at all? The show, I mean."

He ponders this while we inch forward, then says, "The long shoots, being away, inhaling a cheeseburger between Carla's call times, nah, not in the slightest. Not one fucking bit. What I *do* miss, honest to God, is being able to help people that were afraid. I miss being able to tell a frightened mother or some old lady that they have nothing to fear, that the evidence we caught would make them happy, you know? A chance to say goodbye one last time, or that somebody's nice uncle was there watching over them. That stuff. I miss being able to tell people that the things that go bump in the night aren't all bad. Well, at least ninety-nine times out of a hundred."

"Chelsea," I say quietly. "Number one hundred."

"Yeah. That girl—"

"Mike, man, don't start, please? I don't need another lecture."

"I wasn't going to. What I was going to say was, other than the money . . ."

Oh, God. Here we go. Me and my big mouth.

"Which I really need, I'm sure it's our chance at redemption."

Magically, traffic picks up speed for no apparent reason, after having been stalled for no apparent reason, and I nudge the rental faster to keep up. "What do *you* need redemption for? You tried to stop it."

"I didn't try hard enough," he answers, and there's more weight in those words than I've heard in Mike's voice in a long, long time. "One man can't do it by himself. He needs people on his side."

I understand that it's his subtle attempt at telling me I should have been with him two years ago, and not on the side of glory, fame, and television history, but it causes something else to click.

Since the show was forced off the air—since the lawsuits and having my name trashed on every single news outlet—I've felt like I was riding the subway of life alone. I pushed Melanie away and fell into the beds of other women because they were connections that would be with me for an hour, and then I could retreat again. I hired a personal assistant to answer my fan mail because I couldn't bear interacting with too many people. I've worked with dozens of different police departments doing this paranormal private investigator thing, but always alone on night investigations and research gathering, refusing help, refusing to allow anyone to come along.

I don't know why it hits me so hard. Maybe because it's Mike that's saying it. Maybe it's because I finally grasped that I won't be able to take on Chelsea's demon by myself, like I'd planned. Mike or no Mike. Documentary or no documentary.

Either way, that goddamn thing is strong, wherever it is, wherever it went, and whatever is coming, I'm going to need someone on my side.

"You're right," I say, shifting lanes, squeezing between two semis, as I head toward the hotel. "A man certainly does."

We say our goodbyes in the parking lot, the smell of salt air hanging over our heads, poofball clouds drifting west out over the ocean, as Mike shakes my hand, saying, "It's been real."

"It's been fun."

"But it hasn't been real fun." He gives me a thumbs up and steps backward to his navy blue Audi. "Promise me you'll think about the documentary, okay? Carla's not so bad after all those FCC fines. Lightened her up a bit."

I tell him okay, I will, yet I don't believe for a second that Carla Hancock has changed. That cobra will always have her fangs.

As he's getting into his car, I quickly say, "Hey, Mike?" before he closes his door.

"Yeah?"

"Can I send you some audio files to review? I caught something in this old farmhouse back home. Pretty amazing stuff." I leave it at that. I'll tell him what it is when I'm ready.

He considers this for a moment and seems to be weighing whether he wants to get involved again with the almighty Ford Atticus Ford for something other than the documentary, and then says, "Sure. If you send a package instead of e-mail, don't put your return address on it. Toni will have them in the trash before I even know they're there."

"Cool. Will do. You have a safe trip home."

"And you have a good flight. See you on the other side."

I smile because it's reassuring to hear him say our catchphrase that ended every episode of *Graveyard: Classified*.

"Yep." I wave as he drives off. "See you on the other side."

***

I'm late getting to Melanie's condo in the Pearl District of Portland. My direct flight from Norfolk International was delayed due to mechanical issues, so we had to deplane. I sipped free scotch in the Billion-Mile Member Lounge for about an hour and a half, then was sufficiently tipsy enough to pass out and sleep all the way home. I needed it after the previous night's war against—well, shit, I want to call that right-hander Azeraul, even though that's not its name.

As I parallel park my Wrangler—it's essential to have a boxy, compact vehicle while you're trying to park in this city—it occurs to me that Louisa Craghorn's spirit never actually said, "His name is Azeraul." The demon was enraged enough to insist that it wasn't, too, which very well could've been a complete lie. Although, I suspect that we would've gotten an entirely different reaction out of him if it *had* been his name. I'm talking, like, a two-year-old throwing a temper tantrum, lying on the floor and stomping its feet, only this would be an ancient demon slinging a couch like it's nothing more than a sippy cup of juice.

I'm disappointed that I had my own tantrum and gave Detective Thomas the audio tapes before I took the time to convert them to files I could listen to on my laptop. The investigation is a huge, intense, emotional blur, but I seem to recall Louisa's spirit saying something about love and *her*.

I keep referring to the right-hander as a he, but who knows, maybe it's been a female demon all along. You hear it often in the natural world: the female of the species is deadlier than the male.

Don't piss off the mama bear.

Could be that the same goes for the *super*natural world.

It's possible, I guess. Remains to be seen.

The truth of the matter is, I'm not necessarily looking forward to going up against that festering cesspool of evil again anytime soon. I need to recharge my own batteries.

Is there a better way to do that other than unconditional doggie love?

I submit that there is not.

I walk up the brick steps to Melanie's front door, breathing in that damp, mossy scent of Portland, and before I even rap my knuckles against the red-painted wood, I can hear Ulie's snorting and scrabbling claws on the tile just inside her entrance. Melanie's voice follows, and it's amusing to hear her say, "Ulie! Ulie! Who's here? Daddy's home!"

The scrabbling claws intensify, Melanie eases the door open around him, and that beautiful mutt has his paws on my chest and is licking underneath my chin before I can speak to my ex-wife. "Wow," I say, once I manage to get him back down on all four legs. "How come *you* were never that excited to see me when I got home?"

Melanie is wearing a cut-off tank top, running shorts, and her hair is up in a ponytail. She looks amazing. She's always looked amazing, but maybe after Mike's revelation, I'm seeing her differently—or seeing her like I used to, like the Melanie from wardrobe that made my pulse race years and years ago. She squashes my moment by saying, "I don't have enough fingers and toes to count all the reasons, Ford."

I can tell she's joking—with some truth hidden behind it—but yeah, it still burns. I hide it by asking how Ulie did as he prances around me, tail wagging so vigorously that his entire bottom shakes. She gives me the rundown, and it's pleasant, cordial, but I don't see anything hidden in her eyes that would suggest she is still in love with me.

Then again, I suck at reading people. Live ones, that is.

She tells me it's late, she has to be at the news station at 4:00 a.m. where she does hair, makeup, and wardrobe for two local morning anchors, and that she'd happily watch Ulie again if I needed her to. She hands me his things—chew toy, peanut butter bulb thingy, his doggie bed, and a backpack full of food and his favorite treats. I feel like I'm picking up my child after a court-ordered weekend visitation with Mom.

Melanie tells me to have a good night and starts to close the door. I hesitate for a beat and then decide to go for it. Nothing ventured, right? I launch my hand out and catch it before she closes it completely. "Wait, can we, um, can we talk for a second?"

She opens the door fully, eyes narrowed, giving me a confused look.

"Do you think you'd . . . How about a drink one night this week, Mel? You up for it? Hit up McNamara's Pub like we used to do?" I'm strongly aware of the awkward, pleading smile on my face, but I can't shove it into anything resembling smooth. So I wait, my heartbeat creating massive craters on the inside of my chest as she arches an eyebrow.

"A drink?"

"Yeah. Just to catch up." The words trip out of my mouth. I feel like I'm sixteen years old, asking Amy Hemmings to prom, who not-so-politely told me, "Get the hell away from me, weirdo."

Melanie cocks one hip to the side and rests a hand there. "I guess we could. I'd have to ask Jeff to see if he cares, but it shouldn't be a big deal."

"Who's Jeff?" I ask, more incredulous than I intend. Mostly because his name is an atomic bomb in my stomach.

"Actually, it's funny. I've been calling him 'Jeff from the control room' like you used to call me 'Melanie from wardrobe.' We've been seeing each other for a couple of months now. I should really get you two together because he's seen every episode of *GC* at least three times. I made the mistake of telling him we used to be married, and now he won't stop quoting your lines from the show. If I hear 'see you on the other side' one more time, I'm going to vomit."

The only thing I can manage to say is, "Oh, right," and I'm intensely aware of the typical Portland rain that has begun to fall.

"He won't mind, I'm sure."

"Yeah, uh, okay. You check in with him, and I'll give you a call."

Feeling thwarted and defeated, while being jealous enough to fight for what I want, both at the same time, is an odd sensation. Like wearing your shoes on the wrong feet.

"Night, Ford. Nighty-night, Ulie. Auntie Mel will see you again soon!"

I can't even begin to explain how sad I am to hear her say "Auntie" instead of "Mama."

I should've known better.

***

It's a long night of restless sleep. Too much snoozing on the flight home, too many thoughts running around inside my head, and too much love from an excited pooch who can't relax and stay in one spot for more than five minutes. I consider putting him in doggie jail, meaning out in the garage for a while, but I haven't seen him in a couple of days and I don't have the heart. Rather than fighting my insomnia, I get up, brew a pot of coffee, and sit down at the kitchen table, laptop open in front of me. I send a note to Jesse down in Albuquerque telling him to take the day off tomorrow, that I'll review the rest of the backlogged e-mails.

What I'm hoping for is another revelation from someone like Hamster Hampstead telling me that they recorded their Papa Joe talking about Chelsea and saving some people. It'd be nice to have the distraction. New evidence. Something to point me in any direction other than Melanie's true north. I also curse Mike for getting my hopes up and partially wonder if he made it all up just to get me in a lighter mood before he pitched the documentary.

I find nothing of the sort. Instead, I sift through and personally answer about a hundred and fifty e-mails, thanking viewers for being friends and fans, before I find anything of interest, and it's not exactly what I'm looking for.

It's a short note from Caribou, the waitress at that crab shack, thanking me profusely for the flagrant tip I left her and how it was such an honor to serve her television idols. As thanks, she included an attachment; it's a picture of her wearing nothing but a *Graveyard: Classified* bandana and high heels.

There's a single ray of sunshine. Oh, happy days.

I save it in a buried folder called "Taxes 2015" along with a few thousand similar pictures, and then drain the last of my coffee. Out my window, high up here on the hill overlooking Portland proper, the sun nudges through the clouds to the east.

Finally, I'm bushed, even with a pot of coffee screeching its tires throughout my veins. My lonely, abandoned wasteland of a king-size bed sounds like a good idea, and I think again about what Mike said.

A man needs someone by his side.

"Ulie," I say, waking him up where he'd been dreaming and twitching on the floor. "You just earned a spot on the bed."

His ears perk and he hops to his feet.

"But we're not going to make a habit of this, got it?"

He snorts. Plain as day, that's the dog version of, "Yeah, right, whatever you say."

On the countertop, my cell phone sits next to a half-eaten bagel and an empty coffee mug. The ceramic body of it is plain white, while the handle is sculpted in the shape of a provocatively posed naked woman. It's a hideously fantastic gag gift from a detective I worked with in the past, and I don't know why, but coffee tastes better coming out of it. The mug itself becomes a trigger object for my thought processes—Caribou in all her naked glory, a detective—and it makes me think about Detective Thomas back in Virginia Beach.

I check the clock over the stove. It's a quarter to six, meaning it's a quarter to nine back on the east coast. He'll be up and at the office by now. My brain feels like I'm thinking through that sludge on the bottom of a riverbed, which is why I consider calling him to apologize. I've had enough time to calm down, and I'll admit that I probably went slightly diva on him back at the station. Dude was just trying to do his job. Been there, yeah?

This whole line of thinking sets off my synapses and they go tumbling along like dominoes.

Dominoes that lead to the word 'Azeraul' in my mind.

I look at Ulie sitting patiently at my feet. "So we're back to that again, huh? This demon-not-demon bullshit?"

He chuffs and flops onto the kitchen floor, exposing his belly as he rolls over and closes his eyes. Smart dog. He can sense I'm not going to bed any time soon.

It's not out of the ordinary for a demon to lie. I absolutely *know* this and have been privy to it on a number of occasions. So, I'm not sure why I just blindly accepted the word of that assmuncher back at Craghorn's. It seemed serious enough to be offended, yet that's not necessarily proof that it's telling the truth.

I hop up from the table and head over to a small library of demon and spirit guides stashed on a living room shelf. Ten books total, ranging from two hundred years old to being published three months ago. You never know when you're gonna need to look up some ancient demon to uncover his weak spots. Helps quite a bit when you're tackling these things with some electronics, holy water, a crucifix, and a middle-aged bald guy named Mike Long. That's not counting the crew, of course, but in the heat of demonic battle, those guys are nothing but doughnut-gobbling, coffee-chugging cannon fodder.

I flip through each guide—some priceless, some barely worth the paper they're printed on—being dainty with the ancient ones and hasty with the others. Brother Luther's *Guide to Demons of the Realm*. Herr Bonn's *Twelve Levels of Demonic Ranks*. *Life of the Hereafter*. *How to Battle Evil*.

A half an hour passes and nothing comes up.

Nothing. Not a goddamn thing.

Maybe the right-hander in Craghorn's house was telling the truth.

I slam the last book closed and trudge into my kitchen, totally wiped out, fed up, and mentally berating myself for wasting time instead of sleeping. Even Ulie is completely zonked. His snoring sounds like a Harley swallowed a chainsaw.

I flop down at the kitchen table again, ready to give up, but the laptop is open, and Google is sitting there right in front of me. "Why not?" I mumble. It takes every last ounce of available energy to type the name into the search bar, then it occurs to me that I might not even be spelling it correctly.

I take a shot with the following: A-Z-E-R-A-U-L.

It's what I imagined it would be all along, and that's close enough. If not, then yes, Google, your creepily telepathic alternate suggestion will probably be correct.

There's always a chance that someone has heard that name before, so it's worth a look, but there's no way I'm going to sit here for too long browsing through cult blogs and obscure movie references if that's what it comes to. This is nothing but a half-court, half-hearted, buzzer-beater shot before I head into the locker room.

Game over, bro. I'm tired. Man, am I tired. I do the clicky thing on the mousey thing and make the search happen, hardly able to keep my eyes open and then—

"What the—"

On the screen, listed in the search results, accompanied by a picture, is a different kind of demon.

She's tan, with frosted hair pulled back in a crisp, efficient bun, and looks positively radiant in a gold-sequined evening gown, holding a matching clutch at her waist. She's at a charity event of some sort, according to the caption.

Who?

Ellen *Azeraul* Gardner. Wife of the former mayor.

The deceased former mayor who was supposedly having an affair with Louisa Craghorn.

Dear God in Heaven. It's all connected.

I fly up from the kitchen chair and lean across the granite countertop, grabbing for my cell phone, and in a bizarre act of universal kismet, it's already vibrating in my hand by the time I pick it up.

Who in the hell would be calling at this hour? The caller ID shows a Virginia number, with a Hampton Roads area code, to be exact.

There's no doubt who's calling—and I already have an idea why.

Impatient, I answer, "Hello? Hello?"

"Ford?"

"Detective Thomas."

"Sorry to call you so early. I wasn't sure if you were still in town and forgot about the time difference—"

"Ellen. *Azeraul*. Gardner," I blurt, interrupting him. I'm excited and out of breath. The name comes out in punchy gasps.

"Well, holy shit, son. You chase ghosts for a living, are you psychic, too?"

"What? Psychic? No, I . . ."

"Coulda fooled me. Thought I might give you a heads up, but it doesn't sound like you need it. How'd you come by that info?"

I give him the short version of my morning, leaving out Caribou and the "Taxes 2015" folder, and explain how it was a random act of curiosity that led to my discovery. "I'm assuming it's connected, Detective, I just don't know who did what."

"That's what we're looking to find out. Those tapes you gave us—you caught what we needed, though you didn't know it at the time. Or, as you apparently discovered, you gave us a lead that we absolutely can't ignore. I've got some uniforms on the way to Mrs. Gardner's house right now."

"You think she did it?"

"I'll get to that, but first, let me apologize again for not being upfront about Craghorn's history."

"Water under the bridge, Detective. You were doing your job. I get it."

"Not an excuse. I wouldn't put my own men in danger and I can see why you got pissed. I'm at fault here, no ifs, ands, or buts. And besides, after having been attacked myself, and then listening to your investigation files, I realized just how dangerous and careless it was on my part. I'll make it up to you somehow."

"It's certainly not a play-date in the park, but I'm still marking you down for one favor owed."

"Good. Second, I listened to *all six* hours of your audio. Goddamn spine-chilling, Ford, and I can't believe you do this for a living. I wouldn't have a single pair of underwear without brown stains."

"Takes practice. I couldn't be around murder victims all the time like you guys."

"Point made. Anyway, listening to the EVPs, what caught my ear, and what you stumbled on, is the fact that Ellen Gardner, the wife of the former mayor of Virginia Beach, used to be Ellen Azeraul."

"Right. So how's it all connected? Did she kill Louisa?"

"Don't know yet, but I've got a five dollar bill riding on it."

"A whole five bucks? Remind me not to take you to Vegas."

The man has a hearty, genuine laugh. I didn't think he was capable. "The biggest thing, to me, was hearing Louisa's voice saying, 'still love her.' It's a bit disjointed because she seems to be answering questions out of order, like answering something you haven't asked yet or giving a delayed answer to something you asked previously."

"It happens. There are quite a few theories that suggest spirits are functioning within a different realm of time, and they may be experiencing it as a whole rather than a linear progression but—whatever. What does it mean? Are you telling me—"

"That Louisa Craghorn was having an illicit affair with Ellen Azeraul Gardner? It's a distinct possibility. My theory is that Louisa lied about who she was having an affair with in her diary to protect her secret lover. So easy to redirect attention by having the secretary be with the powerful boss. No brainer, even. We can submit your audio as evidence, although I expect the judge will toss it out. Either way, it's enough to warrant bringing her in for a round of questions. Could be the former mayor found out about it and had someone off Louisa, or could be that Ellen was done with her and wanted her gone before she said something. Whatever the case, we'll get to the bottom of it. We may have just broken this thing wide open, Ford. Thank you."

"No problem. I do what I can."

"I'll be in touch. Oh, and don't speak a word of this to anyone. Ongoing investigation and all that. Keep that favor card handy, bud."

The line clicks before I can say anything else.

Dead silence signals the end of another investigation, but there is so much more out on the horizon, out there in the beyond. I should be used to this by now, but the finality of it leaves me speechless, and if I had been able to reply, I imagine it would've been something like, "Cool. See you on the other side."

The Graveyard: Classified Paranormal Series

Spirit World Productions, Inc.

Los Angeles, California
555-682-8307
Contact: Dane Argyle

FOR IMMEDIATE RELEASE

A match made in heaven (or hell) brings America's most popular ghost-hunting team to the silver screen

LOS ANGELES (August 1, 2015) – Spirit World Productions, Inc., is thrilled to announce that it has begun preliminary production of the most anticipated documentary in the history of paranormal investigations. The film's executive producer, Carla Hancock, states, "We couldn't possibly be more thrilled that the former lead investigators of *Graveyard: Classified*, Ford Atticus Ford and Mike Long, have enthusiastically agreed to reunite for this feature-length film. We absolutely can't wait to get started."

Ford, the *enfant terrible* of paranormal reality shows, recently came under harsh criticism and public scrutiny for the events that occurred on the night of October 31, 2012, when then-five-year-old Chelsea Hopper suffered a violent and ferocious demonic attack during a live episode of *Graveyard: Classified*. The upcoming documentary, according to Ford, will once again focus on the Hopper House in Ohio, where he and the former show's technical wizard and co-lead investigator, Mike Long, plan to research, investigate, and clear the house of any "evil entities" that are present.

Long says, "This isn't about us. It's about Chelsea. It's *for* Chelsea. Redemption. Vengeance. We're going to march in there and take that [expletive deleted] thing down. We want the whole world to see us win."

Barring any production delays, filming is set to begin in early September, and in an unprecedented, enthusiastic, team-powered effort, Spirit World Productions has planned for a nationwide theatrical release on December 25, 2015. Hancock says, "We'll be working around the clock. It's a crazy timeline, and nearly impossible, but I'm confident we can pull this off for the holiday season. We fully expect some terrifying consequences to this paranormal investigation because Ford and Mike Long are going to war with a demon, but what better way to celebrate a feel-good time of the year than with two heroes getting much-deserved payback for a little girl?"

The project has yet to be titled, but set aside Christmas Day 2015 to witness history.

***

The Graveyard: Classified Paranormal Series

Desmond Doane

GRAVEYARD: CLASSIFIED
Book 2

THE WHITE NIGHT
Desmond Doane

The Graveyard: Classified Paranormal Series

PROLOGUE

September, 2003
West Ramsey Asylum
Years before the fall of *Graveyard: Classified*

At a quarter past one in the morning, I feel something slide its finger across the back of my neck. It's light, like a dandelion seed caught in a puff of wind, tracing over my skin—ever so soft—but it's there.

I swipe at the trespasser, exploring an inch or two below my collar, finding nothing. I turn and look for the source, seeing only blackness, hearing the rustle of my partner's clothing.

Inside this room, where it's alleged that a former mental patient died after swallowing a bucket of nails, the darkened hour is cloaked in the deepest shadows.

The stench of rotting wood and damp, rusty metal pollutes my nostrils.

Our flashlight batteries were drained of energy hours ago, the first time our ghostly companion tried to manifest. Mike Long and I have yet to learn that we need to always, *always*, bring backups.

Mike says, "Did you feel that?"

"Yeah. It got you, too?"

"I am freaking the hell out, man. Can we go now, please?"

"You want to leave? Are you kidding me?"

"Catching an apparition *once* does not make us paranormal investigators, chief. We're two dudes with a camera and a bit of luck. Do you even have any idea what you're doing? Because I sure as hell don't. What if we, like... what if we get possessed? I can't go home with devil horns or some shit."

"You worried about Toni?"

The decaying floorboards creak at the far side of the room. Neither one of us moved, so we didn't cause it. The flooring groans again, and this time, it's accompanied by what sounds like the *clunk-thunk* of a cowboy boot.

This is our eleventh investigation, and I thought we were having fun with it. I'm charged by the adrenaline rush. Clearly, Mike isn't.

"Damn right, I'm worried," he says. "I've only taken her on, like, three dates. You think she wants me passing a ghost on to her like some demonic STD?"

I scoff and blindly focus on the sound's origin. I think it was in the northeastern corner, but I'm not entirely sure. The sound plays funny in this room—dull, hollow echoes—and it's so pitch black, it's like we've been buried alive. That imagery in my mind tightens my lungs and I take a deep breath. "There's no demon here. You know that. They said—"

"I don't care what they *said*," Mike whines. "We're out of our league."

"Speaking of leagues, you'd step up to the majors with me if we got the call, wouldn't you?"

"The *call*? I don't even know what that means."

"You've seen the insane amount of hits we've been getting."

One of our friends watched our original video capture about three months ago—the one with the full body apparition—and was so amazed that he said we'd be famous if we posted it online. It took a few weeks, but he was right—we're Internet famous, at least. So far, a few hundred thousand people have watched the evidence we've captured, and some nights I sit in front of my laptop refreshing the screen simply to watch the view count go higher. It's incredible that people are so *into* this stuff.

Mike says, "Are you still posting those?"

"Why wouldn't I? People love them. Shit, man, I keep getting messages from total strangers, asking when we're going to post the next one."

"Huh. No kidding?"

Mike thought we'd get a couple of views from friends and then disappear into the grave of long dead videos, the same videos where a baby's trick isn't that impressive and cats that aren't cute enough go to die a digital death.

"Really, man. We might have something here."

"Meaning?"

I wish he could see my teasing smirk in the dark. I bend down in front of his night vision camera, the last piece of equipment with working batteries, and wink. "I hope you're cool with it."

"Whenever you're tired of hoarding information, I'll be here trying to paranormally investigate." Mike yelps, and in the total darkness, I can hear his hands flailing at his face and neck. "Whoever's doing that," he says, "stop it."

We're still pretty new to all of this, but from the research I've done, a lot of the respected paranormal investigators say that passing through spiritual energy can feel like walking into a spider's web. I remind Mike of this and tell him to relax, that maybe it's just trying to communicate.

Mike shudders and says, "God, that's creepy." He tries to ask something else about my news, but gets interrupted. Behind us, a doorknob jiggles and screeches as if something is trying to sneak out of the empty closet.

"Who's there?" I shout.

"Who's in here with us?" Mike asks.

It's a natural reaction. We both know that we're alone—or, at least, unaccompanied by people who are alive, because outside, a chain link fence that's twelve feet high, topped with razor wire, borders this abandoned asylum, and we have a handful of volunteer guards patrolling the exterior in return for a pizza and a six-pack.

When the state board of regulations shut the asylum down back when Jimmy Carter was in office, the fence was left intact to keep out the homeless and other trespassers. A friend of mine, Jake Dunne, bought the place not too long after the events of September 11th, 2001, about a year and a half ago. Really, he got it for pennies on the dollar because the former owners panicked that the States were going to be overrun by terrorists, so they sold everything they had and moved to the Caribbean. Jake bought it because he thought it would be a good place to hide out once Osama bin Laden got prepared to invade the outskirts of Portland, Oregon here in the Pacific Northwest.

Don't laugh. There are some incredible craft breweries back in the city. It would be a great place to set up your Terrorist HQ.

The fence didn't keep out the homeless or the hooligans, but Mike and I know we're in the clear *tonight* because Jake is outside with two of his buddies patrolling the perimeter, ensuring we get a clean investigation. After we showed him the tape of the apparition we caught, he begged us to come investigate his property.

All he needed to say was, "There's some freaky stuff going on, Ford. I guarantee you'll catch something. You keep that shit up, you two are gonna be on TV."

This, ultimately, was what led me to post the video online where we captured a full-bodied apparition of a woman in a white nightgown, pleading for help. Plain as day, you can see her cautiously approach us and hold out her hands for a total of five seconds before her transparent body vanishes.

Mike and I wait in silence for a few moments, scanning the room, giving our visitor a chance to communicate again. Mike finally breaks the quiet and says, "The silence commands you to speak, Ford Atticus Ford. Out with the news."

"Yes, your majesty." I can't see it coming, but I feel a light punch on the shoulder. "Two days ago, I got this cryptic email from a woman named Carla. She said she'd seen our videos and wanted to talk to me. I figured she was just a reporter, maybe looking for a local story, you know? Anyway, she sets up a phone meeting and we talked earlier today. Turns out, and you're not going to believe this, but she's a producer with The Paranormal Channel."

"What? Seriously?" Mike's voice breaks in the middle of *seriously*, which makes him sound like he hit puberty yesterday.

The closet's doorknob rattles violently. So aggressively, in fact, that it falls off and slams against the floor, sending us both retreating by a few feet.

The room goes quiet.

It feels like the skin-prickling energy, the buzz, has dissipated.

It's almost... *normal* in here now. Just two guys hanging out in the dark.

No otherworldly company. Did it burn itself out?

I've noticed this behavior before. Spirit, demon, supernatural entity, it doesn't matter what it is—it takes energy to manifest, and whomever was with us just now has used all that he had, and has left us behind for the time being, slipping back into his hazy limbo, caught in the netherworld until something comes along with enough juice to recharge him. Seems like this guy hasn't quite figured out yet that he can use the energy in our bodies after the batteries have been depleted. Which is entirely possible given that he was in an institution. He might not have the mental acuity to process the possibilities available to him.

Mike says, "You feel it, the emptiness? That thing's gone, yeah?"

"For now. And don't call him a *thing*. He had a body, same way we do."

"Except for the fact that I've never eaten a bucket of nails like it was a three-piece from KFC."

"You know what I mean."

Again, we go silent for a moment, waiting, watching, confirming that our ghostly pal had indeed gone back to the other side.

We're in the clear and Mike says, "So you're not full of shit? She's really from The Paranormal Channel? I thought all they showed was a bunch of crap about aliens and Sasquatch?"

"True, but they're branching out. She was telling me that they had this idea for a show that would be an hour-long collection of home videos—you know, evidence submitted by their viewers."

"I'd watch that. And they wanna use ours?"

"More than that, amigo. They want to use *us*."

"Like for an interview or what?"

"Way, *way* more. Check this out: the producer's name is Carla Hancock. I looked her up on the Internet thinking somebody was screwing with me. Anyway, she's legit and has a list of credits a mile long. Totally, absolutely, completely loved the evidence we captured, said it was some of the best she'd ever seen, and get this... She said the video was fantastic, but what she dug more than anything was how we interacted, talking about how we had great chemistry, good banter."

"And she got all of that from a two minute video?"

"I asked the same thing. Actually, the smell is really getting to me in here. Let's go take a breather."

Entering the empty hall, we step out into the somewhat fresher air of the dilapidated asylum where there's more ambient light provided by the moon. Our feet crunch on broken glass, shattered tile, and the remnants of fallen sheetrock. Out the broken window and a couple of stories below, in the courtyard, I can see Jake sweeping a flashlight across his path. I tell Mike, "Carla said she used to be in casting before she moved over to TPC and always had an excellent eye for a real connection between people. Sounds like she saw something in us that caught her attention. Whatever. Long story short, she *loved* the clip, and she wants us to dig up the scariest place we can find for an investigation—"

"Like your bedroom?"

"Hardy har har, but no. We come up with the scariest place we can find and she'll bring a film crew up here for a test run. She's got some room in her budget to film a cheap pilot, and from what she says, she wants to blow it on us. Reality shows have low production costs, so it's perfect."

"Wow." It's not an excited sound. Mike crosses his arms, turns his eyes toward the moon. The way the window frames his silhouette, he looks like a single-pane drawing from a comic book. "I don't know, man. That's a big commitment, but..."

I knew he would be hesitant—timid, even—because Mike is a creature of habit. He likes things to stay the way they are. The right shoe always goes on first, that kind of thing.

"You don't have to answer now. Just take some time to think—"

"No, I'm in."

I pause, staring at him to make sure he's not screwing with me. "Really? Just like that?"

"Yeah. At least the pilot. I've never been on TV before, so, sure."

"Awesome! I thought I'd have to beg you for weeks, dude, what made you—" I pause mid-sentence, knowing exactly what the reason is. "Toni, huh?"

"I got zero game with her. Maybe being a TV star will help."

I can't help chuckling. "So you'll practically *catapult* yourself out of your comfort zone for a woman you've known for two weeks, but not me?"

"She's prettier. And a knockout ten to my five."

"Fair enough." I clap him on the back, squeeze his shoulder. "This could lead to something big, Mikey Mike. I'm getting good vibes already."

I feel a knock against my thigh, glancing down in time to see a rock skittering across the cracked tiles. Something threw it at me, definitely. The hair on my arms prickles and stands at attention like trees in a haunted forest.

A disembodied voice, deep and distant, says, *"You will fall."*

***

Over a decade later, I have no doubt that something was trying to warn us, even back then.

But how could we have known?

Blindsight becomes hindsight.

1
Ford Atticus Ford

It's early in the morning—too early for normal, sane humans—when there's just enough light to see the world emerging. Born from night once again. Rubbing the sleep from its eyes.

I'm sitting out on the balcony of my rented condo here in Newport, Oregon. It's a coastal town roughly two and half hours southwest from my home in Portland, and the cool thing is, it's far enough away that I actually feel like I'm on vacation, yet close enough that I don't have to spend all day traveling to get somewhere. It's a distantly removed staycation, even though that term makes me gag a little.

I like it here on the coast. It's where I come to pretend like I have a normal life that doesn't involve ghosts, demonic entities, lawsuits, cranky detectives, lawyers who may as well be demons, and responsibility. Here, the misty, rainy grays of the day feel like a comforting blanket to me. It's good napping weather. It smells like salt air and moss. Life feels slower, more measured. Other than sex and pizza, there's nothing better than wrapping a thick, fluffy blanket around your shoulders, plopping down into a cozy chair on a deck overlooking the mighty Pacific, and enjoying a lukewarm cup of coffee while the waves roll in.

But I don't get to do that right now because I just finished reading an email from Jesse, my assistant in dry, sunny Albuquerque, with a subject line that reads, in all caps: OMG! FORD! COOLEST NEWS EVER!

Except it's not.

Not to me, anyway.

The email, which contains the details of a press release from some company called Spirit World Productions, Inc., sits open on my screen. Apparently, I've agreed to participate in the filming of a controversial documentary—without signing anything official, and especially without giving them my permission.

If I could, I'd burn holes through the press release with giant, fiery bolts of white-hot flame from my eyeballs. Instead, I slam my laptop closed, stand up, and twist sideways like a discus-slinging Olympian, ready to hurl the damn thing off the balcony and down the cliff, all the way to the soaking wet sand below. Better judgment prevails because I have important stuff on here and my therapist has suggested in the past that destroying inanimate objects is one of the least productive ways to manage difficult emotions.

The biggest problem is, I don't know whom to blame first.

Should I blame myself for even hinting to my friend and former co-lead investigator, Mike Long, that I may even be *slightly* interested in doing a documentary about the case of little Chelsea Hopper when we were together last, after the Craghorn case in Hampton Roads?

I said *maybe*. I absolutely *did not* agree to it. Not yet. Not in full.

Or should I blame Mike himself, because as sure as the sky is blue, he has to be the one who passed word along that I was interested?

I don't… I just don't know. I can't believe that Mike would do that to me. He knew I needed to think about it. He understood that I was on the fence, that my feelings about Chelsea, her family, and the former *Graveyard: Classified* producer, Carla Hancock—who is mostly to blame for ruining the show's future—were difficult ones to reconcile. That whole situation is heavy, shadowy, and pregnant with nasty possibilities. We're talking, like, a moss green, covered-in-warts imp baby of nastiness.

After Chelsea Hopper, who was five years old at the time, was attacked by a demon on our show, on live television, Halloween night 2012, my world crumbled like a pack of Ramen noodles under the heel of God. Although forgiving Carla would be mentally healthy, because there's already enough darkness swimming around in my head, I don't think I'll ever find the strength, or desire, to absolve her for forcing that situation onto such a sweet, smiling, innocent girl.

Nor myself for allowing it to happen while chasing glory and fame.

So, yeah. I digress. You can see that, in my life, guilt and blame fly around like glowing tracer bullets over 'Nam, but I'll need to make a few phone calls to find out where I should adjust my crosshairs for this particular occasion.

Can you force someone to redact a press release? Probably.

Should be simple enough to issue a correction, right? But the damage will be done. Even hinting at something like this will cause a hurricane of excitement on social media, which normally would be a good thing—except for the subject matter.

After that shit in Norfolk, I'm worried about Chelsea and what might be coming if that demon is to be believed. It's the kind of thing that should be handled in private. Then again, Mike needs this to help his life heal just as much as I do, though for extremely different reasons.

I blurt out a handful of curses, stopping short of shaking my fist at the sky like a crotchety old man and carefully sit my laptop down on the balcony's small glass table. Behind me, I hear the *tic-tic-tic* of dog claws on concrete and turn to see my beloved canine buddy.

Ulie has the only face in the world that I'd like to see at the moment. I brought him with me on this short getaway because I can't burden Melanie from wardrobe—sorry, just *Melanie*—with another dog-sitting weekend. I can only pull water from that well so many times before I feel like I'm taking advantage of her generosity.

As my ex-wife, she's more charitable than social customs typically dictate.

Besides, it's when I'm travelling all across the U.S. that I really need her help. I should probably save my favor cards for when my next case pops up and a befuddled detective needs some paranormal help with an ongoing investigation a thousand miles from here.

Although, I'm sure, to Melanie, keeping an eye on Ulie is considered more of a treat than a chore. I mean, honestly, he's the Bestest Doggie in the Whole Wide World.

Don't tell him, though. It might go to his head.

This dog, man...

One ear that's constantly flopped over. Big brown eyes. White fur around his muzzle that looks like a goatee. The cutest, most mischievous doggie grin that you've ever seen. Who wouldn't want to hang out with this guy?

I left him on the loveseat earlier, legs twitching and upper lip curled, perhaps chasing a bevy of annoying seagulls in his dreams, and now, as he pads out onto the balcony with me, he looks up with a groggy expression. Head cocked as if he's asking, "It's so early. What in the hell are you doing out here, Ford?"

I drop down to one knee and cup my hands around the back of his head, running my thumbs across the inside of his ears. He loves this trick, eyelids drooping in bliss, and it's great to see that he's back to his old self after my third investigation at the Hampstead farmhouse. Papa Joe is a dark, malevolent spirit that rolls in like a thick blanket of black clouds around your heart, and I'll admit that it wasn't the best idea to have that grumpy old bastard serve as Ulie's introduction to the world of paranormal investigations.

And then I had to leave him for a few days and fly east over to the Hampton Roads area in coastal Virginia. That investigation did *not* have the results I expected.

Once again, a spirit will likely change the direction of my life.

It's no secret that ghosts affect my life more than humans, and yet, no matter how much I've been exposed to it, the thought is still strange to me.

Back in Virginia, after my little tantrum in the investigation room, where I practically said, "Screw you guys, I'm going home," and stormed off like a kid on a playground, Detective Thomas was kind enough to send a copy of my audio files back to me when curiosity took over. I spent days reviewing them, staying up all hours of the night, pausing and rewinding, pausing and rewinding, fighting goosebumps, chugging coffee and energy drinks while I sent Mike random, caffeine-infused emails until he finally called and told me to take a break.

"Ford, dude, chill out," he told me last week. "It was the same demon from the Hopper house. I get it. You don't need to convince me. What you need to do is, drop the energy drinks down a notch or two and get a nap in, okay? And take Melanie to dinner. Get your mind off this a while."

You know, it seemed like good advice at the time. At least the part about backing off the energy drinks and getting some rest. What Mike didn't know, and what I hadn't told him yet, is that Melanie was seeing this guy Jeff from the morning news program where she did hair, makeup, and wardrobe. I'd discovered that little tidbit of shitty information when I went to pick Ulie up after the Virginia trip. Sad thing is, I learned it *after* I had made a jackass of myself by asking if I could take her to dinner.

Maybe I looked like a jackass. Take it for what you will. She could've thought it was an innocent gesture. A quick thanks for watching Ulie. Who knows?

The only thing I can say for certain is that I felt my hopes fizzle out like week-old soda in a can, and I left her place that night with my tail tucked between my legs. Ulie had a sympathetic tail-tuck as well, or it could've been that he was just sad to leave Melanie.

Whatever. Doodoo happens.

I mention all that to say this: the trip over here to the Oregon coast was meant to get my mind off Melanie and how I screwed up our marriage. It was meant to give me some mental distance from Chelsea Hopper, her tormentor, and the mental hangups I have about doing a feature-length documentary on her story. Carla wants it for her career. Mike needs the money to heal his life and his marriage, as I've mentioned.

What about me?

That's easy. Redemption. Has been and always will be until I get some closure for myself, and for that sweetheart little girl.

This trip is supposed to be relaxing.

Instead, all it's done is give me more time to think about the crap I should be ignoring for a couple of weeks. My jaws hurt from clenching them so much. I need to be working. I need to be investigating. I need to find something to occupy my mind.

That's exactly why I checked my email earlier. I couldn't sleep, so I left Ulie snoozing while I got up and came out to the balcony. I opened my email in hopes that Jesse had sent me a note with details about a job, any welcome distraction to get my focus elsewhere. Maybe there would be a request from that cop down in Baton Rouge. We left that case open a couple of months and he was supposed to get in touch with me again if he wanted more help.

And then, *blammo*, OMG FORD! COOLEST NEWS EVER.

The thought of it whips up another tornado of anger and nausea in my stomach.

"Damn it." I stand up, grunting as my knees crackle like bubble wrap. I'm getting older, and the sad thing is, I'm probably on the back nine already, on the way down the slide, ready to become one of those who talk to me from the afterlife.

The words of my therapist—and Melanie, too, before we were divorced, crawl into my head. "You can't keep doing this to yourself. You know how you are. Bad news or—or moments of indecision, too much going on in your mind… They're not excuses to start feeling sorry for yourself. Listen to me, okay? It's *life*. It doesn't mean the universe hates Ford Atticus Ford."

Yeah. I get it, but damn if that fist-sized snowball doesn't turn into a massive boulder screaming down a hillside once it gets rolling.

I lean on the balcony railing and feel flecks of rain pitter-pattering against my cheeks and forehead. Ulie whimpers and grumbles when a seagull screeches by, sailing on the drizzle-soaked breeze.

I *have* to find some work. I need to put my mind back in its happy place, and that means I need to go talk to some dead people.

I'll sit back on the press release news. There's nothing I can do about it this very second anyway, and I expect my phone will be ringing, and Mike will be on the caller ID before long. He'll either be apologizing, or asking for forgiveness, or both, and there's no way I'm prepared to have a civil discussion with him.

Right now, at this very moment, as I stand here in my pajama bottoms and a USC sweatshirt, the only question that remains is this: who should a guy talk to if he wants to dig up some trouble with the local ghosts? I've had cases handed to me for so long that I've forgotten what it's like to go out and search for them.

I'm tired, though. I hear the siren call of my bed, but I know if I go snuggle in, I won't sleep. I'll just think everything I'm not doing at the moment to make the world a better place, one that's safer from the powerful right-handers who bear the torches for Satan Himself.

Yeah.

Coffee first. Then trouble.

2
Ford Atticus Ford

Her high heels are a shade of red that exists in nature, but only on the breast of some exotic bird in a South American jungle. That's the first thing I notice. First, the color of her pumps, and second, I'm wondering why someone is so dressed up at half past seven in the morning, standing in line at a petite bakery that would fit inside my master bedroom closet back home.

I'm not disrespecting Le Breadcrumb. They work magic with an oven and some dough, but damn are they tiny.

And the smell in here? If God has air freshener in Heaven, I bet it's the same.

Her appearance boggles the mind on a typical, drizzly day here in Nye Beach. Sure, it's a bit artsy and more trend-*ish* than the rest of Newport, but this ain't Fifth Avenue.

I'll admit, the pumps are sexy, and they seamlessly lead into a pronounced set of well-toned and well-tanned calves. I stop at the hem of her little black dress, which tightly comes to a screeching halt just above her knees, and not because I can't look any further up, but because she catches me.

I'm human. I'm male. Sue me.

Besides, it's not often that you see such classy attire before the sun is barely up.

One of these things is not like the other, right?

I smile over the rim of my coffee, a bit sheepishly, because yeah, I just got caught being a man.

There's a distant sense of familiarity about her too, like it would be *okay* to look because I know her. I'm sure I don't. Ninety-nine percent. I've been here a few days now. Have I maybe seen her at a restaurant? In the wine aisle at the grocery joint up the street?

She's bottle-blonde with a shade of red lipstick that matches the pumps. Black-rimmed glasses—the nerdy sexy kind—accentuate her cheekbones. Nothing about the whole ensemble is an accident. It's by design, and I can only think of a handful of reasons why she's here, dressed like that.

One, she's an escort on her way home—that's *not* why I would recognize her, by the by—or two, this is the walk of shame. Maybe she spent the night with some rich dude who owns an obnoxiously gargantuan oceanfront house, someone she met at a bar or an office party. Or—and God forbid the cliché—she's the personal assistant, she slept with the boss, and she's regretting every second of the hangover, both the moral aspects and the alcohol-induced ones.

But, who am I to judge?

The point is, she's out of place, dressed like that here in this bakery, this early in the morning, and I noticed.

She noticed me noticing.

And, now, we're doing the subtle glance dance… mostly because I'm sitting here with a half-eaten scone and a horrible cup of coffee, waiting on her to recognize me.

I'm not being an egotistical jerk. Honest to God. It comes with the job description of a former television host of one of the most popular paranormal reality shows that has ever graced the small screen. Or any show, for that matter.

Graveyard: Classified was a juggernaut.

And then that thing with Chelsea Hopper happened.

And then it wasn't a juggernaut anymore.

I have no qualms whatsoever about owning up to the fact that I went from A-List Celebrity Extraordinaire to D-List Subterranean Basement Dweller who only gets invited to the big parties when someone is feeling nostalgic.

My ego, my pride… they earned that for me, and I'm man enough to accept it.

However, that doesn't stop me from enjoying the occasional interaction with a superfan, especially when they look like the exotic species now paying for her cranberry muffin, who then daintily picks up her coffee mug—that's been filled too full—and shuffles toward me with a smile baring the brightest, whitest teeth I've ever seen. Really, they're like an exploding star. I can tell that it's hard for her to shuffle in those heels, so I get up, extend a hand for assistance and pull out a chair. Because, obviously, she's coming to sit with me—and then she walks right past and says hello to the elderly woman at my six.

Ouch. *Burn.*

My cheeks are on fire. The knife wound in my dignity is cavernous, and I'm left standing here with my coffee unfinished, my scone half eaten, wiping my sweaty palms on my jeans, wondering if I should pretend like I was simply getting up to leave.

That's the best exit strategy, the safest way to save myself from the moment. I can see Ulie outside, squinting against the drizzle blowing in his face as he sits patiently, waiting for me to bring him one of the baked doggie treats that Le Breadcrumb is known for. Well, at least in the canine world, population: Ulie.

A hasty exit is the only salvageable way out of this, and the wailing screech of metal chair legs on a smooth concrete floor announces my escape to the entire bakery.

Behind me, I hear a radio-smooth voice saying, "Oh, hey, don't go."

I turn around and she's, boom, *right there*. "I'm sorry—what?"

She sets her muffin down on my table, spills some of the too-full coffee, and tucks a loose strand of hair behind her ear. The diamond stud in her earlobe is roughly the size of a hailstone in mid-summer Kansas, and I assume there's a matching one on the other side. She apologizes again and tells me, "That was mean. I was just screwing with you."

"You were? I, uh…"

I don't know what to say to this. It's fairly standard for fans of the show to stumble, fumble, trip, fall, and stutter their way into a greeting, asking for a photo with me or an autograph, whether I'm in line at Target or waiting to speak to a detective at a police station. The general population isn't secure enough to mess with me out in public. That's reserved for Mike Long, Melanie, and other close friends; my guarded circle of people who know the real me—the guy in a t-shirt and flip-flops—not the former *enfant terrible* of paranormal investigations.

"The almighty Ford Atticus Ford," she says, narrowing her eyelids. "You were checking me out."

Wow. The bravado on this one. "I—uh, yeah—I mean, no."

Up close, her perfume dances among the luscious scents of scones, muffins, doughnuts, and brewing coffee, penetrating the moment I'm fumbling through.

She smells like a candy store that also doubles as a florist. If it were possible, it's a scent I would love to taste.

"It's okay," she says. "I don't mind. Happens a bit in my line of work. Yours too, I would imagine."

"Line of work?"

Her jaw drops in mock offense. "You don't recognize me, do you?"

I squint at her, feigning recognition. "*Vaguely.*"

"Don't lie."

"I'm not, I—"

"Whatevs, buddy. We've known each for a long time, even though we've never officially met. I'm Lauren Coeburn. Nice to finally meet you in person."

Oh. My. God.

Lauren Coeburn. I can't believe I didn't figure it out.

Especially since she fucking *eviscerated* me on *The Weekend Report*, that entertainment show where they make fun of all the dumb things said on reality television each week. I used to love it and watched every chance I got, which usually meant a marathon morning in front of the TV on the rare day that we weren't traveling or filming.

I haven't watched it since *Graveyard* got pulled, and not since she repeatedly flashed that single picture of me, taken by Carla Hancock, where I'm looking over my shoulder, grinning nervously. A grin that was taken out of context by every media rep that showed it. It didn't help that you can also see Chelsea Hopper holding my hand, terrified and crying. Irony aside, that photo will fucking *haunt* me for the rest of my days.

Those thirty seconds of *The Weekend Report* are burned into my memory. That image of me, on the screen, appearing and then fading to black, over and over, with the overlaid soundtrack of a heartbeat thumping in rhythm—it stings.

I can recite her words verbatim: "Normally, this show is all about the comedy," said her voiceover. "But today, we're sad to announce the death knell for the almighty Ford Atticus Ford. You know him, you *used to* love him, though I wouldn't blame you for bringing out the pitchforks now. Little Chelsea Hopper, attacked by a demon—and no, I'm not talking about that thing in the attic. Just look at him. The anger in his eyes. The vengeance that he seeks. For what? Why? What kind of monster could do such a thing to an innocent girl? I can tell you this; it takes the frozen heart of someone who's already dead inside to do that to a child. That horrible, rotting, puss-filled shell of a human being should have committed *hara-kiri* in Times Square before this ever became a possibility. So let me ask you this: has Ford Atticus Ford become the monster that he supposedly claims to hunt each week on *Graveyard: Classified*? And, if that's the case, does the *real* question become... should Ford have turned the camera on *himself* a long time ago? We've got the disturbing footage right after the break. You might want to put the kids to bed for this one, folks."

And why, exactly, didn't I recognize her if such an astronomically atrocious attack on my character is still zipping around my synapses?

It's because, like Mike, she's dropped some weight, gotten a tan, gone through a complete makeover, and has pretty much transformed herself into a different human entirely. It's because she's smiling at me. It's because she's being nice to me.

That is why I didn't recognize her.

While Mike went through his transition, I'm assuming, in order to shed a layer that reminded him of anything having to do with *me*, it's likely that Lauren Coeburn's producers had not so subtly suggested that she straighten herself out.

I've been off the Internet and away from social media for close to two years now, but I have been in line at a grocery store, and I've seen the tabloids. I specifically remember seeing her on the cover of *Hollywood Watchlist*, wearing a gray one-piece swimsuit on a tropical beach somewhere, with some awful headline about how an elephant had escaped from the San Diego Zoo. I'll admit that I felt a wee bit of vindication—okay, a whole lot of it—but that's just wrong, man.

Okay, yeah, I chuckled. Poor thing.

Poor her, poor me. Whatever.

Lauren holds her hand out to shake, and I let her get to where I can sense she's getting ready to pull it back. I do this on purpose, and then I grab it during the retreat, squeeze a little harder than you should with a "lady." I make a theatrical show of wiping my hand on my shirt. Not down around my waist or indiscreetly on my side, no, nothing like that, but rather in full view across my chest.

Petty? Yes. Childish? Yes.

Do I care?

Nah.

The only thing I have to say to that is, sometimes it's okay to indulge those tendencies. Staying young at heart doesn't always mean eating an ice cream cone or watching cartoons. Sometimes you have to let go of that inner animal, the one that's been molded and scarred by society, and relish in being the simplest of things: a whiny, foot-stomping brat.

I tilt my head back a bit, which accentuates my flared nostrils and raised eyebrows—an angry, snorting bull, I am—before I flop down into my chair, arms crossed, lips smashed together, in an obvious, edge-of-a-tantrum pouting position.

Lauren appears amused and gestures to the seat opposite of me. "May I sit?"

"Be my guest, Coeburn." I look away. Outside, Ulie remains tethered to the front porch's support beam, only now he's moved down to the microscopic strip of grass between the sidewalk and the street, where he investigates the rear of a friendly poodle being ushered along by an elderly couple.

Two minutes ago, I was daydreaming about doing the same thing to the woman sitting across from me until I found out who she was.

What a world.

I have absolutely no idea what to expect from this, and around someone like Lauren Coeburn, anything I say can and will be used against me in the court of public opinion, so I reserve my right to remain silent. I want her to speak first. That way, I'll know how to proceed.

Either Lauren has the same plan, or she doesn't know what to expect either, because we sit in extended, funeral-parlor silence while she sips at her mug and pinches nibble-sized morsels off the bulbous muffin cap.

In my peripheral vision, I catch the bakery clerk trying to sneak a picture of us with her iPhone. She forgets to turn off the flash, which gives her away immediately, and she apologizes with an embarrassed wave before scuttling behind the metal racks filled with the various loaves of bread that will be gone by ten a.m.

Lauren loses the battle of wills when she finally says, "I heard you might be filming a new documentary."

Damn it. Word spreads fast.

3

Mike Long

Daylight breaks on the horizon. The sun peeks up over the dividing line where green meets blue, and this coffee tastes like complete shit. Why, oh why, do I let Toni buy this stuff? Perhaps it's because she has my testicles poised above the coffee bean grinder, and I have no true say in the matter.

The beach house. Jesus. I don't know why we kept it. The cost definitely outweighs the benefits.

Nah, that's bullshit. I can't even convince myself of that lie. This place is amazing, and that view? Would you just *look* at that view? Pinks, oranges, and yellows quiver along the underbellies of those fluffy puffy clouds. Hot damn. Heaven on Earth right here in North Carolina.

It's warm out already. A nice breeze pushes the seagrass along in rivulets. Out there, maybe a couple of miles, a tanker is sailing northward, probably heading up into the Chesapeake Bay.

It's a good life here. It really is.

Or would be. Could be. Could be better if only Ford will stop waffling and say yes to the documentary. It's not a big deal. Chelsea's parents have already okayed it. *They're* exploiting their daughter more than *we* will. Let them have the guilty conscious. Ford, buddy, *come on*. We're trying to *help* her.

And help ourselves, of course, for reasons so different you could drive a semi through the gap.

I need the money, You need people to love you again.

Well, I mean, like big time love you. Not just the folks you meet at a deli or walking down the street. I know you need to sit on the couches of late night shows and get invited to Eastwood's ranch. Not me. All I need is for Dayton and Ashley to look up to me again, and for Toni to chill the hell out.

I'm trying, okay? Please just get off my ass. I can't *make* people take my ideas for a new series. I can't make the people who sign the checks sign the fucking checks. Don't you get it? This is out of my control. I have no say in this whatsoever. None. And that's exactly why I had to go crawling back to Ford and beg him to do this. He's the talent. He's the show. He's Batman. I'm Robin.

The almighty Ford Atticus Ford *was* the show. He was *Graveyard: Confidential* all by himself. He was the gas, the engine, and the body of the Corvette.

I was the can of soda in the cup holder.

Maybe I had my own little cult following, but the spotcamgirls were never going out of their way to send *me* naked pictures of themselves, no matter how much Ford tried to placate me.

For God's sake, this coffee… Tastes like it's been filtered through desiccated dog turds.

Desiccated. Word of the day right there.

If Ford will just do the documentary—two weeks of shooting, we kick this demon's ass, and then we go home. Little bit of promo around Christmas during the release, sit through a few press junkets, and we're golden. I cash in on a few mil, and then I can disappear again. Maybe the kids will like me. Maybe Toni will stop looking at me the way she does. She doesn't even try to hide the disappointment anymore, not even after I dropped the pounds.

It was never about the fat, was it, Toni? Always the money. I dropped seventy-three pounds for you; the biceps, the pecs, the six-pack, the tan? I thought that's what you wanted, but no, the money. The stupid money. I wish I'd never said yes to Ford back at that asylum.

You will fall.

So many years later, and that continues to pop up in the back of my mind now and again. How did it know? Or did it? Could've been talking about me tripping down the stairs later that night. And yet, here we are, Toni.

Answer me this, *sweetheart*, when did dollar signs replace the love and affection?

Was it after season two, when the sponsorships really started rolling in?

The shoes, the fast food joints, the online investment websites—nobody at TPC headquarters had ever seen anything like it. Such amazing offers right up front for two goobers with a camera and some bad jokes. All we had to do was shill a product, and the bank accounts would runneth over like that Jesus cup thing.

Those were the days, weren't they, Ford?

Looks like the tide is heading out. Should I go to the gym today or take it easy?

It's, what, leg day? Don't be a cliché, Mike, everybody loves skipping leg day.

Up and at 'em, old boy. Get moving. To Do List. To do, to do.

Hit the gym. Check in with Ford, then call Carla. Status update on the documentary.

I should—

"Mike?"

Lost in the randomness of my own runaway thought train, I hadn't heard the patio door open, and Toni's voice scares the bejesus out of me. I jump, spin around to face her, and feel the lukewarm coffee splash on my toes.

"Oh, hey, you're up early."

"You didn't answer the phone."

Hair mussed and sleepy-eyed, she still looks phenomenal in one of my t-shirts and nothing else. Obviously, I don't mind that she's never broken the habit of sleeping in the nude—man's a man, am I right?—and will only throw on a t-shirt to come downstairs if she thinks the kids might be awake. They're old enough to throw out a few jabs of "Gross, Mom," and, "Dad, make her put some clothes on!" but I chuckle and ignore them. It's one of the only awesome things left over from the good times.

The other is her meatloaf.

She mumbles something about the person on the phone.

"Who?"

"I don't know who it is. Just come get the fucking thing." She beckons me over, using the cordless house phone as a lure, and doesn't step out onto the deck.

What happened to us?

Rhetorical question.

She barely acknowledges me when I take it, and then I listen to her bare feet pad across the kitchen floor, around the corner, and her angry stomps fade away the further she gets up the stairs. No matter what's going on between us, that bare bottom remains a symbol of perfection, and I could chew it like bubble gum.

Is that weird? Probably.

Chances are high she doesn't love me anymore, but I'm still attracted to her. Blood through the veins and all.

"Hello. Mike speaking." I have no clue who this could be at six-thirty in the morning.

"Mr. Long?"

"Yeah."

"Mike Long from *Graveyard: Classified?*"

"Yes. Who is this?"

"You don't know me, but…"

The voice is female. Little rougher, could have some age on it, like she's seen things. I'm thinking she could be in her mid-thirties.

Mystery lady says, "God, I'm really sorry to bother you so early, but I haven't slept in days, and I was—this is going to sound like I'm some crazy stalker, but you have your name listed in the phone book, and I was hoping, maybe… hoping you might be able to help."

I told Toni to take our name out of the public phone book years ago. *Years.* She never would. For a while, she was caught up in her own peripheral fame, and having our name in the phone book meant that she could take calls and entertain reporters, sometimes even segueing that whole thing into articles about herself and the interior decorating business she used to own. She even got a few modeling gigs out of it. By the time the phone stopped ringing entirely, I had forgotten that we were publicly listed, and since Toni controls all the household bills and whatnot, I'm guessing she left it out there with wistful hopes on her mind.

When you're in the twilight of fading fame, there's nothing worse than a silent phone.

The woman apologizes again and sounds like she's going to hang up.

"It's okay," I tell her. "I was already up. You know, sunrise on the deck. Bad coffee." I almost whisper those last two words.

Toni is back in bed, in the master bedroom directly above me where the humongous, large-paned windows overlook the Atlantic, but I'm worried she'll hear me criticizing her shopping choices. Yeah. It's that bad. I'd rather avoid the argument. "Can I help you with something, Miss…?" I leave the question dangling at the end of that sentence, prompting her to finally reveal a name.

"I'm Dakota. *Bailey*."

She reveals it in such a way that indicates I should know who she is, simply by her name, but I should keep it a secret that Dakota *Bailey* is on the other end of the line. Are you kidding me?

"Oh, shit. No way! *The* Dakota Bailey? Seriously? Dakota Bailey. On my phone."

For God's sake, Mike, reel it in. It's not like it's the president.

"Yeah," she says. "That would be me."

Dakota Bailey…*the* Dakota Bailey, won the reality cooking competition *Yes, Chef!* three seasons in a row before she retired and went out on top. She's a miracle worker with a blank slate and a silver countertop covered with random ingredients. Give her three onions, a bowl of wild rice, some shrimp, sun-dried tomatoes, and a bucket of strawberry yogurt, and she'll whip up a dish that will blow the ever-lovin' socks off any celebrity judge sitting on the panel.

Chicken cutlets, peanut butter, and a basket full of chocolate-covered walnuts, along with white cheddar and raisins… strap on your seatbelts for the rocket-ride of deliciousness.

It was *all* mouth-watering from my side of the television screen. I never got to sit on the celebrity judge panel, though I tried my damndest to get Carla to pull some strings back when *Graveyard* was the number one show on Thursday nights. Never happened. My star wasn't bright enough. Ford could've gone, if he had wanted to, but he wasn't a fan of the show.

Sacrilege, I say.

Dakota Bailey retired from *Yes, Chef!* about five years ago, and I lost my chance. Last I'd heard she had taken her winnings and started some ridiculously upscale restaurant in New York City, and the reservation list was—literally—two years out.

I *adored* her when she was on the show. It wasn't the same without her, so I stopped watching a couple years back, and she sort of fell out of my memory. Out of sight, out of mind.

Yet, here she is, now, on the other end of the phone.

Dakota Freakin' Bailey.

Now I know what people feel like when they see Ford walking down the street.

Total fanboy moment right here.

I take a breath, or, you know, six deep ones to calm myself down. This takes so long that I hear Dakota say, "Mr. Long? Are you there?"

"I—yeah—I am. Sorry about that. It's just that you're Dakota Bailey."

"And you're Mike Long."

"I am indeed. Just Mike."

"You were my favorite part of *Graveyard*. I'm sure Ford's a great guy off camera, but, you know, you always had the cool gadgets."

That's nice to hear, even if it's a little white lie. I'll take it. "Thanks, I appreciate it." This feels a bit like we're both stroking each other's egos at some schmaltzy cocktail party until I remember that she sorta called me in a panic at half past six in the morning. "So... You needed some help with things, or whatever?" I'm aware of how fumbling and awkward I sound but the words are tripping out of my mouth because I'm talking to Dakota Freakin' Bailey.

"Are you still investigating?" Her tone is full of hope.

"Off and on, yeah. I do some local things around Kitty Hawk for charity organizations. Events like that once in a while. And, believe it or not, last month, I actually helped Ford with a pretty insane investigation up in Virginia Beach. I'm trying to get him to do—" I have to interrupt myself right there.

Unofficially, I'm rambling like a fool.

Officially, I'm bound by a non-disclosure agreement and don't have the privileges to talk about the documentary until Carla and her team send out the press release. I'm told that's any day now. And by 'any day,' it means whenever one of us is able to coerce my former partner into signing the contract. Ford and I haven't spoken in a couple of days, not since I told him to chill the hell out and go take a break, but as of yesterday Carla insisted that he had his fingers wrapped around the pen and was hovering over the dotted line.

"I'm trying to get him to come help me down here once in a while, but you know Ford, always the busy man in the room."

"That's nice," Dakota says. Her end of the line goes silent, and I patiently wait on her to continue. Otherwise, I might begin blabbing about how amazing she was in her third season and how she managed to pull off that incredible win over the guy with the dreadlocks.

I can't remember his name. Nobody remembers second place.

Dakota's raspberry steak parfait must have been out of this world on that final episode. Her voice is hushed when she speaks again. "Sorry. Thought I heard something." The words quiver across her lips.

"Are you okay?"

"No. God, no. Not at all." Her breathing intensifies; it sounds like she's speedwalking. "Give me a sec. Moving to another room."

"Hey, everything all right? Do I need to call the cops?"

"Please don't. I can't—this can't get out to the media. No reporters, no Twitter, nothing, okay? Please?"

"Absolutely. Of course."

Anything for you, Dakota Bailey. Wow.

"Not a word?"

"On my honor."

"I'm just down the beach from you, about half a mile."

"Really?" This is a mind-blowing fact, which sends me instantly daydreaming about walking down Beachfront Avenue, carrying a bottle of my best red wine, and spending the evening with her while she cooks Toni, the kids, and me some of the most delectable food we've ever tasted.

Then I allow myself to be evil for a second and wonder if it's necessary for my family to be there, too. Dakota Bailey and I alone in a kitchen…

Dakota says, "Okay, I think I'm good. I don't know how familiar you are with all the neighbors."

"Not much. At least not that far down."

"I bought this house about a month ago. White with dark blue shutters? You know the one?"

"Didn't the guy who owned it sell all of his Internet companies and buy his own island? Crazy money. You like it there?"

I realize this is sort of a bullshit, throwaway, small-talk question, because something has to be wrong since she's calling me before the sun is fully over the horizon.

"This place is haunted, Mr. Long." Her voice is muffled, like she's holding her hand over her mouth, trying to say something without being heard. If it really is haunted, keeping her voice low won't matter. "I've hardly slept in three days, but I refuse to give this place up. It's my—it's a long story. Would you—is there any chance you could come check things out for me? Or... if you can, maybe get rid of whatever is here? I don't know if you can actually do anything about it. I swear on my mother's grave, there is something *evil* in this house, and I can pay you whatever you want—oh, God, no. There it is! Get away from me! Don't touch me, you—Mike, can you come now, please?"

Click.

I had already decided that I would be helping Dakota Freakin' Bailey, no question about it, but after hearing that, and before I have time to grab any of my paranormal investigation equipment, I'm down the wooden stairs and sprinting south along the sand, cordless phone still clenched in my fist.

The sound of true terror in a person's voice is unmistakable.

4
Ford Atticus Ford

"The hell are you doing here, Coeburn? Are you following me?"

Her thrust, my parry, it's the only defense I could come up with because I'm for damn sure not ready to say a single word about that documentary, much less to this woman with a mouth like a bullhorn on steroids.

"*Sheesh*, enough with the hostility. One, that was a long time ago; two, you earned it; and, three, you *admitted* that you deserved it. I'm not gonna backtrack on something you've already publicly apologized for. Just accept it and move on."

"No."

Yeah, I'm pouting. So what?

She takes a sip of her coffee. Her exquisitely manicured nails match the color of her pumps. "Grow up, Ford. And no, I'm not following you. If I were, you wouldn't know it."

"Bullshit."

Lauren leans back in her chair, one arm propped on the backrest, nonchalant, confident in her smugness. "The press release hit early this morning, and I shit you not, *absolute truth*, one of my producers sent me a text *right before* I walked through the door. And, woohoo, wonder of all wonders, wouldn't you know it, here you are. The stars aligned. Like, literally."

Look at that self-righteous smile. She's proud of her pun. To be perfectly frank, it was a good one, and I'd congratulate her if I didn't want to take the remainder of my scone and smash it all over her face.

"So you just happen to be here, in Nye Beach of all places, dressed like you're ready to walk down the red carpet?"

Lauren lifts one shoulder in a pronounced "meh" gesture. "Local morning show wanted to do a profile on me. Been up since four thirty, and let me tell you something, it's not easy to look like this before the sun is up."

She's not forgiven, by any means, but now I'm slightly intrigued. "You came *here*? What was it? Like one of the public broadcast things filmed on a cheap set? Couple of thrift store loveseats and a coffee table?"

"That's the one." She crosses her arms, leans up on her elbows. "Only it's a legit station and not Wayne and Garth's basement."

"Interesting."

"How's that?"

"I thought that would be beneath you at this point."

"I grew up around here. Just over the hill and past that little Irish pub."

"I thought you spawned somewhere."

"Funny."

But it wasn't. Her smirks emotes *sticks and stones, dickhead*.

The pause in the conversation gets nine months pregnant, and I have no idea where to go from here, so I occupy my hands and mouth with my coffee mug.

I check on Ulie and see that he's curled up on the porch, shivering a little. I feel bad for the guy. It's chilly out there. It's chilly in here, too, but for different reasons.

"So," Lauren finally says, drumming those pristine nails on the tabletop.

"So…" I nod in that uncomfortable way that indicates I have reached the limit of things I can, or want, to say to this woman. She's right, you know. I did publicly apologize, profusely and profoundly, for what happened on that Halloween night over two years ago. Like I said, I *earned* the public's scrutiny, and I'm trying my hardest to get some payback for Chelsea, and for my reputation, and yet, that doesn't mean I have to become instant chums with someone who openly called for me to commit *hara-kiri* in the middle of Times Square.

Her words exactly. She was brutal.

And now she thinks I'm simply going to pretend that the water under the bridge isn't highly flammable gasoline?

As if.

Or, maybe not. Hell if I know. Do I have the energy to fight her? My therapist would tell me it's healthy—this "forgiveness" thing—and that I should sit down with a pen and a sheet of paper, and write a lengthy letter to Miss Lauren Coeburn. I should tell her that I've forgiven her; that I understand why she did it; she had ratings to worry about; she had a team of writers feeding her lines; and I should let her know that I understand how influential a motivated producer can be, because I had gone through that myself with Carla Hancock.

This scampers around in my mind while she takes another dainty bite of her muffin top, which is likely in direct violation of her personal trainer's orders to prevent a different type of muffin top, and I assume that she's desperately trying to savor this dietary break.

"You want an apology, Ford, I'll give you an apology," she says. "I'm sorry. There. But we both know what this business is like. Obligations. Ratings."

"You gutted me," I tell her. "You were like Quentin Tarantino with your wordy violence. Here's you, and here's me." I accompany the last five words with a pantomimed stabbing motion, then imitate a glorified blood splatter.

"Don't be such a drama queen. It's beneath you."

"I thought we—I don't know—I thought we had a thing."

"Meaning?"

"We'd joked around on Twitter. You had reposted some of my crap on Facebook to your fan page. Then you…" I pretend like I'm jabbing a knife into my heart and then I fake a quick death by slumping over in my chair.

"Are we playing charades? Two words, sounds like…giant pansy."

"I'm just saying you could've dialed it back a little."

"Oh, please. It's all part of the game."

"I guess I thought we were buds. Same team, fame team, you know?"

"In this business, we're all playing solitaire. You know that. Regardless," she says, pinching off one last nibble of the cranberry muffin before she slides it across the table. Roughly a tenth of it is gone. That's dedication. I'll give her that much. She continues, "I really am sorry. To a point. We all play solitaire, and we all dig our own graves in this business. I know you got caught up in the moment, and… shit happens."

"Yeah." I have no argument. I pick up the remnants of her muffin and take a bite. It's a helluva lot better than the dry hardtack of a scone I'd been trying to suffer through. I tell her, "That still doesn't change the fact that I'm not saying a word about the documentary. If you'll pardon the pun, that graveyard is… classified."

"Wah-wah-waaaah," she says, imitating the bad-joke horn from ancient cartoons. "Very funny."

"I'm serious, Coeburn. Not a word." I don't know why, but I feel like giving her something. A little tidbit. Just enough to sweeten the tea because maybe, just maybe, if I ever get back in the spotlight, she'll remember I was nice to her once. I wiped the muffin crumbs from my hands. "How 'bout this? I'll give you a little nugget, which is one hundred percent off the record, got me?"

Lauren locks her lips with an invisible key.

"The only thing I'll say is that whoever put out that press release is *screwed* because I haven't even agreed to the documentary yet. No fancy pens, no dotted lines. Not even verbally. I'm trying to decide how I want to approach it."

"Holy shit. Are you for real? They released the news without formalizing it first? Are they mental?"

"Still off the record, okay?" She nods. "Wild guess says that Carla Hancock realizes that I wouldn't mind getting back on camera, and this is her way of, you know, dangling the carrot. Something I can't resist. Baiting me."

"I assume you're going to do something about it."

"That's the thing. I don't know. Ask for a retraction? File a lawsuit? Should I go ahead with the filming and earn a few million? It's all up in the air. And I'm not even sure I *want* to do it. Anyway, I've said enough. There's your nugget."

She may be the host of a reality television review show, but before that she was a standup comedian, and before that, she was a reporter for a mid-sized station down in L.A. Those old journalistic tendencies are crawling out from where she buried them long ago. I can see the curiosity and the excitement in the way she subconsciously licks those fabulous red lips and lowers her voice. "Do you think Mike Long did it? Last time I checked up on him, he was offering to sell whatever soul he had left to the highest bidder. Lots of rumors about his financial situation going around. Maybe he gave the okay to leak it since he'd stand to gain the most."

"No comment." I pick up the remains of her cranberry muffin and take a large bite, as if having a full mouth will block any future words.

"It wouldn't surprise me if Carla did it. Some scummy shit like that has her name written all over it."

I push my coffee away and pick up my worn paperback copy of a Carter Kane novel that I've read at least seven times. "No comment."

"C'mon, Ford. Give me a little. Friend to friend."

If I had any liquid in my mouth, I'm sure I would've comically spewed it all over her face because it's such a ridiculous suggestion. "Friend to friend? You're kidding me, right?"

"At least tell me *something* juicy."

"I gave you a nugget and that's it, Coeburn. No more, no way."

"Something behind the scenes. Something that our readers can really chew on. I mean, *come on*, this is gold. I can get you exposure. We can blow this up. The whole thing. I can help you go public with the fact that they're trying to railroad you into this. It'll be huge."

I stand up from the small table and wince when the metal chair legs screech across the slick concrete flooring. Can't a guy make a dramatic exit without the embarrassing side effects? I tell Lauren, "Nope. Not a chance."

"Please?"

"I'm not going to just *hand* you higher ratings. Apology accepted, yeah, but that doesn't wash away all your sins, and I'll be damned if I do you any favors. Get off my case, get away from me, and take those godawful heels back to L.A. They don't go with that dress. You look like a hooker that's trying too hard."

Cheap shot? Yep. Damn straight. Felt good, too.

But really, they don't go with the dress. That's no joke. The color scheme is way off.

***

I think that's the end of it. Turn out the lights, party's over. Nail in the coffin. Put the baby to bed. Use whatever axiom you can come up with to say that I just ended the conversation on a walk-off homer in the bottom of the ninth.

I couldn't be any more wrong.

I only make it about twenty yards down the sidewalk, with Ulie trotting happily beside me while he licks the remainder of his dog treat from his chops, before I hear the distinct click-clack of platform pumps on a sidewalk.

"Ford!" Lauren calls after me.

Fed up, rolling my eyes, I turn just in time to see her twist an ankle on the curb and go down in a mass of blonde locks, exotic bird colors, and a couple of well-placed expletives. She whimpers a bit, grits her teeth, and puts a hand around her ankle as she rolls up to her butt. Legs splayed out, she doesn't appear to care that she's showing off panties that—you guessed it— match the heels, the fingernail polish, and the lipstick. Talk about coordination. Jesus. I can barely find matching socks each day.

I retrace my steps and reach down to help her up. Ulie, friend to everyone, gives a few sloppy licks to her shin. I tug on his leash when that pink, slobbery tongue goes for her face. She's laughing, but clearly in pain, and takes the hand I offer. She curses again on the way up. The platform pumps come off and she limps over to the nearest street-side trashcan and slings them in.

"You were right," she says. "I hated those damn things but my stylist says I'm a summer."

"A what?"

"Never mind."

The coastal rain has picked up, increasing steadily from a petite shower to plump drops, and Lauren isn't wearing a jacket. Plus, she's now standing in a puddle.

Mentioning the color of her toenail polish might be overkill. Needless to say, it matches.

"Here," I say, wriggling out of my windbreaker. "Take this."

"I'm fine."

"Take it."

Lauren sighs and drapes it across her shoulders without putting her arms through. Her left ankle is already swelling and I'm sure the blues and purples aren't far behind.

"You need to get that looked at."

"Later."

"Suit yourself. Keep the jacket if you want."

That's my singular moment of playing nice-nice because I can't be absolutely certain that she didn't construct the damsel-in-distress moment to manipulate me. Talk about dedication to the craft—she's hardcore, sacrificing an ankle like that.

I back away, and before I can leave her standing, she reaches out with a hand and steps closer. "Wait. Talk to me."

"Forget it."

"The show went over the top. I know we did. Let me make it up to you."

"*No*, Coeburn. Go back to L.A." I'm on the move again, Ulie trotting beside me, oblivious to the drama and happily wagging his tail.

"We can make a deal, okay? Give me inside access while you're filming. Give me the first look, and we'll push the hell out of the documentary for you. Nothing but good things. Millions of fans, Ford. You'll have people camping out for tickets."

"Conversation over. Don't you get it?" I spin to face her, violently enough that it spooks Ulie, and he takes a couple of hesitant steps to the side. "I have nothing else to say to you, and I've already told you too much. You said it yourself, I know how this game works, and I can't trust a damn word that comes out of your mouth. You want a quote? You want something you can take back to your producers? Huh? Then listen to me now... I screwed up. I know I did, and I regret it every single waking moment of my life. I eat, sleep, and dream about screwing up with Chelsea Hopper in front of millions of people. Yes, I earned that shame. Yes, I earned that punishment.

"But let me tell you this, goddamn it, that thing that attacked her? That *demon*? It doesn't deserve to win. It's not going to win. Everything I have done over the past two years, since that night, has been to make my soul right with the world. Yeah, I could use a little redemption. Maybe that's selfish. Maybe part of that is about me, but I have to do that to get through the rest of the days I have left. So I don't care what you think. I don't care what your producers think. I don't care what the rest of the world thinks—if I do decide to do that documentary, if I do decide to get back into the spotlight and take that demon down, it won't be because Mike Long, or Carla Hancock, or you, or anyone else talked me into it. It'll be because Chelsea *deserves* some peace. And just like I earned my shame, I'm going to earn my redemption. It'll be because I worked hard and absolutely not because of exploiting that little girl's story—again—to get it."

I march away, leaving Lauren Coeburn behind in the downpour, regretting everything I just said. Sure as shit, the only thing she'll take out of that entire tirade is me saying, "I deserve it!" That'll be the lead story. That'll be the quote across the top of every tabloid tomorrow morning.

I don't turn around. Ulie does. He whimpers like he knows something.

5
Mike Long

I find Dakota Bailey standing at the bottom of her beachside steps, feet buried in the sand, arms crossed and shaking as she stares up at the large white mansion in front of her. A home. A prison.

Ford was always distrustful of houses, haunted or not, until he'd gotten to know the rhythm of one. It used to bug the shit out of me, like how back during the glory years of *Graveyard: Classified*, he'd insist on arriving at our next shoot at least three or four days ahead of time so that he could familiarize himself with the place we were investigating. Sort of like how you gingerly dip a foot in water, no matter what the temperature, until you get used to it. He never seemed to care that I had a growing family to consider, and all those extra days on the road had deepened the divide between my wife, my children, and me. "Safety first," he'd say. "It's for your own good, dude. We don't trust a place until we do, remember?"

Ford Atticus Ford. Always right, always wrong. I wonder what he would do if he were here right now? Probably try to hit on Dakota.

I can't say I'd blame him.

Disregarding the situation, somewhere down inside my mind, where instinct, hormones, and the desire to procreate with the best of the species intersect, my lizard brain takes over while I take her in. Briefly, I'm overwhelmed by the sheer *celebrity-ness* of her, and then I glance down at her toned and tanned legs in a pair of salmon pink yoga shorts, tracing my eyes up to a matching sports bra.

She looks exactly like she did on the show. Long, lean, beautiful, and ready to run a marathon, which is exactly how she stays so thin, even after working in a kitchen and being around all that delicious food day after day. I remember that from the show, specifically. She's a runner. Boston and New York marathons each year. They did a profile piece during her second season showing how she had qualified for the main Ironman triathlon in Hawaii. Amazing.

There's *her* kind of in shape, and then *my* kind, which is why I huff and puff up beside her. I dropped the extra pounds. I've defined a muscle or twelve, but my cardio sucks.

She's so focused on the menacing house that she doesn't hear or see me coming, and then emits a shrill yelp when I say, "Dakota?"

"Oh, shit, you scared me," she says, putting a hand up to her forehead. She keeps it there, forming a shield over her eyes, as she turns toward the rising sun. The smile is forced, I can tell that easily, because her bottom lip subtly vibrates. "You got here fast."

I salute her, and hold on to my bravado and pride for about three seconds before I double over, trying to deeply inhale my way back to a natural breathing pattern. "You… You okay? On the phone… Sounded like…"

"For now, at least." She puts a hand on my back, pats me. "Hey, raise up straight. You'll never get a good breath like that.

Take it in deep, from here," she says, poking at the center of my abdomen.

I obey the orders, remembering that it'll open up my lungs if I put my hands behind my head. The cordless phone that I managed to haul with me goes into a thigh pocket of my cargo shorts, and I stand there, grimacing. "You saw something in there?"

Dakota squints up at the house, hands on her hips. Her hair is back in a ponytail, minus a few loose strands that flail in the breeze like the beachgrass beside us. A seagull squawks, swoops over the roof, and is gone. Low waves crash, once, twice, three times, and then slide back into the ocean before she finally speaks. "I'm almost scared to even talk about it, Mr. Long—"

"Just Mike." I want her to have that level of familiarity with me. I want to be "Just Mike" to Dakota Freakin' Bailey.

"Yeah," she says, as if it's not really registering. "Mike."

My name sounds fantastic coming out of her mouth. Like honey on a—

Dude. Stop. She's scared. She's vulnerable. She called you for help.

Go away, lizard brain. Business. Professional.

Dakota Bailey needs you.

Right?

It feels good to be *needed*, if only from a distance by someone who is officially a stranger. I haven't felt that in so long. Toni needs me to hang a heavy picture frame or to change the oil on her car. Or to take the kids to school when she has a spa appointment early in the morning. Those are chores, not needs, mind you. It's different.

Feeling like a horny old man, even though we're not too far apart in age, I take one last look for a mental snapshot, then tuck my bestial instincts back down into the recesses of my mind.

Time for business. Yards away, up those rickety wooden steps, then through the double doors bordered by two massive bay windows, there's trouble. What kind and how strong remains to be seen.

"What's up there?" I ask. "Full-bodied apparition? Black, swirling mass?"

When she opens her eyes wide in agreement, nodding, I notice that they're the color of a robin's egg. They glow like a neon sign. They're mesmerizing.

"That's it," she says, voice cracking. "How did you know?"

"Standard stuff for someone who sounded as scared as you did. And you were trying to communicate with it, so, yeah. I figured it had to be something loosely tangible."

She holds her hands up. "Remember how that kid from the Peanuts always had a black cloud hanging over his head? No, wait, even better—on that show, *Lost*, they had that black swirling mass that tore things up in the jungle? It reminds me of that thing, only smaller. Like a baby-sized version of that thing."

"Does it feel threatening?"

"Like it'll hurt me?"

"Yeah."

"It hasn't yet. Whatever it is, it's terrifying."

"I'm sure it is."

She holds her question in for a beat, then asks me, "You've seen things like that before, right?" It's saturated with hope. A plea.

"All the time. I could count off fifteen of them right now." I try to slip into professional mode the way Ford used to do during client interviews. He was always so smooth about that aspect. He'll claim he's not that much of a people person when the cameras aren't tuned on him, but I think that's just an excuse to be an asshole whenever he feels like it. He'd schmooze the clients for the cameras, while I dutifully stood there taking notes and nodding my head.

Later, while Ford would be off somewhere making a van rock with Melanie—back before they were married for a short while—or when he was with another crew member while he was still married to her, I would be busting my ass to get the equipment set up along with the rest of the crew. That was good for me, all the hands-on jobs. They kept me focused and into it.

I rip through a round of questions for Dakota, trying my best to remember what Ford would ask during each episode. You would think that stuff would be carved into my memory like Moses with a sharp chisel. Instead, for a couple of years I blocked out a lot of those memories on purpose. Less anger that way. Rather than dwelling on how Ford and Carla ruined everything for the rest of us, I focused on going to the gym where I lifted heavy things and put them down, again and again. The repetition, the effort, they were my therapy.

Dakota tells me that she bought the house and moved down here for a while because she had been through an atrocious breakup that cast a fat, black cloud over every aspect of her life. She lost interest in *everything*.

In addition to the breakup, the hustle of New York City and the crazy, suffocating energy of her crowded, humming restaurant had become overwhelming. Any time she had tried to get creative with new dishes they sucked donkey balls—her words exactly—and for months they were uninspired and lackluster. A handful of bad reviews had hurt the restaurant's numbers and her pride. She needed out for a while, at least until the city concrete no longer felt like quicksand.

"I didn't quit," she says, "but I handed my spatula over to my sous chef, told her the ship was hers, and that I'd be back one of these days. I thought my investors would flip their minds."

"Did they?" I ask.

"Nope. With the slop I'd been serving for six months, I think they were relieved. I had to get away, so I bought this place and ran. The whole thing was sort of like my *Eat Pray Love* moment. I needed a break from life, and I needed to rediscover myself."

"You just didn't expect to do it with an angry ghost around."

"Not in the slightest. Don't real estate agents have to disclose stuff like that?"

"If they aren't required to, then they damn well should be, huh?"

"Would've saved me some sleep, that's for sure." It's nice to see her smile while she examines her toes and wiggles them in the sand. There's no polish on them, and in fact, her feet look fairly rough. Bruised with broken blisters. I guess marathons will do that to an otherwise perfect example of lean perfection.

Mike, stop. Professional courtesy, please.

After another short round of data-gathering questions, like when she first saw it, had it ever taken on a human form, had there been any sort of poltergeist activity or was it just the black mass and blah blah.

I also ask her why she hasn't left yet, then take a tangential turn before I give her a chance to answer. "That was always, *always*, one of the top questions from our *Graveyard* audience. People wanted to know why on God's green earth some of our clients—the people on the show—why they would continue to stay in a place that was so unbelievably terrifying. Simple answer, though. Not enough money to move, no family nearby. Maybe they can't transfer jobs or just had other obligations, you see.

The easiest response is that they didn't have a choice. *You* do. You've got the money. The freedom. So why stay?"

Dakota points at her house and says, "Because I wanted to beat it."

"Like how? By yourself?"

"I know it sounds ridiculous, and dangerous, but I didn't want to run from anything else. I was sick of myself. I was sick of losing at life. I was a winner for so long, and then I just wasn't anymore. That's a hard pill to swallow." She looks away, flips a broken seashell over using her big toe. "Sorry. You don't need to hear all that."

Oh, but I want to.

She continues, "Honestly, when I left New York, I felt like a coward. Like I'd deserted all the people who were counting on me in so many different ways. Does that make sense?"

"Of course."

"And then I—everybody says to pick your battles, and after all the shit that I had been through, I picked the wrong damn one, you know? What in the hell was I thinking? Fight a ghost? Are you kidding me?"

"I think you did the right thing. You may not have beaten it, or even had the proper *tools* to beat it, but you tried. At least you weren't completely living in fear like so many others I've seen."

"Not exactly. I tried to fight it… I yelled for it to get out of my house. I burned incense. I had a Lutheran pastor come by and say some prayers. I carried a cross around with me. All that stuff, but I was still scared out of my mind. At first, it only showed up every three or four days, just enough to make me think it was gone. Finally, peace and quiet. Hallelujah! Sure enough, I'd wake up in the middle of the night and see it floating over my head like it was watching me. Do you know how creepy that is?"

"Another day on the job, ma'am."

She scoffs at herself. "Dumb question."

"I'll forgive you this time."

She smiles through her embarrassment and says, "You know what I did? I bought the boxed set of your show, all ten seasons, thinking I might get some pointers."

I can't resist smirking. I know how goddamn scary *Graveyard* could be. Even having lived it, there have been times when I'll catch myself watching an old rerun late at night on The Paranormal Channel: I'll say this for Carla Hancock and her team: they were a talented group of people, capable of making something as innocuous as a haunted ice cream parlor seem like it's an open gate to Hell.

I ask Dakota, "And how'd that work out for you?"

"Don't laugh. I was trying to learn."

"Did you?"

"I made it through the whole set. On the finale of whatever season it was—you guys were down in that abandoned subway tunnel. So freaky. I don't know how you did it."

"Practice."

"I did pick up a couple of tips, and watching your show scared me so much, I'm sure all that negative energy made it stronger. Gave it some juice, something. After that, it got worse, started showing up every day, keeping me awake at all hours. Totally miserable. I hit my breaking point and finally called you."

"You did the right thing. We'll figure it out."

Dakota says, "I really don't want to go back inside."

I take another look up at her oceanfront mansion. It looks friendly. It looks like someone's dream home. The graying, sagging wooden stairs could use some work, but the rest looks like it's worth the many millions she paid for it.

The only problem is, there's an uninvited guest.

A dead one.

The Graveyard: Classified Paranormal Series

6
Ford Atticus Ford

What a day already.

The press release, Lauren Coeburn… And it's not even eight o'clock.

I absolutely can't concentrate on anything else. Before I left for the bakery this morning, my sole intention was to find some work and get my mind off Chelsea, the demon, and that ridiculous documentary. All I wanted to do was grab a stupid scone, come back here, and then gorge myself on it while sifting through my messages, hoping Jesse had missed something important.

He gets lazy sometimes, and I've seen an email or two slip by that should've been answered, but he works for sweatshop wages simply for the privilege of saying he's employed by Ford Atticus Ford, and I'm cool with that.

Scone. Email. Work. That was the plan.

Then she showed up and ruined everything.

I have to go for a run.

Next to delicious baked goods, that's the best therapy.

After all, according to Ulie, I am He Who Takes Me for a Run Sometimes.

So, with my trainers on, shorts, a sweatshirt with a pouch on the front and, absent my favorite windbreaker because I gave the damn thing to Lauren, I trot down the rented condo's stairs and into the rain. Ulie, thoroughly thrilled that we're once again outside, recognizes where we're going. As soon as we round the corner, he's barreling down the sidewalk and gallops out onto the sand, tongue wagging and grinning in doggie bliss.

I do the same, stopping short of letting my tongue hang out. I don't run as often as I used to—still, this is a happy place that I can always come back to.

Usually.

It's peaceful, putting one foot in front of the other until I settle into a steady rhythm and the morning's events creep into my daydreams. In order to push them away, I pick up the pace and run harder, focusing harder on proper breathing, and it's enough to push the bullshit to the back of my mind.

Ulie tags along with an effortless trot, and thankfully, the weather is bad enough that we have the beach entirely to ourselves. I don't have to worry about snapping his leash onto his collar if another dog or beachgoer comes along. We're nuts to be out here anyway, and I'm sure the tourists and homeowners on the eastern cliff above us are wondering who the idiot might be that's down here running in this nonsense.

The almighty Ford Atticus Ford, that's who.

The big dummy.

Those people in my imagination, they're right. This is ridiculous. I'm only a couple of miles in before I pull the mental plug.

"Ulie, let's go, bud." I whistle sharply to get his attention, rescuing some poor sand crab from Ulie's snout. Without delay, he sprints after me, and after a couple of loping gallops, he's out front, leading the charge. I don't feel like going back to the condo just yet. A fifteen-minute run, if that, wasn't enough to burn through my agitated energy, and I'm certainly not looking forward to making any profanity laden phone calls. Matter of fact, I've yet to figure out why Mike hasn't called to talk to me about it.

I imagine Carla's sitting in her Malibu home sipping a Mai Tai and congratulating herself. She doesn't have my new number anyway.

Regardless, I would've expected *somebody* to call, somebody other than Lauren Coeburn, to ring me up and ask me what the hell was going on.

I climb the hill, stepping over the street runoff that's rushing past like the mighty Mississippi, while Ulie stops to take a drink. I try to remind him that it's gross water, full of oil, seagull shit, and God knows what else, but it falls on deaf doggie ears. He regularly licks his own butt, so whatever.

"You're not kissing me with that mouth later, I can tell you that much."

He ignores me. Figures.

I spend the next two hours along all the little shops and cafés, drinking too much free coffee because people recognize me and want to give me something in return for gracing their place of business. It's times like this that I enjoy the fame that hasn't quite faded yet, but it's hell on the bladder and the nervous system. I'm shaking like a Chihuahua on a methamphetamine IV drip.

I have to find a bathroom, so I duck into this fantastic little bookstore on Grover Street. I did an impromptu autograph session here once for the owners, Bob and Betty, and we always catch up whenever I'm in town. However, I see no sign of them today. The shop is manned by their son—Dave, I think his name is—and no matter how many times he's seen me here, he flips out like I'm Tom Cruise walking in the door.

"Dude!" he says, stretching the word out for miles. Dave is a middle-aged hippie who would better serve humanity by staying on a perpetual tour with the Grateful Dead or Phish. Yet, here he is, holding a stack of books in one arm and tucking his smoldering joint behind his ear with the other. Smoke wafts up, and I hold my breath, waiting for that shaggy, curly hair to burst into flames.

"Holding down the fort, Dave?"

"Ford. *Atticus*. Ford. My man! First Lauren Coeburn and now you? What a day, *what a day*. Celebrity central up in this place."

Shit.

"Lauren Coeburn was here?" I fire off a quick prayer that she just picked up some books for the road.

"Yeah, man. Beautiful lady, inside and out. You know her? Said she was in town for a few days, needed something to read to her blind grandmother."

Damn.

"I know *of* her, but way out of my league. How's she doing?" I play it off like I'm being cordial. However, on the inside, I'm holding onto hope that Newport is big enough for me to avoid her.

Dave says, "Had a purple grapefruit around that left ankle. Swollen like you wouldn't believe."

Oh, I'm pretty sure I would.

"She moped around here for about fifteen minutes, bought a couple of books and left."

"That's it?"

"You know what's funny? She saw that autographed picture with you and my folks. Asked how well I knew you, and of course, us being buds, I told her all about how you came by whenever you're in town. Never seen such a smile when I told her you usually stay up the hill."

Fuck.

***

I pick up a couple of books, because hey, support your local bookstore, and then I risk running into Lauren again by strolling over for an early lunch at Wanda's Beachside Pub—the best bangers and mash I've ever tasted—and I hang around the bar for a little while, shooting the breeze with a few old timers who have no idea who I am. It's refreshing having a normal conversation about the weather. Baseball. The magnificent set of—well, I'm sure they meant the bartender has a great personality, too. Amazingly enough, she's never seen *Graveyard* either because "Ghosts are too scary," and I don't offer any further detail about the show's history. Nor mine.

Ulie is a hit out on the covered porch, smiling, accepting French fry bribes for affection while he waits on me.

This is why I come here. Normal food. Normal life. Normal beer. The sanctity of the ocean. The hum of the waves pounding the shoreline.

For another hour, I don't have a dark cloud loaded with bullshit hanging over my head.

The beer makes me sleepy, so I pay, bid adios amigos to my compatriots, and head into the downpour, trudging up the hill toward my condo. Ulie scampers along beside me, happy as can be. I'm stopped a couple of times for autographs along the way, which was a ray of sunshine for my ego, and then once we're inside, Ulie gets a scrubdown with a dry towel before he trots off to look for more food. He's a wood chipper when he's hungry.

I take the longest warm shower that any human has ever taken, and after that, I fall face first onto the bed. I slip into dreamland before I have a chance to roll over.

I'm not sure how long I'm out, a few hours, maybe, because when I finally open my eyes, the rainy day has grown darker with dusk's intrusion. I sit up and rub the naptime grogginess from my eyes, uncertain if I actually heard a knock on the door or if I was dreaming about it.

An insistent fist pounds away. "Ford?"

Ugh. Not a dream.

Ulie barks twice, sharply, then goes silent.

I hear "Ford?" again, followed by, "I know you're in there."

No way I'm mistaking her voice. That didn't take long at all.

I grunt and push myself up from the bed, realizing I passed out naked when a short breeze from the window catches me in the right spot, and then rummage around in my suitcase for pair of shorts and a t-shirt.

Her fist rattles the door again.

I shout, "I'm coming, Coeburn, chill the hell out."

Here we go. How do I get rid of her this time?

I probably should've tracked down Carla Hancock, told her to go to hell, and then I'd have something to give Lauren so she'll get off my ass.

"Hurry. *Please.*"

Whoa. That sounded a little panicked.

With Ulie trotting along in strict formation at my side, ears perked up and curious, we head down the hallway. I know it's Lauren, but I take a peek through the eyehole anyway. It's her, and she's brought company that I wouldn't have expected.

Her companion is a hunched-over cotton-top—I mean, what appears to be a sweetheart grandma type who might have seen the last battles of the War Between the States.

Now she's playing the sympathy angle? Hey, here's my dear ol' gran, she loved your show—you know, back when she could *see*—and she'd love nothing more than for you to go back and help that little girl one more time. Please, oh please, Ford, do it before she dies.

Nice try.

"Let's get this over with, huh, boy?" Ulie looks up at me with miles of doggie smiles. I slam the deadbolt to the right and yank the door open. "*What*, Coeburn?"

The sudden noise and my shout spooks Dear Ol' Gran, and she whimpers, cowers, and reaches for Lauren. It's then I remember that Dave said the grandmother was blind, and I feel like an ass for spooking her. It's a miracle the ticker didn't crash right there. "Oh, man, sorry. Sorry. It's—I didn't mean—" As I'm reaching for her, trying to offer a soothing touch, I notice Lauren's red, watery eyes and the rivulets of smeared mascara on her cheeks. "What's wrong? You okay?"

"You need to let us in."

"Uh, okay? Why, exactly, would I do that?"

Ulie takes care of Dear Ol' Gran for me, nuzzling her hand. She coos and allows him to lick her palm.

"This is my grandmother, Ellen."

I exchange hellos with her, shaking a hand that's either wet from dog slobber or old lady sweat—probably the former—and stupidly wave at her sunglass-covered eyes. Idiot.

Lauren is dressed like a normal human now. She's totally out of her exotic bird getup and now wears skin-tight jeans, sneakers, and a University of Oregon sweatshirt. It's a thick, warm hoodie like mine. Her hair is flat and swept around to the front of one shoulder.

Taken down a notch and removed from her on-air persona, she's more beautiful like this, in a natural way, and I catch myself staring for a second. However, the fact doesn't prevent me from reminding myself that pretty things can also be poisonous.

She says, "We didn't know where else to go."

"For what?"

Lauren looks over her shoulder, examining the parking lot, trailing her eyes up the gravel road that divides a row of houses and the condo. I look, too, and see nothing. "Can we just come inside? Would that be okay?"

I hesitate, assessing the situation, trying to decide how far she's going to go with this ruse.

If it's even a ploy. She's clearly spooked about something. She can't stop fidgeting and checking the parking lot.

"Was someone following you?" It occurs to me that Lauren is also a celebrity—one whose star has yet to fade—and it's entirely possible that she ran into some crazed superfan. Differences aside, I feel for her because I had to deal with a few stalkers myself back in the day, and I know how unsettling it can be. "Should we call the police?"

"I'm not sure they can help with what we saw."

"What you *saw*?"

Lauren steps forward and places a cold hand on my bare arm. "I know you hate my guts, but you're the first person I thought about. I'm positive they didn't follow us."

"They? They *who*, Lauren?"

"They were... This is going to sound insane. They were children. Well, boys. One was in his teens and the other was maybe eleven."

"So? Just punks or what?"

"Their eyes were totally black. Like bottomless holes. You need to let us in."

"Jesus. Get in here. Now," I say, practically dragging them both into the condo.

I quickly shut the door, and double check to make sure it's locked.

Then I triple check just to be sure.

Black-eyed children.

Maybe I should check the lock again, just to be sure.

7
Mike Long

Toni is awake, but half asleep, when we get back to my house. Thankfully, she's wearing some shorts and a t-shirt, which is the best thing for everyone involved since I brought a guest along. It doesn't register with Toni, at all—and this is pre-coffee, mind you—that Dakota Freakin' Bailey is in our house.

When Dakota and I first walk in the ocean-side door, from the deck, I can immediately sense the vitriol in Toni's eyes. First, I get a strange phone call from a woman before the sun comes up. Second, I leave for over thirty minutes, and then I come back home with a tall, lean, athletic blonde woman who is wearing nothing more than those salmon pink yoga shorts and a midriff-revealing sports bra.

Believe me, I know what it looks like.

"Hi, hon," I say, approaching with all the tentativeness of a lion tamer holding a rare, bloody steak in front of a ferocious, human-eating feline. "Got some company."

Toni's eyes shoot laser beams through my skull. I'm sure she's imagining my head exploding in a fiery ball of flames, and then she turns the lasers on Dakota and splits her in half, glaring at her all the way up from those bruised and battered feet to the nearly neon blue eyes.

"Hello," Toni says, her tone not quite suggesting she's ready to pull a knife out of the drawer, but way down in the recesses of her instinctual reaction, she's thinking about it. It's easy to pick up on such things when you've been with the same person for so long. Truth be told, I'm not sure why she's so jealous. For a couple of years now, she's been ready to toss me out like a stale cheese puff, in hopes that a screeching seagull would carry me away. And then there was the questionable time with the contractor. And then there was the additionally questionable time with the satellite television repairman. And then there was that time…

Whatever. Do as I say, not as I do, right?

Dakota, barefoot and lithe, with hardened muscles and a deep tan from exercising outdoors when she's not hovering over a grill, moves with poetic grace as she pads across the floor, hand extended outward, all smiles and sparkles as she introduces herself. "Hi, Toni. I'm Dakota. I really love your home. It's so beautiful."

Toni squints and for a moment I'm thinking that she can see through the façade I've created to keep the fireworks to a minimum.

As we were walking along the beach, I informed Dakota that showing up with a strange woman, not to mention an attractive, barely dressed strange woman, would not sit well with my controlling, condescending wife, and that she should diffuse the impending explosion right away by complimenting her on the glorious, fabulous, wondrous interior decorating design.

I'm worried that Toni will know… and that she'll also think I'm guilty of something, and that we're only a couple of seconds away from a detonation roughly the size of Krakatoa's eruption. The resulting aftermath of Toni's anger could send enough ash and dirt into the atmosphere to create a miniature ice age.

Instead, her squint softens into a wide-eyed moment of realization. She sets her coffee mug down on the countertop, brown liquid sloshing everywhere, and her hands fly up to cover her excited, squealing gasp. "Dakota Bailey!" she screeches. "Oh my God, what're you doing here? I mean, like, *here*-here, in our house?"

Dakota looks at me with a mixture of "What just happened?" and "This is a good thing, right?"

Perhaps one could say that I painted too dark of a picture of my wife and the rocky road our marriage has been on. I'll admit to giving Dakota overly exaggerated descriptions of fire-breathing dragons and snake-haired Medusa.

Dakota says, "I'm sorry to come by so early, but I needed Mike's help, and—"

"Oh my God, I love you." Toni bounces on the balls of her bare feet and claps like a teenage girl. You'd think it's 1960 and the Beatles have landed in America for the first time. She looks at me, then back at Dakota in disbelief. "Mikey, sweetheart. You should've told me you were bringing her by. I would've straightened up a bit."

The house is immaculate. This is just a little warning shot to say, "You'll get an earful later when the famous guest that I love so much is gone."

I used to be semi-famous. I've seen wives give their husbands the same look before when a crewmember invited me over for dinner without checking in first.

Unless Ford was along, too, then I'd have to set myself on fire to have anyone notice. Not that I cared, really. I was happy to let him take over the room. I didn't—and still don't—need to have my ego stroked like the Almighty Ford Atticus Ford.

Usually.

Once in a while, it would be nice to be the brightest bulb in the room.

Toni quickly gets back to ignoring me and then speeds through the official pleasantries of Celebrity Entertaining 101, like drink requests, apologizing for only having ground coffee that came from a chain grocery store instead of some upper-end, high-class local market who only sells individually handpicked beans from the indigenous peoples of some tribe in South America. She offers fruits, then pastries, then scolds herself after taking another glance at Dakota's athletic body, saying, "What's wrong with me? Protein bar? How about a protein bar? Mikey, sweetheart, go get the box of peanut butter ones out in the garage."

Who slipped in here and injected my wife with super-hostess stimulants?

Plus, she hasn't called me "Mikey" in years.

Cut the act, Toni.

Mikey Sweetheart is on to your shenanigans.

By the time I get back from the garage, Toni and Dakota are sitting around the kitchen island, drinking steaming coffee out of those blue mugs with the white handles that I hate, and chatting about life as a reality television star.

Actually, Toni peppers Dakota with questions, and she answers politely when she can, and then defers when there are things she can't talk about due to confidentiality agreements. Toni knows exactly what she means, though, because I've been through the same thing, explaining to her how Ford and I weren't really allowed to talk about any of the behind-the-scenes stuff, like *coaching* some of the clients who were more terrified of the cameras than they were of the spirits invading their homes.

If Ford and I ever let it slip that Carla Hancock fabricated storylines to give certain filming locations more *oomph*, she would sue us until she had taken everything, all the way down to the metal in our fillings. More than likely, TPC's big swingin' dick lawyers would argue for the death penalty.

Forget I said anything about that part.

Don't get me wrong, every bit of the investigations were real. Every EVP, disembodied voice, heat signature, floating black mass or apparition that we captured was one hundred percent honest-to-God legitimate. I made sure of that, and so did Ford. We didn't agree on a lot in the last couple of seasons of *Graveyard*, but the legitimacy of our evidence is one thing we never budged on. That was out of respect for ourselves and respect for the other side.

I excuse myself while the two of them chat, and Dakota gives me a glance that says, "Don't leave me here," as I exit the kitchen. Out in the garage, I head to the workshop where I keep all of my equipment, wondering what I should take to Dakota's to conduct a proper investigation.

It smells like a group of sweaty socks got together, ran off a cliff like lemmings, and died in here, and that's probably because it also doubles as my workout room when I don't feel like going out into the world to hit the gym. Lately, that's more often than not. The weight bench, stair-climber, elliptical, and treadmill sit off to the right, stationed in front of a flat-screen television mounted on the wall.

That equipment over there has done more good than thousands of dollars of therapy. I discovered not too long after the incident with Chelsea, the show's cancellation, and the subsequent fallout with Ford, that pushing myself to the point of exhaustion was a happy place for me.

Still is.

On the left side sit three extra large pelican cases, relics from the early days of the show when the filming budget didn't have room to supply us with quality equipment. Ford and I bought all three of these together, along with the ancient digital voice recorders and camcorders that sit on the shelves or hang from pegs. Most guys have hammers, saws, wrenches, and other tools hanging from a pegboard in their garages. Mine holds an SB-11 spirit box, thermal imaging cameras, EMF pumps, laser-light shadow detectors, and a whole host of experimental equipment that never worked during testing or simply didn't have a necessary function that we thought applied to an investigation.

Like this thing right here—this little black box with four red lights that supposedly detects when a spirit farts.

My hand to God, that's what it was designed to do.

True story, Ford and I went by the inventor's place while we were on location outside of Dallas. The guy's name was Teddy Carmichael—wiry white hair that swayed in the breeze like seaweed underwater—and he owned a couple of rental properties down the block, one of which was haunted by a spirit with extreme, uh, *flatulence.*

You can't make this up.

We took off down the street with this guy, Ford and I chuckling behind his back, unable to comprehend what we were actually about to do, right? Fifteen minutes into this little mini investigation, the lights on Carmichael's black box start blinking left to right the way that talking car used to do with Hasselhoff. And wouldn't you know it, we listened to the digital voice recording; sure enough, right when we marked the time where the lights fired up, it had recorded the loudest fart EVP that none of us heard with our own ears.

I remember looking at Ford, trying to contain my laughter, and then I couldn't. We guffawed like teenage boys infatuated with lowbrow humor like dicks, butts, boobs, and poop. Carmichael hadn't seen the humor in it, obviously, but he insisted we take the device anyway, telling us that he hoped to see it on the show one day.

Never happened.

As I stand here looking at the thing—what we labeled the CF-1000, with the 'CF' short for 'Carmichael Farts'—I'm struck by a suffocating sense of remorse and regret.

All I ever wanted by doing the show was to impress Toni. That's it. I balked after the first season—didn't want to sign again. Felt like one was enough. There are only so many ways you can walk into a dark house and ask if anybody is there.

Ford convinced me to stay on, again and again. Eventually, all the long hours and long nights away, all the interviews and conventions, all the autographs and selfie poses, they became a part of me. It *was* me.

And then Ford fucked up.

And then I lost the thing that had made me *me*.

Rather, it was ripped from my hands.

As I stand here looking at my collection of equipment, some bought with my own money, some bought using money from the deep coffers of The Paranormal Channel that they never made us return, maybe it's not regret and remorse I'm feeling. Maybe it's longing.

A couple of weeks ago, working the Craghorn case with Ford, man, that was what it's supposed to feel like.

Energy. Anticipation. Fear. Wonder. Excitement. Just like the memories I was fond of when *Graveyard: Classified* was an infant, rather than a lumbering juggernaut concerned with sweeps week and landing monster sponsorships.

Ah, the glory days.

I finally realize that I want to do the documentary for the experience, too, not just for the cash that might keep my disappointed family happy.

I also understand how odd it must be for Ford that I'm the one trying to talk him into coming back for another round. Should I call him?

My watch says it's not much past seven a.m.

He's still snoozing, for sure. I'm tempted to call and get his ass up anyway. I want to share this moment with him. I want to tell him that I'm about to go on another legitimate investigation and that it'd be great to have him along if he was here.

I've been drinking the venom called blame for two years. It's time to let go.

Besides, this is my chance to prove to the universe that Mikey Sweetheart has the juice to face demons on his own.

I figure that's probably both literal and figurative, depending on what's haunting Dakota's house.

8
Ford Atticus Ford

Dear Ol' Gran—sorry, *Ellen*—sits in the recliner. The sliding door is open and she seems to be fine listening to the roar of the wind, the hammer of rain, and the wailing ocean. She rocks peacefully while my overly affectionate pooch slurps her like he's trying to get to the gooey center. How many licks will it take, Ulie?

Meanwhile, Lauren Coeburn, former arch nemesis turned quivering mess, tells me to stop once I've poured her about four fingers' worth of expensive scotch. In the tiniest way, I feel like I'm wasting it on her. However, it may be worth it because I've heard stories about the black-eyed children from all over the world; this is the first time I've actually had a chance to speak with someone who has seen them in the flesh.

Lauren lifts the tumbler of scotch—no rocks—and drains it, which she then follows with two beckoning fingers. I'd like to tell her that she just guzzled about fifteen dollars. Instead, I pour her another, and she downs that one like she's drinking a fraternity kid under the table. She wipes her mouth with a sleeve. "That should do it."

"You sure?"

"Explain what in the hell I saw, and I'll let you know."

I'm not in the mood for scotch, so I pop open a beer for myself and stare at her, still wondering if she's coming at me from another subversive angle, trying to get the scoop on this documentary. Ah, what the hell, black-eyed children are interesting enough that I'll bite.

I ask, "You want the long version, or the short one?"

"Long, because unless you kick us out, I'm not going back there for a while. Maybe never. And what am I gonna do about her?"

I look back at Ellen. Ulie has his head in her lap. "Hard to say."

Lauren leans across the counter, takes the scotch, and pours herself another round. "Story time, Ford."

I gulp down about half of my IPA, and this is what I tell her:

Nobody really knows what the black-eyed children are, other than what details you get from urban myths. However, like Sasquatch, the Loch Ness Monster, the Mothman, or the Chupacabra—name your weird entity of choice—there have been too many sightings for them to be a fluke or simply nothing but a legend made up by your neighbor with a good imagination. From the UK, to China, to Ethiopia, to some town populated by three hundred citizens in middle-of-nowhere New Mexico, these things have come up in reports all over the world.

Are they aliens? Are they supernatural beings?

It's anybody's guess.

The way the stories go, you'll get a knock on your front door, or see these kids outside of a window, or maybe run into them in a deserted parking lot in the middle of the night. You've heard that old adage about how eyes are the windows to the soul?

Well, then, if that's the case, these things are absolutely soulless, because they have the deepest, darkest black eyes, hollow and void of anything good.

Witnesses have reported that the black-eyed children range in age from eight to sixteen years old. They're dressed in black pants, a white shirt, and a black tie. Or, on rarer occasions, hoodies and jeans. It varies. I've seen reports of both.

"Actually," I tell Lauren, "you're pretty much wearing what they wear. Jeans and a hoodie."

"Are you trying to freak me out even more?"

I wink at her, slightly enjoying an obnoxious bit of payback from her stunt earlier.

I take a swig of beer, and continue where I left off.

Black-eyed children speak in pointed, quick sentences with a flat, monotone voice, usually asking if you have any food or if they can come inside.

No matter what, do *not* let them inside.

That's the first and only rule that will keep you alive.

Lauren interrupts me to say, "That's exactly what he said!"

"Tell me you didn't let it in."

"No. God, no."

I continue: no paranormal researcher has ever been close enough to study them, nor has anyone ever caught evidence of these kids on camera. They exist, but I've yet to see proof, which is so baffling to me. It's almost like they know how to avoid security cameras, things like that.

Not a single person has ever gone on record about what happens if you let them inside, and it's my educated guess that they didn't live to tell the tale.

The best hypothesis I've heard, and the one that makes the most sense to me in all my years covering the paranormal, is that they're definitely something alien that's chosen a host. Maybe they want information or maybe they want to do some anal probing—no idea.

See, the alien-host possibility seems to be the most plausible, at least to me, because how many children vanish each year, never to be seen again? And if anyone actually has recognized one from the back of a milk carton, they haven't come forward to announce it.

On the other hand, they *could* be powerful demonic entities, like the right-hander we fought in Norfolk, who have discovered a way to walk the earth, looking for more souls to devour.

Disguised as children.

Creepy. Makes my skin crawl thinking about it.

Regardless of what they are, if it's some form of possession, whether it be alien or demonic, the thing doing the possessing has yet to realize that people are generally freaked the hell out by black, soulless eyeballs.

Am I right, or am I right?

That's about as smart as a serial killer showing up on your front porch wearing a t-shirt that has *I'M HERE TO EAT YOUR LIVER* in big, bold letters emblazoned across his chest.

So, that could be why there are no reports of someone letting them inside. Nobody is that dumb.

But I doubt it. I don't have that much faith in humanity. *Oh, hi, honey. Are you really hungry? Have some lemonade. Maybe it'll put some color in your eyes again, you poor thing.*

Would not surprise me in the slightest.

Out of all the paranormal entities I've encountered over the years, the black-eyed children probably scare me the most.

It's the fear of the unknown, because there's simply so little information about them.

Loch Ness Monster? Easy. Giant lizard-like dinosaur.

Sasquatch? Missing link. Huge, hairy ape dude.

Aliens? Little green men in spaceships.

The Mothman? An extremely convenient, monstrous bird. Well... close enough.

But black-eyed children?

I'm clueless, and there's just something about evil-looking children that makes me want to hide in the corner and suck my thumb.

I think it's the idea of corrupted innocence, black blood pumping behind an angelic smile.

And those soulless eyes.

Jesus help me.

My hand goes up to my crucifix necklace, and I close my fingers around it.

"That's insane," Lauren says. "God, I need another drink for this conversation."

"Have at it." I watch her pour more scotch. Her hands have finally stopped shaking. "Easy, though. I don't do well with puke."

"Don't worry. This is like a normal breakfast."

I leave that one alone. I remember the mornings before we would film. No matter how many locations or episodes, I would get the shakes. It was natural, and besides, I always figured that if I ever *didn't* get nervous, there was something wrong. Being 'on' in front of the camera takes a lot of work and mental acuity—nerves of steel, especially when you have an audience as large as the one for *Graveyard*. Lauren too. I know millions of people watch *Weekend Report*.

"Your turn," I tell her. "What happened?"

"Everything you said. Just like that."

"Details, Coeburn."

"Do I have to?"

I cross my arms and nod.

Lauren's eyes go blank as she looks past me, absently shaking her head. She's staring at a memory in her mind. "I went back to Grandma's house—"

"What's that, honey?" Grandma Ellen is leaning up in her chair, sunglass-covered eyes turned in our direction.

"Nothing, Grandma. Just talking to Ford."

"Okay. Let me know if you're hungry. I have cereal."

Lauren grins at me and mouths, "Sorry about that," and with another glance into the living room, she adds in a whisper, "Blind and almost deaf. Poor thing. I don't know how she manages."

"The kids, Coeburn."

"Right. Um, okay. After you so gallantly left me there with a broken ankle," she says around a smile, "I went by the bookstore and then back to Grandma's to ice it." She points north. "She lives up the hill, that way, about half a mile. Great little house right along the street. Still got a view, even with all these condos and hotels going up. She raised my dad there. So, yeah, I'm in the kitchen, putting ice in a big plastic bag, and something catches my eye out the window. The kitchen is around back, and from over the sink, you can see into the yard. It's pretty small but it's fenced in, so it kinda spooked me because I'm freaked out that something got inside the gate. It was big, and I'm standing there thinking that maybe a dog got into the yard somehow, then wondering how in the hell that could happen because there's no—I'm rambling, sorry."

"You're fine. Keep going."

She clears her throat and leans in. "I went over to the sink and looked, right? Gone. Nothing. Empty yard, which spooked me even worse because I *know* I saw something. Here I am with a sprained ankle, a ninety-year-old blind grandmother, and we're about to get robbed. That's what I'm thinking. Then I thought maybe somebody had seen the local show this morning, and he's out there stalking me. I'm panicking, trying to find anything I can use as a weapon, just in case, and the first thing I can think of is the broom. I look around and it's propped up right beside the back door. I scrambled over to grab it, and, oh my God, Ford, I *literally* pissed myself. Literally. Pee came out. It really did because when I reached for the broom, he popped up right in the window, right there in the middle of the door."

"No shit?"

"Yeah, like he was waiting on me. I screamed like a goddamn maniac. There was pee running down my leg. I tripped over the broom. If it hadn't been so freaking scary, it would've been comical. Then I realized it was a kid, just like you said, but those eyes. Those horrible, black little eyes."

"Wow. You *actually* saw one."

"From what you described, yeah."

"Look at the chill bumps on my arm." I've seen some crazy ass shit in my time, I'm one of the most well-known paranormal investigators in the world, and yet, my goosebumps have goosebumps. I might need another beer for this.

"It didn't register at first that it was something *paranormal*. Grandma's blind, so that's the first place my mind went, and I thought he might be some neighborhood kid. Like a little blind buddy."

"Makes sense."

"Then again, I'd never seen or heard about anybody being blind quite like that. I'm standing there with pee on the side of my leg, pee on the floor, and there's this kid staring at me. I opened the door and asked him what his name was. He goes, 'You need to let me inside.' We go back and forth a couple of times like this; what's your name, let me in; no, not until you tell me who you are and stuff like that. I ask if he's here to see

Grandma Ellen—'cause that's what all the neighborhood kids call her—and he stares at me and I swear, it felt like he was freezing my soul. He finally smiles and says, 'I'm hungry. I need to come in so you can feed me.'"

"Matches everything I've heard. What'd you do?"

"I'd had enough of the little fucker's shit, so I slammed the door in his face."

"Good for you."

"Even then, I hadn't registered that it was paranormal or that I should be afraid. I mean, yeah, he was kinda scary looking and maybe he's autistic too, doesn't have social skills. Something like that. It's not until another one—shit, man, I can still feel how many back flips my stomach did when I saw the second one come around the corner."

"Same thing? Like twins?"

"No, totally different. This one was older. Around fifteen, sixteen, maybe? Definitely bigger. Dressed the way you described."

"What'd you do when the second one showed up?"

"Locked the door and told them to go away. What else could I do?"

"Did the bigger one say anything?"

"Same flat tone as the other one, right off the bat. He looked at me—no, more like *through* me—and he said, 'Let us in. We're hungry. You need to let us in. We have to come inside. Let us in.' The longer I stood there, the more insistent he got, but he never got louder or angrier. Just like, 'Let us in. We're hungry. Let us in, let us in, let us in.' I screamed for them to leave or I'd call the cops, then Grandma starts yelling from the other room, asking what was going on, was I okay."

"Then what?"

Lauren stares into her scotch glass, swirls the liquid around, watches it spin in circles.

"Lauren?"

She wipes a tear from her cheek and looks up at me.

"Promise you won't make us leave?"

"I... guess, yeah."

"Promise."

"Fine. I promise. You can stay."

"No matter what I tell you?"

"Yes. Really. If you're worried about earlier... I was already in a shitty mood and I overreacted. My fault. I shouldn't have taken it out on you." I place my hand on the counter, palm down, and swipe it in a wide arc. "Slate clean. You're still an asshole for gutting me two years ago, but we'll forget that for now."

"I'll make that up to you. That's *my* promise. But about the kids... I kinda lied a little." She tentatively nibbles her bottom lip and waits on my reaction.

You *have* to be kidding me. I fell for this? Really?

Exactly what I expected. She made up some bullshit story to get close to me again. Yet another attempt to squeeze blood from a rock. She's not getting anything from me. I'm going to string her along, though, because I haven't come up with the perfect comeback yet, and whatever it is, whatever the words are that finally come out, I want them to absolutely destroy her.

"It wasn't so much of a lie—more like an omission of certain... details."

"If you're making all of this up just to ask about the documentary, so help me God—"

"I'm not, Ford. Just listen."

"To what, more of your bullshit?"

"I'm trying to tell you the truth. All of it. You were the first person I thought of because they, um… they specifically mentioned you by name."

"Nuh-uh. Shut up." Wasn't expecting *that*.

"Hand to God, the little one said, 'Tell Ford we're waiting for him.'"

9
Mike Long

Back in the kitchen, Toni and Dakota are whispering and giggling over something like a couple of teen girls at a pajama party. I haven't seen Toni smile like this in months, if not a year or more. Maybe since before *Graveyard* was cancelled.

Dakota's laughter is throaty and full of life, like she has nothing against the world. That's what real happiness sounds like. Not the forced chuckles I push out once in a while.

"What's so funny?" I ask as I lay a small pelican case on the black marbled island where they're sitting on hand-crafted stools that cost more than the annual GDP of Cambodia. Way back when, in the days of sponsorships and big contracts, I didn't blink when Toni begged for them, saying they'd really bring the kitchen together. Now they're a symbol of an excessive past that I both wish I had again and thoroughly hate at the same time. It's a weird sensation.

My wife and my celebrity crush go silent and try to contain themselves, sharing in their secret humor, and I have to admit, I feel a bit betrayed by Dakota.

Not a bit. A lot.

I thought I gave her an appropriate description of the cold shell my wife had become. Why is she actually enjoying Toni's company? Boggles the mind.

Toni snorts first, followed by Dakota, and then they both explode in cackles.

I feign my best dismissive, "Oh, you two," and occupy myself by re-checking every item of equipment I have in my case. For an initial investigation, I only brought the essentials, like an EMF detector, a digital video camera, and a couple of DVRs—digital voice recorders—in hopes of catching some EVPs, or electronic voice phenomenon.

It's obvious that I'm annoyed once I slam the lid closed.

Dakota lifts both eyebrows and Toni lowers hers.

Toni asks, "What's gotten into you?"

"Nothing," I say. "Frustrated. Haven't brought any of this stuff out in so long, most of the batteries are dead."

"There's some in the garage, next to that giant box of toilet paper. You know that."

I disappear for a few minutes and hang out, waiting, pretending like I'm taking the time to find all the right batteries while I take a breather. Okay, fine, fair enough. They hit it off. No big deal.

Breathe, Mikey Sweetheart. That charm is why you fell in love with Toni in the first place. You know she's magnetic when she wants to be.

Pockets full of batteries, with my cargo shorts hanging low on my hips from the weight, I head back into the kitchen one last time. Dakota is at the door, one foot on the deck like she's ready to leave, and Toni stands beside her, arms crossed and flashing that million-watt-sparkle of a smile.

I ask Dakota, "You're not coming, are you?"

"I can't let you go back there alone."

"What? Of course you can. I did this for a living, remember?"

Obviously I *want* her to come back with me, but we can't let Toni know that, now can we?

Toni says, "Why don't you stay, Dakota? I'll show you around." She pats me on the bottom. I definitely haven't felt that in two years, then she ruins it by saying, "I'll tell you more secrets about chubby Mikey before he turned into a meathead."

So that's what they were laughing about. Thanks, Toni.

Dakota grins. "But look at him now, huh? Lucky you."

Now I'm uncomfortable. And shy. And probably blushing.

When I get back, I'm sure Toni will come at me with her jealousy guns blazing after a comment like that. She surprises me with another gentle touch as she affectionately replies, "Yeah, he's not so bad."

I risk a kiss on her cheek and she doesn't pull away. Could our relationship be salvageable after all?

Dakota backs onto the deck, and says, "Ready?"

"You're definitely coming?"

"It's not like you're gonna stop me."

"Can't argue with that. Off we go."

"Don't bring anything home… and be careful," Toni says, shutting the door behind us, and for a moment, I think she actually means it. Which leaves me wondering if bringing Dakota around sparked Toni's territorial claim. Could that have been enough to rekindle something?

Dakota and I are silent as we walk along the beach. She looks determined, striding with her spine straight and shoulders back. Ford always loved that episode in the ghost town where we marched down the dirt-road main street, dressed like gunfighters preparing to assault the OK Corral. Admittedly, that's one of my favorite episodes too.

That was one of the times when the spirits were truly malevolent, and it legitimately felt like we were the vanguard marching headfirst into a battle of good versus evil.

Have I mentioned I miss that shit?

Dakota gives a quick glance back at my house and says, "All right, I think we're far enough away."

"For what?"

"For me to tell you I was totally faking."

"You were?"

"The laughing. At you. It wasn't bad, actually, she was just poking fun about how you used to be a little overweight and—I think the word she used was 'fluffy'."

"Clouds are fluffy. I was fat," I admit.

"She really does seem proud of you. It's just a shame that you're…unhappy." I'm looking at Dakota when she says this, and I don't know why, but I can sense there's something else hidden in her tone the way it drifts off, the way she looks out at the ocean, pensively, like there's more she wants to tell me.

I leave it alone. That's a discussion for another day. Besides, talking about my wife's erratic emotions is not something I'd care to partake in right before I investigate Dakota Freakin' Bailey's multi-million dollar beach home.

We have a ways to go yet, so we chat about some of the episodes of *Graveyard* that she'd seen, and I ask about all the incredible meals she fixed on *Yes, Chef!* and if she prepares those any more.

It's a gentle, easy conversation. It's fun, and we don't have to try.

This is what it should be like.

I remember how it used to be that way with Toni so many years in the past.

Good times gone.

"Back again," Dakota says once we reach her steps. They're faded and gray and splintery and will likely get smashed and sucked into the ocean if The Big One ever comes. Meteorologists keep talking about how global warming is getting worse, and hurricanes are getting stronger. I say let them come to wash all this excess away, my house included, so we can start again with reasonable lives.

I follow Dakota up, trying to pretend I'm not some tongue-wagging cartoon wolf as I check out her calves and that ridiculously incredible bottom. I believe in God, and I believe that he created yoga shorts for lonely men in bad relationships who still need proof that the downstairs equipment is alive.

Horrible, just horrible, Mike. Control yourself.

Human nature, bud, whispers the devil on my shoulder.

I turn my attention to the massive mansion at the top of the steps. Bay windows line the ocean-facing side, perfect for that morning experience of watching the sunrise. There's another deck up on the second level, and I can see the tops of chairs pushed up against the wall. To the left of that is another boxlike structure of rooms, and then up and to the left of that, another, smaller box. Imagine a set of stairs going down from left to right, that's what the house is shaped like; an odd conglomeration of designs, like the architect wanted to experiment while high on some designer drugs, yet she mentioned earlier that she paid about four and a half million dollars.

If I recall correctly, the prize money Dakota won from *Yes, Chef!* only amounted to about three million. Then there were some sponsorships, which I'm no stranger to, but they wouldn't pay enough for this place. Her restaurant must be killing it up there in the Big Apple.

How she affords it is none of my business.

The Graveyard: Classified Paranormal Series

I bought *our* beachfront home when the *Graveyard* contracts were renewed after the fifth season. Back then, *Casa de Long* was worth around two-point-five, and I paid for it with a single check. Now I cringe whenever Toni brings home two-ply toilet paper because I feel like we're on the precipice of pinching that final penny. Toni knows this, and doesn't seem to care.

My saving grace will be convincing Ford to do the documentary, after which I'll be able to breathe without feeling like I'm a thousand feet under the ocean surface.

Breaching the top of the beach stairs, we stroll across a small expanse of sand and seagrass before we reach the ground-level deck. It's painted a greenish-gray color and sits completely empty except for two large pots. They're filled but flowerless, and the dirt looks so old and void of moisture that it couldn't grow a cactus.

Dakota notices me taking in the barren wasteland of a deck and says, "I'll get some stuff out here soon. Haven't been here long enough to really decorate yet."

"Lots of potential," is my pathetic, small talk reply.

She points overhead and says, "I'd been here for about a week before the ghost-thing showed up for the first time. I mostly hung out on the upper deck where I didn't have to—" She stops midsentence and unsuccessfully tries to hide an embarrassed smile with her hand. "This is silly. I don't even know why I'm telling you this stuff. Maybe it matters. I don't know."

"Like what?"

"Since it—what's the word? Oh, manifested. Since it manifested the first time, I've had this sort of gut feeling that it was—I don't know—*into me*, if that makes any kind of sense whatsoever."

"Gut reactions are usually right, and a lot of entities have sexual motivations, believe it or not."

"Really?"

"Yup. And I don't mean to get too personal, and I'm not accusing you of anything, not in the slightest, but do you think you might've done anything to provoke it?"

"Not intentionally, no. The thing is—the hell with it, this is what I was gonna say earlier. My ex *hated* tan lines, like he was a freak about it. Some habits stay habits, and besides, I'm at the beach. That deck is sorta private and most of the neighbors are hardly ever here. Why wouldn't I lay out with all this sun?"

"Right," I say, and I won't deny where my mind goes with the mental imagery.

Mike! Chill.

Okay, fine.

I will say this, however: that little devil on my shoulder is furiously working on stronger forearms because he hasn't felt an actual wiggle downstairs in a long, long time.

"I stopped for a couple of reasons. The ghost is one." Dakota scoffs and puts her hands on her hips. "I feel so ridiculous admitting this stuff, but the neighbor's kid—the one over there in the gray house?"

"Yeah?" I look to where she's pointing at an equally impressive mansion. It's a lighter slate color with white trim, black shutters, and a balcony that wraps around the entire second floor.

"I'm fairly certain it was the same day the black mist showed up, but I caught the creepy little shit with a video camera. Standing right up there, up on top of the house where they have a sun deck."

"No way. You tell his folks?"

"Nah, no real harm," she says with a dismissive wave. "My fault for being out there naked. Obviously he's going to look. Birds gotta fly."

"But he was recording you. Aren't you worried about it showing up on the Internet?"

"I doubt he knows who I am, and even if he does, that's when you know you've made it, right? When strangers care about seeing you naked?"

I admire her levity. It's refreshing.

Although, that fact doesn't prevent me from feeling a twinge of overprotective jealousy and envisioning myself punching some teenage punk in the nose.

She adds, "All it took was me standing up and flipping him the bird. He ran like I'd pointed a gun at him."

"Funny."

Dakota takes another step closer to the house, but doesn't go any further, silently surveying the interior of her home through all the spotless windows. She's looking for the entity, and I am, too. Rather than seeing a floating, swirling black mass, I spot a single couch in the living room to the right. A blanket is wadded up and hangs limply over the ocean-facing arm. I suspect she's been sleeping there because it's a faster escape. A television the size of a small drive-in theater screen is mounted on the wall and a wilted fern rests underneath it. There's no artwork hanging. It's decorated less than a dentist's waiting room.

Over in the kitchen a lone coffee cup rests on the glass table—a petite four-top that she probably bought just to make the place feel like home. No pots and pans hang on hooks over the island counter, nor does anything like a toaster oven or microwave populate the rest of the long counters that angle around the far walls.

The refrigerator seems to be about the size of the Titanic, and I'd bet a hundred bucks that it's empty too—even for a world-class celebrity chef.

I'm certain I'd win that bet because the trashcan is overflowing with fast food bags. Burger joints, tacos, subs. When she said she needed a break from her old life, she was more serious than I thought.

Dakota catches me looking at the artery-clogging remnants and says, sheepishly, "That's our secret. And who would eat a five-star meal here if I fixed it? Me and the ghost?"

"Zipped lips." I take one final glance around. Seems safe. Then again, it's the quiet houses you have to worry about. "Should we go in? Get started?"

She rubs her arms like she's cold, and I know it's not the temperature outside. Feels like we're in the high seventies already. Not even the breeze is chilly enough to cause gooseflesh like that. "I think maybe you should go in. Alone, I mean."

"Positive? It's not every day you get to hunt a ghost with a world famous paranormal investigator."

Shifting her weight from foot to foot, daintily nibbling her bottom lip as she tries to make up her mind, Dakota eventually takes a single step closer to the gorgeous, beachfront mansion that she so desperately wants to call home. "Okay," she says, the single word shuddering itself into pieces. "I can—I can do this."

"*We*," I remind her, raising my voice like Ford used to do during so many investigations. He'd put on this locker room speech before filming, every single time, and the crew loved it. So did I, honestly. It got everyone revved up and ready to rock, and I'd like to do the same for Dakota. "Let's go in there and kick some ghostly ass. Let's go tell this piece of shit where he can shove it, and let's take your home back, because you're Dakota *Freakin'* Bailey."

"Damn right," she squeaks, without a single bit of confidence.

10
Ford Atticus Ford

It's easy to be a good person, and it's also easy to be a bad person.

Making the right decisions is the line that divides the two.

And sometimes that line is blurry.

The choice I have to make at the moment is whether to believe Lauren Coeburn or call complete bullshit whilst throwing her and her dog-slobber-covered Grandma Ellen out of my condo and into the ferocious rainstorm. Ellen—I'd probably be cool with her hanging around. She's nice, gentle, low maintenance, and has never completely gutted me on national television in front of millions of people.

Am I a humongous jerkface for holding a grudge? Depends on your angle, I suppose.

My therapist, bless his pointy little goatee, wire-rimmed glasses, and fatherly tone, always suggests that forgiveness will open my heart to the light of the world and fresh possibilities. I generally try to follow his advice; then again, he doesn't really know what it's like to stand across the kitchen counter from a woman who slid a sharp blade across your reputation's throat.

What she just now told me is so thoroughly unfathomable that my brain can't even comprehend the enormity of it.

The Graveyard: Classified Paranormal Series

Tell Ford we're waiting for him.

I—seriously? For real?

First, Hamster Hampstead's grandfather, Papa Joe, called me out by name in that abandoned farmhouse.

Then, the demon right-hander that had attacked poor Dave Craghorn—and we're fairly positive it was the same one from Chelsea Hopper's house—that bastard knew me and knew my name as well.

I mention this to people all the time. The police detectives I work with on a regular basis, the families I try to help… I try to make them understand that it's all connected. There's sort of a universal *energy* out there, and you can look to George Lucas and *Star Wars* for a fancy nickname for the thing that binds everyone together, living or dead, earthly or otherworldly. My theory is that information can travel across this plane of energy in the spiritual world, which is exactly how Papa Joe—grumpy old cuss that he is—was trying to warn me about what's coming, especially in relation to Chelsea Hopper and that all-too-powerful right-hander.

But this? Black-eyed children, some of the least known and least researched paranormal entities sending me a message, by name?

Well, color me stunned.

It's terrifying, confusing, and bowel-loosening, all at the same time.

And I don't want to believe it.

Because what's next? Will I get an email from Bigfoot?

Ford! Dude! Let's grab beers this weekend. This amigo of mine, he lives up the hill and has some wicked cavebrew going on. You need to try it, yo!

Except that I might actually enjoy having a couple of pints with Bigfoot, rather than some cross-dimensional demonic entities out there trying to throw down.

What I prefer to believe is that Lauren Coeburn is lying out of that succulent mouth of hers, right between those pristinely bleached teeth. What I would also prefer to believe is that she did some research—probably remembering some interview I did five or six years ago where I mentioned how spooky the black-eyed children are—and now she's here to play against my fears, sidle up next to me, and pickpocket whatever info I have on Carla Hancock and Spirit World Productions.

If that's the case, I'm might go caveman on her, grab a handful of hair, and drag this screaming blonde pixie out of my condo where I'd deposit her in the deepest puddle in the parking lot.

Ellen might get shown the door, too. I'd be gentler, though—like maybe an angry piggyback ride.

That would be so much easier than the difficult decision I'm about to make.

I'm going to trust that Lauren is telling the truth for the time being.

The black-eyed children have tossed out a vaguely concealed threat, and I'm not one to back down from paranormal fisticuffs.

Lauren says, "Ford?" which shreds apart my mental seesaw and yanks me back into the kitchen.

The beer bottle is cold in my hand. The tiles are cool under my feet. And when it comes to the woman occupying the stool across from me, it seems like my heart isn't as frozen as I thought it was.

Open yourself to forgiveness, Ford. People make mistakes. The world isn't made up entirely of demons and belly-crawlers.

Lauren asks, "You heard what I said, right? He mentioned *you*. By *name*."

"Wouldn't be the first time."

She flattens her lips together and considers my statement, then spins around on the stool to check on Grandma Ellen, who has dozed off with one of Ulie's floppy ears gently curled up in a bony hand. He appears to be enjoying the affection and unwilling to move and disturb her at the same time. Lauren hooks a thumb over her shoulder. "I can't take her back there. Not until it's safe."

"Definitely not."

"Then what do we do?"

"We?"

"I can't call the police, especially not me. They'd think I'm crazy. Next thing you know, I'm on the news. All those L.A. frenemies of mine would see it; goddamn story goes viral in a heartbeat, and boom, they yank me off *Weekend Report*."

"Imagine the horror."

She's quick, this one, picking up on my sarcasm right away. She reaches across the counter and touches my arm with a clammy palm. "Sorry. You know what I mean."

"Yup."

"Everybody in the business, we all have to tiptoe around everything we do now, and it just completely sucks."

"Yup." Preaching to the choir, sister.

"Did you read about Kaylynn Simms last week?"

"I have no idea who that is."

"The cute redhead on *Smile High Club*."

"That's a TV show?"

"Where have you been? It's that Thursday night dramedy about the promiscuous flight attendants? Really? You haven't seen it? You are so missing out. It's—"

I hold up a hand to interrupt. "What about her?"

Lauren wiggles her bottom on the stool and claps her hands in glee. "It's so good. You have to watch it. Anyway, my point is, some 'razzi took a picture of her last week wearing this t-shirt. Only thing it said was, 'I drink orange Jews' underneath a cartoon orange wearing a yarmulke."

"So?"

"So? Ford, it's a fucking t-shirt that's actually kinda funny, and it only took about six hours for people online to go ballistic. The Internet blew up about how Jewish people are still being persecuted and when will it ever end, the whole nine. She apologized, but it was too late. Rumor is, they're reshooting the next episode of *Smile High* to kill off her character."

"Seems a bit excessive for a t-shirt."

Lauren throws her hands out wide. "Thank you. That's what I've been saying, too. It's not like she got a five-year-old girl attacked by a demon, right?"

"Ouch."

"I'm just making a point. No harm intended."

"You sure?"

"I just meant it's not quite on the same level, and..."

"I get it, Coeburn."

"Give me a sec, will ya?" Lauren stands up from the stool and wobbles a little. Looks like breakfast finally caught up to her. She plays it off like a pro, however, apologizes again, and excuses herself to go to the bathroom.

Which leaves me standing here in the kitchen, wondering what to do next. I don't have the slightest bit of paranormal investigation equipment with me. I'm supposed to be here relaxing, so yeah, I'm severely unprepared.

Then again, these little black-eyed bastards are kinda front and center. I won't need much to have a face-to-face conversation. Any sort of camera would be nice for proof, and I figure my cell phone will have to do for that. I'm not about to run down to the nearest superstore and walk out of there with a few cameras and voice recorders. There's too much risk of being recognized and drawing attention to the fact that the almighty Ford Atticus Ford is up to something.

Aside from a smartphone, what does one take into battle against a paranormal entity that appears to be flesh and blood, but may not actually be alive?

I don't carry a gun. Never have. Even when my celebrity star was at its apex in the sky, I didn't carry any heavy-duty protection with me. I figured if a stalker or some overly excited fan got a little too rowdy, I'd trust my instincts and charm.

What to do? What to do?

This condo isn't mine, so I spend about thirty seconds rifling through cabinets and drawers, looking for something to use as a weapon besides a kitchen knife. How about a lighter and some cleaning spray? Or maybe I could throw a handful of flour in their eyes and then use some karate-chop action. I find a half full bottle of canola oil over the stove and get a slightly hilarious and cartoonish image of pouring it on Ellen's steps, then watching them hilariously slip and slide off the edges.

I'm bordering on absurd now. What else is there?

All this shit is scary as hell, but sometimes it's so unbelievable that all you can do is laugh at it and at yourself.

Perhaps Ellen will have something useful at her house. I'm not above using a kitchen knife to protect us.

I feel awkward about the possibility of stabbing a child, yet if there's a demented alien or upper-level demon possessing its host, one that has its sights set on dragging me down to hell, I might just have to find out if these things bleed.

Lauren enters the kitchen from the hallway, looking fresher. She says, "I'll have to leave a thank you note for the owners. I feel a little more like myself."

"How so?"

"Fully stocked drawers."

Finally, I see what she's talking about. She has on a touch of makeup now and it suits her well. Much subtler and normal than the garish, exotic-bird tones she was flaunting this morning. Little bit of lipstick, little bit of eyeliner. I'm not sure what the need is because she's here, in jeans and a sweatshirt, and she doesn't know it yet, but she's about to go confront some terrifying paranormal entities.

Hey, I said I'd forgive her—I just didn't say I'd be entirely nice about it. I'm not letting her hang out here while I go parlay with the beasts by myself.

***

We drape a patchwork quilt over Ellen and leave her behind with Ulie. I like the idea of him staying behind to protect her rather than risk being exposed to the unknown potential. He's my little buddy, you know? I feel like I'm the overprotective parent, doing my best to guard him from harm.

Lauren isn't too thrilled to be going back. I understand why, obviously, and she relented once I told her that this could go a long way toward retribution in my eyes if she's sincerely apologetic about her actions two years ago.

We rumble along in the Wrangler, its fat, knobby tires thrumming along on the blacktop, hissing over the layer of rain covering the streets. The waterfall downpour hammers the canvas soft-top, and it sounds like we're sitting inside a snare drum. It smells musty in here due to all the small leaks in the canvas ragtop. Maybe I'm driving a jalopy into battle instead of a tank, but I wouldn't trade it for an armored car shaped like a crucifix.

I focus on the road, trying to see past wipers that can't handle the deluge, while Lauren can't keep her hands still in nervous anticipation.

She says, "I think I'm gonna be sick."

"From nerves or the scotch?"

"Both, probably."

"Don't hork in here, please. I'll pull over."

"What're we gonna do, Ford?"

"You're asking if I have a plan?"

"Yeah. It's not like we can invite them in for tea."

I ease up to a stoplight. Ellen's house is three blocks away, and I'm more than a little freaked out. I have shit for plans and no qualms about delaying the inevitable. Sitting here for thirty seconds longer is not a problem. I'm also not going to tell Lauren. She needs to be reasonably calm in case the black-eyes feed off of—and get stronger with—negative energy.

"We wait," is all I tell her. The downpour slams against the soft-top overhead, the repetitive, slightly muted ratta-tat-tat on canvas heightening my anxiety.

"We wait? For what? For them to kill us?"

"No. To talk. To see what they want."

"It can't be good, can it?"

"You never know. Could be like a singing telegram."

"This is not the time."

"I'm serious. They're not going to hop up on the front porch and sing a jingle, but maybe they have a message for me." About three molecules in my brain actually thinks this might be a possibility, simply because Papa Joe had asked for me by name then granted me a Class-A EVP with some vague details about Chelsea Hopper.

"You don't actually believe that, do you?" Lauren leans up against the window and stares out into the night.

The light turns green, and I allow the Wrangler to drift forward.

I don't answer her.

Lauren says, "So this is how we die, huh? I was hoping to go out with a pool boy in my lap and a martini in my hand, but I guess you'll have to do."

11
Mike Long

"I'm going to change," Dakota tells me as we tentatively step across the threshold and into the breezeway. "Funny how I don't mind running in this out in public. Now I just feel..." She shakes her hands like she can't find the right word.

"Exposed?"

"Exactly, especially with a ghost around."

I understand, and somehow I manage to hide my disappointment.

If I haven't fully acknowledged it yet, this is the part where I finally grasp that it has been an *excruciatingly* long time since an attractive woman was nice to me. It's emotional as much as it's physical. Sure, fans of the show will say hi while I'm in line to buy a soda somewhere, but that's different. This is up close. Personal niceness.

Dakota heads for the stairs and stops three steps up. She looks back at me and asks, "Coming?"

"Right behind you."

I won't lie—in the porno movie in my head, the head that should be focusing on the impending ghost hunt instead—this is the way it would go down. The mustachioed, giant-sideburnhaving investigator gets invited in, magic happens, and hallelujah, Mikey Sweetheart is singing like a choir of angels.

Bow-chicka-bow-bow.

Just as quickly as the imagery flashes through my mind, I mentally flick myself in the testicles, which works, somewhat.

Horny old man. Good grief, dude. She's scared. She needs you.

I have a job to do here, for someone I admire, who is terrified of the black, floating, unholy mass in her home, and here I am letting my imagination turn into an X-rated funhouse.

Wow. I'm totally acting like Ford would. Two days with him in Hampton Roads and Captain Penis is saluting the first woman that smiles at me.

Ghosts. Ghosts. Ghosts.

Grandma on the toilet.

Roadkill.

The smell of spoiled ham.

Yuck.

Okay, that did it.

Back to business.

We breach the landing, and she stops at the second set of stairs leading to the master bedroom one floor up. She pauses, looks over her shoulder at me. I can tell she's worried about being alone.

"Need me to come up with you?" I ask. Dakota raises an eyebrow and the opposite corner of her mouth. *Is she flirting with me?* And in the amount of time it takes me to realize how stupid that idea is, I get flooded with warm mortification. "Oh, shit, no—uh, I mean—like wait outside the door. You know, for the ghost and stuff." Hand goes to forehead and eyes go to the ground, embarrassed.

"Hah, relax. I'm messing with you. Just gonna throw on some shorts and a t-shirt. Hopefully I don't get possessed in the two minutes that'll take. Wish me luck."

I tell Dakota not to worry and jokingly suggest that her fearless protector will be right down here, adding that I'll do some recon work while she gets dressed.

She steps back over to me. "What kind of recon?"

"Eh, just boring stuff. Baseline EMF reads, things like that."

"I'd like to try that. Will you wait on me?"

"I... sure," I reply, sounding unsure.

"I'm serious," she says. "After watching you and Ford, I always wanted to see it firsthand."

"But that's the boring part. Just staring at numbers."

"No, it's fascinating to me, at least. It's like tracing the outline before you color in the picture, right?"

"I never thought about it that way. Okay, Picasso, I'll be here."

She holds up a wait-a-sec finger. "Two minutes. Have a look around, but there's not much to see."

And then she's gone, climbing the stairs to the master bedroom—that box on top of a box on top of a box. I hear her footsteps overhead, and it reminds me of the thousand or so investigations that I did with Ford. I've lost count of how many times we heard footsteps on the floors above us, knowing full well that we were the only two living human beings present. I still get chills thinking about it.

When Ford talked me into doing the show, on that ancient night when we investigated that asylum back in—what, 2003?—all I ever wanted was to impress Toni, the former college cheerleader that I had a massive crush on, and say to her, "Hey, look, I'm gonna be on television!"

I figured we might have a good run at a single season; the producers would soon be on to our shenanigans and the fact that we had no clue what we were doing. By then, Toni would be so madly in love with me and so thoroughly impressed that her future hubby was on television that we'd stroll happily into the sunset.

A second season came around, and a third. We got married in the middle of filming the fourth season. The Paranormal Channel put everything they could behind *Graveyard,* and the show scored well right away. Then we hit some magical tipping point before the start of the fifth season, and after that, all aboard the gravy train.

Like I've told Ford a hundred thousand times, he was the face, the talent, and the reason we did so well in the first place.

I started calling him the 'Almighty' Ford Atticus Ford way back when, and it's always been the truth. His onscreen presence turned us into worldwide megastars, and I can't say I didn't enjoy parts of it—like the money, mainly—but yeah, all I ever wanted was to impress a girl.

And that girl is no longer impressed.

I hear the toilet flush up in Dakota's bedroom and decide that I should be down at the far end of the hall, pretending like I had already given her some privacy. The bulk of the mansion is downstairs, but the second floor has a lot to offer, especially if you have plenty of overnight guests or about thirteen children. There are at least five spare bedrooms on either side of the hall, each as empty as the last, and plain white walls with a cream colored carpet so plush you could sink into it and get lost. You'd need a machete to hack your way out.

No pictures or decorations yet, which doesn't surprise me. The bedrooms on the eastern side of the hall would be preferable since they have a sweeping view of the Atlantic.

A few miles out to sea, hovering over an oil tanker, I see a fat, dark storm cloud.

If I were the dramatic sort, I'd pretend it's an omen.

But I'm not, so it's a cloud, from which rain falls.

I find her office and it's nearly as empty as the rest of the house. There's a desk pushed up against the wall. On top of that sits nothing more than a closed laptop and a lamp.

Some paranormal cases have a clear reason why the house is haunted. Say, for example, a curious teenager and her friends have a sleepover. Tina Teenager brings along a Ouija board for fun and a group of giggling teen girls unwittingly and accidentally unlock a gateway to Hell, thereby opening up all of that youthful energy for something to cross over to our side. Seen it a couple hundred times. Those are easy to figure out.

Other times, someone has passed on, whether specifically in the home or not, and they have unfinished business. Messages to send, guilty consciences to allay, reassurances that they're fine if only the intended recipient could hear them. Often, if Ford and I were able to communicate with the spirit in an intelligent haunting like that, they would be satisfied and go into the light. Whether that light was cast down through the pearly gates or lit by the flames of Hell was for them to find out.

If it's intelligent, you can potentially communicate with it—human or demonic.

If it's a residual haunt, it's nothing but leftover energy imprinted on the film of time, and you can't do anything about it. Ford used to describe it as a looping video, replaying throughout infinity. It's not going to hurt you, and those footsteps you hear at three in the morning, every single night, will be there long after you're gone.

Based on what Dakota told me, the entity in her home isn't residual, so it'll be my job to uncover the reason it's here. Today, during the daylight, we can do some baseline checks and try to communicate with it via digital voice recorder. Later, I might run into town and see if I can dig up the history of the home, like whom the previous owners were, before the billionaire, or if there have been any violent deaths on the property.

Then, the real investigation can begin with nightfall.

Unless Dakota wants to participate, I'll probably send her to a hotel, but definitely not back to hang out with Toni. That's an invitation for trouble, and I'm all out of RSVP cards.

Bad joke, dad joke.

Dakota is whisper quiet as she enters the office, which is why I don't hear her come in at first. She says, "Hey," sharply, and I launch an inch off the ground, clutching the DVR in my hand like a sword.

"*Gah.* Jesus, you scared me." My free hand goes up to my chest, pretending to check for a heartbeat. I grin at her around a raspy laugh.

She pats me on the shoulder. "Nerves of steel on the famous ghost hunter, huh? Couldn't resist. You find anything yet?"

"Nah. I was just processing. Getting a feel for the place."

I'm definitely disappointed to see that she's dressed like a normal human being now, rather than an elite athlete, and yet, she looks amazing in a simple white tank top and a pair of tan shorts that show off her quads. Looks like Dakota hasn't skipped leg day in a long time. Her hair is now pulled back in a ponytail, which is awesome, because it shows off her fabulously long neck and sleek jaw line.

I process all of this in about a third of a second to keep from staring at her, and then proceed to ask her some more of our—I mean Ford's—standard questions, like does she know of any deaths in the home, was the former owner into Satanism, is *she* into Satanism, or has she conducted any séances lately that might've involuntarily invited something into the home.

The answer to all of these is no, of course, and I knew it would be. It's always a good idea to ask, just in case, because sometimes you can catch an untruthful person through their body language. Ford was better at this part than I ever was. Still, I learned enough by watching him to know that Dakota isn't lying.

The only thing she says is, "The guy who owned it before me, maybe he sold his soul to the Devil to get that kind of money, right?"

I say, "I wouldn't be the slightest bit surprised," though I stop short of telling her that I would've sold *mine* to hang on to what I used to have. I don't, because that's not the impression I want to give Dakota. The money was good, but not everything. Then again, you get used to a certain lifestyle. Woulda coulda shoulda. I add, "We talked about this a little earlier. Did your real estate agent mention *anything at all* about him or the history of the home?"

"Nope. Nothing other than the fact that he was selling this place and moving to his private island. Makes you wonder if he left *because* it's haunted."

"We could always ask. Best to cover our bases."

"True. I'll call my agent later. She might know something or know how to get in touch with him. I think he's somewhere in the South Pacific, so he may not even have access to a phone."

"I doubt he went dark. Billionaires like that, they can't stay unconnected."

Dakota steps over to the window and swipes a bit of dust off the windowsill, rolling it between her fingertips. "This place... All I wanted was an escape. I left one prison for another."

I move over beside her. "Don't get discouraged. We haven't even started yet. I'll get it cleaned up. Promise."

"You know what's funny? I already feel safer. With you here, I mean."

I can feel the instinctual longing down there in my subconscious, wishing there was a deeper meaning to that statement. I know she's talking about the fact that she has an experienced paranormal investigator around.

Dakota adds, "It feels lighter in here now, like that thing isn't around."

I lean up against the window with my shoulder, turning to face her. Man, she looks amazing in the early morning light. "Don't tempt fate. It's probably just taking time to recharge. Matter of fact, I should probably check these batteries."

As if I had flashed a signal in the sky to call it to us, from down the hallway, the loud crash of a shattered mirror sends Dakota into my arms.

The Graveyard: Classified Paranormal Series

12
Ford Atticus Ford

Lauren and I decide to do some recon work around Ellen's property before we go inside, and when we cruise past the front, it occurs to me that I'm somewhat familiar with this old house.

I've seen it a bunch of times on my way to and from the condo during my vacation trips of the past. I even remember Melanie pointing it out one time, years ago, when we were here on a mini-vacation before we starting filming whatever season that was.

Like the ass I can be, I was already in the midst of numerous affairs by that point, and I specifically recall feeling like a huge douche-pickle when she pointed out that Ellen's house would be a perfect little retirement home for us once the show had finished its run.

I keep that bit of information from Lauren. Anything I say has the potential to be used against me. I do, however, tell her that I've seen her grandmother's house before, and have always been envious of the view.

"Incredible, isn't it?" Lauren says, wistfully.

"I'd *live* on that front porch, if she'd let me. Just give me a sleeping bag and a cardboard box."

Ellen's house sits up on a hill, and I examine it closely as we circle the block three times looking for anything suspicious. Unless they're hanging out in the backyard, there's no sign of the beastly creatures waiting on us, giving me time to observe what's soon to be our fort for the night.

It's dark and pouring. Most of what I'm able to piece together comes from the wet view I have now, coupled with daylight memories. The exterior, when the sun is shining on it, is painted the color of a bluebird sky that you get on a cloudless summer day here on the coast. The shutters are white, and the awnings are white.

In fact, it reminds me of a dress shirt I once owned—blue, with a white collar and white cuffs. I left it in Hawaii about seven years ago. Funny that should pop into my head now because that was the first time I'd heard about the black-eyed children. It was a hotel maid who mentioned it. Sadly, we never had time to go investigate her home, and given the circumstances, I'm wishing we had, just so I could come into this with some experience.

Ellen's home is craftsman-style with a wraparound porch that skirts the south, west, and northern sides. In back, facing east, the yard is fenced in by tall, wide slats pressed so firmly together that you couldn't slip a sheet of paper between them.

The home itself is fairly plain, and Lauren tells me that it's because Grandpa has moved on to the great beyond, and with Ellen's eyesight nearly gone, it's less trouble. I can specifically remember when there were gorgeous, lush flowerbeds along the foundation, and huge, round pots standing along either side of the front steps, guarding the stairway like terra cotta sentinels.

"Shame it's sorta going to waste," I say. "It's a great place."

Lauren tells me that her parents are living down in San Diego where it's warmer and they can be closer to their daughter. I ask forgiveness for prying, but I'm curious as to why they're not here where their ancient, blind matriarch lives, who would appear to need more care than their wealthy television host of a daughter.

She answers, "Mom and Grandma never got along, never ever. And with me living so far away, it was the perfect excuse for her to escape. My dad dug his heels in for about seven or eight seconds, but you see where that got him. Happy wife, happy life. They pay for a nurse to come by few times a week, and don't tell my mother, but I spring for extra care when the nurse they hired isn't around."

"You're such a heathen."

"Hell in a handbasket." We drive back around to the ocean-facing side of the house again, and Lauren tells me to slow down. "Park here," she says, pointing to a spot in front of a compact sedan. I can tell by the corporate bumper sticker that it's her rental.

"Have any of the nurses ever seen these things here before?"

Lauren rolls down her window. Thankfully, the rain is shooting in from the west, so the drops fly right over the top of the Jeep, and the only thing that enters is the salty scent of the ocean. She tells me not that she knows of, and none of them have said anything to her parents either during their weekly reports. She leans out the window, and I can't tell what she's looking at.

"What're you doing, Coeburn?"

"Trying to see between the slats."

It's pointless, I know, but I can't fault her for trying. "You think they're still in back?" My tone comes off a bit too incredulous, because she flicks her head around and narrows her eyes.

"How should I know, Ford? Where do black-eyed children hang out? The YMCA?"

"Point taken, though I doubt even supernatural monsters would be out in this."

"You're kidding, right? Something tells me they're not very discriminating when it comes to the weather."

"Hey, who's the world famous paranormal investigator here with all the first-hand knowledge?"

"If you say so."

A nearby streetlight flickers and goes dark, adding an extra layer of depth to the shadows. Was that chance or a deliberate act? I've been doing shit like this long enough to know that *actual* coincidences are rare.

I ask Lauren if she's ready to go in, and she gnaws on the loose skin of a knuckle. A deep breath later, she finally says, "I can't. At least not until you check it out." She hands me a single key with a rabbit's foot dangling from the ring. "Here. Please?"

"You're gonna stay here? By yourself?"

Her voice quivers when she says, "Leave the keys in the ignition." It's more of a question than an order.

I relent. If she's not legitimately scared to death, somebody should give her an honorary award.

And the Oscar for plucking Ford's heartstrings with the pouty-lip sadface goes to... Lauren Coeburn! I'd like to thank my agent, God, and Ford, for being a sucker.

I zip up my jacket and flip up the collar. "Last chance for the truth. If you're fucking with me about this..."

"I'm not. I swear."

"Then I guess I'll turn on the porch light for the all clear, okay?"

She snatches my hand, squeezes it, and tells me to be careful.

Funny. I think she actually means it, and it peels away a single layer of steel from around my heart.

***

At first, I hustle up the walkway because of the weather then change my tactical approach.

I remember why I'm here and slow down, succumbing to the urge to crouch. I've been around enough detectives and patrolmen to pick up some habits, so I slip up to the front of the house, climb the stairs, and then back up against the wall. The front picture window, which will have an incredible view of the ocean from inside the living room, is unblocked by curtains or shades. I dip to my left to take a quick peek. It's dark in there, but I spot no movement.

It's full of what you would expect for a house: a couch, a recliner, a fireplace, and a coffee table, with a variety of knick-knacks sitting around on shelves, and end tables. I spot a television that might have been brand new when Gerald Ford was in office. Other than the TV that should probably be haunting anyone here, the room is free of anything paranormal.

To my right, the porch disappears around the northern side of the house. I sidestep over and for the briefest of moments, while my back passes by the closed door, I feel my stomach clench, waiting on our demented friends to yank it open and grab me.

It's not possible, obviously, because Lauren didn't invite them inside, and supposedly these things can't enter unless you tell them it's okay. Kinda like how a vampire needs to be given permission to enter, but the black-eyed children aren't quite so obvious about their paranormal ambitions.

Still. You never know.

Nothing shatters the picture window and grabs me as my exposed back crosses in front of it. I exhale, my gale-like relief getting lost in the wind. I pause at the corner, count to five, then spin around to my stomach and flatten myself against the wall. I can feel the wind whipping raindrops underneath the porch roof and onto my jeans.

Slowly… Slowly… And goddamn, I didn't know it was possible to move so slowly… I'm slow like molasses fresh out of the freezer as I lean and ease one eye around the corner.

Shit!

I've never been afraid of spiders but when the rain-drenched wind pushes that little bastard forward, slinging him at my face, almost landing on my eyeball, I yip like someone stepped on a Pomeranian, and then have to catch my balance before I tumble back into the railing.

I mutter, "You little jerk," around a chuckle.

Back in the Wrangler, Lauren calls out to me, asks if I'm okay and if I see our guests. I wave her off and tell her I'm fine, hiding the fact that I'm on edge, man.

For real.

Little white lies are preferable to big black ones.

I just told Lauren a little white lie.

Melanie got a lot of big black ones. There's no question about why she left me.

Given Lauren's Hollywood cutthroat nature, I wonder how many lies she's told during her life and career. Living under the roof of subterfuge is probably so natural to her, she expects it.

She yells up to me, "Think it's safe for me to come up?" Her words are scattered through the cacophony of Mother Nature's wrath, yet I can make it out enough to suggest that she stay put. I tell her I'd like to check out the back first and then I'll come get her. "Wait for the porch light. I mean it!" I yell, and she waves as she cranks the window back up.

The backyard fence adjoins the blue siding about halfway back. The tops of each slat are pointed, reminding me of a long, jagged saw blade. In the low ambient light, even with the streetlamp still out, I can make out their rough-cut edges. They're high enough that I'd have to jump, grab the top, and pull myself up. So, being the soft-skinned pansy that I am—and not too fond of splinters—I find a flimsy deck chair, one of those rickety plastic ones that cost about four cents to manufacture, and park it as close as I can get to the fence.

It wiggles when I climb onto it, and, my heartbeat flitters like the wings of a butterfly in a wind tunnel. First, I'm worried this plastic piece of crap will collapse and I'll break an ankle. Second, what if I put my hands over the top and one of those damn things is over there waiting and tries to bite me? I don't fancy my fingers disappearing the way a drunken college kid plows through a whole bucket of buffalo chicken on ten-cent wing night.

You've waited years to see these guys, Ford. Put up or shut up. They're only fingers.

A blend of fear and morbid curiosity sends my tentative hands up, and then they retreat.

Reach, retreat. Reach, retreat.

Do it, Ford!

I grab the peaks of the fence—lightly of course, to avoid the splinters—and pull my weight up on my tip-toes, poking my head over the top.

It's empty, thank God, and I feel both silly and relieved at my hesitation.

It's nothing more than an empty yard—a deep, lush green from the Oregon coast rainfall—and on the far side, I spy the wide open gate.

Easy enough. No baddies.

I dart around, emerge through the gate, and up to Ellen's back door. Using the key that Lauren gave me, one that has been rubbed smooth by time and spare change in someone's pocket for decades, the tumblers eventually relent with some wiggling and shimmying.

The interior of the house smells and looks just how you'd expect a prehistoric cottontop's house would. Kitchen grease, liniment oil, and probably mothballs, if I'm correctly remembering the scent from Grandma Ford's home. The paint has faded on the walls and some of the historic furniture would fetch quite a high appraisal value on *Antiques Galore* every Sunday morning. Paneled walls, sagging cushions, rabbit ears on top of the television—I feel like I've traveled back in time.

Aside from a miniature grandfather clock that stands resolute on the mantle, ticking like a hammer against steel, it's silent in here. I give my eyes a few seconds to get adjusted to the even blacker shadows inside, and even though it's theoretically impossible for the demonic shitheads to be in here, I decide to clear the upstairs first, because if anything is down here, I want the advantage of higher ground.

It makes sense in my head.

I tiptoe up the creaking steps to the second floor, then sneak from room to room. The master bedroom, spare bedroom, and reading room are all clear of paranormal thingies that go boo in the night.

Good, I think. Looks safe up here. Supposing the downstairs is okay, we can fortify the place a bit and wait on the punks to come back.

Fortification would be incomplete without weapons, and I try to think about what I could use, barring the materialization of a beginner-savvy firearm. I'm not a fan of guns, so I need something long, something that I can swing from a distance. I wonder if Grandpa Coeburn might've been a golfer.

The hallway closet is void of devices that would create bruises or fleshy holes, unless I beat the shit out of somebody with a rolled up hand towel, and I'm about to give up looking when I find an item that's totally unrelated to causing pain.

An old video recorder, VCR-style, with those brick-sized tapes. Nice. I haven't seen one of these things in years. I can set this up and try to catch evidence.

The batteries are dead, no surprise there, but eureka and hallelujah, I find the plug-in cord on the shelf, along with a box of unopened blank tapes sitting next to another one with hand-labeled videos. I twist them around into the available light and read the fat, blocky handwriting.

LAUREN CHEERLEADING MAY 1988.
MOM DAD FISHING TRIP JUNE.
HANDS OFF – PRIVATE.

The last one gives me a chuckle and I'm fairly certain what's on it.

Sometimes skeletons in the closet are made up of adventurous couples.

Oy.

Thing is, if the recorder actually works, it occurs to me that if I tell Lauren about it, she'll try her damned best to use it on *me*.

The almighty Ford Atticus Ford, on a private home tape, on an actual paranormal investigation, with a princess of Hollywood.

Imagine her ratings for *Weekend Report*.

The desire to catch the black-eyed children on camera is overwhelming, so I'll have to keep it hidden from her as best as I can. I find an outlet in the hall, plug in the recorder, slip a tape into the side carriage, and check out its operability.

Damn if it ain't perfect.

Sometimes you catch a break and the universe tips its hat at you.

Go get'em, cowboy, it says.

I remember the large bookcase I saw in the living room and scamper downstairs where I do my best to use some hardback novels to conceal it on an upper shelf. I can barely see the lens, and an angled copy of *Moby Dick* hides the blinking red light. If we keep the lights low, it'll be perfect. I don't have a plan for getting the tape out of here in case we do manage to get them into the shot, but I'll deal with that when the time comes.

I'm giddy with the possibilities, images of my former glory catapulting through my mind, when there's a knock on the front door. It spooks me, ruining the daydreams, and I murmur a handful of curse words when I see Lauren standing outside on the porch.

Yanking the door open, I say, "You were supposed to wait for the light. That's the all clear, remember?"

She's soaked and looking miserable. "You need to let me in."

"Fine, whatever, get in here," I say, frustrated as I step to the side. "It's your place, do whatever you want."

13
Chelsea Hopper

Chelsea Hopper is seven years old now and will be eight in two more months.

She often wakes from horrible nightmares where she is back in the old house, the one that other people call the 'Hopper House.'

The Most Haunted Place in America.

She dreams of claws and fangs and darkness and the scent of rotten eggs. She feels fear that loosens her bladder in her dreams, but not in her bed, thankfully. At least not yet. She's proud that she's never wet herself, unlike that boy Gordon in her class, the one who always smells like moldy dirt and cat litter.

Often, when she wakes from these dreams, she rises from bed, as she does now, and patters down the hallway into the bathroom. The nightlight plugged into the wall helps assuage her fright, but it's never enough. She flips on the overhead lights, a gloriously bright row of seven bulbs over the mirror.

And in this mirror, she stares at her reflection, first checking her eyes, then touching her cheeks, pushing the puffy skin around to make sure it's still soft and bendy. She pulls her lower lip down first and then pushes the upper one toward the ceiling, checking her teeth. Next come her ears, then her fingers and toes, her nails.

Finally, she pulls open the front of her pajamas and holds her breath as she looks down, breathing a sigh of relief that she hasn't grown a scaly, shriveled penis.

Chelsea is relieved to see that she is not the boy demon she becomes in her dreams—that evil, vicious creature with grotesque, pebbly, raised skin made of scales. Eyes yellow and slit like the stray tomcat that sleeps underneath their back porch. Fangs, long and sharp, which dig deeply into the flesh of Mr. Ford and Mr. Mike. Pointed ears that lay back against her head, listening to their screams.

This happens to her practically every night. It's terrifying, yet it has happened enough that it's almost normal. The dreams were never this bad before, not even when she lived in the Hopper House. These violent nightmares have been happening for months, even before her parents mentioned the movie that Mr. Ford and Mr. Mike might be making about her life. They had asked her if it was okay, if she minded. She had said she was scared and wasn't sure.

They needed the money, they told her. They needed it, and it would be good for the family. They could pay for her school when she got older, and maybe now, too, if she wanted to go to a different place, maybe a less crowded one where not as many people knew her, where she could concentrate and not answer questions about ghosts and demons.

I have friends here she had told them. *It's okay, Mama, and don't worry, Daddy. I'll try to do better in school. I promise.*

I'll do better in school, and I won't tell you about the dreams yet, because maybe they had forgotten how horrible it was in that house when she was so little.

Would they make her go back in the house with Mr. Ford and Mr. Mike?

Carla, that super nice lady from Hollywood, the one who had given her candy corn and chocolate on Halloween night the last time, had said that Chelsea wouldn't have to go back in the house. Never ever never again. Never ever.

Mama and Daddy had said okay, Carla and her people could make the movie, but only for lots of money and as long as Chelsea wasn't in danger.

Chelsea almost told them about the dreams then.

But if she did, if she told them how scary it was to become that demon and use her horrible fangs to bite the hearts of Mr. Mike and Mr. Ford every night, they would send her back to that awful man, Dr. Slade, who had breath like rotten fish and hands that were rough like sandpaper when he touched her skin.

She kept her secrets to herself, and now she revisits the same place each night—that pitch black hallway in her old home. She climbs from a deep, dark place, claw over claw, for what feels like a hundred years until she breaks through the floor, smashing the wood and smelling the soot and ashes, feeling the flames licking at her heels. She gets to her knees and spreads her leathery black wings, then stands to her full height, towering over the two men she thought were her friends. Big, strong guys who were supposed to *protect* her from this thing that she has become.

Satisfied that she's not a demon—a horrifying, disgusting *boy* demon—Chelsea drinks a glass of water from her cup decorated with pink cartoon puppies and steps back from the bathroom mirror. It's pure habit as she reaches for the light switch, then draws her hand away, just as she does every night. It's better to leave them on.

Chelsea sneaks a furtive peek out the door, looking left and right. Spying nothing in the short hallway now illuminated by the bathroom, she turns left and darts toward her bedroom. She flies through the door, imagining she's like the older girls at her gymnastics class as she plants her feet and jumps, twisting, spinning in the air, landing on her soft, comforting mattress. The sheet and pink puppy comforter go up over her head for protection.

She knows it won't do much good if the demon ever comes for her again.

That's what the spell is for.

Chelsea whispers:

The white night is bright with light and love.
Put the pedal to the metal and
Swing your sword with grace at his face.
Keep me safe in this place.
The Demon Killer is my savior,
May he protect me forever and ever.
Thanks, Jesus.

Her teachers, her parents, her parents' friends, aunts and uncles, older cousins, all tell Chelsea how smart she is. Knowing this, she understands that her little incantation is silly, but so far, it has worked, and she has not been attacked by a demon in real life—not like at the Hopper House—and only her dreams have been damaged.

Those are bearable, for now. As long as she can keep them to herself, she'll be okay, and she only has to do it until Mr. Ford and Mr. Mike kill the thing in her dreams. She just hopes she's not inside of it when it happens. She's not ready to die, but the thing in her dreams is strong and will hurt a lot of people if they don't do something. The movie with the demon killers and that nice lady, Carla, will make it all go away.

September will be here soon. She can make it until then.

Chelsea slides her hand underneath her pillow and tightens her grip around the handle of a knife. Her mother thinks it was lost in the trash.

Chelsea tries to take it with her into her nightmares.

One day, it might work.

14
Mike Long

We both listen to the plinking, scattering sound of shattered glass bouncing off a countertop and the bathroom tile.

I gotta say, Dakota feels good in my arms, soft but solid. Strong.

She says, "Fuck! What was that?" before pulling away.

Wait, come back! "Mirror. Down the hall."

She starts for the office door, and I grab her wrist, telling her to wait, to let me go check first.

"You think it's the—the *ghost?*"

"Probably," I say, the word sounding more like a question than I intend. After all, I'm supposed to be the one who knows what I'm doing.

I insert my ear buds and press 'Record' on the GS-5000, my bitchin' digital voice recorder that allows me to listen to what's being recording in real time, while also being able to rewind and review captured evidence as it continues to record. I love this thing. Out of every piece of equipment I've ever used, even that damn spiritual fart detector, this is my favorite.

Capturing video evidence and watching a spirit walk across an empty warehouse, asylum, or a football field—that's cool, that's chill-inducing—but to me, uncovering the real humanity comes from being able to hear what a spirit has to say. Their words make them authentic and give them an identity. Seeing a hazy shape on a screen… I don't see it as being much different than watching a television show with some sophisticated CGI. Hearing the emotion in their words, that's what does it for me.

It's a different story hearing something demonic or listening to the vitriol of a malicious dead guy who's yet to let go of his murderous rage, and yet, it makes them genuine, almost corporeal. The bad ones can be terrifying—case in point, that right-hander that attacked Chelsea and Dave Craghorn—but it gives them a measure of tangibility.

So yeah, this particular device is like my ghost-hunting security blanket.

Toni once said, "If you love that thing so much, why don't you leave me and marry it?" I don't doubt there was some truth behind her joke, and believe me, the idea wasn't, and isn't, entirely out of the question. I'm not sure how the law regards marrying electronics—procuring joint insurance would be a problem, I'm sure.

I hold my finger up to my lips. Dakota nods through anxious breathing, blowing through pursed lips, fanning her cheeks, trying to calm herself.

At first, I hear nothing but the gentle hiss of silence through the miniature speakers in my ears.

The white earbud strings tickle my neck as I creep into the hall, straining to pick out any obvious noises that don't belong, that aren't innate to the home. I wish I'd had extra time in here to get more familiar with the place—and as much as I hate to admit it, Ford's annoying habit of spending a couple of days surveying a location before he would even consider investigating it would be helpful here. I'm not accustomed to the particulars of Dakota's home, like what sounds it makes when the lumber is settling, the creak of loose floorboards, or whether the grill over the air vent vibrates when the air conditioner kicks on.

Knowing that stuff would be immensely valuable.

Instead, I'm storming the castle with no plan and no idea where the archers are hiding along the soldier's walk.

I glance behind me and hold up my palm, then point at my eyes and finally toward the hallway bathroom, silently signaling that Dakota needs to wait while I check it out.

Thumbs up from her.

The GS-5000 is so sophisticated that it picks up on the squish of plush carpet under my bare feet as I slink down the hall.

I hear nothing.

I see nothing.

I smell nothing.

I don't *feel* anything unusual, either, like a static charge in the air or random cold spot. Given that, I am scrotum-shrinkingly unprepared when the black, swirling mass explodes out of the bathroom.

I scream, "Shit!" and duck from pure shock. I've faced worse—much, much worse—but it caught me by surprise. Behind me, back in the bedroom, Dakota shouts, "Mike?"

My eyes stay locked on our intruder. It hovers there, ten feet away from me. Floating, swirling, the tendrils of blackness climbing on top of each other like snakes in a pit. I feel my neck muscles tightening. I sense that it's hostile, and yet, curious, like it's sizing up the new opponent.

It nudges closer, ever so slightly, undulating, rippling, slowly moving from a malleable mass of blackness, smoke-like, into the shape of a man. Broad-shouldered, no arms or legs, but large and bulky; it's the size of an NFL linebacker and just as intimidating.

I ask, "Who are you?" as I hold the GS-5000 closer to it, adding, "I'm not afraid of you," like this thing would actually give a shit.

That's when I hear it—an EVP in my ears, not a disembodied voice that emits from nowhere within the room, and thank God, because I wouldn't want Dakota to hear this thing laugh. It's booming, throaty, and vile, sending shivers down my arms. There's something wicked behind it, as if this bastard knows that I am nothing in its presence. Maybe it's stronger than I thought.

"What's your name?" I ask.

Dakota, still in the bedroom, says, "Are you okay?"

"Fine. Stay there. Don't look," I tell her, which is the absolute worst thing to say to stubborn curiosity. A beat later, she gasps, curses, and then it sounds as if her voice is rising up from the floor, like she dropped into a carpeted foxhole.

She calls out to me, "That's what I saw before, Mike! Get back here. Hurry."

"I'm good. We're good. Right, Mr. Ghost?"

Mr. Ghost? The fuck?

It growls at me—literally growls like I've put my hand too close to its food dish—and I step back. My bladder feels bulging and warm. Growling, especially something so dark, as if it's seared by hate and ashes, could easily be classified as demonic.

I'm not buying it. Dakota hasn't mentioned any of the typical signs like claw marks showing up on her skin in threes—a mockery of the Holy Trinity—or any of the other indicators like childish voices and shredded Bibles.

It doesn't *feel* demonic. My guess is that it's masquerading as something bigger and stronger, much the same as a human lifting its arms and shouting to appear more intimidating over a dangerous animal.

Assuming it's posturing, and weaker than it actually is, well, that's my first mistake.

***

My second mistake is feeling like I need to be Billy Badass in front of Dakota and impress her with my ghost-demolishing skills. Peacocking, so to speak.

I don't have a crucifix with me, so what I do is, I raise my forearms and lay one over the other, in the shape of a cross. I shout, "Back, ye heathen devil!" and immediately feel like a gargantuan dork in a late night B-movie. Ford was better at this part than I am. Viewers told us our banter made the show what it was, but he knew how to put on a performance, man.

The thing is, it's taken me over two years to forgive him for ruining *Graveyard* and screwing up Chelsea Hopper. What never wavered, though, was my belief that his presence made us what we were. It didn't surprise me in the slightest when I approached all those producers without him along. They acted more interested in the dog crap on the soles of their expensive loafers, especially if they knew I'd be prone to shouting stupid stuff like, *Back, ye heathen devil!*

It laughs at me again. Roars, really, at my childish attempt.

I try a different tactic, attempting to channel the almighty Ford Atticus Ford at his best. I can remember his speech from an Irish rectory in season six, word for word, and begin to recite it: "Whether you are a child of God, or a child of Satan, this home is not yours. Listen to me, and understand me. You do not belong here. You will leave this place on my command and you will never bother this woman again, do you hear me? What is your name? Do you know that there is power in a name, you pitiful, pathetic weakling?" I raise my voice, one click of the dial below shouting, and continue, "What is your *name*, you bastard?

The Graveyard: Classified Paranormal Series

My named is Ford At—shit, I mean, my name is Mike Long, and I command you to leave now in the name of God. Leave now and never return!"

The mist diminishes in size, losing its shape of a man, churning in a slow circle like black muck down a bathtub drain.

Victory is on my lips, forming the word, when I hear it speak one of the most chilling EVPs I've ever heard.

"*I know you want her. She's... mine.*"

The black cloud swishes around like Batman making a dramatic exit with his cape and then poof, it evaporates. Gone as fast as it arrived.

Son of a bitch!

It takes me around two-point-seven seconds to decide I don't need, nor want, Dakota to hear that EVP. This scenario is already too messed up for her, and I can't have my schoolboy-slash-lonely-middle-aged-dude crush complicating the situation any further. I rewind roughly twenty seconds back on the GS-5000 and then record the silence over top of the EVP. This pains me to do so, because in over twelve-plus years of being involved with the paranormal world, that was one of the cleanest EVPs with proof of an intelligent haunt that I've ever come across.

During *Graveyard*'s amazing run, Ford was often accused of reading too far into the language of EVPs, trying to fit meaning relatable to the situation into nonsensical ghost blathering. I never came right out and told him this: I agreed. That was his deal, more or less, and I never argued with him over creative control. It was what it was. Ford developed the "story" behind the investigations. I was there to be the tech guy and provide straight man humor to his over-the-topness.

Frankly, I wish he were here now. My vibrating hands and shaky knees are proof that I'm out of practice when it comes to doing this alone.

Chin up, chest out, Mikey Sweetheart. You got this.

"Is it gone?" Dakota's voice is fifteen feet behind me and timid.

I look back to see her peeking out of the office. "For now. I think."

She eases through the doorway, head, shoulders, and arms first, in slow motion. She's so tall and lean and muscular that it reminds me of a video my daughter watched online where someone had filmed the birth of a baby foal.

Yup, that'll do it.

Nothing will put a damper on a horny crush faster than a loathsome spirit and the thought of horse vaginas.

I tell her again that it's gone—for a while—and we should take this opportunity to get out of the house and let it recharge, adding, "There's no need in doing any baseline checks. I got a visual. You're not imagining things."

"You thought I *was*?"

Whoa, backtrack. "No, no, not at all. I meant I'm positive you don't have anything else going on in here, like a fear cage where the EMF stuff is so strong, it can give you hallucinations."

"EMF stuff? Is that the technical term?"

"Official. Got it out of the guidebook."

Dakota giggles and it's a melody. I want to make her laugh for the rest of her life.

And mine.

She hugs herself and tentatively studies the hall and the nearby rooms.

I reassure her, "I don't think it'll bother us. At least not for now."

"For now? *Ugh.* And did I hear you say you wanted that thing to recharge? What in God's name for?"

I explain the whole principle of spiritual beings needing and expending energy to manifest or communicate with the living world. "And by taking the time to recharge, he's drawing on any available sources, like the spare batteries in my pockets, your fear. I mean, seriously, right now you're probably a walking Tesla coil just shooting off lightning bolts of ghost juice."

"And this is supposed to make me feel better?"

"Just the facts, ma'am."

"Right."

"We should go. Get you out of here and let it fill up on something else."

"Tell me why—this recharge thing you're talking about."

"Because it's easier to communicate once he builds up enough power to step over to this side again. When he does, he's at his most potent, but also his most vulnerable."

"And that's what we want? Strong but vulnerable?"

"When you put it that way, it makes him sound like Ryan Gosling, but yeah, essentially."

She nods, resigned, and looks away. "Now what?"

"Research. We need to find out who it is."

"*Was*," she reminds me.

15
Ford Atticus Ford

Lauren steps into Grandma Ellen's house and takes a look around like she's never seen the place before. Initially, this seems like an odd reaction, then it occurs to me that she's probably freaked out and expecting her black-eyed buddies to pop up from behind the couch and yell, "Boo!"

"It's okay," I tell her. "All clear. I checked."

That's a small, possibly harmless fib, because I got so involved with setting up the antiquated video recorder, I didn't have a chance to thoroughly check the bathroom down the hall or the linen closet beside it. Or, you know, both bedrooms. Besides, I'm still in the mindset that if she didn't invite them in, it's all good. That tingly sensation I get when something paranormal is present isn't firing off either.

We're fine.

I hope.

At least until those things come back.

And then what?

Pray? Let them in? Let the host of *Weekend Report* interview them?

No clue, but I'm going to trust my instincts when the time comes.

The Graveyard: Classified Paranormal Series

Lauren stops in the middle of the living room floor. She's soaked. Her wet hoodie and jeans and limp bottle-blonde hair all drip onto the throw rug that bears a picture of the local seascape.

"You okay, Coeburn? You seem *off*."

"No, I'm good. Just feels strange being in here after... them."

"Why were you out in the rain?"

"Checking around the house. Helping."

"You didn't need to do that. I had it." And for someone who was so terrified, that's a damn ballsy move, so I should give her some credit. "Thanks, though. Pretty brave."

She nods and pulls her soaked hair back. "So we're safe? You're positive?"

I tell her I think so and that we should be good until our visitors return.

"How long?"

"Until they come back? Hell if I know. Ten minutes? An hour? Never?"

"Good."

"Why?"

Lauren ignores my question and snatches her sopping wet hoodie at the hem and then whips it up and off. Before I can grasp what she's doing, I see a perfectly taut tummy and full, round breasts that, upon a microscopic glimpse, appear to be a little too perfectly round. My educated guess says that pushup bra isn't necessary.

Typical male, yeah, but I'm also a gentleman—sometimes—so I grunt, "Whoa," and turn away. "How 'bout a little warning?"

"Chill, Ford. It's not like you haven't seen breasts before," she chides, zipper hissing down, followed by mumbles and wiggling as she tries to peel off her painted-on jeans that must be astronomically harder to remove now that they're wet.

Yeah, I've seen lady parts before, but does she have to strip down right here, though?

I get my answer why when she says, "The dryer is in the kitchen. Avert your eyes if you must, gallant Sir Ford."

Curiosity trumps my gallantry, and I *have* to look, because telling me to avert my eyes is like putting me in an empty room and telling me not to push the giant, red, DO NOT PUSH button. While I used to hate her guts with the passion of a million stars gone supernova, it's hard to ignore the fact that all the weight she's lost has really done wonders. She looks *good*. Capital G good.

Although, as she's walking away, I note that her bra and thong don't match. I don't know why this amuses me. Maybe it's because I expected the ultra-pristine television persona to be as put together off camera as she is on. In the dim light, the bra appears to be something of a cream shade, and the thong looks midnight blue.

Could be purple, could be black, but not that I care because her butt is amazing.

I wonder how much she squats?

Shit. I'm an asshole.

Or am I human?

Frustrated, I grind my teeth and look out the bay window. Whitecaps cover most of the angry ocean. It's mental behavior like this that sent my relationship with Melanie hurtling and flaming toward the ground like a meteorite. It landed hard. That's for damn sure, and it left a huge crater in my heart.

Why do I do this?

My therapist says I shouldn't punish myself for my intrinsic male tendencies. Everybody looks, he says, because it's *biology*. The difference is, you gotta have the common friggin' courtesy to not act on your animalistic impulses. Your partner—the person you *love* for many reasons other than sex—deserves that respect.

I'm working on it.

Lauren's shenanigans, unintentional or not, and my reaction to them, makes me think of Melanie. I feel regret bubbling and growing warm in my stomach like a simmering pot. One day, it'll boil over, and I'll either drink a million gallons of beer to dull the memory or carry my heart up to her front door and beg forgiveness.

Jeff from the control room be damned. I'm pretty motivated when I need to be.

If she'll have me. I've learned that's another aspect of common courtesy in a relationship. Respecting the needs of others.

See?

I might get a boner if the wind blows the right direction, but I'm trying to keep the train on the tracks.

In the kitchen, the dryer door slams and I hear Lauren call out, "Coming through." I close my eyes—out of respect for Melanie, not Lauren—and hear my counterpart scamper from the kitchen, through the living room, and down the hallway. A bedroom door screeches shut and a moment later, she emerges wearing, yet again, a new pair of form-fitting jeans and a hoodie.

"How many sweatshirts did you bring?" I ask.

"I pack comfy," Lauren answers. "And you've seen the weather here, haven't you? Pouring rain, hoods. No brainer." She pulls her hair back tight against her scalp, deftly twirls it into a bun, and straps it down with a hair band. Then she rolls up her sleeves and snorts, a mama tiger prepped and ready for battle, ready to protect her territory.

Speaking of battle, I ask, "Do you have anything here we can use as a weapon? Golf clubs? A baseball bat? Anything you can swing?"

"When was the last time you swung either of those?"

"Last… decade. But it's better than nothing."

"Fair enough." Lauren twists at the waist, hands on her hips, chewing the side of her lip while she evaluates our options. "Not that I can think of. Grandma's blind. She doesn't need much." She holds up an index finger. "*Oh*, hang on a sec."

Back down the hallway she goes, this time to a different bedroom, and returns carrying a small, green lockbox, roughly the size of a paperback copy of *War & Peace*.

I remember seeing that book on the shelves earlier. Who has the time? Maybe that's why Ellen went blind. Trying to read that brick would do it, no offense to Tolstoy.

"What's this?"

"A .22 pistol. Belonged to my grandpa."

"Uh, yeah… *no*."

"What? Why?" she asks, incredulous.

"Not my thing, guns."

"You'll beat some paranormal creature thing over the head with a baseball bat, but you won't *shoot* it?"

"Bats or clubs can't accidentally go off and shoot someone in the foot. Or the face, or the head, or the chest, or—"

"Or the nose, or the knees, or the ears, I get it, but can't we—"

"Not a chance, no." I take the lockbox from her, step over, and place it in the middle of the bookshelf. My eye goes up to the video camera. It's still hidden well, yet I catch the tiniest glimpse of the little red light blinking. I can't risk an attempt to hide it more, so I try out some misdirection. "It's a thing I have.

The Graveyard: Classified Paranormal Series

With guns, I mean. You've kept up with what I'm doing now, right? The whole paranormal private investigator gig?"

"Yeah. Why?"

"Just, you know, wondering what you thought about it."

"It might come as a shock that I don't think about you all the time."

"Meaning?"

"*Meaning* I don't have an opinion."

"But what do you *think*?"

"You're being weird, but fine." Looking past my shoulder, she longingly eyes the lockbox on the shelf, and I'm afraid she'll look up and see the camera. I nudge sideways and block her view as she says, "I've heard some stuff. Let me guess. You're greasing the gears for a shot at another show?"

"The thought crossed my mind, but that's not entirely the reason, no. Just helping out, working on a little soul redemption. After Chelsea, I mean." It occurs to me that I've gotten exactly what I wished for earlier this morning. I haven't thought about Chelsea, the documentary, or Carla Hancock in hours.

You can't miss Lauren's eyeroll. It's the stuff of television legend, and part of her signature persona on *Weekend Report*. I'm on the receiving end of it as she says, "Whatever."

"It's true."

"Uh-huh. Anyway, what's it got to do with you and no guns?"

Here's where the full misdirection lie comes in: "One of the first official investigations I did was with this detective down in New Orleans"—I pronounce it *Naw'lins* to give it some authenticity—"and this guy, he was caught up in such a horrible case with this family. The dad was a drunk, the mom was on drugs. You make your own luck, yeah, but these people had gotten the shaft over and over. Turns out, one of their neighbors had died of—well, supposedly of an overdose, right there in their living room. Graybeal, the detective, wasn't convinced it was an accidental OD, so he brought me in to see if I could communicate with the dead neighbor's spirit. Long story short, the dad and mom both were so strung out when we got there for the investigation that they tried to attack us both. Graybeal ended up shooting the dad between the eyes right in front of me. Boom, bullet. Dead and done."

Lauren cringes and sucks air in through her teeth. "Jesus. That's sad."

"Yeah."

In true Lauren Coeburn fashion, the sympathy disappears, and she's right back to the story. "How come I never heard about this? Especially with *you* involved? Why wasn't that all over the national news?"

Oh, shit. Good point.

"Um, they swept it under the rug. Total cover up. You get that kind of treatment when..."

"When you're *you*?" She can't hide her snide incredulity. "You're a piece of work."

"Hey, I didn't ask for it, but yeah, since that day," I say, shaking my head with feigned remorse, "I don't want to be near a gun. That image is burned in my brain. The blood, the way his head rocked back. Gives me the shivers. You get that, right?"

Lauren lifts a shoulder, drops it with an exaggerated pout. "If you say so. No guns." She points past me with her chin. "Just in case, the combination is one, twenty-nine, seventy-four if you change your mind."

"Got it."

"And now you know when to send me something for my birthday. Don't forget it."

"Note taken."

Lauren steps over to the large bay window, surveys the outside, and says, "The anticipation is killing me."

I move over, floorboards creaking underneath my boots. "Tell me about it."

"I wish they'd get it over with. I hate waiting."

"You'd never make it as a paranormal investigator then. That's all we do. Hurry up and wait."

A strong rush of wind whips below the awning and across the porch, bringing with it the sharp pitter-patter of rain against the glass.

She uses her forefinger to trace the rivulets. They capture the distant light from the southern streetlamp, the nearest one that's shining, and refract it with shimmering color. "You have a plan?" Her voice sounds empty and flat.

"I hate to say it, but no, I don't. I've never had the chance to see these guys up close. The only thing I can think of—we wait and see what happens. Maybe we invite them in, ask what they want me for. Don't look at me like that. I already know it sounds stupid."

"Stupid? Those six letters don't do that idea justice."

"With a situation like this, I gotta trust my instincts when it happens."

Lauren watches the storm. She says, "I'm hungry. Can you find me some food?"

I look sideways at her, eyebrow raised. "Uh, sure, I guess. You'll take first watch?"

Peculiar request from her. However, she's in a peculiar situation, thinking about her safety, her grandmother's safety, while relying on a guy who might seriously consider pushing her in front of a moving train.

Not that I would, on a good day, but I'd say she had a legitimate reason to be acting weird.

Anyway, off I go into the kitchen. The dryer is humming back in a little alcove, accentuated by the *clink-chink* of the metal button on Lauren's jeans tumbling inside. It smells like fabric softener in here, remnants of past laundry exploits released with the current heat. A streetlight to the east shines through the kitchen window, giving me enough ambient light to see and move around. The linoleum under my feet crackles in spots. No black-eyed children are sneaking up on us from *this* direction.

Earlier, when I eased in through the back door, eyes alert, waiting on something to pounce, I hadn't noticed the half-eaten meals on the kitchen table. Sandwiches with small bites taken out of them sit next to glasses of dark, flat soda. The generic "cola" two-liter is off to the right, cap unscrewed.

They left in a hurry, apparently, which leads me to a question I had forgotten to ask earlier. With the black-eyed children right at the back door, and so close, how had Lauren gotten her nearly blind grandmother moving fast enough to make an easy escape? They left their uneaten meals behind, yeah, but had Lauren really stopped long enough to lock the front door behind them?

Acting out of habit? Afraid the black-eyed children would try to get inside while they were gone?

Sure. Maybe.

I need to ask her about that.

First, food.

In the refrigerator, I discover some leftover munchies, perfect items to whip together a makeshift picnic; a pack of sliced, dry salami, sliced havarti cheese, and an open bottle of Chardonnay go onto a serving tray conveniently stationed nearby on the counter. Crackers from the cabinet too, once I check the date and ensure they're not as old as Ellen.

Wine glasses. Can't forget those.

The Graveyard: Classified Paranormal Series

Napkins. Check.

Salami, cheese, and wine. You'd think we should be smack in the middle of Napa Valley, not setting up perfect appetizers for a night of paranormal frivolity.

I balance the tray on one hand, like back from my days waiting tables, and stroll into the front room where Lauren remains stationary at the window. "Tasty snacks for m'lady," I say, setting our mini-meal down on the coffee table.

Lauren has light in her eyes again. "Oh, yay," she squeals, clapping.

It's weird, you know? Like I don't feel as if either one of us is as scared as we should be, given what we're facing. Or what might be coming. Lauren seems to be swaying back and forth between normal and cautiously strange, and, I have to admit, there are a few molecules inside me that remain skeptical of her story.

That said, it catches me totally unaware when Lauren, mouth full of cheese and salami, asks me the scariest question I can think of:

"Are you ever going to get married again, Ford?"

16
Mike Long

We retreated to my place, and now I'm standing here in a confused daze.

By the time we got here, the kids had left for the Daltons' house, friends of ours who live up the street and also have an in-ground swimming pool with a diving board. Dayton and Ashley spend more time there than anywhere else—which is completely alien to me since they have an entire ocean to swim in mere feet away. Not that I care, it's just that sometimes I'm burdened by an adult's logic. Aren't we all? Most of us, anyway.

Toni gave me no jealousy-fueled argument about leaving again with Dakota, and in fact, she almost seemed excited by the idea that I'd be out of the house. She didn't even beg Dakota to hang around and take a tour of *Casa de Long*. She had on makeup, dangling earrings, and that skirt with the revealing slit up the side that I love so much, offering minimal details about a 'meeting' she was late for.

"You might see me designing for a new client," she'd said. "Wish me luck!"

Stranger still, Toni also kissed me goodbye when she left, which I'm sure was just an act in front of Dakota, and whisked herself out the front door in a flurry of perfume and dramatic flair. She called back over her shoulder, "The kids are going to spend the night at the Daltons, so take all the time you need. Be careful, Dakota!"

Then she was gone.

And now Dakota stands beside me in the living room, studying me with an arched eyebrow. "Evil Medusa, huh?"

I snort in disbelief. "I have no idea who that person was. Keeping up appearances for you, I guess."

"She doesn't seem so bad."

"Give it time."

"That skirt, though. I'm jealous of her legs, that's for sure."

"*What?* Don't even go there. You're—" I cut myself off. The conversation—my brain, rather—is heading down a playground slide coated in lard. I gotta stay on track. Dakota is attractive, yes, and I'm married—final word. Perhaps not *happily* married, but still, I have principles. I am *not* Ford. I'm a dedicated father and husband, not a cheating horndog.

I stammer something dismissive about her looking great, smile awkwardly, and make a hasty exit, telling her I'm going to put my paranormal equipment out in the garage, charge the batteries, and then we can go to the library for some research.

So, yeah, that entire interaction just now was like watching a crash-test dummy take a hit at sixty-five mph in slow motion.

What had poured water on the hot 'n' bothered flames of my once-stagnant libido was that black, floating-mist-spirit thing blatantly noting that I *want* Dakota. If I'm projecting enough of that energy for it to be picked up all the way in the goddamn afterlife… then I need to back the hell off.

Jus' sayin'.

What I really need right now is a hard workout—Old Faithful—to burn off some of this mental garbage. I need to go pick up heavy things and set them down, over and over, to wash my sins clean.

I check the wall clock and see that it's not much past eight-thirty in the morning. Best bet is, Ford's asleep out on the west coast. It'd be nice to ask him how he'd approach this scenario—the investigation, I mean, not about being Don Juan with Dakota—because he always had the best ideas. You know, theories, angles, or a way to come at the spirits that would elicit the best response. He was so amazing at assessing a situation, creating a scenario as if it were a movie or a play in his mind, figuring out how these people had lived, what motivated them, what would be best to use as a trigger object.

The one and only time he royally screwed up was with little Chelsea Hopper.

One unheeded warning—mine—sank an entire ship like a midnight iceberg.

***

Toni took the Audi, and that's cool by me. Dakota and I hop into the BMW sedan, my first true gift to ourselves when the show got renewed for a second season. I love this damn car—bangs, knocks, rattles, and all. Loveable warts that remind me daily of so many good memories. I'll drive this thing until the wheels fall off because there in the passenger side floorboard is the perpetual stain where Toni spilled an entire glass of red wine. Above Dakota, the cloth material is torn in a lightning shaped pattern, evidence of Toni's stiletto heel and a particularly adventuresome, uh, *event* a long time ago when money wasn't required as an aphrodisiac.

The buttons on the CD player have ancient crumbs wedged between them where Dayton tried to see what his PB&J would sound like. Behind me and in the seatback pocket, there's a miniature shovel that we brought back from the beach one afternoon a few years ago. We had no idea to whom it belonged, and none of the four of us had any clue where it came from. It simply showed up among our collection of toys.

General consensus, at least from my side of things, was that a ghost had been trying to get our attention that day. I never discovered a reason, and since spirits can get attached to objects, I brought it out here to the car rather than unleashing a spiritual stowaway on our brand new home back then.

I didn't have the heart to throw it in the trash, because it's a kid's toy, and, well, you know, child spirits tug on the heartstrings.

Over in the passenger seat, Dakota seems distant, distracted. It's muggy, but not quite air conditioner weather, so we have the windows down. Wisps of loose hair, somehow escaped from the Alcatraz of her hair band, drift around in the thirty-mph wind.

"Dakota?"

She turns to me.

"You okay?"

"Yeah, why?"

"I dunno. Seems like you left us there for a bit."

"Just thinking."

"About?"

"Mostly about how I got here. I mean, like, *here* here. It's funny, you know, how I just randomly decided one day to go audition for this new show because I was bored at my old job. I absolutely could not hang around and plate up my old chef's bland steak, his stupid, lumpy potatoes and his limp, soggy, disgusting salad. Not anymore. It wasn't what I went to culinary school for, and I was completely wasting my life. I got bored with a song and changed the station, right over to an ad for auditions on the radio.

"Instead of going to work, I made a left turn, and here I am. My life took an entirely different direction because I got bored with a song. That amazes me."

"You don't think you would've ended up here eventually?"

"Destiny? Could be. But the point is, I'm in a place where I have more money in the bank than I could have ever imagined, a humongous house on the beach—that happens to be haunted—and, honestly, I feel like such a first-world cliché. Beach house, nice cars, a few extra zeroes in my bank account... All great to have, yeah, but you saw my kitchen. I'm eating burgers and fries, pizza. I'm not even cooking anymore. I haven't in *weeks*, and I feel like I've lost sight of doing what I loved."

"And this just hit you now?"

"Earlier. Something clicked, maybe after you mentioned Toni wasn't happy after the paychecks stopped coming. God, if I ever got to that point, shoot me. I'd rather a hurricane come through and wash this all away than let money rule my world."

My stomach flutters with pride and admiration.

Same team, Dakota and me. It's like she's been reading my mind.

She puts her head down into her hands, takes a deep breath, and says, "Ignore me. I shouldn't be unloading on you like this. It's just that I haven't talked to anybody about something other than food or fame in so long."

"No, I get it, definitely. And *unloading*? Please. It's a conversation. It's how normal people interact." I hesitate to tell her that I've been feeling the same way about wanting to wipe the proverbial slate clean. That's too close to the sun, Icarus. Save that conversation for some other time, like when she's not in soul-baring mode. "Really," I tell her. "It's no big deal."

"This is crazy. Cray-zeeeee. Poor, poor pitiful me, right? My multi-million dollar beachfront mansion is haunted. I literally sound like I should be on your show."

"Yep. You'd make a perfect season finale."

"It's… Jesus, Mike, it's been exhausting. I've barely slept, I'm eating like shit, and the only thing that's keeping me sane is exercising."

True dat, sister. "It's a good thing. At least you're doing that."

Dakota sits up straighter in her seat, like she's pouncing on an idea as she slaps her lean thighs. "Fuck it. You know what? I need to cook something. Let me cook you dinner tonight."

"You'd do that?"

"If you don't think your wife would care, yeah. It'll be the most gourmet home-cooked meal you've ever had. That's how I can pay you back! Does that sound good? Gourmet meal from the multi-season, not-humble-at-all winner of *Yes, Chef!*? Would that work for you? In exchange for bug-zapping the bad guys?"

Have I died and gone to heaven? Funny, it looks more like the inside of a BMW than I thought it would. "Abso-freakin-lutely. Are you kidding me? I've literally daydreamed about that, like, five thousand times. Deal." Then, reluctantly, I have to address the situation because the smart, yet tentative, side of my brain understands that if this happens without Toni and the kids along, my bed for the next, oh, century or two, would consist of the rickety Adirondack chairs on our deck. I'd take up permanence residence in the doghouse.

I tell Dakota, "I have to invite Toni, though. She'd stab me with a butter knife in my sleep. A dull butter knife because it'd hurt more."

"Sure, sure," Dakota says, not entirely hiding the flicker of disappointment I can hear in her voice. "Of course they can come."

"Come? Oh, you mean do it at your house?"

"That's where all my supplies are."

I chuckle. "Don't get me wrong, I'd love to, but I don't want you to be under any kind of impression that all we have to do is say a few magic words and your house is footloose and demon-free. There's a chance it could take a while."

"I know." This comes with a narrowed glare that insinuates, *dipshit.*

"And you *still* want to do it?"

"Yes," she says, matter-of-factly. "That's the whole idea. A big fat middle finger to that jackass in my house. I'd like to take my life back."

"Okay. Sure."

"You don't sound so sure."

I lift one shoulder. "I'm not, to tell you the truth. This shit is *dangerous.* If we're focused on anything other than this floater, we could be in trouble. It takes time, and patience, and a lot of in-depth concentration, especially if it's malevolent. Technically, I shouldn't even have you around the house, it's that risky. You could get possessed. You could be scratched, attacked… anything. As much as I'd love to eat one of your meals, time is a limiting factor here."

"Mike?" She grins.

"What?"

"You do remember the format of the show, don't you? Cook the perfect dish in forty-five minutes or less?"

"Right, but—"

"And who was the champion three years in a row?"

"You, but—"

"No more buts. We got this. You and me. And your wife, and your kids, and a ghost, and, hell, invite the whole neighborhood. Bottom line is, I feel safer with you there, and I need this little win. Does that make sense?"

"Oh, I get it, but I'm not bringing my kids to your house. And Toni"—I can't believe Boy Scout Mike is actually going to say this—"what she doesn't know won't hurt her."

"So just us then?"

"Yep. Ghost hunting on a full tummy. No better way."

"Now you're talking."

I turn left, changing streets. The trees are green and lush this time of year. They sway in the breeze, casting early morning shadows on the squat buildings on either side of us; the surf shops and crab shacks, the banks and drive-through beer stations, they're peacefully empty. The real crowds are at the restaurants where the tourists are filling up on pancakes and good southern grits before heading out to the beach to get bad sunburns and drink one six pack after another.

It's a beautiful morning, really, and I have a crazy lady sitting beside me.

Determined, but crazy.

I like it.

This might be one of my most favorite investigations ever.

Tonight will be a good night.

What could go wrong?

17
Ford Atticus Ford

Lauren takes a sip of her wine, staring at me over the rim with a hint of smug satisfaction in her gaze.

I cough and sputter a barrage of *ums* and *uhs* like I'm firing them from a Gatlin gun, then finally manage to squeak, "Married again? Me?"

"Why not?"

"I—it's complicated."

"You're not a Facebook status, Ford. Give me words."

I fill up my wine glass and drain most of the chardonnay before I reply, "Tell me why you're asking."

"I don't know. Just curious. I heard about your, uh, issues. With your ex, I mean."

"Oh you did, huh? Issues? Like what?" Obviously, I know exactly what she means and my past infidelity problems weren't really a well-kept secret, considering loose lips are great for making out and sinking ships. Tabloid fodder, I was.

Given the troubles with Chelsea *and* my infidelity, I'm surprised people didn't throw rotten vegetables at me in the streets.

"You know exactly what I'm talking about. I've seen your ex, dude. She's gorgeous. What were you thinking?"

"As if I was thinking at all?"

"Good point."

"I have a lot of soul redemption that needs to happen for reasons other than Chelsea Hopper."

"At least you're owning up to the fact. And, I'll admit, you sound reasonably sincere."

"I am," I insist. "I was an idiot."

"Is that on the record?"

"Coeburn—"

"Relax, Ford. Kidding. Besides, it's kinda refreshing."

"My dad always told me that honesty is like a sugar-coated razor blade, real sweet until it cuts you deep."

"Smart man." Lauren moves away from the bay window and over to the couch. She sits, picks up a cracker, and studies it before putting it back on the tray. Can't risk the extra carbs, I suppose. "So what made you do it?"

"It?"

"Cheat."

I turn my focus back to the rainy world outside. The feeling that this entire shitstorm is a setup comes hurtling back, and I'm now positive that I'm on some kind of interview. I'm severely tempted to go exploring for the digital voice recorder that she probably has stashed behind a throw pillow. "Coeburn, am I gonna end up on your show again, or are we here to hunt some fucking paranormal shit?"

"We're talking. That's it. You said you didn't know how long we'd have to wait, so here we are. Old friends telling stories."

"Why aren't you acting more scared?"

"Of course I'm scared."

"That's not what I asked. I swear, if you're setting me up—"

"Setting you up? For what?"

"Asking me about marriage, cheating on Melanie. Feels to me like you're trying to get a scoop."

"Jesus H., Ford. Stop with the paranoid bullshit," she says, eyebrows pinched together as she slaps an arm of the couch. Her offense seems genuine. Then again, everyone in Hollywood is an actor, so…

"*Really*," she insists.

"Then don't be so glib when we have some of the least-researched paranormal beings out there stalking us. I have no earthly clue what we're getting ourselves into."

"Look at me."

I feel exposed with my back facing the window, but I look anyway. Lauren pats the couch beside her, saying, "Yes, I'm freaked out. You're here though, so it's not that bad. I trust you."

"You probably shouldn't. The last time someone trusted me, I lost my show, my friends, and my life."

"Fuck that albatross around your neck. Let it go."

"I can't—"

"*For now*. Forget it, just come sit. We'll have some wine, and we'll wait."

I glance down at the empty glass in my shaky hand, the chardonnay's finish sitting sharp and tangy on the back of my tongue. "I shouldn't be drinking anyway. Dangerous to go up against something nasty when you have dulled senses."

I'm partly talking about her, partly talking about the black-eyed children.

"The doors are locked, right? Front door, back door? Garage? Nobody is getting in here. And besides, didn't you say we would actually have to invite them in before they could come inside? It's just the two of us hanging out. *Mano a womano*, if that's a thing."

"That's not exactly what it means, unless we're in direct conflict."

"Then it seems about right to me."

I'm pretty damn sure this is an attempt at an interview now.

Ass.

Hole.

Both of us, actually, because I fell for it. When will I ever learn?

Moron.

I tell her, "We have to be insanely careful. Most of the evidence we have is anecdotal. Pure hearsay."

"Whatever. The doors are locked. Come sit. Tell me more about the almighty Ford Atticus Ford while we wait."

"You are *relentless*."

"Nervous, actually. I get chatty and excitable when I'm on edge. Talking helps. Why do you think I do it for a living? I'm never more anxious than when I'm in front of a camera filming, and yet it's when I'm on top of the world."

"Funny thing." I know precisely what she means, and I'm not going to admit it to her. I don't want her to sink her claws into some flimsy psychological bond we might share.

I pour myself another splash of wine and plop down on the couch beside her, then get an idea.

I might as well get *her* drunk, throw off her game, and then make my escape.

Sometimes I'm a genius.

Sorta.

"More?" I ask, holding up the bottle.

"Absolutely." Lauren holds out her glass, and I listen to the *glug-glug* of a heavy pour. "Whoa, cowboy," she says.

I lean back against the soft cushions of Ellen's ancient couch. This is what I love about old furniture—the fact that it's broken in. Just when you get used to something, get it right to where you want it, it's time to throw it away.

Reminds me of *Graveyard: Classified*. I've always wondered if I didn't somehow subliminally self-sabotage my life when my screw-up happened. Maybe it was my brain trying to tell me it was bored with the routine and needed to shake something up.

Yeah. You just keep telling yourself that, Ford. Shattering ratings and sealing your place in television history didn't have *anything* to do with it, did it?

Lauren wiggles around sideways on the couch and pulls her legs up in a criss-cross position, getting cozy.

It's strange, her vibe. Her level of familiarity feels like we're maybe somewhere between the third and fifth date, and this is the precursor to the first time. Meaning, that fumbling, awkward, pathetic attempt at whoopee when you have yet to uncover the other's natural rhythms, favorite positions, or hot spots.

Feels like it. Ain't happening.

The reality is, this is probably the interview right here.

There should be lights and cameras strategically placed around the living room. We're supposed to pretend as if we're simply relaxing like two old friends while she grills me about my love life and what the *real* Ford Atticus Ford does in his downtime.

Lauren says, "So. Marriage? Again? Ever?"

I close my eyes and gently press on my temples. Deep breath in, deep breath out. I might as well get this over with, at least until she passes out, and I can sneak away. "I don't know, honestly. I had my time with Melanie, and I screwed it up. I'm— maybe I'm afraid I won't ever be able to handle monogamy."

Which is a total lie, but it plays into what Lauren is looking for in her "scoop."

The low-down dirty of it all.

"What made you do it?"

"You tell me. What makes anyone stray?"

"Boredom. Lack of respect. Sex addiction?"

"Are you asking that about me?"

"Maybe?"

She allows a slight *gotcha* grin to slip through when I lie and say, "Oh, definitely. I couldn't keep it in my pants. I was horrible."

"That poor girl."

"She's fine now, though. Probably the best thing she could've done was to get away from the likes of me."

"Oh, stop. You're not so bad."

"More wine?" I ask, hoping to change the subject. Melanie isn't someone I want to be thinking about right now.

Why?

Hurts too much.

After Mike got my hopes up, and she used a pin to pop my hope bubble once I got back home from the Craghorn case, I have yet to get over it. I could've taken a monster step toward redemption, and then, *whoosh*, there went the rug, right out from under my feet.

Lauren looks down at her glass. She's only taken a couple of sips so far. "I'll have a little more, sure." I refill it, and then before she takes another sip, she asks, "Here's something I've always wanted to know, Ford."

I hold up my palm. "If it's about Chelsea and my reasoning, that's off the table. I don't have any new responses to that question."

"No, no. I wasn't going to. The ratings and fame were obvious motivators."

"Then what?"

"In all those years doing *Graveyard*, did you ever actually get scared?"

"Hell yeah, all the time."

"Like pee your pants scared?"

"I might've dribbled a time or two."

"Gross."

"You asked."

Lauren leans back against the armrest both hands cradled around her chardonnay held close to her chest. "If that's the case, then here's what I *really* want to know. If you got scared, if you dribbled pee-pee into your panties like a big boy, then why the fuck did you constantly tell those families that they had nothing to worry about, that whatever was in their home couldn't hurt them?"

She's pointed out something that always bothered me, too. I *had* to do it. The data from The Paranormal Channel's test audiences suggested that the viewers loved seeing that our clients were going to be fine once the white knights rode out on their equally white horses.

That's not something I want Lauren to know. It's too much juicy insider info that'll make its way out onto the Internet. Instead, I say, "Because more often than not, they *were* fine. If somebody's grandma passes away—take Ellen, for instance—if she steps over to the other side but sticks around to haunt this place, it might be freaky at first, but you'd get used to it, and you'd understand that she wasn't going to do anything to harm you. Maybe the spirits were too weak to do anything physical and *yes*, the families would be okay."

"But what if they weren't? What if it was one of the times where you really were scared shitless? I watched *Graveyard* constantly—I had to, because you were such good fodder for *Weekend Report*—and yet, I can't ever remember an instance where you told some terrified family, 'Hey, you need to pack your shit and get the fuck outta Dodge.'"

"True, but at the same time, you're forgetting that faith is a powerful weapon."

"Don't feed me that bullshit, honey. I know better. If *you* were scared, the greatest ghost hunter who ever lived, then yeah, those people had every right to know that they were in extremely real danger."

I break away from her gaze and study the loose button on the couch cushion beside me.

"I think, maybe, *that* might've been one of the reasons I was so hard on you when *Weekend* ran that piece. I'd been holding onto a lot of this, I don't know, distant anger. Like you deserved what you got because you weren't always this bastion of good vibes. Don't shake your head. You know what I'm talking about. The Keenes, the Richards family with the lighthouse, those poor nuns down in New Mexico."

"Good memory." That's a partial list of investigations where I was definitely scared out of my mind. Guess I conveyed more than I intended during filming.

"I saw the look in your eyes in each one of those episodes, then you sat right there and told them they had nothing to worry about. Then Chelsea happened, and I… It pushed me over the edge. I wanted to hurt you."

"You succeeded."

"Truth time. I mean, yeah, the producers pushed me toward it, but it was mostly me. I felt like, a couple of years ago, if karma's a bitch," she says, holding out her hand to shake, "then hi, nice to meet you. I'm Karma."

"You should write bumper stickers."

"It wasn't right of me. Who the hell am I to judge? I'm no better, am I? I rip people a new one every single weekend. So,

I'm trying to say I'm sorry." I mumble a slight acknowledgement, and she adds, "I'm serious. I took it too far."

"And so did I. Producers. Ratings. Contracts. I've been there."

"Still doesn't make your disinformation the right thing to do. Anyway. You know what they say about hindsight." She gulps the last of her chardonnay and motions for the bottle. Instead of refilling the glass, she squeezes it around the neck, brings it to her lips, and tilts her head back. She wipes her mouth clumsily. The alcohol's effects are creeping up on her like dusk on a slow afternoon. "I didn't need to be so hard on you. You already had enough of that shit from everyone else. I could make amends somehow."

I let the silence stretch out a bit, since I don't know how to respond to that.

Outside, the ocean wind howls under the eaves. Rain drives through the hazy glow of a single street light, sheet after sheet.

Lauren slides her foot across the middle couch cushion, puts it against my thigh, and uses her wiggling toes to get my attention. "One other thing I always wanted to know."

I scoot to the side, moving my leg just out of her reach. "What's that?"

"Say you're a husband and wife on an episode of *Graveyard*. If you're absolutely positive your house is haunted, how would you ever have sex in it without feeling like some pervert ghost is watching you? What if he's off in the corner cranking one out while you get busy? How do people do that?"

During our decade of investigations, the question always plagued me, too. I'd never been brazen enough to ask. It always seemed too personal. "I dunno," I tell her. "Maybe in the heat of the moment, you forget?"

"You *forget*?"

"Best I got."

She turns the bottle up, spills a little out the sides of her mouth, then wipes her lips with a hoodie sleeve. "Maybe you learn to be an exhibitionist," she says, numbly looking around the living room. "This place is haunted. Did I mention that?"

"Who's here?"

"My great uncle Gabe lived here for a few years and then died of a heart attack. It has to be him. I can smell his tobacco."

And then something clicks. At first, it was a flicker in the back of my mind, like an EVP from a weakened spirit many planes of existence away, back when she put her delicate toes up against my thigh.

I could make amends.

How do people have sex when a house is haunted?

This place is haunted.

I shove up from the couch, slamming my knee against the coffee table, and stumble to the side. "Sorry, I can't."

"Can't what?"

"Are you kidding me with this? You're trying to *seduce* me?"

"I—*seduce* you?"

"Is this some kind of long con, Coeburn? You come to me with a sob story about your blind grandma and these black-eyed kids because you knew that'd get my attention, and then what? Bring me back here, bump uglies? You show me a good time, and I finally cave? Nope. The afterglow is a myth! And Ellen probably isn't even blind, is she?"

Incredulous, Lauren shoots up from the couch and says, "They were *real*, Ford. They were here. And I came to you for help." She marches over to me, slams a finger into my breastbone, one, two, three times, accentuating each word. "We. Needed. Help."

She crosses her arms. "And I'm not trying to get you into bed." The quiver in her voice betrays her anger. "I just needed you to let me in. I needed you to feed me with—with your soul."

I feel like I'm on some paranormal soap opera. "Oh, God. Gag me, please," I say, flinging my hands into the air. "You've got an hour. If those little bastards don't show up by then, I'm gone, and you're on your own." I spin on my heels and stomp down the hall.

"Where are you going?"

"To take a piss, if that's okay with you."

I jerk the bathroom door open, step inside, and slam it closed behind me.

The small window above the bathtub is open. Flecks of rain flitter inside, carried on wind that shoulders up against the solid shower curtain, billowing the looser folds of purple cloth, and then I remember, I didn't check in here earlier. I had been too busy trying to get the ancient camcorder set up.

I'm sure it's fine.

Next to "Hey, y'all, watch this!" I'm certain that "I'm sure it's fine" ranks high on the list of famous last words.

18
Chelsea Hopper

The Graveyard: Classified Paranormal Series

Chelsea opens her eyes, having dreamed of claws and fangs. Darkness and the scent of rotten eggs. Always the same.

She hears the scrabble of sharp nails on a hard surface, and for a moment, she believes that her nightmares may have become reality. She gasps and blinks hard, once, twice, and then shakes her head, finally taking stock of her surroundings. She's in her classroom at school and the noise is Mrs. Hill scribbling on the chalkboard.

Chelsea squints at the writing, manages to make out something about 1492 and Columbus. She needs glasses but hasn't told anyone, doesn't want anyone to know she has a weakness. Her parents have told her she's strong for so long now, it's second nature. She's the girl who bears the scars of a demon's hand. That makes her legendary, according to the magazine her mother showed her, and legendary people aren't weak. At least she thinks they aren't.

It also makes her a target to some of the kids her age—not only in her class, but in her entire school. She would be okay if it were only the couple of boys sitting across the room—Logan and Dylan—who pick on her, but there are more of them. Everywhere. All day.

In the hall. At lunch. At recess. In the restroom.

If it weren't for her best friend Tania, who stands a head taller than everyone else, Chelsea would have ran away long ago.

Tania is fun. Tania is nice to her.

Tania can punch harder than the older boys when it's necessary.

Tania protects her when she can, but she can't always be there.

Chelsea hears a hushed whisper to her right.

"Earth to spacegirl. Wake up."

Chelsea takes her eyes away from the board and sees Tania's welcoming smile. Tania, with her dark skin, her curly hair, and teeth whiter than bleached sheets; she's a guardian angel. The sight of her relaxes Chelsea.

She's had the dreams for ages now, but never at school, never in the middle of the day. And still, when Tania playfully sticks out her tongue, Chelsea knows that she won't need to check her reflection in the bathroom for fangs and horns. She won't need to pull open the front of her jeans and check for demon boy parts.

Chelsea's grandmother loves Tania, calls her, "The safest port in Chelsea's storm."

Chelsea isn't sure what that means. She just likes the sound of it.

From the front of the room, up near the chalkboard, Mrs. Hill says, "Ladies? Attention, please."

Chelsea and Tania say, "Yes, ma'am," in unison, then giggle when they both whisper, "Jinx, Pepsi!" at the same time too.

As soon as Mrs. Hill returns to scribbling the white letters on the chalkboard, something hard slams into the side of Chelsea's head. She shouts, "Ouch!" as a small rock bounces across her desk and tumbles to the floor. To Chelsea's right, Dylan and Logan snicker, trying desperately to contain their laughter.

Mrs. Hill snaps around as Chelsea rubs her head. When she pulls her hand away, she sees fresh, slick blood on her fingertips.

Mrs. Hill says, "That's it, Chelsea. Out."

"But I didn't do any—"

"Out!" Mrs. Hill points at the classroom door. "*Out*, I said. Take the empty desk into the hallway."

"I'm *bleeding*. They hit me with a rock."

"And what did you do to provoke them?"

"Nothing! They're being mean!"

Tania shouts, "She didn't do anything!"

"Quiet, or you're out, too. You know the rules, Tania. One more detention means you're suspended, and if I were you, I'd think long and hard about my next words."

Tania lowers her head, mutters, "It's not her fault," under her breath, then goes silent.

"Well, Miss Hopper? I'm waiting."

Mrs. Hill is older than Tyrannosaurus Rex. All the kids say so. She's mean, too. She's never been on Chelsea's side, thinks she's a little girl that uses her fame for special treatment. At least that's what her parents say about her. They tried, many, many times to get her into a new classroom, but that would mean leaving Tania behind. Besides, Principle Cage said no anyway, refusing to give her any kind of special treatment.

Mrs. Hill raises her index finger. "I'm going to count to three. Take the empty desk into the hall, then go see Nurse Miller. Come back when you're patched up, sit in the punishment desk, and we'll discuss this later with Principle Cage. If you're finished with being the center of attention, *go*. One, two…"

Chelsea stands, feeling blood trickle down the side of her scalp. "Wait until I tell my parents," she says, then darts for the door when Mrs. Hill glares at her, cheeks flushed with anger. Chelsea yanks the "Bad Chair" with her, not caring when the legs screech across the tile.

Behind her, Mrs. Hill slams the door closed, the tiny square windows rattling in the center.

Chelsea shoves the empty desk up against the beige-tiled wall and marches toward the nurse's office. She pulls her arms up, cradling herself, trying to hold back the inevitable tears, refusing to touch the blood trickling along her neck.

Her sneakers squeak on the freshly waxed black tiles. They sound like the screams of a dying bird.

At least she gets to see Nurse Miller, who is friendly and treats Chelsea like the normal child she should be, instead of the celebrity that everyone thinks she is.

Nurse Miller says, "Come in!" when Chelsea knocks.

She steps inside, bottom lip protruding, shuddering, barely holding back the emotional dam, the cracks growing wider with each tear that leaks out.

It splinters and explodes when Nurse Miller looks at her with pity and tender concern, asking, "Oh, honey, what happened?"

Chelsea balls up her fists and rubs her eyes through the heaving sobs. She pushes broken words out. "She's so mean. They all are. I hate it here."

Nurse Miller is impossibly tall, and to Chelsea, it seems like days pass before the nurse bends all the way down and puts a hand on her cheek. "I know, sweetheart. I know. Let me look at you." She nudges Chelsea lightly to her left and clucks her tongue, shaking her head, as she lifts the soft blonde hair and examines the wound.

"Is it bad?" Chelsea asks. "Somebody threw a rock and Mrs. Hill blamed me." *Me* slides out in a helpless squeak.

"I know, honey. I know."

I know. That's what she always says. Chelsea has lost count of how many times she's been to see Nurse Miller, and even though she's pretty and nice, and as tall as an NBA basketball player, Chelsea expects to hear, "I know, honey. I know."

But at least it's comforting. At least she sounds like she cares.

She asks Chelsea to sit down.

The Graveyard: Classified Paranormal Series

The chair is cold against Chelsea's legs. She tugs at her shorts, trying to make them longer. She sniffles and wipes her nose, then pushes leftover tears from her cheeks.

Nurse Miller asks Chelsea to be still while she cleans and bandages the wound, but it's hard.

It hurts. Chelsea has to pee. She wants to run as far away as she can. She wants to burst back into her classroom, grab Tania's soft, plump hand, and run.

Run as hard as they can down Parker Street, where they would go right onto Larder Road, the one with all the beautiful maples trees along the sidewalk. The leaves are a gorgeous green now, and in the fall, they'll be full of amazing oranges and reds. She pays attention to the colors around her now more than she used to. That man, the therapist, the smelly one who made her uncomfortable—if he had any good ideas, any at all, it was suggesting that Chelsea should learn how to paint. He had said it would quiet her mind and "give her a creative outlet," whatever that meant.

Thankfully, her parents loved the idea, and that day, they bought her an easel and paints, brushes and a smock that made her feel like an official artist. They bought her some DVDs, too. It was an entire series about painting pretty landscapes by some guy with hair like Tania's. Big, curly, and bushy, like a poofy ball on the top of his head.

Chelsea loves watching the videos nearly as much as painting. He seems like a loving, calm soul, with his lilting voice that caresses the very air that his words cross. He seems at peace, unlike Chelsea, and first she would sit for hours watching the masterpieces he created with a simple flick of his wrist and a daub of his sponge. It seemed so easy. Chelsea was sure she could do it.

Her first attempt looked like somebody had dipped two angry cats in paint and then let them roll around and fight all over a canvas. It was so horrible, she almost gave up right there. *You'll get it*, her parents had said. *It takes time. Practice!*

And she did. She kept going. Not because her parents said so, but because for the first time—ever, probably—she felt like her world was as it should be. No demon claws, no haunted house, no children picking on her for being on television before.

Lost in her memories, she's snatched back to the present with a wince as Nurse Miller touches her scalp with a stinging cotton ball. She jerks away.

"Hold still. One second, sweetheart. You don't need stitches, but it's a pretty nasty cut. Honestly, I can't believe that Mrs.—never mind. It's not my place."

"Tell me," Chelsea pleads.

Nurse Miller is silent for a long time, dabbing at the cut, pushing Chelsea's hair out of the way, and breathing hard through her nose. Finally, she says, "Do you know what secrets are, honey?"

Chelsea almost giggles. What a silly question. "Uh…yeah? *Duh.*"

Nurse Miller *does* chuckle. "I know you know. Just checking. I shouldn't even be telling you this—Chelsea, listen to my words, please."

Chelsea sees that familiar look of pity in the nurse's eyes, along with something extra in her gaze. Anger, it feels like, and she hopes that the nurse doesn't think she did something wrong, too.

"Pinky swear me," Nurse Miller says.

"Okay." Her tiny finger is swallowed by the massive pinky. It's fleshy and comforting.

"You may not—really, I can't believe I'm telling you this. This is *our* absolute secret, okay? Remember you pinky swore."

Chelsea fakes a serious sigh. "Okay, sheesh. I promise and you can break my pinky if I tell."

Nurse Miller inhales deeply and lets her shoulders slump. Chelsea smells old coffee on her breath, but that's fine. It's a comforting scent, like when her dad kisses her before he leaves for work each morning. "Here goes. The only thing I'll say is, you may not have to put up with Mrs. Hill for much longer. There have been plenty of...*complaints*. That's it. Lock it up, throw away the key."

Chelsea jumps up from her chair, feeling the skin of her scalp pull against her small bandage. It hurts, and yet, she's so excited, it doesn't matter. This is like a birthday and Christmas all coming together at once. "Holy cow! Really?"

Nurse Miller tries, unsuccessfully, to hide a smile. She stands, going up and up, higher and higher, like a construction crane towering a hundred feet over the ground, like the one Chelsea saw downtown last week. The smile remains even though she pretends to sternly shake a finger. "Not a word, you understand? I'll have that pinky mounted on my wall."

"Yes, ma'am!" Chelsea salutes her. It seems like the right thing to do.

"Not even your parents, and I'll probably regret that I ever said anything. You needed some good news, huh? Everybody does once in a—"

Beside them, the door to the small infirmary slams open with enough force to shake the boxes of bandages and bottles on the nearby shelves.

Mrs. Hill storms inside, her bony, claw-like hand gripped tightly around Tania's arm. Chelsea gasps when she sees so much blood coming from her friend's nose.

"This one," Mrs. Hill says between clenched teeth, shoving Tania forward. "Her, too. As soon as they're both cleaned up, send them straight to Cage's office. Never seen such lack of respect." Mrs. Hill flings her arms in the air and swishes out the door, her black skirt fluttering as she goes.

Tania smiles, showing off her blood-stained front teeth. "I got them both for you," she says. "I got them *good*."

It's nice, what Tania did for her, but look at what those boys did to her friend.

Chelsea thinks about the dark creature in her dreams, and almost wishes it wasn't a nightmare.

She might ask it for help.

Just this once.

The Graveyard: Classified Paranormal Series

19
Mike Long

The exterior of the library is insanely quiet, which seems off to me, and like a hilarious summer-movie pratfall, I walk straight into the sliding glass doors that don't open on my approach.

I stumble to the side, momentarily dazed and confused. "What the hell?"

Dakota asks me if I'm hurt, then breaks into a grin that she had no chance of hiding. She chuckles and puts her hand over those perfectly lush lips and stunning white teeth. I have to laugh too because, of course, I hadn't been paying attention, instead choosing to focus on my lovely cohort.

Glancing down, I note the small sign indicating the library won't open for another hour.

"What? Not until ten?"

"Maybe they think people don't read early?"

I cup my hands around my eyes and try to peer through the tinted glass doors. "I see someone in there already. Is he working?" A thin guy with horn-rimmed spectacles—really, you can't call them anything else than that archaic term—walks by pushing a cart full of books, I.D. lanyard dangling from his neck. He looks over and sees us, offering an apologetic frown as he taps his wrist, then holds up both hands, fingers splayed.

He mouths, *Sorry, ten o'clock.*

I back away from the glass doors and wipe a thin layer of sweat from my forehead. "Well, shit. What now? You hungry? Grab a bite while we wait? There's an awesome greasy spoon diner a couple blocks that way—"

Before I can finish, I hear the clatter of keys against glass, followed by the fat, fumbling, metallic clunk of a lock tumbler. Horn Rims is eagerly trying to get the lock open, smiling at us, telling us to hang on like he thinks we're going to run away from him. "Just one sec," he says, his voice muffled by the doors.

"Changed your mind, huh?" Dakota asks him.

Horn Rims gets the latch free and worms his fingers into the crevasse between the doors, grunting as he shoves them fully open. "Oh my gosh! You gotta be kidding me. Sorry about that. If I had recognized who you were I would've come over right away but I couldn't see with the shadows and the—never mind. *Mike Long* and *Dakota Bailey*? Together? *Here*? I don't even know... I'm Preston. And you're Mike. And you're Dakota. Wow, I'd heard people say that you guys lived here in town but—wow. Sorry, I'm Preston. Did I say that already? I'm babbling. Babbling Preston. I mean, yeah, I'll shut up now. Wow."

Dakota flashes the sparkling smile that charmed America for three seasons, steps forward, and extends a hand to shake. "Hi, Preston. Nice to meet you."

He reaches for her hand and halts like it ran into an invisible forcefield. "Wait, can I give you a hug? Sorry, it's just that I've always wanted to do that. Is that weird? It's weird, isn't it?"

This guy is too much, in an amusing way, of course. It's been a long damn time since I've seen this level of fandom gone wild.

Chuckling, Dakota says, "Sure, why the hell not? Bring it on, dude!"

And it makes me adore her all the more.

Babbling Preston dives in and squeezes her tightly, saying, "My friends will never believe this." Chin on her shoulder, he glances over at me with expectant eyes and a knowing grin. "I'm coming for you next, big guy."

"Right. Arms open wide, chief." Might as well. You gotta be good to the evangelists like this, the ones who will tell a thousand people on Facebook and Twitter about how amazing you are in person.

Preston lets go of Dakota and leaps over to me, wrapping one arm up over a shoulder, and the other around my side and back. Total "bro hug." We slap each other on the back like old friends, and I'm already thinking about how I need to come down to the library for some promo if I can talk Ford into the documentary.

Always thinking, always on.

Anyway—setting my dreams of a bank account in the black to the side—it's cool that Preston has so much enthusiasm. I really do miss it.

He steps back from us, hands at his waist, huffing from the excitement. "Wow. So cool. What can I do for you? Did you guys want to come in early?"

I have this thing where I'm always worried that I'm on the verge of inconveniencing a total stranger, so I wave him off, tell him he doesn't have to do that for us just because we're, well, *us*.

That gets me a hearty *pshaw*, like I'm being utterly ridiculous, and we find ourselves following him inside before I have a chance to protest again. He squirms around us to shove the glass doors closed under his own power and secures the lock once more.

After a couple more rounds of assuring us that we're not going to get him in trouble, we learn that he's the only one here, and he'd be thrilled to give us a tour or help us find something if we need it.

"But can I just ask something first? Be totally nosy for a second?"

Dakota says, "Sure," before I can hedge the discussion with subtle misinformation.

"What're you guys doing here? I mean, like, together?" He must recognize the squint I'm giving him as a sign that this is probably too far over the line. "No, no. I don't mean *together*. I just meant, like, do celebrities hang out with each other all the time? You know, because you don't really have anything in common with the little people?"

Dakota says with measured amusement, "We're not too far from common ourselves. It just so happens that I'm having some—what would you call it, Mr. Long? Ghostly...*troubles*?"

Ah, shit. That's exactly what I didn't want her to say.

Preston's eyes can't possibly get any wider. "Holy crap! Really? That's like a season finale episode of *Graveyard*. Or maybe some sort of crossover episode on *Yes, Chef!*, like you would have to cook a masterpiece while you were terrified of the spirits in your house. How cool is that?"

I raise an eyebrow at Dakota. "Sound familiar?"

She nods. "You should make him a producer."

Before Preston can explode into an excitable mist of giddy glee, I ask him about public property records or if those microfiche things still exist so we can do some research on Dakota's house, past occurrences there and the like.

Sometimes fate, chance, or luck smiles down upon you, while a choir of heavenly angels sing a tune so sweet that you can't help but feel like the universe is blatantly moving the chess pieces around for you.

Preston's entire demeanor changes. His smile droops. His hands go to his hips. He briefly checks the first floor, and it makes me wonder what he's looking for, considering the fact that we're supposed to be the only three in here. He lowers his voice and says, "To answer your question, public property records—you might need to go to the courthouse to find what you're looking for. Probably? Microfiche, yeah, but can I make a confession first?" He waits until I nod assent. "Don't think I'm a creepy weirdo, okay? That was—I mean, I know who you guys are. I was trying not to be an obsessive stalker fan or anything."

So that was just an act? Damn, he's good. Dude has a career waiting for him in the theater.

Preston continues, "It's not like we were spying on you."

"We?" I ask.

"A friend of mine thought he saw Dakota moving into Damon Healy's old beach house." He turns to her. "Is that true?"

Dakota doesn't hesitate to tell him it is—though I wish she would've—and she adds that she hasn't been there long. "You're not creepy," she reassures him. "I'm not keeping it much of a secret."

Preston says, "That place is bad news, and I've been wondering how long it would take before someone showed up here. After Healy sold it, I mean. Never in a million years did I think both of *you* would. You're *here*. You're actually here. What are the odds?"

"Given the fact that you work at one of two places where people go to dig up local history, I'd say they're not that astronomical." I wink to let him know I'm just yanking is chain.

"Good point. What I meant was, what are the odds that I know something you'll want to hear?"

"Higher, but when you've been balls deep in the paranormal for as long as I have, coincidences are a permanent part of the equation."

"True."

"If you expected us, then why didn't you come looking for me, specifically?"

"It's not the kind of thing I'm willing to broadcast."

"What changed your mind now?"

"I'll get to that." Preston pushes his horn rims up where they rest on top of his skull like a headband, holding his curly mop back out of his face. His eyes dart left and right as the corners of his mouth lift. It's completely a look that suggests, *I have a secret to share*, and, *Wait until you get a load of this*.

We're the only ones in the library. Half of the lights are off, and while it's filled to the ceiling with books, computers, magazines, without the hullaballoo of readers marching to and fro, it feels empty and hollow. And yet, he lowers his voice further, barely audible, whispering, "You ready to hear some crazy shit?"

***

Preston made sure all the doors were securely locked before he led us upstairs to the second floor, turned left, and practically scampered behind a shelf of young adult books, leading us at a brisk pace toward the northwestern corner. "We can go in here," he says. "You know, for privacy." He uses his jangling set of keys to open a solid oak door that reads, "Study Room 1" in bold white lettering on a black wall plaque.

The study room is starkly empty of everything but a basic table and four uncomfortable chairs, along with brass pegs on the wall for coats and backpacks. The walls are painted a soft mushroom color. The chairs and desk are a single shade off for variety. Seems like the decorator was a total wild man.

"Sit, sit," Preston begs, pulling the chairs out for us.

We do, and he sits down on the opposite side, lifting his eyes to the ceiling, shaking his head. "Okay, here goes. I *can't believe* I'm going to tell you this. Unless, of course, you guys already know what I know, but then I doubt that would be the case because you probably wouldn't be here if you did and—"

"Preston?"

"Yeah?"

"We don't know anything."

He leans across the table. "You didn't hear this from me. Not a word of it, because this is some storybook plotline stuff right here. Dangerous, too."

"Sounds juicy." Dakota leans up on her elbows.

Preston dips his head to the side, clucks his tongue once. "Not the word I would use, but yeah."

I feel a bit lost because I forgot to bring a notebook with me. That was my role on the show; I was supposed to follow everyone around with a notebook and act like I was taking notes. Occasionally I would mumble something in the affirmative and look like what I was scribbling down was terribly important.

You know what I was really doing?

Playing Sudoku.

No lie. I'd have Ambrosia or one of the other interns print out some game sets for me, cut the boxes out, and tape them to the yellow-lined paper. You'd probably wouldn't be surprised how many of those you can go through during a particularly grueling and boring B-roll film day.

Anyway.

Preston clears his throat and trips through a handful of false starts before he finally sputters through his top-secret info. And what he tells us about Damon Healy is like a jackhammer to my sternum, which means my earlier instincts about Dakota's infiltrator were off by miles and millennia.

Goddamn, was I ever wrong.

"Damon Healy," Preston says, knocking on the table, "was into some stupid scary stuff. Séances, animal sacrifices, Ouija board parties with other Fortune 500 CEOs. I haven't told a soul about this, and one of the reasons is that who would fucking believe it?"

I say, "Come on, now." He's right, because for a moment, I'm feeling like we've been totally duped, and this dude just wants us to listen to his nonsense because when is he ever going to get the chance to say he lied to Mike Long and Dakota Freakin' Bailey, right?

I push back from the table. "Dude, *really*? You're not gonna give us some 'sold his soul at the crossroads for money' silliness, are you?" Though Dakota and I had joked about it earlier, I didn't think I would actually hear it as a reason.

The hurt in his expression is evident.

Wow. He's honestly wounded.

"No way, Mr. Long. This is a hundred percent truth."

Dakota nudges me under the table with her foot.

"Sorry. Old habits."

"I get it, but the thing is, that's exactly what it was."

I snigger in disbelief and rock back on the chair's hind legs. "I'm—sorry, continue, please."

Seems like I might be working my way onto Preston's Shit List, because he turns away from me and tries Dakota. "They would have these meetings there at least once a month, sometimes more. They dressed up in robes and lit these blood-colored candles. If you were out on the beach, especially at night, there were so many candles going that you could see it from a quarter of a mile away. It sits up so high—of course you know what I'm talking about, you live there. It sits up high enough that nobody could ever look in to see what was going on, right?"

I ask, "How do you know this?"

"That friend I mentioned, his dad was there once."

"And he told his son about some secret robe-wearing ritual?"

"I know, I know. But don't forget, the truth is sometimes stranger than fiction."

"And this friend of yours believed his dad?"

"Well, yeah, why wouldn't he?"

"Uh, *proof*, maybe?" I let the chair drop back on all fours, then lean on the table, elbows propping me up. "Man, I'm really not trying to bust your chops here. Honest to God. And, look, Dakota is already freaked out. First and foremost, I'm trying to protect her, especially her emotions about all this, and to tell you the truth, I've seen and heard all of this before, especially with movie stars and musicians—"

"Sean Franks," Preston interrupts. "That episode in Hollywood where he lied to you about what was going on in his house."

"Exactly. Dude was playing us for exposure. Somehow his producers learned what our production schedule would be, right? Turns out, what they'd done was bribe somebody at TPC headquarters to find out when his episode would air so he could promote his movie."

Dakota interjects, "Which was a piece of shit, by the way. I remember some critic saying a statue could've given a better performance."

"Yup. Total waste of three hours. Anyway, my point is, we heard these stories constantly. Souls sold at discounts prices for fame and fortune. Meet me down at the crossroads after midnight."

"There's nothing for me to get out of this, Mr. Long. The opposite, actually. I could lose, well..." Preston's voice trails into silence. That buried-secrets look returns to his face as he reaches into a pocket and pulls out his cell phone. "You want proof? My buddy's dad managed to get a picture," he says, using his thumb to swipe across the screen, going from photo to photo. "He was looking to dig up dirt on one of his competitors, made some connections and managed to score an invite to one of these little billionaire jerk-off sessions. He pulled some real James Bond type shit to take pictures with these fake glasses he ordered online and—anyway, here, see for yourself."

He hands the phone over to me and adds, "It's like an episode of *Crime Watch Nightly*, right?"

I hold my hand over the screen, not looking yet because I want to see where he's going with this.

Dakota asks, "Why do you say that?"

"Brandon's dad got that picture out, and two days later, they found him *dead*."

"Oh no, that's horrible. Murdered?"

"*Supposed* to look like a suicide," Preston says. "Lots of detail at the scene. But Brandon and I, we had *that*, so we knew better."

I wave the phone around. "And now *you* have the proof? Aren't you afraid?"

"Hell yeah, I am."

"If it's all true, trusting you with this is pretty heavy, wouldn't you say?"

"Yup."

"So why do you know?"

Preston shakes his head, like he simply can't believe the shit hand that life has dealt him. "I got drunk at a party one night, and poof, wouldn't you know it, Brandon's sister ended up pregnant. She lost the baby, but this is still my penance. I'm the dead man's switch if anything ever happens to Brandon." He notes the confused look on Dakota's face and explains, "A dead man's switch basically just means I'm supposed to open the floodgates if he dies—gets murdered."

I ask, "And he wants you to do that why?"

"Exposure. Publicity." He takes a long second before he adds, "Bribery."

"How so?"

"I'm not telling you how much, but Healy deposits a healthy amount into an untraceable account each month. If that stops, or if anything happens to Brandon…let it rain."

Dakota says, "Is that why Healy sold the beach house and moved to whatever island he bought?"

"I'd say so, yeah. Doesn't mean that Brandon isn't always looking over his shoulder. His hair is falling out. He's lost about sixty pounds. The stress is eating him alive."

"If Healy's payoff money is going into an untraceable account, send your buddy into hiding. What's the big deal?"

"He's gone already, but this is like trying to run away from cancer. You can't escape your own paranoia."

I shake my head and push Preston's phone back across the table. "If what you're saying is true, we shouldn't even be here. I don't want any part of it. I'm not going to spend the rest of my life hiding from some billionaire on a mission. Besides, what does any of this have a damn thing to do with Dakota's house being haunted?"

"I thought—" He stops himself, rubs the bridge of his nose. "I thought, eventually, whoever moved to that house after Healy left might show up here, just like you did, to check on the place's history. Then, I could use them as a cover to get to you."

"To get to me? What do you mean?"

"I was trying to be careful. I figured it would set off alarms if I started asking around about where you lived or how I could get in touch with you."

"I'm in the goddamn phonebook."

"Who uses a phonebook anymore?"

Point made, so I drop that line and ask, "What were you hoping I could do?"

"Totally a long shot, but I kinda hoped that if I got to you, you'd hear this story I'm telling you, and then send that demon thing that's in the house to wherever Healy might be since he conjured it up. If something was haunting him, maybe he'd forget about Brandon, and I could get this fucking picture off my phone. I don't want to be a failsafe anymore."

I stare at him in disbelief for so long, Dakota touches my arm to bring me back around. I've had enough. This is insane. "What the immortal fuck are you talking about? Are you fucking with me? Do you know how many holes are in that plan? What if you weren't working the day somebody came to look for information? What if nobody ever did? What if, what if, what if. And did you really think I could just call up this demon and hand him a map to the south Pacific and tell him where to go? You're kidding me with this, right? I don't know that I've ever heard a stupider plan—"

"Mike," says Dakota, "relax. It's all right."

"No, it's not. He's screwing with us."

"Hey," Preston says, jamming a finger at me from across the table. "I'm under a lot of stress too, okay? I said it was a plan, I didn't say it was a good one. You have to sign in to use the microfiche, so I check the records every day."

"Fake names. Or what if we'd gone to the courthouse and found what we wanted?"

Preston sighs. "I was going to wait a couple of months, or until I couldn't take it anymore, and then come looking. I didn't—I didn't think it through. What else was I supposed to do?"

"I don't know, but what you're asking isn't possible. So, yeah, I don't care what kind of proof you have, if it's as dangerous as you say, we don't want any part of it.

Dakota says to me, "But what about my house?"

"Maybe you just leave it. Sell and get away."

"I can't," she says. "No way I can do that to somebody else. We *have* to fix it."

"Dakota—"

"*Please*. Not for him, for me. For everything we talked about before."

Even with Preston's absolutely flabbergasting bullshit, it's impossible for me to say no to her pleading eyes.

Preston tries to convince me as well by saying, "*Nobody* knows I have this. Nobody but Brandon. If something happens to him and his copy of the evidence disappears, I'm mailing this damn phone to the local paper and going bye-bye. Vanishing like a ghost, so to speak."

"Probably not the best choice of words."

"You get my point." He gingerly nudges his cell phone back in my direction.

Dakota says to Preston, "If I were you, I'd walk out the door right now, and don't look back. Go start a different life somewhere. Just get away as far as you can. No matter how unbelievably ridiculous that plan was, you're smart enough to know you'll have a better chance of making it out of your twenties elsewhere. Move to Montana. Raise a herd of cattle. Disappear. I'm sorry, but that's what has to happen."

He nods, lips flattened, frowning.

She adds in a motherly tone, "If you need a voice of reason to tell you what to do, that's it."

I tell her, "We *can't*. We can't become a part of this. What if Healy finds out we know and comes after *us*? It's a legitimate concern."

"You're not saying a word, are you, Preston? Because if you do, and he finds us before he finds you, I'll have no trouble blabbing your name."

"Not a peep, ma'am. My hand to God." Preston puts his hand on his chest.

It doesn't comfort me in the slightest, but Dakota seems to believe him.

Then she says to me, "At least we'll know what we're dealing with, Mike. Right? Séances, Ouija boards, even animal sacrifices? That sounds serious."

"It's damn serious. And it means I was wrong about how dangerous this thing can be. Who knows what in the hell they could've conjured. And I mean that literally. You mess with shit like that, you're bringing something up from actual *Hell*, like proper-noun Hell. Matter of fact, I'm surprised it left so easily this morning." I yank the phone from underneath Preston's fingertips. "It was toying with me. Had to have been. If we're going to do this... Whatever. It'll be for you. Not him."

Abject frustration and the cramped nature of this study room makes it feel like we're sitting inside a pottery kiln.

And yet, when I hold the phone up to get a closer look, my skin goes cold.

The Graveyard: Classified Paranormal Series

20
Ford Atticus Ford

The shower curtain is a dark purple color. It might as well be solid steel, an inch thick, because I can't see behind it.

Droplets of rain slip in through the open window. I feel one splatter against my collarbone as the sporadic breeze causes the shower curtain to billow and flutter again.

I stoop sideways, bending down to lift the toilet seat and lid. I should look first, shouldn't I?

It can wait. I have to *go*. There are plenty of reasons why there's nothing behind that goddamn shower curtain. And besides, my grandfather, in his late days when he had minimal control of his continence, used to say, "A bladder in need is a bladder to heed, my boy."

I unzip and begin to relieve myself. Body water hammers against toilet water. I use my peripheral vision to mind my aim while warily staying focused on the purple cloth. I should've looked first. *Dummy.*

Suffice it to say, I'm certain this is the first occasion where I've ever given this much consideration to peeing. Tolstoy likely spent less time writing *War & Peace*.

Bladder empty, I zip, flush, and manage to take one step toward the tub before I hear BLAM, BLAM, BLAM behind me.

I screech and whip around, glaring at the door as Lauren says, "Ford? You okay? You need to let me in."

"Fucking hell, Coeburn. What're you doing out there? You scared the piss out of me." Which isn't entirely true since it's already gone. She knows what I mean.

I imagine her standing in the hallway, and if she was truly trying to seduce me, maybe she's naked. Or maybe she's out there now, having taken the time to slip into something more comfortable. Ye olde cliché. Cue the porn music.

"You need to let me in."

Irritated, I fire back, "*Hang on*. I need to check something really quick. Just a precaution."

"You need to let me in."

"I heard you, and no, I *don't*. Whatever you're doing, go put some clothes on. I mean, you know, if you're naked or whatever."

"You need to let me in."

"I—"

Wait. Why does she keep saying that?

The pause feels like decades pass. The silence squeezes at my lungs.

I step over and put my ear up to the door. "Yo. You okay?"

There's a soft knocking on the other side.

Tap. Tap. Tap. "Ford?"

"What?"

Her voice is a whimper. "You need to let me in. I'm hungry."

What the hell? "And you think I have food in—oh shit."

Oh shit, oh shit, oh shit.

You need to let me in. I'm hungry.

The sense of panicked realization warms my thighs, sends ripples of nausea through my stomach, waves of skin prickling up my back.

I didn't see it. My God, it totally went right past me like it was wearing an invisibility cloak.

I slink away from the door, going toe-heel, toe-heel, as quietly as I can.

What—how did—I missed it. I can't *believe* I missed it. She's—

BLAM. BLAM. BLAM.

She lands booming blows on the door with such ferocious intensity that I can hear the daunting sound of splintering wood.

My pulse rages in my ears, matching the sound of Lauren thrashing against weak wood.

Eyes darting around, I instinctively look for some kind of weapon or an escape route. Toothbrush in the eye? Jam the toilet scrubber down her throat? Spray that flowery smelling stuff in her face as a distraction? Will any of that have an effect?

I glance around, looking up and over my shoulder. The window is too small for me to escape. I'm trapped. A mouse in a cage with a hungry cat outside, trying to find its way inside.

BLAM. BLAM. BLAM.

"You need to let me in, Ford!"

"Go away." I hesitate mid-step, trying to think of what to say or do next, and it costs me. The thick sole of my black boot catches on the purple rug in front of the toilet, folds underneath my foot, and trips me. I stumble backward, arms flailing, twisting, trying to catch my balance.

Reaching for the shower curtain, I clutch it in my fist, hoping that it'll be strong enough to hold me upright.

The foolish dreams of a falling man hinge on two letters: if.

I hold tight, feeling gravity take me, unrelenting, as the curtain rod gives away. In the next gasp, I'm hurtling downward. I throw my body forward, using my shoulder as a wedge to block my fall—not block, but temporarily pause as I linger there, hanging over the bathtub, and then it happens. The bathmat slips from underneath my foot, and I go down.

I land on something soft. I feel it give under my weight. It's a pile of—what? It feels like there are peaks and valleys, hard and soft, as I roll onto my stomach, pushing up and away.

Please let that be dirty laundry.

Please let that be dirty laundry.

Behind me, Lauren is hurtling her body weight into the door. She's screaming that I need to let her in, that I need to feed her.

I yank the shower curtain back and away, unable to delay this any longer; my supposedly irrational fear is coming true. Something was behind the shower curtain all along.

I feel faint, dizzy, and nauseated when I see it.

Them, I mean.

Two boys. One younger. One older. They're dressed in the traditional black-eyed children attire of a white shirt, a black tie, and black pants for the younger, and the older one is in a hoodie and jeans. Their mouths are slightly open like they're simply in soft slumber. Their dark hair is combed to the side. Clumps of it are missing. My eyes go down to their hands. Both of the boys bear deep claw marks on their skin, the scratches disappearing inside their sleeves. Signs of a struggle. Something, or someone, struggling against them.

Any air I have remaining in my lungs escapes me as I look into their eyes. I don't know what I expected. It's not this.

Their eyes are black, but not for the same reason.

The sockets are hollow, empty like freshly dug gravesites. A black trickle has dried at the corners, near the bridge of their noses.

It comes to me in a surge.

Let me in. Feed me.

The black-eyed children, when they say these things, they're not talking only about the homes of their victims. That much is clear.

You need to let me in. They mean into the body as well as the house. They need a new host.

I'm hungry. Feed me with your soul.

My own soul, the one I've been trying to redeem since the night of Chelsea's attack, curls into a fetal ball and retreats deep inside my chest. I can feel its essence pulling away.

I step back from the tub. A hand goes over my mouth.

Maybe to hide my quivering lip, maybe to hold back the vomit that's clawing its way up my throat.

I can't hold it in.

Wine. Cheese. Salami.

They all go into the toilet as I lose my insides to fear, disgust, and terrified understanding.

I grasp how vulnerable I am in this position as Lauren Coeburn—no, whatever that *thing* is—on the other side of the door rams it with her shoulder, raising her voice ever higher, demanding that I let her in. She's hungry. She needs to feed.

What now?

I try to recall everything I've read in the past about the black-eyed children. Is there anything that can be done?

Not that I can remember. There's simply not enough available information. It's not like I can fashion a stake to drive through her heart or hope to miraculously find silver bullets for that pistol in the living room.

Now I wish I had that damn thing.

Good time to change your mind about guns, Ford?

I invited Lauren in. Goddamn it, she knocked on the front door at my condo and I let her in. I let her in here, too. She specifically said, "You need to let me in," and I stood to the side and watched as she entered.

I'm in such deep shit here—not to mention the fact that my fear is like quicksand, dragging me further and further down. Thick, brown, gooey quicksand made of poop. That particular image doubles me over again, and I retch into the toilet again.

I wipe my mouth with a hand towel, praying the door will hold long enough for me to formulate a plan.

The two boys to my right—no, the *hollow shells* in the bathtub—*they* knocked here earlier. She let them in.

BLAM. BLAM. BLAM.

"Ford!"

"Go back to hell," I scream. "I know what you are!"

As absolutely petrified as I am, I can't help but think this would've made a goddamn amazing episode of *Graveyard*. This would've topped the night we spent in that Italian restaurant in season nine, and I didn't think that was possible.

For the life of me, I can't figure out why Lauren would've let these two inside. She had to have seen their eyes and that something was wickedly off about them.

Then, I see my reflection in the mirror.

I *see*.

The connected dots finally form a picture.

Ellen let them in. She's almost completely blind. *Holy shit that makes sense.*

She never saw them for what they were, and by then, it was too late.

Whatever is inside the bodies, it jumped from them to Lauren and—

No. Damn it, no.

As if I can bear any more, crippling regret weakens my knees.

Ulie.

I left him at the condo with Grandma Death Eyes.

I left him there to protect her.

I left him there to die.

The center of the door splinters and shatters as Lauren manages to break through the cheap particleboard. The hole is the size of a baseball, yet it's plenty enough for the creature out there to put her black, soulless eye up to it and look in the bathroom.

She giggles and it's so haunting, I immediately reach for my crucifix necklace.

Jesus, save me.

Is this worse than Chelsea and Craghorn's demon?

Yeah, quite possibly. I'm all alone, unlike past experiences where I had Mike or a crew at my back. When it comes to dealing with the paranormal, there's something to be said for reinforcements, even if it's just a cameraman and a sound guy.

Lauren giggles again, louder this time.

"Peekaboo, I see you!" she says.

The thought that the paranormal entity, whatever inhabits her body, has been inside her and around me since she came to the condo sends my stomach twirling again. It was baiting me. Waiting patiently. Controlling her. Allowing Lauren to be Lauren until the time was right.

She watches me through the hole with that single black eye as I stand here, gulping short, shallow breaths, begging the universe, God, or common sense to hand me a logical plan.

"Ford," she says in a lilting, sing-song voice. "You need to let me in."

"Go away."

Go away? Pathetic, but it's all I have.

What happens next is both innocuous and normal, but it literally sends me two inches off the ground, accompanied by a childish yelp.

My phone buzzes in my pocket.

I've lost track of time, but it seems odd that anyone I know would be calling at this hour, and yet, it gives me an idea. I jam my hand into my pocket and jerk the phone out, only taking my eyes off the door long enough to check the caller ID.

The name surprises me. I answer and creep back toward the far corner, whispering, "Melanie?"

"Oh God, you're alive," she says, the relief evident in her voice.

"What?"

"I woke up from this horrible dream, and I know that it's probably because I watched an old episode of *Graveyard* tonight, but wow, it was all so freaking scary. A demon had attacked you and you died and I was at your funeral with Mike. It was so real I *had* to call."

"Melanie," I whisper. "I *am* in trouble. Swear to God."

"What? Are you okay?"

"Call 9-1-1 for Newport, right now."

"Ford—"

"Hang up and call them. Get the cops here."

"What's going on?"

I recite the address. "If that's wrong, tell them to look for my Wrangler. Light blue house. White shutters. They need to bring backup for a dangerous suspect."

"Okay, just stay on the—"

I hang up. The phone goes back into my pocket as I stand, wiping my drenched, sweaty palms on my jeans.

I have no clue what the average response time is for a call to the Newport, Oregon emergency system, but best guess says that I have to last about three to four minutes.

Black-eyed Lauren howls and throws her body at the door. The hole in the center splinters and opens wider. The entrance to my fortress isn't going to last that long.

I only have one choice.

I crouch, weight leaning forward on my right leg, left toe of my boot planted firmly against the linoleum.

What in God's name am I doing?

I say, "I'm coming for you, asshole. You ready for the almighty battering ram?"

Our fans would've loved that.

Lauren unleashes an ungodly howl and backs away to get a running start. I wait until she charges, her shoulder slamming into the door. A hinge breaks free from the molding.

With every bit of strength I have, I drive my legs forward, launching myself.

Dressed in black pants, black shirt, black boots, and with jet black hair, I'm like a goddamn human cannonball, plunging ahead, throwing every ounce of my weight into the broken door, into Lauren, and into freedom, I hope.

21
Mike Long

I press down harder on the accelerator. I don't know why I'm in a hurry to get back to my place. I'm in even less of a hurry to get back to Dakota's.

"Horns," I tell her, unable to temper my disbelief. "The thing had the most insane horns I've ever seen."

"I saw it too," she says. "Remember?"

I informed Preston that extra copies had to be out there, because of the way smartphones these days will automatically back things up to a cloud server somewhere in the middle of nowhere. He'd reminded me, then, that there were only two—now four—people with the knowledge of the events of that night. All it took was one of us to get the phone into the hands of a person with media access.

That falls to him. I refused to let him give either of us a copy.

Let me say this: Dakota is a wonderful human being, and I'm at the point where I'll do any thing humanly possible to help her out, but I desperately hope beyond hope that this doesn't come back to bite us in the ass.

A billionaire with a desperate secret out there?

Metaphorically selling his soul at the crossroads with a cadre of powerful people—it all sounds so insane, and I never would have believed it if I hadn't seen that picture.

And believe me, I studied the hell out of that thing. Over the years, I got quite adept at spotting digitally altered photos, especially when a potential client was trying to convince us to come film at their location. Getting approval from us meant a boatload of free exposure, plus the stipend The Paranormal Channel paid them to allow us to film. Win-win for them all around. More often than not, they were legit. When they weren't, the fakes were easy to spot.

Granted, I had to zoom in to study Preston's picture on a small iPhone screen, so I didn't have the best possible situation, and there's always the possibility that I could've been experiencing something known as matrixing.

Matrixing is where your eyes see an image, and the brain tries to put it in terms it can understand by applying a similar image to it. The quickest example that comes to mind is looking at a cloud and seeing a fire-breathing dragon instead of puffy balls of condensation in the atmosphere.

That said, I couldn't pick out a damn bit of digital tampering.

In the photo, six men stand in a circle, in what Dakota now uses as her master bedroom. The seventh is from the viewpoint of Brandon's father who is apparently trying to take a picture with his James Bond super secret spy glasses and do his damage. The carpet is rolled back, up against the eastern facing wall, and at their feet, blood red candles burn around a white symbol that I don't recognize. It's not a far leap to assume it's something satanic or demonic in nature. It's made up of circles, swirls, star-points and what looks like two crossed scythes. An angry skull snarls in the center.

The men are dressed in dark colored robes, all except one, who I assume is Damon Healy, and his cloak is obsidian black. His disciples, for lack of a better word, hang their heads, holding clasped hands at their waists in a posture of prayer. Healy holds a staff in his left hand, held high up over his head, where flames arch up from the end. In his right hand—and I swear to this—he's holding what looks like a human heart.

It's a bit distorted in the photo once you zoom in at a certain level, but the heart shines as if it's wet.

Could it all be fake or maybe nothing more than a demented play date?

Possibly.

And yet, a local businessman with more money than sense, who couldn't let a grudge go, was so intent on getting this news out into the world that he was willing to risk his life for it.

Poor bastard.

Which leads me to the worst part of it.

The ritual sacrifice? I can deal with that, no problem. To me, doing what I've done for so long, that's part of the standard operating procedure. It's like going to the grocery store. Another day, another dollar.

Ford and I saw enough in our time on *Graveyard* that I understand what we're going up against. We had clients describe stories like this to us all the time. We were always present when we had local actors film reenactment scenes just like the one in the photograph. We even had one episode where we recreated something eerily similar, as a trigger event, in the sub-levels of some eastern European catacombs.

Usually, nothing comes of it. Some adventurous teens try to freak each other out after they've procured a couple of dad's beers from the downstairs refrigerator. They say a few words they heard in a movie once, feel the Ouija board planchette move around a little, spook themselves all to shit, and they're done.

Some folks go the extra mile and play dress-up, trying to be serious. Literally *trying* to conjure up a demon. Morons. I wish people, no matter what they believe, would understand the significance of what they were trying to unleash upon the world. If they're unsuccessful, then throw an extra dollar in the offering plate and thank God for looking out for us.

Could be because they said the words wrong, or maybe they sacrificed a goat that believed in the Big Man Upstairs and the holy goat blood dripping on the satanic symbol thingies didn't work because the life juice was tainted with the love of Jesus.

Beats me.

Then, you get people like Dave Craghorn, that sad, lonely, infected man in Virginia who simply wanted to feel *less* alone, and in the process, managed to invite a demon—our demon, Chelsea's demon—into his home by meddling with this shit.

Finally, there are these guys. Hardcore, real deal types.

When you're sitting on top of a few billion dollars, you can afford to hire the best people to do their worst.

All that to say, when I looked at the picture, I knew we were in some deep, *deep* trouble.

I shiver just thinking about what I saw.

Dakota notices and asks if I'm okay.

I smile my okayness, as if that's an acceptable answer.

Dakota is comforting. I'm glad she's here.

That fact doesn't help me get the image of that thing out of my mind.

A dark, murky mist pools behind Healy, extending roughly a foot out on either side of his body. It puffs up and out behind him, almost like a mushroom cloud, yet not as defined in its form. Right in the center—and I'm absolutely positive this isn't matrixing—is a sharp, pointed face, with angular jaws and long fangs bared in a scream. Where the eyes are supposed to be, there are two hollow pits that are more than empty caverns. Staring at them long enough leads to a morose, pulling sensation, as if you were being led along by a tether, drawing you deeper into the depths of darkness, blacker than ink, horribly void of heat and light, love and anything good in the world.

Horns. My God, the horns.

Traditional pictures of Satan and his minions depict creatures with two horns, one above each ear. Left. Right. Pointing skyward or at a slightly forward angle.

That's what we think of when we picture a demon, right?

This thing, or at least the image it projected in the photo as it tries to manifest, has six horns, each one jagged and broken. Not quite antlers, not quite traditional horns, but something in between. Branches, possibly, from say, a tree growing outside of the demon's rental unit in Hell Central.

Branches doesn't do it justice.

Knives. Razor blades. Needles.

My stomach goes numb picturing what those horns would do to a human body.

"Mike!" shouts Dakota.

I come back from the dark place my mind had gone, barely in time to spot the stoplight and the rapidly approaching taillights up ahead. Tires squeal as I skid to a stop, inches away from the trailer hitch of a massive pickup, the kind you would expect to have a fake pair of bull testicles hanging from the bumper.

I see the guy look up in his rearview mirror. He turns, looking down at us through the back window, and shrugs, holding up his thumb and forefinger, signaling "This close, bud."

I wave and mouth my apologies while Dakota pats her chest, trying to get her breathing back to normal.

I apologize, she tells me it's fine, and asks me what happened.

"Thinking about tonight and that thing," I say. "I'm..."

"Scared?" she asks.

I agree without meeting her eyes. I hate to admit it, but I'm truly not ready to take on something like this on my own. It's always been with Ford around. The crew as well. We had people nearby carrying sophisticated equipment. Backup. There's no way on God's green earth that I'm allowing Dakota to come with me tonight, not after what I saw in the picture, and I have nobody else to go with me.

I consider tracking down a local paranormal group, which would be the best possible scenario, but with something this treacherous lurking around, I can't risk it with a greenhorn group of people who don't have enough experience to know how to guard themselves properly.

I have to face this alone.

So, hell yeah, I'm scared.

A small part of me considers the possibility of Chelsea's demon being in the area. It's not *here*, is it?

We thought that was a ridiculous possibility in Craghorn's house, and you saw how that turned out. Once you consider the distance, the Outer Banks really aren't that far away from the Hampton Roads area. If that right-hander can jump from Ohio to the Virginia coast, then there's nothing saying it couldn't have sauntered a couple hours south.

Particularly if a group of obnoxiously wealthy Satan worshippers—with monetary access to all the best bad people—were literally putting out a flashing neon sign that read OPEN.

I'm going to say that's too much of a damn coincidence.

Besides, that fucking thing hates *Ford*, not me.

Dakota says, "Green light."

"Hmm?"

"Gas pedal is on the right."

I look up to see the monster pickup already fifty yards ahead of us and picking up speed. "Yep, got it."

I hit the gas too hard, prompting Dakota to say, "Maybe we should get home in one piece, huh? Or would you like to kill us before we get there so the demon doesn't have to?"

"Lost in thought," I admit. "This is infinitely bigger than I expected, and holy shit, how was I so far off earlier? I thought for sure this would be—maybe not harmless, but easier."

"So what do we do?" She turns to me with a concerned, expectant look, the creases between her eyebrows creating furrows over her nose.

"*We* aren't doing anything," I answer. "The best thing for you to do is go rent a hotel room somewhere, or," and I'm stunned that I'm offering this, "maybe you could go hang out with Toni tonight. Let me handle this."

She throws herself sideways in the seat, puts her back up against the window. "By yourself? Absolutely not," she says. Her tone tells me I won't have much success with an argument. I recognize this tone because Toni uses it all the time.

Dakota crosses her arms, not pouting, but angry-like. "You can't do this alone."

"I can and I have," I lie. "You saw that thing in the picture, Dakota. I'm not letting you anywhere near it."

"And you're forgetting that I've been living with it for weeks. We might as well be roommates."

"All the more reason to stay away. You're already weakened to it, and one bad night could tip you into a place that you're not climbing out of. That's all it would take. Trust me on this."

"Wouldn't you agree that having two *positive* sources of energy—the two of us together—that's better than you alone, right?"

"I guess."

"See?"

"Don't confuse my agreement for an invitation."

"I can feel something changing already by having you around. Getting me out of there, your positive vibes. It's a *good* thing. I feel like, emotionally, I'm getting stronger. You could use me. You *need* me."

"Dakota—"

"Besides," she interrupts, plowing straight through my reply with her miniature tirade, "I don't want to hang out with your wife and her boyfriend." She stops, a surprised look of "Oops, shit!" yanking her eyebrows high as she gasps, "I'm sorry." Her hand flies up to cover her mouth.

"My wife and her *what*?"

Dakota turns her attention elsewhere. "Forget I said that."

"Huh-uh. You don't get to hold out, not after that." I whip the BMW into a grocery store lot, sidle up next to a beige minivan, and slam the shifter into park. "Tell me."

Dakota reaches for me. I think about pulling away, and instead, I let her take my hand.

"Tell me it's not what I think."

Who am I kidding? I've suspected it for ages.

She says, "It's none of my business."

"You say that *now*? Wait, you acted like you didn't know her. Were you...were you hiding this all day long?"

"I didn't *want* to. You deserved to know, it's just that—I didn't know if I should, or if you'd believe me. People get protective over stuff like this. I've had friends in the past who got pissed and ended up hating the person who told them more than the spouse doing the cheating." She clamps her other hand on top of mine.

"Tell me everything."

"You're sure?"

"Yes."

"When I can drag myself outside to actually go running, I've seen her a few times. With another man, I mean. This morning I recognized her as soon as I walked in the door, and it was her, and you weren't the man I'd seen her with, and, yeah."

"Why didn't you say something sooner?"

"I told you why. But, mostly, I didn't want you to hate *me*."

I don't even know how to process this. I'm angry. I'm sad. I'm relieved.

My muscles are knotted ropes.

I'm surprised. I'm not.

I bite down on the back of a knuckle, tightly pinching the skin between my teeth.

The pain is a good release.

I hold it for as long as I can.

I tell Dakota, "We'll talk about this later."

"Okay."

"I'm serious. I'm pissed that you didn't say anything."

"I understand."

"I can't do anything about it right now."

"I know."

"Besides, it's been over for a long time." It's true. And yet, that doesn't mean I'm not hurt.

"Yeah."

"Later." I'll swallow the pain with a bottle of scotch later. "I'll concentrate on it when we're done."

"You just said 'we.'"

"I'm not thrilled about it, but after *this* conversation," I say, pointing at her and then myself, "I might not be in the best place. Your positive energy might be a necessity."

She lets go of my hand and starts picking at a hangnail. She looks up at me, timidly. "I promise I didn't do that on purpose."

"I know you didn't."

Dakota asks, "What now?"

"Only one thing to do. We go get your house back, right?"

"I thought you'd never ask." She grins at me sheepishly.

I reach to put the car back in reverse, then pause. "What's that thing you used to say on *Yes, Chef!* right before you walked into the competition kitchen?"

"If you were really such a huge fan, you know exactly what it was."

I put the car in gear and take my foot off the brake. As we ease back out of the parking spot, I tell her, "I wanted to hear you say it one more time."

"Fine, just for you." Dakota affectionately squeezes my shoulder. "*Boom* go the bombs. Time to light this motherfucker up."

Man, it's so much cooler to hear it without the network's censoring *bleep*.

22
Ford Atticus Ford

I plow into the door, all one hundred and ninety pounds of me hitting it at full throttle. Well, with as much momentum as I can muster across seven feet of bathroom floor space. I hit it with the force of a dump truck barreling through a papier-mâché wall, my body pushing the door into Lauren, knocking her back, sending her hurtling completely off her feet. Her back slams into the cheap sheetrock wall on the opposite side, leaving a dent, and then she falls forward, face down.

I watch it happen as my awkward fumbling carries me ahead, tripping over the downed door at my feet, gravity doing its job, pulling at me as my arms windmill frantically. One boot catches in the hole Lauren had made while my knees buckle and I drop, hard. I get my arms up in time to prevent a faceplant, but barely.

I push up hard, scrambling for safety.

The front door. If I can just make it to the front door, I can get away.

I don't even come close.

Her hand latches onto my ankle, and holy shit, is she strong.

I fall again, unprepared this time, and my face smashes into the floor. I blindly reach for an anchor, anything to prevent her from dragging me back. There's nothing. I try to dig my fingers into the hardwood, but it's too slippery, worn smooth by shoes and the passage of time. I press harder with my fingertips while the howling, possessed, television host tightens her grip around my ankle, yanking me.

She digs her claws into my skin and tugs repeatedly, like a coyote pulling a stubborn piece of meat from a carcass.

I'm going to die, aren't I?

This is how it happens. This is the end.

After twelve years and countless hours of tempting, testing, and antagonizing the more atrocious aspects of the paranormal afterlife, I'm about to go bye-bye at the hands of a soulless blonde woman with black eyes.

Come to think of it, I've actually dated a few of those in the past.

She's strong. So strong, and no matter how hard I kick, I can't break free of her grip. What will happen? The thing inside her already has a new host. What good will I be to it?

Unless...

Unless it needs me to spread like a paranormal virus.

What will it feel like when it happens? Will I go cold? Will I feel black and void on the inside, the same way I felt when The Paranormal Channel informed me that they would be indefinitely removing *Graveyard* from the air?

I roll onto my back, hoping for better leverage, as I plant my hands for support and kick her forehead, again and again. It doesn't help. Her clutch is too strong.

Lauren, or the thing she has become, bares her teeth and growls at me.

The sound is threatening, unholy, and I whimper.

I steady my hands against the floor and shove, twisting my body sideways. The wrenching momentum works, and hallelujah,

I'm free long enough to dive for the wooden couch leg and grab it, thinking I can pull myself away and up to freedom.

I'm too slow.

The she-beast lunges, her fingertips burying into my calf. I can feel her nails through my jeans.

I wrap both hands around the couch leg and lock my fingers, holding on with everything I can manage. It works, briefly. She's unnaturally strong, but not strong enough to pull me and the couch too.

While she struggles, it gives me a moment to plan, to frantically search for something I can use as a weapon. There's nothing within reach, not unless I get all Superman and manage to cut off a leg of the nearby coffee table using laser beams from my eyeballs.

I'll never make it to that pistol in the lockbox.

One. Twenty-nine. Seventy-four.

If only.

I glance back at her when I sense movement, the lessening of a struggle with my legs. She smiles maliciously. She's toying with me. Instead of pulling me to her, she uses my leg like a rope and pulls up along my body, hand over hand, progressing a few inches at a time.

"No. No. No," I snarl through gritted teeth. "Get off me."

I get brave for about half a second and hold still, you know, like that scene in Braveheart where Mel Gibson is shouting, "Hold!" while his ragtag army hides their spears. I wait, shaking with fear, until she gets just close enough to put her hand on my thigh.

Then I bring my free knee up and slam it into her temple as hard as I can, using all the leverage I can muster. It's one final attempt, one last-ditch effort, and I'm just as surprised as the advancing English army that Gibson's plan worked.

She tumbles over, temporarily dazed, letting go as she flops to the side, groaning up at the ceiling.

I thrash away from her, rolling to my right, pushing up on my knees, then spring to my feet. I'm perched to bolt for the front door when I hear, "Ford Atticus Ford," in a voice that is nothing like Lauren's.

It's a voice like black tar covering a bed of nails, thick and sharp at the same time. A devilish hound growling at me with broken glass lodged in its throat.

I should run. Goddamn it, I should take a stuntman dive through the large-paned picture window instead of fooling with the door.

But I can't.

The sound of that thing's voice freezes me in place, petrified.

I'm like a USPS mailbox, one of those squat blue ones on a street corner, with my feet bolted to the concrete. I'm not going anywhere. A small rodent, frozen in fear, at the sound of a superior predator lurking near me.

"What do you want?" I croak.

"We were sent for. We are messengers."

"For who?" I can't *not* look in Lauren's direction. My need to know is like a ringing phone. I *have* to answer its call.

She's on all fours now, sneering, slowly swaying side to side to a rhythm I can't hear. She puts one hand in front of the other and crawls six inches closer to me.

I smell fire, smoke, and sulfur.

"I'm not letting you in," I say. "I'm never letting you in. You'll have to take me."

"There are no doors between us now. You are free. Open to me."

"No."

"Mine if I want you."

"You can't. I'll—"

"Silence, child!" she shouts, getting to her feet. "Master has a message."

"Wh—who—who's your master?" I retreat, inching away from her.

"You already know." She steps closer, arms at her sides, breathing heavily. I look at her feet as she takes another step—instinctual reaction—and I see that her perfectly manicured, pristine nails, the flawlessly polished red ones that I remember from this morning, have grown into gnarled claws. The tips click on the hardwood floor.

"Chelsea's demon?"

She says, "Him, yes," then lowers her voice to a whispering hiss. "Master."

I'm nothing if I'm not trying to catch some supernatural entity off guard, to get them to reveal themselves, to give me workable information—it's what I'm good at. It's in my nature, so on pure impulse, I ask, "What's his name?"

It's a foolish hope that Lauren's possessor will accidentally reveal some information, because there's power in a name.

The Tier One right-hander that we were calling Azeraul, that son of a motherless goat has a name—*everything* has a name, and it's a damn disgrace that I won't live long enough to use it, in it's presence, accompanied by the words, "What a humongous goddamn asshole you are, *blank*."

She doesn't take the bait.

Instead, she tilts her head back and erupts in charred, smoldering laughter. "You will never know his name."

So it's definitely a he. That's one step in the right direction. If only I had more time.

Time.

Time!

In my panic, I completely forgot that I asked Mel to call 9-1-1. How long has it been? How long have I been struggling to get away from Lauren? What feels like hours has most likely been a couple of minutes. On a great day, in fantastic weather, I'm guessing the police would be here in another minute or two. Then again, I suspect that Newport's abilities aren't perfection personified—not that I doubt the ability of their emergency response teams—it's just that it seems like a slightly underprivileged town, like many along the coast of Oregon, with little access to big budgets and...

For the love of God, why is this shit traipsing through my mind when I'm about to die at the hands of Unlovely Lady Death right here?

Focus, Ford.

If I can wait her out, if I can stall for just a little while longer, I might be okay.

"What does he want with me?" I ask, my voice cracking, tripping across my tongue. "What did I do?"

"You stole," she growls.

"Stole what?"

"Her. Master's plaything. You took her away. And you took him away, you pathetic human slug."

"You mean Chelsea and Craghorn?"

"Yes," she says, the long s slithering out of her mouth. If she shook her ass, would it sound like a rattlesnake? "The girl, so young and delectable. Fresh meat. Delicious. She would have been perfect for him. A suitable host. So blood red on the inside. Her skin, the purest white of innocence. He was preparing her, and you took her from him. You stole what wasn't yours. And that man, the little worm. He begged for a new life. He got down on his knees and he renounced your Creator. He wasn't pristine like your darling little friend, but he was willing. His soul was searching for salvation like an infant begging for a teat."

"That's not true," I say, stalling. "He just missed his wife. He was trying to call her back to him."

"You mortals, such imbeciles. Believing the written word of a desperate man. He was a liar. You all are. You don't deserve your Creator's generosity. You ate the apple, every single one of you, and then you expect your pitiful Maker to give you more. More. Always more. Gluttonous heathens. All of you belong at the feet of my master, and *his* master, while your skin fries and your fat boils in the fires below."

"Like I didn't already know we're doomed? And why Lauren? Why use her? Why didn't that piece of shit tell me face to face? You're killing her to tell me something I already know? What a waste. And you wanna accuse *us* of gluttony?"

"Why use her? Master knows all. Master is everywhere. Of the seven deadly sins, lust has the shortest path to travel. And for you, Ford Atticus Ford, lust is in your heart. She could get close, quickly."

"Lust? For *her*? Then Master doesn't know everything."

Maybe I can get away with that fib.

Laughter explodes from her chest. "See? Liars, all of you."

Maybe not.

"If you're going to kill me," I say, "do it now. Let's finish this. Send me down there so I can talk to him in person and tell him where to shove it. Maybe I'll set up shop, take over, then I can be the one calling the shots, huh?"

Does reverse psychology work on a demonic entity?

Nope.

The coffee table is made of heavy oak, with a thick plate of glass sitting on top of it. The Lauren Thing picks it up with one hand by the support bar underneath the glass. She holds it high over her head, glaring at me, and I'm certain that this is it.

Me and my big mouth.

How many times have I said *that* in my life?

Seems fitting that's what will send me out of this world, too.

She winks—the fucking thing actually winks at me—then flicks the coffee table through the picture window as easily as tossing a magazine on a kitchen counter.

Shattered glass peppers the porch outside as wind whips through the gaping maw left behind, bringing with it sheets of rain and the salty smell of the ocean beyond.

"I'm not going to kill you," she says. "He just wants you to know that he's going to take her back. She will be his again. No matter what you do. No matter where you go or where you take her, he will find her and reclaim what he rightfully owns. He knows of this woman Carla and her plans for his youngling. Master will wait, if he must."

I shout, "Why wait? Why not take her now? Why not take her before? If he's so goddamn sure of himself, why hasn't he gotten to her already?"

"Does a cat eat the mouse right away? No. It toys with it. Prepares it for a meal."

"So? If he can take her any time he wants, if he's just playing with her, why tell me? The fuck do I care?"

I really gotta stop this reverse psychology thing. It's not working.

"Because," she says, lengthening the pause, teasing me with her secret, "you've been a burden for far too long. *You* will be the end of Chelsea."

"Yeah, right. The girl I've been trying to *save*?"

The wailing sound of sirens drifts through the shattered window.

Thank God.

"*You* will damage Chelsea. *You* will prepare her for his return, and *you*, repulsive maggot, will finally burn for your meddling intrusions. You'll be ripped from limb to limb in the eyes of humanity and thrown to the snarling wolves, bloody and crying."

The sirens howl, less than a mile away now. In the corner of my eye, I spot a fireplace poker leaning up against the stone. I inch closer to it.

"Whatever," I say, sneering, "you and what army?"

"I don't need an army," she replies, stepping forward. "I only need to get inside you. Master will do the rest."

The woman I previously knew as Lauren Coeburn plunges at me in brutal rage, a blood-curdling scream screeching out of her throat, teeth bared, fingernails like talons reaching for my throat.

I reach for the poker, leaning over, moving as if I'm swimming in cold molasses, drifting, flowing to the side. I wrap my fingers around the cool metal handle and spin, bringing it up, holding the base of it against my shoulder for support, the other hand high on its neck, aiming it at the base of her throat.

The black-eyed Lauren Thing understands too late. She tries in vain to halt her momentum, yowling in fear a split-second before I feel the sharp tip puncturing soft skin. Her wail becomes a choking gurgle as the poker slides easily through the tissue, glances off her spine, and protrudes out the back of her neck.

It sounds like stabbing Eve's proverbial apple with a knife. What a nauseating noise. I tumble backwards, onto my rear, as she continues to slide down toward me. I squirm to the side, pushing the twitching body away.

I hear a wet, final cough coming from the Lauren Thing, which is then followed by hurried steps coming up the front porch.

The undulating red and blue lights on the ceiling fill my chest with relief.

Help. Thirty seconds too late.

The Graveyard: Classified Paranormal Series

23
Mike Long

If a lot of this seems vaguely familiar, it's because it is.

Black swirling masses, demonic entities, Ouija boards and séances.

It happens more often than you would think.

Ghosts, demons, paranormal thingies that go bump in the night, they all have a myriad of ways to manifest once they've managed to cobble together enough energy. That said, they'll often choose the path of least resistance if they're an intelligent haunt—rather than a residual one—because why not? If the easiest method gets the point across, then so be it. If they don't choose to take a physical form, or if there isn't enough energy available, they'll communicate via EVPs or by knocking a book off a shelf to either make a point or let you know they're present, and that they do, in fact, exist.

Back in Dakota's home earlier, when I felt like the entity was junior class, no big deal, I totally screwed the pooch on that one. I should've known better.

Ford would have noticed something was off, damn it.

Ford would've taken one long look at that thing and said, "Yep, get out the holy water, it's gonna be a long night."

I fell for the oldest trick in the book: I allowed that dickwad to convince me that it was relatively harmless before I had done my homework. I consider myself lucky that it didn't pick up my soul by its scraggly, bony fingers and swallow it whole like an unlucky goldfish at a frat party.

Stupid, stupid, stupid.

I was so caught up in All That is Dakota earlier that it could have done some major league damage. That's the last time I'll go into a potentially dangerous investigation with my shorts down around my ankles and a bullseye painted on my butt.

Then there's the matter of Toni and—well, I'm guessing it's the contractor, Armando, from Dakota's description—which will have to be shelved until later. I had expected it, honestly, and I feel like I should be more outraged, but I'm not.

It's like you're playing shortstop in a baseball game, right? The Paul Bunyan-sized first baseman from the other team steps up to the plate using a sequoia tree for a bat, and he wallops a ninety-mile-per-hour fastball into a line drive, straight at your face. You stand there and watch the ball spinning, hurtling at you in super slow-mo, and you let it wallop you right in the honker.

I'm upset that it hurts, yet I can't necessarily be pissed at the baseball for hitting me when I stood there and didn't take action to protect myself.

Anyway. Lots of shit on my mind that I need to push out of the way so I can be properly focused on this demonic asshole squatting in Dakota's beachfront mansion.

Speaking of Dakota, she's still sitting over there in the passenger seat, trying to tell me that she is *most certainly* helping me tonight, that I shouldn't be doing this alone, especially not without Ford around.

I hadn't been entirely listening until that part.

"What?" I snap. We're sitting at the last stoplight before our coastal street that will take us past homes that cost way too much for what they offer. I flash an annoyed look at her. "You think I can't handle this on my own? Let me tell you something: I do *not* need the almighty Ford Atticus Ford to hold my hand, okay?"

Dakota, bless her, understands that I'm operating on an accelerated level of stress, and the snarky, pissy version of me that she's seeing right now isn't the standard Mike Long. My hand is on the shifter. She covers it with hers, soft skin soothing me.

"That's not what I meant," she says. "Put the guns away, Tex. I know you're on edge, but you of all people know that you can't go into an investigation with so much negative energy fogging up your windows. Season five, episode nine, remember? 'Rule number one, folks, surround yourself with positive, white light.'"

"You saw that one, huh?" She's got me there. We were on that decommissioned navy ship in North Carolina, and Ford was pissed about something—I can't recall what—and a particularly angry spirit, a former sailor, feasted on his negativity. It soaked up all of that damaging energy and scratched the absolute shit out of the docent during our initial tour. Last I heard, the guy quit the next day and never set foot back on deck.

"Top of my list," Dakota says. "One of the few times where you took charge. You looked good in the captain's seat."

The light turns green. I have a little extra lead in my foot. "Flattery will get you everywhere, Miss Bailey."

***

"You've probably seen enough episodes to know how this works, yeah? That stuff earlier was just preliminary. This is the real deal, now that we know what's in there."

"I got this," she says. "I think."

We're standing outside of Dakota's front doors, the tall glass ones facing east out over the Atlantic, suited up and armed like a couple of badass SEALs getting prepped to storm a terrorist stronghold.

Not really. I'm carrying a few pieces of ghost hunting equipment with me—I left the paranormal flatulence detector behind—along with a Batman-style utility belt. Okay, really, it's one of Toni's running belts that carries four eight-ounce bottles of water for drinking on long distance runs.

Only this water is blessed. Holy-fied, if you will.

After our big scare back at Craghorn's place a couple of weeks ago, where Ford and I went into that investigation with some decade-old holy water I had lying around, I decided it might be a good idea to stock up again. I visited a Catholic priest I know in Kitty Hawk proper, a fellow by the name of Father Duke, and had him bless a gallon of tap water I brought along. I'm not sure if the Pope and his many minions would necessarily approve of that process, or if, like, that's Catholically legal, but Father Duke has been a fan of *Graveyard* from day one.

Just don't tell his congregation.

So, I have two digital voice recorders on me, a full spectrum camera, and digital video cam, one of the sophisticated bastards we used to call spotcams, which led to Ford's infinitesimal supply of spank bank material when thousands of spotcamgirls took it upon themselves to flood his inbox with pictures of ladies in various stages of undress.

That's four pieces of equipment for me, and not nearly as many photos of naked fans.

Dakota carries an EMF detector, the thermal imaging camera, and a digital camera.

Seven pieces total, which is really about half of what I'd like to go into this place with, but here's my thinking: less equipment means less batteries, which leads to less available energy for the demon to access. There's no doubt that he'll try to chomp on the batteries like a handful of synthetic energy pills, along with the spares I brought with me.

However, we should be able to get a few hours of investigation time in, or it'll be just enough to provide him with energy to manifest, albeit weakly, on top of whatever else he's drawn from.

The less time we have to spend in this house, the better.

Well, strike that. I'd love to hang out here all night and discuss life, liberty, and the pursuit of happiness with Dakota.

Just not under this particular set of circumstances.

Dakota takes one of the small plastic bottles out of the running belt, examines it, and slips it back into the empty slot. "Nice fanny pack. Only thing you're missing are some black socks pulled up to your knees."

Eyeballing her sideways, I fire back, "Hey, you're the tourist."

"Not in my own house."

"Yeah, but we're on *my* investigation. You're just along for the ride, sister."

She playfully pokes my shoulder. "Try to keep up, Fanny Pack."

It's fun, this gentle, friendly bickering. I really enjoy it, which scares the absolute doodoo out of me since I'm about to take this awesome human being back inside the prison of her own home.

You know, where it's entirely possible for her to become demonically possessed.

No biggie.

I feel the sweat leak out onto my palms, hesitating to touch her with the clamminess as she fiddles with some dials on the thermal imager. "Just in case," I say, "if anything happens to either one of us, my cell phone is in my back pocket. Don't go fondling my butt if you need it—"

"*Pfffft*. Gotcha." The surprised sputtering is real, genuine. I love her laugh.

"I'm serious, though. We gotta promise to do this for each other. There's a Catholic priest in my contacts. His name is Father Duke, same one who blessed the holy water. I've known him for years and we even had him on the show once—"

"*That* guy? The short round one with the glasses?"

"Yep."

"I remember thinking he looked like an owl. He seemed nice on the show. And, appropriately concerned about the sanctity of your eternal soul before they'd allow you through the Pearly Gates."

That's what he said on the show, almost word for word. She's good.

"He's a good guy. Loved *Graveyard*, not that he necessarily approved of us playing with hellfire, like you said. Anyway, I'm more worried about you than myself, but if anything—and damn it, I mean anything—goes funky with me, you call him. Understand?"

"Mikey's back in the captain's chair. I like it."

"I'm serious."

"I know you are. It won't, but if it does, what if I can't get the phone out of your pocket? Like you become this crazy, evil, fanny pack wearing version of yourself and I can't get near you?"

"Good point. We can move it room to room during the investigation. Always within reach."

"Aye, aye, cap'n." Dakota salutes me, and then slaps my bottom like we're about to take the field. I feel like I'm blushing, but damn, the camaraderie is endearing, which scares me even more.

I've done this enough to have a certain shiny veneer of confidence, yet the idea of Dakota having to deal with a haunted version of Mike "The Exterminator" Long, especially now that I have a well-defined muscle or two, leaves me shaky and unsure, again, about allowing her to come along.

It's not a battle I'm going to win, I know this, so I resolve to take every precaution necessary to keep her safe.

Which is a nice idea, in theory.

***

Thirty minutes pass. Dakota and I maintain radio silence as we execute our pre-determined game plan. I don't allow her to leave my sight, but we individually accomplish our own tasks. She runs EMF checks while I use my GS-5000 to listen to the background noise and search for any signs of something demonic that Damon Healy might have left behind. I mean, like, hidden symbols, decapitated squirrel bones. The standards.

We haven't been in here long, but so far, we're coming up empty. I would've expected more, sooner. I'd rather this son of a bitch manifest on its own, without needing to provoke it, for a couple of reasons: first, spewing all of that negativity out of my mouth can cause negative energy to grow and mutate, even if you don't mean for it to happen. Positivity begets positivity. Negativity does too. I want to keep the latter to a minimum.

Second, I've never been sure that it matters, nor has Ford, but if this demon manifests without me taunting and cursing its good name, that scenario is preferable to some supremely pissed off entity storming through the gateway to hell, angry and combat ready, because I insinuated that he enjoyed sodomizing his mother.

When we finish the first stage of the game plan, which entails fully scouting the first floor, I call out to Dakota on the far side of the kitchen, "Anything?"

"Flat. Everywhere. Had a reading of zero-zero the whole time."

"Figured as much. He's hiding out upstairs."

Dakota is over by a couple of the larger, ocean-facing windows. She asks if she can open the blinds, maybe let some light in.

"Um…"

"I know you guys always liked it pitch black for your investigations, and I know it'll be night soon, but maybe—I might feel safer with more light."

I nod my assent. "Of course." *Anything for you, Dakota.* "We only did that to make the equipment more effective anyway. Although, upstairs needs to stay darker. That's where the cameras need to be at their peak."

Dakota stops in mid-pull. The clattering of the blinds goes quiet, their weight keeping her arm suspended. "So this is pointless?"

"'Fraid so."

She mock pouts, bottom lip drooping dramatically, as she lets go and walks over to me. Jokingly, she says, "If we have to be in the complete dark, are you gonna hold my hand?"

"'Fraid so."

It's easy to see how delicate flirtations can lead to a major downfall in so many different ways.

The Graveyard: Classified Paranormal Series

24
Ford Atticus Ford

I'm here at Newport's police station, sitting in a suspect interview room, and the lights overhead burn my eyeballs as if they're scrubbing them with bleach. They're too bright, too white, for my darkened mood.

My chair is your standard, uncomfortable plastic piece of crap, purchased with taxpayer money on a limited budget, and I squirm to get comfy. I've been waiting here for over three hours. Maybe longer. I've lost track.

I have a room-temperature cup of coffee sitting on the table that someone brought five minutes after depositing me here, though I doubt that'll do any good for the nausea roiling in my gut like a volcano bulging on the eve of eruption.

Why the nausea? Well, a couple of things: thinking about the squishy crunch of that poker sliding through a used-to-be-human neck, combined with the fact that I am absolutely torn up about the fact that they won't tell me if Ulie is okay. I tried to have them get word to Melanie, to let her know that I'm okay, and they've yet to give me an affirmative on that as well.

Matter of fact, I'm surprised she doesn't have a lawyer here yet. Although, more than likely, knowing Melanie, she hopped in her car and is on the way here.

I risk a sip of the coffee. It tastes even worse with the lack of heat. I grimace and think about how Lauren will never get to drink coffee again and my stomach spins around the uneven bars like a drunken gymnast.

I feel horrible about what happened to her, I really do.

I had so much stale hatred for her, but I was coming around. Could be that I'm feeling sentimental and sad now that she's dead, but no matter what I thought about her past transgressions, I'll admit that I could've learned to enjoy her company.

Eventually.

You know, like how you despised broccoli as a kid, and now as an adult you can tolerate it as long as it's seasoned properly.

Anyway. Lauren was more than broccoli, and it's so damn unfortunate that she had to go out like that. I've been sitting here wondering if I could've done anything for her, and I've come to the conclusion that no amount of spiritual antibiotics would've cured what ailed her, so she's in a better place.

Or, at least she's in a *different* place. Let's hope her soul travelled the right direction.

That gets me to thinking about Ulie again and I feel a lump well up in my throat.

Dogs are heaven-bound, no matter what. If anything happened to him...

Ugh. Man, this sucks.

Ulie is the child I never had. My heart aches that much.

I left the poor guy cooped up inside the condo with Grandma Death Eyes.

I was mentally wavering on the way here, but I specifically remember babbling about my little buddy and that he was in terrible danger.

I shout at the two-way mirror, "Can somebody please find out what happened to my dog?"

As expected, the silence continues.

Before they tossed me in the squad car, while I was sitting at the kitchen table, hands cuffed behind my back, I also managed to remember the camcorder, mentioned it to the uniformed officers, and then prayed like I've never prayed before that it caught everything.

There's also the matter of the two empty black-eyed children in the bathtub, and I have no fucking clue how I'm going to explain what they were doing there. I also realize how patently insane it'll sound if I try to truthfully explain why *I* was there, and how the celebrity television host and beloved local girl, Lauren Coeburn, had gotten possessed and then tried to kill me, which resulted in her lying on the living room floor with a poker sticking out of her like she was a demonic corndog.

The only reason I'm not cuffed now is that the uniforms and the detectives in charge, Carson and Jaynes, recognized me as "that guy, the one from the ghost show—you know, *Graveyard Something or Other*." This was followed by a round of whistles and exaggerated *oohing* and *aahing*, along with a knowing set of smiles.

Then they promptly shoved me into this austere room with a single table, two chairs, and a two-way mirror. There's a camera up in the corner watching my every move. Not that they need it. The only thing I've been able to do is sit here and relive the last few minutes in the movie of my mind, over and over.

Again, the whole scenario is further proof that it's all connected.

The afterlife, I mean, and the energy that bonds it together.

Master, whatever his actual name might be, had sent messengers.

Our demon, my nemesis, wanted to tell me he's taking Chelsea back, and because he's an all-powerful sumbitch and thinks he can do whatever he wants, he throws down the gauntlet, basically challenging me, wanting me to know that just for funsies, he's going through me to get to her. And if the Lauren Thing is to be believed, Master's intent was to stick his hand up my butt and use me like a puppet.

I'll tell you what, dude—over my dead body.

He's calling me into the ring.

And I've never been one to back down from a fight.

You know, except for that time in elementary school when Danny Delp wanted to fight me by the swings during recess.

I was a shy, quiet kid growing up. During art class, the other rugrats would fashion crowns out of construction paper and shove them on my head, calling me the Nerd King.

So, yeah, I kept to myself a lot. Imagine that.

One day, in a rare moment of peeking out of my antisocial shell, I had tried to stop him from picking on Cindy Moss—who bore a striking resembling to Chelsea Hopper, come to think of it. The teachers intervened, and Danny was far from happy about that. I had taken his toy away from him, and now it was my turn in his spotlight.

I didn't meet Danny by the swings that day because I was smart, and because he was about three times my size. He ruled the school. He had dozens of friends and lackeys that he could order around. Totally a genuine cliché.

He always booted homeruns in kickball and won every arm-wrestling contest.

I was the weird skinny kid who watched The Exorcist over and over.

Danny and his friends taunted me for several weeks after, called me a pussy and pushed me into lockers. Knocked my lunch tray out of my hands.

I couldn't take it anymore, so you want to know what I did? My dad, Bill Ford, was ex-military, a real badass with a high-and-tight haircut and muscles that had muscles. He used to beat up hippies back in the sixties for shits and giggles, and among the remnants of his past was a set of brass knuckles that I found in a cardboard box in the corner of our attic. They were easily hidden in a backpack all morning, and then under my jacket during a game of dodgeball.

Danny started his crap and one good pop was all it took. He left for the hospital with a fractured cheekbone and never bothered me again. That is, once I got back from my month-long suspension and my parents paid his medical bills.

Plus, if you look closely enough, you can still see the scar on my right ass cheek where my dad's belt buckle landed instead of the strap like he intended.

Needless to say, not many people have examined my ass to that extent.

It's not that I enjoyed watching Danny Delp lying there in the mud on that rainy Thursday morning, clutching his cheek and bawling as he writhed on the ground. I didn't like that part at all—okay, maybe a little—but I came away with something different.

Whenever I tell this story, I still get chills. That day awoke something inside me. Not necessarily a fire, just...a different level of perception about the world and my role in it. I *could* be strong. I *could* fight back if I wanted to. I had the power to change things if I wanted it badly enough, or if something had pushed too far.

I was entirely too young to fully grasp the enormity of my realization, but now I can look at it like this: if you go back to the metaphor of Adam and Eve's apple, I held two of them, one in each hand. One of the apples was made of a life that I could create for myself. The other apple was made of a life that was handed to me by external events.

One tasted sweet. One tasted bitter.

One was fulfilling. One left me famished and empty.

The choice was simple.

Somewhere along the monumental run of *Graveyard: Classified*, I went back to eating the wrong one.

I sit up straighter in the chair and cross my arms, feeling a hint of realization beginning to manifest somewhere in my mind.

I think back to that Very Special Live Halloween Episode, and the days and months leading up to it, when I kept trying to convince myself, Chelsea, and Mike—*especially* Mike—that if Chelsea stood up to the demon and beat it, then she would be a changed person for the rest of her life, ready, willing, and able to take on anything. That was me taking a bite from both apples, the old Ford desperately trying to regain control.

It's like wiping the condensation off a fogged up bathroom mirror when the understanding finally settles in.

I suppose I was channeling myself from the third-grade, and trying to reconcile that with Chelsea's situation. Deep down, floating around in my subconscious was a well-intentioned desire for her to experience that kind of awakening, too.

Eat the right apple, Chelsea.

I had good intentions, but what I didn't take into account was the fact that there's a fuckload of difference between a bully named Danny Delp and a Tier One right-hander who probably plays darts with Satan every other Saturday night down at the local watering hole.

Whatever Master's actual name is—let's call him Boogerface for now—whatever Boogerface has in mind probably involves lots of planning, lots of deception, a tactician's dream.

Why go through all the trouble?

Boogerface has an eternity on his hands. He has time to entertain himself. Even if we send him back where he came from, he'll still be down below, boiling in the fires of Hades for thousands upon thousands of infinite years to come.

It's not a far-fetched concept to assume that demons get bored.

This is all a game to him. Chelsea is a pawn. Maybe I'm a knight. Mike's a knight.

And Boogerface is simply moving his pieces around.

I wish I could figure out what's so special about Chelsea, you know? Why her?

I think about what Grandpa Joe said back in the Hampstead farmhouse, about how Chelsea is the key to everything. I kept thinking that perhaps he meant that Chelsea was some sort of catalyst to this spiritual war that's about to take place.

Could be, though now I'm starting to think it might be far simpler than that.

This is Cindy Moss all over again.

Boogerface is pissed off because I took his toy away from him.

Sure, Chelsea got hurt in the process when he lashed out and attacked her, which was probably his way of saying to me, "Now look what you made me do!" and to be perfectly honest, so did Cindy back in the day, but what it all comes down to is this: he wants revenge, and has been setting up his pieces since Chelsea's parents took her away that night.

If that's the case, then why didn't he follow her to her new home when she left the first time, before we even filmed the Very Special Live Halloween Episode?

Maybe he did, at least a small part of him. She kept having those horrific dreams.

Maybe he had to stay behind in the house, close to his portal to hell. I can't say. I can't pretend to know the mind of a demon.

And then we brought her back that night. We brought people, and cameras, and batteries, and the black heart of Carla Hancock. We brought energy, millions of subliminal watts of paranormal energy from all around the world with so many people focusing everything they had on that one singular location.

Trust me, I know my shit, but sitting here, in this empty room as I wait on somebody to come talk to me, I think I'm just now realizing how lucky we got that Chelsea's attack wasn't far worse.

We didn't necessarily save Chelsea from Boogerface forever, much in the same way that my intervention didn't stop Cindy Moss from getting picked on again, but we put our noses where they didn't belong.

And, again, much in the same way that Danny Delp and his heathen cronies taunted me mercilessly for weeks on end, often slapping and shoving Cindy Moss right in front of me, asking, "Whatcha gonna do about it, huh, pussy?" it's plainly obvious that Boogerface has the same motivations.

He's a playground bully.

With an extremely powerful right-hander like that, he can have Chelsea anytime he wants, and anywhere he wants. It's not necessary for the *Graveyard: Classified* crew or me to be within a thousand miles of the Hoppers for Boogerface to take control of Chelsea again.

This is about exerting control.

I'm the weird skinny kid who dared to defy him, who dared to stick up for his prey, and he wants to teach me a lesson before he takes Chelsea back.

Fucker. I get it now.

Know what this means?

Mike will get his wish. I *have* to do the documentary.

What better stage for David to take on Goliath?

It's the perfect showdown, and I'm bringing a set of paranormal brass knuckles with me, Boogerface.

***

Another fifteen minutes pass before I hear a short rap on the door and in walk the two detectives, Carson and Jaynes. Carson reminds me of John Madden, all the way down to the wiry eyebrows sprouting from his forehead like a ball of cotton stuck a fork in a light socket. He's tall, round, and gives off the impression of a jovial grandfather who's ready to pull a lint-covered piece of candy out of his pants pocket. Don't let that fool you, though. This guy is sharper than he looks. I picked up on that earlier when they shoved me into this human-sized fishbowl.

Jaynes is short, stout, built like a small refrigerator with close-cropped salt and pepper hair. She didn't smile or speak once earlier.

I bet she's fun at parties.

Carson takes the lead and offers Jaynes the lone remaining chair. She silently declines with a raised hand and backs herself into the corner, standing with meaty hands buried in her pockets. Nonchalant. Staring. Or glaring, I should say. There's a measure of suspicion and anger there.

I pry my eyes from her and turn back to the more welcoming grin of Carson. I'm probably wrong about that, too. I doubt it's welcoming. More like, 'I know something you don't.'

I know what tricks are coming, but I don't feel like playing games, so I relent and speak first.

"Detective."

"Mr. Ford."

"Anybody check on my dog?"

The corners of his mouth dip as he looks down and away.

I feel my heart burning with dread. "Is he okay?" I ask, leaning forward.

Thank God, he nods. Hallelujah. "He'll be fine in a few days. The vet said he's a little banged up and scared to death whenever anyone tries to get close to him, but Animal Control has him on sedatives down at the pound. Hate that for you. Got a sweet little poochie myself."

"Thanks."

"Damn shame when trauma like that happens to a good animal."

"Trauma?"

Carson angles his head backward, scrunching up his forehead. "They didn't tell you?"

"Tell me what?"

Over his shoulder, he says back to Jaynes, "Goddamn it, Sheila. They did it again, didn't they? Lazy sons of—never mind." To me, he adds, "I see you got coffee. Need anything else? Water maybe?"

"I'm fine."

He intertwines his fingers and props himself up on the table. "Somebody was supposed to come in and brief you. It's the young kids these days, you feel me? I can't get nobody to do right by anybody." He shakes his head in disgust, looking up at the ceiling like he's reminiscing about the good ol' days when people actually did what they were asked.

Has that ever been the case?

I don't know whether this is a legitimate show of consternation, or if he's simply playing Good Cop and trying to ease me into his news that I'll be arrested for murder.

Carson clears his throat. It's long and rattling, like he's shaking something loose after years of smoking. He says, "Anyway, your dog will be fine eventually. Sorry we left you waiting so long. Had some things to check out before we had a chat, like looking at the condo. Nice place you got there, right up on the ocean like that. You own it?"

"Rental."

"Ah. Shame. Nice place from the outside, but when we got up to your floor, the door was open, the place was torn all to shit like somebody set off a bomb inside a hoarder's house, and there was no sign of Ellen Coeburn. Who knows how he did it, but by God, your petrified pup had somehow managed to work himself under the sofa. You see how big I am. I'da smashed him if I'd sat down."

"We wouldn't want that," I mutter, already tired of the banter. Now that I know Ulie is okay, let's get to the business of proving my innocence. I ask the detective, "Are there security cameras there? Any idea about what happened to her?"

"She's ninety years old and blind, Mr. Ford. She didn't get that far." I almost give him a derisive snort, wanting to tell him about how much he doesn't know. Instead, I nod in mock acceptance. "But you wanna know the craziest thing? They picked her up knocking on some scared neighbor lady's door, talking about how she needed inside and was hungry. Miss Lane, that's the neighbor, she was scared to let her come in on account of how weird her eyes looked. You wouldn't know anything about that, would you?"

I lift one shoulder and let it drop. He knows something strange is going on. He knows who I am and what I do—or did—for a living. I think I need to know where I stand before I admit to anything.

He stares at me so long, I become aware of the watch ticking on his wrist. This time, I wait him out. He eventually says, "Those two boys in the bathtub. Horrible. Just horrible. Know anything about them? Who they are? What in the hell happened to them?"

"They were already there. I found them that way."

"Uh-huh. Uh-huh. Okay. And did you notice anything about their eyes?"

"I should probably get a lawyer before I answer much more."

Carson's beaming smile comes back. "*Naw*, no need to do that. We're just having a conversation."

"Are you going to arrest me, Detective?"

Carson turns to Jaynes. She dips her chin, indicating her agreement with some unspoken directive.

"In all my years, Mr. Ford, I don't know if I've ever quite seen anything like this. Being who you are, and seeing as how you do what you do, I'd expect some cooperation with such strange matters. You are one lucky so-and-so, you know that?"

"How so?"

"Detective Jaynes and I reviewed your video evidence, and we both agree that it's enough to show that you acted in self-defense, at least when it comes to Miss Coeburn. Not to mention the fact that we ran some quick tests and found the boys' DNA underneath her fingernails. The scratches on their arms connect the dots there."

"So you're saying she murdered them?"

"We're not saying anything of the sort," he says. "Not yet."

"But you're not accusing me of anything?"

"Depends."

"On what?"

"Cooperation." He flicks a look over his shoulder at the two-way mirror. "Help. Things like that. Seems as if you might hold your future in your hands."

Shit. No *he's* handing me the bitter apple. But I have to eat it. This time, at least.

I ask, "Am I free to ask questions?"

"Be my guest."

"Are you looking for the boys' families?"

"Trying. It'll be a while. You wouldn't believe how many kids go missing each year." He leans back in the chair. The flimsy, plastic construction groans in protest. "So the question remains—*questions*, actually—why did you set that camera up to begin with, what language is she speaking, how did she get up again, and what's the deal with their eyes? All four of them. They got Ellen down in holding and her eyeballs are blacker than coal. All of the eye. The whole thing. And then the deceased individuals—the two boys and Miss Coeburn, hollowed out sockets. Black liquid crusted around them."

"Whoa," I say, sitting straighter. "Did you say she got up again?"

"Yes, sir. After they put you in the car. Apparently you were a couple of blocks away by the time the EMTs were getting ready to zip her into the trash bag. Miss Coeburn popped straight up off the ground and rushed my boys, poker sticking out of her neck. They fired two shots in self-defense, purely reactionary. One bullet centered her forehead and dropped her. We can show you on the video later. Helps your case that we didn't find that until after the fact. Stress does things to a man, but had we listened to your incoherent babble upon arrival, we might not have that evidence available, except for eyewitness accounts and what not."

"She got up. Jesus."

"I'm fairly certain he had nothing to do with it."

"Yeah, I hear that a lot. And you asked *what language* was she speaking? What does that mean?"

"The language Miss Coeburn is speaking in your recording."

"It wasn't English?"

Carson presses his lips together, flicks a look at Jaynes, then back to me. "You understood her when she was talking?"

"Yeah. I mean, I think so."

"Mr. Ford, one of the reasons we were delayed is because it took us a while to find a linguistics expert at this hour. Tracked down a professor up at Oregon State and he says he's never heard it before, but it sounds ancient. Biblical, even. Or probably older. As in, from what he can tell, there are no earthly languages existing today that are a derivative of what she's speaking."

"I—uh. Wow. I don't know."

"And you say you understood every word of it?"

"I thought I did. It's possible she had me under—" I almost say 'hypnotic spell' but that would sound even more ridiculous that everything we're discussing. "Under, um, I mean on… on drugs?"

"You're not exhibiting any signs."

"I don't know. I really don't."

"What in the hell are we dealing with here, son?"

I take a deep breath and hold it, exhaling. "You really want to know the truth? I need some kind of guarantee. Something in writing, especially without a lawyer here. That's probably not possible but—"

"Hang on." Annoyed, Jaynes finally speaks up from her perch in the corner. "We're not going to arrest you, Mr. Ford. We're familiar with your history, and we're familiar with what you've been doing with other departments since your unfortunate event with the Hopper child. We're asking for your help, and when you give it to us, you'll be free to go."

I sense an opportunity here. Should I take it? What do I have to lose?

"And I'm asking you for a written guarantee. Whatever you can do that'll hold up in court, if it comes to that."

She says, "We'll see what we can do."

I start to protest, but Carson interrupts me, saying, "That'll have to be good enough for now, Mr. Ford. We're good people. Trustworthy."

"Fine. So, we're looking at a little pro bono work in exchange for maybe overlooking some of the gray areas of my involvement?"

"Careful," Jaynes says, smirking, "verbally confirming that could be construed as an attempt to bribe an officer of the law."

I hold up my palms, feeling that intense, nervous urge to piss. That backfired.

"But I didn't hear a word of it," she adds. "You, Carson?"

"Not a bit, no, but if I *had* heard something I'd say it sounded like a fair deal."

"One more question first."

"Shoot."

"Lauren's a celebrity. How're you gonna approach the news of her, uh, *death*? Publicly, I mean."

"It'll be handled. If *this* is what you're asking, your involvement will be…minimal."

I lift my eyes to the video camera mounted in the corner of the room. "Is this going on record?"

"Maybe not all of it."

"Okay then." We shake hands. I feel slightly sleazy for trying to protect myself at the expense of Lauren's death, but if I'm going to save Chelsea from a Tier One demon, I need the freedom to move about.

Coeburn, I'll say an extra Hail Mary for you.

Jaynes says, "Tell us a story, Mr. Ford."

Well, shit. Here we go. Let's see how open-minded these two can be.

"Have you guys ever heard of the black-eyed children?"

25
Mike Long

Hours pass with no action.

This is not what I wanted.

The longer Dakota's unwelcome visitor hangs back without manifesting, the longer he's able to store up energy for when he does come through the portal and graces us with his presence.

Jerk.

We move from room to room, checking and rechecking the thermal imager, asking questions, trying to elicit a response. So much uneventful time crawls by that I begin to consider taunting him simply to see if that will create some kind of reaction. With demons, however, taunting is never a good idea, even with an experienced team like Ford and me. Those guys over on "the other channel," those dudes from *Ghost Bros & Company*, they found out firsthand what can happen when you taunt a demon with inexperienced members along. I think that poor dude that took the strongest hit might still be hanging out in a padded room, wearing the latest straightjacket designed by Martha Stewart.

Anyway. We're bored. You can't make something manifest, so Dakota invites me to the kitchen for a snack, and on the way down the stairs, she asks, after she's been tortured by this thing for weeks, why isn't it showing up now when we need it to?

"In the world of paranormal investigations, you take what you can get and be thankful for it. They don't operate on our schedules or on our planes of existence. That said, I'm starting to think that this is just going to be one of those nights where nothing happens. Ford and I hated that shit with a passion, and it occurred more often that we like to admit.

"There were times when we'd go into an investigation that promised a freakin' *goldmine* of evidence based on the strength of a witness's testimony, and then, zilch. Twelve hour days over a week's worth of recording to get one shitty, grainy, garbled EVP that may have been a barking dog somewhere else in the neighborhood. Set up, break it down, do it all over again, and you get static and hours of video of a high-backed chair sitting in a bedroom. Whoopee!"

We reach the bottom floor, turn right, and head back into the kitchen. The blinds are open, just as Dakota left them earlier, and the moon provides enough light for her to move about without flipping any switches. She pulls two plates out of a cabinet, asks me if I'd like some coffee, and pulls a couple of mugs down from an upper shelf.

She starts pulling a snack together while I go on blathering about fruitless investigations. "The Paranormal Channel would be out an ungodly amount of money paying for the whole crew to travel to the location, plus the equipment transfer costs, the stipend they paid to the witnesses and all that stuff. Somehow, Ford and I would end up taking the heat for it, no matter how often we tried to explain to the suits writing the checks that we couldn't *make* ghosts show up no more than we could ask the sky to turn pink on command."

Dakota has one of those fancy, single-cup brew devices, and by the time I'm finished with my mini tirade, she's already handing me a cup of black coffee. I decline sugar and sweetener both.

I take a sip and get back to it.

"Actually, I know why they'd pin the heat on me and Ford. Carla threw us under the bus every chance she got. I'm sure I hate her as much as Ford does, and after we screwed up Chelsea's life, I swore on *my* children's lives that I would never work with her again. And yet, here I am, trying to talk Ford into doing this goddamn documentary, canoodling with that she-demon in Louboutin pumps, because that's where the money is." I put a spoon in my coffee and stir it, pointlessly, since it's free of additives, while I wait on her to tell me it's okay to sell my soul.

Instead, she jokes, "I'm just surprised you know what Louboutins are."

"You're aware of the woman I married, right?"

"Ah, that explains it." Dakota plops down at the kitchen table with me, sliding a bowl of hummus and some carrots in between us. As I'm contemplating how well that'll pair with coffee, she licks her index finger and says, "Can I ask you something?"

"Sure."

"Might be a touchy subject."

"I doubt you can offend me."

She sips from her coffee mug, eyes me over the rim. She sputters through a number of false starts, then says, "You *do* understand that if Toni's cheating on you, you don't have to compromise your principles to keep her happy with the new money, right? Just hire a private investigator, get some pics of her and this Armando guy together, and boom. No court is going to deny that. You sail off into the sunset free of the gold-digger with your kids in tow."

"While that may be true," I say, mouthing the words around a crunchy carrot, "there's no money left. At least nothing substantial. Living expenses and some decent royalty checks from syndication. That's about all. It's barely enough for her to keep up appearances. And, supposing the courts miraculously decided to side with the mother after evidence of infidelity—no, trust me, she'd probably fight for negligence since I was gone for so many years—the kids won't have anything. Not what they *could*, anyway. They'd likely go with her anyway because Dear Old Dad will be the pitiful sap who's too broke to pay for the Xbox and smartphones. Hell, I don't even know what 'tween kids are into nowadays. Anyway, if she wants a divorce, so be it. Let her have it. I hardly have half of anything for her to take, regardless, and the least I can do is spend some time filming this documentary, as long as I can talk Ford into it, and then take whatever I earn to set up a trust fund for my children. I'm sure some of our lawyer fans of *Graveyard* could figure out how to protect anything I earn from the movie so she can't get to it. I'm not even betting on that, to be honest. The main goal is to make sure the kids are good."

Dakota nods, but doesn't say anything. I think she gets it, yet she seems sad.

"What's wrong?"

She taps a packet of artificial sweetener into her coffee and stirs it before answering, "Maybe I have no right to be, because really, we've only known each other for less than a day, but I'm worried about you."

I wave her off and say, "Nah, don't be. It's like I'm sad, but not really, because I kinda saw it coming from a mile away. I *tried* to salvage things, and actually wanted it to work on some level because there really were some good times in the past. I guess—it's just—when you know it's time to move on, it's not that bad. I'll be fine."

"Fine speech," she says, grinning slightly, "but that's not what I meant. I'm talking about going to war with—what did you call it? Chelsea's right-hander? What happens if you get possessed while you're filming? What happens if they commit you to some asylum like that kid from *Ghost Bros*?"

The lady knows her trivia. I reassure her that it won't happen, that even if I convince Ford to sign on, we're experienced, and we know our limits. Besides, now that we know what we're dealing with, we're primed to win.

Irritated, Dakota says, "But *what if*, Mike. What if something happens? How in the hell am I going to cook you dinner if they won't let you have a fork in your padded cell?"

Oh. *Ooooh.*

I see it now. She's *that* kind of worried—like, don't screw up the possibilities by having a demon go *nom-nom-nom* on your soul.

Damn, that's not at all what I expec—

Crash!

Crash!

Crash!

"Behind me. Now," I order, springing up to my feet, taking Dakota's arm, and slinging her back to where I can use my body as a shield. Across the kitchen, over the coffeemaker, three of the glass-paned cabinet doors have shattered like some pissed off teenager put his fist through them.

And, seeing as how there's no mop-haired brat around, my best guess is that Dakota's interloper drew in ample energy to make himself known.

Three more glass panes in the cabinet doors disintegrate—*crash! crash! crash!*—in rapid succession, coming closer to where we stand.

Dakota screams and tries to hide her face between my shoulder blades, her fingers clutching my t-shirt, wadding it up in her fists. I reach around, put a hand on her lower back and pat her, urging her to retreat into the next room. "Go, go, go," I whisper, realizing that we foolishly left all of our equipment on a hallway table where we were last investigating. We're blind to any kind of attack. I order Dakota upstairs and follow along behind her, sprinting up them, taking them by twos as the stairwell curves around and opens on the middle landing.

"Back to the office. Get the thermal cam ready," I tell her. "Take one of these." I yank a four-ounce bottle of holy water free from the runner's fanny pack and shove it into her hand. "Stay right back in the corner, with the thermal cam focused on the doorway, and if you see it coming through—"

"How will I know?" She can't hide the quiver in her voice.

"Remember what I told you? About the different colors for different heat signatures? You'll know. You can tell. Just keep repeating the Lord's Prayer and douse it with the holy water."

I move to leave. Her free hand whips out and wraps around my wrist, fingernails digging into that soft spot where you check for a pulse. "Wait, what're you doing?"

"Going to get rid of it."

Her eyes widen to the size of sand dollars. "No, don't leave me here. Not by myself."

"You're staying. End of story."

"No—"

From some far off corner of Dakota's beachfront mansion, a door slams, and then another.

"Stop," I say, stepping closer to her, cupping my hands on her shoulders, soft and reassuring, "I know this seems like some Hollywood ending where the hero leaves the leading lady behind and runs off to beat the bad guy—"

"Don't go."

"Just stay. Please. You'll be fine. I'll be fine. A few prayers, some holy water cocktail, and I'll send this dude packing."

From downstairs comes the thrashing, clattering sound of a kitchen chair flung across a tile floor.

The living room television cuts on at full volume. It shuts off again.

On again, off again.

"Ted, what we" ... *"going on"* ... *"the Republican party absolutely can't..."*

"Really? Political talking heads?" I say, trying to bring some much needed levity into the moment.

"Do *not* leave me here," she says, and it's a mixture of anger and fear.

"I have to. You know how you're worried about me and Chelsea's demon? Same thing. I can't let anything happen to you. I couldn't live with myself. I know how to handle these things, and you have to trust me."

"You said it was stronger than you thought. Those awful horns, remember?

"And I did, but that doesn't mean—whoa." The lights in the stairwell flicker like a strobe light at some juiced up rave party. "Gotta go."

I pull away as Dakota lets go of me, mouth pursed, her breath forced and heavy through her nostrils like she just finished a marathon. She pounces, surprising me with a kiss on the cheek.

I might have about seven seconds to relish the soft, tender touch of her lips on my skin before the demon is upon us, and I plan to use every single one while I stand here, gawking at her. I lift a hand and—

Outside of the open office door, a disembodied voice that sounds like the scream of a thousand souls being forced through a wood chipper says, "Hello, my pretty one."

Dakota says, "Oh shit," and tries to pull me into the corner with her.

I yank my hand free and reach for the remaining holy water containers. The spare one goes in my pocket and the other two are in my fists, locked and loaded.

A black, misty shape appears about head high, the smoky tendrils wrapping around the doorjamb like fingers clasping onto it. The shape grows. A head and shoulders peek around the edge, billowing, swirling, pulling itself into the room.

The voice changes to a haunting, childish tone as it emanates from everywhere and nowhere at once when it sings, "You want her. You can't have her. She's miiiiine!"

Then it hisses, unbearably loud, and pulls itself into the room.

Dakota screams.

The mist moves with so much speed.

My hands fly up and I clamp down on the bottles of holy water, squeezing as hard as I can, shouting, "Our Father, who art in Heav—*ungh!*" as it hurtles into my chest. I feel as if someone has reached inside my lungs and replaced the air with boiling gasoline.

I blink, once, twice. Unsteady. Off balance.

I feel invaded.

I feel murky. Cold.

And then a voice in my head tells me to face Dakota.

***

Dakota watches every terrifying second in slow motion. Her head has grown thick with pressure, as if she's submerged and can't reach the surface. Her heartbeat thumping in her ears sounds like the inside of a womb. She loses the feeling in her hands as the black, swirling mist surges into the room, and the small, seemingly useless bottle of holy water slips from her fingers. She hears the faint plunk on the carpet when it lands at her feet.

She screams, covers her mouth.

The entity hurtles straight at Mike's chest as he slings holy water at it.

He tries to pray—stops with a grunt—and goes eerily hushed for a moment before he begins turning around slowly, as if he's controlled by something else.

The dark mist is gone. Now it's only her and Mike.

She can sense that his energy has changed before he has fully turned to face her.

The warmth she felt from him, that schoolboy crush that had her pretending she didn't notice all day long, is now gone. It's replaced with a black longing. Not a crush, not affection, but an angry, lustful desperation—not want, *need*.

"Are you okay?" she asks.

His eyes have changed—before, they were droopy with exhaustion. He was a man whose life had been shredded apart by others through no fault of his own. There was a subtle desperation in the way he looked at the world, silently asking for something to finally go right again. His eyes held history of someone who had it all, lost everything, and had learned to accept his fate.

Yet whenever she had smiled at him, a trace of hope would lighten them.

All of that is gone, replaced by threatening *intent*.

"Mike?"

He takes a step closer. "Hello, my pretty one." It's Mike's voice, but polluted and strange. "Mine. All mine."

"Get out of him," she says, delicately at first, testing the reaction. When nothing comes, she raises her voice, demanding that the demonic entity leave. Yet again, there's no response, only the deliberate, hushed movement closer. She screams, "Mike, fight it! Don't let it take you!"

Mike's hands come up to chest level, hands spread apart, fingers curled.

"No," she whimpers.

He lunges, arms swinging wide, closing in as Dakota ducks at the last instant, grabbing empty air.

Dakota drops to one knee and grasps the last remaining bottle of holy water. She had made fun of Mike earlier for the ridiculous contraption around his waist, and now, what remains might not save her life, but it may give her a singular chance at escape. Her fingers tighten around it as she rolls forward on one shoulder, rotates, and springs up to her feet, continuing the motion, spinning to face him.

As Mike—no, not Mike, the demon inside him—whirls around, she squeezes the tiny bottle with both hands, the thin stream going straight into his eyes. She says, "Our Father, who art in Heaven, hallowed be thy name…" And she can remember no more.

It wouldn't matter anyway because he roars with rage, head turned to the ceiling, teeth bared and fists clenched.

"Uh oh." Dakota sprints for the office door, and before she darts into the illusion of escape, she sees a small black rectangle next to a lamp.

Mike's cell phone.

She grabs it, slams the door behind her, and trips. She breaks her fall with her hands and pushes up, driving her legs, feeling the muscles forcing her ahead.

In the same instant, the door booms as Mike's body pounds into it.

The handle rattles. The door is wrenched open.

It's then that Dakota realizes she has gone the wrong direction.

A wall of muscle, bone, and demon stands between her and the staircase. Behind her is nothing but empty room after empty room.

One of which has an extra patio door leading outside.

Dakota sprints.

All of her training, her conditioning, the marathons and triathlons, years spent burning away stress because it worked better than alcohol or prescriptions, has led to this moment. She knows she can outrun him. *It*.

If she can make it outside, the only question that remains is, how far is the drop off the balcony?

There's nothing but sand and brush below, but it's dark, and the second floor balcony hangs over a hillside, which could mean as little as ten feet at the rear and as much as twenty or more at the front. Possibly higher? She can't remember. She's never paid that much attention to it. She's only been out there to sunbathe, and then that ended when she caught the creepy teenager trying to film her.

I can do it, I can make the jump, she thinks as she flees. *I have to.*

She ducks into the last bedroom on the right and then makes an immediate left.

The sliding glass door is fifteen feet away.

Freedom.

***

Fire. Rage. Ashes and smoke in my lungs. I see her running. When she looks back, the fear in her eyes is fuel for the overwhelming ache for her that invades and engorges every cell in my body. It's a cold fire in my veins. I have images in my mind, memories of a past that doesn't belong to me. The flames of hell aren't orange. They're black. They lick up the walls, the rocky floor, and across the bodies of millions of damned souls screaming for eternity.

I run. I reach for her, grabbing her ankle as she tries to climb over the wall.

Mine. She's mine. Now and forever.

"Hello, pretty one." I dig my fingers into her strong shoulders and pull her closer. My lips go to hers as she struggles, screaming for me to stop.

My tongue feels forked as it invades her warm, inviting mouth.

She retches and—

***

Dakota sprints across the open upper deck. The smell of salt air and the remaining warmth of the day provide her with no comfort.

She begs God to save him.

Sweet, caring Mike. A good man.

No more. At least not right now.

How far will he follow her?

She's positive she can run fast enough. She's not as in shape as she was weeks ago, before this started, but she can do it. She can get away.

If she can escape him, maybe long enough to call Father Duke, they could do something for Mike. But, it's late. Would the priest answer at this hour? Would he even hear it? Did he have a hotline for demonic possession emergencies?

Dakota shoves Mike's cell phone in her back pocket, and then grabs the top railing that runs the length of the low wall. She looks over the edge, hesitating a second too long to see how far the drop is, and says, "Fuck it," as she tries to pull herself up. It has to be at least fifteen feet from this spot. Drop down to the soft sand, land lightly on the balls of her feet, and roll with the hill. Let gravity do the work.

One foot goes up to the railing and—

There's a hand on her ankle, pulling her back. She screams at his touch, his palm rough on her skin. Mike whips her around, squeezing hard as he jerks her close.

"Mike! Don't!" she screams.

And then his mouth is on hers.

She had thought about what a kiss might be like throughout the day, considered the possibilities. They had bonded over shared fame and their public image, celebrity and the burdens of maintaining a positive public image. She was vulnerable and scared. He played the part of her flawed hero well, even though he may not have known it at first.

She had sensed his attraction, caught him looking, and had felt it, too. It had been so long since anyone looked at her that way. Then, Toni. She had recognized her, seen her time and again, around town and along the beach at odd hours with a man who was not this man. She had kept quiet, deciding it was none of her concern.

A day spent with him did not constitute a chance at something more—she was old enough to recognize reality and responsibility—but there had been no harm in briefly fantasizing about his lips on hers, much in the same way you daydream about time spent on warm, sandy beaches with the handsome stranger who held the door open.

Fleeting moments about *what if* had twisted and snarled the question into *what now?*

This close, she can smell the sweat on his skin and feel the heat of his body against hers.

His tongue, stiff and wet, forces itself between her lips and deep into her mouth.

Dakota gags, not because of Mike, but because of the entity inside him. She considers biting his tongue, clamping down as hard as she can, severing the slithering muscle in half.

But she can't. Somewhere deep inside, the real Mike is trying desperately to regain control. He has to be. He would never do this to her, would never allow it to happen. She hasn't known him long, but she knows that much.

Instead, Dakota silently apologizes to Mike, wherever he may be in there, then distracts him first with a slap to the side of his head, followed by driving her knee up between his legs, hoping beyond hope that pain is a motivator for the demonically possessed.

A guttural *oooph* erupts from his mouth, blowing into hers, and he lets go, hands flying down to his crotch.

Dakota shoves him away, staggers a few steps back toward the house, and comes to an abrupt halt when he clamps onto her wrist. He's down on one knee, using her resistance as a counterbalance to pull himself up.

She wrenches sideways, twisting at the hip, bringing her arm up as she spins. Her sole intent was to hit him hard enough to break free, but luck helps the point of her elbow to land just behind his eye, instantly knocking him unconscious. Mike crumples into a heap.

Dakota gasps in relief, wonders how long she has.

Just hurry, she thinks. Find something.

A minute later, she's kneeling over him, binding his wrists and ankles together using shoestrings from abandoned sneakers, multiple pairs that she had worn out from years of training.

Mike groans as she pulls the cell phone from her pocket.

She scrolls rapidly through the list of contacts and finds the number she needs. She calls, and she prays.

One ring. Two rings. Three.

Fading hope tightens her chest.

Then, a groggy voice answers, "Hello?"

"Father Duke? I need help. It's about Mike Long."

***

A hundred yards north, a grinning teenager can't believe what he's just captured. Thank God for rich, pushover parents and a strong zoom.

He had seen weird lights in Dakota Bailey's house. Flashlights going from room to room. Then rapid, sporadic flashing, illuminating various parts of the house. So he began recording, curious, not expecting much.

Minutes later, Dakota hurtled onto the balcony, the same one where he had filmed her sunbathing so many times—in the nude—and sold those videos and pictures to his friends for hundreds of dollars.

The man followed. What would this lead to? The teenager could only cross his fingers and wait.

Even in the green hue of night vision, it was easy to see that Dakota's aggressor was Mike Long, one of the former hosts of *Graveyard: Classified*.

This was worth more than a few bucks from his friends.

Tabloids would pay thousands.

Or YouTube. Millions of hits. *Millions*.

Yes. There it is. That's what he'll do.

He backs away from his window and sits down at his laptop where he connects a USB cable.

He crops the video to only use the best parts, uploads it, then waits for the page to go live.

Minutes later, he emails his friends, and absolutely cannot believe his good fortune. He'll be on the front pages of the Internet by the time he wakes up.

That is, *if* he can sleep.

26
Portland, Oregon
Ford and Mike Long

I'm not quite sure how many times I've apologized to Ulie, and in the past couple of weeks, I'm positive he's put on a doggie pound or two from all the treats I've been giving him.

He's fine around me, because I'm the one and only Foodbringer. I'm the Light of His Life. I'm the One with the Stick. I am the Thrower of All Things.

I am Pillow. I am Chew Toy. I am He Who Takes Me for a Run Sometimes.

I am also He Who Will Never Leave My Dog Alone Again. Unless he's with Melanie.

He gets slightly skittish when I come into the room unannounced, but other than that, we're best buds. When we venture outside the house, it's elderly ladies that spook him the most. Can you blame him?

We've been going to a dog park down the street while I slowly try to reintroduce him to the outside world, away from the security-blanket comfort of his cozy bed in the corner of my living room. He does fine until the little old ladies with their yippy growlers try to come over and see if he wants to make friends with whatever puffball abomination they're dragging around on the end of a leash.

I make up excuses for Ulie, tell them that he's just super shy around other dogs. There would be no conceivable way to explain the following: "He's wary around wrinkly old ladies like you because he thinks you're going to eat his soul for breakfast."

One thing that's puzzled me since I had my revelation about Lauren Coeburn is the fact that animals are supposed to be sensitive to the supernatural. Ulie should have been able to pick up on something as soon as she and Grandma Death Eyes walked into my condo. I have no reasonable explanation for why he didn't. The only thing I can assume is that the entity piloting a black-eyed person has evolved beyond nature, and is undetectable by standard methods like doggie intuition. It can lie dormant until it's time to act. If it doesn't have an objective, then it'll emerge once it's sapped the available energy from its current host and needs to feed.

Ford, I'm hungry.

You need to let me in.

I can't blame Ulie. I like to think of myself as sensitive to the spirit world. Perhaps not as much as an animal's innate abilities, but regardless, I missed it too.

I still get shivers thinking about Lauren being that close to me and how close I came to having *my* soul devoured.

That would've sucked.

I stayed in Newport for another three days working with Detectives Carson and Jaynes, trying to explain to them everything I knew about black-eyed children, which wasn't much. I speculated enough to write a book.

We read report after report online, emailed witnesses and had web chats with those willing to talk to us. It was the same thing, every single time.

No, they didn't let them in.

No, they didn't have proof.

Yes, they were absolutely positive of what they had seen.

They weren't able to uncover the identity of those poor boys either. There were no fingerprint matches in the national records, no DNA, no dental records. Nothing. Nor were there pictures of missing children that matched. Some came close. Dark hair, light skin, thin builds, but nothing definitive. It was odd that they didn't exist anywhere, and when I suggested that perhaps there was a mother unit somewhere pumping out fleshy shells to be used as cute and approachable hosts, Detective Carson lifted his palm and said, "I can't take any more, Ford. This shit's all too weird for me. We'll take it from here. You go on home, get some rest. But, hey, keep your phone handy. We might stumble across something else."

So here I am. I gave Jesse some time off. He wanted to leave Albuquerque for a while anyway and do some traveling, and I told him to go before life and his own demons got in the way.

I've been ignoring calls from unrecognized numbers, letting them go to voicemail, which is how I know that Carla Hancock has been blowing up my phone.

In a rare move for the cutthroat she-devil, she apologizes again and again for issuing the press release and announcing my commitment to the documentary before getting the official okay from me. Still, she wants to know if I've made a decision. The numbers she offers for my involvement get higher with each successive call. Why bother telling her that, for me, it's not about the money?

Although, I *do* enjoy listening to her voice get that tiny hint of desperation each time she raises her bid.

The Graveyard: Classified Paranormal Series

I've been resting, answering emails, and filing away the raciest picks from the spotcamgirls under a new folder called "Mom's Cornbread Recipe."

I'm not entirely sure why I do that since it's just me living here, and it's not like I'm going to corrupt Ulie's young mind if he goes snooping around my laptop.

Well, yeah, I do know why. I scared Melanie so much that night, she's been coming around to check on us. She brings meals for me and rawhide bones for Ulie. She stays a little longer each time, and it could be because Jeff from the control room is no longer in the picture.

Ironically enough, he was too controlling.

I'm not getting my hopes up, but we even had lasagna *together* the other night and watched a rerun of *Yes, Chef!* on that twenty-four hour food network. It was the one where Dakota Bailey concocted a ham and peach tart so amazing that it made the bald judge get up from his little table of superiority and shake her hand.

And speaking of Dakota Bailey, that thing with Mike?

Dude.

***

The very first news I heard about his situation came by way of Glenda Harrison, that "nothing but the hard facts!" lady on one of the political news channels. You know the one. She pounds the desk and yells at people when she thinks they're lying to her—that one.

I was still in Newport and had moved from the contaminated condo to a cheap hotel room. I'd had a long day of talking to witnesses, so I ended up mindlessly flipping through channels when I heard this:

"Tonight! More news from Graveyard: Classified. *Are the famous paranormal superstars possessed, or simply cursed with bad luck?"*

There was some mention of my state of affairs. Evidently an anonymous source had leaked news to the media that I'd had a lover's quarrel with Lauren Coeburn while on a secret celebrity retreat to the Oregon coast. I left her behind and she proceeded to get high on whatever designer drugs she had available, had a violent reaction, went batshit crazy, and essentially committed "suicide by cop."

(The "official" autopsy report stated that it was a rare biochemical reaction that affected the nervous system. In addition to that, we were ridiculously lucky in the fact that Lauren had designated that she wanted her eyes donated to science, given Ellen's blindness. That solved the lack-of-eyeballs thing before Carson and Jaynes had her body shipped back to L.A.)

Lover's quarrel. Abandoned Lauren.

Screw Glenda Harrison.

I flipped a cheap chair and the pathetic coffee table in the hotel room, and thought about suing Glenda Harrison from here to the end of time. But then, she commended me for keeping cool and calm in such an unfortunate situation.

If she only knew.

Also, thankfully, whoever leaked the news had graciously decided to leave out the bit about the hollowed out shells of two former black-eyed children.

That whole case is going so deep into the file room that they'll need an archeologist to find it.

I owe Carson and Jaynes, big time.

And then, Mike.

Man, I didn't even know what to think when I first heard it. I was stunned.

The Graveyard: Classified Paranormal Series

Since I had been so involved with the detectives and Lauren's situation, I hadn't been online. Nobody had said anything to me either. How and why someone at the station failed to mention it is beyond me, and I can only assume that Carson and Jaynes kept the information from me so I would be able to focus on helping them.

In the video—the one being broadcast *everywhere*—even with the green hue of night vision, accompanied by an incredible zoom feature, you can plainly see that it's none other than Dakota Bailey. She's running across the second-level deck of her beachfront mansion, pursued by my friend, partner, and brother-in-life, Mike 'The Exterminator' Long.

Mike grabs her, forces a kiss. The low wall blocks what happens below their waists, but based on his reaction, her knee goes up to his crotch, giving her a long second to break free. He grabs for her again, she spins, delivers an elbow, and my buddy drops like his parachute failed to open.

The video already had two million hits before the national media began to get wind of it.

"And get this, folks," Glenda Harrison said, "Miss Bailey must be a saint, because she's *not pressing charges*. What's the world coming to? I don't know about you, but I'm not buying that whole 'he was possessed' excuse for a second."

Then, for the next two weeks, since I left Newport and came home, Mike has been getting drawn and quartered all over the place. Social media, nightly news, cable shows filled with talking heads, all of them talking about how fame and fading stardom can do strange things to people. This was despite Dakota's best efforts to dampen the critics' fire. Interview after interview, she defends him and insists that she bears no ill will toward Mike Long, that it wasn't his fault, and that she had enlisted his help to eliminate the evil spirit in her home. If anything, he should be labeled a hero for facing down such a sinister entity.

Mike's only saving grace has been the fact that he has fought demons in the past, possibly adding a hint of credibility to Dakota's story.

It doesn't change the fact that there are plenty of grievances, people griping online, asking, "Why is she protecting him?"

I hate it for him. I really do. I know what it's like to be the target of such vitriol.

And yet, maybe now he can understand what I went through with the aftermath of Chelsea's incident.

The craziest thing is, I was positive this shit would put a big fat damper on the documentary. We would be able to move on, and I'd have to find some other way to protect Chelsea from Boogerface.

Instead, I'm going to postulate that it increased the interest for a reunion by about seventeen million percent, which has doubled the calls from Carla, and brought even more attention to Mike, Dakota, and the video captured by that damn peeping tom.

The teen jerkhole is eating it up, by the way, making the rounds on the interview circuit. I heard he reportedly got a six-figure offer to do his own reality series. When will it ever end?

I've tried to call Mike. Cell, home, his former agent, Dakota's agent, mine, even Father Duke, but he's not answering, and nobody knows how to get in touch with him. I did get a note from a fan who insists she saw him at a gas station in Kansas. Throughout the day, three more emails arrived from fans in the same town. They all wanted to know what was up with Mike, why was he in Kansas, and asked if I would be willing to tell them.

So, at least he's alive. If I can't get in touch with him within the next couple of days, I'm calling in a private investigator to track him down. Less attention that way.

Bottom line is, for now, I'm in the clear and Mike's not.

It's strange being on this side of things.

***

I'm putting the finishing touches on my world-famous mushroom bacon burgers out on the deck when I hear the faint ding-dong of my doorbell.

Curious, but not curious enough to go rushing for the door, I take my time, wiping my hands as I stroll in from outside, through the living room and kitchen, up the elevated flooring, and then past the library and bathroom. It might be Melanie, though she hadn't mentioned that she would be coming by.

I open the door to find Mike looking like he's been living under a bridge for about five years. He has dark bags under his eyes, scruffy cheeks, about a week's worth of stubble on his normally shaved head, and plenty of stains on a plain white t-shirt. His shorts are wrinkled. One sneaker is untied.

"Mike! You're alive."

"Hey, Ford."

"The fuck have you been, man? I've been trying to call you for days. Get in here."

Mike nods and steps inside, rubs his hands together and looks around. "I like what you've done to the place."

"No bullshit small talk. We're heading straight for the alcohol because you look like you need a beer. Actually, I should say you look like you need *another* beer. Maybe something stronger? Whiskey?"

Mike follows me, saying, "I'm fine, Ford. I already got one mama."

He leans up against the kitchen counter while I pull a local-brew lager from the refrigerator and pop the top off. He takes it, salutes me, and gulps a long pull from the bottle.

I ask, "How you holding up?"

Burp. "Been better."

I want to ask him a million questions, but I don't know where to start. I *do* know Mike, and if the past two weeks haven't completely changed him as a human being, he'll get around to the details when he damn well pleases.

He takes another pull from the bottle and then examines the label. "That'll put some hair on your chest, huh? Not like I need it."

I grab one for myself. "So."

"So."

I chuckle and nonchalantly ask, "Anything new?"

I feel like he's going to hold out on me. He'll keep his chin up and chest out, we might skirt some details, and then I'll get some truth out of him later once I've gotten him hammered.

Nope.

Without warning, and totally unlike Mike 'The Exterminator' Long, he sets his beer on the counter, hangs his head, and opens the floodgates. Shoulders bobbing, tears streaking down his cheeks, mouth twisted sideways in abject anguish.

Holy shit, that's an ugly cry if I've ever seen one.

It makes my heart ache. "Aw, buddy," I say, moving over to him.

Nobody ever said that bromances couldn't involve hugs. I put my arms around Mike's shoulders and pull him in, letting him rest his forehead on my collarbone. "It's gonna be fine, dude. If anybody can sympathize over what this feels like, then you're snotting all over his shirt. It sucks balls, big hairy ones, and it feels like someone is squeezing your lungs every time you take a breath, but it'll pass. It really will."

We hold that pose until his sobbing subsides, and then he pulls away, gently headbutting my clavicle a couple of times in bro-like acknowledgement. He gives me an embarrassed grin and wipes his cheeks. "I don't know how you handled it for so long. I'm sorry, man. I…"

"You don't have anything to apologize for."

"It felt good to let that go."

"Always does."

"Do I smell burgers?"

"Yeah. But you'll have to fight Ulie for the second one."

And that's the end of the Time That Mike Long Cried.

We eat. We chat. We get slightly buzzed on what few beers I have. He declines when I suggest that I could call a delivery service. "Too tired," he says. "I'll be out by sundown. You know how long the fucking drive is out here?"

I learn that Toni has been cheating on him—I'm not surprised—and yet, she'll get anything he has left because of the video. He's positive of that. He compliments Dakota and her resolve; he says that they had a little talk before he left.

"She's amazing, and it'll be good," he says, "one of these days. But now it's weird, you know? For me, I mean. Seeing myself in that video, remembering the things I saw while that fucker was inside of me. I need to cleanse myself first. I feel dirty."

"What'd you see?" I ask.

"Hell. I *literally* saw what hell looks like. Black fire. Screaming souls. What everybody imagines, you know? I don't know if maybe I was recreating an image I'd seen before in my mind, but goddamn, did it ever *feel* real."

I've been holding onto this for a couple of hours now, figuring I should wait for the right time. I tell him about Lauren Coeburn and the black-eyed children. I tell him what the Lauren Thing said to me right before I jammed a fireplace poker through its neck.

"Son of a bitch," Mike says. We're leaning over the balcony, looking down at Portland proper below us. He reaches over and slaps me on the back. "Sounds like Boogerface wants you to meet him down at the OK Corral. Showdown at high noon, right?"

Here it is. Here's the true reveal. What's behind the secret door?

"Let's do it, Mike."

"Do what?"

"The documentary. I'm in."

I thought he would've been more excited. Instead, he continues to peel the label off his beer bottle. "A week ago, I would've kissed you on the lips. But now? Sure, if that's what you want. Let's fight the bastard and be done with this shit."

"That's the plan. It's all about Chelsea now. I can't believe I'm actually going to give Carla Hancock what she wants, but we have to protect Chelsea. That's priority number one, no matter what. Priority number two—now that we both could use a little redemption in the eyes of God and everybody underneath him, let's kick some demon ass and ride off into the sunset like heroes."

"Win and walk away?"

I nod. "Win and walk away."

We shake on it, and I take the opportunity to rub the scruff on his head. "What in the hell is up with your hair? Looks like somebody got after a pair of bull's balls with a set of dull clippers."

"Hey, don't knock it. I'm trying something new."

Later, we move into the living room and flop down on the couch on opposite ends. The TV goes on, and I hurriedly flip through the channels, careful to avoid anything that might be talking about Mike and that damn video.

I settle on yet another rerun of *Yes, Chef!*, this one also featuring Dakota—it seems like they all do—and it's one I haven't seen before.

Mike says, "Watch what she does with this porterhouse, Ford. She could make a grown man weep for joy." I look over at him and watch the corners of his mouth pull up into a soft smile, flush with pride and admiration. "She's a magician. It's like she's David Copperfield with a filet knife."

Nice.

It's good to see him on the other side.

And by that I mean the right side of happiness.

At least for the time being, because God only knows if either one of us is truly prepared to take on Boogerface.

EPILOGUE
Chelsea Hopper

Chelsea wakes up, having dreamed of fangs and smoke in her lungs, black fire and claws, people burning alive in a pool of yellow, foul-smelling water. The dreams are getting worse. Horrible, ghastly dreams that leave her legs shaky as she pushes herself up from her bed. It's still dark out, but her nightlight illuminates the room and she's relieved to see that she doesn't have cloven hooves like in the nightmare.

She *wants* to be strong, *is* strong for her age. People tell her all the time.

She's so tired, though.

And angry. The dreams fill her belly with hatred.

For her school, her teacher, and her principal.

Tania has been gone for a week now. She won't be back for a long while.

Dylan's mouth is wired shut. He looks so sad, so pathetic.

People feel sorry for him.

The entire school has turned against her.

Chelsea leaves her bedroom and drags her fingers along the wood paneling through the dark of night until she feels the opening of the bathroom, hoping she doesn't wake her parents.

She enters, shuts the door behind her, and turns on the lights above the sink.

In the mirror, it's her.

Of course it is. It's always her.

Her hair is blonde, hasn't been burnt away. Her ears don't rise into sharp points. Her fingers aren't long, bony, and tipped with razor-sharp claws. Her skin is fine. It's white, like it's supposed to be, rather than gray and pockmarked with craters and blisters, oozing with pus.

She pulls open the front of her pajamas.

No gross parts have sprouted like those of a filthy, disgusting boy demon.

In a way, she's disappointed.

Chelsea lifts her gaze and stares at the young girl looking back at her.

She opens her mouth, baring her teeth, spit glistening on her gums.

Chelsea hisses, tasting ashes in the back of her throat as the mirror splinters, shattering her reflection into a thousand jagged points.

She giggles.

Soon.

***

Desmond Doane

GRAVEYARD: CLASSIFIED
Book 3

THE BELLY OF THE BEAST
Desmond Doane

The Graveyard: Classified Paranormal Series

May all your nightmares come true…

Desmond Doane

PROLOGUE

THE MAN, THE MYTH, THE ALMIGHTY
A conversation with the enigmatic Ford Atticus Ford
by Jessie Lynn Wade
September Issue
Portland Paranormal Quarterly

It's dusk, in that hazy time when the horizon is minutes away from swallowing the last morsels of daylight. The brilliant pinks, purples, and oranges lining the wispy clouds are gorgeous. The sky is, and has always been, a canvas for nature's paintbrush. Once the color drains away, darkness wraps its black cloak around the hum of life while mothers tuck children in beneath cozy sheets. Fathers say goodnight and kiss soft foreheads. Streetlights fight for command of their territory, barely winning the battle for a small patch of space along empty sidewalks.

Hours later, after we mere humans have slipped into blissful slumber, one man—along with his partner and a team of technicians—steps forward to protect us against scary things that go bump in the night.

At least that used to be the case, and that man, my friends, is the almighty Ford Atticus Ford. A hero to many before committing an egregious mistake that had his hit television series ripped from the coveted Thursday night lineup.

Almighty. It's a term he once accepted with pride, but it would seem he hasn't felt so omnipotent over the past couple of years. Not since The Incident with the Little Blonde One.

You know what I'm talking about, as does nearly every person who is aware of Ford's existence. There's no need to belabor the mistakes made during that live episode on Halloween night two years ago. One could say entire forests have been destroyed with articles written about the occurrence and its consequences—this magazine included—and with this being Portland, Oregon, we're trying to hug as many trees as possible.

Portlanders unite! Save the trees! Save the ink!

Try as we might, eventually the topic of Ford and Chelsea Hopper comes 'round again, inevitably made partners, a graveyard and a tombstone. Attempting to talk about one without the other is an exercise in futility.

As Ford sits across from me in this tiny café in the Pearl District where the scent of roasting coffee beans is subdued only by shouting baristas. It's obvious that the man dressed in his signature black outfit is emotionally burdened by past failures, but will forever have a love of the game.

For now, he remains passionate about the paranormal, visibly thrilled when I share my own personal ghost story, and yet, whenever the conversation drifts near Chelsea Hopper, a melancholy weight settles over him, pushing his shoulders down, eyes averting, examining the minuscule wording on a sugar packet as if he's truly interested in the fine print.

It's impossible not to discuss her, given the motivations behind his current project with his partner, co-host, and bosom buddy Mike Long, but going into the interview, I didn't want to push him away, so my intentions were to focus on what was always his favorite topic in the past.

Himself.

Ford Atticus Ford was a womanizing glory hound during the impressive primetime reign of *Graveyard: Classified*; he'll readily admit to that fact because he seems determined to right his wrongs. Yet when I suggest that maybe you can't change a zebra's stripes, he scoffs and tells me the colors of a zebra have nothing to do with motivation and the desire to be a better person.

Noted, Ford, but how does one respond to those who say forgiven, but not forgotten? Those impressive shoulders—he's been working out, you know—lift and drop. A resigned shrug is his only answer.

Has Ford atoned for his sins already? Perhaps and perhaps not, depending on whom you ask.

These days, he offers his spooky services to police departments, functioning as a paranormal private investigator, getting paid in peanuts and smiles. He's fighting the good fight. He still gets recognized in public and poses for photos. He still has female fans sending him racy pictures. He still gets calls from celebrity acquaintances asking if he'll lead paranormal investigations for curious groups of A-listers. It's easy to say no to those, he says, because it feels like it would be disrespectful to the citizens of the spirit world.

And ten seasons of exploiting them on television wasn't?

Once you become a social pariah, Ford tells me, you have a lot of time to think about the past, and what you might have done wrong, or what the catalyst was that might have changed things. If you can identify the switch, you can see another problem coming.

Rather than condensing our conversation into meager paraphrasing, I thought it best to let the discussion with Ford Atticus Ford play out as it happened. What I noticed during our interview is that the Almighty has some inherent characteristics that will always remain the same—there's the whole zebra and his stripes thing—but the man sitting across from me was just that: a *man*.

Finally.

Gone was the *enfant terrible* of reality television, the womanizing adolescent in an adult's body. In its place sat a mature adult willing to own up to his mistakes and claw for redemption.

That is as long as it doesn't completely smother the occasional ego trip.

Or prevent him from winking at the cute barista behind the counter.

The following is a partial transcript from our brief interview—he's on a tight schedule, of course, with the upcoming documentary—and it's the first in-depth look at the man, the myth, the almighty, in well over two years.

Enjoy, and I'll see you on the other side.

Jessie Lynn Wade: Hi! Thanks so much for coming, Mr. Ford.

Ford Atticus Ford: What's with the 'mister,' Jessie? You've known me for, like, eight years.

JLW: Just responsible, professional journalism.

FAF: As if you've been accused of that in the past.

JLW: Hey!

FAF: Kidding. Kidding. Good to see you again. And before I forget, happy birthday. (*Editor's Note: Mrs. Wade reached the forty-year milestone on the date of the interview.*)

JLW: Aww, thanks. I managed to survive another year.

FAF: Sometimes that's more of an achievement than it sounds.

JLW: True. So, let me start here, because I've always been curious… Do you ever wonder if people are calling you by your first name or your last name when they simply address you as 'Ford'? For me, I think that would lead to some sort of identity crisis.

FAF: (*chuckles*) It's all part of the mystery isn't it? At least it's better than, "Hey, dickhead!"

JLW: Seriously, though, I'm not criticizing your parents here, but I think everybody has wondered what in the world their thought process was like when they decided to name their kid 'Ford Ford.'

FAF: They're interesting people, certainly. Both hyper-intelligent. Caring to a fault. Wicked senses of humor. My dad finally retired after thirty years in the military, and my mom is getting ready to pull the plug on her tenured career as an astrophysics professor. How they ended up with a TV personality who chases ghosts is anybody's guess. If the apple doesn't fall very far from the tree, I should be barking orders at baby-faced recruits or creating diagrams of planetary alignments. Anyway, there's no *real* mystery behind my name. Dad had this gorgeous '67 Ford Mustang, candy apple red with white racing stripes, and Mom always joked that he loved it more than her, which he obviously denied. So when I came along, here I am, a gurgling bundle of joy, and he told her that if there was anything he'd ever love more than her, it was me. Took her about two seconds to start referring to me as 'the other Ford' and it stuck. The 'Atticus' part is easy. She was reading *To Kill a Mockingbird* in the hospital and liked the sound of it.

JLW: Mystery solved.

The Graveyard: Classified Paranormal Series

FAF: *Zoinks!*

JLW: (*laughs*) Funny, Shaggy. Which, I might add, is fairly appropriate considering I've heard the scuttlebutt about your new canine companion.

FAF: You mean Dog Atticus Dog?

JLW: You're kidding... Right? Tell me you're joking.

FAF: Yes. His name is Ulysses. Ulie for short. My own little bundle of joy.

JLW: Should we move on to some serious topics? Anything out of bounds?

FAF: I've got a strict non-disclosure agreement with Spirit World Productions, so any specific details about the documentary are off limits. Broad generalizations are fine.

JLW: Anything else?

FAF: I'm sure you have a pretty good idea. Some questions are more painful than others.

JLW: Responsible, professional, *easy-going* journalism, that has to be my *modus operandi* here?

FAF: I didn't say that. Just no knees to the groin. Respectful. How 'bout that?

JLW: Fair is fair. Oh, but you know what? I've been dying to tell you this for ages. Can I share my own ghost story?

FAF: Of course!

JLW: My husband and I just moved into this new house across the river. Small fixer-upper, needs lots of work, but I adore it. It's what we always wanted. Two stories, creaky hardwood floors that remind me of my grandmother's house. Beautiful place, but we're positive that the man who lived there before us never left.

FAF: Intelligent or residual?

JLW: Residual would be my guess. No response to any EVP or spirit box sessions or anything like that, unless he's shy.

Mostly what we hear is a clear set of footsteps going up to the second floor about every six hours.

FAF: Nice! (*Here he spends five excitable minutes offering detailed advice about possible approaches to capturing evidence.*) That is, if you want to go that route.

JLW: We thought about it, but really, we're kinda content with letting him be. From what we've learned, his wife was sick for a few years and he was diligent about keeping to a schedule with her medication. When she finally passed, he wasn't too far behind her.

FAF: Yeah. Lost his reason for staying on. So sad, huh?

JLW: Sad? It's *heartbreaking*. Ugh. I get choked up just thinking about it.

FAF: (*silence*)

JLW: Does it ever get to you like that?

FAF: Like what?

JLW: Thinking about all the investigations you've been on. All the death you've been around. Some of it violent. No reason for others. Any regrets that you didn't do enough for someone on either side of life? All those hauntings. I mean, they were *people*.

FAF: Not all of them.

JLW: Oh, you mean… The one at the Hop… Um, that one.

FAF: Yeah. And others. (*silence*)

JLW: I'm sorry. 'Regrets' isn't exactly what I meant. Not in that sense. Everybody already knows you have regrets about… her.

FAF: Can we, um… Let's not.

JLW: Absolutely. Yeah, moving on, then. Here's something I've been dying to know. Everyone is familiar with the story about how you and Mike Long captured that full-bodied apparition on film, and that was the genesis of your rise to paranormal fame. Yet you've hinted about an experience when you were younger that piqued your interest in the supernatural. I spent *days* reading every print and televised interview of yours that I could find, and not once have you discussed it. Any reason why that is? And would you care to share it now?

FAF: (*Remains uncomfortably silent for twenty seconds*) Fine. (*smiles*) Why not, right? I did have an experience, and I've never shared the details for a couple of reasons. One, it was part of the intrigue, like what could've *possibly* happened to this guy to scare him into chasing ghosts for a living, that sort of thing. Two, you get to the point in the *business of celebrity* where nothing is sacred. Your home, your meals, your vacations, your relationships. Cameras, fans, autographs. Even inside the supposed privacy of your house, you never really feel like you have anything of your own because there could be some paparazzi photographer out there with a telephoto lens, trying to grab a shot of you walking around in your underwear. So, I never shared my story because it was the one thing that was mine, something that I could hold onto.

JLW: I can understand that. If you'd like to keep it private, that's okay by me. I don't want you to feel like I'm dragging it out of you.

FAF: No, I'll share. I'm a different sort of 'me' these days. I have a lot of things that are mine now that I didn't have before. Anyway. I can see it in my head, clear as day. I was seven years old, and I was in bed. My nightlight was on and I called my dad into my room to ask him to get the moths off the ceiling. Every night, without fail, every flying insect in the house would flock to my room. Freaked me out thinking I'd wake up with a moth trying to climb into my nose. Okay, so Dad left, and I was lying there in bed, just about to drift off, and the closet door opened by itself. I sat up to see what was going on, and the damn door swung shut like I'd caught something trying to sneak out. It scared me so much I couldn't speak. Totally froze. And even if I could've moved, I would've had to pass by the closet door to leave the room. Wasn't happening. A minute or two later, it creaked open again, and a young girl about Chelsea's age poked her head out. Kind of transparent, kind of not. She smiled and waved at me, then ducked back into the closet and closed the door. Thirty-odd years later, here I am.

JLW: Wow.

FAF: It's not the most incredible origin story.

JLW: I think it's fantastic!

FAF: Regardless, I never saw her again. Never slept in that room again either. Being the military and sciencey types, my folks didn't believe me, but they let me sleep on the living room couch for the next three years until we moved.

JLW: Do you think, subconsciously, that the child spirit is maybe why you have such a connection with Chelsea Hopper?

FAF: Nah. I was seven. I had a visitor. (*shrugs*) Chelsea getting attacked was my fault, and I've been through some experiences lately that suggest her demon tormentor isn't finished with her. Or me.

JLW: Care to explain?

FAF: I can't. Let's just say that revenge is not confined to humans alone, and we're hoping the documentary will convince the believers and doubters to be careful, no matter what.

JLW: So what *can* you tell me about the documentary?

FAF: Not a whole lot, I'm afraid.

JLW: Rumors have been swirling that you and Mike Long are headed back to the Hopper House—

FAF: I can't, Jessie. Sorry. Next question.

JLW: You're not going to like this one very much either.

FAF: Go for it.

JLW: You had a highly visible public breakup with your ex-wife, Melanie, due to your infidelity during your time on the show. I mean, you were shameless back then, if the rumors are true.

FAF: Is there a question in there or...

JLW: You've always said you felt like you were sort of crucified in the public eye after the, um, the *incident*. Do you think that the media helped that explode because of the cheating playboy image you had? Maybe some reasonable retribution?

FAF: So the question is, were they justified in tearing me down because I was such an asshole to Melanie?

JLW: Close enough.

FAF: (*long moment of consideration, punctuated by heavy sighs*) Yeah. I think they were.

JLW: So you *agree* with what happened to your public image? You deserved it?

FAF: Look, I screwed up. I know I did. I had fame and fortune shoved into my lap and into my bank account. I'd always been the dorky guy next door and suddenly women were throwing themselves at me. I began to accept that I was owed this all along for taking so much shit growing up. That's not an excuse. I had control of my decisions, but I abused my positioning in the universe. I've apologized to Melanie, profusely, I might add, and we're back on speaking terms. Maybe even more than speaking terms. Don't print that. Or, screw it. Print it. She's amazing, we're talking again, and I won't screw it up this time.

JLW: Are you sure? I mean, I don't doubt you, really, because you seem headstrong when you're motivated about something, but what if a zebra can't change his stripes?

FAF: (*scoffing*) C'mon. I know what you're getting at. Once a cheater, always a cheater? Is it *inherent*? Genetics, like the color of a zebra? That has nothing to do with free will, motivation, and the desire to be a better person.

JLW: Duly noted.

FAF: Sorry for the tone. I just—I'm *trying*. Melanie has forgiven me in most respects. I doubt we'll be walking down the aisle again any time soon, but it's all about redemption. Trying to atone. For Melanie. For Chelsea. Will I ever be truly forgiven? Only God can answer that.

JLW: Or, on the other hand, what about forgiven, but not forgotten? Is that something you can accept?

FAF: (*shrugs*)

JLW: That's it? Just a shrug?

FAF: The media has a short attention span, but history has a long memory. Ask me again in fifty years if they've forgotten.

JLW: Good point. So.

FAF: So.

JLW: Since you're not allowed to talk about the documentary, what else are you up to these days? Confirm some of the rumors for us.

FAF: Well, I don't know if they're rumors, per se, but most everyone knows I've been working with various police departments around the U.S. as a paranormal private investigator, helping solve cases when they hit dead ends.

JLW: No pun intended.

FAF: (*chuckles*) None at all. That's mainly it.

JLW: I heard you're thinking about starting some celebrity ghost hunting tours. Something like that?

FAF: (*rolls eyes*) Don't believe everything you read online. Totally got blown out of proportion. Some Hollywood buddies of mine wanted to get some ghost tours going, you know, groups of super famous people, and they wanted me to lead them. It wasn't easy to tell these powerful people I couldn't do it, but I had to say no.

JLW: Why?

FAF: Because it's disrespectful of the dead.

JLW: And exploiting them on television for ten seasons wasn't?

FAF: "Exploiting" is a bit harsh, but I'll let it slide. We didn't start out that way. Definitely not. Look, once you've become a social pariah and you're afraid of showing your face in public for a while, you have a lot of time to think about the past and what you might have done wrong, or what the catalyst was that might have changed things. If you can identify the switch, you can see it coming again.

JLW: What was yours?

FAF: Allowing people to massage and inflate my ego. That I was *almighty*, for God's sake. Mike started that as a joke, and it turned into this *thing*, which led to believing everything the media said about me.

JLW: (*laughs*) Now you're blaming us?

FAF: No, I'm saying I'm just a guy. I've *always* been *just a guy*. There's nothing special about me except for the fact that paranormal creepy-crawlies are attracted to the energy I give off. From here on out, all I really want to do is right my wrongs and ride off into the sunset, knowing at the end of the day, I did what I could to redeem myself for what happened to Chelsea, and for what I did in the past to screw over the people I care about most.

JLW: Admirable goal. So what comes next? After the documentary, I mean.

FAF: Hopefully, I'll be enjoying a private beach, somewhere warm, with a drink in one hand and holding Melanie's with the other. Fresh start, clean heart, and a good woman at my side. Right now, I can't think of anything better.

JLW: Do you think that's possible?

FAF: I don't know. Check back in a few months. You'll either have to look me up or dig me up to find out.

(end of interview)

The question becomes do I believe him? Should I? Should you?

I'm not sure that's for us to answer.

Whether you call it life or fate, chance or universal decree, God or Satan, something out there has a way of handing out the appropriate judgment, and unless he comes back to haunt us, Ford will be the only one to know the result of that decision when he crosses over.

And perhaps he'll be the one going bump in the night.

The Graveyard: Classified Paranormal Series

THE FIRST ACT

1

It's been over two years since I've seen Carla Hancock in person, and she hasn't changed much. She's pale to the point of translucence. Her hair matches mine, black as night. Her lipstick color reminds me of a vampire who has just finished feeding and hasn't bothered to wipe her mouth. The color of her eyes—coal. Perfume, subtle and flowery; it's quite possibly the only thing soft about her presence. Her high heels could skewer a still-beating heart. Her pantsuit is crisp, sleek, and wouldn't be out of place on an undertaker.

She makes my skin crawl. I'm not afraid of too many *living* people, but I sure as shit wouldn't want to run into her in a dark alley.

Carla stalks around her home office, heels clicking against the tile floor, punctuating every pissed off step she takes. She uncrosses her arms and leans against the window, palms and forehead flat against the surface.

I'll wait her out. I'm good at that.

On any other day, she might look like she's admiring the mighty Pacific, the setting sun. We're at her modest mansion, and while it's a beautiful sight up here in the hills overlooking the ocean, she couldn't give a damn about the view right now. She's pondering my proposal.

Unhappily, I might add.

I dropped a bomb on her ten minutes ago. I put myself in her shoes before I walked in, and I understand the scope of what I'm asking for. It's insane. Totally insane. I expected yelling. Anger. I got it, for sure.

And now that it's subsided, I wait, and I hope, because my plan makes sense.

Part of me wonders if she's actually considering it. The other part wonders if she's choosing the words she'll use to tell me to go to hell, and to take my demons, both literal and figurative, along with me for the ride.

She emits an audible sigh over by the window, and I glance up in time to catch the circle of breath fog fading away, retreating from those blood-red lips.

Carla turns around, pinches a small piece of lint from her lapel, and crosses her arms again. Her movements are slow and deliberate, everything calculated, showing me that she's not pleased, but maybe willing to listen.

"Explain it to me again," she says, "in slow, simple fucking words, Ford, *why* you think this is such a good idea. I don't have to tell you it's going to cost the studio a lot of money. A lot. And I also don't need to remind you we've already been in pre-production for—"

"And the crew is already there in Ohio, and it's what we promised the fans, and blah blah bullshit bullshit bullshit. I get it." I'm okay with interrupting Carla even though she's the one pulling all the strings. First, she knows she needs me. No Ford, no documentary. Second, she's awful, and I don't suffer assholes. Not anymore.

Carla squares her shoulders and narrows her eyes, stays silent.

I'm not going to tell her the real reason. I'm not going to give her *all* the details about what my partner, Mike Long, and I learned on a research trip to Ohio. If I do, she'll never agree to what I'm proposing. She'll insist that we stay at the Hopper House.

I have to stand up. It creeps me out when she's towering over me. She's a crow sitting on top of a telephone pole, waiting to swoop down and devour the carrion I'll become.

Once I'm on my feet, I move closer to her. Then I take another step forward, closing the gap, leaving an uncomfortably small space between us. Am I trying to intimidate her? Yeah, probably. Will it work?

Doubtful. She was born without that particular gene. I guess that's one of the reasons she's been so successful here in L.A.

I lower my voice—not quite to a whisper—and say, "Let me tell you something about demons." I hold up my index finger. "They're nasty fuckers. Dangerous, Hancock, with a capital D. Particularly the one that was in the Hopper House. If we go back there, we're not just risking demonic possession. We're risking lives."

The second finger goes up: "And why is that important? Because given the right circumstances, a demon as powerful as Boogerface could make the Pope leave a brown stain on his white robe. You hear me? God's beacon himself would hide in the best place he could find. This is not a joke. I'm scared, worried, and I want every advantage possible."

Finally, the third finger: "Demons really, *really* don't like change."

It's a simple statement—what Carla asked for, honestly—that represents a significant part of my plan.

"Carla, listen to me. This is the truth. Mike and I spent the last two weeks researching the Hopper House. The history of it,

I mean. It's a death trap, and I refuse to risk lives. Absolutely refuse. Sure, it's a great location, it's scary, fans are familiar with it, but Mike and I *strongly* believe people could die. Murder. Suicide. All from demonic possession because that house is where Boogerface is the strongest. If any of that happens, this thing never makes it to theaters, and boom, hundreds of millions, gone. Vanished."

You have to put it in terms these Hollywood types can understand.

I didn't tell her everything, and I almost said too much.

"Relocating will give us the advantage we need. It'll put Boogerface off his game, make him angry and confused, prone to mistakes. I honestly wasn't sure about this before—he's *so* damn powerful—but this way, I think we can win, and that's what the viewers *want* to see, right?"

Carla studies me with her arms crossed. Lips pressed together in a thin red line.

And then a small crack forms in her hardened shell.

She says, "You're positive you can get this Boogerface—I seriously despise that name, by the way—you think you can get him there? To that old farmhouse in Oregon?"

"Yes. It's complicated, though. There's this whole underlying band of energy that gives us the ability to communicate across time and supernatural boundaries and planes of existence and—"

"Don't preach to me in nerd. Just tell me how I spin this to the board and the investors. If, and that's a huge if, I decide you're not batshit crazy, then I need a damn good reason for the people who sign the checks."

"Tell them I'll back out if they don't go along."

Carla shakes her head. "It doesn't work that way, Ford. They're already prepared for you to pull that card. They'll take their money and they'll walk."

"Might not be such a bad thing."

"Nope. Uh-uh. You back out, there goes Mike's money and any hope of rebuilding his life. There goes your chance of getting any more fawning blowjobs from those—what did you call them? Spotcamgirls? There goes any hope of Chelsea having a good future. How long do you think it'll be before your silly little demon eats away at her soul? How long do you think it'll be before she slips out of the public eye and a few years later, bye-bye cash, here come the drug addictions and dying in a gutter with a needle hanging out of her arm?"

I raise my hand to shush her. "Chill with the doomsday speak, Hancock. We both know I'm not going anywhere. I've already figured it out. Here's how you pitch it to the investors: Before you do anything else, you get Spirit World Productions to subversively trash my reputation for being *fearless* when it comes to the paranormal."

"That's the stupidest thing I've ever heard," she says. "Why?"

"I'm getting there, listen. Slowly start spreading rumors that I'm too afraid, that the *Almighty* Ford Atticus Ford is too scared to go back to the Hopper House. I'm terrified. I'm refusing. Spin it so that it seems like production might fold on the documentary. Leak it to all your television sources. Spread rumors on social media. The whole works. The fans will be so bummed, they'll start signing petitions and creating websites and doing candlelight vigils. You get the idea. We give it another month—"

"Another month?! We'll never make the Christmas deadline by then."

"You were never going to make it, Hancock. Besides, a Christmas release was idiotic. Movie watchers want sappy fluff and Oscar bait in December, not something reminding them how shitty the world can be. If my plan works the way I think it's going to work, you could release this thing on a random Tuesday in the middle of February and it wouldn't matter. If you pretend to take it away from the fans, they're only going to want it more.

"Once the despair fully sets in, we come back with the news that it's on, I'm in, and I'm only going to do the documentary if I can do it on my terms. We tell them it's my fight, my battleground, and then we reveal the Hampstead farmhouse as the new location. Of course they'll wonder how I'm going to get Boogerface to meet me there, right? We don't tell them that Mike and I can use the underlying energy of the universe to send paranormal telegrams. That's boring. Instead, we'll say that we're using Chelsea as *bait* to draw him in to that location."

"You mean bring her back?"

"In a way. Sort of." I leave it there. No more detail than necessary.

Ever so slowly, one corner of Carla's mouth creeps upward into a knowing grin.

"Sometimes I don't know whether you're a genius or certifiably insane, Ford."

"You've met me, right?"

She relents. "Okay."

"Okay, meaning we can do it?"

"I'll *try*. I can't promise you anything, but we'll see how it goes." Carla points toward the front door with her chin. "You can see yourself out. Let me make some calls, and I'll get back you."

Interesting. This might *actually work.*

The truth is, I have no intention whatsoever of using Chelsea as bait. I'm not letting her within a thousand miles of the Hampstead farmhouse. I've already learned that lesson.

You ever see a teaser for a movie or TV show and there's one part that you really, really like and then when you watch it, the moment is nothing like what they led you to believe? That's what I'm hoping to do with Chelsea. We'll find a rickety old farmhouse somewhere in Ohio, shoot a few minutes of side footage of her walking in through a ramshackle door, we'll have that big blaring horn that you hear in every movie trailer these days, and then fade to black with a little girl's scream trailing off into the background.

We got accused of this constantly during the entire epic run of *Graveyard: Classified*, but this will be the first time ever that we'll dupe our audience. I abhor that concept, and yet, if it draws in paying theatergoers and keeps Chelsea out of harm's way, I'm willing to do it just this once. Mike is on board, too.

It's a risky play, and I'm absolutely trashing any future chances I have at returning to Hollywood on a regular basis. You know what? I'm not sure I care anymore.

This will lead to bridges burning, I'm certain of it.

My thinking is, the upper level suits, the executive producers and big timers with funding money, they'll be pissed and threaten to take their ball and go home if I pull another switcheroo on them—*sorry, no Chelsea!*—at the last minute, but they know the game. They know how this works. They know more delays means more money flushed. They want this documentary in theaters something fierce because their studies and focus groups are predicting a colossal payday, and they'll make concessions for it to happen.

I *think*.

What happens if they come back with their own set of demands?

I'll run with it. I'll figure it out.

I'm a man of absolutes. Research. Evidence. Numbers.

But this is a gamble. Sometimes you gotta cross your fingers, squeeze your eyes closed, and hope your dreams into reality.

***

The next morning, I wake up to Melanie gently shaking my shoulder. She has the hotel room shades open already and the rising sun reflects off the Pacific waves. Far out in the distance, a container ship catches my eye as it cruises north. I have a distant recollection of an upsetting dream lingering in the back of my mind. It flutters and vanishes before I can recall what it was about.

And then Melanie refreshes my memory.

"You okay?" she asks. "Sounded like an awful dream."

I groan and roll over, certain that my dragon breath is killing flowers on the opposite side of the hotel room. We split two bottles of cabernet with dinner last night, and the aftertaste lingers on my tongue. "Was I talking in my sleep?"

"Moaning. Whimpering. You said something about it being dark and looking at yourself in the mirror."

Images begin to crawl their way back into my mind. She's right. It was dark. There was a hallway with a single nightlight. And then a bathroom. That's right. I remember waking up and needing to use the toilet.

But I was little. Young, actually. I had to reach *up* for the light switch.

"That's right," I tell Melanie. "I was a kid and in this house I didn't recognize. No, wait. Like it was my house but it wasn't."

"You were repeating a—I don't know, something like a poem?"

The rest of the dream floods back. I remember everything. "*The white night is bright with light and love.*"

"Yes!"

I'm a young blonde girl, staring in the mirror. I recognize that face. I'm Chelsea Hopper. What? I feel evil. I feel darkness in my heart. I feel male, which is strange, because I am a male in real life, I know this, but in the dream I'm a girl feeling *male…something like that. I pull open the front of my pajamas to check for boy parts. Good. Still a girl. I raise my eyes to the mirror to make sure I'm me. I'm not me. My face shifts. I'm becoming someone, some*thing, *else. A crack appears in the corner, creaking and slithering across the mirror. Then everything goes black to the sound of shattering glass. In total darkness, rage consumes my soul. I want to swallow hot coals. I want to scour the earth with acid, burn it with oil and gasoline. I want to rip wings from the backs of angels.*

Melanie says, "I'm not sure that I've ever heard you whimper like that in your sleep."

"Pretty crazy," I say. I rise up and pretend to rub the night's lingering effects from my eyes. What I'm really doing is trying to wipe those images from my mind.

I change the subject, ask what we're doing for breakfast, because I don't ever, *ever,* want Melanie to know what I saw.

Later, I'll try to check in with Chelsea Hopper's parents to make sure she's okay.

First, I need a croissant and some of that stuff that passes for coffee down at the continental breakfast.

Melanie has other ideas. In her best poor-baby voice, she says, "Let's get that scary nightmare out of your head before we go down. Maybe work up an appetite?" Her hand slips beneath the sheets.

Yup. That'll do.

After all, it was only a dream.
Wasn't it?

2

How That Came to Be – Part 1

Not long after Mike arrived on my steps looking beaten, broken, and as if he'd been knocking on death's door instead of my own, we sat down to come up with a plan. How in the immortal hell were we going to take on Boogerface and win given what we'd both seen and recently experienced?

My time with the black-eyed children was bad enough. Mike, however, had been invaded. He'd been possessed, and therefore his defenses were lower, like how your body isn't in top shape after you've been sick for a while. Not only that, he was worried about Dakota Bailey and how the media had been treating her. He was concerned about his own reputation. He was upset that Toni was going to rip his life apart in the upcoming divorce proceedings.

We were both weak, and we knew it.

We had to come up with a plan to take on Boogerface that didn't result in us being dragged down into Satan's living room. We had both seen and experienced the demon's power, and we were certain that what had happened so far was only the beginning.

The Graveyard: Classified Paranormal Series

At first, we were all talk and bravado. *Rah-rah, sis-boom-bah, kick the demon's ass! Gooooo team!*

(Mike jokingly asked if a "holy" touchdown should automatically be worth seven points instead of the standard six.)

The more we shared, the more we talked about our recent experiences, the more times we reviewed the evidence from the Craghorn investigation and the Very Special Live Halloween Episode—both aired and not—the fear spread in our souls like a decaying fungus.

We were positive that the Tier One right-hander had only been toying around with us pathetic humans, and whenever he grew bored, we'd be dispatched to a Satanic display case, our heads mounted next to possessed Little League trophies and other past conquests. You know, like coming in first place in a Helling Bee.

Demonic. Demonic. Can you please use that in a sentence? D-E-M-O-N-I-C.

So, we started looking for an advantage, a legitimate one.

It gave us something to do other than sit around my house, waiting for the production crew to finish prepping in Cleveland while we fed off of each other's fear. It was an odd sensation. We had been scared in the past, spooked and jumpy, but it wasn't a big deal because we were professionals; we were confident in our ability to right paranormal wrongs and wash our hearts clean, but we had never really and truly been...*afraid*. We didn't start that way, but the more we uncovered in the evidence, the more we got to that point.

Perhaps we were psyching ourselves out, picking up on negative energy and allowing it to fester, creating our own two-man hive mind. Hard to admit, easy to recognize.

We read and reread every paranormal guidebook we could get our hands on: *A Dark Afternoon With the Paranormal*;

Ellsworth's Guide to Spirits and Hauntings; *Hell in Spades, One Man's Journey to the Underworld*; and *Demons and Death, A Guide to Life Post-Rapture*.

We looked for clues that might give us information about Boogerface's origin, especially his *true* name.

Why?

If you recall—there's power in a name, and there aren't many things a demon hates worse than having a weakness exploited.

We filled notebooks with scribbles, jotting down what might be important, what we might be able to use, anything to give us a one-percent advantage against the house. In the end, we found nothing substantial. They were just a handful of old tricks that we hadn't used in a decade, yet they were nothing but fun memories. The advancement of paranormal technology has left those tactics far behind.

It wasn't until we began researching the deep, full history of the Hopper House online, and made a trip to Ohio in person, that we understood how unprepared we were for the upcoming war, and how goddamn stupid we had been the night we were there for the Very Special Live Halloween Episode.

We'd gotten lazy by then. Production schedules, filming, press tours, interviews with late night TV hosts, all the things that come with being a celebrity left little room to do the investigation prep work we had once handled on our own.

Well, not necessarily lazy, per se, but ten years in, we simply didn't have time to do everything like back in the old days. I remember we assigned the Hopper House historical research to some underpaid and overworked intern—Ambrosia, I think—who assured us that the family's testimony had checked out, and longtime neighbors agreed that there had been trouble at the frightening abode for as long as they could remember.

Ambrosia hadn't taken the time to get *deep* into the home's history. She hadn't given us a detailed report about the decades of pure evil that had gone on there. What we got was a brief write-up that explained how there had been reports of paranormal activity there going back to the 1850s, and that was it.

Remember how wary I was of the Craghorn house itself, how I described the way homes, too, can feel like malevolent entities just as much as the thing haunting the inside? It was almost as if the house itself was a conduit for evil.

The more Mike and I uncovered, the more we came to understand how fortunate we had been to get out of there alive. It sounds morbid and insensitive to say it, but Chelsea's attack—the incident that ruined our careers and a juggernaut television show, and left a young girl scarred and mentally damaged—amounted to us getting off easy.

What we found in regards to the Hopper House's past was a veritable what's what of everything that can happen to make a domicile a bastion of evil: animal sacrifice, devil worship, bloodletting, *human* sacrifice, séances that opened doors to other realms, Ouija boards with unholy symbols painting on them in blood.

And it was all right there, available in online archives, black and white photos, and information we gathered during interviews with retired policemen and medical examiners.

I've lost count of how many homes, museums, abandoned asylums, hospitals, lighthouses, schools, and, yes, churches, where similar things have gone on, but not all at once. The Hopper residence had your standard wicked mischief congregated into one location.

That simple, unassuming, faded pistachio colored house had been a megastore dedicated to wholesale horrors: Hell-Mart, The Demonic Depot, Dead, Bath, & Beyond the Graveyard.

What made the Hopper House the worst one I've ever seen, and a paranormal warhead capable of leveling humanity as we know it, was the message we uncovered in an unknown language written on the basement walls. It had long since been painted over, and the Hoppers had no clue that they were sitting on top of Satan's front door.

Three days before my visit to Carla Hancock's L.A. office, Mike and I had taken a trip east, and found ourselves in the basement of the main Cleveland police department, digging through cold and closed case files. Being able to browse through ancient evidence isn't exactly kosher when details haven't been made available via public record, but there's a certain amount of celebrity privilege that comes with being the Almighty Ford Atticus Ford and Mike 'The Exterminator' Long. Not to mention the fact that the guys at the station had heard about all the good work I'd been doing with other police departments around the country—all it took was a handful of autographs and the promise of some *pro bono* assistance in the future if and when they needed it.

Blind eyes were turned.

And then Mike and I found the photo.

We were going on the third hour of Day Five. We'd spent that time in libraries and the courthouse, conducting interviews, asking questions and following leads before we migrated to the evidence room where we began pulling down boxes, coughing and sneezing from herds of dust bunnies the size of real rabbits. We combed through file after file. I hate to say it, because I don't want to badmouth our boys in blue, but holy shit were their organization skills lacking.

We were warned. I scoffed that it couldn't be that bad.

I ate those words with a side of slaw as we rummaged through what felt like miles of shelved boxes.

And there we were, not coming up with anything useful as a weapon against the most powerful monster we had ever encountered.

Mike was at the far end of the long table, head down on his crossed arms, studying the back of his eyelids instead of doing what we came for. I let it go. We were tired from reading and saying, "Holy shit, did you see this? I can't believe we weren't seriously hurt," over and over.

We had gathered enough historical evidence to understand that we, nor anyone else, should ever go back inside the Hopper House ever again. Exorcisms, Native American rituals, holistic blessings—none of them had worked in the past and wouldn't in the future. Boogerface held too much power there, and the best choice for humanity would be to raze the structure to its foundation and seal it off for good.

The ice had melted in my lunchtime soda, and Mike remained asleep by the time I grabbed the folder that would cement our decision to take the fight elsewhere.

I opened it and caught my breath in the same motion. On top of a stack of papers sat a single black and white image. Someone had used an ink pen to mark it "Johnson residence – 1957 – language unknown – Dr. Keller confirmed" along the border. The folder wasn't identified as being from the Hopper House, but I recognized the Johnson name and a unique, decorative feature of the basement wall.

It was your standard red brick construction from the mid 1800s with immaculate masonry work. Three rows of bricks were angled in peaks and valleys as a form of decoration. At some point in the past, the house had shifted and a vertical crack extended five feet upward toward the low ceiling. It ended at the edge of a white stripe that looked to have been painted by one of the previous owners. It served perfectly as a message delivery surface.

The writing would be hard to describe to someone who hadn't seen the inscription with their own eyes. I wouldn't even call them letters; they were symbols, unlike any I had ever seen. They appeared to be grouped together in a sentence-like structure.

I haven't studied ancient languages, not enough to be a scholar, but I've had experience with them in the past. You have to in this line of work. Sanskrit, prehistoric Sumerian, anything dating back to the Old Testament and beyond, cave markings—they have all been involved with our investigations over the years.

These markings were unique in every way possible.

All but one.

An upside down cross punctuated the primordial sentence like a taunting exclamation point.

After everything I've seen, after every paranormal creepy-crawly that I've witnessed and captured, I'm still surprised at how anxiety and unrelenting curiosity can coexist in my mind. I didn't want to know what it said. I *had* to know.

"Mike?"

He grunted and raised his bald head. The last vestiges of an interrupted nap lingered. He squinted against the fluorescent lights. "What?"

"Come see."

Mike protested with a heavy grunt, then pushed himself upright. Flip-flops slapping against his heels, echoing throughout the spartan records room like small arms fire, he trudged over and took the photograph from my hand.

"You ever seen a language like that before?"

He studied it, frowned, and shook his head. "Nope. I'm guessing you have? This is one of your tests where you pretend not to know something just to see if I do?"

"I haven't done that since season three."

"Yeah, well."

"See anything in there you recognize?"

"Upside down cross, that's about it."

"Exactly."

"And?"

"Mike, seriously. That doesn't get your sixth sense all tingly?"

"My sixth sense is being able to pinpoint a taco stand from three blocks away. To me, this just looks like some random crap. I mean, like, literally crap. Some insane dude dropped the kids off at the pool and then used one of them like a crayon to blabber some nonsense."

Perturbed, I snatch the photo from his hand. "First, *eww*. Second, it's more than that. I can feel it." Then it occurs to me: "What if this is the *written* form of the language that Lauren Coeburn was speaking in that video?"

"The one from Newport?"

"I understood every word in real time and then in the film, it sounded like gibberish."

"If it's the same, shouldn't you be able to read this?"

"Who the hell knows. Maybe it doesn't work like that."

"Yeah, so, say it's the same. What're you thinking? Devil worship? Satanic rites?"

As soon as those last four words came out of Mike's mouth, the lights dimmed and buzzed. A freezing puff of wind blew past us.

The Mike of old, the one who would put a Boy Scout to shame in his paranormal preparedness, had returned. He pulled a digital voice recorder from a pocket in his cargo shorts and said, "You want to do the honors?"

"Leave it," I said, standing. The chair legs screeched across the floor. "It's probably a cop who can't leave the job behind. We got better things to do."

"Like what?"

"Finding this Dr. Keller. Maybe he knows more than what this picture can tell us."

Mike hesitated, wanting to protest. Instead, he resigned with raised palms and followed me across the room, up the stairs, and back into the light.

***

We sat in the rental car bickering like an old married couple over directions and whether we were at the right place.

I showed him the notes I'd taken on my phone. Again. "This is what the desk sergeant said. 2103 Dobson Avenue."

"You sure you didn't get the numbers mixed up? Doesn't look like anybody's lived here in years. See? Broken shutters, waist high grass. If he's in there, he's been dead for a decade and nobody claimed the corpse."

"Then we do what we always do."

I opened the car door and stepped into the Cleveland heat. Even with the nice breeze and acceptable humidity level, I often wish I'd chosen something other than black for my trademark persona color, maybe an off white to give myself a heavenly look. It's something to consider for the documentary.

Mike was right. The house looked abandoned. Missing shingles. Shutters with slats broken. A screen door hung limply from one hinge. I figured I'd need a brown hat, a whip, and a sharp machete to navigate through the jungle that used to be a yard.

The desk sergeant had said this was the last known address for Dr. Addison Keller, the linguist who had consulted with the police in 1957 regarding the unknown language. "If he's alive," he'd said, "looks like Keller would be a hundred years old now. No public record of his death from what I can see. No next of kin listed either. Wife died in 1988. No kids or siblings. S'all I got." He'd offered an apologetic shrug before he wished us luck.

We stopped at the front gate, a chain-link job about four feet high, rusted through in spots. When I pushed it open, it emitted a screech that would rival the occupants of any medieval torture chamber.

Beside me, Mike winced and rubbed an ear. "*Gah*. There goes that eardrum. Good thing I've got a backup."

We braved the untamed wild of the yard, watching for snakes and Bengal tigers, then climbed the rickety steps. They complained with loud creaks under our weight until we reached the porch. A mop bucket filled with crushed beer cans—bearing a faded Miller logo that I recognized from the early '90s—sat to the right of the main door. Next to that was a broken flowerpot overflowing with bottle caps. Coca-Cola, mostly, from what I could tell. On the opposite side sat a large, dusty, hard plastic toolbox. The black had dulled and the other color might have once been yellow.

I'm a curious sort, so I opened it, gagged at the stench of hundreds of cigarette butts floating in a soup of murky water, and slammed it closed while Mike laughed.

When Satan hosts his book club on every second Tuesday of the month, I imagine that's the sort of drink he serves.

Trying not to retch, I coughed out, "Shoulda known better."

"Wouldn't expect any less, Ford. Nose always where it doesn't belong."

I ignored that and tried to take a peek through the windows before knocking. The roll-down shades were pulled, preventing any snooping.

I knocked. We waited. Rinsed and repeated until we were certain that the place was truly abandoned.

"Lost cause," Mike said. "Pardon the pun, but we're chasing ghosts here."

"Funny you should say that… You still got that DVR in your pocket?"

He flicked a look at me, face contorting into a whine before the words formed on his tongue. "C'mon. No."

"We have to. There might be something we can use against Boogerface."

"*Ford*. We're trespassing, and besides, this place is a death trap."

"Again with the puns."

"You know that's not what I meant."

"Just a couple of questions to see if he's around."

"And what if he's not? What if the guy's alive and in some nursing home?"

"Then we'll do more research, but while we're here, we might as well check. Thirty minutes, tops. If he moved on, good for him. If he's here, maybe we can get some answers." An idea occurred to me, and thankfully, it was enough to convince Mike. "What about this? What he couldn't decipher in life, maybe he can in death. We know it's true. We know that ghosts and demons can communicate across paranormal planes. We also have proof that time and language don't matter."

The second season, episode nine, that Catholic Church in Texas, the one along the border of Mexico. Remember?

The Graveyard: Classified Paranormal Series

We asked every single question in English, and every response was in Spanish. Translated, it was evident that differing languages were not a barrier on the other side.

Mike said, "Whatever. If it'll get us out of here faster, we can try. But remember, those were *human* languages. Who knows what—"

He halted abruptly as the front door shuddered and crept open.

It stopped flat against the wall. Nobody greeted us. The hallway, empty.

No breeze had blown it open. The wind was comatose.

I smiled at Mike and gestured toward the entrance. "I'd call that an invitation."

3
How That Came to Be – Part 2

The smell.

Oh, dear God, the smell.

It was so awful that I expected to trip over the bloated, decomposing body of Dr. Addison Keller.

Prayers answered, that didn't happen. What we did find was seven dead pigeons, a puddle of water in the middle of a sagging hardwood floor, and a random box full of AA batteries that had gotten wet, split open, and then some of them had rolled into said puddle, corroded, and leaked acid. One would think that pigeons would be smart enough to not drink contaminated water. Apparently, one would be wrong.

Best guess was, the avian graveyard was the source of the horrific odor, but they looked like they'd expired long ago, and I wasn't positive. Could have been a rat in the crumbling walls. There was no way to be certain, and those weren't the dead things inside the house that we wanted to communicate with anyway.

I asked Mike if he also had an EMF detector—a device that measures the presence of electromagnetic fields that can indicate the presence of a spirit—and he informed me that he did not. Strike one for the paranormal Boy Scout.

"Besides," he said, "this place probably hasn't had power in years. The whole goddamn house is decaying, you know? Nobody *alive* has been here in ages."

I found the nearest light switch and flipped it a few times just to check. *Nada.*

"Good enough," I told him. "If it's been fully disconnected we won't have to worry about fear cages or interference."

Mike quizzically arched an eyebrow. "Like I don't know that?"

"Right. My bad. Slipped into show mode there for a second. I guess doing all that research ourselves fired up the old mental hardwiring."

"Sounds like you got a residual haunting in your brain, bro." Mike patted my back and pulled the DVR from one of the many pockets on his cargo shorts. "Let's get this over with so I can go snort about fifty bottles of perfume."

Once we were recording, we stayed close together and moved softly from room to room. The bones of the home—the walls, the floorboards, the steps to the second floor—moaned and groaned each time we advanced. I stopped verbally tagging every manmade noise because the evidence would've been filled with nothing but the sound of my own voice.

With the downstairs fully explored, and after hearing no intelligent or residual responses in the replay, we went upstairs, going from bedroom to bathroom to bedroom. We found boxes of junk in one room where someone, perhaps a distant family member or friend, had started packing away Dr. Keller's things, only to abandon it halfway. The bathroom was filthy, grown over with mold on the tiles and in the tub, the result of yet another leak in the ceiling.

More of the same was in the second bedroom: half-packed boxes full of knickknacks, empty picture frames, and a number of educational books on linguistics and the history of language. I thumbed through a couple of them, spotting yellow highlights and handwritten notes in the margins that appeared to be where Dr. Keller had prepped for something, maybe teaching a class, maybe taking notes for a research paper. The next box of books proved to be more interesting.

Mother's Tongue: From Europe to the Americas, A Comprehensive Examination of the Advancement of Our Language, by Dr. Addison Keller.

Tribes: Dissecting the Language of Indigenous Peoples, by Dr. Addison Keller.

The Death of Clear Communication: Generational Gaps and the Slow Erosion of Proper English, by Dr. Addison Keller. I noted that this one was published in 1985 and briefly wondered if the good doctor had lived long enough to be horrified by the current age of LOL, IDK, and TTYL.

I was about to give up and ask Mike to start an EVP session when another one of Keller's own paperback books caught my eye.

Languages of the Righteous and the Damned: An Uncommon Guide to the Linguistics of Heaven and Hell, by Dr. Addison Keller.

"Neato" didn't do it justice. My hands went numb. While Mike fumbled through a box of junk, the room took on that muddled, cottony feel, the biological response to overwhelmingly important information flooding your body.

On the cover was a picture of God on the left and Satan on the right. Both wore confused expressions with the speech bubbles over their heads containing differing scribbles, an artist's representation of "language."

God and Satan floated above massive armies charging one another in the background, spears and swords raised overhead as they sprinted across the open green of a battlefield. I assumed the intent was to show how differing languages could cause communication issues, thus leading to the war between Heaven and Hell.

I opened the front cover to find a handwritten note underneath a printed message that read "Uncorrected proof. Not for sale."

The note read as follows:

Dr. K,

First, please allow me to say what a joy it was to work with you on this project. For a first-time editor, this was a baptism by fire, if you'll pardon the joke, and I loved every minute of it. Your mastery of the subject matter is enthralling, and I devoured your words. In truth, I read it as a fan as much as I am your editor. Bravo, good sir.

Yet here I must profusely apologize. From what I've been told, it's unusual for any publisher, my employer included, to cancel a project this late in the process, especially for someone of your caliber and sales record. You and I have discussed this via telephone, but let me again reiterate that I don't agree with their reasoning for a moment.

If anything about this book is too inflammatory, it's the fact that there aren't more of them like it. In my best guess, a handful of senior management members made an eleventh hour decision based on some nudging from their high-ranking clergy connections. I had also heard rumblings that some of the suits on the floors above were concerned about your assessment that God was just as guilty of miscommunication as Satan and the outcome it would have on the house's reputation as the publisher. It's a bold statement, and while I may not necessarily agree with <u>all</u> of your views

100%, I think you made an excellent case for the point you were trying to prove.

I'll close here by saying that this proof copy is a small consolation for what could have been a blockbuster. I'm certain of that fact. Please accept my sincere condolences, and I look forward to working with you again in the future.

*All my best,
Carter Kane
August 3, 1976*

PS – I almost forgot! Recalling the chapter about the Johnson house in 1957 still gives me the creeps and while we were forced to cut it, I must tell you that I slept with the hallway light on for a week. With your permission and blessing, I have some ideas for a novel that might prove interesting.

"Oh my God." I looked closer to make sure I had read that signature correctly.

(To date, Carter Kane, one of my heroes who played a large part in my budding fascination with the supernatural, has published twenty-one paranormal suspense novels. I own all of them in hardback, fourteen of which have been personally autographed by the man himself. I can say with certainty that the signatures in mine matched the one in my hands.)

Mike poked his head up from behind a stack of boxes. He looked like a curious gopher. "What?"

I flipped the proof copy around and showed him the cover art.

"What's that?" He stood fully.

"One of Keller's books that never made it to publication. Guess who his editor was?"

The Graveyard: Classified Paranormal Series

"From the looks of that cover, I'm going to guess it was Jesus?"

"Hardy har, but no. Carter freakin' *Kane*, man."

"Um...cool?"

"Hell yes, it's cool. You know I'm obsessed with him, and he's—"

"Almost entirely responsible for your interest in the paranormal, as long as you don't count your own supernatural experience as a child," Mike said with faux exasperation as he nearly quotes the past-me word for word. "I've heard it a thousand times in a thousand interviews."

Clearly, Mike didn't share my amazement. I thought it was such an incredible bit of Kismet that life, in its many circles of fate and intersecting lines of chance, had connected my apex of inspiration with an obscure man who was a puzzle piece in our current investigation. To me, this was six degrees of separation on steroids.

I was also a bit surprised. I thought I knew everything there was to know about Carter Kane. I'm a superfan, though. Unlike the multitudinous *Graveyard: Classified* groupies who sent me racy pictures over the years, I stopped short of sending Kane photos of myself in frilly thongs. Believe me, I was tempted.

You know, as a joke.

Honestly.

Anyway.

I knew that Kane had been an editor prior to his meteoric rise to author mega-stardom, and I thought I'd read everything he'd edited in addition to the works he had written. The name of Dr. Addison Keller hadn't fired any synapses when I first heard it, but then it occurred to me that if Keller's book never made it to publication, then I wouldn't have.

You learn something new every day.

It was a damn shame that the chapter on the Johnson/Hopper residence had been removed because I would have loved to read Keller's assessment. That was precisely why we were there at his home.

Good Thing Number One: We were experts at communicating with spirits, and if he happened to be lingering, we could potentially get the information we wanted.

Good Thing Number Two: Carter Kane wasn't dead, far from it, and with a couple of phone calls to my agents, I could be talking to him within the hour. All I had to do was cross my fingers really hard that he remembered what Keller had said in the missing chapter from almost forty years ago.

Mike said, "Hey, space cadet. You coming back?"

"Huh? What?"

"You know you're getting worse with these moments of flying off into la-la land." He paused a couple of seconds, considering something. "Damn, remind me. How many times you been possessed?"

"Like full-on, need a priest possessions or just minor attachments?"

"The big ones."

"I lost count. Why?"

"Nothing major, just wondering since that thing got inside my head back east at Dakota's house…"

"Yeah?"

"You think it'll make me want to put gel all over my head and start staring off into the wide open yonder?"

Beside my free hand was an empty cardboard box. I slung it at Mike's chest. "Fuck off," I said. Not angry, simply snorting my annoyance. I mean, I got what he was saying. I did (do) have a tendency to get lost in thought, like any other human with two firing brain cells, but I tend to fully disappear inside my mind movie, oblivious to the rest of the world, when I'm trying to process something. Mike has joked about it since our days of sitting in a classroom together.

He caught the cardboard box and flung it back at me. "Just busting your chops."

"You're a child."

"Always."

I saw that his digital voice recorder was clipped to his belt. "Should we do another EVP session while we're up here? Maybe use some of Keller's books as trigger objects?"

Mike picked up a ceramic kitten out of a plastic container and turned it over and over in his palms. "We can try. I don't know about you, but I'm getting *nada* in this place. No tinglies, no prickly hair. Feels dead. It's nothing but a gross old house."

"Worth a shot. We've captured evidence from less."

He considers this, breathes deeply. "Sure. Fifteen more minutes won't hurt." Mike reached for the DVR and pulled it free from the clip holster. He began recording. "Ford Atticus Ford and Mike Long, EVP session number two, gross old house belonging to the potentially former Dr. Addison Keller. Mark time, beginning of session."

Stepping around boxes, moving to the center of the room, I said, "Hello? Dr. Keller? Again, my name is Ford; this is my buddy, Mike. Thank you for allowing us to visit your home. We apologize for the intrusion, though it did seem like you opened the door for us downstairs. Was that you inviting us in?"

I paused here for a moment, thinking back to the black-eyed children and Lauren Coeburn. *I'm hungry. You need to let me in.*

I'll never forget it. My skin prickled, which is typically a sign of a supernatural presence nearby. Not this time. It was the images in my head of those empty eye sockets. Lauren throwing her body against that bathroom door. The squish and crunch of a fireplace poker sliding through her neck.

I shook my head. Cleared my throat. It was the closest I could get to ridding my mind of the memories.

Mike said, "You okay?"

"Peachy keen," I answered. Then: "Dr. Keller, if you're here, please give us a sign of your presence." Right back to business. And so it went for another quarter of an hour. I read aloud from his books. I asked questions about his personal life, what little I knew. I mentioned that it probably was a lovely home at one point. I asked about his wife and how much he loved her.

Finally, Mike asked *me*, "What are you stalling for?"

He had noticed my reluctance. Damn it. I thought I was hiding it better.

In truth, I *was* worried about asking Dr. Keller things regarding the Hopper House—or, what used to be the Johnson house back in his time. What if I asked him questions about the strange language written on the wall and it somehow alerted Boogerface that we were poking around? What if I insinuated that I knew where the scrawled message had come from (Hell) and that I knew who left it? Would that be like a drop of blood in the water for a shark demon? Could a Tier One right-hander smell my fear? We were, in fact, in Cleveland, and the Hopper House was no more than a few miles away. It wouldn't have surprised me in the slightest if my questions sent Boogerface racing in our direction.

Cue the *Jaws* music.

Duh-dun. Duh-dun. Duh-dun. Boo!

"I'm—uh—I'm just…" I stammered.

Mike paused the recorder, glancing down to my shaking hands. Palsy would have been less evident. "You're scared? Of Keller?"

I tried to sugarcoat it. "*Pffft*, no. It's nothing. Too much coffee and it's so quiet in here that I feel like we're cranking the handle on a jack-in-the-box."

"Bullshit. What's wrong?"

"Mike—"

"What. The fuck. Is wrong?" He accentuated each block of words with a sharp poke on my shoulder. "We agreed years ago, dude. No bullshit on an investigation. Not when our souls are on the line."

He's right. We did. He deserved to hear the truth. "Boogerface."

"What about him?"

"I'm freaking out because what happens if he hears us talking about him, like across the paranormal Pony Express and he shows up here? That's a war I'm not ready to fight. Not today. Not when we're armed with nothing more than a recorder. We need holy water, Father Duke, cameras, crosses. A million pounds of garlic and silver bullets."

Mike considered this for a moment. "We got all those dead pigeons downstairs. We could use those like grenades."

I chuckled. It helped.

A little.

"Besides," Mike added, "you just said his name, so we're screwed anyway. My advice? Let's quit fucking around, ask Keller the right questions, *if he's even here*, and then get the hell gone."

"Right. You're right. Let's hurry." I pointed at the DVR. "Fire it up."

I'm losing my mojo. I'm actually afraid.

That thought was the genesis of an idea, one I might pitch to Carla Hancock.

"Recording."

"Dr. Keller, back in 1957, you were asked to consult with the police regarding a strange message in the Hop—uh, Johnson house. It was an unknown language at the time. Were you ever able to figure out what it was?" Pause. "If you were able to uncover which language it was, what did the message say?" Pause. "Was it an actual human language, or gibberish, or…"

I couldn't bring myself to say it. The final words would *not* come out of my mouth.

"Something demonic?" Mike asked.

We waited. I took slow, measured breaths while Mike fidgeted and looked nervously around the room. A crisp, cool spot of air pushed through the space between our shoulders.

No windows were open.

"Did you feel that?" Mike asked.

"Something's here."

"Doesn't feel evil, does it?"

"Not really, no. Dr. Keller? Is that you?" I paused. Waited.

A floorboard creaked in the hall outside the room, then nothing more. "Give it a sec, and then we'll check the recording."

We replayed the entire EVP session, listening for any signs of communication, and true to what we had felt physically, there was nothing until the final seconds when the cold spot scurried by.

Four words. A Class-A, top o' the line EVP. As clear as glass.

But it had nothing to do with the questions we asked.

"*She will … betray you.*"

The Graveyard: Classified Paranormal Series

4
How That Came to Be – Part 3

I made two calls, one to my agent, and one to Carter Kane's agent.

At a quarter past five the next morning, Mike and I were on a flight out of Cleveland Hopkins International Airport, riding coach because that's how we roll nowadays, and a few hours beyond that, we pulled our rental car up to the gated entrance of *Shatterbone*, Carter Kane's magnificent estate in the Hamptons.

If you're wondering, it's named after his third novel, *The Shatterbone Children*, which is the specific work that made him a household name. It's the best-selling paranormal suspense novel of all time at fifty-three million copies sold worldwide; the film version—far inferior in my opinion—was nominated for seven Oscars and cemented Kane's status as *the* premier wordsmith of all things spooky and fearful.

Shatterbone is also ridiculously haunted.

Over the years, Mike and I tried, unsuccessfully, countless times to get Kane to allow us to film an episode there. While he was familiar with *Graveyard: Classified*, and a fan of the show—he told me once while autographing one of my hardback copies of *The Faceless Name*—he didn't want to disrespect the spirits he cohabitated with. He was so familiar with the ghosts of *Shatterbone* that they were like the family he never had, and out of respect for the tormented souls who hadn't crossed over yet, he couldn't allow us to go poking or prodding.

Back in those days, we didn't hear 'no' that often, but our discussions always ended cordially with Kane's unfulfilled promise to write me into one of his novels, or at least name a character after me, while I would promise to bring him on the show one day—a promise I never had a chance to keep.

We were not boon companions by any means, but we were on good terms with Kane, and yet we still had to convince his agent that we weren't requesting an audience to beg for another chance to film there. We had to namedrop Addison Keller, have the agent relay the message, then wait for Kane's enthusiastic, yet curious, reply before we were allowed an in-person visit.

So that's how we ended up sitting at an iron gate blocking the driveway of one of the world's most well-known authors, speaking into a small metal box, then cruising along a short, winding road bordered by seasonal flowers, fresh cedar mulch, and stone statues of gargoyles attacking cherubs, vampires with their teeth buried in the soft-looking skin of fainting damsels, and a six-headed dragon rising out of a manmade pond.

"Jesus," Mike said, amazed.

"More like 'Jesus wept.' Look at all this. Spooky."

I steered the rented Mazda around a dilapidated green pickup parked on the right side. It was full of rakes, shovels, buckets, and two push mowers. The gardener waved as we drove by, Mike returned the greeting with a salute, and the man went back to pruning a bush.

"We had money," Mike said, "but we never had hire-your-own-personal-gardener money."

"That's a luxury I couldn't care less about."

"As if you've ever had dirt underneath your fingernails."

The house—no, check that, the *mansion*—came into view once we rounded the next bend. I'd seen pictures in magazines but they never do a house like that justice. Three stories, beige colored stucco siding with more paned glass windows than a hospital, along with a second story balcony overlooking a circular driveway and the coastline off in the distance. I guessed maybe thirty rooms, but once we got inside, I found out how conservative that estimate was.

We parked, climbed out of the rental, then left the paved surface of the driveway and walked along a path made of bleached and broken seashells that resembled the remnants of shattered bones.

Shatterbone. Clever.

We rang the doorbell and while we waited, I asked Mike if he had his DVR in the pocket of his shorts.

"Always."

"Do me a favor. Leave it off in here. I know this place has been high on our Wish List for years but don't try to sneak it out for EVPs."

Mike arched an eyebrow. "Hadn't planned on it, but why, exactly?"

"I don't want to piss Kane off, especially if he knows anything about Keller's lost chapter."

I heard the metallic clunk of a deadbolt disengaging, followed by the clatter of mechanical door parts as it swung open, revealing a tall gentleman dressed in the pressed, splendid attire of an old world butler. His tuxedo was immaculate and crisp, unlike the sagging skin around his neck, along his cheeks and under his eyes.

"Barnes!" I said.

"Yes?" came the guttural, grumbled reply.

If he was surprised that I recognized him, or knew his name, he didn't show it. Fenworth Barnes had been Kane's longtime butler since back in the 80s, imported from Merry Olde England. The man himself had been the subject of numerous lifestyle interviews in magazines and newspapers, mostly concerning what it was like to wait hand and foot on one of the world's wealthiest authors, and being the Kane Junkie that I am, I'd learned enough about Barnes to feel like we were at least on a last name basis.

The air he presented, staring down the bridge of his long, hooked nose, judging the simple cretin that stood before him, gave him a regal, authoritative presence that required a similar response in return. I said, "Please allow me to introduce myself," then bowed. "I am Mr. Ford Atticus Ford, here with my partner Mr. Michael Long, requesting an audience with your employer, Mr. Carter Kane."

I could sense Mike's attempt at stifling a chuckle.

"Ah," Barnes said, "you're expected. Right this way, please." Once we were through the arched entrance, he eased the door closed behind us and added, "You were made aware of the rules, I presume. No attempt will be made to contact the spirits residing here. Do not touch anything that appears to have value. Do not waste Master Kane's time. If you are caught in violation of these terms, you will be removed from the property."

Mike made a click-click noise of acknowledgment with his tongue and gave Barnes a thumbs-up. "You got it, dude."

Barnes studied Mike, nose upturned, not hiding his disdain. "Very well, *dude*. Please have a seat. Master Kane will be with you shortly." His exit was so effortlessly fluid I could have sworn he floated away.

Mike waited until Barnes was out of sight before he whispered, "You could shove a piece of coal up that guy's ass and have a diamond by the end of the day."

"Now there's a mental image I could have done without."

We sat. We waited in silence.

Mike tapped his toes and fidgeted, eyes darting around the cavernous room. I don't know what he was looking for. Ghosts, maybe? And while his gaze flittered from statue to photograph to the bay window the size of a NFL football field, I sat with my hands in my lap, studying a painting that hung over the fireplace. I had seen this one in some art magazine years ago and had always been curious about it. Supposedly, in addition to being one hell of a talented author, Kane spent his downtime learning to paint like a Renaissance master. He'd been at it for twenty-five years if I remembered correctly, and he had referred to the fireplace painting as his breakthrough piece.

A hulking demon—charred, black skin and muscles like Conan the Barbarian—was presented in such exquisite 3D-detail that he appeared to be marching directly at the viewer, coming off the canvas head on. Its flame red eyes matched the background and felt as if they were boring directly through mine. Blood dripped from a single, razor-sharp horn protruding from the left side of the demon's skull. One hand held a sword high, its edges jagged and erratic, like a sawblade missing some teeth. In the other hand, the demon held the ankle of an unconscious nude woman, dragging her over the ragged volcanic rock under his feet.

It's an image from the plot of Kane's second novel, *Soul Harvester*, and at six feet tall and four feet wide, it's an imposing one that seared itself into my memory.

I shuddered. I had to look away.

A beat later, Carter Kane appeared through a door on the eastern side of the sitting room, all smiles in a sunflower yellow polo shirt, khaki shorts, and sailing loafers that squeaked with each step against the spotless white tile under our feet.

Kane didn't look a bit like someone who had scared the living daylights out of hundreds of millions of people over a thirty-year career. He reminded me of my Grandpa Garfield—my mother's father (and don't tell anyone, but he was my favorite of the four before he passed back in 1997).

At seventy-six years old, Kane looked sprightly for his age. He was distance-runner fit, trim like he hadn't had a cheeseburger in decades, head shaved bald with a razor, a white mustache like an albino caterpillar, and a matching set of diamond earrings. He'd gotten a tattoo since the last time I saw him in person—and it wasn't just any tattoo. It was a full arm sleeve that depicted an angel falling through so many levels of a fiery hell.

Interesting. Gotta stay hip when you're his age. You know, instead of breaking one.

Kane is also *fabulously* gay and has been out since before it was cool. I read in an interview one time that he struggled with his sexuality growing up. Having gone through so many dark places in his life, looking for answers and acceptance wherever he could find them, that was the fuel for his demented, paranormal-influenced imagination.

Also, he had been emotionally wrecked by a vindictive lover in the late '60s and remained single since, which, I assume, is partly why he was so attached to the spirits in *Shatterbone*. Not to mention the fact that any partner who chose to be with him would probably have a hard time sleeping soundly next to the man who wrote *A Knife in My Dreams*.

Kane opened his arms wide and said, "Gentlemen! So lovely to see you both again."

We exchanged handshakes, hugs, and double-cheek kisses, then Kane motioned for us to follow him into the breakfast nook where Barnes had hot tea and scones waiting for us.

Kane seemed to really take notice of Mike for the first time. "My word, look at you. So much weight gone. Muscles look good on you, my friend. I'll tell you what, if I was thirty years younger…"

Mike blushed and joked, "Well, I *am* getting a divorce."

"Don't tempt me, sweetie," Kane replied.

"Be careful what you wish for with this one," I said, sitting down at the white breakfast table bordered by four white chairs. Underneath the tri-window that overlooked the rose garden was a handcrafted bench; on it sat white cushions and pastel pink pillows. "Anyway, Mike's love life aside, I'm not sure how many times we've met, or how many times I've told you this, but it's an honor. Thanks so much for having us, sir."

"*Sir*," he coos. "Oh, please."

I've rubbed elbows with a plethora of Hollywood A-listers in my day—no big deal—but Carter Kane is the one person that gets me starstruck every single time.

Gawking like I'm a teen girl who just met The Beatles for the first time, I managed to fumble out, "I'm sure I've told you this too. I love your work. *Love* it. You've been scaring the shit out of me since I was a teenager."

"Yes, every time we've met." He winked. "Whenever someone tells me that, I don't know whether to thank them or apologize."

"Same goes for us," Mike said.

"I'd imagine."

"But nothing like what you've had to deal with, I'm sure." Mike, eager to get down to business, added, "And speaking of scaring the shit out of people, the reason we're here is, we came to ask you about—"

"*Tsk, tsk*," Kane interrupted. "Small talk first, then we'll titter like a bunch of hens. Besides, Barnes went to so much trouble getting these scones just right. Try one. The man deserves a medal." Kane took a bite, eyes rolling back in pastry-induced orgasmic delight.

Too starstruck to be hungry, but wanting to appease one of my heroes, I reached for the top scone and paused, hand frozen in mid-reach as the chair next to me began to shake violently, dancing around on its legs before it shot across the breakfast nook and slammed against the wall so hard, one of the framed ocean paintings rattled and fell off its hanging nail. It was only a canvas stretched across the frame, no glass, but I cringed regardless as it hit the floor and bounced underneath the bench.

With a raised, frustrated voice, Kane scolded, "Margie! You stop that right now. I'll have you know that these gentlemen are our *guests*, thank you very much."

If it had been anyone else, and if we hadn't been involved with the paranormal for the last twelve or thirteen years of our lives, it would have seemed an odd sight, watching this little old man reprimand an invisible person.

"I'm so sorry," Kane said, crumpling his napkin and slinging it onto the table. "I warned them all that you were coming, but they're just so belligerent sometimes. That's mainly the reason why I never allowed you to investigate my home. They would never forgive me, and then what would it be like around here? Oh, dear, I don't even want to imagine." Kane pushed his wire-rimmed glasses up and pinched the bridge of his nose.

They are the seven spirits who inhabit *Shatterbone*; supposedly, according to the modicum of information that Kane has released about them, they're a family who was lost at sea and returned to their former residence. Unable, or unwilling, to move on from the last place they were the happiest. The family consisted of a mother and father, and their five children; three girls, two boys, the eldest of which was Margie.

Kane sighed and took a deep breath with his eyes closed. "Okay, she's gone. Probably up to her room to pout."

I've mentioned that I'm sensitive to spirits—tingling skin, goosebumps whenever something is near—and at that moment, I felt nothing either. The three of us were alone again, except for Barnes lurking in the distance, waiting to be summoned.

We spent the next hour catching up, filling each other in on our lives. Mike's troubles, my own, what we were up to now, our romantic situations, what manuscript Kane was working on, and all manner of general chitchat. In that time, I watched a spoon float up and out of Mike's teacup—a product of Paul, the youngest spirit, and his mischievous nature. I felt two fingers caress my cheek. Kane assumed it was the middle daughter, Anna, who was the flirtatious one. A nearby cabinet door opened and closed by itself. Kane informed us that the youngest daughter, Mary Beth, and the eldest boy, Homer, were fond of playing *Monopoly* and he'd had to hide the set from them because they never cleaned up their mess.

It was all quite charming and I never once felt threatened or scared.

It was so casual; I could have been visiting a grandfather's home for brunch. It also made me realize that filming an investigation there would have been fun for us, but the activity had been so tame, our fans would have gotten bored and changed the channel.

With the three of us in the same room, you couldn't have possibly thrown together a more perfect triumvirate of people who were completely comfortable in the midst of such continuous paranormal activity.

Until I finally brought up the name of Dr. Addison Keller.

The lights dimmed on their own.

A deep chill blanketed the small room.

I jumped when I felt the sharp edge of a fingernail slide across my jugular vein.

"Oh my. Oh no." Kane sat up straighter, hand shaking as his fingers touched his lips. "I was hoping it wouldn't come to this."

The Graveyard: Classified Paranormal Series

5
How That Came to Be – Part 4

Mike pushed his chair back from the table and stood up, hand diving into the pocket of his cargo shorts. He removed his DVR and before I had a chance to say anything, Kane touched Mike's arm and said, "No, no. I know what that is, sweetie. Put it away."

"But—"

"No buts. It'll make it worse."

"Make what worse?" I asked. So far, the paranormal activity in *Shatterbone* had been lighthearted and playful, minus my scratch, minus Margie's jealous fit when we first sat in the breakfast nook. The air felt decidedly different now. Charged. Intense. The scrape on the side of my neck burned.

Kane replied, "Keller's name has come up a few times over the years, and in every single instance, it feels *black* in here for a couple of days. The activity picks up. Gets malevolent. Whomever it is—whatever it is—is most definitely not a fan of that poor old man."

"But you knew we wanted to come talk to you about Keller and invited us anyway?"

Kane urged Mike to sit down, to fill his mind with positive energy, before he explained. Mike obeyed, and Kane went on. "It was the weirdest dose of kismet when you called about him. Just yesterday morning, I was up in my attic, rifling through some boxes that I hadn't been through in years. I was looking for some pages of an old manuscript that I'd buried God knows how long ago. I couldn't find them, but I managed to dig up Keller's unpublished book on ancient biblical languages."

"The one you edited."

"Yes. I can't believe you found his copy with my note in it. What a strange, small world we live in." He accentuated it by cupping his hands as if he were holding a tiny Earth. "That book was so profound. Such an absolute shame that they shut it down before it changed the way a lot of people viewed religion. Keller was a genius."

At this mention of the doctor's name, heavy footsteps thumped down the stairs with the measured precision of someone calculating each step.

Thump. Thump. Thump.

Barnes stood in the kitchen entryway, gaze stuck straight ahead, either unable to hear what was coming, or too rigid to break out of his professional character. He reminded me of a redwood. Tall, regal, and motionless. Enduring. So he wasn't the source of the noise. As far as I knew, the four of us—and the spirit family—were the only ones in the mansion. I pointed over my shoulder. "Is that…"

"One of the family members?" Kane asked. "No. But it won't hurt us. At least I don't think so."

Thump. Thump. Thump.

Despite Kane's shaky assertions, it made my skin crawl.

Not many moments are spookier than the sensation of being stalked by something you can't see.

"Shall I go on?" Kane asked, turning from Mike to me.

Mike nodded silently. I answered yes. I had to know what Keller learned.

I said, "The chapter they removed, the one about the Johnson house. What was in there?"

Kane looked out the window with that thousand-yard stare of reflecting on the past. He tapped the table with his index finger then pushed his half-eaten scone away. "I put two and two together, you know, back during that Halloween episode when that little girl got attacked. I hadn't thought about that house since the late seventies."

I noted that he said, "got attacked," not, "you let her get attacked." Add one bonus point of admiration for Master Kane.

He continued, "I thought I recognized the home as soon as you did that flyby intro piece, but I had to go find Keller's book just to be sure. I skimmed through and the details brought up so many memories about that missing chapter that I tossed the book into the attic without looking and forgot about it."

"Let me get this straight," Mike said, leaning forward. "The guy who's managed to scare half the goddamn planet with his books was afraid of somebody else's?"

Keller smiled warmly. "I write them as a way to deal with my fears. I never said I wasn't scared of things that go bump in the night. No, Keller's lost chapter had me shaking in my loafers back then just as the thought of it does now."

At the mention of Keller, again, the stalking footsteps resumed. Slower this time. Getting closer to the ground floor.

Thump.

Thump.

Thump.

Mike kept looking over his shoulder, fidgeting until he finally moved around to a different chair. He said, "Sorry. Having my back to the door makes it worse."

Kane said, "When I realized where you were during the Halloween episode, I was so worried for you guys. For that child too. I knew what was in that house. I knew what you were up against. I was shaking like a Chihuahua in the middle of a snowstorm because I was so distraught. But I couldn't warn you. You were live. And what was I going to do? Play phone tag with fifty different people just to relay a warning that you probably wouldn't have heeded anyway? It was already too late."

"Yeah, that train was on a downhill slope with no brakes at that point. I couldn't have said no if I wanted to."

"Yes, you could have," Mike interjected.

"Not now," I said, my tone one notch away from scolding him like a child.

Mike's version of an apology was a silent nod and pressed lips. He knew it wasn't the right time. Old habits, I guess.

I asked Kane, "The important question is, what in the hell was in that chapter? Was he ever able to decipher what that message said? I mean, like, decode the language? Because I'm positive I heard something similar recently. It's a long story, but I had a confrontation with some black-eyed children—"

Kane slapped the table. "You did not."

"Yeah, in Newport, Oregon."

"They're *real*. I knew it!" He grimaced and rubbed the sting from his palm, adding, "You'll have to give me details, but for now, go on."

"If you had seen what I did, you wouldn't be so excited about it, trust me. The short version of the story is, I had this encounter and in the evidence video, the woman who attacked me was speaking this godawful, skin-crawlingly spooky language that sounded *ancient*. I'm talking, like, pre-recorded history. The police and I spoke with a linguist and tried to have him identify it, but no dice. Nobody had ever heard it before. The real kicker is, in the heat of battle, real time, I was able to understand every word of it. I can't say for sure, but I believe that the message in the photo is the written form of the language I heard."

"It makes sense," Kane agreed. "What doesn't make sense is, if you could understand the spoken form, why can't you read the written version?"

"I asked the same question," Mike says.

"My wild guess is that it—them, they, whoever—*wanted* me to understand in that moment, and that's all."

"What did it say to you?"

"That there's a war coming, basically. Chelsea's demon is calling us out."

"Like an O.K. Corral showdown? High noon in the streets?"

"Something like that."

Kane nods thoughtfully. "Keller studied that message written in blood for nearly two decades before he came to a conclusion."

Thump.

Thump.

Thump.

The third step was followed by a loud crash—the distinct sound of a vase shattering against a tile floor. I've been around enough poltergeists and angry spirits to recognize the sounds various items make when they're destroyed.

Kane whipped his head to the side and leaned back, eyes searching. "Barnes! Please go do…something."

I watched Barnes hesitate. He inhaled deeply. Frowned. The stoic façade was broken.

He was scared.

So was I, but it didn't compare to the surprise that came next. I mean, I had an inkling of an idea, but…

"Barnes!" Kane said.

"Okay, okay."

Barnes's hand fluttered like the last leaf on a branch as he blindly fumbled for something out of sight behind the nearest wall. His arm emerged, holding a broom, which he promptly wielded like a baseball bat. He took one step forward, then froze in place, as if someone had hit the pause button on his life, as the crash of yet another vase vaulted out of the nearby sitting room.

Barnes stammered, "Carter, I—I can't."

"Barnes, please."

"I'm—I'm—I can't *do* this."

"Yes, you can, honey." Kane halted, considering what his next words should be. 'Honey' wasn't an absentminded term of endearment, that was *affection*. Instead of speaking to the rattled butler, he addressed me and Mike. "Well, shit. I slipped, so you might as well know. Husband. Husband," he said, pointing to himself, then at Barnes. "Now you're the only two carrying that secret, other than his family. Just please keep it out of the tabloids. My better half over there has this image he insists on keeping pristine."

Mike nodded. I nodded.

I said, "Your secret's safe with us."

Kane said to Barnes, "And now they know. So will you please spare our guests the drama and go see what's going on? At least take that broom and sweep up the mess."

"They're the ghost people, have them do it," Barnes fired back.

"*Now*," Kane ordered.

The flaming anger shooting from the butler's eyes could have melted stone, but he listened, marching away somewhat bravely, holding his weapon at the ready.

I guess his resignation was akin to happy wife, happy life?

"Where were we?" Kane asked. He crossed his legs and clasped his hands around the bare knee. "Oh, yes, the lost chapter."

He put on a good front, but the twitch in his cheek and rapid breathing betrayed the fear he was trying to hide.

I asked him, "First, who—or what—do you *actually* think is out there?" I listened for any sounds coming from Barnes, worried that he might have been shoved directly into the demonic lion's den.

"Yeah," Mike adds, "that doesn't sound like something a broom can swat away."

"I honestly don't have the slightest idea, but it's not friendly."

"Obviously."

"It hasn't physically attacked anyone yet, so there's that."

Much in the same way I was afraid to say Boogerface's name back in Keller's abandoned home, for fear of him hearing me and showing up, I wondered if something similar was happening here. Maybe there was even more of a chance since Keller was the connection between Kane, the indecipherable message, and Boogerface.

I asked, "You said it's been here before, and then it, what, just goes away?"

"Eventually. We pray a lot. We ask the family to intervene. The spirit family, I mean. Like they're fighting whatever it is from the other side. It's probably happened ten times over the past twenty years. A couple of them, we've packed some bags and took off for the Belize estate for a month or two. It's always been gone when we get back."

Barnes grumbled in the next room. Next came the scrabbling noise of shattered vase pieces being swept into a pile.

Mike said, "Maybe we should just discuss what Kel—uh, what the doctor discovered and get out of here. Right, Ford? We don't want to cause you any more trouble."

"That's right," I agreed. "We don't need the full history. Here's what we already know; the chapter was removed because he had spent however many years trying to decipher that message, he had it figured out, and whatever it said was so goddamn terrifying that the publishing house pulled the chapter, and the whole situation freaked out enough people that they decided to yank the entire book out of the lineup. Is that pretty much it?"

"Minus a few details, but essentially, yes."

"And what did the message say? What did Dr. Keller discover?"

The name was out of my mouth before I realized what I'd done.

In the next room, the swish of the broom disappeared, replaced by Barnes shouting, "Argh!"

"What happening in there?" Kane said.

"Son of a bitch bit me!"

Kane flew up from his chair. "What? Oh no. I'm sorry. I'm so sorry. I'm coming." He turned at the doorway and said to us, "You two, outside with us. Hurry."

Mike and I were right behind them a second later, darting for the front door. It reminded me of the fifth or sixth episode of the first season when that poor sound guy named George ran screaming from a library in the middle of an investigation. We scolded him so much that he quit the next day. I felt guilty for running out of Kane's mansion, and childish, but we didn't know what we were up against. With the connection between Kane, Keller, and Boogerface so prevalent, it wasn't beyond the stretches of my imagination that the badass right-hander had made a house call.

The look on Mike's face suggested he felt the same.

The four of us stopped in the circular driveway fifty feet from the front door. Barnes bent at the waist, hands on his knees, just on the verge of hyperventilating. Kane rubbed his back and apologized again and again.

"Where did it bite you?" I asked.

The butler righted himself and pointed at his left cheek.

I winced as I examined the blemish—a red, broken circle of teethmarks like a dashed line that didn't exactly portray that the entity doing the biting had once been human. I'd even go as far as suggesting it appeared supernatural, possibly even demonic. I've never looked in a demon's mouth, but the jagged wound—contusion, no blood—formed marks that resembled a rocky outcropping, not the smooth edges of a human's front teeth.

I debated sugarcoating the truth, reassuring Kane and Barnes that it was no big deal. I didn't want to frighten them beyond their current state, but it's dangerous to give someone false impressions about a possible demonic entity. Going back in that home with their guard down could lead to some disastrous consequences.

"How bad is it?" Barnes asked.

"Not, um, not good."

Kane said, "Meaning what?"

I looked back at the mansion, hoping better words would come to me.

They didn't.

"I think it's demonic, but my gut instinct tells me it's not powerful enough to be Boogerface." That was as close as I dared to go with glossing over what I suspected. Also, if it was really

Boogerface, I would have suspected him to go straight for his true enemies, not Barnes and Kane.

"Booger who?"

"Sorry. Chelsea's demon. Could be one of his underlings. Could be something that had a connection with Keller while he was researching the Hopper House message. It's hard to say."

"What should we do?"

"If it's always left in the past and hasn't harmed you, maybe you're fine going back in if you take some time away. Go to Belize. Take a trip to Bali. Whatever. Just now though, I'm guessing we poked the badger too much and it lashed out because whatever that is, it's *really* not a fan of Keller. I'm not sure I could recommend it in good conscience, but if you want to keep staying here, get rid of anything that has any ties to that man. Books. Notes. Pictures. *Anything.* Never mention his name again. The attachment could fade over time."

"And we'll be fine?" Kane asked.

"*Could.*"

"What do you think, Mike?"

Mike rubbed his bald head, scratched his neck. "Ford's right. If I had anything to add, I'd say stay the hell away. We know what we're doing; we've been fighting this shit for years. Given your books, you've done your homework, so you should realize how dangerous it could get. Even if Ford's also right about it not being Chelsea's demon, I'm not a fan of having you stick around. Whether it's an underling or not doesn't matter. Demonic is demonic, and small fish attract bigger fish."

"So you're suggesting we leave. For good." Kane crossed his arms and looked forlornly at the front door. "Shame. I do so love this house."

Barnes touched the bite marks on his cheek with one hand and took Kane's with the other. "I'm not going back in there.

Never again, Carter. I've asked for years. Enough is enough. And with your health—we can't."

I noticed the quick glance that passed between them, secret information relayed in a blink. I wondered what it meant.

"You're right." Kane kissed the back of his husband's hand. "Then it's settled." He let go and moved away from Barnes, stepping closer to the mansion. He balled his fists, shook them at the front door, and shouted, "You win, you loathsome asshole. I hope our family in there drags you back down to the diarrhea-infested, semen-stained, piss-soaked bowl of Hell's toilet that you crawled out of. *Fuck. You.*"

Kane quivered with anger.

I could certainly see where his books got their colorful language.

I gave him a moment to regain his composure, then said, "Maybe it's not the best time, but Mike and I have a lot of work to do before filming. We need to be prepared. We need to know…"

"The message. Yes. Let's at least get Barnes out of the sun and then I'll explain everything."

He put the stamp on our exit by flipping the bird at whatever might be watching.

6
Back to the Present

"*She will ... betray you.*"

Believe me, I've been trying to figure out who "she" is since Mike and I blessed ourselves, said a few prayers, and slowly backed out of Dr. Keller's abandoned home days ago. I'm thoroughly convinced that Keller—Kane positively identified his voice after we played the EVP recording we had captured—was aware of something happening on the universal timeline that we don't have access to and was trying to tell me to be careful.

Mike, Melanie, and I'm pretty sure Ulie as well, are all convinced that it was nothing. Since we left the Hamptons, Mike tries to reassure me daily, tells me to stop stressing out, and that after reviewing the recording for the two hundred and sixty seventh time, his intuition says it's a residual EVP, not an intelligent one.

Mike has even been calling while Melanie and I are down here in California. I'm just hanging up on him when she steps out of the bathroom wearing nothing but a towel on her head.

She smiles at me. I feign rolling my tongue back up into my mouth, kiss her on that ticklish spot at the base of her supple neck, and then we discuss our plans for the day. Another meeting with Carla for me and the beach for her since I promised that our entire jaunt to southern California would not involve me working.

"Play soon," I tell her. "Cross my heart."

"You should've brought Mike with you and let him handle your negotiations."

I scoff at the suggestion. I know better. I know she knows better.

I learned a long time ago to never let Mike negotiate anything. Ever.

Our drastically reduced perks during the filming of the sixth season were a direct result of Mike, his temper, and me stepping out of the meeting room for ten minutes to take a phone call.

"I got a text from Carla while you were showering. She spoke to the suits and wants to discuss what they said. If you can decipher anything from a couple of lines, her language sounded positive."

"And then that's it?" Melanie wraps her arms around my shoulders. My hands go to her waist, skin smooth and inviting under my palms. "One meeting with the Devil Herself and then margaritas out by the pool?"

"As many as you can handle."

This pleases Melanie. She kisses my cheek tenderly and then leaves me standing, watching her walk naked across the hotel room, humming some pop tune I don't recognize as she shuts the bathroom door. A beat later, the hairdryer roars and I picture her standing in front of the mirror, still naked, still gloriously brown and—

I gotta go before Little Ford wakes up.

"Bye, Mel. Wish me luck," I yell at the bathroom door. There's a muffled response and I'm gone, prepping myself for another round with Carla.

***

Traffic is miraculously light and about forty-five minutes later, I'm in downtown L.A., riding the elevator up to Carla's office, which is strange, because you usually go *down* to meet the Devil.

An open bottle of champagne sits in a metal bucket filled with ice. Next to it, two flutes of golden liquid bubble and fizz. Evidently we have good news. And yet, knowing Carla, this could very well be her attempt to soften me up before she slides the dagger of betrayal between my ribs.

"You should smile more often, Hancock. It looks good on you."

She winks, grins wider, and hands me a glass of bubbly, clinking it with her own.

This—*this* is the woman I remember from the early days of *Graveyard: Classified* before she turned into Mega Wench 3000 while chasing ratings, pushing limits, and causing undue stress on the entire crew. To be fair, she had a lot of pressure on her from The Powers That Be. A juggernaut program like ours had no one to compete with but ourselves, which meant that we didn't have to do the minimum to beat second best; no, we had to outperform *ourselves* each and every week, each and every season. Otherwise, that whole thing about how "the bigger they are, the harder they fall" would have manifested like a nasty demon.

I'm not making excuses for Carla Hancock. How she handles stress, and in turn, spreads the shit sandwich around to everyone else, that's all on her. How you choose to act and react to stimuli is the beauty of free will.

The beauty or the beast of it, I should say.

Prefacing a statement with, *"I'm not trying to be an asshole, but—"* does not absolve you from being an asshole. It just shows that you took a couple of seconds to think about the repercussions of what you're going to say or do, and then decided to go through with it anyway.

Stuff like that started early with Carla. A decade later and by the time we got to the Very Special Live Halloween Episode, she had devolved into growling her demands and shrieking when I touched a crucifix to her bare skin.

Not forgiven, and not forgotten either, though with time removed, it's possible that I can find a gnat-sized nugget of goodness inside her. I'd have to get out a shovel to dig it up, mind you, but it might be there after all.

Carla says, "How does it feel?"

"How does what feel?"

"Winning." She takes a sip, eyeing me over the rim of the champagne flute.

"Like a big surprise, honestly. Did you expect it?"

"Not in the slightest." She raises her glass and we clink. "But, I need your cooperation on some things."

Uh, what in the hell does that mean? I should have known.

Today she's wearing a cobalt blue pantsuit. It fits her perfectly, trim in the right spots, buttoned just below her breastbone, accompanied by a pair of nude pumps so high, we're almost seeing eye-to-eye, a strange concept in more ways than one. It's then I notice she's not wearing a top underneath the jacket. The spectacular curve of pale, and, um, *enhanced* breasts are on full display between the lapels.

Abort! Abort!

She catches me looking as I shove my stare elsewhere. Over her shoulder, a white camisole rests across the back of her desk chair.

I'm already planning my exit when she notices that the color has vanished from my cheeks. I'm positive that my heartbeat is also visible in my neck.

Carla inches closer, and I can only imagine that the rapacious expression on her face is the exact same one that Boogerface wore while he was stalking me down that hallway at the Craghorn house. It's a look of salivating victory. The predator has won.

I've already made up my mind that I'll face the lawsuits and the fines, that I'll destroy any chance I have at a future career in the paranormal, and Mike's as well, before I let her put her blood red lips anywhere near mine. Not a chance in hell I'm selling my soul for that. Nor am I going to betray Melanie again.

Carla smells like strawberry cream, though, which is nice.

She leans in and underneath the fruity perfume is the hint of bubbly booze on her breath. I'll likely associate that with demonic sulfur for the rest of my life.

Before I can speak, before I can get my mouth fully open in protest, she whispers, "You couldn't handle me anyway," and bursts into a round of cackling, howling laughter, punctuated by deep snorts that could trigger the Rapture. I let it go, softening with relief, letting her relish the I-got-you-good moment. It dissipates into an easy giggle before she finally says, "Oh, God, your face. You looked like you'd seen a ghost!"

I've heard the joke innumerable times since the show's inception, but I'm so relieved to not be sleeping with Carla Hancock to have my documentary needs met that I begin to laugh, too.

She waits until she's able to catch her breath before she says, "I spilled coffee on my top. My assistant, the little mouse-faced girl? She's out picking up a new one." She shakes through another small fit of giggles. Wipes the corners of both eyes. "Did you think I would—or would you really have—forget it. That's a question neither of us wants to hear answered."

"Right."

Thank you, Jesus.

"So, back to business." She takes a deep breath to stifle more laughter. "They agreed, but with some small stipulations."

Here's where I'm getting nervous. Could my plan actually have worked this easily? My pops always said that if something is too good to be true, then it probably is. I'm holding my breath in anticipation, but I manage to ask, "What's the catch?"

"There's always one, isn't there?"

Is this it? Is this the moment where the prediction of Keller's ghost comes true? Betrayal in its finest?

***

It wasn't betrayal, but shit blew up on me.

In a big way, and I never saw it coming.

"They want us to do *what*? That's about as fucking far from *small* stipulations as you can get, Ford."

I feel his frustration. I did the exact same thing to Carla back in her office.

Melanie sits over by the pool, frowning at me over her margarita, because I'm supposed to be relaxing beside her in a cozy lounge chair instead of trying to convince Mike that this is fine, that we can work through it.

I motion to Melanie that I'll only be another minute and say to Mike, "Trust me, dude, I had the same reaction with Carla. I understand how crazy this sounds, but if we want to relocate to the Hampstead place, where we can at least attempt to control the outcome of this war, then this is the only way they'd go for it. It's frustrating. I never expected them to—"

"*Frustrating*, Ford? That doesn't even come close. This is bullshit. Complete and total bullshit. You promised it wouldn't come to this. What did you say to Carla when you pitched the idea? You told her this wasn't an option, didn't you?"

"I said nothing that would give them this idea. I dangled falsely using Chelsea as bait, and this is what Carla came back with. I tried to refuse and she wouldn't budge. She played me better than I thought she could. Like I said earlier, we had three choices. Agree to their terms for the farmhouse, keeping the filming at the Hopper's old place, or get tied up in court from here to eternity for a breach of contract."

"Fuck me sideways."

"I'm sorry, bro. I had no choice."

The catch?

Yeah, about that.

We had to give a lot to get a lot. In order for the suits to meet my requests, or better known as demands, they had one major request of their own.

Guest investigators.

Not a big deal, right?

Wrong.

We'd had them on *Graveyard* in the past, and while it might have been fun to see a handful of my A-lister friends get spooked all to hell when a breeze blew a door closed, behind the scenes it threw off our rhythm. Mike and I got to the point where we despised bringing someone else in, even for a minor cameo.

Why?

Because we were purists. We loved the thrill of the investigation itself. Gathering evidence to prove to the world that we weren't a hoax. Talking to the other side. Battling evil. Punching a demon right in his scrawny, shriveled nutsack.

The Graveyard: Classified Paranormal Series

Whenever a celebrity guest host finagled their way into an episode, we knew we were in for a long night of placating egos and reassuring the next Hollywood "It Girl" that she wasn't going to go home with a spooky paranormal attachment that might ruin her budding career.

Fun for the audience to watch their heroes squirm, while we seethed at having to humor someone who'd earn twenty million for their next film.

Carla told me that the upper-level suits were going on data analysis. Celebrity guest episodes had been some of our highest by far throughout our enormous run at TV history. "It's all about the numbers," she said earlier that morning. "Data doesn't lie."

A sparrow swoops down, landing a few inches away from my feet. It has enough time to hop around, scope the pool deck for dropped scraps, and explode in a flurry of beating wings before Mike replies, "Son of a bitch. We specifically had them modify the contract for no celebrity guests before we signed."

"Which they likely resented and now they're using it against us. They've got the lawyers drawing up an addendum already. Carla says she'll have it faxed to us before three this afternoon." Mike is back at my house, where he continues to be my roommate until all of the divorce nonsense is finished with Toni. Dakota Bailey, the former queen of an ultra-popular reality cooking show, *Yes, Chef!* and Mike's unofficial new flame, is there with him this weekend. Publically, things calmed down surrounding Mike's "issue" with Dakota—meaning the press moved on to something else, which has given them a chance to pursue what may come.

In the background, I can hear Dakota talking to Ulie. I hated to leave him behind with someone other than Melanie, yet the evidence is proof enough. His excited bark is all I need to know that she'll make a great doggie aunt one of these days. I inform

Mike that he has to keep an eye on the ancient fax machine in my office. "No hemming and hawing. They need it signed and returned today. I'm doing mine here through the hotel office."

"This really blows, Ford. We had such a great plan. There's no other way?"

"Not if we want to keep our souls out of hell or endless courtrooms. We knew there was a risk, man. We were prepared for it."

"But I never expected it to happen. We shouldn't have brought up her name."

"Hindsight."

"And the celebrity guests? As if that's not going to be distracting enough?"

"The good news is, they're only requiring us to have three, and we get to pick two of them."

"All right. Three I can handle. Well, two and…her."

"Yeah." If a word with typically positive connotations can carry a thousand pounds of negativity, it's "yeah" wrapped in a demoralized sigh.

"I wish you'd called me first. We can't do this to her, man. Not again."

The *her* in question? I'm sure you can guess.

Devastating.

"I thought about it, but we agreed that if we want Boogerface away from the Hopper House and on our home turf then I had to swallow the bitter pill before things got worse. I hate it as much as you. Probably even more. We'll do everything possible to keep her out of the line of fire."

"And they got her parents to agree to it? Again? That's what baffles me. That's—like I just want to punch them both square in the mouth *so hard*. When Carla and the other producers first talked to them about being involved, all they wanted was to be interviewed off site and have it coincide with the memoir's release."

"Preaching to the choir."

"What in the hell changed?"

"Money. It's all about the money."

"Bastards."

"And finding peace for their daughter, I hope."

"Like we promised them the *first* time. As if that giant clusterfuck wasn't enough. How much did they offer?"

"From what I can gather, it's an ungodly amount."

"*Must* be an ungodly amount for them to risk their daughter's soul. That can't be the only reason, Ford. It just *can't*. I'm not buying it. I'm a parent. I can feel it in my chest. No money is worth that. There *has* to be something else."

"I was thinking the same. Like somebody holding a gun to their heads."

"I wouldn't put it past Carla," Mike says.

"She didn't have time to fly back East, otherwise I'd say you're right. We can try to find out, even if it means showing up on their doorstep to ask them what in the fuck they're thinking. In the meantime, Chelsea will be—look, I can't promise she'll be fine, but it's our best chance at ending this. We'll take every precaution possible and keep her involvement to the absolute minimum that we can get away with. And...I need you to know this, hear me and understand me; I had nothing to do with it. This is not about me or my ego. It's not about me wanting to get the ratings higher, or me wanting the world to validate my existence, whatever. None of that psychoanalytical bullshit."

"Then what's it about, Ford?"

"Ending it. Forever. The more we dig up, the more we learn"—there's that whole matter of Keller's translation of the

Hopper House message to consider—"the more terrified I feel, but it's for Chelsea. From now on."

Mike says the same six words that came out of my mouth when Carla delivered the demands this morning: "My God, that poor little girl."

***

About that translation; an elaborate description of the "how" of Keller's translation crusade doesn't matter. Carter Kane condensed it for us back before we left *Shatterbone*, and I'll do the same.

Vigorous research. Multiple trips to holy lands overseas—Israel, the Vatican. The remnants of satanic rituals. You name it, Keller tried to uncover it, study it, dig it up and bury it again. The search became an all-consuming obsession, and eventually the linguistics expert managed to decipher the symbols. Possibly. He may have been right. He may have been wrong.

Given that Keller seems to have mysteriously vanished from the face of the earth, I'm willing to bet he was correct, and someone, or some*thing*, punished him for it.

The message?

"*The blood of the meek shall feed my horror.*"

Shiver.

7

Here's the thing—as little as a couple of years ago, Mike would have rejected the idea of bringing Chelsea back with the burning passion of a thousand stars gone supernova.

Why did he reluctantly agree this time?

He *really* needs the money.

It's always about the money, right?

After the video surfaced of him attacking Dakota while he was possessed, and made the rounds on national media, there's a good chance Toni's not just going to get half of everything during the divorce proceedings. She'll have the ammunition she needs to go after every last cent, right down to the loose change under his car seat.

Then why do the documentary if it's only going to hand over more cash to his bitter, soon-to-be ex-wife?

Because Mike is a good guy, and regardless of what happens between him and Toni, he wants his kids to have an excellent future, even if it means handing it over in the form of a signed check.

He'll need whatever his lawyers can scrape up in the violent aftermath just to get back on his feet and maybe buy a few cases of Ramen noodles. Of course, Dakota has money, but Mike is one proud son of a bitch, and mooching off anyone—except for me—is an abhorrent state of existence.

This is why I find him on my living room couch, passed out, with a nearly empty bottle of my best scotch tucked underneath his arm. He's cuddling it like a stuffed animal, arms wrapped around it as he snores.

On the television, I see that he's been watching a recording of that Very Special Live Halloween Episode. It's paused right at the moment Chelsea came bounding up the stairs when everything was still somewhat right with the world.

Before I sent her up the attic ladder.

Before she was attacked by Boogerface.

Before my life was reduced to ashes after the fiery, explosive fallout.

Chelsea is all smiles in the frozen image, unaware of what's about to happen.

As I relive the memory, my heart aches for her, for her lost innocence.

I did that. Carla convinced me—hell, practically ordered me to do it—but I could have said no. I could have taken Mike's advice that night and walked away.

It's still painful, you know? So much time and so many therapy visits later, the regret continues to pool in my stomach. It's burning, acidic, like that puddle full of corroded batteries and dead pigeons back in Keller's abandoned house.

I wiggle the bottle from Mike's snuggle grip, careful not to wake him, and sit down on the leather recliner. A soft *kush* of air escapes the cushion as I sink in and take a swig of the remaining scotch. A morose blanket sinks over me. I know exactly what Mike was thinking and feeling. The evidence is paused right there on the television screen.

But Chelsea's involvement has to happen. I was honest with him on the phone. This isn't about me or my ego any more.

Matter of fact, fuck my own redemption.

I earned this pain.

(I *could* say no to Carla, again, I realize that, but I just don't have the energy to face the future years of courtroom drama. It's selfish, so selfish, and I understand how awful it looks on paper. And yet, what does it say about our legal system that I would rather fold against The Man and subject a child to another possible demon attack, than spend the next ten or twenty or thirty years fighting off recurring lawsuits? The way I see it, I'm more confident in my ability to battle with a demon than take on some three-piece suited prosecutor with a law degree.)

Maybe I'll forgive myself one day. For now, I can only assure Mike and my own shaky psyche that we're taking this bastard right-hander down. I'm sick of Boogerface. I'm sick of him ruining the lives of people I care about, and I'm sick of being afraid.

You heard that right. Ford Atticus Ford is *actually* afraid.

Oh, how the almighty has fallen.

I take another swig, wince at the burn slithering into my stomach, study Chelsea's paused face on the television screen, and then come to an understanding with the warring emotions inside my heart and head.

Come hell or high water, this is most definitely the end. My time with the paranormal is finished once I drive a holy stake through Boogerface's forehead. Let some young gunslinger step into the role; somebody who isn't tired; somebody who hasn't risked a child's life; somebody who isn't carrying around innumerable tons of regret like Atlas with the world on his back.

So, it's settled. Fight and retire, or go out swinging my fists all the way down to my reserved room in Hotel Hell.

Melanie and I had taken an early flight back from L.A., and the rising sun is searing through my wide picture window. Far down below, Portland proper glows warmly, light reflecting off wet rooftops and cars. So many people living normal lives, so many haunted by remorse and guilt, haunted by spirits, real or imagined, haunted by their own personal demons, or those from the underworld.

It's both beautiful and gloomy at the same time.

Or maybe it's just my mood.

I hear the garage door open, a quick "Daddy's home. Go give him some love, Ulie," followed by the rambunctious, excitable scrabbling of doggie feet on the kitchen floor. I had been so lost in thought that I had momentarily forgotten about the Best Dog Ever and Ever, Amen, along with his new running buddy, Dakota Bailey. A machine-gun blast of clicking claws later, and he's rounding the corner, launching himself from the top step down into the sunken living room, then comes at me like a furry missile, all slobber and flopping jowls.

I'm smiling, laughing, greeting him, trying to thwart the onslaught of drooling love. He manages to get his tongue so far into my mouth that I can feel him lick a molar. I finally get him off me, and he stands there, doggie grin a mile wide, tail swishing back and forth faster than windshield wipers on high.

Mike is waking up as Dakota comes into the living room. She's carrying a fresh bottle of water from the fridge and glistening with sweat on her chest and arms. Her yellow sports bra and pink running shorts are the color of that amazing strawberry and banana saltwater taffy I used to buy over at the coast.

Also, you could crack a walnut on her abs.

I fight off another slurp from Ulie's tongue—this time across the bottom of my chin—as Dakota greets me and insists that she's too sweaty for a hello hug, adding, "You're back early."

Mike grumbles something unintelligible about a hangover and rolls onto his side, facing away from the brightness outside the picture window. I point at him and tell Dakota, "That's what I was hoping to prevent. Looks like we didn't make it fast enough."

"He started on that bottle at about eleven last night," she admits. "Where's Melanie?"

"Her place. Unpacking."

"You don't sound too thrilled about that."

"Meh. She's not too thrilled with me at the moment."

"Because of Chelsea?"

"Mike told you?"

Dakota points to him. "Obvious, much?"

"Right. So, yeah, Mel understands, but, you know, bad decisions beget more bad decisions. She probably just needs time to go find a picture of me and draw devil horns on it, black out...a few teeth."

I almost said "black out my eyes" but the memories made me shudder before I could say the words. *I'm hungry. You need to let me in.*

Dakota points down at Mike, then silently mouths for me to come talk to her in the kitchen. I oblige, and with Ulie only a couple of inches off my heels, I follow her. We make it out of earshot, supposing Mike is even awake, before she says, "He's really stressed out about this whole thing with Chelsea. Like to the point I'm worried he's going to give himself a stroke before you guys make it to filming."

"I'm not too far behind him. I even paid for a couple of calm-my-nerves drinks on the flight, and then dealing with Mel's frustration on top of it. Rough morning."

Dakota unscrews the lid on her water and downs half the bottle.

Ulie trots away and inspects his food dish. He's lapping up a few remaining morsels when Dakota tells me, "I haven't been a part of your lives for long, Ford, I get that, but I'm not thrilled about it either. I rewatched part of that live episode with Mike and couldn't take it. I had to leave the room."

"No, I get it. We're in such an awful position."

"Isn't there some way out of using her? Loopholes in your contracts, maybe? I can't imagine it's going to go over that well with the public. The media is going to eat you alive."

"No such thing as bad press. Not that I'm condoning it, obviously, but they've done the research. The focus groups tested off the charts when they were asked about Chelsea's involvement again. Once Carla's bosses reviewed the data, they had to have her, and it seemed like they'd been holding that ace up their sleeve until I came at them with any kind of ridiculous demands. It was so simple for them, like they were waiting there, ready to say, 'Sure thing, Ford, you can do whatever you want as long as you bring Chelsea back. Thanks for falling right into our trap, dumbass. Mwahahahaha.' Seriously, how did I not see that coming?"

Dakota leans against the countertop, hooks her thumbs into the straps of her sports bra, and nods knowingly. "I was on the other end of that a few times. God, it sucks, doesn't it? Being powerless?"

"Always. Five or six years ago, I could have told them where they could shove it and gotten my way. But now, not a chance. Being a pariah removes any bargaining goodwill I might have had."

Dakota finishes her water and drops the bottle into the recycling bin. I kind of feel like that bottle, honestly. Finished, tossed into the recycling, and then melted down and molded into a weaker version of myself. She asks, "So who are you thinking for the other two celebrity guests?"

"I'll tell Mike when he gets up, but I've already called Carter Kane. He agreed in a heartbeat."

Dakota seems surprised. "No kidding? I thought after what happened at his house, he wouldn't want to get anywhere near another demon."

"Revenge is a powerful motivator."

"Yeah, I guess," she responds with a shrug. "Who's in mind for the other slot?"

"I have a list of people that I put together on the flight. Guests we had on *Graveyard* back in the day, a few A-listers that begged to be on the show, people like that. Nobody seems quite right, though, and even if they did, it's going to be dangerous as hell. What happens if some Oscar winner like Merilyn Street gets possessed for a while and then sues the shit out of me? You can't get any more game over than that."

"I know people, too," Dakota reminds me. "I could make some calls."

"But who? What's the right play?"

"This is going to sound callous, okay? Let's lay it out there. As much as you both would be happy driving this thing into the ground just to piss off Carla Hancock, on some level you need it to be a success, right, even if it's simply to get a message out there?"

"Yes. For Mike, his kids. To warn people about how dangerous this shit really is."

"Okay, so, first, you've got Chelsea, which means you'll have all the movie-going family demographic tied up. Parents aren't going to forego rubbernecking the mistakes of another family like the Hoppers. They'll show up just so they can sit there and be judgmental, pointing fingers and swearing they'd never do something similar. Second, you'll tap into the paranormal-loving portion of fans because it's you guys *and* Carter Kane. That's *huge* right there."

"Exactly."

She grins. "Tell me what you're missing."

"I have a feeling you have an idea already."

"*Teens*. Early twenties. They're notorious for going to theaters over and over. They'll go back *multiple* times. You hit that market and you're talking half a billion dollars in ticket sales worldwide."

"You really think so?"

"I used to study this stuff a lot when I was on *Yes, Chef!* You said it yourself, data doesn't lie. Invite some young star on and you're golden."

"You already have someone in mind, don't you?"

Dakota bites her bottom lip as if she can't wait to tell me.

I remind her, "It would have to be someone that I wouldn't mind getting possessed or dragged down to hell, just in case."

She blurts, "Gunnar Creek."

"Whoa." Teenagers, early twenties, those kids love his smushy, lovesick lover music. It's an unhealthy obsession, while at the same time, most people over the age of thirty would pay good money to have him dropped in the middle of the South Pacific on an empty lifeboat. Or, to watch him struggle with a demonic possession and secretly cross their fingers. "Dakota, that's genius. Do you know him?"

"Not personally. We have mutual connections."

"Connections with who?" Mike interrupts as he joins us in the kitchen.

"Morning, sleeping beauty. You look like hell."

"Feel like it." He rubs his bloodshot eyes and asks what we're talking about.

We fill him in on the picks for our celebrity guests. As predicted, he goes along with it, saying, "I figured you'd want to ask Kane regardless, and who wouldn't want to see Gunnar Creek piss his skinny jeans?"

"I'm totally open to suggestions," I say, "just as long as we pick Carter Kane and Gunnar Creek."

Mike rubs his temples, trying to ease the hangover headache away, and yawns without taking the bait. "Fine by me."

Dakota scoots next to him and puts her arm around his waist. "You okay?"

"Just this dream I had. Seemed so real that I can't shake it."

My entire body tenses when Mike adds, "I was walking down this hallway, like in the middle of the night, and it was my house, but it wasn't at the same time, and I felt evil—so evil. And the weirdest thing about it was I was a little blonde girl that looked a helluva lot like Chelsea. There was some song or poem she kept singing about white nights."

I say quietly, "The white night is bright with light and love."

And then every speck of color drains from Mike's face.

8

When you have a modicum of clout in TV or film, it's amazing how a few simple calls can set up an entire scenario. Carter Kane was already on board, and with a couple of favors cashed in around Hollywood, using Dakota's connections, my people got in touch with his people, short discussions ensued, and Gunnar Creek became our second major celebrity guest before lunch. In fact, the pretty boy punk was so thrilled about being asked, he posted something cryptic on one of those social media sites I typically ignore, and the rumors began to spread before Carla's team had a chance to draw up his contract.

Not that I really care, and there will likely be some stricter limits set up in his contract to deal with things like breaking a non-disclosure agreement, but it would have been nice to put that news out there ourselves.

We also have two more things to accomplish before I'll give Carla the official green light to shift the production crew to the Hampstead farmhouse. Mike and I need to spend a night or two there, make contact with that cranky old bastard Papa Joe, and then ensure that our message gets delivered to Boogerface across the energy airwaves. It's time for a showdown, you big ugly bastard, no matter how frightened and worried I am.

What happens if he doesn't fall for our trap? My heart withers every time I think about the prospects, but if Chelsea is going to be there, then we'll have to make do with my original lie to Carla about using that poor child as bait.

It became a self-fulfilling prophecy, goddamn it.

That's what I get for putting the thought out into the universe.

Speaking of Chelsea, that's Item #2 on the list. We have another important stop to make before informing Carla we're ready.

***

We left Dakota, Melanie, and Ulie behind. They'll have fun bonding some more while Mike and I fly back to Ohio to ask Rob and Leila Hopper why in the immortal hell they decided to get their daughter deeply involved again instead of peripherally. There's no choice—we have to do it in person. It's too easy to hide the truth behind twenty-five hundred miles of separation and a phone call.

Remember Detective Thomas, the gent working the Craghorn case back in Virginia? The one who promised to do me a solid if I needed it? I had indeed kept that favor card handy, and cashed it in with him. More calls were made, records were checked, perhaps illegally—I'm not suggesting that, and he isn't either—and we were on our way to the new, and, we hoped, *not* haunted Hopper residence.

We touch down at the Cleveland airport after a bumpy flight, Mike nearly got down on his knees to kiss the solid, stable ground, and forty minutes later, we're hauling ass in a rented Ford Mustang because I allowed Mike to choose the upgraded option. He's making zooming noises, laughing as we juke and jive our way through slow-moving nighttime traffic, and I *think* it's a defense mechanism—distracting himself from the fact that we both had the same demonic dream about Chelsea.

(It had severely freaked us out earlier. We chose to accept it as an indication of the war to come, as if Boogerface was taunting us, calling us out into the street just as Carter Kane had alluded to, and then we attempted to put it aside. We had work to do, and it led us to the outskirts of Cleveland at midnight.)

We arrive at the hotel, unscathed, and I'll admit to peeling my fingers loose from the door handle after Mike's insane driving. It was too late to call on the Hoppers, and besides, I'm wiped. Mike is running on an adrenaline high, and I don't know if it's because he's exhausted or his body is trying to burn away a level of fear that I've never seem in him before.

Ten minutes later, he's knocking on my room door, telling me he needs to go for a drive, and then he's gone.

I don't bother asking why or where. Sometimes Mike needs his space, and I let him go unchecked.

We don't meet up again until the next morning, seven a.m. sharp at the continental breakfast in the hotel lobby, and he looks like he got run over by a garbage truck, and then that garbage truck backed up and drove over him again about six or twenty times. We barely speak, shovel a few morsels of stale cereal and rock-hard bagels into our mouths, bypass the coffee dregs, then hit the road. We want to catch the Hoppers before they leave for work.

It's not until we get in the car that I officially ask him if he's okay.

"Shitty sleep," Mike grouses as the Mustang rumbles down the street. "Like two hours of nothing but dreaming I was Chelsea again. Goddamn thing was on repeat."

I don't tell him that I got a solid five hours and had nothing but deep slumber visions of sun, sand, Melanie in a thong bikini, and oddly enough, a pet penguin that enjoyed the heat. "Where did you go last night?" I ask him.

Mike changes lanes rapidly, coming so close to a lumbering pickup that you would have a hard time slipping a sheet of paper between the side mirrors. Egypt's pyramids were built with less precision. "Honestly? I was too scared to sleep. That's why I was so jumpy and agitated."

"Oh, good. I thought you were being an asshole for the fun of it."

Mike acknowledges this with a sideways glance. "No more than usual. It's just that I'm freaked the fuck out about Boogerface getting inside my head. Like, gun shy, I guess, after that thing got in me back at Dakota's."

"Bad news is, he's already in there," I inform him, "even if it's only a little. Where do you think the dreams are coming from, *amigo*?"

Mike takes his eyes off the road long enough to flash me an astonished look. "I get it, but you call that dream a *little*?"

"Dreams, man. That's all they are," I say, trying to placate him. I know it's not the truth.

"Don't bullshit me, Ford. I know better. The fact that we both had the exact same dream, right down to checking to see if we had a winky in our pants—"

"A winky?"

"Yeah, that's what Dayton called it when he was a toddler. Don't interrupt. It's too much of a coincidence to be nothing but a dream."

"Meaning?"

Mike takes the time to process, weaving around soccer mom vans and delivery trucks. Trees lining the road whip by in a green blur. A blackbird swoops in front of the Mustang. A cloud passes over the sun, creating a temporary shadow. Mike finally says, "I wouldn't say it's necessarily a message, because he's not really telling us anything, right? It's just—oh shit."

"What?"

"He's showing us Chelsea."

"Right, Dream Chelsea," I reply, with a hint of 'yeah, *duh*!'

"No, it's more than that." Mike shakes his head adamantly. He might kowtow to my assertions and decisions—or did, on a regular basis in the past—but I learned way back when we were filming the first season of *Graveyard* that when he actually balks, when he cares enough to put up a fight about something, he's usually right, and there will be no changing his mind. "I'm telling you, Ford. Our dreams are her reality."

"No," I say, in slight disbelief. It makes sense though.

"You know damn well that girl has had horrible dreams about this asshole in the past. She was having nightmares about 'the dark man' back when she was five, before we even brought her on the show."

"He never left her, did he?" I had hoped, perhaps foolishly, that once the Hoppers had gotten out of that godforsaken haunted house, Chelsea would have found some peace. Now, it seems, Boogerface has been attached to her this entire time, perhaps lying dormant, but not quite, waiting for the perfect opportunity. "You think her folks realize it? Like that's why they signed on to have her in the documentary?"

"It's possible, but… I don't know, man. Something seriously feels off."

"Best thing to do is ask."

"If they let you anywhere near her, you mean?" Mike's phone chirps with verbal directions. He flips on the blinker and turns right into a quaint neighborhood with tree-lined streets and immaculate lawns. "Let's not put that idea in their head, you know? Not at first. What's it called when lawyers try to ask sneaky questions to get people to admit to something?"

"Leading the witness?"

"Bingo. No leading the Hoppers. We go in there asking questions, offering suggestions, subliminal or not, they could tell us what we want to hear, instead of the truth."

"Makes sense. So are you the good cop, or am I?"

"I'd say as much as they hated us after she got attacked, we're both playing bad cops."

Mike mumbles the address and slows down. We both check the house numbers as we pass single family homes that are well-maintained. Lush green yards, beautiful arrays of multi-colored flowers in beds, white-picket fences, with two-point-five kids playing in the driveways. You know, typical American suburb. Mini-vans. Swing sets. An older gentleman walking a droopy-eared basset hound.

It looks like the perfect place for a young family to raise their possessed daughter.

Mike's phone informs us that we have arrived at our destination.

"There is it," Mike says, whipping the Mustang over to the curb. He parks, and we sit in silence for a moment, staring at the one-story home with cream-colored siding. There's a porch swing. Hanging potted plants gently drift from side to side in the morning breeze. A pink bicycle lies on its side in the front yard next to a birdbath, which is currently populated by two sparrows flinging water, the spray catching sunlight and glistening.

Inside the Hoppers' new home, I see movement through the window.

It looks like a large figure, and I imagine that's Rob Hopper heading for the kitchen where he'll inhale a breakfast bar and pour a mug of coffee. No, wait, I remember now that he's a green tea guy. One of those small details that I might be able to use to establish a connection with him, because I have absolutely no idea how they're going to respond to us showing up at their front door, unannounced.

Worst case scenario, there's a good chance they'll call the police and try to have us arrested for trespassing, such was the intensity of their hatred for all things Ford and Long from two years ago.

Best case scenario is that they'll invite us in for—you guessed it, green tea—and we can have a civil discussion about their intentions.

There's an untold number of possibilities ranging between those two options, but we have to try. Like I said, it's harder to hide the truth in a face to face conversation. At the very least, I want them to hear and see my sincerity firsthand; I want them to know how sorry I am, and I want them to understand that I'm going to do whatever it takes to protect their daughter, even if it means shouting it at them while I'm being dragged away in handcuffs.

The figure moves past the front window again and Mike says, "Um, that's strange."

"What's that?"

"You saw that, didn't you?"

"Yeah. Probably Rob getting ready for work."

"Nope."

"Huh?" I check again, straining to see if the figure walks by once more, trying to make out some details. "That's not Rob?"

"Nope," Mike repeats.

"How do you know?"

With his eyes on the rearview mirror, Mike lifts his chin toward whatever he's seeing. "Because he's walking down the sidewalk with his wife and daughter."

I whip around in the passenger seat to get a better look. The Hoppers are happily strolling through their neighborhood, wearing workout clothes and running shoes. Sweat drenches both of their shirts, and they're all smiles. Rob has put on quite a few pounds since I saw him last—stress will do that to you. Leila, on the other hand, appears to have gone the opposite direction. Back during the filming of the Very Special Live Halloween Episode, she still hadn't quite lost her post-pregnancy weight, five years later.

She looks great now. Her hair is a different color. It's longer and pulled back into a ponytail. Her grin is the exact opposite of the last time I saw her face in person. Joy looks good on her.

And then my eyes drift down. Walking in between her parents, holding hands on either side, is little Chelsea Hopper. Somehow, my heart simultaneously melts and breaks at the same time. I want to leap out of the car and run to her. Wrap her up in a bear hug and beg forgiveness for what I did and what we're about to do in a couple of weeks.

After this, Chelsea, it'll be over, I promise.

The Hoppers certainly don't look like people who have committed to sending their daughter into another fight with a demon. Maybe they *are* the psychopath pageant parents that do anything to their children to obtain fame and fortune, to pick up where they failed in their life's ambition.

Or, they could be trying to put on a good face in front of their only daughter before they tell her that she has to go visit the Dark Man again in a house that's far, far away.

Only one way to find out. Ask and see.

But a more pressing question begs to be asked: "If they've been out, then who's in their house?"

"Could be anybody," Mike answers. "Friend sleeping over. Family in town for a visit. Who knows. They're both still working, aren't they? Maybe it's a babysitter."

I take another look at the Hoppers approaching, then survey the house once more. The dark figure hasn't passed by the window again. "Doesn't feel right, dude. My sixth sense is going off." I glance down at my arm. "Goosebumps. It's—"

"It's nerves," Mike interrupts. "Let's go talk to them before they get inside. Less of a chance they'll shoot us in the face out here on the street."

I take a deep breath. Maybe he's right. I haven't been in contact with the Hoppers since that fateful night. What's the likeliest scenario? That they have a friend or family member staying with them, or that this house is currently being visited by the Dark Man himself?

The problem is, in my mind, they're both possible and hold equal weight.

***

"Let me go first," Mike says. "My gut says they hate me less."

"You think so, Sherlock?"

Before I can follow it up with a request to *ease* into questioning their sanity, Mike is out the door of the Mustang, walking around the front of the car, waving and smiling as if he's their best buddy.

Nice move, Mike. Kill them with kindness.

He says, "Hi, guys! Long time no see," and I shift in my seat to observe Rob and Leila's response. It's a mutating mess that goes from curiosity, to surprise, to reactionary anger, which slowly melds into smiles that show in their lips, but not in their eyes. Playing along, so to speak.

I watch through the side mirror and listen.

"Mr. Long," Rob says. "Been a while, huh?"

Chelsea recognizes Mike right away, and her smile is genuine. "Mr. Mike!" She jogs to him as Mike drops down to one knee and accepts a hug coming in at a full sprint. Her weight barely moves him when she crashes into his chest.

"Sorry for popping in on you like this," Mike replies over her shoulder.

Leila says, "I'd guess it's few thousand miles out of your way to pop in."

"Something like that," Mike admits. He stands but keeps his hand on Chelsea's shoulder. She looks up at him with admiration. They had a good relationship back then—you know, before a Tier One right-hander scarred her for life. "We wanted to talk to you about some things before filming starts. Figured it'd be best to do it in person."

"We?" Rob and Leila ask in unison.

Mike nods at the Mustang. "I had to bring him."

I take my cue, open the car door, and step out onto the sidewalk.

When I'm fully upright, I don't know which concerns me more, the look of venomous rage coming from Leila and Rob Hopper, or the black figure with bright red eyes now watching us from inside their living room.

9

Fear digs its claws into my abdomen, and my stomach sinks with that feeling of spotting your high school bully in the hall while you're both alone. I want to turn. I want to walk—no, run—the other way, and I'm at odds with myself because that's such a foreign sensation. For over a decade I've encountered every kind of paranormal entity, from simple ghosts to black-eyed children to full-fledged demons, and I can't recall a time when the panic grips me as much as it does now.

And I finally understand why.

Just as I told Mike earlier, while I was trying to calm his nerves, Boogerface is already inside our heads.

Only a little, yet it's enough.

Granted, we're not as susceptible as Chelsea Hopper. We've been doing this a long time. We have strong defenses built up around our hearts and minds—scar tissue that forms a wall.

But it's not impenetrable.

These dreams, showing us what he's doing to Chelsea is the equivalent of implanting a virus in our heads that's not quite strong enough to accomplish what he wants.

Which tells me at least one thing: he's underestimating us, and that's a good sign.

That doesn't mean that it's not doing its job in manufacturing fear.

I see the bright red eyes staring back at me as soon as I climb out of the car.

Chelsea shouts, "Mr. Ford! Yay!"

"Leave, Ford," Rob says.

Chelsea bounces over and takes my right hand in both of hers.

"Hi, Chelsea. One sec, sweetie. Mike," I say. "Look."

He follows my stare and gasps as the figure and its menacing eyes shoot off to the right, out of view.

I turn to Rob and Leila Hopper. "Did you see that?"

"See what?" Leila asks.

"In your house. That... *thing* with the red eyes."

They appear confused, hesitant, as if they're trying to decide if I'm bullshitting them, and probably torn between calling the police and taking a Louisville Slugger to my shins on their own.

Leila, her latent anger momentarily forgotten, asks, "What? Red eyes?"

Rob says, "You mean like a de—" and stops himself short with a look down at his smiling daughter. He mouths "demon" with his eyebrows raised as a question mark.

"I think so."

"Stop," Leila demands. "Do not do this to us again. You need to leave, right now."

Mike backs me up. "I'm afraid he's right," he says, his stare never leaving the front window.

"How long has it been in there? Have you seen any signs?" I ask. I'm finding it hard to hide the dread and panic in my voice.

Rob shakes his head in disbelief and answers, "Never. Not yet. Not that we've seen."

Leila accuses us of bringing a demon here to frighten them. Mike and I both deny it, and then it occurs to me, there's a chance she's partially right. Perhaps Boogerface trailed us here.

Only one way to find out.

God, my hands are shaking like one of those paint mixers at Home Depot.

When did this start happening to me, this fear?

You know when, dummy. The dream. The supernatural virus in your head.

I take a chance on hope. "You guys don't have someone staying with you, do you? Nobody that would try to pull a prank?"

Leila ignores my question and says, "I really think you should leave."

Thankfully, Rob answers my question. "Nobody we know would do such a thing. Especially after what we've been through."

"Give me your keys. Let us go in first." I hold out my hand.

Chelsea innocently asks, "What's going on, Daddy?"

Rob bends down to her level and rests his hands on her shoulders. "Nothing, honey. Mr. Ford and Mr. Mike are here... Well, I'm not sure why they're here but they're leaving soon. You'll see them at the—"

"Rob!" Leila scolds. "Not yet."

A wave of realization takes my breath. They haven't told her. She doesn't know that she'll be in the same house with the Dark Man again. What the hell? I understand why—that regret, that anticipation of putting your sweet daughter in harm's way has to be an overwhelming feeling in your chest, but my God, they need to prepare her.

Insistent, I say, "Give me your keys."

"Why?"

"Because *we're here*, Rob, and unless you want things to get a lot worse, you need to let us get rid of it."

Get rid of it is the understatement of the century.

Part of me feels like Boogerface isn't going to wait until we call him to the Hampstead farmhouse. He's showing us that he's ready and willing to throw down right here.

"No," Rob replies. "No way. There's nothing going on"—which sounds so forced that I don't believe him for a second—"and besides, we've had the house blessed and—"

"I saw something," I interrupt. "And it's not safe for you guys."

"We had a Native American shaman come by and do that smoke thing with the sage and the chanting throughout the whole house. I promise you, it's as safe as we could make it."

Mike points at the picture window and asks, "You swear you didn't see it?"

Rob and Leila shake their heads, defiant.

Chelsea asks, "See what, Mommy?"

"Nothing, honey." Leila strokes her daughter's perfect blonde hair and sighs in defeat. "What are you doing here, guys? Honestly."

"We'll talk about it later, but for now, I really think Mike and I should—"

"No," Rob says, growing more agitated. "You are not going in our home. At least not until you tell us why in the h-e-l-l you're here. It's because of the movie, has to be, but I wanna know why. What business is it of yours if we choose to have..." He flicks a quick look down at Chelsea again, searching for the right words to hide what's to come. "To have her... involved. Huh? Tell me that. What *business is it* of yours?"

Mike wears a deep tan these days, but the red plumes in his cheeks. "Are you kidding me? *Seriously*? What business is it of ours? We're doing the damn thing—"

"*Language*," Leila warns.

"Sorry. But guys, it's a d-e-m-o-n, and we're risking our lives for her, which is *exactly* why it's our business. And if I'm guessing right, she doesn't know, does she?" Mike asks. He picked up on that vibe, too.

Rob and Leila exchange worried glances.

I keep looking past Mike at the front window, expecting to see something glaring back at me. For now, it stays hidden, building up energy. Crouching. Waiting.

I'm anxious to get in there and discover the truth. I'm scared, yes, but my overpowering need to protect this family that I have wronged in the past is screaming for me to go break down the front door.

But I relent, trying to empathize, realizing they need information as badly as we do. We showed up unannounced, and now we're claiming there's a demon in their supposedly safe home. My need to know why they decided to put Chelsea through this horror again must match their need to know why we had the audacity to show up and challenge them on it, with a demon in tow.

"Guys, I get it," I say, addressing Rob and Leila. "It's nuts that we showed up here uninvited."

"Nuts," Rob scoffs. "*Insane*."

"We had to know."

"Had to know *what*, Ford?"

I let my shoulders droop, hang my head, and pinch the bridge of my nose. "Why?" I ask. "Why do it? I thought you were only selling your story rights, not bringing her back. It doesn't make any sense to us. If it's about the money..."

"Don't you dare," Leila says, pointing at me. Anger chokes the rest of her words. She looks away.

Chelsea reaches over and tugs on my hand. She scrunches up her nose and grins. The beautiful thing about children is that sometimes their fear can have a short life-cycle. I would be willing to bet that she's mentally blocked the terror of her old house and what happened to her from her memory, only for it to resurface years from now in a therapy session discussing why she feels the need to draw Satanic shapes and cut symbols into her thighs with razor blades.

For the moment, she sees Mike and me as the fun guys who offered her peppermint candy and chocolate chip cookies over two years ago. "Bring me where?"

I freeze. I don't want to lie to her, but I also don't know how to answer, nor is it my place.

"Bring me where, Mr. Ford?"

She's seven now and slightly more self-aware. She has a better grip on the world and how it works, to a point. She's naïve, yet she can tell that something is obviously wrong.

I look at Leila, then Rob, pleading with my eyes, begging for help, wondering if they're really going to leave it up to me to deliver the bad news.

I watch Leila capitulate. She huffs through her nose, uncrosses her arms, and takes Chelsea by the hand. Just when I think she's going to reveal the future atrocities to come, she pauses, then changes course. "Come on, little lady. Let's go play in the treehouse out back. Your best friends here need to talk to Daddy a minute."

"But, Mom—"

"Go with you mother," Rob says, voice deep with alpha-male authority.

"I'd rather you didn't get out of sight, but please be careful," I remind Leila. "Don't take her in the house. Not until—"

I catch Chelsea squinting at me curiously, wondering why they can't go in.

I clear my throat. "—not until we can look around, okay? Promise me that?"

Leila nods wordlessly and pulls Chelsea away as if she's dragging a pet on a leash against its will. Chelsea, in between balking against her mother's instructions, asks us not to leave without saying goodbye.

And for the briefest of seconds, I see something in her eyes before they walk away.

It's a glimmer, a hint, merely the way her lids narrow, nothing more, and yet it gives me the chills. There's understanding in there that isn't coming from Chelsea. I don't know how I know that. My sixth sense picked up on a feeling, and before I can fully react, I feel Rob's hands on my chest, shoving me, quietly saying, "What the fuck are you doing here, Ford?"

Unprepared, I stumble backward, never taking my eyes off Chelsea and her mother as they disappear down the side of the house, between the outer wall and a row of bushes separating their property with the neighbors.

Mike reaches for me with one arm and puts a hand over Rob's heart with the other, keeping me from falling as I trip over my own feet. Mike has been working out like a crazy person for two years now—he's got some beefcake going on—and his bracing arm easily stops the big man where he stands. "Whoa, Hopper, don't start. We're on your side, dude. Same team. Stop it. Do not shove him again. Same. Friggin'. Team."

I hold my palms up. "You don't want us here, I get that. We suck. I suck. We did a horrible thing, and I can never apologize enough—"

Rob takes an aggressive step forward, balls up his fist, and stops when Mike steps in front of him.

"Same team," Mike reminds him again. "We have to be."

Rob shakes his head and pushes his hair back. Hands to hips, he backs away, walking in a small circle on the sidewalk.

"Rob," I say.

He ignores me.

"Rob."

Again, no eye contact.

"I never got to officially apologize, and I'll go to my grave with that."

"Good."

"I sent cards. And money. I tried, man. I promise."

"Straight into the trash can."

Really? God only knows how many thousands of dollars they probably threw away. Good thing that college fund I set up for Chelsea is in an untouchable account that won't transfer to her until she's eighteen.

Mike says, "What he's trying to say is, we fucked up. We know we did. Ford especially—"

"Thanks," I say, not hiding the cynicism.

Mike continues, "—but really, it was both of us. I could have tried harder to stop it. I could have talked to you and Leila more, explained what it was that you guys were getting into. I could have done something insane right in the middle of filming to stop production, but I didn't. I gave in, and I gave up. The machine was too big, and when I realized that, I wouldn't have been able to stop it anyway. But I could have tried harder. So hate Ford as much as you want… you gotta hate on me, too."

Rob stops pacing and sits down on the rock wall bordering the sidewalk. He puts his head in his hands.

Mike seems to have better luck with speaking, because tensions flare the moment I open my mouth, so I pat him on the back and motion for him to go ahead. Meanwhile, I'm going to step back and survey the house, moving to the side slightly, hoping I can also keep an eye on Chelsea and her mother.

Mike says, "We both screwed up. We all did. Ford, me, the producers, the networks; we should have known better. That was our fault. We did that." Mike moves over and sits down next to Rob. He puts a hand on his back. "But you have to understand, agreeing to bring Chelsea back for another round against that goddamn thing in your house? That's not us. That's on you."

Rob sits up straight, nostrils flared.

"It's hard to hear," Mike says, lowering his voice, trying to smooth the accusation in his words. "I can see that. You don't want to hear it, but it's the truth, and that's why we're here. We needed to talk to you. We need to know *why* before we do it. And you can trust me on this, we'll be better prepared this time. We have a better understanding of what we're up against, and we'll do everything humanly possible to keep that beautiful girl of yours safe. I can't promise she'll be okay, but we'll do our level fucking best. I'll protect her like she's one of my own children. You get that, bro? You understand?"

Rob nods, wipes an errant tear from the side of his cheek. "Yeah."

I glimpse movement in the window. It's not much. Maybe the shadowy outline of an arm, and it's gone. Did I see it again? Or was it a trick of the light? A breeze blows a branch overhead and a similar shadow flickers across the window.

Okay, so that wasn't it. Debunked. Nerves taken down a peg.

I can't explain it in simple terms, but I feel a sense of awareness coming on. A knowing. An understanding. I can't grasp what it is. Not yet. I step toward the Hopper's new home, attempting to discover the source of inexplicable energy that I feel.

Then, I see it again. The tree-shadow theory gets flushed as fast as it appeared.

The shape of an arm and shoulder, a swirling mass of black, manifests at the window's edge. The figure leans out.

First one red eye.

Then the other.

My breath catches in my chest.

I'm stone motionless, watching it.

The red, glowing orbs are surrounded by a black so deep I can't see beyond it—the clearest sign of a demonic possession you can get. They aren't looking in my direction. They're focusing on Rob and Mike.

And then, the muddled sense of understanding presents itself like a slap to the cheek: Boogerface is here, and he's trying to spy on the Hoppers.

Rob's assertion earlier that things were fine, when I saw that he was lying, had some weight to it. He knows, and Boogerface wants to see if he'll tell us.

"No," I whisper, unable to find the full depth of my voice. Maybe we don't want to know. Not here. Not now. Maybe it'll make things worse for the Hoppers until Mike and I are prepared to fight the war.

I can't break away from the figure in the window as I hear Mike say, "Why, Rob? Why get her involved again? It's not the money is it?"

"No."

"If you want this fucker gone, if you want me and Ford to have a real shot in kicking its ass back to hell, then we have to know why. Knowledge is power for us."

I whisper again, "Don't." Fear chokes my words. They can't hear me.

Rob says, "He did it. He made us do it."

"Who?" Mike asks.

"That demon. Everything had been fine until a couple of weeks ago."

I force my feet to move toward them.

If my voice won't work, maybe my body will.

Rob continues, "He, um—he invaded her one night."

"Invaded her?"

"Out of the blue. Possessed Chelsea. She was acting so strange, her eyes got this blank look to them, and then this horrible, growling, demonic voice just sort of exploded out of her and said, 'When they ask, you say yes. Say no, and she's mine, forever.' And then poof, it was gone. Chelsea collapsed, and we had no clue what it meant until Carla Hancock called us the next day, asking if we'd reconsider the level of Chelsea's role during filming."

The door to the Hopper's new home swings open and slams shut so hard that the picture window next to it cracks, a sliver going from the lower right corner to the center.

Three heavy thuds, like a sledgehammer on thick wood, boom against the door.

Immediately after, coming from the back yard, I hear the dual screams of Chelsea and Leila.

Time slows. Mike, Rob, and I move in a blur, sprinting toward the house.

The Graveyard: Classified Paranormal Series

I'm terrified, but I keep going because that's what heroes do—like a paranormal firefighter running headlong into the flames of hell.

10

Now I've seen some shit, but let me tell you, what we encounter when we round the corner of the Hopper's home and hurtle into the back yard really and truly sends some of the worst chills down my spine that I've ever had.

Black, swirling mist.

A thin blonde girl, seven years old now, hanging upside down in the middle of the air.

Twisting. Flailing her arms and legs.

Screaming.

Her mother stands at the edge of the dark cloud, grasping for a leg, reaching upward, fear and rage contorting every facial muscle.

It has to be Boogerface. I've heard plenty of urban legend stories, but I've never seen anything this powerful before, not in all my years of paranormal investigations.

Rob bellows, "Let her go, you son of a bitch!" He drops his head and lunges forward like an NFL linebacker, arms and legs pumping—pistons driving him to save his daughter.

Leila jumps and tries to grab a tiny hand.

Rob thrusts his body ahead and three steps away, a portion of the dark mist rapidly forms into a thick cylinder, a swirling mass thick like a steel pipe, and swings sideways, catching Rob in the rib cage. He hurtles to his right and sails into a pink and white princess house. The flimsy plastic crumbles under his weight, and he hits the ground hard and lies there motionless.

This all happens in a matter of seconds. Mike and I are still moving, running toward this evil black cloud, yet once we grasp the magnitude of its power, tossing Rob like an old rag, all two hundred and twenty-five pounds of him, we back off a step. We arc around to our left, flanking the undulating mass, yelling for Leila to get away, that it could hurt her.

She either doesn't hear us, or ignores us, and if it's the latter I wouldn't blame her. If I were a parent, I couldn't back away from my child being attacked by a Tier One demon. We stop five yards back, flabbergasted, looking at each other, silently asking what to do now, what comes next?

I'm at a loss.

Undeterred, Mike acts first by slowly inching closer to Leila. He calls her name, once, twice, three times, and she doesn't look back. She's screaming, reaching for Chelsea who is dangling five unreachable inches above her mother's fingertips. On the other side of the demonic cloud, Rob pushes himself to his feet, stumbles to the side, groggy and dazed.

Mike wraps an arm around Leila's waist, yells over her screams that it's too dangerous, and pulls her away.

Leila fights to get away from him. She throws elbows at his head and neck, driving her heels back into his shins, wailing in anguish and anger for him to let go.

I'm roughly a foot taller than Leila, I know I can reach Chelsea, so I make a decision to go for it. Possession be damned, I have to get that child away. She's unconscious from the shaking, from the blood running to her head. To my left, I spot a wheelbarrow between an herb garden and a shed. As Rob rubs his face and staggers toward the dark form, yelling something unintelligible, I dart over and grab the wheelbarrow, drag it back, and then flip it upside down.

Backing away a handful of steps, I take a deep breath and shout at the abomination, "She's not yours, asshole!"

And then I run.

Like an Olympic sprinter in the hundred-meter dash, I'm at full speed by my third step and a second later, I use the wheelbarrow like a ramp—and if this weren't such a harrowing situation, I could imagine hearing the blare of the General Lee's horn from *The Dukes of Hazzard*. Arms outstretched, flying over the yard below—what feels like a chasm between two worlds, standard and haunted—I crash into Chelsea and grasp her tiny body, clutching it against mine.

For a holy-shit second, Boogerface hangs on, and I dangle with her, floating inside a pure personification of evil, and then we drop. I land with a hard *thunk*, feeling my ankle twist underneath me, and the two of us go down. I wrench myself sideways, quickly, using my body to shield Chelsea from the ground.

My head bounces on the packed soil and the impact blurs my vision, but not so much that I can't see Rob standing over me, swinging a yard rake like a medieval sword, bellowing for the demon to go away, to leave them alone. "The power of Christ compels you!" he adds, and though I've rarely seen that work, ever, the swirling mist hisses, compresses itself into a black orb the size of a baseball, then shoots straight into the ground where it vanishes.

Behind me, Leila sobs as she orders Mike to let her go. Mike says, "*Un*. Real."

***

Mike and I sit next to each other on the Hopper's love seat, too close for comfort, but we've been in tighter spots.

Over on the sofa, sit Rob and Leila, with Chelsea in between them, protected on both sides. She seems slightly dazed, looking blankly around the room while she sips chocolate milk.

After that attack, it didn't take much for Mike to convince the Hoppers to allow us into their home—one, to do some more baseline readings with the equipment he brought along just in case, and two, to ask Chelsea some questions because we're the "experts."

Mike explains that after a brief investigation, the home shows some unusual readings on his EMF detector, but there are no other signs of paranormal activity. He adds, "The higher than zero reading on the EMF could be due to inefficient wiring, which could also be acting as a battery for the bad guys, like a charging station. If you plan to stay, get an electrician here as soon as you can. Don't let apathy contribute to the problem."

Rob says, "Ignorance does not equate to apathy."

While I feel like reminding Rob that he should have known better, after all they've been through, I don't. Instead, I survey the room we're in, trying to recall if it's anything like their old house. Spirits can attach themselves to objects, and it makes me wonder if the Hoppers brought something *with* them from the last place.

You know, *other* than Chelsea.

To the best of my memory, nothing in here looks familiar. It's definitely a different couch and coffee table. I recall that much. The pictures on the wall seem to be encased in new frames, silver now, instead of the polished wood in the past. Lamps? Maybe? They seem new.

This all could be an exercise in futility, but perhaps not. The Hoppers walked away from that Very Special Live Halloween

Episode with quite a bit of money, plus the fact they've sold the rights to their story to a big-time New York publishing house. It stands to reason that they totally abandoned their former home and bought all of this stuff fresh off the shelf.

As Mike finishes, Rob leans forward, elbows on his knees, and thanks us for saving his daughter.

They've held onto such a strong hatred for me for the past two years that his sincerity surprises me.

"You're welcome," I reply. "Part of the job. Maybe some recompense that will never be enough."

"Five-dollar word of the day," Mike says.

I ask Chelsea how she's doing. She blinks and sips at her chocolate milk, unresponsive.

Addressing Leila, I ask, "Is all of your furniture new in here? I mean, like, everything?"

Mike grasps where I'm going with this and says, "Spiritual attachments to objects have the potential to be extremely powerful."

Leila confirms what I had suspected. "Everything. Right down to the spoons and nightlight in the hallway. We never wanted to set foot in that godda—" she glances at the semi-catatonic Chelsea—"that stupid house. Never again. We used the money to start completely fresh."

Rob says, "Which is why we thought that thing was gone, you know? At least to some degree. We've done enough research to know that possessions and hauntings can drag on for years, those bastards can latch on and follow you from place to place, no matter where you go, but this place... this house *felt* clean. It's fifty years old, but it seemed new, you know? And then it happened, the message I told you earlier."

"Yeah, about that," Mike says. He looks to me for confirmation, and I nod for him to go ahead. We had asked the

Hoppers to stay behind, outdoors, while we performed a hit-the-high-spots investigation of the house, and discussed the details in private, agreeing that it would be best for Mike to do the talking and the convincing. "It doesn't surprise us at all, but it seems odd that Boogerface—"

"*Who?*" the Hoppers ask in unison.

Mike points to the back yard. "Him. Your demon."

"*Boogerface,*" Leila says. "I'll never understand boys."

Mike continues. "So, yeah, it seems odd that it would just suddenly pop up out of nowhere and deliver that message. Like you'd said, attachments can drag on for years, forever sometimes—*not that Chelsea's will,* not as long as we're alive and breathing—but they usually manifest in some way, shape, or form. Has she said anything about seeing him? Anything at all?"

Leila strokes Chelsea's hair, watching her with a concerned look as Rob answers, "Not a peep. She's had some trouble at school. Small things, like fights and getting sent to the principal's office. We assumed it was because she's had a touch of celebrity, and the other kids were picking on her for being 'famous.' She's been fine since a therapist gave her some ideas on how to handle her emotions when her classmates behave that way. Stronger than before, and really kind of amazing that a girl her age has already learned to take the high road, come to think of it."

Mike flicks another look my direction.

Ask them, is my subliminal response.

Mike does. "Is there any chance, at all, she could be hiding something from you?"

Rob and Leila both raise their chins, curious looks lifting an eyebrow each, tugging the corners of their mouths down.

Leila stops short of baring her teeth like an angry mama bear when she says, "Are you suggesting she's lying to us? Don't you think I know my own—"

"Ford and I both have had the same dream," Mike interrupts, and then apologizes for doing so before he adds, "and we think that the demon is showing *us* what he's showing Chelsea, or how he's controlling her under the radar. Something like that. It's too hard to say."

Rob squints and shakes his head. "Meaning what?"

I have to chime in here. You know me—it's hard to keep my damn mouth shut for this length of time. "We think," I say, catching the icy glare from Leila, "that she's been having dreams, or that he's guiding her to do odd things."

"Like what?"

"Like what, we don't know. Maybe asserting control? The dream," Mike says, edging out on the couch cushion, "is just weird. Bottom line. We've both seen the exact same thing. We wake up in the middle of the night and, actually, I can't believe I didn't notice this earlier." He leans over and studies the hallway leading to two bedrooms, a bathroom, and then an office at the far end. "Ford? That look familiar to you?"

In fact, it does. The hallway is familiar to the dream, but not quite the same. I suppose it's the difference between dreamland and the real world. It's diverse enough that neither of us made the connection until we began discussing the dream.

"Almost the same," I admit, and a herd of goosebumps slither down my arms.

Mike tells the Hoppers, "Okay, so, the dream goes like this; it's the middle of the night, we wake up and start walking down a hallway, we're both saying some sort of prayer or reciting a poem? Not quite sure. We feel like ourselves, but not, because we can tell that we're a young girl, and then we think we're— well, we get the sensation that we're a male demon. That's the best we can describe it. Even though we're a girl. Sorry, I'm rambling. We check inside our pajamas to make sure we don't have, you know, male parts, and then after that, we look at ourselves in the mirror, do this sort of rage-filled, super evil hiss, and a crack starts running across the mirror. That's where it ends and we wake up. It's happened to us both a number of times."

At the mention of the cracked mirror, Rob and Leila go white, all color draining from their cheeks.

Rob clenches a fist and points at us, nostrils flaring, "Let me ask you A-holes one question. Tell me the truth when you answer, because if I find out you're lying, I won't even bother suing you, I'll find a sharp machete and I'll gut you in your sleep."

Leila gasps. "Rob! Little ears, please."

"Do you guys have cameras in here? Serious question."

Stunned at the allegation, Mike and I rock back on the love seat, then lean forward again. "God, no. Why do you think we would?" I ask.

Rob hesitates, and I suppose he's making up his mind about believing us.

Excruciating seconds tick by on the wall clock.

Finally, he stands and says, "Let me show you something."

We follow him down the hall and into the bathroom. Rob turns on the light, then steps out of the way. He points at the mirror. "It happened a while back. Chelsea woke us up screaming. We thought she'd been sleepwalking, that she woke up in here, and it freaked her out. Then we saw the mirror."

A slithering crack runs from one edge to the other, splintering like lightning.

Rob says, "And that has happened three different times. The guys at the glass company said maybe the house was settling and causing it. I'm going to ask you again—did you install cameras in here? Are you spying on us?"

Again, we reassure him, profusely, that we haven't been.

"Looks about the same as the dream, though," Mike says, hands on his hips. "Is that what you see, Ford?"

"Almost exactly," I agree. My stomach sinks down to somewhere near the soles of my shoes. Mike's theory was right. Boogerface is taunting us, showing us Chelsea's reality and how easily he can manipulate it.

Seconds pass as all four adults stare into the bathroom, grasping to make sense of everything. And then behind us, we hear the soft, angelic voice of little Chelsea Hopper saying, "The white night is bright with light and love. Right, Mr. Ford?"

The Graveyard: Classified Paranormal Series

THE SECOND ACT

11

Before all of this started, the first trip to Ohio, the trip to Carter Kane's home, the subsequent trips to L.A. and back to Ohio, Mike and I had consulted with Hamster Hampstead and her parents and were granted permission to film at the family's abandoned farmhouse.

Due to insurance, budgeting, and a million miles of red tape, we were certain that we wouldn't be allowed to have Hamster, in all her teenage angst and emoticons, investigate the property with us during filming, even though she begged. What we did promise, if we could pull it off, was to first have her and the family members interviewed for the documentary. A decent spot in the lineup, if contracts are negotiated properly, can lead to a pretty fantastic paycheck. We put the family in touch with our agents, and they begrudgingly agreed to sign them on if we were able to finagle the scenario we wanted.

Second, we promised to bring Hamster on an investigation with us at the farmhouse, one where we would attempt to make contact with Papa Joe so he could spread the message to Boogerface over the paranormal energy airwaves. In my mind, I had this image of some cranky old man sitting down in front of a microphone, donning headphones, and screaming, "Good morning, Paranormal Land!" in the style of Robin Williams in *Good Morning, Vietnam*.

And now that Mike and I are here, sitting on the front porch waiting for Deanna Hampstead's mother to drop her off, I'm one hundred percent positive that this is a horrendous idea and we're about to get sued into oblivion.

We've parked ourselves on the top of the porch steps, sitting patiently and running through our routine equipment checks while we wait. EMF detector, check. DVR (digital voice recorder) in operating order, check. All manner of equipment with screens and lights and buttons gets the once over as we ensure they have fresh batteries, that they squeak and honk and beep like they're supposed to.

Mike has been silent for the last fifteen minutes, looking up only when headlights appear from the north, the direction the Hampsteads will be coming from. It's not unusual he's quiet; this is more par for the course, our old habits of getting ready for an investigation like we used to do, back during the first couple of seasons when the budget wasn't as healthy as it would become years later, back before we had interns and lackeys do all of this stuff for us. During the early days, it became almost a meditative state for both of us.

You've seen professional athletes sitting on the sidelines, pre-game, I'm sure, where they're hanging out on a bench, headphones on, lost in their own world while the stadium around them is going nuts.

That's what it's like.

A pre-game warmup. We're getting in the zone.

And yet, I can't help but feeling a sense of morose sadness hanging over me, a small, dark cloud roiling above, like Pig Pen in the *Peanuts* comic.

Nothing is wrong. I know this.

At least not here, with the two of us. Mike and I are on better terms than we've been in ages. Bosom buddies again, you know? Soon, this place will be the site of an epic paranormal war, and you want your ultimate bro at your side. Back home, Melanie and Dakota are asleep, and I'm sure that Ulie is hanging out in the hallway between them. "Doggie in the middle," we say now that we're essentially two couples living together in my mansion. Our own commune, if you will, made up of two guys who don't really deserve the wonderful, understanding women who have chosen to be a part of our lives, regardless of our past indiscretions or the mistakes we're likely going to make over the next couple of weeks.

Things are looking up. Some of them.

Then why am I so morose?

I'm worried about Chelsea. That's the main thing. After we inspected the bathroom mirror and Chelsea told us what she had been doing as well, which more or less matched scene for scene with the dreams Mike and I have been having, I put in a call to Father Duke—and though he would have done it for free—I offered him a hefty chunk of change to travel to Ohio, bless the Hopper's new home, and then remain nearby and on call until the Hoppers were set to arrive here at the farm for filming.

It's not only that; Papa Joe, and whatever other entities might be in there—I'm positive he isn't alone—can pick up on my fear, my worry over Chelsea, and that negative energy is like a generator. I can sense the spirits. They're out here with us, soaking up the negative juice I'm emitting. It's going to happen whether I like it or not, and that's a fact I'm used to.

My legitimate fear grows every time we have to face the supernatural. Further evidence that it will be time to walk away from this life after the war, supposing I'm able.

Carla and Spirit World Productions have been leaking stories that I'm too afraid to proceed with filming, and the falsified inside scoop is working its magic. We're all lined up.

The Graveyard: Classified Paranormal Series

Things are in order, both professionally and personally. We've gotten approval from all sides. Contracts have been signed. The Hampsteads have an agent and will get paid for allowing us to set off a supernatural nuclear bomb on their property. Home team advantage. Melanie and I are great. Dakota and Mike are in what I've been calling teenage love mode, cooing at each other, feeding each other grapes; it's kinda gross, honestly. Since the incident with Grandma Death Eyes, Ulie finally seems like he's relaxing again, and that's also a good thing. Carla and the remainder of the crew are on standby, ready to come here and set up as soon as we give them the green light. The only thing left is to deliver the message to Boogerface.

Yo, Boogerface, you rotten, slimy, disgusting piece of Satanic excrement, we'll be riiiiight here, waiting on your filthy ass.

Big talk from somebody who is shaking in his proverbial shoes, to be honest, but that's the message we have to send. However giant the lie may be, we have to put on a charade of fearlessness, taunt him, get him riled up and angry so that he'll make a mistake.

A guy can dream, can't he?

Mike shifts where he's sitting. The porch boards creak underneath his weight as he clears his throat. "Hey."

"Yeah?" I don't even look up. The EMF detector I'm holding isn't registering quite right, and it's holding my attention. I've already replaced the battery, so it must be an equipment malfunction.

"Hey," Mike repeats.

"Yeah?"

"Look at me."

I pull my eyes away from the needle dancing around erratically and glance over at my friend, my partner, my brother. "What?"

"I'm proud of you," Mike says. He looks elsewhere, out into the night sky. Unless it's him blowing off steam when he's really angry, he rarely exhibits emotion like this, an attempt at peeling back the layers he so desperately holds against his chest.

The fact that he's able to say it out loud surprises me more than him being proud of me. I draw my head back and squint at him. "Who are you, and what have you done with the real Mike? Wait, you're not already possessed are you? We haven't even gone inside yet."

"Shut it. I'm trying to be real here, dude."

I put the malfunctioning EMF detector on the porch beside me, and shift sideways to face Mike.

He says, "I'm serious. I'm proud of you."

"And?" I drag the question out, as if doing so will pull the answer from him like a magician pulling an egregiously long handkerchief out of his mouth.

"Back there with the Hoppers? When Boogerface had Chelsea swinging her around?"

"I was there."

Mike stands and puts his hands in his pockets, looks as if he's contemplating the moon rising over a distant hill. "I hesitated."

"Meaning what?"

"You didn't, man."

"You were right there with me, running around the house as fast as I was. And you grabbed Leila and dragged her away." I stand up beside him and cross my arms. "Didn't look like hesitation to me."

"I could've done more. I could have—"

"You kept her away. Kept her safe. You did the right thing."

"No, I—I stayed back on purpose. I haven't wanted to admit it, but, goddamn, man, I'm scared. Not in the way we've been before. Not just *spooked*, you know? Now I have Dakota in my life and, aside from my kids who still treat Dear Old Dad like an empty ATM, she feels like the best thing that's ever happened to me." His hand goes up and rubs an eye—not a strong attempt at hiding what might have been a tear.

"It takes two, bro. You did your part. I did mine." I rub his head, a quick shot of *attaboy* that I hope will cheer him up. "It's okay to be scared. I'm starting to realize that. We all need a healthy dose of fear; it's what keeps us from dying by doing stupid shit, yeah? Like a few days ago, I was at the athletic center near the house, the one up on Carter Road?"

"Yeah."

"I'd been swimming and stopped to take a break when I look over, and I see this middle-aged dad, maybe around forty—"

"Which means *we're* middle-aged, Ford."

"Good point. Anyway, he had his toddler with him, such a happy blonde kid, maybe three years old, and at first he seemed fearless."

"The kid?"

"Him, yeah. Jumping into the water, swimming like Michael Phelps at that age, already knew how to do the butterfly and backstroke. I was impressed, and then a few seconds later, something happened, and he came up coughing and choking. The dad lifted him out of the water and rubbed his back until he stopped. I went back to my laps but I'd look up every so often, and the kid was still sitting there on the side. The dad, he was trying. Kept pointing at the water, saying something to his son, and boy would shake his head. Nope, nope, nope. And it was fear, obviously. He got too close to his own personal sun, and Icarus got burned. I'll tell you what though, five minutes later, the next time I looked over, he was back in the water. Not quite as confident as he'd been, but he was in there."

"So you're saying I'm a toddler that needs to get back in the kiddie pool."

"Not even the kiddie pool, bro. They were down at the deep end. Short and simple, when we get back in there," I say, hooking a thumb over my shoulder at the front door, "and we take on Boogerface, we're back in the deep water, but it's that healthy dose of fear that's going to keep us alive. I've been thinking about it a lot, and honest to God, Mike, we were stupid all those years. It blows my mind that we didn't come out of it any worse than what we did. For all intents and purposes, we should be six feet under, chained up for eternity while Boogerface uses us as a double-ended dildo."

"There's an image I'll never get out of my head."

I chuckle. Seems like my miniature motivational speech worked because a smile slowly appears on Mike's face, too.

He says, "Before we get too far off track, let me finish my thought; you were like this crazy, spikey-haired superhero—"

"Leave the hair out of it."

"You're trying something new, I get it, Captain Porcupine, but what I'm trying to say is, even if you were about to shit your pants, you were brave, man. Courageous."

"You know what I read one time? Courage isn't the absence of fear. Courage is being scared and choosing to run at danger anyway."

"Point taken." He sits back down on the porch and motions for me to join him. "That was one reason I'm proud of you."

"There's more?"

"One more, and don't get used to it." He holds up an index finger. "You haven't mentioned any regrets, not for a single second, about not having a camera rolling while Boogerface had

Chelsea dangling up there like a rag doll. I mean, good Lord, dude, that was one of the most insane things we've ever seen in all our history together. That topped Italy. That topped the lighthouse in South Carolina. That topped the mental asylum in Pennsylvania. It was unbelievable, and you haven't said a word about missing the chance to capture evidence. All you've talked about since we got back was hoping that she's okay. Do you know how huge that is? You're changing, bro. You've evolved into, well, you've evolved into a human fucking being. Good for you."

It hadn't occurred to me until he mentioned it. I sit stunned for a moment, thinking about that and studying my arms and hands, as if the evolution is physical.

Nothing about my body has changed. Same as I ever was.
Reality and maturity are finally playing nice together.
Wow.
You know what?
I'm proud of me too.

A chilly breeze pushes between us, and for a moment, I wonder if it's Papa Joe or one of the other spirits from inside coming back for another hit off the energy crack pipes known as the 'Almighty' Ford Atticus Ford and Mike 'The Exterminator' Long.

It's not paranormal, it's simply Mother Nature. Her breath puffs against the trees, leaves shaking and rattling in the wind— breath that brings with it the fat scent of distant rain, reminding me of the first night I brought Ulie here with me. That seems like an ancient memory. It was only a couple of months ago. So much has happened in that amount of time.

And so much more will.

Desmond Doane

12

Mike and I turn our ears toward the clap of distant thunder after a small flash of lightning illuminates the southwestern side of the property. Storms of this nature are such a rare occurrence here that we give each other a high five and smiles. It's a good thing, because electrical storms bring with them more energy for supernatural entities to draw on, meaning we'll have a better chance of connecting with Papa Joe tonight.

There's no way on God's green earth that I would want a storm during our filming of the documentary, when we're battling Boogerface—he doesn't need to get any stronger than he already is—but tonight… tonight's okay for storms. Preferred, even.

We see headlights arcing around a bend and wait. Hamster and her mother are fifteen minutes late, and we're on the verge of starting the communication attempt without them.

This particular vehicle slows down and turns onto the gravel road that extends roughly a quarter mile out from the farmhouse. Finally. We gather up our equipment, tuck instruments into various pockets on our vests and pants, and shove some of them back inside the hard foam slots of our pelican cases. These we'll carry inside with us for later use.

The Hampstead's rusted pickup rumbles to a stop next to a decrepit shed. Deanna 'Hamster' Hampstead hops out, and her overweight but jolly mother follows suit. We exchange our greetings in the front yard, and even though we've spoken on the phone, this is the first time I've met two of the Hampstead clan in person. Hamster's mother is starstruck and having a tough time communicating with us without shaking.

Hamster, on the other hand, is not quite what I expect. She's small, as the nickname suggests, but I had pictured her as a teeny bopper teen with a ponytail on the side of her head and pink sandals. I don't know why that is, other than the fact that her email communique sounds like she should be coated in pink apparel and with cute teddy bear cartoons on her socks.

She's nothing of the sort. She has the total goth *chic* thing going on. Black boots, black jeans, black t-shirt, black lipstick and eye shadow, and a dark hoodie, the hood of which is covering dark hair cropped short.

Her smile is another story. Her pristinely white teeth reflect off the glow of the flashlight, and her joy cuts through the angst-ridden image she's trying to convey.

Granted, I wear all black, but I do it to project my television persona. What I've never understood is teenagers trying so desperately to convey a certain image of themselves, especially goth-style clothing during the middle of July. It must suck giant donkey balls to feel as if, in order to be accepted by your clique, you have to wear all black, head to toe, when it's ninety-five degrees outside.

We promise several times to take care of Mama Hampstead's baby girl, and even invite her inside with us to join the investigation. She refuses with so many 'nuh-uh' hand gestures that I'm worried she'll sprain her wrist. "You're not getting me in there," she says. "Not after what y'all have seen. No, sir. No thanks."

"And no problem," I assure her. "Come back in two hours at the least. She'll be fine, especially since Papa Joe is family."

Mama Hampstead nods and hugs Hamster, insists that she be careful, and then ambles over to the truck.

Mike and I, along with our temporary ward, head for the porch and wait until the pickup has reached the main road and trundled away. The less noise pollution, the better. That thing sounds like a pile of rocks clanking around inside a clothes dryer.

Hamster says, "Sorry we're late. My stupid dad decided at the last minute he didn't want me coming."

I steer clear of telling her to respect her elders and choose to identify with her instead. "*Pffft*. Adults, am I right? How'd you change his mind?" I ask.

Hamster shrugs in the "I dunno" way that only teens can use to convey apathy before responding, "Didn't, really. We waited until he passed out on the couch."

She can tell I'm worried this might cause a problem for tonight's investigation if some drunk, pissed off father shows up, waving around a shotgun and demanding to know what we're doing with his daughter. To be fair, dropping off a fifteen year old girl with two strange men, celebrities or not, sounds damn shady on the exterior. Before I can express my concern, she assures me, "He'll be asleep all night. Once he's out, you couldn't wake him up with a stick of dynamite."

Mike chuckle-snorts. "That so?"

"My older brother tried one time. Didn't work."

Through the flashlight's glow, I watch Mike's eyebrows arch in shock as he says, "Well, okay then." Without anything further to add—because, really, what can you say to that?—he asks if I'm ready, then Hamster.

Two affirmatives later, we're standing at the front door, discussing our investigation plan, when the entire house shudders under our feet.

And thank God, it's the result of nothing more than thunder erupting the same time a lightning strike hits a tree two hundred yards east. I'll take Mother Nature's wrath over supernatural posturing any day. Doesn't mean it's not a small shock, and all three of us duck and cover our heads.

As cliché as it sounds, like those overdone scenes in movies, with the gigantic thunderclap comes a waterfall downpour, as if the heavens burst at the seams.

We're sheltered underneath the porch roof, and that's a good thing, because—I shit you not—it's like Noah's Flood out there. I've never seen anything like it for as long as I've been living here in the Pacific Northwest.

Lightning crackles and races across the sky, reminding me of the mirror shattering in the Hopper's bathroom.

Mike says, "Maybe we should get inside, huh?"

"Yes, please," Hamster whines. "I hate storms."

I put an arm around her shoulder. "Your guardian protectors are here to save you, ma'am." Thunder slams into the home again, rattling the windows on either side of us, and Hamster sinks into me. Oddly enough, it's a comforting feeling, being the protector, and the thought of having kids with Melanie skitters across my mind.

First things first, Ford. Papa Joe. Message Sent. Mail Delivered.

Try not to shit your pants while you go to war against the strongest demon anybody has ever seen in modern times.

I checked in with some of my paranormal investigator colleagues, giving them the low-down, asking if they'd ever seen or heard of anything so powerful. They confirmed they indeed had not, though one suggested talking to this demonologist he knows. Apparently back in the 1700s, a suspected demon shut down half of London's east side for three days. All conjecture derived from shaky historical accounts, but it wouldn't surprise me if it were true.

Besides, I've seen this shit firsthand.

I let go of Hamster and reach for the front door. The century-old iron knob is cool to the touch. I twist it and the ragged, decaying wood swings inward on its corroded hinges. The screech makes my eardrums tingle.

We march inside, single-file like three good little soldiers, and then leap inches off the ground when it slams closed with enough force to crack the closest window.

Rarely have I seen Mike shake from fear. He squeaks out, "The wasn't the wind, was it?"

"No," I say, sighing, "no, I don't think so."

Hamster whispers, "Maybe this wasn't such a good idea."

"You got this," I tell her. "No worries, 'cause you've got the two best paranormal investigators in the world standing right beside you."

I say that, though these days, I'm not so sure. Fear has invaded us, and the inability to maintain positive energy during these situations is bad, bad news.

I'm almost to the point where I'm not wholly certain we'll both make it out of the documentary without a minor possession at best or dead at the worst.

God, I hope that's not psychic foreshadowing.

I'm sensitive to the supernatural. I've mentioned that, and I've had more than one time where I hoped what I had sensed would never come true.

And there's Keller's warning: *"She will … betray you."*

Could he have meant Hamster Hampstead?

Good grief, now I have another possible suspect to worry about, in addition to Melanie, Dakota Bailey, Carla Hancock, Chelsea Hopper, Leila Hopper, my mom, and the nice lady who makes my cappuccino the way I like it at the coffee shop around the corner. I don't know how many "she's" could be possible suspects for betrayal, but I'm thinking those eight are enough.

I ask Mike, "Why don't you run a quick baseline sweep and see where the numbers are sitting?"

"Sure," he replies. "You've been here before. Any wiring issues to worry about, any fear cages that'll throw off the EMF detector?"

"No power to it. You're good there. Hamster and I—"

"Deanna," she interrupts. "I'm just Deanna now."

"Deanna and I," I say, acknowledging her insistence, "will hang out here and get the spotcams set up, then start an EVP session."

"Roger that. Back in a few."

Mike and I should have set up the spotcams earlier, when there was more light outside. We chose not to because we didn't want to upset the spiritual feel inside here.

Short version: We didn't want to muddy the waters before we began the main investigation.

Lightning, both strikes and flashes, is doing a good job of illuminating the downstairs, in addition to our flashlights. Deanna and I get the two spotcams up and running in quick succession. One by the front door, facing the stairwell going up to the second floor, then another in the western corner of the adjoining kitchen to capture most of that room and this one at the same time.

She and I stand side by side, hands on our hips, surveying our work.

She's trying to appear confident.

It's not working well.

Her façade begins crumbling seconds later when we hear knocking on the kitchen door behind us, the door leading out to the back yard.

Tap, tap, tap. Tap, tap, tap.

"What's that?" she gasps.

"*Who* is more like it," I reply.

"What do you mean, *who*? Nobody would be stupid enough to come out in this."

"Ummmm, yeah, I don't mean human. At least not one that's alive."

"Oh," she says quietly, moving back a step. "Right."

There it is again.

Tap, tap, tap.

A large cold spot begins to form in front of me. I can feel a twenty-degree temperature difference on my hand.

I step closer to the door, and Deanna begs me not to answer it. I tell her I have to investigate; I have to at least look out the window. It's long been thought in the paranormal community that if you open a door for something, then that's an invitation.

Since I'm positive that Papa Joe is already here, I have no desire to *invite in* whatever might be *out there*.

I peek out the window and study the back yard when a bright bolt of lightning streaks and scatters across the dark, roiling clouds.

One, two, three, I count in my head, as the thunder comes barreling through.

I see nothing. No one is waiting out there. Just overgrown grass, an ancient tractor with four flat tires, and the skeleton of a dead cat that I focus on with my flashlight beam.

I turn to reassure Deanna everything is fine when I feel it on my shoulder.

Tap, tap, tap.

I yelp, twitch, and spin around at the same time Deanna screams, "Get off me!"

"What? You okay?" I reach for her.

"Something pulled on my hair. Ugh, so creepy."

"You're fine," I promise. "It'll be fine. Let's run an EVP session and see if it communicates with us."

"Okay," she replies, not sounding like it really is at all.

"More than likely," I explain, "I'd say it's members of your family, so they won't hurt you. Wait, how long has it been since you investigated here?"

"Me and my friend, Em, we used to, but she moved away, and I haven't been back since the last time I emailed about how we caught Papa Joe asking to speak to you."

"Then whoever's here is just getting used to us again. No big deal. Okay? Family won't hurt you."

She tucks her hands into her armpits and nods. Even in the darkness, after I turn the flashlight off and when the lightning briefly takes a rest, it's easy to see her bottom lip quivering in the ambient glow from the spotcam screen close to her shoulder.

"We can do this," I tell her. "Nothing to be afraid of, yeah?"

Those words quickly become a false promise as Mike plunges down the stairs, taking them by twos until he lands on the ground floor. He flicks his flashlight back upstairs and huffs, "Son of a bitch, that scared the shit out of me." The cone of light from his flashlight flicks around the room as he looks for us. "Where the hell are you—oh," and he scrambles around the rickety furniture to join us at the kitchen entrance.

I ask him what happened, and he twists sideways, pointing at his neck. "Felt like something bit me. You see anything?"

"Like a mosquito?"

I get a giggle out of Deanna. It's good to see that her instinct and gut reactions can overcome her fear. Besides, it's hard for me to resist the easy and obvious joke.

"I'm not kidding, bro."

"Let me see."

Deanna scoots next to me, clenched hands covering her mouth as she whimpers. I shine my beam on the back of Mike's neck.

He's right.

Only it's not a bite.

Three claw marks, a demonic mockery of the Holy Trinity, slash down in a bright red angle across his skin.

"Dude?" he says.

I don't have anything to say, and that's rare.

I was *not* expecting this level of malevolence.

Tap, tap, tap.

Tap, tap, tap.

13

Why does it seem like a *natural* storm is in the vicinity whenever I'm the most frightened by the *unnatural*? It's almost as if the universe is sending me a warning signal, waving signs, flashing its lights, telling me to watch the hell out.

Mike, Deanna, and I all huddle together in the middle of the rundown living room, our backs together, guarding against a rear attack while covering all the visible area with three sets of eyes. Our flashlights circle and sweep in thin swaths of light across a sheet-covered couch, a rocking chair that has twice now moved on its own, and a grandfather clock with the pendulum somehow stuck at an odd angle. A gun cabinet sits in the corner with its door open, the firearms inside long gone, either stolen by looters or taken away by family members.

This place holds a bevy of stories within its walls, tales about lives once lived.

Well, those lives appear to continue here, only on another plane of existence.

We've tried our EMF detectors, our digital voice recorders, our spirit boxes, and yet, *nada*. Nothing, no evidence captured. We only have anecdotal moments that we can't prove happened. We heard and felt the taps, Mike got scratched, the rocking chair has moved on its own, and that's it.

Not too scary, right? So why are we guarding each other in a reverse huddle?

Precautions.

My gut is telling me there's more to come, and whatever may be in the rest of the house is soaking up the ambient, natural energy each time Mother Nature flings a bolt of lightning out of her fingertips.

Deanna whispers, "Didn't you catch the most activity upstairs, in their old bedroom?"

"I did," I say.

There's a long, pregnant pause filling the room before she asks, "Then why aren't we up there?"

"Mike got scratched for one. Two… well, I don't have a two."

Mike insists he's okay and suggests we get this over with. "We'll get this Joe Schmoe guy to deliver our message, then we can come back when we're better armed."

"Better armed?" I ask. "We brought almost every piece of equipment we own."

"I'm talking, like, holy water. Father Duke. Maybe ten or fifteen more priests and the Pope. Grenade launcher. Simple stuff."

"The big guns would be nice," I reply, though I know taking on Boogerface is never going to be simple, no matter how well prepared we are. "Upstairs we go. Deanna?"

"Yeah?"

"Stay close. Keep yourself guarded. On the inside, I mean. Don't invite anything in. Don't tell the spirits they can use your energy, nothing like that. You're here to observe only, got it?"

"I'm good," she says, then quietly adds, "I think."

"Stay that way. We take you home with an angry visitor in your back pocket, your folks might not let us off your property alive."

I lead the way upstairs. Deanna follows, with Mike trailing her. It may not work, but I'm more comfortable having her in the midst of a safety sandwich. We can at least give her the illusion of protection.

The wooden steps, once polished but now dingy and scuffed from a hundred years of boots and shoes scraping across their surface, now creak and cry with every step we take upward. It sounds like a rickety March of the Ants with all three of us ascending at the same time.

We reach the second floor landing. A bedroom door is open to my left. Inside, the glass is broken on the westward facing window. The storm pushes a damp gust of wind through. Crumbling eaves wail against the wind outside.

Mike bumps into Deanna, and she yips, startled.

"Sorry."

"S'okay," she whines.

I ask Mike if he was able to do enough of a baseline sweep before he got scratched, and he replies, "Not a hundred percent, but it was running flat as a pancake until this." He points at the back of his neck.

"Did you taunt? Anything like that?"

"That's your gig, chief. I asked a couple of questions to see if I could stir something up. Nothing major. Who's here, anybody with us, what's the score of the Giants game, the usual."

"Gotcha."

You wouldn't think that one floor up would make much of a difference, yet when the lightning crashes and the thunder explodes overhead, it feels as if God himself is screaming in our faces.

"Deanna? Take my hand."

She does, and it's cold. Shaking.

"Let's go straight to the source. I know where he hides."

"Usually," Deanna whispers.

I turn to face her, pointing the beam of my flashlight at about chest level. "Usually?"

"We went in the basement once. It's so scary down there."

Mike snorts. "Perfect."

I shake my head. "Not tonight. We'll get Papa Joe up here." Pointing to the master bedroom, where I've captured the most evidence in my past visits, I tell my somewhat brave companions we're heading there, to say some prayers if they want, and we're off.

Crossing the expanse between the stairs and the main bedroom can't be any longer than twenty feet, and yet it feels like we're walking a country mile through the entrance to Hell.

The hand-hewn floorboards, crafted with love and passion, now screech, sob, and moan as if they're lost souls hanging out in this hallway to Hades. Each step we take is more unnerving than the last.

We pass the first bedroom on our left.

The bedroom door to our right, five feet ahead, slams with violent ferocity, and we freeze in place. Deanna clenches my hand hard enough to hurt, and I can literally hear her teeth chattering from fear. I tell her it was probably the wind, nothing to be afraid of, then I ask, "Were you this scared when you came with your friend?"

"No way. We were just, like, goofing off, trying to spook each other. NBD."

"NBD?" Mike says, molding the letters into a question.

"No big deal."

I smirk and think about the linguist, Dr. Addison Keller, turning over in his grave.

Deanna says, "Tonight—it feels different. Like *real*. Like there's something here that's not happy with us."

"Spirits like your Papa Joe rarely are," I inform her. "We're lucky Mike's neck is the only thing getting—"

"Ouch!" Deanna yelps. "What the shit was that?"

I spoke too soon. She yanks up the sleeve of her hoodie.

These scratches didn't even need time to bloom bright red. They already are.

Sure enough, there are three of them, and I'm wondering if Boogerface is already a step ahead of us. Is he here?

Deanna's breathing grows rapid. Good arm up to her forehead, she takes a step backward and stumbles into Mike. "I can't get a full breath. I'm—" She slumps into my partner's arms. "So exhausted. Like all of a sudden I can't…"

I fumble for the tiny penlight I keep in my jeans. Once I find it, I shine the light in her eyes, checking her pupils, feeling her pulse, finding the erratic beat is weak underneath my fingertips. Breath after breath after breath peppers my cheeks, and I'm worried she's going to faint.

"Out of here, Mike. Get her gone."

"No," she mumbles, "I want to help."

"Your night's done, Deanna." I squeeze her arm twice, trying to reassure her. "I promise we'll do a rain check, okay?"

She's barely able to nod. Mike and I exchange a silent, burdened glance detailing everything we need to say.

"Stay with her. Don't let her back inside."

Mike scoops her up in his arms with all the effort of picking up a kitten, and then they're gone, thumping down the stairs.

I wait. I watch. I listen to the front door slam and hear their muffled voices underneath the blustery, raging storm outside.

"Good," I say out loud.

But maybe not so good.

Now I'm all alone.

And the energy in here is extremely different than my previous visits.

I may have shut myself inside an abandoned farmhouse with an ancient demon.

Not one of my brightest moments, among the many, but what am I supposed to do? Allow Deanna Hampstead to stay in here and have another repeat of the Chelsea Situation?

If I take her home possessed, soaked to the brim in evil, vomiting demon puss, and spitting pea green soup all over the house, I'm dead in so many different ways. I can't go through that again. I can't allow it to happen twice. My guilty conscience would plant me in a mental ward, staring out a closed window and drooling all over my straight jacket.

So, yeah.

Here I am.

Back to the basics; might as well attempt another EVP session.

I sigh. "Here goes nothing."

I push the red Record button, mark the time and the location, and then gingerly, cautiously, step from room to remaining room, staying out of the master, because I haven't quite built up the jujus to head in there. I introduce myself, again, ask all the standard questions like 'Who's here with me tonight?' and 'Papa Joe, if you're here, will you give me a sign of your presence?'

I do this for ten minutes and then do a live review session before I tackle the last bastion of evil in the Hampstead farmhouse.

Ten minutes of my questions.

Ten minutes of no replies.

Shit.

Downstairs, the front door opens, and Mike calls up, asking if I'm okay, asking if I need him to join me.

"Not a chance," I bark back. "Stay with her. *Please.* I'm good here." Though I'm positive my shaky voice betrays me.

"Okay. Yell if you need me."

Another deep breath. Here we go. Second verse, same as the first.

Not really, because I can feel this place taking on a life of its own now, as if the house itself is breathing, the walls expanding and contracting each time it inhales and exhales. It's huge, crouching, and bestial. Throat rumbling, fangs bared, their sharp points glinting with each flash of lightning, while I crawl around inside the belly of the beast.

I shiver thinking about it.

And this is just the beginning.

We're only here to send a message.

What's it going to be like when this place is crawling with cameramen and crew, each one of them like a goddamn supercharged battery with energy that can be soaked up to power a raging, angry, revenge-fueled demon?

Okay, Ford, stop freaking yourself out.

One thing at a time. One day at a time.

"You've done this more before," I remind myself, and then I press on.

I would like to say I bravely march toward the master bedroom door. Instead, I kinda run to it like a chickenshit coward.

I grab the doorknob, twist, and for a second, it feels cold on my palm.

Then my brain catches up with my sense of touch.

It's so hot that it feels cold at first, confusing the synapses sending signals.

I haven't felt something similar since the Craghorn house.

I scream obscenities, push it open farther, and then jerk my hand away, trying to shake it free of the pain.

Downstairs, Mike must be eavesdropping because he once again yells up and asks if I'm okay, if I need him.

"*No*," I shout back. "I got this."

"What happened?"

"Doorknob is about a million degrees. I'm going in."

"Be careful, please," Mike begs, and then I'm through the door.

It's so hot in this room, I'm surprised Satan isn't sitting in the shredded easy chair by the window. Up near the headrest, two springs have broken through the thinning purple material, and they remind me of jagged Devil's horns.

Thanks, Ford. Didn't need that imagery.

I breathe deeply, calmly—as best as I can—and for ten full minutes, I stand in the bedroom, enduring the heat, trying to use each piece of investigative equipment I have with me and watch as, one by one, the fresh, full batteries die. The entity, or entities, present are soaking up everything I'm throwing at them.

Sweat beads race down my back and sides like wet snakes slithering along my skin.

I search my pockets and find one last set of batteries, choosing the digital voice recorder for my final round in the chamber. I spend another five minutes addressing Papa Joe, explaining what we're up against, but only revealing part of our plans in case there are prying demonic ears that might run home to Daddy Master and tattle on us.

Then I play back the recording.

The first voice I hear, in between my yammering, is Papa Joe, finally.

But gone is the cranky old bastard that I've spoken to before.

It's the voice of a man cowering in a corner, holding up his hands and shaking his head before he meets his fate.

"*They're here...*" Papa Joe whimpers through the speaker. "*They can ... tell him. No. No, please.*"

It's one of the clearest Class-A EVPs I've ever caught. Instead of being on the other side, he sounds as if he's directly in the room with me.

"*His ... minions. Can't you ... see ...*"

My voice, having not heard this in real time, continues to blather, asking if he can send a message to Boogerface for us, it would really help us out, and blah-blah.

"*They ... know. They're coming. He's coming.*"

With each passing word, his voice grows more and more frightened on the recording while I fumble with my words. A second or two here, a second or two there, Papa Joe talks over my questions, addressing me directly, telling me that a portal has opened. He can see a wave of lesser demons howling, flying up, up, and up.

And then my voice stops for a moment. I had paused to give him a chance to respond.

"*Tell everyone ... I'm sorry,*" his voice says, then Papa Joe screams in such abject terror, I can feel gooseflesh flood my entire body at once.

My voice again: "If you could send that message, it would help." Short pause. "Oh, and if there's any chance you know his name, could you maybe tell me? Please?"

"*Mirror, mirror,*" is the last clear EVP I hear, and then his horrified voice fades as if something is dragging him away.

Or down.

If it's possible, the room has grown hotter, and I decide it's long past time to leave this place for the night.

You've heard the expression, 'Going to hell in a handbasket,' right?

It takes me a moment to fully comprehend I just listened to a spirit being dragged into a pit of raging fire, and it is certainly possible Mike and I aren't far behind. When the time comes, I'll probably have to save Mike a seat in the handbasket.

This is bigger than us.

I know that now. I understand we're out of our league, *completely*.

My only consolation is that Father Duke has agreed to join us, along with Carter Kane, who, aside from Mike Long, are two people I inherently trust to handle the demonic. We'll have some quality backup the next time we're here.

Until then, maybe I can figure out what Papa Joe meant by '*mirror, mirror.*'

I don't take my time descending the steps, pausing only at the bottom to look back once, regretting I didn't ask Papa Joe if he knew what "*The blood of the meek shall feed my horror,*" referenced.

Aside from what could be construed as a doomsday prophecy.

14
One Week Later

Gunnar Creek.

Two words. First name. Last name.

Three syllables that elicit a look of annoyance, disgust, and mild rage in anyone over the age of thirty. Rather than working hard like most overnight successes that took two decades to come to fruition, the dude was nearly handed his fame in a week.

For the first fifteen years of his life, he was a cute kid with bleached blonde hair, bright blue eyes, and real, rare talent with a guitar. He learned to play when he was six. When I was six years old, I was picking my nose and seeing how many Matchbox cars I could fit into my mouth at one time.

Then, YourVideo appeared on Ye Olde Interwebs, Gunnar's mother uploaded a couple of recordings where he performed excellent cover songs of popular Beatles tunes, and boom, honey, *viral* ain't even the word for it.

The short clips shot around the Internet, garnered millions of positive votes in a handful of days, and a month later, he performed an original song on *Sherilyn*, the super popular daytime talk show hosted by the queen of comedy, Sherilyn Jones. In between interviewing the Hollywood elite, Sherilyn likes to play games, give away coffee roasters, and scare the crap out of her celebrity guests around Halloween.

Not long after, Gunnar Creek was on posters in every single teenage girl's bedroom from Seattle to Mongolia, a worldwide sensation who grew up in a trailer park outside of Mobile, Alabama. He went from eating string cheese for dinner every night to earning north of two hundred million dollars in his first three years of performing to sold out shows across the globe.

You'd think the Beatles landed in the U.S. for the first time again with the way crowds react to Gunnar Creek's arrival.

Fame, and all the nasty vagaries that come with it, took its toll on young Gunnar, and he spent two years getting arrested, being photographed with a rolled up dollar bill stuck in his nose as it hovered over a white powdery line, to having a raucous public breakup with another teeny-bopper songstress named Kayla Carmichael after some paparazzi snatched a photograph of Gunnar cozying up to a naked supermodel—also with a line of white powder stretching from nipple to bellybutton below Gunnar's distorted, stoned grin.

His publicists have been working double-time to repair his image, and so far, I'm not entirely sure it has been doing any good. He's still an entitled prick who treats waiters poorly and racks up the occasional speeding ticket while berating the beleaguered officer unfortunate enough to pull him over.

If I had my druthers, I'd avoid him like a leper in the buffet line.

What I mean is, the dude's a humongous asshole, and anyone with a modicum of maturity sees him that way. In the Over Thirty Crowd, he might be the only person in the U.S. who has a poorer public image than I do.

Er, *did*. I hope.

And yet, he's going to be in our documentary, because the Under Thirty Crowd absolutely adores him. In their eyes, he can do no wrong.

Asshole? Not a chance, Grandpa. My boy up on that stage has the voice of an angel.

A twelve-step angel, but an angel nonetheless.

As Dakota had said, the Under Thirty Crowd will go watch the documentary multiple times because he's in it, while the Over Thirty Crowd will go just to see him scared shitless—and cross their fingers really, really hard that he wets his pants.

The numbers sent over by Carla's data guys have suggested that including Gunnar Creek in the celebrity lineup will raise worldwide profits by an estimated three-hundred million dollars.

We'll see. That's all I can say.

For the time being, Mike and I had some serious discussions about his involvement after we exchanged a handful of phone calls with his representatives and Gunnar himself. He was a major fan of *Graveyard* and sent out those tweet things constantly before the show got pulled…

…are you sensing the *but* here?

He has never been on a paranormal investigation before, which could pose a problem.

We had uninitiated celebrity guests on *Graveyard* in the past, but none of them were quite on the same level of popularity as Gunnar Creek. Nobody would care if Dane Kowalski, the standup comic who starred in that movie with the talking cat, ended up possessed after a night spent in a haunted asylum with us. Nor would they mind much if Lucy Lanyard, the host of the ultra-conservative news show, *Today Tomorrow*, found herself sitting in a corner, sucking her thumb for the rest of her life because she got groped by a dead sex offender.

There is no such thing as a Big Loss when it comes to B- and C-level celebrities.

A Big Loss of Gunnar Creek, on the other hand, would raise the ire of a few billion people on Earth, perhaps even alien planets, if someone committed him to the loony bin, post demonic encounter. We would have nowhere to hide.

So, armed with the fear of reprisal from about a billion teenage girls, Mike and I decided that Gunnar needed the experience of at least one investigation, and we had an adequate location in mind.

There's a place in Oregon we always wanted to investigate but never had the chance. It was actually on the docket for our eleventh season—and we all know how that turned out.

Once all the calls were made and details arranged, we caught up with Gunnar Creek and his entourage in Bend, a small city in central Oregon, home to amazing scenery, professional athletes, and a number of celebrities, both retired from the public spotlight and others actively engaging in selling their soul to Hollywood. It's a fantastic area if you love the outdoors, being active, consuming mass quantities of microbrews, and enjoying three-hundred days of sunshine each year.

The snot-nosed brat insisted we stay the night and dragged us from local brewhouse to local brewhouse until we finally threw in the white towel around three a.m. Evidently Oregon's serving laws don't apply to Gunnar Creek.

I'll have to admit, the conversations were somewhat entertaining in the fact that while almost every person on the planet knows who this young guy is, he gushed over us like he had met a couple of superheroes. We spent the night drinking gloriously excellent IPAs, pale ales, and wheat beers, all while recanting stories about our past investigations and trying to curb Gunnar's expectations. "It's not going to be *Ghostbusters*," we told him time and again, "because this is some serious shit. We're taking on a demon—an actual, real, live—well, dead—demon."

Having him fawning over us didn't totally change our opinions of him, by the way. He'll always be a dipshit with an entitled attitude problem, but we were able to see how he'd been molded into such a jerkhole by his parents and his handlers.

Anyway, Gunnar's life story aside, we're now riding in the lead SUV of a celebrity motorcade that could seriously rival the President's, while traveling northeast through the beautiful, rolling hills of the Ochoco Mountains. The mounds remind me of piles of brown sugar, dotted with pine trees and weathered rock outcroppings. We roll through farmland in the valleys, which often feels as if we're running a livestock gauntlet what with the number of cattle on either side of the road.

Mike and I are somewhat alert, being old and wise enough to know when to quit drinking to avoid a massive hangover, while Gunnar dozes in the far back seat of the SUV, trying to sleep it off. You would think his tolerance level would be higher than the cruising altitude of a 747, and yet, when he walked out of the hotel this morning, he looked like he'd fallen out of a tree and hit every limb on the way down.

I can't remember the driver's real name; he goes by Bomber, and he's the monstrous head bodyguard who spent time in the Marines, then the Middle East working as a private security contractor before he moved stateside to kick ass and take names for the upper echelon of celebrities in southern California.

We don't speak much because Bomber quietly hinted that if the "mental toddler"—his words, not mine—in the back didn't get his beauty rest, he'd be impossible to handle for the next thirty-six hours.

Point taken and duly noted, Mike and I spend the four and a half hours from Bend to Sumpter, Oregon communicating with each other and our respective partners via text, chuckling at goofy pictures of Ulie that Melanie and Dakota keep sending along, and reading up on the history of Sumpter and the haunted hotel where we're staying.

Ghost Bros and *Terrible Tales* have both been there before and captured some terrific evidence, but, the hauntings have seemed like they're *tame* for lack of a better word, and, to us, that sounded like the perfect place to indoctrinate Gunnar Creek into the world of the paranormal.

The trip seems to get longer and longer as each passing mile reminds me that even in a heavily occupied state, unsettled areas remain, holding onto the feel of a settler making his way west to seek fortune and a place to call home. If I look out to my right, down a steep embankment, down to where a river carves its way through multiple layers of soil, I can imagine a pioneer with his wagon parked off to the side while he pans for gold in them thar hills. Then, looking up and up the other bank, I imagine a line of Native Americans cresting the ridge while they glare down at the interloper below. Cue the music of doom inside my mind movie, and there's one dead settler with a spear sticking out of his chest.

Fun. My brain is imagining death before we get to our destination.

Finally, we arrive at the middle-of-nowhere town of Sumpter, Oregon, population three hundred and four if you count the pets, too. It's a borderline ghost town, but back in the day, according to historians, this place was a hopping gold mining metropolis of close to four thousand people. The easily accessible gold dried up, an enormous fire destroyed over ninety percent of the buildings, and the citizenry moved on to seek the yellow, malleable metal elsewhere.

From what I read online, nowadays the townspeople spend their time cruising around on ATVs and entertaining tourists who come to take in the history, ride a fully functioning steam train, and try their luck at digging up some gold wherever they can find a bit of land to do it legally.

Bomber strictly obeys the speed limit of fifteen miles per hour as we drive along Sumpter's main street, giving me time to take in the scenery. The town seems like it has two more saloons than necessary, in addition to antique stores, restaurants, and a different hotel with a wooden fence built around it and made to look like an Old West fort.

Mike leans up from the middle row and taps on my shoulder, whispering, "Dude, look over there. Not all of the streets are paved. What year is it again?"

How's that for a step away from civilization, huh? Gravel roads right in the middle of town.

The GPS on Bomber's phone barks an order, and we turn right up a slight incline, gravel scrabbling under the tires and bouncing of the SUV's underbelly. The noise is enough to wake Gunnar, and he grumbles his displeasure from the far back as the Sumpter Hotel & Spa looms above us. Two stories tall, painted forest green on the sides and celebrity-teeth white on the front, it looks ominous already, and we haven't stepped inside yet.

You know me and buildings—I don't get comfortable until I've had time to discern whether it's the structure itself or the entities inside that are causing the biggest issues.

The hair stands up on my arms and my supernatural sixth sense is pegging in the red before Bomber pulls the SUV's reins and stops in front.

Interesting. Our research indicated this would be like serving Gunnar a haunted cupcake instead of tossing him directly into the shitstorm sandwich of the Hampstead farmhouse.

Gunnar, acting like he's five instead of twenty-one, climbs over the back of the middle seat and flops down next to Mike. He runs a shaky hand through his ratty bleach job and asks if anyone has a cigarette. When we tell him no and he begins to whine like an *actual* five-year-old, Bomber rolls his eyes so hard I'm sure they'll pop out of his head, then reaches into his jacket pocket and tosses Gunnar an unopened pack of Marlboros.

We had planned on giving Gunnar a briefing on the Sumpter Hotel & Spa, and what to expect during the investigation, but that opportunity vanishes because he's out the side door and bounding up the stairs, flicking his cigarette ashes into a potted plant before we're able to open our mouths.

Anyway. Bomber warned us that the kid would be difficult to control, and I'm cool with that. My only goal here is to keep him out of the psych ward and get him prepared for the insane, supernatural shenanigans—now there's an understatement—of an unnamed, Tier One demon who may very well sit at the right hand of Satan Himself.

Mike, Bomber, and I climb out of the SUV, along with the remainder of the entourage parked behind us. They pour out like multiple clowns from a small car. Security guys, onsite makeup specialists because you never know when the 'razzi are going to be hiding in the bushes for a photo op, and three young women we met when we stopped for a burger a couple of hours ago—a blonde, a brunette, and a redhead, a rainbow of flavors for our Dear Leader.

It's a sight to behold and reminds me of our days at the height of *Graveyard*'s popularity.

More bodies means more energy for the dead, and it worries me that if this place is as haunted as my supernatural radar suggests, then every one of these damn people, whether they're here because it's their job, or tagging along because they hope they might be "accidentally" photographed in bed with Gunnar Creek, are nothing more than paranormal cannon fodder.

It's gonna be a long night.

The one saving grace is that we invited Carter Kane along, you know, for funsies, and he's just now rumbling up the hill on a Harley, looking badass and ready to eat some ghosts for dinner.

Amen to that.

The Graveyard: Classified Paranormal Series

15

Established in 1903, the Sumpter Hotel & Spa used to be the area's first hospital. According to the brochures, various plaques around the walls, and my short form internet research, it came equipped with all the modern facilities a gold miner with a case of the sniffles or an arm that got crushed in a cave-in could want.

It served as the hospital for a while, spent some limited time as a brothel—because in a gold mining town, why not?—then became a Masonic lodge before it finally settled into its current role of half hotel and spa, half bed and breakfast. Reviews on the internet report some of the most amazing huckleberry pancakes anyone's ever tasted.

But I'm not sure we're going to make it that far unless Gunnar Creek stops bouncing around the joint like somebody gave an ADHD-suffering child a caffeine enema with a chaser of speed. He's already broken an antique vase, spilled cola on a pistol from the late 1800s, and knocked the same photograph from a shelf three different times.

When I quietly ask Bomber what the little prick is on, he replies, "They're blue. That's all I know."

And speaking of the owners, they're amazing. Mack and Bonnie, two salt of the earth type folks I'd happily adopt as honorary grandparents. They're calm, gentle, and quite tolerant of Gunnar ping-ponging around the main downstairs doubling as a sitting area and dining room, complete with red and white checkered tablecloths.

I try to subtly apologize for Gunnar's behavior while he's plastering fingerprints all over an antiquated wheelchair, and they wave me off, whispering their grandson is a toddler with ADHD too.

Well, then. Familiar territory, it would seem.

It smells old in here, and for a building with well over a hundred years behind it that's not surprising. The scent is distinct, and it takes me a half an hour to realize it reminds me of my grandmother's farmhouse. It's the combined scent of paperback books turning yellow, woodstove smoke soaked into the walls, and a hundred years of sweat, meals, and pipe tobacco all combining to douse the joint in a heavy pile of nostalgia.

Gunnar's posse, along with the three tagalong girls that I've secretly dubbed One, Two, and Three, stays behind in the main area while Mike, Carter Kane, Gunnar, Bomber, and I all take a tour with Mack. Bonnie, I assume, is hanging behind to ensure the gaggle doesn't destroy anything valuable.

The six of us ascend the wooden staircase to the second floor, each step whining under our weight, particularly Bomber's, and I suspect he's about one gigantic cheeseburger away from falling through.

The popping and cracking of the wooden steps is overruled only by the snickering and giggling of One, Two, and Three, as they watch longingly after Gunnar's ascent. I see Two lick her lips and recall the days when that was an everyday part of my life and Mike's too, I should note, but to a lesser extent.

Mack gives us a short tour of the upstairs, pointing out the individual details of each of the eight bedrooms. The Sunflower

Room. The Black & White Room. The Cary Grant Room. You get the idea. Each has its own flavor and style. Some are equipped with modern items like digital clocks and air conditioners. Others, depending on your requests during reservations, are more rustic in nature. Quick shots of time travel back to a different era: oil lamps, wooden bedframes, and goose down blankets designed to give the guest an "old-timey" experience. Never fear, because you can walk right out into the main sitting area upstairs and find a flat screen television and satellite TV.

The charm is delightful, and that's a statement I never thought I'd hear coming out of my mouth.

What concerns me is the sixth sense feel that I'm getting up here. Downstairs, I was cool. It felt fine: no vibes, just an old building with its individual quirks and oddities.

Upstairs, the hallway leading to the sitting area is closed-in, claustrophobic almost, and then the sitting area is… off. I feel the tingling sensation of being watched. Mike has noticed it too because his eyes are flitting from room to ceiling, to the rear door, to the staircase behind us. His curious glance settles on mine. Something is going on here.

"Mack," I say during a lull in Gunnar's endless supply of chatty questions, "just how haunted is your place? I've heard stories, and some of the other paranormal crews have been here, but what's your take?"

Mack replies, "Straight from the horse's mouth, you mean?" I nod. "Straight from."

"Well." Mack clears his throat, tucks his thumbs in his belt loops and arches back as if he's going to launch into his story, as if he's the ammunition in a giant slingshot. "If you ask Bonnie and me, we try to keep an open mind. We've seen things, heard things. Stuff gets moved around. There's a ghost cat that scratches at the door now and then."

Gunnar blurts, "Anything bad ever happen here?" though it comes out in a jumbled mess, like '*anythingbadeverhappenhere?*'

"No," Mack answers. "Not evil bad, really. But you got to remember, this place was a hospital, and the gold miners around here, they'd come in with some gruesome injuries, and as one might suspect, not all of them made it out of here alive."

"Creepy," Gunnar says, with a delight in his eyes that's both excited and diabolical.

Once Mack resumes his tales of woe and grief that happened here over the past hundred-plus years, Kane taps me on the shoulder, points at Gunnar Creek with his chin, and silently mouths, "Him? Really?"

I whisper that I'll explain later, and then move an antique lamp to the side before Gunnar knocks it off a nightstand.

Did I mention that it's going to be a long night?

***

"Okay, gang, here we go." I motion for Bomber to turn off the lights behind us and then ask Mike to do the same thing upstairs.

Thank God, there wasn't enough room for the entire entourage to spend the night here, and doubly so, not all of them have the guts, desire, or testicular fortitude to hang around for a paranormal investigation. The Good Riddance Gang is staying down the street, at the aforementioned hotel that looks like a fort, leaving Mike and me here alone with Bomber, Gunnar, and Carter Kane, along with One, Two, and Three, who seem like they would literally strip naked and swim in a pool of rotten buzzard doodoo just to stay close to their crush. I can't count how many times I've heard them say things like, "People are *so* not gonna believe this," and, "Like, he's just so hot," and, "They'll all be totally jelly, the wenches."

So, there are eight of us. (Minus Mack and Bonnie, who have retired to their small studio in the back of the building. They're separated by a soundproof wall and insist they won't be able to hear a thing.)

By my advanced mathematical capabilities, eight means six more people than I'm used to conducting investigations with.

At least in the past couple of years since *Graveyard* has been off the air.

Anyway. Adapt and move on.

We're rolling with a couple of different devices tonight that can't be as easily contaminated. Mike and I figured a digital voice recorder would be practically useless with so much noise tromping around here, so that one is gone. The EMF detector sweep showed some minor fluctuations during our initial run, which means that it will be good to have along to indicate energy spikes. We left the thermal imaging camera behind; too many warm bodies, too much potential for contamination, even if we split up.

To sum up, we've brought the EMF detector, digital video cameras, a few flashlights to do the yes/no trick, and the SB-11 Spirit Box, which, if you'll remember, cycles through all the available radio stations, in reverse, at a half-second per station. Words, phrases, and voices, when captured using the SB-11 device are particularly awesome because of the way it operates. Hard to fake something like, "The butler did it in the green room" over individual radio channels being played in reverse.

It becomes obvious that we will need to split up the moment all eight of us try to trundle up the rickety staircase together. It's just not going to work.

In a perfect example of boys being boys, Mike is head over heels in love with Dakota, but he also has a pulse. He—ahem—*volunteers* to stay downstairs with One, Two, and Three, who are quite attractive, honestly, and immediately gets on their good side when he mentions that he used to be on television, too.

How they didn't know is anybody's guess, but if I had to make one, I'd say they were too enthralled with Gunnar Creek to notice.

Mike, green from the night vision setting on my camera, grins and winks at me on the monitoring screen. "Captain Exterminator to the rescue. We'll trade up later if you want."

"Nah, I'm good. Be careful."

The resulting expression on Mike's face suggests that he's found another reason to be proud of me. In the past, I would have broken down walls to spend time with three twenty-year-old groupies.

Now? Not a chance. I know that Melanie is who and what I want.

Nor is there any danger of Mike ruining what he has with Dakota.

Over the years, he'd always said of his marriage, "Just because I'm on a diet doesn't mean I can't look at the menu."

He never bought a thing off it.

That's why all of this is so crazy. In a minor role reversal, Mike is taking advantage of a little bit of harmless confidence, which I'm sure he hasn't felt in years, and I'm passing on the opportunity to hang out with some beautiful groupies.

Holy shit! Maybe we're both possessed.

***

Whatever mind-altering substance Gunnar was on has worn off, and so far, Bomber has refused to give him any more. This is good for us, but bad for the mood in the room. Gunnar sulks around, ignoring my advice, and generally giving off enough negative energy to power the lights in a football stadium.

That's bad.

Forty-five minutes in, Bomber whispers something to his ward, and the botched bleach jobber lifts his head as I watch on my camera's screen. Gunnar allows a smile to creep out. He has pristine teeth, but in the green of night vision, the coating of saliva provides them with a malicious feel, along with a devilish glint in his eyes, the kind where you know something bad is about to happen to someone.

I don't care to find out what Bomber said, and I don't really want to know.

But intuition tells me that I should have One, Two, and Three sleep in a different room.

That's an issue to deal with later.

Right now, I'm curious as to why the activity up here seems so absent, especially when the vibe felt so strong and strange earlier.

Then, Carter Kane offers the understatement of the night: "So, what's happening here, Ford? Calm before the storm?"

"I think they're gone," Gunnar says. "It's not—I mean, right, Ford? Doesn't feel like it did earlier."

Bomber says, "And since when are you the expert?"

Alrighty then! Maybe the kid *has* been paying attention. As much as it pains me to say it, given my distaste for him that's nearly as strong as my hatred of tomato pudding, he's on to something.

For now, I should say.

"He might be right, Bomber. I'm not feeling it—" For a split second, I see it coming, but I can't react fast enough. The antique canoe oar, previously hanging on the far wall, flies off its mounting hooks like a wooden missile and slams into my forehead.

***

Watching the video later, multiple times, reveals that I'm unconscious for three minutes and thirty-nine seconds, completely knocked cold. While Carter Kane, Gunnar Creek, and Bomber Something, react to paintings sailing off the walls, ceramic cats levitating and then smashing through the windows, and the television blinking on and off, blaring static and white noise at full volume as if the other side is trying to communicate by Morse code. Further analysis shows that that wasn't the case—more like a possessed television with Tourette's Syndrome.

(If it didn't hurt so damn much, it would almost be comical how many times I've been knocked out in recent months, though I guess that comes with the territory when you factor in angry spirts, demonic entities, and best friends who are furious with you for ruining their lives. One thing is for certain, multiple hits to the noggin aren't doing me any favors. I should wear a helmet.)

At the three minute and thirty second mark, for a full nine ticks on the clock, five black shapes—Mike believes they're female because they appear to be wearing flowing dresses—march single file out of the Gold Mine Room by the back door.

On camera, Kane can be seen shaking me, whispering, "Ford, you okay? We're seeing full-bodied apparitions over by—"

He screams, as does Gunnar Creek, when the five black masses surge forward with ridiculous speed, the same way the wooden oar flew at me.

Bomber has enough wits about him to grab my arm and drag me out of view as my boot hits the camera. The screen spins three hundred and sixty degrees, and the five figures are gone.

I hate that I'm unconscious for such an amazing firsthand experience, but we captured it on film, and we were able to save it. You can never have enough proof for the naysayers.

Later, when everyone else is asleep on the floor downstairs—because of safety in numbers—Mike and I stay upstairs to review the video footage again. We pass the part where Bomber whispers in Gunnar's ear.

Mike asks, "What'd he say to him right there?"

"Something about pink pills."

"Which do what?"

"According to Bomber, they're antacids."

"What?"

"I was worried they were going to roofie those poor girls. I hinted around to Bomber about an interaction of theirs being on camera, and the dude spent ten minutes bullshitting me, but he finally admitted he lets Gunnar think they're aphrodisiacs."

"That's hilarious. What for?"

"Record company has Bomber on the payroll, trying to keep their gazillion dollar cash cow from riding the dragon's tail to the other side."

"Cool. Good for him. Earns him a few extra bonus points."

"Tons."

We turn back to the video, and there it comes, the oar hurtling at me. In super slow motion, you can see the eyes of my confused companions reacting to a noise they couldn't see in the pitch black.

Something in the video sparks a memory—could be a sound I hadn't noticed yet, could be the look in Bomber's eyes, could be anything triggering it—but I clearly see it in my mind's eye. While I was out, I dreamed of Chelsea, that terrifying walk to her bathroom, and seeing her scream in amplified rage as the mirror cracks, splitting her reflection into jagged pieces.

Only this time, I'm able to see more, like an extended director's cut going beyond where the dream typically ends.

It's fleeting, and blurry, but I may have an idea about what Papa Joe meant by "*Mirror, mirror.*"

You know, before the poor old bastard was dragged down to the fiery pits of Hades.

I don't mention what I might have glimpsed to Mike.

I know, I know. We're supposed to have full disclosure, no secrets, all that nonsense, but this… this is different. It could give him hope, and if what I saw doesn't actually come to pass, or if it was just another one of Boogerface's trickery attempts, then it could cause Mike to come crashing down.

Hope is a dangerous thing to lose.

The Graveyard: Classified Paranormal Series

THE THIRD ACT

16

Filming day.

And I swear on everything that is holy, and everything that I hold dear, I'm more scared now than I've ever been in my entire life.

No shit!

It's strange because I've faced down other demons—maybe not quite a Tier One right-hander with the strength of Boogerface, but demons nonetheless. I've had knives and samurai swords thrown at my head. I've been possessed—literally—a few times, and that feels like you have a million maggots crawling around inside your body, each and every one of them a tiny pocket of hate that exists to fuel your rage against humanity. I've seen full-bodied apparitions. I've listened to EVPs that have called me out by name and insisted that I would die in my sleep. I've had priests, Father Duke included, who have informed me that my soul is a millimeter away from being too far gone to save—that is unless I decide to walk off the field and hang up the cleats.

Which, really, is exactly what I plan to do once this is all over, supposing I walk out of the Hampstead farmhouse alive.

I'm kind of at the point where I don't even have to be Grand Champion Victorious. All I want is to make sure Chelsea is safe and that she'll be able to live a normal life.

I want that for her. I really do.

In some of our recent phone conversations, Carla Hancock has mentioned that studio execs are snooping around, hinting at the possibility of a series of feature film documentaries, maybe even another shot at a show like *Graveyard*.

The Phoenix could rise again. Out of the ashes, out of the flames, and Carla suggests if the numbers are good, Mike and I could have the potential to spread our wings and fly again.

Nah.

I'll pass.

Mike and I, along with Melanie, Dakota, and Ulie, the Bestest Doggie Pal in the Whole Wide World, have had many long discussions about the future, and we all agree that it's time to walk away.

This shit puts a heavy burden on your psyche. It damages your heart, your motivation, and your perception of reality.

I'm not solely talking about the paranormal world—I mean life in the public eye. Having to perform, having to be on point every single time you step into the spotlight, having to rise above and beyond what you've done in the past. This interview, this appearance, this investigation, this feature documentary which is expected to earn two hundred million on its opening weekend, all have to be better than the last thing you delivered to your fanbase.

The moment you falter, or stumble, or put out a product that doesn't best what you've done before, you're toast. People question your talent. They wonder if they've wasted years of their lives cheering you. They grumble and complain. They tell their friends over drinks and across the table at dinner parties that they lost interest. "It's just not the same," is a good one. Or, "It used to be so much better before they sold out."

Constant criticism messes with your confidence. It keeps you debating your relevance in society, keeps you questioning if you still matter to people.

The impression of significance in this life, like hope, is also a dangerous thing to lose.

But you know what? I don't mind that I'm not relevant anymore.

It took a motherfucking Tier One demon picking a fight with me to realize love and relevance don't come from millions of adoring fans, not even close, brother. It comes from that person standing next to you with her fingers intertwined in yours. It comes from that fluffy, furry ball sitting at your feet, looking up with a wagging tail and admiration in his eyes so deep, you wonder if you might be his version of God.

It doesn't come from a packed folder—named "Mom's Meatloaf Recipe"—full of thousands of risqué and XXX-rated photos of the groupies known as spotcamgirls. It comes from the satisfaction of a job well done.

It doesn't come from extra zeroes in your bank account; a number that includes more than one comma. It comes from knowing you did right by someone less fortunate than yourself.

It doesn't come from appearances on late night television or getting invited to the best parties in Hollywood.

It comes from realizing you have the willpower to choose your honor, dignity, and peace over the devil sitting on your shoulder telling you that life isn't worth living without the naughty side.

It comes from reaching up, taking that pesky dickhead by the horns, and tossing him into the toilet.

Flush. See ya on the battlefield, chump.

Cue the Almighty Ford Atticus Ford stepping down off his soapbox.

Like I said, I'm terrified, and I can't beg God, the Force, or the Universe enough to let me know that I'm making the right decision by going up against a demon twenty times (fifty? a hundred?) stronger than anything we've ever faced.

But, I have business to attend to, a child to keep safe and save, and I've never been one to back down from a fight, even when I'm afraid.

Speaking of fear, Carla and Spirit World Productions ceased their viral campaign about my reluctance to film the documentary a week ago with a press release stating that Mike and I had bowed to the public pressure for our return, and filming would begin immediately.

That portion of my original plan worked. Social media is abuzz with delight. Word is spreading. The anticipated opening weekend numbers have taken the express elevator up toward the clouds.

Too bad we might not live to enjoy the aftermath.

***

It's a quarter past two in the afternoon, birds are chirping, the crew is hustling about, and the Hampstead farmhouse doesn't seem so intimidating when you're on the outside looking in.

Under the blazing hot sun—finally, not a cloud in sight!—the two story home looks like nothing more than century-old craftsmanship that's seen better days. I'm not sure I've ever paid attention before, but it appears to be listing a couple of degrees to the left, like the Leaning Tower of Hampstead. The windows are all pockmarked with holes, reminding me of impact craters on the moon's surface. The steps sag. Shutters hang limply. Missing shingles align in a jagged Picasso pattern on the roof.

To somebody driving by, it's simply a house, nothing more. It's a decrepit, dilapidated structure that looks as if it could topple over at the behest of a stiff wind.

To us, it'll be like walking into a meatgrinder, or stepping directly in front of the full barrage from a Gatling Gun. After the attack at the Sumpter Hotel and Spa, which I anticipate to be infinitely worse, I considered borrowing riot gear from a fan I know on Portland's S.W.A.T. team.

We've repeatedly asked Carter Kane and Gunnar Creek if they're positive they want to do this, and they insist they're prepared. My biggest concern is that they don't truly understand what's coming. Mike and I can only explain so much. At some point, you gotta see demonic, paranormal insanity with your own eyes.

Carter's butler—er, I mean *husband*—stands quietly by him. The tall man's arm rests on his beau's shoulders, and they stare at the farmhouse together.

Gunnar Creek sits in the bed of a rented pickup the crew brought to haul equipment. He chews his fingernails and swings his legs back and forth. Nervous, it would seem, distracted only by the arrival of One, Two, and Three. He's really taken to them. Three in particular—I think her name is Andrea—and I can only hope that maybe he'll find love and relevance in her arms instead of the three billion teen girls clawing for a one-second glance. The rest of our crew, sound and camera guys, unpaid interns, producers, directors, and the Devil Herself Carla Hancock, all ignore him. They've been around enough celebrities to understand fluttering eyelids and effusive praise will get them nothing more than a smile and a joint selfie.

Besides, they've got work to do.

Mike and Dakota stand by the catering truck. They're eating buffalo chicken wraps and chatting with Father Duke while the poor man sweats himself thin in his dark suit.

Mike looks calm, but I know he's shitting himself on the inside. He told me earlier he's trying to put on a brave front for Dakota so her worries won't boil up and bubble over.

The Hoppers? They're late. Flat tire on their rental, they said earlier, and I pray they're not getting cold feet, maybe coming to their senses and shipping Chelsea off to a nunnery where Boogerface has no dominion.

Might not be such a bad thing.

As for me?

I'm sitting under a shade tree, sweating profusely in my own trademark black outfit, feeling the gel in my hair combine with sweat and run in rivulets down my forehead, along my temple. I'll have to hit Makeup again before we officially start filming the investigation.

On my left is Ulie. He's exhausted from sprinting around the farm, chasing sparrows and squirrels, barreling after tennis balls thrown by the camera guys who don't have much to do until we're ready.

Ulie rests with his head in my lap. He's asleep and dreaming about something nice, evidenced by the doggie grin, playful growl, and twitching legs.

As always, I am Foodbringer. The Light of His Life. I am He Who Takes Me for a Run Sometimes. I am Chew Toy.

I am Pillow.

To my right, and thank the Good Lord above she's here, is Melanie.

My rock.

It's impossible to put any numerical measurement on the regret I feel for destroying our relationship the first time around.

Man, I was a dumbass, and, man, she's a saint for giving me another chance.

Today she's wearing a light sundress, one I bought her last week because it matches the color of her eyes, and the fabric compliments her tan skin. She has her knees pulled up to her chest. Neon pink toenails peek out from underneath the hem of her dress as she shoos a fly away from her elbow. I ask her if she misses all this—the setup, working with a familiar crew, flirting with me way back when, before we were lovers, before I became a giant asshole.

"Do I miss the long hours, the traveling, the awful pay, and sleeping in shitty hotels with Geraldine the Snore Monster as my roomie? Not a chance," she answers, and then she pats my forearm. "And, to be perfectly honest, you weren't *that* much of an asshole."

"You're joking."

"Well, yeah," she replies, feigning like she's pondering her memories with a finger over her lips, "you were, actually. But that's in the past and, despite the raging objections from my feminist friends, I… I want you to know, before you go in there, I've forgiven you. Look at me, Ford. It's true."

You might be surprised to learn that, since we've been seeing each other again, this is the first time she's uttered those specific words, and it's such a relief to hear that I have to swallow the lump in my throat.

"Which means," Mel adds, "you're going to walk out of there the same way you walk in, understand? If we're going to start over, I need you on this side of the ground."

I lean over, careful not to disturb the slumbering Ulie, and kiss those soft, forgiving lips. "You don't have to tell me twice."

"Whatever happens in there, don't give up. Don't you dare give up. I didn't fight through all the anger and lonely nights, all the weird charges on our credit cards, all the racy pictures you kept on your laptop—"

Embarrassed, I snicker and look away. "You found those?"

"Don't name a folder 'Recipes' if you don't want me to look into it, dummy."

"Fair enough. Sorry." I make a mental note to delete the other folders when I get home. Lately, like the recent addition from Caribou, the waitress in Virginia, I've kept pics from the spotcamgirls more out of habit than any real need to feel desired by groupies. If I do march out of here alive, those pics are gone. Done.

"What I'm trying to say is—there's a future here. You're different now, and I can feel that in my chest, Ford. No more sleeping around. No more betrayal. That's not you anymore."

Betrayal.

The EVP we caught at Dr. Addison Keller's home comes screaming up out of my memory bank. "*She will ... betray you.*"

And now I have something else to worry about.

17

A handful of the braver souls on the crew have been here for a couple of days already, setting up spotcams inside the farmhouse, filming picturesque shots for the B-roll footage, and doing family interviews, along with members of our team walking through the local library and museum researching the Hampstead farm's history. Mike and I watched some of the raw film this morning, and they captured some thoroughly intriguing content, but the real meat of the story will be our investigation.

Normally, and people in the paranormal reality industry will rarely tell you this, we'd spend a couple, maybe three or four nights at a location to gather enough evidence to create an hour-long episode.

But here, now, this evening?

One night only. That's all.

I've explained to Carla Hancock and the other producers and directors that this is a one-time deal. We are *not* coming back again. She'd rolled her eyes at me and asked what happened if we didn't catch anything, adding, "Then what, dumbass?"

To which I had replied, "No danger of that. I know it. We'll be fine."

Maybe *fine* in the fact that we'll get enough footage to last a lifetime, if my assumptions are correct, but fine as a whole, overall, spiritually—I haven't the slightest.

That was an hour ago, and the crew spends the remaining daylight prepping, checking equipment, and testing batteries. The usual.

Finally, the Hoppers arrive.

As they creep up the gravel driveway and find a place to park next to one of the sound vans, I whistle at Mike and motion for him to follow me. He gives Dakota a peck on the cheek, and joins the short walk to their car. The tiny donut wheel is proof positive they had a flat.

Rob greets us as he climbs out of the driver's side, apologizing profusely, and explains that the original spare was flat as well, then they had to wait on roadside assistance and—

"…blah, blah," Rob finishes. "They didn't have a matching tire, so they brought another rinky dink spare… Anyway, sorry again. Hope we didn't hold up filming too much."

"Not at all," I tell him. "We're prepped, ready to go. Just waiting on the sun to go down. Carla wants you guys to meet her over by the barn for some preliminary B-roll interviews."

Rob nods his acceptance, hands on his hips, then proceeds to remove some chairs and bags full of blankets and snacks from the trunk while Leila helps Chelsea out of her booster seat.

And there she is. The little blonde girl. The catalyst that led us all here to this moment.

Chelsea rounds the back of the car, smiling and waving. She's carrying a stuffed bunny under one arm and a can of soda in her free hand. She dashes up to Mike and me, wraps an arm around Mike's leg, then mine, and greets us with a smile, tells us she's missed us.

She doesn't look afraid at all, and that's concerning.

Leila calls her daughter over to help with an overnight bag, and once she's out of hearing range, I arch an eyebrow at Rob and ask, "You guys have explained what's happening tonight, haven't you?"

"Yeah."

"She doesn't look scared."

"Weird, right?"

Mike adds, "Weird ain't the word for it."

Rob says, "On the way over, she kept talking about how she'd had a dream about you and had shown you something, and you were going to protect her. Stuff like that. We kept trying to tell her tonight might be pretty scary, but she insisted she had to come help you, so… here we are, I guess."

My jaw drops at the mention of her revealing something to me in a dream. I try to hide my surprise because Mike knows me well enough to pick up on that, and then I would have to explain to him, etc., you know the drill. Besides, I haven't decided when, or if, I'm going to tell him about what I saw until it's time.

Why? I'm not absolutely positive it's viable.

Rob whispers, "You guys, seriously, you've got this under control, right? Because this is all suddenly sounding like a fucking incredibly bad idea."

Understatement.

He continues, "He—the demon, I mean—I told you what he said, that he'd take her away from us if we didn't do this, but tell me right now, face to face," then puts an index finger on my chest, "do we have any other options? Any at all?"

I gently push his finger away, then cup his hand in both of mine. A gesture of calmness, caring, and I tell him, "No. As much as I hate to admit it, this is the right thing. It's the worst possible option, but maybe if we cut the head off the snake then we might have a shot at giving her some peace."

Rob checks for Leila and Chelsea, sees them on the opposite side of their rental, and then his bottom lip quivers with the speed of a sewing machine needle. He holds back the tears with all the effectiveness of a screen door in a submarine, yanks me in for a bear hug, and says through gritted teeth, "Please take care of her, you son of a bitch."

It's a promise I shouldn't be making, because there's no way for me to guarantee that, but I reply, "At all costs, man. No matter what."

He claps me on the shoulder and backs away, goes to his family. I hear Chelsea ask him, "Have you been crying, Daddy?" He says something was in his eye, then she informs him, "It'll be okay. I know it will."

God, I wish I had her confidence.

It'd make things a helluva lot more interesting if she is actually psychic.

Mike says, "So, now what?"

"Now we wait for sundown. Strap on the armor. Say our goodbyes."

"Anything happens to me, make sure Toni does right by my kids, okay?"

"It won't, but I will. Pinky swear."

Another promise I shouldn't be making.

***

Night comes.

So does the sinking feeling in my stomach, a giant tumor of worrisome anticipation in my gut weighing a thousand pounds.

The plan is for Mike and me to go in first, do some sweeps on our own, and then bring in Carter Kane, followed by Gunnar Creek, then Chelsea accompanied by Father Duke for the grand finale. We'll film from ten p.m. to five a.m., just as the sun brightens the eastern horizon, and walk out of here with our souls uncontaminated.

Yeah.

Right.

Good luck, says the voice of reason in the back of my mind.

We stand on the bottom porch step, staring up at the front door awaiting our entry.

Behind us, two cameramen and a sound guy carrying a boom mic wait on us to get our shit together and get moving, but I can't do it.

"You guys can't come in," I say, turning around. "I'm changing my mind."

Cameraman One—I think his name is Tommy—says, "The hell you talking about, chief? Clock's ticking."

Mike says, "Ford?"

"Too dangerous. I'm serious. I don't care what Carla says, it's only the two of us going in."

"But—"

"Do the three of you want to go home to your wife and kids, or do you want your souls to burn for eternity in a lake of fire and acid? Because that's a real possibility, considering what we're dealing with inside."

Tommy and Cameraman Two make eye contact and shrug while the sound guy retreats, shaking his head. Tommy says, "I'd rather get there on my own time, honestly. Your neck, chief. I'll let Carla know," and then the three of them walk away.

I tell Mike, "Let's get in there before Carla erupts like Krakatoa."

"Serving up our souls in three, two, one." Mike presses the record button on his handheld digital camera. "Rolling."

Is it a good move, sending them away? I'm not positive. Safety in numbers, right?

The thing is, those guys have families—wives and daughters and wagging tails to go home to—and I can't risk having more broken homes and possessed families bearing down on my wounded conscience. Mike and I can take care of ourselves. Carter Kane is close enough to the paranormal that he knows what he's doing. He wants to be involved. He's not here because there's a paycheck coming. We'll protect Chelsea with everything we can muster, and it'll help having Father Duke along. I'm not confident, but I'm okay with that.

Gunnar Creek? I won't necessarily mind if he sprints out of the house with some lower-tier demon hanging onto his hoodie sleeve.

But for the people who don't have to be involved? I'd like to preserve their souls before they have a chance to be eternally damned, thank you very much.

Look at me, all caring about other *people. Who is this new man?*

Behind us, I hear the door of a production van slam, followed by Carla shouting, "Ford! What the—Ford! Get over here, now!"

"Time to go," Mike says.

"Yep."

We take the rickety steps in twos, push through the front door single file, and then close it behind us because we know that Carla won't follow us inside. She has millions upon millions to earn and Hollywood elite to rub elbows with, so she's not going to risk giving all that up to fight with me over filming decisions.

She's like the president of the United States—more of a figurehead—while Mike and I are the Senate and Congress. We're the ones actually running things.

Carla's shouts continue for another thirty seconds, clawing their way through the cracks in the walls and the holes in the broken windows. She finally ends with a resounding, "You're such a pain in the ass. I never liked working with you!"

This sets off such a barrage of giggles between the two of us that it's a wonder we're able to recover five minutes later.

We desperately needed a bit of stress relief.

God, did we ever need that.

Mike wipes the corners of his eyes, turns the camera on himself, and says, "Ladies and gentlemen, that was only the second worst demon we've ever encountered." It'll wind up on the editing room floor, no doubt, but it sets off another round of belly laughter leaving us short of breath and grasping our sides.

On the tail end of a final chuckle, Mike asks, "Jesus, Ford, how in the hell did we end up here, huh?" as he surveys the room. His tone is almost pensive, regretful, like he knows it's the end of something, and he's not all that happy about the journey it took to get here.

I turn my camera on his face. He glows green against the black shadows. This should be good footage for the editing guys to work with later. "If you had a choice, would you do this all over again?"

"Meaning this investigation or our careers?"

"Careers."

He bites the side of his lip, scratches his temple. "We had some bumps, bro, but yeah. Here we are. I'd rather be drinking a rum and Coke on the beach somewhere, but man, what a ride it's been."

I move away from Mike and turn the camera up to the second floor. "Ladies and gentlemen, the ride is about to get bumpier."

For the next ten minutes, Mike films me downstairs while we run some baseline checks, and I explain the history of the home and what we're doing here instead of the original Hopper House back in Ohio.

"As you will see later," I say, "the real danger of this haunting resides upstairs in the master bedroom. You'll remember him from that Very Special Live Halloween Episode. How could anyone forget the demon we've nicknamed Boogerface? The evil, rotten, pus-filled maggot who hurt that beautiful girl. I've spent the last two years trying to redeem myself for what happened, and it's done little good. He haunts her dreams. He won't leave her alone. He insists that she belongs to him, and he's picked a fight with us just to prove it."

I move over to the stairwell, but I remain on the bottom landing. I dive into more detail about the message left on the Hopper House wall. I stare directly into the camera, making eye contact with anyone who will be watching in the future. "The blood of the meek shall feed my horror. That's what we're up against."

Mike then films me shouting up to the second floor.

"Know this, demon! We're here to take back the night. We're here to drive a stake through your putrid heart and end your reign of terror. You will no longer sink your claws into Chelsea Hopper. She belongs to us. She belongs to everything good in the world. She belongs to God. You picked a fight with the wrong motherfucker, asshole! You wanted a war, well, guess what? You fucking got it. Did you hear me, you piece of shit? I want you to bend over, pucker up those rancid lips of yours, and kiss your own ass goodbye!"

After my tirade, I can only hope that Mike was filming my face, because my hands won't stop shaking.

I'm also positive some pee dribbled out.

Mike closes the camera screen and sighs in feigned exasperation. "Did you have to?"

"What?"

"Push buttons. Make it worse."

"You didn't expect us to go up there with a tray of cupcakes, did you?"

"We could've put tiny crucifixes on them if that had been an option."

"What kind? Red velvet?"

"Is there any other?"

The banter, while unrecorded, is good, because it gives me a second to calm down and catch my breath after essentially poking the demonic badger caged upstairs in the master bedroom.

And a second is all it lasts, because the war begins with a violent hiss two inches away from my face.

18

It's not the first time I've been hissed at by a paranormal entity, and after tonight's investigation, I kinda hope it'll be the *last* time something hisses at me, barring the occasional cat or unruly toddler.

The sound was so close, I could literally feel its rotten breath on my face. It's powerful too, because I feel hands shoving me, hard, as it drives me into the wall at my back.

Mike gasps and says, "What the fuck, dude?" and I hear him fumbling with his video camera. "I missed that."

Rubbing my chest, eyes wide, I push myself away from the wall, upright, and say, "Oh, no biggie. Just got attacked by a demon is all."

"Rolling," Mike tells me. His cues will be edited out later.

"Who was that?" I shout. "Did you hiss at me? Did you shove me?"

The answer is not quite so obvious, because my tingling sixth sense tells me that wasn't Boogerface. The energy, a swirling mass of negativity, is here, filling the downstairs living room now, but it's not strong enough. Since Boogerface has been dipping in and out of my mind with these dreams, I dare say I've developed something akin to a bridge across worlds with him, a psychic bond between host and parasite.

This energy belongs to something else, perhaps one of his underlings acting as the vanguard in the attack.

I can't explain it. I just know.

Mike continues to film my reaction, muttering to himself, taking shaky breaths. I'm doing the same, shivering with fear on the inside, though trying to put on a strong image of fearlessness for the camera. The audience has an expectation of the Almighty Ford Atticus Ford, and I want to do my best to give it to them.

That fact occurred to me seconds before the attack. While I'm ready to move on, get away from this life, find peace in a new one and give the same to Chelsea Hopper and her family, the dedicated fans who stuck with us all those years, and got us to where we were—and are today—deserve the hero they've built up in their minds.

I can try.

I can't promise.

"Boogerface," I shout, stepping down from the stairs, "we're here. I'm here. That's Mike; I'm sure you remember him. Did you send one of your pathetic minions to attack me?"

In the presence of a paranormal entity, one will feel the presence of a cold spot—I'm sure you know this by now—because the spirit or otherworldly being is sucking up the available energy to manifest.

This time, instead of being enveloped by a pocket of cold air, I feel a thick wall of moist heat surge around me, as if I've stepped inside a steam room full of naked old men, and then it rockets away.

Mike exhales with a heavy '*ooopb*' and a beat later, he's on his back, handheld camera clattering across the wooden floor. He rolls to his side, trying to push himself up as I dart over and kneel down. My hand goes to his forearm.

"You okay, bro?"

He groans painfully, as if the impact had left a crater in his chest, and winces when he sits up. "Goddamn, that hurt. Landed on a DVR, too. Take this for a sec. Make sure it's okay."

Mike hands me a small digital voice recorder that had been clipped to his belt. I grab it, examine it, and shove it in my shirt pocket, snapping the button closed to hold it in place. Then, I'm almost surprised to find my digital camera is still in my other hand, its weight a foreign entity. I flip open the viewfinder screen and begin recording. "Show the audience. They have to see what we're dealing with here."

Mike lifts his shirt—and this is the point where the spotcamgirls and adoring lady fans will gasp in the theater, because not only are there two handprints on his chest, they're visible right above his six-pack abs. A few years ago, we joked that he was carrying around a keg. Now you could hike through those muscular peaks and valleys. He and Dakota make a good pair.

Even though he's sporting a dark tan from his time spent at his former beachfront property in North Carolina, the handprints flush brighter. I turn off night vision, turn on the regular light, and inform our future audiences that this is what it looks like when you get attacked by a demon.

"See those claw marks?" I ask. "Right up there at the tip of the fingers."

I switch back to night vision, and turn the camera on myself.

"You want to know the worst part? That wasn't the big one. That wasn't even the demon we're after. You'll probably recall from our ten seasons on The Paranormal Channel—we believe each energy source, from both natural and unnatural entities, has its own unique signature, or vibration, similar to a fingerprint. The thing that just attacked us is weaker than its master. Trust me on this." I stand and pull Mike to his feet.

While he feels around on the dark floor for his camera, I continue: "We explained earlier"—meaning an introductory sequence which we'll film later and add at the beginning of the documentary—"that we chose to move our investigation here, to the Hampstead farmhouse, because it's our home turf. Unfortunately, our cameras may not have captured what happened to *me*—I don't know, we'll have to check the footage in a bit—but you saw what happened to Mike. We think, and let me stress *think*, the demon we call Boogerface is a Tier One right-hander, meaning he could literally be one of the superior beings who sits at the right hand of Satan himself. He had chosen the old Hopper House as his—let's call it his demonic headquarters, a place where he could reign over his dominion. That's why we're here, to get away from that. Anyway, sorry, I'm still in shock a bit, and I just needed to point out we moved our investigation here to throw him off his game. But I'm not entirely positive it made a goddamn bit of difference. If the weak ones are that powerful, we can imagine how much stronger Boogerface has become since the night of Chelsea Hopper's attack? We're here to find out so you don't have to."

I go on to explain exactly how we lured Boogerface here, citing our beliefs and evidence that clearly indicates there's some sort of paranormal Post Office able to send universal messages across time and space over on the other side.

Most of my rambling will likely end up in the Bonus Footage section of the DVD, but I'm out of practice filming for an audience. Plus, I'm a wee bit petrified of taunting these sons of bitches at the moment. I blather when I'm nervous.

It's in this moment that I feel the energy shift, like someone changed the radio station. There's a different vibration to it. The hair on my arms stands at attention.

Player Two has entered the game.

Who's this now?

"Found my camera," Mike says in the middle of the living room. "How'd it land all the way over here? Do you think it's still—"

With his back to the kitchen, Mike can't see what comes next.

A black mass, darker than the deepest shadows in the room, darts from left to right across the kitchen doorway, and in the middle of Mike's question, it shoots around the corner, flies straight at Mike's back, halts abruptly, and unleashes one of the most ungodly howls I've ever heard. It's fueled by rage, the fires of hell, hatred, corroded souls, and the poison known as hazelnut coffee.

I have nothing to equate it to, honestly. Imagine a dragon. Now imagine a dragon the size of a United States Navy aircraft carrier. Now imagine it on steroids.

That's how loud and heart-stopping it is.

On the shaky screen of my viewfinder, I watch Mike duck, cover his ears, and sprint toward me like a Vietnam soldier running under the glowing tracers of machine gun fire.

"Oh my God, dude," he screams, and dives at my feet. Then, for the first time ever, Mike scrambles up and hides behind me, using my body as a shield.

I can't take my eyes off the screen. The black mass swirls against the moonlight seeping through the kitchen windows, and then launches itself straight up through the ceiling with another vicious hiss.

It's gone.

I turn the camera on my face once more. "Did you hear that? I've—I've never—I... we need to take a break."

"Thank you." Mike exhales in relief.

The cameras go off. The flashlights come on.

"Should we leave?" he asks. The tone in his voice suggests *please?*

"Not yet, no. It'll be too dangerous to show any more fear than we already have."

"Um, bro, I'm not sure that's possible."

"Fair enough."

"You caught that, right?" Mike asks.

"Every bit of it."

"Let me guess, black mass, red eyes, mouth like a cannon filled with razor sharp teeth?"

"Just the swirly stuff. No eyes, no physical manifestation." I run my hand across my forehead, wiping away a mixture of sweat and hair gel. Then, a terrifying thought occurs to me: "You know what I don't get?"

"Laid?"

"Really? Now?"

"Trying to break the tension."

"Right before you were attacked—I mean those handprints on your chest—my sensitivity meter started going off, and I was absolutely positive it wasn't Boogerface. It wasn't strong enough. It wasn't his energy signature, and then that thing, just now, that screaming. The vibration felt right; it was him, I'm positive, but so much *stronger*."

"Meaning what?"

My fingers and toes go numb. "Somebody's been holding back. What if…"

This is bad, the worst possible realization to have. We're not ready-- not in the slightest.

We would never be ready for something like this.

But we don't have a choice.

"What if *what*, Ford?"

"It can't be," I say, pointing at the ceiling where the demon exited. "What if Boogerface isn't just a Tier One—"

"No," Mike says immediately. He's shaking his head, shifting toward the door, rubbing a hand nervously across his bald scalp.

"It could be. I'm just saying—that was Boogerface turned up to ten. He's been playing possum, I'm sure of it. That message in the Hopper House, bro. The blood of the meek shall feed my horror. *My* horror. Not his horror. Mine. Doesn't that sound like something coming from—"

"Nope. No way. I refuse to believe it, because if it is, Ford, we don't stand a chance. We're worm food."

"It means we *have* to, Mike, now more than ever. For Chelsea."

"We should walk away, man. We *need* to walk away."

"Mike." I move closer to him, hand outstretched.

"I have kids," he says. Emotion chokes his breathing. "I have Dakota now. There's a future out there for me. You have one, too."

"We can't run."

"Oh, yes we can. Watch me." Mike moves for the front door, and I grab him by the arm. He pulls, and I squeeze tighter.

"We have to do it for her, for Chelsea. It's my fault we got her into this situation. I should have said no. I should have stood up to Carla, but I didn't, and I'll go to my grave with that, which might actually happen tonight, and the only way to find out is to do the job." Mike tries to pull away again. "I need your help. She does. We all do if the big boy upstairs is who I think it is."

"Lucifer," Mike whispers. "all this time?"

A new, confirming fact surges to the forefront of my mind. "When Lauren Coeburn became one of the black-eyed things, when she gave me the message, she kept calling someone

'Master,' and I assumed she meant Boogerface and that he's a lower demon just because—seriously, who would expect the top dog to be up here doing some dirty work?"

"*That's* who? You're literally telling me that *Satan* is here?"

"Yeah, I am. The language she was speaking, the Hopper House message Dr. Keller deciphered, and his book, holy shit, his book! The whole thing was about the war of language between heaven and hell. It was right on the cover! God and Satan both. Son of a—"

Footsteps thump overhead.

"*Sshhh.*"

"I got it," Mike whispers, pressing buttons on his handheld camera. "Rolling again."

Thump, thump, thump one direction, and back again. This continues for three full minutes, back and forth, back and forth, as if it's impatiently waiting.

When I'm sure it's finished, I turn on my camera and look into the lens. "We're back," I say, swallowing the growing ball of fear in my throat. "And we've just figured out something that we should have known all along. The demon we've been calling Boogerface—we *thought* he was a Tier One right-hander, but it's more powerful than that. Infinitely more powerful, and we may be dealing with the one who was kicked out of Heaven. Yes, that one. We explained the history of our interactions, and the thing is, after the power in that scream you just heard, we now believe he's been toying with us all along. We never saw it coming. It didn't matter if we fought the war here, or at the Hopper House, or in the middle of Wrigley Field. We've been screwed since Chelsea fell out of that attic so long ago. But we're not going to walk, are we, Mike?"

His long, *long* pause will make for good onscreen drama—not that I'm concerned with that right now—and eventually, he flattens his lips and gives an affirmative nod.

"So, then," I say, panning the camera slowly around the room, taking in every inch of rotten wood, furniture ensconced in white drop cloths, and the grandfather clock stuck on permanent midnight. "We have a little girl to save, and now that we know what we know, it's more important than ever. He doesn't get to have her. He thinks he already owns her, but we have news for that nasty bastard; we're prepared to die to save her."

Behind me, a shocked Mike mumbles, "Not really, no."

The audience will love that.

I film the stairs, where, again, we'll be going up into an annex of Hell.

"Nobody ever said I was original, so I'll borrow a line from Shakespeare: 'Once more into the breach, dear friends.' Now, folks, it's time to introduce you to them, our guest investigators. Carter Kane. Gunnar Creek, and"—I have to pause here so I won't start crying—"little Chelsea Hopper, our secret weapon."

Up on the second floor landing, we hear disembodied laughter.

A swirling mass manifests at the top of the stairs. Two red eyes open and then narrow into slits.

A voice growls, *"Bring her to me,"* and the eyes close, followed by the clomp of retreating footsteps and the thundering boom of my pounding heart.

My only consolation is that Chelsea showed me something in that dream.

It might help. It might not.

And then those same four words come 'round again: *"She will ... betray you."*

Desmond Doane

The Graveyard: Classified Paranormal Series

19

Mike and I cinch up our gusto, find a modicum of professionalism among our frayed nerves, and investigate for another hour, downstairs only. I get the sense that the main action is only going to happen on the second floor; he's waiting for us up there, using whatever portal that master bedroom might be to refuel himself.

No pun intended: it's dead in here.

Well, I shouldn't say dead, not completely, it's just that things are *tame* compared to the earlier onslaught of paranormal activity.

We use every piece of equipment we brought and capture some evidence that would be the highlight of the episode on *Ghost Bros*.

We capture a couple of Class-A EVPs from spirits we assume to be Hampstead ancestors. To us, they sound like residual voices, because no intelligent spirit in its right mind would hang out in this house while The Big Guy Downstairs has a summer home up on the second floor.

We film a small blob of light in the corner. It's shaped like a cigar, hovers for five seconds, and then darts out the window. My guess is that it was something on the other side curious enough to come check out the supernova-like ball of negative energy that has to be permeating this joint. It snuck in, the record player scratched its warning, and then it wisely left.

This is all good footage that we can use to fill the ninety-minute running time the studio has planned, but it's not the real fight the audience will be anticipating. I hate to show you how the sausage is made, but what will probably happen is, the technician team will perform some fancy-schmancy editing on the back end, they'll put this evidence capture up at the beginning of the documentary, and then build up to the big battle from there.

It's only when Mike notices another set of red eyes spying on us halfway up the stairs that we decide it's time to go take an actual break. You know, maybe grab some caffeine pills, a snack, and then let Father Duke dunk us in a vat of holy water.

We're walking across the front yard when Mike says, "I've changed my mind, Ford."

"About what?"

"Chelsea." He stops me before we reach the gathering crowd who will want to ask us how things are going. "We can't. I can't. We're back to the Halloween episode. I... It's not right. Not with kids of my own. If you were a parent, you'd do the same. I wish you could understand. We can't send her in there. Not again. You gotta do something. Talk to Carla. Call the suits."

"I—Mike, c'mon." My hands go to my hips. I sigh. "Maybe."

"I *know* you better than that. You wouldn't send Ulie in there; imagine your child. There's no way on God's green earth you would send your own kid in there. Maybe if we were dealing with nothing more than a demon, even if it was a Tier One fucker, but the Devil? Satan? Lucifer? Shitsucker Numero Uno? No way, man. The Hoppers only agreed to do this because they were afraid."

"He said he'd kill her if they didn't."

"And that's probably true, but not if we get to him first. We're her last, maybe her *only*, hope. Honest to God, I don't know if the Church can do anything about him because they've been trying for a few thousand years. If we can find some sort of edge, maybe we stand a chance, you know? Something. *Anything*. Kane's probably done more research on Evil—with a capital E—than anyone we've ever met. Maybe he knows something? Maybe we don't beat the Devil, but what if Kane can help us break the chains on her?"

Mike has a point; we could use an advantage now more than ever, and I never wanted to send Chelsea inside in the first place.

We do have one detail he doesn't know about: I have a secret shown to me by a seven-year-old angel.

However, it's not that easy. "Dude, we have contracts. Legal obligations. Did you even read the fine print before you signed it?"

"Yeah, but—"

"Carla's got us by the short and curlies. We do anything to screw with the legal shit, we're toast. There'll be lawyers circling overhead until the end of time."

"Ford." Mike steps closer to me, holds a hand up and waves off an approaching intern carrying two bottles of water. "Please. I begged you not to do it the last time. I'm begging you again. Screw the contracts. Screw the lawyers. Fuck Carla Hancock. Let's figure out how to save Chelsea's life without handing her back to Satan like she's some stuffed animal that he dropped."

"But—"

"No buts."

A dog barks in the distance. A car roars by. Crickets chirp. And I think. And think.

Okay. He's right. Mike's always been right.

Honor supersedes the resulting circumstances.

If I had only said no the first time, maybe none of this would have happened. Could be the Hoppers finally had enough and moved away on their own, never to hear from Boogerface again. Or, could be he would have tagged along no matter where she went.

Woulda, coulda, shoulda.

We're here at this spot, this specific moment, for a reason. Every act, decision, and flicker of thought we have made in the past has led us right here to this farmhouse.

To save Chelsea Hopper.

But we don't have to use her as a weapon to do it.

"You're right," I tell him. "She's out."

His relief is visible, like a doctor just told him the cancer tests came back negative. "Good. Thank you. Thank God."

"Just because I agree doesn't mean we can make it happen, but let me go talk to Carla. I have an idea."

We walk toward the crowd. I quickly explain my plan to Mike, and he agrees that, in theory, it should work, though we'll be misleading our viewing audience for the first time ever if Carla allows us to go through with it.

I also decide it's finally time to tell him what I saw in my dream.

Wouldn't you know, I don't get a chance because the throng of technicians, sound guys, camera operators, producers, directors, interns, and Carla Hancock begin to gather around.

Then the unexpected happens.

Behind us, the Hampstead farmhouse shakes violently and a guttural roar rises and fades.

Mike and I whip around, just in time, and see the walls of the Hampstead farmhouse expand and contract once, as if the house itself is breathing.

The belly of the beast, once again.

It goes quiet, and a collective gasp of relief swishes around the group.

Somewhere among all the warm bodies, I hear Gunnar Creek's voice. "Whoa! Cool!"

The poor bastard has no idea what he's getting into.

Nice. If any of us survives this, and the documentary makes it to theaters, Gunnar's underestimation of this satanic haunting will make for some fantastic filming.

We spend the next fifteen minutes talking with the crew. We explain what we saw, what we captured on film and audio, and then sit in the back of a video monitoring van with our mouths shut while Carla hands out a tongue-lashing for our earlier behavior, and for the fact that we walked out of the house an hour ahead of schedule.

"I hope to Christ you got enough footage, knuckledraggers. You know how much we have to cut and pare just to make a forty-two minute primetime show. We're looking at ninety here, maybe even a hundred or more."

"*Relax*, Carla, we have the interviews, all the B-roll content. We're—"

"Shut up. Listen to me."

Off she goes again, so angry she's almost speaking in tongues, speaking in run-on sentences. When she's finished— indicated by the slower breathing, wiping a drop of spittle from her chin, and the general lack of vitriolic words flying out of her mouth—Mike looks over at me and says, "Good luck." He pats my thigh, stands, and offers Carla nothing more than a thumbs-up before climbing out of the van and slamming the door in his wake.

Carla crosses her arms. Her face is tinted red from the glow of various buttons and lights. Put a couple of horns on her, give her a spiked tail, and, well, you know. She says, "Good luck with *what?*" She spits out *'what'* as if it tastes awful.

"Sit, please," I say, pointing at Mike's empty chair. "I need to talk to you."

"About?"

"It's important, and you need to be sitting to hear it."

"Why?" She stands her ground.

"Mostly so you can't kick me in the neck when I tell you this."

Carla scrunches up her nose, pinching her lips together. She huffs through expanded nostrils, and surprisingly, takes a seat beside me. Exasperated, she hides her face behind her hands and a muffled "What?" escapes between her fingers.

"We can't take Chelsea in there. Not after—"

Carla slaps her legs. "I fucking knew it. You goddamn—"

"*Not after* what we just learned," I say, raising my voice to stop hers. "I don't care what the suits say. Or you. Or the lawyers. Or whatever language is in the contracts. We'll keep filming—stop, let me finish—we'll keep filming. We'll get you your movie, I promise, but if you try to force us to take Chelsea inside that house, we'll walk. I swear to God in heaven, Hancock, we'll take off through that field out there, and you won't see us again until the deposition room for whatever bullshit you and Spirit World tries to hit us with. Dead serious. Hundreds of millions, gone."

"You won't stand a chance."

"Maybe not, but I can't imagine any judge on the planet will rule against us for preventing reckless child endangerment."

"Contracts are binding. Even if he sees it that way, you're doomed. You and Mike, you're done. Careers gone. You'll never work in television again."

"Not that I care, and I'm pretty certain Mike doesn't either."

Carla almost seems sad. Maybe she knows I'm right about the moral issues. Maybe she knows she has lost all power when we cease to care about the legal repercussions, cease giving a shit about the money.

"Why, Ford? Explain it."

"Because inside that house, that's *Satan*. It's not some rinky-dink demon, even if it might have been a Tier One right-hander. The devil is inside those walls, and that's the truth."

Carla laughs and rolls her eyes. "You and your stupid theatrics. We're not on camera."

"It's real."

"Whatever. Say I believe you, even if it's for a second. Why would—I can't believe I'm feeding into your delusions—why would Satan stoop low enough to fight with an insignificant poop stain like yourself?"

"Because I tried to take his plaything away. And that's not cool."

"Not cool? That's how you describe it?"

"I don't have time to get into all of the reasoning or explanations, Hancock. Here's my proposal: Chelsea is out, but we'll find a way to get her into the documentary. This is what I originally wanted to do after we talked down in L.A. We'll scout some locations and film her in another crumbling, ancient farmhouse. We cut it just right, shoot all the right angles, have your editing wizards wave their magic wands, and nobody in the audience will ever know the difference. You agree to that, Mike and I will walk back in there with Carter Kane and Gunnar Creek, and we'll get you the most impressive paranormal footage you've ever seen because the motherfucking *Devil* is in there, Hancock. Maybe we survive, maybe we don't."

"And what if you don't?"

"How many millions of extra people are going to sprint to the theaters to watch The Almighty die on camera?"

There's the catalyst.

The dollar signs begin blinking in her eyes.

She smiles, deviously. "It's that serious?"

I dip my chin, acknowledging that indeed it is.

Carla sits back in the metal chair, laces her fingers behind her head and stares at the roof of the van. While she ponders the new development, thoughts race through my mind. What happens if we actually get what we want?

It'll be the end of our careers. Mike will lose his last penny in the divorce settlement. He won't have anything extra to give his children. (Privately, Dakota has told me what she's worth these days; through some intelligent investing and being smart with her money, she's loaded, and generations to come will be, too. If she and Mike stay together, he'll be fine, and so will his offspring.)

Me, I don't need the money.

Matter of fact, screw the dollar signs.

Humanity. Heart.

Soul preservation.

That's what it's about.

A week from now, I'll wake up with my conscience clear.

Earning that for *myself*. That's the secret I've been missing. I've been looking to redeem my image in the public eye for the past two years.

Wrong angle, my friend. What I've really needed all this time is the realization that *I* need to forgive *myself*.

So if Carla agrees to this, what do we have to lose?

Not much.

Other than our lives.

And that seems worth a lot more now than it has in the past, especially since the night of the Very Special Live Halloween Episode.

"I like it," Carla agrees, almost too easily. "But I have some stipulations."

I reply, "I wouldn't expect any less," too concerned about these "stipulations" to be relieved just yet.

20

I find Mike over by the catering van, where else, chatting with Dakota and the Hoppers. At first, when I walk up, I'm worried he's been making promises I hadn't been granted yet, but instead, I hear him talking to Rob and Leila about his children and how precocious they were at Chelsea's age. Who, by the way, seems to be smitten by Dakota.

The older, blonde grownup sits criss-cross-applesauce on the ground beside the younger blonde child, and I feel like I might be getting a peek into Mike's new future. They're giggling and playing some sophisticated version of patty cake that I would never have the coordination to master.

Melanie also sits beside Dakota as she wrestles with Ulie's leash, trying to keep him away from the buffet table. She glances up at me and smiles.

Everybody seems content on the outside, yet internally, it's another story. I can tell by the way Mike holds his posture. He's antsy. Worried. Leila clasps her hands at the center of her waist, fingers fidgeting as she rocks from foot to foot. Rob pretends to listen, but his smile is vacant, and his eyes focus past Mike's shoulder; he's looking at something in his mind.

"Everything okay over here?" I ask, my tone nonchalant, making conversation as if we're not all standing three hundred yards away from Satan's current hostel.

The adults focus on me.

Chelsea shouts, "I win," once Dakota stops paying attention. She hops up to her feet and plucks a handful of blueberries off the seemingly endless catering spread.

Mike says, "How'd it go?"

Asking, but not revealing his intentions, and not letting the Hoppers know there might be some hope.

"She agreed," I tell him.

Mike fist-pumps the air. "Holy shhh—"

"Little ears," Dakota warns quickly.

"Right. Sorry. So we're good then?"

I tell him yes, though he can sense it's not that easy.

"What?"

Rob asks, "She who? Agreed to what?"

Leila adds, "Are you talking about Chelsea?"

"What's the catch?" asks Mike.

"We lose a few percentage points on the back end profits."

"That's it? Fine by me," Mike says with an accepting shrug.

"And by a few, uh, I mean *all* of them."

That's what I had to agree to in order for Carla to say yes to leaving Chelsea out of the lineup. It's the difference in a couple million apiece for our upfront appearance fee and possibly tens of millions if the documentary takes in the gargantuan profits everyone expects.

Surprisingly, Mike considers this for all of two seconds—I expected more—before he says, "Done."

"Your kids and their future? You're cool with that?"

Mike's hands go to his hips. He looks down at the ground, then back up to me. "They'll be fine. Toni will get everything I have already. Apparently the new boyfriend comes from old money down in Brazil—or maybe it's Florida. Either way, they should be set, and they're not leaving much room for Dear Old Dad in their lives anyway. Sucks giant donkey balls, but money ain't everything."

Leila and Rob approach us. She says, "What're you guys talking about?"

Rob asks, "What happened?"

I take Leila's hands in mine and look into those terrified, troubled eyes. "Chelsea's out. I pulled a miracle out of my backside and just renegotiated our contracts on the spot. Carla should be on the phone, waking up the lawyers as we speak."

The Hoppers squint at me, so confused.

They listen while I explain our plan.

And then they tell me I'm insane.

"I'm sorry, what?"

Rob inches up to me, and I can't tell if it's an act of aggression or if he's trying to keep Chelsea from overhearing. She's over by Dakota and Melanie, sharing a handful of chocolate covered strawberries, so I'm sure there's no chance of that happening. He says, "We told you what could happen, Ford. He—that demon thing in there—he said he would take her away from us if she wasn't involved. That's why we're *here*, dumbass, and you're trying to get her *out* of it? Excuse my ignorance, but what the actual fuck, man? Do you *want* our daughter to die?"

Leila tries to take him by the arm, and he jerks free.

"You already tried once," he spits. "You can't possibly think we're going to let you get away with it again." Rob grabs the front of my t-shirt and twists it, yanking me close enough to smell his coffee breath between gritted teeth. "I will bury you, asshole, and you can go to hell with that bastard."

"Please, Rob, just calm d—"

"Don't tell me to calm down," he screams.

Heads are turning our way. Curious. Watching to see what I've done now.

Thankfully, Mike steps in and attempts to ease him down, back him off me with gentle words and insistence that "This isn't helping." And when that doesn't work, he hooks a forearm in Rob's underarm, pulls him around and away, using the bigger man's weight as leverage.

"Stop," Mike orders. "Listen to us. We know what we're doing. We know what's in there now, and we know how to beat it."

Eh, I'm not entirely sure that last part is true, but at least Rob surrenders with his palms in the air.

"Daddy?" Chelsea says. "Everything okay?"

"Not too many strawberries, sweetheart." Rob lifts his chin at Dakota and Melanie. "Maybe you can take a walk around with Dakota and Melanie? Looks like Ulie needs to find a bathroom."

He's not really *asking*. Dakota recognizes this right away. She has good parental instincts, this one. She tugs on Chelsea's ponytail and asks her if she'd like to see if one of the cameramen can show her how he's able to hold that big device up on his shoulder.

"After Ulie goes potty," Melanie reminds her, playing along.

Chelsea agrees, smiling over her shoulder at us as Dakota leads her off into the night, Melanie and my loyal pup in tow.

"Talk," Rob says.

And yeah, he's not *asking* me either.

"It's all about Chelsea's dream, or, our dream, I should say," pointing at her distant figure, then Mike, then myself. "I had the same dream the other night, and I saw something, or maybe she showed it to me, I have no way of knowing. If it's what I think it is, then we have a chance of giving her a normal life. Maybe."

"So you're not sure," Rob says. He puts his arm around Leila's shoulders, pulling her closer. Two distraught parents, wary of putting their faith in the guys—or guy, I should say—who made a lot of empty promises the last time he held their daughter's fate in his hands.

"No more than I was before. There's never a guarantee. Never was, never will be, but I can tell you this—wait, Mike? Did you already explain what we learned inside?"

"Nah, I was waiting for you. You're the general in all this. I'm just Private Goober, reporting for duty."

The subtle attempt to lighten the mood doesn't work. The Hoppers don't take their eyes off me.

"Inside that house," I say, "is something far bigger and stronger, more evil and vile than I expected. Deception is the Devil's greatest weapon. I don't even know how we ended up here, in this situation, or what he's doing out of Hell—"

"He who?" Rob says. "What in God's name are you talking about?"

"Not God's name," I reply, shaking my head. "We could use him right now if he's out there listening, but this, over there in that farmhouse? It sounds too unbelievable to be true, but that's *Satan*. Like, the real one. The eight-hundred-pound gorilla downstairs."

Leila gasps. "What? You're joking."

"I wish I was. Like I said, I have no earthly clue how we ended up at the point where we're actually going to go to war with *the* granddaddy of them all."

Rob points at my chest. "But you said it was just a demon. Maybe a powerful one, but not—not this... How—what—why? I don't even have the words to tell you how insane this sounds."

I anticipated this reaction. The Hoppers have enough experience with the paranormal, having been on the receiving end of it for so long, to be aware of the dangers and consequences. Yet, until you've been on our side, the side of *Graveyard: Classified*, having seen and done nearly everything possible in the paranormal field, the abstract, the ridiculous, is difficult to accept until you've seen it yourself. To counter his reaction, I hook a thumb toward the Hampstead farmhouse and tell him I would be happy to take him inside and prove it.

Rob eases up on the bravado, snorts and looks away. "No, I'm good, it's just—why Chelsea? Why us? Why you? It doesn't make any sense at all."

Mike says, "It doesn't have to. He—You Know Who—doesn't play by those rules. He doesn't play by any rules at all, Rob. The only thing that we can think of is that your original home in Ohio may have been, like, the Highway to Hell. Like that old AC/DC song, remember? You were right in the middle of the road, he was on his way to some demonic beach, and got sidetracked by a pretty little girl. You know how celebrities go out in public with sunglasses, and hoodies, hats pulled way down over their eyes? Could be he was disguising himself this whole time. Then, we come along and mess up his game, try to take his plaything away. It doesn't necessarily work because me and Ford screwed it up so much, but he's still pissed. Holds a grudge. Finds a couple of new toys to fuck with just for having the balls to try and take him on the first time, even if we didn't understand that we were stepping into a mountain of shit a mile high.

"So, yeah. Here we are. Ford and I have an out. We think. If it works, perfect. We're all good, end of story. If it doesn't, we're dead. Or not dead but we walk out of that dilapidated shack we call a farmhouse carrying a load of Lucifer in our souls, and the next thing you know, we're batteries for the undead, and they're siphoning energy off us, and probably you, and probably Chelsea from now until they put us in an urn or six feet under. So what I want you to do is this: back the hell off, trust that we know what we're doing, trust that we know what we heard, saw, and believe, and show some freakin' respect for a couple of guys who are risking their lives to save your daughter. Did you even hear what Ford said earlier? We are walking away from tens of millions of dollars that would set up our families for the rest of their lives, just so we can try to save yours. Okay? Got it? Now, please, say thank you so we can get this over with."

Rob hesitates for two breaths, looks to Leila for confirmation, and agrees. Leila uses her knuckle to dab away a tear. She leaves her husband's side, hugs Mike, then me.

"Thank you," she whispers. "We trust you."

"We'll do whatever it takes," I remind her.

A minute later, after more reassurances and promises we may not be able to keep, the Hoppers leave in search of their daughter.

Mike and I stand alone. He shoos a moth away from a bowl of potato salad.

I tell him, "Looks like you just got a promotion, Private Goober. Where'd that giant set of balls come from?"

"They were never going to listen to you, not after last time. You could've told them the farmhouse was infested with nothing more than a cute, cuddly pile of demonic bunnies, and they would've fought you every inch of the way. In steps the voice of reason."

"Right."

Mike picks a pastry from the catering table, takes a giant bite, and says around the mouthful, "I'll tell you the same thing I told him. Please, say thank you so we can get this over with."

"Thanks, Mike. I don't know what I'd ever do without you."

"Sarcasm's not a good look on you, bro."

"Remind me to rethink your promotion."

"Sir, yes, sir."

As we walk toward the equipment truck, where the interns and crew have been steadily working to ensure our devices have fresh batteries and remain operational, I look down at the half-eaten pastry in Mike's hand. "You sure you want that thing sitting in your gut? It's gonna hurt like hell coming back up once Satan gets inside you."

"I'd rather it be this than pea soup."

We laugh quietly, and it's a refreshing moment of calm before the absolute funhouse of terror that we're about to walk into.

First things first, we remember the matter of capturing some footage with Carter Kane and Gunnar Creek.

Oh, boy. Given what we know about our "visitor" inside the farmhouse, won't that be fun?

21

I wish I could say it was eventful.

I had my worries, my fears, and many hesitations about taking one of the world's most popular authors and inarguably the world's most popular pop star into a house that was currently Hell Central.

We caught some small bits of evidence—a couple of balls of light flickering in the downstairs corners; an oil lamp from the 1800s moved two inches right in front of Gunnar Creek; the grandfather clock, which apparently hasn't worked since 1903 according to Hamster's mama, began to chime—three bing-bongs, and that was it. Carter Kane was subdued and knowledgeable, providing some excellent commentary about the world of the demonic and your plain-old, garden variety paranormal activities. He lost his temper once, shouting obscenities the same way he did back at his Hamptons mansion, when something touched the back of his neck.

Gunnar Creek, as much as I can't stand the annoying whippersnapper, put on one helluva show for his fans. There were times where I couldn't tell the difference between him being legitimately spooked and him being the pretty boy entertainer for his billions of teenage admirers. He yelped when he was supposed to, flicked that bad dye job hair to the side more times than I cared to count, and seemed genuinely respectable to the spirits we were interacting with on the first floor.

After reviewing some of the footage we captured with our celebrity guests, Mike and I noted they did exactly what they were supposed to do: put on the appropriate persona for the markets they're trying to capture. All in all, it might have been more exciting and outrageous if we took them upstairs. But even before we entered the farmhouse, they had both agreed—off camera—that they still wanted to continue with the investigation, but they sure as shit didn't want to walk out of there with any demonic stowaways hiding in some dark corner of their souls.

So, now, here we are. Three o'clock in the morning. The "witching hour" when—if you'll pardon the cliché—all hell is supposed to break loose with all things supernatural.

Mike and I stand shoulder to shoulder, facing the front door of the Hampstead farmhouse while the director films some content for the B-roll. We wield pieces of paranormal investigation equipment in our hands like they're boxing gloves; the cameras at our back film this pose to enhance the image of our bravery. It will show that we're heading into the final battle of this war, and we're going to kick some serious demonic ass. For roughly five seconds, I have a wave of goosebumps racing across my arms, across my shoulders, and down into my back because I can imagine the musical overlay the sound team will add during their time in the studio. It'll be something strong, badass, with a seriously angry guitar riff that'll make us seem like mighty warriors, undefeated, rescuers of humanity, saviors to little girls, and heroes to puppies from the pound.

And yet, I feel like anything but.

I think, think, *think* we might have an edge. My confidence dissipates with every passing second because I keep going back to it, again and again…

What if that wasn't Chelsea revealing something in her dream?

Boogerface, or, you know, motherflippin' *Satan*, has been inside her head for so long already he's practically purchased real estate in there. Some shitty bungalow to call his own. He's briefly dipped inside Mike's head and mine, bragging and laughing, not doing any real damage, only proving to us that he can.

What if he showed me something that will end humanity as we know it?

It had to be Chelsea. She was so confident.

This reminder does not instill my own confidence.

We have to take the chance and use it as a weapon.

It's the only shot we have.

Father Duke, the portly priest who was supposed to come with us to help protect Chelsea, has chosen to stay uninvolved for two reasons: First, now that Chelsea doesn't have to face her tormentor, he's not necessarily needed. Second, he had signed a separate contract from ours, one that gave him an out, the right to rescind his involvement in the project, if "extenuating circumstances that would mar his ability to perform his role for the Catholic Church" arose.

Once Father Duke learned the identity of our opponent, he thanked us for the opportunity to be a part of something historic, blessed us, dabbled some holy water on our foreheads, told Carla Hancock to go screw herself in the PG-rated version, and hauled buns down the driveway so fast he left a swirling cloud of dust behind.

But not before he told us, "Boys, good luck, I wish you the best, and I hope to see you on the other side—and I think you know which one I mean," as he pointed skyward.

Then, whoosh. Dust. Gone.

So much for being the Great Protector of all the sheep in His Holy Flock, but I get it. If I didn't have to be here, I wouldn't risk it either.

Behind us, the director shouts, "Okay, cut! We got it, people."

I feel a chilly palm on my forearm. It's Carla.

"What?"

She says with a smile, "You two go take thirty. They want to set up for a couple of new shots, and I told them that'd be fine."

I sigh and let my shoulders droop. My nerves can't take another delay, and here we are, being shuffled around like dolls at a tea party while the kids playing the game control all the shots. "Whatever."

"It won't take long," Carla promises. "Besides, you might as well go give your girlfriends one last kiss goodbye."

"Thanks," I say, sarcasm so thick you'd have to heat it up in the microwave before you could spread it.

Carla cocks her head to the side, feigning sincerity. "Or, maybe you could just pucker up and kiss your ass goodbye?"

"Thirty minutes, Hancock. Won't be long before the sun starts peeking over those hills." I'm saying this to her back. She's already stomping across the yard in her high stilettos; I imagine the sharp heels puncturing the hearts of unsuspecting mice and moles who happen to get in her way.

Mike rolls his eyes. "How did we ever put up with her for so long?"

I rub my thumb and forefinger together. "You know why."

"If I'd known…" He *tsks* at himself, tilts his head toward Dakota and Melanie, and says, "She's probably right though. Let's go."

My heart pounds in my chest. It's nervous energy. I can't calm down. Mike and Dakota hold hands and sit next to each other on the bed of a crew member's pickup while Ulie remains under the care of Chelsea, adoring every second of the girl's attention, Melanie and I embrace in the Longest Hug Ever, I'm talking like Guinness Book of World Records hugging, and then we walk over to one of the equipment vans and sit down, leaning up against a dusty rear tire. Morning dew has already begun its slow march across the grass, toward daylight, and I can feel the dampness through my jeans.

We sit in silence, Melanie's head leaning against my shoulder, my hand in hers, feeling the warmth of her palm, the life in her body, the sanctity of her soul.

This calms me. My heartrate slows. It no longer feels like the veins will burst in my neck.

It's good. She's good. I'm good.

This is it, right here. I've made it this far.

I can see the light of self-forgiveness shining at the end of the tunnel, and for once, holy shit, it's not the headlight of an oncoming locomotive instead.

I never want this moment to end.

And yet it does.

Ulie trots up to us, alone, leash dragging in the grass alongside him.

Melanie glances at me. "Ulie? Where's Chelsea?"

Then, a distant question: "Hey, Ford? You out there, buddy?"

I emerge from my peaceful trance, almost sleepily, and recognize the voice of Darren Ellis, one of the cameramen who worked with us on *Graveyard*. Believe it or not, it's not that simple to find camera operators willing to walk into complete darkness, stand unprotected with their backs to an approaching supernatural entity, and then film our reactions. Since the cameramen aren't going into the house with us, they're stuck doing busywork, like monitoring the video and sound feeds.

"Yeah," I reply. "Right around the corner, actually."

"You might want to come see this." His tone suggests more than a hint of *uh-oh*.

"Coming."

Melanie pulls away so I can stand and then follows me, brushing the grass off the back of my jeans as she bends to take Ulie's leash.

I round the corner, and Darren motions me up into the van with quick, waving hands, followed by an index finger over his lips. His eyes are wide as he sneaks a look outside, beyond the van's rear doors, and then whispers for Melanie to hurry and get in if she's coming. She climbs in. Ulie follows and flops on the floor.

"What's going on?" I ask as Darren pivots in his chair.

"I need to show you something."

In front of us is a bank of monitor screens, each displaying a certain area of the Hampstead farmhouse interior—cameras placed inside by ignorant, or desperate interns—some screens are in black and white, some display the green hue of night vision. Six total. Dust flies across the image like it's snowing inside the house.

"Where..." he mumbles, his voice trailing off. "Shit."

"Darren?"

"Did you authorize her to go in?"

"Who?" I feel that worrisome shot of adrenaline prickle my skin.

"Carla came in and asked me to cut the feed to the spotcams—"

"Why?"

Uh-oh.

"She said the whiny bastard she brought in to direct this thing felt like they weren't filming the best spots, and he demanded to do some rearranging. I reminded her we didn't need to fully cut the feed to all of them while they were doing that, and—"

Fear of the unknown grips me, yet I have a sinking feeling about where this is heading. "Oh, God. What'd she do? What's happening?"

"Here, just quickly—she said she would radio back and tell me when it was cool to fire all the feeds up. I got curious and turned a couple back on to see what in the shit she was doing, then—"

"Oh no. Oh my God," I say, moving closer to the bank of monitors. On the far left screen, showing the live feed from the kitchen camera filming the stairs, is Chelsea Hopper moving into the picture. She's holding Carla's hand, looking up at her expectantly, tiny eyes glinting against the black and white. I can't hear anything, but Carla is clearly talking. She bends down, gives Chelsea a hug, and walks away, leaving the child behind. Ambient light from the moon floods the living room as the front door opens off camera, and then Chelsea is encased in pitch black once again.

She slowly begins climbing the stairs, pauses at the third step and looks around as she chews on a fingernail. A moment of indecision, and then she takes another step.

I feel like I'm going to throw up.

I can't move.

This is it. This is what he was talking about.

She will ... betray you.

I whisper, "Carla. She promised."

It was a promise that Carla had no intention of keeping.

Melanie gasps and snatches my arm, fingernails digging into my skin, but I feel no pain. I'm petrified. Terrified.

A walkie-talkie bleeps on the table. Carla's voice says, "Okay, turn'em back on, Darren. Let's get a few minutes of this before we send the boys back in. Anything you see for the next ten minutes is strictly off the record."

Darren has one quizzical eyebrow arched. "Chelsea's not supposed to be in there alone, is she?"

"She's not supposed to be in there at all."

Melanie says, "Hurry, baby. Go!"

The rear doors of the van slam against the sides as I burst through, land, and immediately hit a full sprint.

"Mike!" I scream, checking the crowd for my partner. "We gotta go, man! Hurry!"

He's pushing himself out of the truck bed and chasing after me as I spot the Hoppers off to my right, coming around the side of another white van. "Chelsea," Leila shouts. "Chelsea, honey. Mommy's looking for you."

Rob bellows his daughter's name and then sees the two of us sprinting toward the farmhouse. "Where you going? Where's Chelsea?"

"Did you tell Carla she could take her inside?" I shout over my shoulder, not breaking stride.

Another two hundred yards to go.

"Inside where? The house? *No.* She said she wanted to take her for a walk and then disappeared," he yells back, and then he's running, too. Leila joins her husband.

I don't slow down. Neither does Mike. They'll catch up.

A hundred and fifty yards remaining.

A hundred.

My arms pump. My legs drive my body forward like pistons. My lungs burn. My pulse throbs inside my ears.

Fifty yards left.

Chelsea is inside that house, and we have to catch her before she gets upstairs.

I'm both enraged and curious about Carla's motives. How in the name of all that is holy did she think she could get away with this?

Didn't she know? Didn't she realize I would never allow it? Didn't she think the Hoppers would sue her into oblivion?

And then I understand...

Our agreement was only *verbal*. She promised Chelsea didn't have to be involved. She promised the studio's lawyers would get to work right away.

But there were no witnesses. It's her word against mine. The original contracts we all signed are probably sitting in a locked file cabinet down in Los Angeles.

She never had any intention of keeping those promises.

She caught me napping. She let me feel safe.

She betrayed me.

She will ... betray you.

How could I have ever been such an idiot, stupid enough to trust her?

I thought, for the sake of money, all the zeroes Mike and I would be losing, I thought it would be enough to motivate her into some level of sanity.

But you know what?

Money, power, fame—sometimes they aren't enough for the evil, greedy heart.

The Graveyard: Classified Paranormal Series

22

I spot Carla rounding the back side of the house, and she sees me at the same time. She pauses—freezes dead still, rather—with a surprised look of being caught with her hand in the cookie jar. I point as I sprint by her, yelling, "You! Later!" and then I'm gone. Not a lot of clarity in that, though I'm sure she understands.

We didn't run fast enough, because when all four of us explode through the front door like running backs breaking through the offensive line, hitting the hole hard, my eyes immediately go to the stairs, and Chelsea is nowhere to be seen.

From upstairs, I hear the hard crash of a bedroom door slamming, and my heart drops to the floor, along with my stomach, and any remaining sense of confidence I might have had.

Rob and Leila scream for their daughter and frantically scatter throughout the living room and kitchen, looking for her on the first floor. I tell them she's not here, she's upstairs, and that they should *really* stay downstairs.

"Like hell we will," Rob growls, and he's rushing for the stairs with Leila right behind him. "Move," he shouts, pushing into my chest.

I hold my ground. Rob is a big guy, and yet, the adrenaline coursing through my veins gives me an advantage. I throw my hands to his chest and stop him there. "Don't," I tell him. "Do *not* go up there."

"Out of my way," he orders.

"Please," Leila begs. "Chelsea."

Mike gently touches her shoulder, trying to be comforting.

"Our daughter," she whimpers.

Rob slaps at my hands and attempts to shove past me. I sidestep, block his path, and put my hands back on his chest, demanding that he stop right here.

All of this happens in seconds, and it feels like an eternity. It feels like we're wasting hours, days even, while Chelsea is up there with the Dark Man, where he's already doing his worst to her.

Rob reaches across my arms and grabs the opposite wrist, he twists, using leverage against me, and before I can recover, I'm on the way to the ground. I land face first, popping my forehead against a lower step. My vision blurs. Sparkles dance in my line of sight. Still, I'm able to grab his ankle as he's clambering over me. He goes down on the stairs, popping his shins and knees. Behind us, Leila is crying. Mike holds her in place as she struggles to free herself.

I shake my head clear and then crawl on top of Rob, straddling him. He's holding his side, perhaps bracing a broken rib—I'll owe him a sincere apology for that later, but for now, he *needs* to understand the severity of the situation.

I clasp both hands on the side of his head and pull his face up to mine. "I said, do *not* go up there, Rob. Not unless you want all three of you to walk out of here carrying Satan in your soul. You're not *strong* enough, and neither is Leila. You have to stay here. Mike and I will go. We can do this. We know what we're doing. You go up there, either of you, and it's the end, man. You got me?"

Rob's face twists and contorts like clothes spinning in a washing machine, folding this way and that as he races through so many emotions, rage and understanding finally joining hands. "She's our daughter," he says, baring his teeth.

"Hurry," Leila says between sobs.

Mike says, "Ford," and the urgency is evident.

I tell Rob the best thing they can do for their daughter is stay strong, and stay down here. "Be ready for her. No matter what happens up there, if we can get her away from him, then we'll find a resolution, but I can guaran-damn-tee you that if you and Leila disobey and come upstairs, you could wind up possessed by Satan, and if all three of you are sporting horns and hooves, you're done, and you won't even know it."

Rob's breath snorts out through flaring nostrils, then eases as he inhales deeply, fingers loosening their grip on my shirt. I climb off him, stand, and offer a hand to help him to his feet.

Mike and I leave the Hoppers behind, standing at the base of the steps, holding each other, desperate for this to end well. Their restraint is phenomenal. Their trust is off the charts. What must it take inside their minds to listen to the man who caused all of this in the first place? How strong do they have to be to give in and accept that we will do what we claim we can?

Truth be told, if it were my child up there, I don't think I could do it, no matter how many promises and reassurances were made.

God bless the Hoppers.

They're gonna need it.

***

Second floor. Mike on the left, me standing like a sentry on the right, fists clenched, abs tight, chest held up and out like a shield protecting my soul.

I'm reminded of the time I first brought Ulie here, when the permeating darkness was blacker than the bottom of a well. That night, a warm gust of wind scampered through an open window as Ulie whimpered down the hallway, aiming his twitching snout in the direction of the room we're about to enter.

Mike is slightly higher on the evolutionary scale than Ulie, but I swear, he lifts his nose, angles it down the hallway, sniffs the air, and gives off a slight moan like Ulie's whimper. I would have laughed if I wasn't scared out of my mind. He says, "You smell that?"

I do the same. "Sulfur."

"Yep. But stronger, you know? Like sulfur and spoiled chocolate milk that's been baking in the sun for a few days."

"Oddly specific."

"I know what I know."

"You think it means anything? Since he's stronger than we thought?"

Mike waves his DVR toward the room. "Could be exactly that. Big Man Downstairs has the body odor of a rotting cow carcass, nothing more. Or, could mean he's brewing up something big in there. I can't even begin to—"

"Hurry," Leila screams. "Go!"

"On it," I call back.

Rob adds, "The fuck are you waiting on, assholes? Get her back, now!"

Mike says, "Man's got a point. You ready?"

"Will I ever be? No."

"Then here we go."

Mike actually takes the lead. Rarely does 'The Exterminator' part of his personality come out, but in the past, they were some of our highest rated episodes because the fans went crazy whenever the slightly shy, reserved sidekick broke free from his chains of quietude. From the corner of my eye, I notice a spotcam in the bedroom with the open window and briefly wonder if he saw it too and was playing to the crowd. Maybe, just this once, Mike is thinking about the footage we're capturing.

Nah.

Mike?

Doubtful.

I'm sure he's thinking about the Hoppers, his own children, and steeling himself to kick some Satanic ass.

It's motivating, I'll be honest. Not in a competitive sense, like I can't let my bro outdo me in the world of paranormal search and rescue—no, it's more like, if he's not showing fear, or doing a fantastic freakin' job of hiding it, then I need to step up to my A-game of old. Find the Ford that Ford used to find in situations like this, back when I felt comfortable referring to myself as The Almighty.

Deep breath in, deep breath out.

Here we go.

We're walking down the hallway, slowly, deliberately, one foot in the front of the other in unified precision, at least until we reach the bedroom door when Mike reaches for the handle, and I don't.

"Wait," I say, grabbing his wrist.

"Why?"

"What's our plan?"

"Do we need one?"

"You don't think we do?"

"I mean, shit, Ford, we step inside," he says, pulling a small bottle of water from the pocket of his cargo shorts, "we squirt some holy water on anything that manifests, you yell your thing, and then we grab Chelsea and get gone."

"Right. My thing."

"It's not much, but what else do we have? Like you told the Hoppers, if we get her back, we always have a chance. We're not *beating* Satan at anything, so we do the best we can, which is grab Chelsea, and take her someplace safe."

"But then what?"

"The hell do you mean, then what? The fuck should I know? They move to Vatican City? I don't know. What I do know is, there's a terrified girl in there and—"

BOOM. BOOM. BOOM.

Three heavy thuds pound against the master bedroom door from the inside, and Chelsea screams. It's the first sound we've heard from her since we entered the house, and the next is even more heartbreaking. "Mommy! Daddy! Help!"

"Go, go, go," Mike says, grabbing the doorknob.

I can literally hear the hiss his skin makes a beat before he yelps and jerks it away, flapping and flailing it like a wounded bird. "Son of a bitch, that's hot."

I suspected that, which is why I cover my hand with my shirt, twist the knob rapidly, and shove the door open where it slams against the interior wall.

"Chelsea!" I spot her over by the window facing north, stuck to the wall, upside down, arms out as if she's on an inverted crucifix. No nails pierce her hands and feet and I thank God for that. She appears to be mounted by nothing more than the ultimate demon's willpower. She struggles and screams.

There's a strange, orange glow in the room, like it's illuminated by a fiery light source.

Before I can take a step, Mike puts his hand across my chest like my mother used to do when she slammed on her brakes in the car. "Whoa," he says. "Look down."

"Chelsea, honey, hang on, we're coming," I tell her, then glance where Mike is pointing.

Below us is one of the most incredible things I've ever seen.

Real, imagined, it doesn't matter. It's insane.

Smoke swirls in a circle along the wall in thick black ropes, down, down, into a fiery, boiling pit that's growing wider, and coming closer, with each rotation of the smoke.

I had speculated that the room was a portal to Hell, and assumed that was what happened to Papa Joe. Looks like I might have been right, except... something is off about what we're seeing.

Chelsea screams for help, screams at us to get her down.

"We're coming, sweetheart. One second. We just have to—Mike, wait. Hang on."

Mike bends down to the floor and reaches out. I'm a split second away from screaming at him, petrified that he's going to get sucked into the void, or that something will reach up out of there, grab his wrist, and drag him into eternity.

Instead, his hand thumps against the wooden floorboard and he grunts in response. "Ow," he says. "It's not real."

"Huh?"

"It's—I don't know how to describe it. Fake. You're seeing the same thing, yeah? Swirling smoke, open pit down into Lucifer's bedroom?"

"Yeah, but—"

"He's inside our heads. He's screwing with us. That's what the Devil does, right? Messes with your mind?"

A deafening roar erupts from below. It's so loud that it shakes the foundation of the home. The walls rattle and shimmy.

Ancient picture frames, empty of photographs, fall from pegs and shatter. The glass pieces come to rest on the floor, but appear to float over the gaping maw of Hades. Jagged rocks encircle the walls of the hole all the way down—scraggly teeth that would rip us to shreds if we actually fell.

I can't be sure of how far down it is, where the fire pit bubbles and surges upward, coming closer to us, but I spot movement. It's a pointed horn carving through the surface like a shark fin. It dips below and then appears again with its partner, the tips of which slowly rise up, growing with each second. As far below as it appears to be, whatever they belong to must be enormous. I have a pretty good idea who's coming.

I ask Mike, "This is all in our heads, right? You're sure?"

"Are you seeing that down there?"

"I am. Hang on. I need to find something."

Chelsea sobs and begs Mike and me to come get her. He promises we will as soon as we can. Behind us, at the top of the staircase, I hear the Hoppers pleading with us, too. I glance back, see them standing a couple of steps from the top, and order them back to the first floor. They refuse. I don't blame them.

But I also can't focus on them at the moment.

To my left is a bathroom, one that I've investigated in before, and if it's still here—yes, there, a random two-by-four length of wood, approximately five feet long that stood in a corner. For what purpose, I don't know, but now it has a purpose.

Mike moves out of my way, asking, "What're you doing with that?"

"Making sure."

I lift it over my head and swing it downward, like chopping wood with an axe, as hard as I possibly can, and it occurs to me an inch away from the floor—what if I break through like it's glass and Chelsea falls?

No—

Too late.

The two-by-four slams into the floor with a resounding thud, and the reverberation shoots a stinging blast of pain through my hands, forearms, and all the way up into my shoulders.

Another horrid, wailing roar erupts from below. The glowing, swirling, superheated liquid surges up and up, burying the crown of the head, the horns, and then they appear again, the tips glowing red from the intense heat of Hell's lava, fueled by millions of tortured souls.

"Move, Mike. Go. *Go!*"

Mike drops his head and powers forward. I'm an inch off his heels, telling myself not to look down.

And yet, I do. The vertigo is intense. I sway and stumble. I know the floor beneath our feet is solid wood, that the Devil is playing tricks on our minds, yet it doesn't stop me from feeling like I'm walking on clear glass, on air, and that I'll fall at any second.

The sulfur smell grows stronger. It clogs my nose and claws at the inside of my lungs when I breathe.

Chelsea struggles against the wall. The beast below spins her once, twice in rapid succession before Mike reaches her.

I can feel the heat coming through the soles of my boots.

Mike wraps his arms around Chelsea and tries to pull her free.

It doesn't work. He tugs her again and she yips in pain.

"Get her legs," he says. I do. We pull. Nothing happens.

"Our Father, who art in Heaven," I say, trying the first thing that comes to mind. "Hallowed by thy name." Mike joins me in reciting the Lord's Prayer.

Halfway through, the floor shudders, the room becomes awash in fresh heat, and the image of Hell trying to swallow us whole appears beneath our feet again.

We finish the prayer, Mike says, "Amen," and the moment the word is out of his mouth, the gaping hole below us vanishes, and the master bedroom returns to normal once more. Chelsea falls into Mike's arms upside down, and flings her arms around his neck when he flips her upright.

"Go, Mike. Get out."

Mike runs for the door, but I can't move. Something is holding me in place as if my feet are encased in concrete. The image of Hell returns, then vanishes, blinking in and out like a slow strobe light, switching between the scorching, sharp-toothed orifice to Hell, then back to normal.

Hell.

Normal, and then—it's almost subliminal it's so fast—I spot the most horrible, haunting thing I could imagine.

It's there, then it's gone. My stomach roils like it's full of boiling acid.

The vision of hell returns. The flaming pit is empty. No creature arises from the liquid flames.

I don't think it's a good thing. I don't think it means we beat him.

It means he's here.

Finally, the room blinks back to its natural state of existence and stays that way. Moon glow shines through the windows. I spot the blinking red light of a camera mounted in the upper right corner of the wall, placed there by some unpaid intern desperate enough to enter this home and try to please Carla

Hancock. Regardless of my current mental state, where I stand on caring about anything but rescuing little Chelsea Hopper, I can only hope the camera was able to catch something, just for the sake of my own sanity. I need proof of this. I need evidence that it isn't all in my mind.

For now, all is calm.

All seems safe.

Everything is dead silent.

23

Down the hallway, I can hear the distant shouts of Rob and Leila Hopper through the open door, asking if everything is okay, asking if we've rescued Chelsea.

Mike stands beside the door, holding a quivering Chelsea against his chest, "Is that it?"

"I—um—I don't know. Why are you still standing there? Get her gone, man. Now." I stare at the floor, hands out, palms up, examining them to make certain they're real. Solid. That this isn't a dream.

"I'm not leaving you here. I saw it, too."

I do a double-take. "Him? The thing with the…?" Chelsea doesn't need to hear a description.

"We have to go. That's not—we can't—Ford, buddy, I don't even have the words."

"Don't forget the—you know." I don't want to say it out loud. Not yet. Not until we know for sure.

"That's a big risk. We don't—"

"Just go. We're wasting time. Get her out of this fucking house. I'll be right behind you. This will only take a second." I go to them, put my hand on his back, right between the shoulder blades, and push him toward the master bedroom door.

Reluctantly, he moves, asking, "You sure?"

"Positive."

"Bro, I don't know about this. I can't leave you—let me give Chelsea to her folks, and I'll be back, okay?"

"Whatever, Mike, just go!"

Then he's out the door, and I can hear the Hoppers sobbing and shouting with joy as I slam it closed behind him. I turn the deadbolt.

There's no way he's getting back in here. Distant and disconnected though they may be, Mike has a family. Mike has multiple reasons to stay away, stay alive, and stay free from the Devil's harm. It won't be the first time I'm making a decision for him, but it might be the last.

What about me? What about Melanie and Ulie? I have reasons to stay alive, right?

I do, but this is all on me. I started this shit, and I'm going to finish it, no matter how strong the fear is, no matter how strong my urge to turn and run, no matter how low my odds are of walking out of here after facing Satan Himself. I have to try, and I'm not taking anyone else down with me.

People have called me an idol. They dedicate books to those who go bravely into the night. They look up to me. They want to emulate me. They want to trust that I am a real hero.

Maybe it's time I give them a reason to believe it.

Seconds later, Mike hammers on the door, jiggles the handle, and shouts, "Ford! Open up, man. Don't do this. Don't be a martyr. It's not worth it."

"Chelsea's life is worth it, Mike. Yours, too. Go deal with Carla. I'll be out in a minute."

"Ford!" His fist pounds and pounds on the unforgiving wood. He starts throwing his body weight into it, but nothing budges. The good thing about handcrafted homes from yesteryear, the damn things were built to last. He'll never break through that solid oak. "Don't do this!"

"Go, Mike!"

I turn away.

And there he is.

Him.

It.

The vile thing I saw a minute ago.

Satan.

Lucifer.

The Devil Himself.

Standing directly in front of me, in the center of the bedroom, bent at the waist, legs coiled and ready to pounce, hands out to his sides with the tips of his claws glistening in the moonlit reflection of whatever substance drips off of them.

Black skin. Ragged. Filled with cracks and pockmarks, warts and open wounds oozing pus. It covers thick, powerful muscles that heave and ripple with each apparent breath. I retreat two steps as my disbelieving gaze travels up his arms and I try to recall everything I've ever read in the field of paranormal research about this guy right here. History books. Common guides to the undead. Encyclopedias detailing all the known demons.

Some had advice. Some speculated.

But when it comes to encountering Satan, it's unlikely that anyone who ever did lived to explain how they escaped.

Don't look him in the eye? Don't touch the skin? Don't open your mind to psychic suggestions? I have no idea. He's already been inside my head, playing around. Shit, he might be in there right now.

A forked tongue lashes out like a whip from a hole in his neck and then retreats inside with an audible, moist slithering.

I thought about this often in my days of paranormal investigations, but it's true, the eyes are the window to the soul. In this case, though, they're windows to the soulless. His irises are blue. I'm not sure what I was expecting.

Slime-green? Blood-red? Shit-brown?

Perhaps they're a reflection of my own.

He hisses, baring yellow, gray, and black fangs, rotten breath wafting past me. My knees weaken from the ungodly stench of decay and waste. At the corner of my peripheral vision, I see his hands clenching into fists, and yet, I can't look away from his face. The skin, burned to a crisp by thousands of years of fire and ash, stretches tight across blackened bones peeking through gashes along his chin and cheekbone.

The horns. Oh, God help me, how do I describe the horns?

Sharp, piercing tips with thick bases; they're angled and twisted, multiple offshoots like burned branches in a forest fire, sharp as blades, jagged as lightning in a night sky. In some spots, I notice carvings—symbols, language maybe—or it could be a running tally of all the souls he's consumed since breakfast. Am I to be another notch in his belt?

The son of a bitch smiles at me, baring those horrid, serrated teeth, tongue flicking out of the hole in his neck, and he licks his lips.

The anticipation is excruciating.

It sounds like a death wish, but I almost want him to attack me to break the growing, seething tension. Do something. Say something. Quit staring at me.

"Why Chelsea?" I squeak. "Why me?"

And I wait.

I suspect that outside the door at my back, Mike continues to beat against it and throw his shoulder at the hinges, trying desperately to break inside. I suspect he's radioed back to the crew, asking for help. I pray the Hoppers are running as fast as they possibly can. I pray they're safe forever.

If it's happening, I hear none of this.

The atmosphere is thick in the room, swollen, as if a thousand pounds of feathers are sitting on my chest, covering my face, smothering me and dulling the clarity of the world. I know it's him. I know he's doing it.

"Why?" I repeat, one tick of the dial louder.

He swings an arm, and I have no time to react. It catches me in the side with such force, it's like stepping into the path of a speeding dump truck—white flashes across my vision from the pain—and I slam into the wall. He points at me with a single, hooked finger, waves it up and down, left and right. My arms are pulled out wide, one foot goes over top of the other, and I find myself in the same crucifix position as Chelsea, hanging upside down.

Lucifer arches back, chest pointing at the ceiling, arms and legs flexed, muscles rippling under the scorched skin, and then he roars. It's the sound of endless souls screaming while they burn in a lake of fire. It's the battle cry of the most wicked entity to ever exist, nails driven into human flesh, witches burned at the stake, all combined into one, thunderous shriek.

My chest shakes from the reverberation. My vision darkens for a second, and returns. It's then I realize, I'm already dead. I'm not walking out of here alive.

I once saw a documentary on World War II, and one of the surviving soldiers was asked how he did it, how was it possible to run toward the sound of gunfire, to run between howling machine guns, bullets flying everywhere, to rescue a fallen friend? How was it possible to wake up and fight every single day, knowing that any minute could be your last?

His response?

"I opened my eyes each morning accepting the fact that I was already dead, and every second I had left was time borrowed from God. Might as well make the most of it while I could. Take a life. Save a life. Nothing to lose, everything to gain."

Sounds about right, huh?

So, if that's where I am now, if you're out there, Lord, I could use some help. Give Melanie a good life. Keep an eye on Ulie. Let Mike find his happiness. Oh, and maybe put Carla Hancock in jail for eternity. Not too much to ask, is it?

"I didn't take your toy," I say to the sadistic monster standing before me. "And you want to know why, you filthy piece of dog shit? She was never yours to begin with."

He chuckles.

The son of a bitch actually laughs at me.

I didn't suspect he was able, nor is it comforting.

Wind, with the strength of an approaching tornado, blasts through the room, riding on a wave of heat. Curtain rods rip from the walls. Windows shatter. Closet doors swing violently and crack.

Lucifer speaks. The tone is harsh, unfathomable, and burnt with hatred. "She has always been mine."

"Bullshit. She's an angel. A child of God."

"The blood of the meek shall feed my horror."

It must be the blood rushing to my head, creating a hint of temporary insanity, because I find strength I thought was long gone. "Maybe you didn't hear me, you revolting fucking dog turd. Why her? Why that poor girl? Leave Chelsea alone."

"Pathetic weakling. You are an ant. I am eternal. You dared to step inside my lair."

"I didn't know it was—"

"Silence, worm. Your crime was arrogance. You challenged me. Her scars are the price she paid for your transgressions, you wretched mortal. You revealed me to the world."

"Hate to break it to you, chief, but it's not like you're a secret."

"Weaklings watch. Weaklings care. Weaklings *pray*." He waves his hand in a small circle, pushes against the air, and then a hole explodes in the far wall. Splinters and shards rain down both inside and out, and far beyond, a few hundred yards away, in the din of multiple headlights, I can see the Hopper family standing behind a semi-circle of crewmembers, all trying to protect Chelsea. There's no sign of Mike.

The ultra-demon bellows, "Those rodents think they can take her from me? Ignorant fools. I will end you all."

"I don't get it. I don't understand. I need to know, *why her?* Explain yourself!"

"Corruptible purity is the most powerful weapon against love, kindness, and that thing you call a god," Lucifer says. "She will be my scepter. My wife."

"Your *what?*"

Look, if I'm already dead, I might as well go for it.

"Let me get this straight, Lucy."

He hisses angrily, doesn't appreciate my clever nickname.

"I exposed your stupid plot to take over the world with the blood of the innocent, a plot that began by hanging out in a young girl's house and making her your wife because she's, what, she's some kind of obsession of yours? If knowledge caused the fall of man, what's your vice, dickhead? Pedophilia?"

A low growl emanates from the depths of his chest. He takes a single step closer to me, his cloven hoof clunking against the floor. The wind continues to whip and howl around the room. Orange tongues of flame flicker near the baseboards and lick up the walls.

I dare to take my eyes off of him and look outside through the exposed hole. Smoke lifts and twirls past the opening.

Oh, shit, he's not planting the images of flames in my mind. The house is on fire.

And I'm trapped inside it with the Devil.

"Why Chelsea?" I ask for the…hell, I've lost count of how many times.

"Reason is the bastion of simple minds."

"Reason keeps the world from falling into complete chaos."

"Evil, without reason, creates the purest fear in the heart of man."

"Is it an understatement to insist that you're fucking crazy? Or, you know what? Maybe I am. Maybe I'm nuts, and this is all in my head. Am I going to wake up any second now? Am I seriously hanging here, like an upside down crucifix, trying to rationalize the nature of humanity with the Devil?"

He begins to pace around the room, hooves clunking with each step. "A fight you will never win. You die. She's mine. And this miserable place that you mortals call home will burn with my wrath. The blood of the meek shall feed my horror!"

"Yeah, you keep saying that. Broken record much?"

"I have waited an eternity to rule what is rightfully mine, and you, *you*, I have let live too long." He pauses in the far corner, twenty feet away. The air floods with heat, and it's hard to tell if it's from Satan's seething wrath, or the fact that the freakin' *house is on fire*.

"Well, now, hold on a second, because this is how I see it… This whole scorched earth policy is kind of ridic—"

"Your words mean nothing!" He lifts a hand. A fireball blooms in his open palm. Flames dance from his fingertips. He could crush me at any moment.

It's time.

I can wait no more.

Chelsea's secret is all I have. It's either a weapon against the strongest evil known to man, or it's a keyword that will bring about the thousand-year reign of Satan on this dirtball we call home.

***

When I was knocked unconscious, back at the Sumpter Hotel & Spa, Chelsea, bless her adorable heart, appeared in my dream—her reality—as we walked down the hall together, reciting the poem she had written to protect herself from malevolence:

> *The white night is bright with light and love*
> *Put the pedal to the metal and*
> *Swing your sword with grace at his face.*
> *Keep me safe in this place.*
> *The Demon Killer is my savior,*
> *May he protect me forever and ever.*
> *Thanks, Jesus.*

She looked up at me with an angelic smile accompanying a mischievous twinkle in her eye and said, "Let me show you something," as we turned on the bathroom light. We stood next to each other, her head nearly even with my hip. Maintaining her hold, she squeezed my hand and pointed. Another Chelsea—I'm assuming the original one from the original dream—checked inside her pajama bottoms for boy parts and sighed with relief.

She lifted her gaze, stared at her reflection in the mirror, and then unleashed a violent scream so shrill the mirror cracked.

Before, that's when the dream had always ended; now, we watched as the mirror clicked and clattered, a quieter version of land buckling under the shifting power of an earthquake, and the Chelsea beside me whispered, "See? I can only show you here, in your dream."

"Show me what?" I replied.

"He'll know if I say it out loud. Goodbye, Mr. Ford. I'll see you on the other side."

She vanished. Blink. Gone.

And that's when I looked in the mirror.

The cracks had splintered into a word, into the language found in the Hopper House decades ago, the language spoken by Lauren Coeburn on the coast house footage. I don't know how I knew what it was, I just did. Perhaps Chelsea left the truth behind in my psyche, tucked away in a hidden corner only she could find.

What was the single word? What am I laying the hopes of humanity on?

The true name of Satan.

In the language of the damned.

Not Lucifer. Not the Devil. Not Satan. Or Beelzebub. Or Dancer. Or Prancer.

None of that. Nothing created by human minds.

There's power in a name.

***

The creature we came to know as Boogerface, before the truth was revealed, raises the flaming ball higher, up over his head, then lifts the other hand, cups it from the outside, and stretches them apart. Fire swirls and undulates, grows, and sets the ceiling ablaze.

"Death to the weak. I will drag you into the dark," he growls, leaning, arms surging forward, and I'm about to bite the big one in what appears to be a satanic version of dodgeball.

This, I fear, is my one and only chance. My merely human mind, my simpleton grasp of this moment, has no clear understanding of how to pronounce his name. I have no phonetic knowledge to equip me, but I feel the truth in my soul.

Please, God, let this work.

"I know thy name, demon! Burn in hell, *AXCLALKAX!*"

His name leaves my lips. For the briefest of seconds, nothing happens. Time slows and continues to march ahead, crawling sloth-like, and clarity shatters my expectations. This is what it feels like when you must return the time you borrowed from God.

Death to the weak. I should have known. I'm not strong enough to fight Satan. What have I been thinking?

Then it happens. A miracle. Ask and ye shall receive.

I fall away from the wall, catching myself before I land on my skull, and look up.

Axclalkax, or Boogerface, since that's easier to pronounce, halts like a speeding car driving headlong into an immovable steel wall. His body begins turning to stone, gradually at first, starting with his hooves, then swiftly ascending up his legs as the ball of flame dies in a whisper and vanishes. Stone consumes his worldly form, leaving behind a vicious-looking statue that could only exist in the imagination of Carter Kane.

Somewhere distant, far beyond the boundaries of this life, this side of the supernatural, I hear the rage-soaked, roaring howl of defeat and despair, falling away and down, down, down.

I inhale smoke, coughing as I cover my mouth and nose with my t-shirt. My eyes deceive me because it looks as if the portal to hell is opening again beneath my feet. The floor shakes and I stumble to the side, finally understanding that the Hampstead farmhouse has reached its ignition point.

It's not Hell. The floor is burning.

Another strong shake comes as the foundation weakens.

The stone statue of Boogerface teeters, falls, and shatters into thousands of pieces when it hits the floor.

Time to go. Time to find a way out.

Flames everywhere. The hallway. The stairs. The other bedrooms.

I'm trapped. Smoke soaks into my lungs.

Maybe this *is* Hell.

I spot the hole in the wall, the one blasted open by Boogerface.

One chance to live the life I've earned.

I run. I jump.

I fly.

But there are no angel wings to soften my fall from twelve feet up.

Both ankles snap when I land. The dual cracks are sharp, like a pool stick angrily broken across a biker's shin, and the intense pain shoots swirling, sparkling fireflies across my eyesight.

I roll onto my side and vomit—from the smoke I swallowed, from the pain, from expelling the evil that had once been inside of me.

It's over. It's done. Chelsea is safe.

I crawled out of the belly of the beast.

I'm still alive, and I owe a thousand prayers to God.

The Graveyard: Classified Paranormal Series

Desmond Doane

EPILOGUE

You're listening to KWAL 92.9 FM, rocking you from here to the end of time, with Crazy Dave Barker on this dark and sultry Monday night. Joining me today is our guest from the recently released documentary blockbuster, The Belly of the Beast, *the one, the only, Mike 'The Exterminator' Long. Thanks for being here, brother, and why don't you give us some background on what you've been up to lately? I heard you and the Almighty Ford have faced some challenges getting this thing to the big screen, huh?*

Thanks for having me, Dave. And we did have some trouble, that's right, but here's the thing…

Every story has to end somewhere.

Mine. Yours. The guy sitting beside you in a crowded movie theater, inhaling popcorn as you wait on *The Belly of the Beast* to start again—it's your third time seeing it, but he won't get another chance because he dies abruptly in a car crash on the way home, killed by a drunk driver.

That's how life goes, you know?

This movie is the final chapter of what felt like a never-ending road, but it has to. Stories end. Books end. New adventures, and new chapters, they begin with the turn of a page.

I could spend days telling you about the years leading up to filming this thing, or the time between the Hampstead farmhouse collapsing into a fireball and all the release delays for the documentary, but where's the fun in listening to me ramble on about bullhockey like that?

I mean, yeah, we faced quite a few production issues. People quit, just walked straight off the job because they were too scared to even look at the footage we captured.

I heard some major comeuppance slapped around your executive producer. Any truth to that?

I'm not sure what I can legally tell you. The short version is, after we were finished filming, Ford found a digital voice recorder in his shirt pocket that had been running for something like two hours—we were so distracted by the evidence during our investigation, and everything that happened with Chelsea, he'd totally forgotten about it. That didn't so much as capture paranormal proof, but we had Carla Hancock on record promising she wasn't going to send Chelsea Hopper into the house. That led to her eventual arrest for child endangerment, and then they let her go because of some contractual loopholes. The Hoppers filed a lawsuit against Spirit World Productions that was thrown out too because of the same issues. You know the drill.

Then there's the matter of the missing evidence you guys captured. That caused more delays. Any theories there? Conspiracies or otherwise?

Yeah, so much footage and data from the investigation vanished. Like, it just went *poof,* and it was gone. Ford and I have our theories about what happened, and most of them are slightly terrifying, in a paranormal sense, but it took weeks for some computer gurus we hired to retrieve the data. Backup cameras, backed up data files that for all intents and purposes looked absolutely corrupted, those guys sorted through everything, around the clock, and hell, they might still be looking. They scraped enough together for us to create a solid ninety minutes.

How do you feel about the finished product? I've seen some of your recent interviews and you don't sound so pleased about how things turned out. Given that, would you maybe say that all the negative reviews are justified?

Am I dissatisfied with the film? No. The end result is fantastic. It's some of the most incredible evidence we've ever captured. What I disapprove of is the studio's handling of the press and marketing once some of the back story came to light. Honestly, to suggest *Ford* alone has been the quote-unquote bad guy all along, and that he was trying to falsify paranormal evidence just to sabotage the movie because of a feud with Carla Hancock is utterly ridiculous. They're just passing the buck, you know?

There were certainly better ways for them to handle it and I can tell you for dang certain I won't be working with Spirit World again once all this is over. Granted, I'll admit that Ford was also caught on tape suggesting we should falsify Chelsea's involvement, in addition to Carla's promises, but it *never happened*. We suggested an alternative scenario to protect a seven-year-old girl, who had been threatened with death by Satan if she didn't show up at the Hampstead farmhouse. Still, let me be perfectly clear, it didn't happen, we didn't fake *a single second*. Everything you see in the documentary is one hundred percent real. All of our evidence, Carter Kane's reactions, Gunnar Creek's reactions, they're all genuine. I'm not giving anything away by saying this—

Spoiler alert!

The Graveyard: Classified Paranormal Series

Right, I'll keep the details to a minimum. Everything we captured in that final scene, with Ford in the master bedroom and the, you know, that situation, it's all real. No special effects. No fabricated evidence.

But you weren't in there with Ford. You didn't see it yourself.

And yet I trust him completely. Ford isn't without his faults—I've known the guy for a quarter of my life—but when it comes to the supernatural, he's nothing but serious, and he risked his own life to save Chelsea Hopper's because he felt completely responsible for what happened to her on that live Halloween episode. He's a good man, and I'm happy to call him my brother.

Despite the negative reviews—I don't know if you've seen this or not, but you guys have a morbid rating of eight percent out of one hundred on SweetOrSucks.com—despite all of that, you guys are absolutely, positively thrashing every known record for a documentary release, let alone films released in February. It's only been out for two weeks now, and Tanya, our intern, she's seen it five times already. To me, that sounds like it's sweet and it sucks at the same time. How're you reconciling that?

It's hard, man. See, the biggest thing is, we put *so much* effort into trying to save Chelsea Hopper. When we originally began our talks about coming back one last time to do this documentary, that's all it was. A cash-grab for the studio, maybe a chance for Ford to redeem himself in the public eye, and—well, I had my own private reasons—

Alimony, I'm guessing.

Like I said, my own private reasons, but it turned out to be paranormal war where we were fighting against supreme evil, all to save a child, to give her a chance at a future free from a demonic possession and, more than likely, to keep her out of padded rooms for the next eighty years.

For that, I would have done it for free.

Ford, too, for that matter.

How's Ford healing, by the way?

You mean emotionally? Mentally? Physically? You'll have to ask him about the first two, but yeah, his ankles are good, casts are off. Sounds like he'll be back to running marathons any day now. But, see, that's what drives me insane, Dave. Ford literally stood inside a burning farmhouse and then launched himself from twelve feet high because he waited until the last possible second doing what needed to be done. Then these critics, who have only seen the footage the editors cut into the film, have the motherfu—sorry, the ignorant audacity to sit there in their cushy desk chairs and criticize Ford for faking that fall, and then chastise him for his horrible acting. I have the X-rays.

Right, right.

I mean, for real, the guy from the *Times* who suggested Ford's shot at an Oscar went up in flames like the farmhouse? What a jerk. If you're listening, *Art Daniels*, come on an investigation one day and we can show you what it's really like. They say character is what you are in the dark. Well, let me tell you this, we've spent our careers and lives in the dark. Don't question our character. Not ever.

Was that the same dude who said the magic was gone, and you guys looked like nothing more than a couple of morons shouting at bogus special effects?

Different guy. Same offer. Come experience it firsthand.

Okay, looks like we have time for one last question, Mike. I've ran my mouth enough and there's a caller on the line. Whaddaya say, man? Brave enough to take a question from a stranger?

Go for it.

Caller? You're on.

Mike? Can you hear me?

I'm here, ma'am. You had a question?

This is so awesome. I can't believe I'm talking to Mike Long! I'm Olga from Portland, and I wanted to tell you this first: I don't care what the reviews say. They can't all win Academy Awards. Sometimes you have to give in and enjoy things at face value.

Thank you. My point exactly.

Just know that all your fans are out here supporting you and Ford, every day and always. The movie absolutely rocked, and I was on the edge of my seat the entire time. I didn't breathe for ninety minutes. Anyway, my question is—I'd just like to know how Chelsea Hopper is doing now after so long. Is she still okay?

She's—you know—it's hard to say much without spoiling the documentary. I'm sure you've seen that she and her family have been in hiding since the internet mafia discovered her parents were sending her back into a house to face a demon. People were typing in all caps everywhere without knowing the real story, without knowing what that family was subjected to. But, yeah, she's good. Their book is coming out soon. They're in an undisclosed location. So far, so good.

Duhn-duhn-duhn. So far, he says. I'm Crazy Dave Barker, and that's just as good of a place as any to send Mike 'The Exterminator' Long out the door and into the night. Give the Almighty Ford Atticus Ford our best, wherever he may be. Oh! Also, a hearty congratulations on your upcoming nuptials to Dakota Freakin' Bailey.

I'm a lucky man, in so many ways.

There you have it, folks. I'd say keep your nose clean, but in your case, brother, I'll send you off with this… Keep your soul clean.

Thanks for having me, Dave.

Say it. Go on, you know you want to. Send us off like the good old days of Graveyard: Classified.

Nah, that's Ford's line. I'll let him do it if he ever shows up again.

***

I turn off the internet radio and smile at how awesome Mike handled the interview. My boy's all grown up.

"Ford, honey, you want some more rum punch?" Melanie asks, holding up a clear glass pitcher full of bright pink liquid that nearly matches the color of her string bikini.

"I'll take another half glass, sure."

She pours, smiles, and kisses my forehead.

I twist the gold band around my ring finger. We haven't told anyone yet, and I'm enjoying this secret that's ours alone.

I have to admit, commitment looks good on me.

Better than all black, that's for damn sure.

By the way, New Zealand is amazing. I don't know if anyone has ever mentioned that before, but I gotta tell you, I'm fairly certain we're never going home again.

Months ago, I told Jessie Lynn Wade of *Portland Paranormal Quarterly* that once all of this was over, I wanted to ride off into the sunset with my arm around Melanie and Ulie trotting along and wagging his tail close by.

Which is exactly what we did.

We spend our days reading, relaxing, and ignoring the rest of the world, with a few dog walks thrown in.

I hear the documentary has been getting panned by critics, but the box office numbers are staggering. I expected that, really, and it's almost a good thing Carla Hancock betrayed us and left the original contracts as they were. If the predictions hold true, who knows how many zeroes our royalty checks will have in them. Who knows how many children's charities will benefit from my donations when the time comes.

Carla's been blacklisted by Hollywood and is living in Alaska, according to my sources. I've also heard that she's currently staying in a ridiculously haunted house, where she's scared to death both night and day, and I can't promise I'm not responsible for getting the word out to a few "friends" of mine.

Mike, bless him, has been a real trooper, handling all the press and interviews. I don't think he minds much. He's never been an attention seeker, but after more than a decade of standing by in my shadow, he says it's nice to be asked and have the opportunity to answer questions in my absence.

Gunnar Creek and Carter Kane have seen a massive surge in popularity, which I didn't think was possible given their celebrity status pre-Satan.

As for Chelsea…

She's great. Learning Italian. Eating amazing food. Sleeping soundly for the first time in years. I won't say where she is, other than the fact that she's closer to Vatican City, just in case, than she is to Cleveland.

How was she able to show me the true name of Satan?

I don't know, but here's what I suspect…

Ultimately, it came down to this: Boogerface had spent so much time inside Chelsea's mind that she was able to sneak a peek inside his. The bravado, the pride, the uncontrollable rage, they caused his downfall, which were probably some of the unspoken reasons he was kicked out of Heaven to begin with. He was so blinded by his quest for power on Earth that he didn't account for the exceptional strength, innocent wisdom, and unwavering perseverance of a determined child.

The blood of the meek shall feed my horror?

As if.

Never forget it, boys and ghouls, *the meek shall inherit the earth.*

And I'll be over here on the sidelines, laughing, cheering, and sipping a cocktail while it happens.

See y'all on the other side.

The Graveyard: Classified Paranormal Series

Printed in Great Britain
by Amazon